Nelson DeMille was born in New York City in 1943. He grew up on Long Island and graduated from Hofstra University with a degree of Political Science and History. After serving as an infantry officer in Vietnam, where he was decorated three times, DeMille worked as a journalist and short story writer. He wrote his first novel, *By the Rivers of Babylon*, in 1978 and has gone on to write many other international bestsellers, with sales of over fifty-five million copies in twenty-four languages. He lives on Long Island.

For more information on Nelson DeMille, go to:
www.nelsondemille.net

ALSO BY NELSON DEMILLE

By the Rivers of Babylon
Cathedral
The Talbot Odyssey
Word of Honour
The Charm School
The Gold Coast
The General's Daughter
Spencerville
Plum Island
The Lion's Game
Up Country
Night Fall
Wild Fire
The Gate House
The Lion

Mayday (WITH THOMAS BLOCK)

NELSON DEMILLE
THE PANTHER

sphere

SPHERE

First published in the United States in 2012 by Grand Central Publishing,
a division of Hachette Book Group, Inc.
First published in Great Britain in 2012 by Sphere
This paperback edition published in 2013 by Sphere

A CIP catalogue record for this book
is available from the British Library.

ISBN 978-0-7515-4754-2

Typeset in Centaur by M Rules
Printed and bound in Great Britain by
Clays Ltd, St Ives plc

Papers used by Sphere are from well-managed forests
and other responsible sources.

MIX
Paper from
responsible sources
FSC® C104740

Sphere
An imprint of
Little, Brown Book Group
100 Victoria Embankment
London EC4Y 0DY

An Hachette UK Company
www.hachette.co.uk

www.littlebrown.co.uk

To the memory of
Joan Dillingham,
who maintained her Viking spirit
throughout her beautiful life

AUTHOR'S NOTE

Regarding the spelling of Arabic words in this novel, I've used a variety of sources in transliterating. There is no standard transliteration of Arabic script into American English, and in some cases I simply used phonetic spelling to make it easy for the reader. I mention this up front with the hope that I can persuade the reader not to send me an email saying I spelled an Arabic word wrong. However, if you see an English word misspelled, let me know.

— ■ — PART I — ■ —

Marib,
Yemen

CHAPTER ONE

A man wearing the white robes of a Bedouin, Bulus ibn al-Darwish by name, known also by his Al Qaeda nom de guerre as al-Numair – The Panther – stood to the side of the Belgian tour group.

The Belgians had arrived in a minibus from Sana'a, four men and five women, with their Yemeni driver, and their Yemeni tour guide, a man named Wasim al-Rahib. The driver had stayed in the air-conditioned minibus, out of the hot August sun.

The tour guide, Wasim, spoke no French, but his English was good, and one of the Belgians, Annette, a girl of about sixteen, also spoke English and was able to translate into French for her compatriots.

Wasim said to his group, 'This is the famous Bar'an Temple, also known as Arsh Bilqis – the throne of the Queen of Sheba.'

Annette translated, and the tour group nodded and began taking pictures.

Al-Numair, The Panther, scanned the ruins of the temple complex – over an acre of brown sandstone walls, towering square columns, and open courtyards, baking in the desert sun. American and European archaeologists had spent many years and much money uncovering and restoring these pagan ruins –

and then they had left because of tribal suspicion, and more recently Al Qaeda activity. Such a waste of time and money, thought The Panther. He looked forward to the day when the Western tourists stopped coming and this temple and the surrounding pagan ruins returned to the shifting desert sands.

The Panther looked beyond the temple complex at the sparse vegetation and the occasional date palm. In ancient times, he knew, it was much greener here, and more populous. Now the desert had arrived from the East — from the Hadramawt, meaning the Place Where Death Comes.

Wasim al-Rahib glanced at the tall, bearded Bedouin and wondered why he had joined the Belgian tour group. Wasim had made his arrangements with the local tribal sheik, Musa, paying the man one hundred American dollars for the privilege of visiting this national historic site. Also, of course, the money bought peace; the promise that no Bedouin tribesmen would annoy, hinder, or in any way molest the tour group. So, Wasim wondered, why was this Bedouin here?

The Panther noticed that the tour guide was looking at him and he returned the stare until the guide turned back to his group.

There were no other tourists at the temple today; only one or two groups each week ventured out from the capital of Sana'a, two hundred kilometers to the west. The Panther remembered when these famous ruins attracted more Westerners, but unfortunately because of the recent reports of Al Qaeda activity in this province of Marib, many tourists stayed away. He smiled.

Also because of this situation, the Belgians had arrived with an armed escort of twenty men from the National Security Bureau, a paramilitary police force, whose job it was to protect tourists on the roads and at historic sites. The tourists paid for this service, which was money well spent, thought The Panther. But unfortunately for these Westerners, the policemen had also been paid to leave, which they were about to do.

Wasim continued his talk. 'This temple is also known as the Moon Temple, and it was dedicated to the national god of the Sabaean state, who was called Almaqah.'

As the Belgian girl translated, Wasim glanced again at the bearded man in Bedouin robes who was standing too close to his tour group. He wanted to say something to the man, but he was uneasy about him, and instead he said to his group, 'This was one thousand and five hundred years before the Prophet Mohammed enlightened the world and vanquished the pagans.'

The Panther, who also spoke English, nodded in approval at the guide's last statement.

He studied the Belgian tourists. There were two couples in their later years who seemed to know one another, and who looked uncomfortable in the burning sun. There was also a man and a woman, perhaps in their early twenties, and The Panther saw they wore no wedding rings, though they were obviously together, sometimes holding hands. The remaining man and woman were also together as a couple, and the girl who was translating appeared to be their daughter or a relative. He noted, too, that the women had covered their hair with hijabs, a sign of respect for Islamic custom, but none of them had covered their faces as required. The guide should have insisted, but he was a servant of the non-believers.

They were all adventurous travelers, thought The Panther.

Curious people, perhaps prosperous, enjoying their excursion from Sana'a, where, as he knew, they were guests of the Sheraton Hotel. Perhaps, though, this excursion was more difficult and adventurous than they had been told by the tour company. So now, he imagined, they might be thinking about their hotel comforts, and the hotel bar and dining room. He wondered, too, if a few of them were also thinking about security matters. That would be an appropriate thought.

Again Wasim stole a glance at the Bedouin, who had intruded even closer to his small tour group. The man, he thought, was not yet forty years of age, though the beard and the sun-browned skin made him appear older. Wasim also noticed now that the man was wearing the ceremonial jambiyah – the curved dagger of Yemen, worn by all males in the north of the country. The man's shiwal, his head covering, was not elaborate nor was it embroidered with costly gold thread, so this was not an important man, not a tribal sheik or the chief of a clan. Perhaps, then, the Bedouin was there to ask for alms from the Westerners. Even though Wasim had paid Sheik Musa to keep the tribesmen at a distance, if this Bedouin asked for alms, Wasim would give him a few hundred rials and tell him to go in peace.

Wasim again addressed his group. 'This temple is believed by some who practice the American Mormon faith to be the place to which the Mormon prophet called Lehi fled from Jerusalem in the sixth century before the Common Era. It was here, according to Mormon scholars, where Lehi buried the prophet Ishmael. And when this was done, Lehi built a great ship for himself and his family and sailed to America.'

Annette translated, and one of the male tourists asked a

question, which the young girl translated into English for Wasim, who smiled and answered, 'Yes, as you can see, there is no ocean here. But in ancient times, it is believed there was much water here – rivers, perhaps – from the Great Flood of Noah.'

The young woman translated, and the Belgians all nodded in understanding.

Wasim said, 'Follow me, please.' He ascended fourteen stone steps and stood before six square columns, five of which rose twenty meters in height, while the sixth was broken in half. He waited for his group to join him, then said, 'If you look there to the west, you will see the mountains where the local tribes believe the Ark of Noah came to rest.'

The tourists took pictures of the distant mountains and didn't notice the bearded man climbing the steps toward them.

Wasim, however, did notice, and he said to the Bedouin in Arabic, 'Please, sir, this is a private tour group.'

Al-Numair, The Panther, replied in Arabic, 'But I wish to learn also.'

Wasim, keeping a respectful tone in his voice, replied to the Bedouin, 'You speak no English or French, sir. What can you learn?'

The Panther replied in English, 'I am a poor man, sir, who comes to entertain the tourists in my finest tribal robes.'

Wasim was taken aback by the man's perfect English, then replied in Arabic, 'Thank you, but Sheik Musa has assured me—'

'Please, sir,' said the Bedouin in English, 'allow me to pose for photographs with your Western friends. One hundred rials for each photograph.'

Annette heard this and translated into French for her compatriots, who had seemed anxious about the exchange between the two Arabs. Hearing now what this was about, they all smiled and agreed that this would be a very good thing — an excellent souvenir photograph to take home.

Wasim acquiesced to his clients' wishes and motioned to the Bedouin to proceed.

The Belgians began posing alongside the tall, bearded Bedouin, individually at first, then in small groups. The Bedouin smiled for each photograph, and he was very accommodating to the tourists as they asked him to move around the temple to set up various shots with the ruins in the background.

One of the older men asked him to draw his dagger, but the Bedouin explained almost apologetically that if the jambiyah is drawn, then it must be used. On hearing the translation of this from Annette, the older Belgian said to his compatriots, 'Then we will not ask him to draw his dagger,' and they all laughed. But Wasim did not laugh.

Wasim glanced at his watch. Though they had left Sana'a at eight in the morning, the bus had not arrived at the nearby town of Marib until after noon. The tourists had lunched, too slowly he thought, at the Bilqis Hotel tourist restaurant, and there Wasim had to wait too long for Sheik Musa, who demanded two hundred American dollars, saying to Wasim, 'The other tribes are making problems, and so I must pay them to allow you safe passage on your return to Sana'a.'

Wasim had heard this before, but he explained to the sheik, as he always did, 'The tourists have already paid a fixed price to the travel company in Sana'a, and a price for the police escort. I can ask no more of them. And there is no profit for me if I give you more money.' But, as always, Wasim promised, 'Next time.'

The sheik and the tour guide from Sana'a had agreed on the one hundred dollars, but Wasim had decided there would be no next time. The road from Sana'a to Marib was becoming unsafe, and it was not only the tribes who were restless, but also this new group, Al Qaeda, who had entered the area in the last year. They were mostly foreigners – Saudis, Kuwaitis, people from neighboring Oman, and also Iraqis who had fled the Americans in their homeland. These people, Wasim thought, would bring death and unhappiness to Yemen.

In fact, Sheik Musa had said to Wasim, 'These Al Qaeda people are becoming a problem. They are attracted by the American oil wells and the American pipelines, and they gather like wolves waiting for a chance to strike.' The sheik had also told Wasim, 'You cannot buy those people, my friend, and the police cannot protect you from them, but I can. Three hundred dollars.'

Again, Wasim had declined to make the extra payment, and Sheik Musa had shrugged and said, 'Perhaps next time.'

'Yes, next time.' But Wasim was now sure there would be no next time.

Wasim al-Rahib, a university graduate with a degree in ancient history, could not find a job teaching, or a job anywhere, except with this tour company. It paid well enough, and the Western tourists were generous with their gratuities, but it was becoming dangerous work. And also dangerous for the tourists, though the tour company would not say that. All the guidebooks – written years ago – said, 'You cannot leave Yemen without seeing the ruins of Marib.' Well, Wasim thought, they would have to see them without him.

Wasim watched the tourists, talking now to the Bedouin through the English translation of the young girl. The Bedouin seemed pleasant enough, but there was something unusual about him. He did not seem like a Bedouin. He was too at ease with these foreigners, and he spoke English. Very unusual, unless perhaps he worked for the Americans at the oil installation.

In any case, it was now past three in the afternoon, and they had not yet visited the Temple of the Sun. If they stayed here much longer, they would be traveling the last hour to Sana'a in darkness. And it was not good to be on the road after dark, even with the police escort, who themselves did not want to be on the road after dark.

Wasim spoke in English to the young woman, and to the Bedouin, 'We must now leave. Thank you, sir, for your hospitality.'

But the Belgians wanted a photograph of the entire group together with the Bedouin, taken by Wasim. So Wasim, thinking about his gratuity, agreed, and took the photographs with four different cameras.

Wasim then said to the Belgian girl, 'I think if you give this gentleman a thousand rials, he will be very happy.' He made sure she understood. 'That will be about five euros. A very good day's pay for this kind man.'

Annette collected the money and handed it to the Bedouin, then said to him, 'Thank you, sir.'

The Bedouin took the money and replied, 'You are very welcome.' He also said to the girl, 'Please tell your compatriots that

Bulus ibn al-Darwish wishes them a happy and safe visit to Yemen.'

Wasim was looking to the north where the minibus had parked on the road behind the army truck that carried the security police. The bus was still there, but the truck was not. In fact, Wasim could not see any of the National Security police in their distinctive blue camouflage uniforms.

Wasim made a call on his cell phone to the police commander, but there was no answer. Then he called the bus driver, Isa, who was also his wife's cousin. But Isa did not answer his cell phone.

Wasim then looked at the Bedouin, who was looking at him, and Wasim understood what was happening. He took a deep breath to steady his voice and said to the Bedouin in Arabic, 'Please, sir . . . ' Wasim shook his head and said, 'This is a very bad thing.'

The tall Bedouin replied, 'You, Wasim al-Rahib, are a bad thing. You are a servant of the infidels, but you should be a servant of Allah.'

'I am truly his servant—'

'Quiet.' The Bedouin raised his right arm in a signal, then lowered it and looked at Wasim and at the Belgians, but said nothing.

The four men and five women were looking at their guide, waiting for him to explain what was happening. Clearly, something was wrong, though a few minutes earlier everyone had been smiling and posing for pictures.

Wasim avoided the worried stares of his group.

Annette said to Wasim in English, 'What is wrong? Did we not give him enough?'

Wasim did not reply, so Annette said to the Bedouin in English, 'Is there something wrong?'

Al-Numair, The Panther, replied to her, 'You are what is wrong.'

The Belgians began asking Annette what had been said, but she didn't reply.

Then one of the men in the group shouted, 'Regardez!' and pointed.

In the temple courtyard below, where they had been standing, a group of about twelve men suddenly appeared from the dark recesses of the ruins, wearing Bedouin robes and carrying Kalashnikov rifles.

At first, all the tourists were silent, but then as the Bedouin began running up the stone steps, a woman screamed.

Then everything happened very quickly. Two of the Bedouin pointed their rifles at the Belgians while the others bound their hands behind their backs with tape.

Annette shouted to Wasim, 'What is happening? Why are they doing this?'

Wasim, whose wrists were also bound, was at first afraid to speak, but then he found his voice and said, 'It is a kidnapping. Do not be frightened. They kidnap for money. They will not harm us.'

And as Wasim said this, he hoped it was so. A tribal kidnapping of Westerners. It was a common thing – what was called a guest kidnapping – and they would spend a week, perhaps two, with a tribe until money was delivered. And then they would be released. These things usually ended well, he knew, and Westerners were rarely harmed, and never killed unless the army intervened and attempted to free those who were taken by the tribes.

Annette, though she was terrified, said to her compatriots, 'It is a kidnapping. For ransom. Wasim says not to be—'

'Shut up,' said the tall Bedouin in English. He then said to Wasim in Arabic, 'This is not a kidnapping.'

Wasim closed his eyes and began praying aloud.

Bulus ibn al-Darwish, The Panther, drew his curved dagger and moved behind Wasim. With one hand he pulled Wasim's head back by his hair, and with his other hand he drew his curved dagger across Wasim's throat, then shoved the man forward.

Wasim fell face first onto the stone floor of the Temple of the Moon and lay still as his blood flowed quickly and spread across the hot stones.

The Belgians stared in horror, then some of them began screaming and some began crying.

The armed men now forced all the Belgians to their knees, and The Panther moved first to Annette, coming around behind her, and said to her, 'So you don't have to watch the others die,' and with a quick motion he pulled her head back by her long hair and sliced open her throat with his curved dagger, then moved on to the others.

Some cried or begged for mercy, and some struggled, though it was futile, because the jihadists held them in a tight grip as The Panther cut their throats. A few accepted their fate quietly. Only one prayed, an elderly woman whom The Panther saved for last so she could finish her prayers. It was interesting, he thought, to see how people died.

In less than two minutes, it was over. All nine infidels and Wasim their servant lay on the floor of the temple, their life blood flowing freely onto the ancient stone.

Bulus ibn al-Darwish, al-Numair, The Panther, watched the infidels as, one by one, they went into a final death throe, then lay still.

One, however, the man who was the father of the young woman, suddenly stood, his wrists still bound behind his back, and began running down the stone steps. He quickly stumbled and fell face first onto the stone, then tumbled down the steep steps and came to rest at the bottom.

The Panther said to his jihadists, 'I hope he was not injured.'

The men laughed.

The Panther stared at his jambiyah, red with blood, then slid it into its sheath.

He retrieved one of the tourists' cameras and looked at the digital images on the small screen, which made him smile.

He called to one of his men, 'Nabeel,' and handed him the camera to take pictures of the slaughter.

The Panther looked at the dead Europeans and said, 'So, you came to Yemen for adventure and for knowledge. And you have found both. A great final adventure, and a great knowledge of this land. You have learned that in Yemen death comes.'

PART II

New York City

CHAPTER TWO

I f the earth had an anus, it would be located in Yemen.

And speaking of assholes, my boss, FBI Special Agent in Charge Tom Walsh, wanted to see me, John Corey, at 5:15 P.M., and Detective Corey was now five minutes late. But not to worry — my wife, Kate Mayfield, who also works for Walsh, was on time for the meeting and had undoubtedly made excuses for me, like, 'John is in a passive-aggressive mood today. He'll be here when he feels he's made his statement.'

Right. Another five minutes. I logged off my computer and looked around the empty cube farm. I work on the 26th floor of 26 Federal Plaza, which is located in Lower Manhattan in the shadows of the Twin Towers. Well ... not anymore. The Towers, I mean. But I'm still here.

It was Friday — what we call Federal Friday — meaning that by 4:30, my colleagues in the war on terrorism, mostly FBI agents and NYPD detectives, had left to beat the bridge and tunnel traffic, or they'd gone off on special assignments to the surrounding bars and restaurants. With any luck, I'd be joining them shortly. But first I had to see Tom Walsh, who is in charge of the New York Anti-Terrorist Task Force. And what did Mr Walsh want to see me about?

His email had said: *John, Kate, my office, 5:15. Private. Subject Yemen.*

Yemen? Typo, maybe. Yemex? A new kind of explosive? Maybe he meant 'Yes-men'. Too many yes-men in the organization.

Walsh doesn't usually state the subject of a private meeting – he likes to surprise you. But when he does state a subject, he wants you to think about it – he wants it to eat at your guts.

If I thought this out, I could conclude that Tom Walsh wanted to assign Kate and me to the Yemen desk. Do we have a Yemen desk here? Maybe he just wanted us to help him find Yemen on the map.

Another possibility ... no, he was *not* going to ask us to *go* to Yemen. No, no. I'd been there for a month to investigate the USS *Cole* bombing. That's how I found out it was an anal cavity.

I stood, put on my jacket, straightened my tie, and brushed the chips off my shoulders – a well-balanced detective has a chip on *both* shoulders – then made my way toward Walsh's office.

A brief history of this elite organization. The Anti-Terrorist Task Force was founded in 1980, when the word 'terrorist' was not synonymous with Islamic terrorist. The ATTF in those days had its hands full with Irish Republican Army guys, Black Panthers, Puerto Rican separatist groups, and other bad actors who, to paraphrase William Shakespeare, thought that all New York was a stage, and every bad actor wanted to play Broadway.

So the first Federally funded Anti-Terrorist Task Force was formed here in New York, made up of ten FBI agents and ten NYPD detectives. Now we have a lot more people than that. Also, we've added a few CIA officers, plus people from other Federal and State law enforcement and intelligence agencies. The actual number is classified, and if someone asks me how many people work here, I say, 'About half.'

The New York Task Force experiment worked well, and prior to September 11, 2001, there were about thirty-five other anti-terrorist task forces across the country. Now, post-9/11, there are over a hundred nationwide. A sign of the times.

The theory behind these task forces is that if you mix people from various law enforcement and intelligence agencies into a single organization, you will get different skills and mind-sets coming together to form synergy, and that will lead to better results. It sort of works. I mean, my wife is FBI and I'm NYPD and we get along and communicate pretty well. In fact, everyone here would get along better if they slept with one another.

The other reason for including the local police in the Federal Task Force is that most FBI agents – my wife included – are from non-urban areas, meaning the 'burbs or the boondocks. So in a big city like New York, it's the local cops who know the territory. I've instructed new FBI agents on how to read a subway map and I've pinpointed for them the location of every Irish pub on Second and Third Avenues.

In any case, I'm actually a contract agent here, meaning I'm a civilian. Until five years ago I was NYPD, but I'm retired on medical disability as a result of being shot three times in the line of duty, all on the same day. I'm fine physically (mentally maybe not so fine), but there were other reasons to take the offer to retire. Now, like a lot of ex-cops, I've found a new career with the Feds, who have zillions of anti-terrorist dollars to spend. Do I like this job? I was about to find out.

CHAPTER THREE

My boss and my wife were sitting at a round table near a big window that faced south with a good view of Lower Manhattan and the Statue of Liberty in the harbor; a view now unobstructed by the Towers, though on the window was a black decal of the missing buildings with the words 'Never Forget'.

No one, myself included, commented on my lateness, and I took a seat at the table.

I am not overly fond of Mr Walsh, but I respect the job he does, and I appreciate the stress he's under. I'd like to think I make his job easier, but ... well, I don't. I have, however, covered his butt on occasion and made him look good. He does the same for me now and then. It's a trade-off for Tom. So why did he want to send me to Yemen?

Tom informed me, 'Kate and I haven't discussed the subject of my memo.'

'Good.' Bullshit.

Kate is career FBI, which is maybe why she likes the boss. Or maybe she just likes him, which is maybe why I don't.

A quick word about Special Agent in Charge Tom Walsh. He's young for the job – mid-forties – good-looking if you like store mannequins, never married, but in a long-term relationship with a woman who is as self-absorbed and narcissistic as he is. Did that come out right?

As for his management style, he's somewhat aloof with his own FBI agents, and he's borderline condescending to the NYPD detectives under his command. He demands total loyalty, but he's forgotten that the essence of loyalty is reciprocity. Tom *is* loyal to his superiors in Washington; everyone else is expendable. I never forget that when I deal directly with him. Like now.

But human beings are very complex, and I've seen a better side of Tom Walsh. As a for-instance, in our last major case, involving the Libyan terrorist Asad Khalil, a.k.a. The Lion, Walsh exhibited a degree of physical bravery that matched anything I've seen in my twenty years with the NYPD and my four years with the Task Force. If it wasn't for that one act of incredible courage, when he put his life on the line to save thousands of innocent lives, I'd now be thinking about another job when my contract expires next month.

Tom got right to the point and said, 'Let me get right to the point.' He glanced at an email in front of him and informed us, 'Two overseas postings have come down from Washington.'

I inquired, 'Paris and Rome?'

'No,' he replied, 'two jobs in Sana'a.' He reminded me, 'That's the capital of Yemen.'

'Not happening,' I assured him.

'Hear me out.'

Kate said to Tom, 'If my husband is not interested, then I'm not interested.'

Actually, she didn't say that. She said to me, 'Let's hear this.'

Thanks, partner. Kate is always putting career and country

ahead of her husband. Well, not always. But often. I have notes on this.

Also, my detective instincts told me that Tom and Kate had, in fact, started without me. FBI people stick together.

Walsh continued, 'One posting is for a legat, and the other is for an ERT person.' He added, 'Both in Sana'a, but with some duties in Aden.' He informed us, 'The Sana'a embassy currently has no Legal Affairs Office, so this is a new position, beginning next month.'

He then went into an official job description, reading from a piece of paper. I tuned out.

A legat, FYI, is a legal attaché, attached to the US Embassy in a foreign capital, or to a US consulate office in a major city. In this case, it would be Sana'a and maybe Aden, the only two cities in Yemen as far as I knew.

Kate, like many FBI Special Agents, is a lawyer, so I, as a detective, concluded that the legal job was hers. The ERT is the Evidence Response Team – the Fed equivalent of forensic or crime scene investigator – so I concluded that that was to be my job.

The crime in question, I was certain, was the bombing of the USS *Cole*, a warship that had been refueling in Aden Harbor. This took place on October 12, 2000, which was why I had been in Yemen in August 2001. The investigation of this terrorist act is ongoing and will continue until everyone involved is brought to justice.

As for Sana'a, the capital of Yemen, the word in Arabic means A'nus. And by the way, the port city of Aden is no treat either. Trust me on this.

Mr Walsh continued, 'As John knows from his last visit, the Yemeni government will issue only forty-five-day visas to our ERT personnel who are investigating the Cole bombing. But with some pressure, we can usually get this extended for up to a year.'

A year? Are you kidding?

Walsh editorialized, 'The Yemenis are being cooperative, but not *fully* cooperative.' He explained, 'They're walking a fine line between pressure from Washington and pressure from sources inside and outside of Yemen who want the Americans out of their country.' He further explained, 'The government in Sana'a is currently going through an anti-American phase.'

I informed him, 'I don't think it's a phase, Tom.' I suggested, 'Maybe we should stay home and nuke them.'

Tom ignored my suggestion and continued, 'Kate's job with the embassy comes under diplomatic rules, so she can be there for any reasonable length of time.'

How about five minutes? Does that work?

Tom further briefed us, 'Bottom line, you can both figure on a year.' He added, 'Together.' He smiled and said, 'That's not so bad.'

'It's wonderful,' I agreed. I reminded him, however, 'We're not going.'

'Let me finish.'

This is where the boss tells you what's going to happen if you say no, and Tom said, 'Kate's time here in New York is approaching a natural conclusion in regard to her career trajectory. In fact, Task Force headquarters in Washington would like her to transfer there. It would be a good career move.'

Kate, who is from someplace called Minnesota, did not

originally like New York, but she's grown fond of being here with me. So why wasn't she saying that?

Tom continued, 'If Kate accepts this overseas hardship assignment, the Office of Preference will move her to the top of the OP list.' He explained, unnecessarily, 'Meaning, after Yemen, she can return to New York — or any place she chooses.'

Kate nodded.

Tom said to me, 'If you accept this assignment, your contract, which I understand is about to terminate, will obviously be renewed for the time you're in Yemen, and we'll add two years afterwards.'

I guess that was the carrot. I think I liked the stick better — don't renew my contract.

Tom had obviously thought about that, too, and said to me, 'Or, after your return from Yemen, you can have a Federally funded job with the NYPD Intelligence Unit.' He assured me, 'We'll take care of that.'

I glanced out the window. A crappy February day. It was sunny in Yemen. I looked at the nearby brick tower of One Police Plaza. It would be nice to be back on the force, even as a Federal employee, though I'd be working in intelligence rather than homicide. Still, I'd be out of 26 Federal Plaza, which would make me and Tom equally happy. Kate and I could fly paper airplanes to each other from our office windows.

Tom seemed to be done with the carrot and the stick, so I asked the obvious question. 'Why us?'

He had a ready answer and replied, 'You're the best qualified.' He reminded me, 'You've already been there, and the team in Yemen would appreciate someone with experience.'

I didn't reply.

He went on, 'You two work well as a team, and the thinking is that a husband and wife might fit in better.'

'I'm losing you, Tom.'

'Well ... as you know, women are not fully accepted in some Islamic countries. And professional women and unmarried women run into many obstacles. But Kate, as a married woman traveling with her husband, can move about more freely.' He added, 'And more safely.'

Neither Kate nor I responded to that, but I was getting the feeling that he wasn't talking about Kate's work as a legal attaché at the embassy.

In fact, Kate asked, 'What's this about, Tom?'

He didn't reply directly, but said, 'You both may be asked to go beyond your official job descriptions.'

I inquired, 'Do we have to kill somebody?'

He didn't laugh and say, 'Of course not, you silly man.' In fact, he didn't say anything, which said a lot.

Tom stood and went to the sideboard. He returned with three glasses and a bottle of medicinal brandy. He poured, we clinked, said 'Cheers,' and drank.

He turned and stared out the window awhile, then said, as if to himself, 'There were seventeen American sailors killed – murdered – when a boat pulled up beside the Cole in Aden Harbor and the suicide bombers on board detonated a large explosive device that blew a hole in the side of our warship. Thirty-nine sailors were injured, some very badly.' He added, 'A multi-million-dollar warship was put out of service for nearly two years.'

Right. That was almost three and a half years ago, and the ongoing investigation has had mixed results.

The Evidence Response Team in Yemen, by the way, has long ago discovered any existing forensic evidence, and the crime scene — Aden Harbor — has been dredged, and the USS *Cole* is repaired and returned to duty. So this is an Evidence Response Team in name only — a designation that our reluctant Yemeni allies can live with. In fact, the ERT team in Yemen interrogates suspects, witnesses, and informants, and is actively involved in hunting down the perpetrators. That's what I did when I was there. So maybe that's what Tom meant about us going beyond our job descriptions. Or ... he meant something else.

Walsh sat, then confided to us, 'We have identified one of the masterminds of the attack, and we have good intelligence that this individual is now back in Yemen.' He added, 'The focus of our team in Yemen is to find and apprehend this man.' He looked at Kate and me and said, 'You would be part of that effort.'

Neither of us replied, so Walsh continued, 'This assignment could take you out of Sana'a and out of Aden and into the tribal lands.'

I thought about that. The tribal lands, otherwise known to the Americans there as the Badlands, or Indian Territory, were basically lawless. Also known as dangerous.

Walsh said to us, 'As John knows, this could be risky.'

Right. Now I knew the answer to 'Why us?' Walsh wanted me dead. But he liked Kate. So ... maybe I would be the only one riding a camel into the Badlands, looking for this guy.

I pointed out to Walsh, 'You're not making this job sound very attractive.'

He replied, 'I'm not going to sugarcoat it.'

'Right. I appreciate that, Tom. But I just don't see what's in this for us.'

'Why is it always about you?'

Well, that made me feel bad. Tom knows how to do that. So I said, 'Look, Tom, I'm a patriot, a soldier in the war on terrorism, and I've never backed away from my duty or from danger—'

'I know that. Both of you are brave, dedicated—'

'Right. But I sort of like my danger in an urban setting. Like here.' I reminded him, 'I've been there. We slept with our boots on and our guns in our hands.' I assured him, 'I'm not thinking of my own safety. I'm thinking of Kate.'

Kate, of course, said, 'I can take care of myself, John.'

'Right.' *You* go.

Walsh told us, 'You would need to report to the American Embassy in Sana'a no later than next weekend. So I'll need your answer Monday at nine.' He added, 'If you say yes, then I can give you the classified details of your assignment. Once you have those classified details, you are committed to the assignment.'

'In other words, we don't know what we're saying yes to until after we say yes.'

'Correct.' He assured us, 'If you say no, there will be no record of this meeting and no adverse entry in your file.' He reminded us, 'Your careers will take a normal course.'

Right. I'd be unemployed in New York, and Kate would be in Washington.

Walsh continued, 'This assignment – if you choose to accept it – will ensure your futures—'

'Shorten our futures?'

He ignored me and continued, 'Even if this mission is not successful. If successful, you and the other members of the team who are already in Yemen will be appropriately honored by a grateful government. That's all I can say about that.'

Honored where? Arlington National Cemetery?

He had some good news. 'Your assignment in Yemen would actually be over as soon as you apprehend this man.'

Good incentive to wrap it up in a week. The other side of that deal is that our assignment could be over if this guy found us first.

Tom looked at me and said, 'This assignment will give you ample opportunity to demonstrate your sometimes unorthodox methods, which are not always appreciated here, but will be invaluable over there.'

How should I take that? Loose cannon makes good in Sandland?

Kate said, 'We'll think about it.' Then she asked Tom, 'Can only one of us say yes?'

He nodded.

Well, I was seeing the old handwriting on the wall here. What did I do with my desert duds from my last trip to Sandy Arabia?

Tom stood and we also stood. He said, 'I'll see you both here in my office, Monday, nine A.M. Have a good weekend.'

We shook, and Kate and I left.

On the way back to our cube farm, I suggested, 'Let's get a drink.'

She didn't reply immediately, then said to me, 'John, we have to do this.'

'Absolutely, and we'll have dinner, too. Where would you like to go?'

'We have to go to Yemen.'

'Why not Ecco's?'

'I'm going.'

'Good. Should I call ahead for a table?'

'And I'd like you to go with me.'

'I wouldn't let you drink alone.'

'Are you listening to me?'

'No.'

We grabbed our coats, rode down in the elevator, and exited the lobby of 26 Federal Plaza onto lower Broadway.

It was windy and cold on the street, but I like the cold. Good drinking weather. Yemen was hot and alcohol was illegal.

On the plus side, I could, as Tom said, and as I had discovered myself in Yemen, be free of the bureaucratic bullshit here, and free of the political correctness that permeated 26 Federal Plaza. I could be me. Nuts.

Also . . . I had the feeling that someone in Sandland needed to be whacked. That could be interesting. I mean, I never had or wanted a license to kill – but I could conceive of a situation where this might be necessary and right. Especially since 9/11.

This was a lot to think about, and I think better at the bar.

We got to Ecco's on Chambers Street, and as we made our way to the crowded bar, Kate said to me, 'We're getting into a rut here. I'm ready for a change. An adventure.'

'Let's go to a different bar.'

'We'll appreciate our lives and jobs more when we come back.'

'Right.' But not everyone who went to Yemen came back.

CHAPTER FOUR

E cco's is an Italian restaurant, but the bar is sort of old New York, though the prices are new New York.

The place was hopping on this cold Friday night after work, and most of the clientele were lawyers, judges, police officials, and politicians whose wallets hadn't seen the light of day in years.

Kate and I found a place at the bar, said hello to a few people we knew, and ordered the usual — Dewar's and soda for me, a Pinot Grigio for the lady.

Kate asked me, 'Are there any places in Sana'a or Aden where you can get a drink?'

'Is that all you think about?'

My ex, Robin by name, is a high-priced criminal defense attorney, and she introduced me to this place years ago, and she still comes here. I don't care, and I don't dislike her, but I don't like her life's work, which is defending the scumbags I spent twenty years trying to put in jail. That caused some strain on the short marriage. Now I'm married to another lawyer. As I often say, I like to screw lawyers.

Kate and I clinked and said grace. 'Thank God it's Friday.' There was a piano in the corner, and the player was just getting started. I said to Kate, 'Ask him to play "Midnight at the Oasis".'

She rolled her big baby blues.

A word about Kate Mayfield, a.k.a. Kate Corey. We met on the job when we were both working on the first Asad Khalil case. FBI and NYPD are different species, but we fell in love, married — about four years ago — and it's still heaven.

Kate is a little younger than me — actually, about fourteen years — and the age difference is not an issue; she's mature beyond her years, and I can't seem to grow up.

She's originally from Minnesota, as I said, and her father is retired FBI and her mother is a loon. They both hate me, of course, but being from Minnesota they're really nice about it.

Also on the plus side, Kate and I have been shot at together, which is good for any relationship, and she's cool under fire. If she has any faults, aside from her divided loyalty, it's that she doesn't fully appreciate my NYPD work habits or methods. Also, the Feds are almost humorless, while cops are funny. I'm trying to get more serious, and Kate is trying to see the funny side of terrorists.

Away from the job, we get along well. I wondered, though, how we'd do in Yemen, where we'd be on the job together 24/7. Maybe she'd appreciate my cowboy style better in a place where the only law is a man with a gun. Better yet, maybe we'd never find out.

I asked for a table and was happy to learn it would be a thirty-minute wait. 'Another round,' I said to the bartender. Can't walk on one leg.

Kate said to me, 'If we don't take this assignment, your contract may not be renewed, and I may wind up in Washington.'

'He's bluffing.'

'He's not.'

'I don't respond well to threats,' I assured her.

'It's not a threat. It's a transfer.'

'Whatever.'

'Would you live in Washington?'

'I'd rather live in Yemen.'

'Good. We'll be together. In a year, we'll be back in New York.'

'Right. It's that year in Yemen that might be a career killer.'

She didn't reply.

Regarding my last visit to Yemen in August 2001, the same month I was there, Kate was in Dar es Salaam, Tanzania, as a legat investigating the 1998 US Embassy bombing, which was an Al Qaeda attack, planned by Osama bin Laden, whose name was then unknown to most of the American public. A short time after Kate and I returned from our respective overseas assignments, Osama bin Laden and Al Qaeda both became famous for murdering three thousand people.

Our separate assignments overseas, by the way, were a sort of punishment – or a warning – resulting from my and Kate's unauthorized snooping into the mysterious mid-air explosion of TWA Flight 800. So off we went. Kate to Dar es Salaam, which was not such a bad place to be, and me to Yemen, which is like the Siberia of the Task Force, though I did feel like I was doing something useful. We returned to New York a few days apart, as I said, just in time for September 11. Tom Walsh was not the boss then, so I can't say he was now making another effort at adjusting my attitude. So what was he up to? Kate was taking this at face value. I was not. Tom doesn't do things *for* people; he does things *to* people. Also, this came from higher up. John Corey has to go to Yemen. But why?

Anyway, all this was running through my mind as I stood at the bar in Ecco's, observing Western civilization at its best or worst, thinking about my career, my marriage, my country, my life, and my future.

I normally don't reflect on any of this, and I pride myself on a low level of introspection and zero self-awareness. But I'd just been unexpectedly presented with a life-changing choice, and I needed to think about my response.

Kate asked me, 'What are you thinking about?'

'There's a new Monet exhibit at the Met.'

She looked doubtful, then said, 'John . . . if you don't want to go, I will understand.'

I said to her, 'You should take my word that this is not a place you want to be for a year.'

She reminded me, 'A lot of our people are or were there. And we have troops in places like Iraq and Afghanistan who are making great sacrifices every day.' She informed me, 'You can't pick where you want to fight a war. You have to go where the enemy is.'

'They're *here*, Kate,' I reminded her. 'We're manning the ramparts of Fortress America.'

She thought about that, then said, 'We've done a good job here. But now we need to go into the belly of the beast.'

'The asshole,' I corrected.

Our table was ready, and as we made our way through the restaurant, who should I see but my ex, sitting with yet another beau. I mean, this lady has had more mounts than a Pony Express rider.

She saw me and waved, so I went to her table and said hello and got introduced to Mr Right Now, who looked like he was about halfway through a sex change operation.

Kate, who is cool about this, said hello to Robin and her date, and Robin asked us, 'How's the war on terrorism going?'

I informed her, 'The alert level is still yellow.'

Robin didn't respond to that, but said, 'God, sometimes I think they're going to blow this place up.'

Kate had a nice comeback and said, 'Why would anyone want to kill lawyers, judges, and politicians?'

Robin wasn't sure how to take that and asked me, 'Are you still in the apartment?'

The apartment in question is the former marital residence, a very expensive place on East 72nd Street that Robin had lived in when I met her. She'd signed over the long-term lease to me on her way out, a very nice gesture that took care of most of my monthly income. I said, 'Still there.'

'Good. I wanted to send you both an invitation for a fund-raiser I'm running. It's for the Downtown Association for the Arts.' She explained, 'To raise money to commission artists to create murals and sculpture in Lower Manhattan.'

More shit.

'It's at the downtown Ritz-Carlton. Black tie. March twenty-sixth. You'll be my guests.'

I found myself saying, 'Thanks, but we'll be out of the country.'

'Where are you going?'

'Classified.'

'Oh … well … good luck.'

'Thanks.'

We followed the hostess to our table, and Kate asked me, 'Does that mean you'd rather go to Yemen with me than a black-tie fund-raiser with your ex-wife?'

'You know I'd follow you to hell.'

'Good. We leave next week.'

CHAPTER FIVE

It was Saturday, and Kate and I agreed not to discuss Yemen until Sunday evening.

Kate went to the office Saturday morning to clean up some paperwork and to identify cases that she would need to hand off if, in fact, she was going to Yemen.

I had an appointment with a guy named Nabeel, who coincidentally was from Yemen. I didn't know Nabeel, but he'd called the ATTF office, using only his first name, asking for me by my full name, and saying to me that we had a mutual friend. I doubt that, but that's how I get half of my contacts in the Muslim community; my business card is all over town. Well, Muslim neighborhoods. It pays to advertise.

My brief phone conversation with Nabeel revealed that his legal status in the country was a little shaky, and he wanted some help with that in exchange for some information he had. Nabeel worked in a delicatessen in Brooklyn, so I wasn't sure what kind of information he had for me. Phoney baloney? Exploding beans?

A little-known factoid is that many Yemeni immigrants work in delis in Brooklyn and Queens. Why? Who knows? Why do the Turks own so many gas stations? Why do Indians own all the 7-Elevens? Who cares as long as the Irish still run the pubs?

Anyway, I told Nabeel to meet me in Ben's Kosher Deli on West 38th Street, a place unlikely to be frequented by others of the Islamic faith – though, ironically, kosher food is halal, meaning okay for Muslims, so this works.

And here I was now in Ben's, sitting in a booth across from Nabeel. He had to get back to his deli in Bay Ridge, Brooklyn, so this was going to be a happily short meeting.

Nabeel looked to be about mid-thirties, but he was probably younger, with a scruffy beard, dark skin, and teeth stained green by khat – a narcotic leaf that keeps ninety percent of the male population of Yemen perpetually stoned and happy. I wished I had some now.

Nabeel ordered tea and a bagel with hummus, and I had coffee.

I asked Nabeel, 'Where did you get my name?'

'I tell you on phone. From friend.' He also reminded me, 'Can not tell you friend.'

'Was it Abdul?'

'Who Abdul?'

'Which Abdul. Who's on first?'

'Sir?'

'Talk.'

Nabeel talked. 'There is big plot from peoples of Al Qaeda.

36

Saudi peoples. No Yemen. All Saudi. Plot is to make bomb exploding in New York.'

'Can you be a little more specific?' And maybe grammatical?

'Yes? What more?'

'Bomb where? When? Who?'

'I have all information. I give you. I need work visa.'

Maybe I could give him my visa to Yemen. I asked him, 'You have ID on you? Passport?'

'No.'

They never do. I really didn't want to speak to this guy unless I could see his passport, so I said to him, 'I need you to come to my office.' I took a card from my pocket and asked him, 'What's your last name?'

He gave me a scrap of paper on which his name was written in badly formed Latin letters — Nabeel al-Samad — saying to me, 'I copy this from passport.' He said proudly, 'I can sign name.'

'Wonderful.' I wrote on the back of my business card, *Nabeel al-Samad to see Det. Corey.* I signed it, dated it, and handed it to him, saying, 'I'll have an Arabic translator and I'll have someone from Immigration for you to talk to. Capisce?'

'Yes? You arrest me in office?'

'No. I can arrest you here.' And fuck up my day. Not to mention yours.

'Talk here first.'

'Okay. Talk.'

Nabeel confided that he was in contact with people who knew more about this bomb plot, but he needed more time — like a six-month visa — to get the details. Sounded like bullshit. But you never know.

Finally, he agreed to come into the office on Monday if he could get the morning off. These guys work twelve-hour days, six or seven days a week, and they send what amounts to a fortune home to their wife and ten kids. A deli in Brooklyn is like a gold mine in Yemen.

I asked him, 'Where you from in Yemen?'

He named some place that sounded like 'Ali Baba.'

'You like it there?'

'Yes. Beautiful country. Good people.'

'Then why do you want to stay here?'

'No work in Yemen. I go home, two months. Three months. See family. Come again here. Go again Yemen.'

A Yemeni jet-setter. I tore a sheet out of my notebook, gave it to him with a pen, and said, 'Write your info.'

Unfortunately, he couldn't write English beyond his name, so I said, 'In Arabic.' No luck. Illiterate in two languages. 'Spanish?'

'Sir?'

Three languages. I asked him the name of his deli in Brooklyn, his place of residence, and his cell phone number.

He spoke — slowly, please — and I wrote in my notebook, saying to him, 'I want to see you Monday morning at 26 Federal Plaza or I'll send a police car to pick you up. Have your passport with you. And your visa — expired or not. They'll have your name at security. Bring my card. Understand?'

He nodded.

I dialed the cell number he'd given me and it rang in his pocket. Trust, but verify. I threw a twenty on the table and left.

I was supposed to meet Kate at the Met to see the stupid Monet exhibit. I should learn to keep my mouth shut.

I had some time, so I began walking the forty blocks. Good exercise.

I thought about Nabeel. Most informants have or can get you some information, or they wouldn't come to you. All of them want something in return. I've never seen a Mideastern inform- ant who just wanted to do their civic duty to their adopted country. In Nabeel's case, as with most of them, he wanted per- manent citizenship or a green card in return for ratting out someone. Sometimes they just wanted money. Money for inform- ants was easy – green cards not so easy. Meanwhile, I still can't figure out why they want to live here. Could it be that their beau- tiful countries suck?

I have a theory about immigration. Wherever you were born, stay there.

Kate and I made cell phone contact and met at the Met. We had lunch in the museum restaurant, then went to the Monet exhibit. Was this guy going blind? Or do I need glasses? Saturday night we joined two other couples at Michael Jordan's Steak House. This is a cool place. Cholesterol and testosterone.

The restaurant is located on the balcony above the Grand Central Station Concourse, with an overhead view of the famous clock under which lovers and others meet. I watched the mass of humanity arriving and departing by train – a scene that hasn't changed much in a hundred years, except now there were soldiers and police watching everything. No one seemed to notice them anymore; they were part of life now. That sucks.

Cops tend to hang with cops, but I've expanded my social circle since joining the Task Force, and tonight we were with Feds. Fortunately, the two guys, Ed Burke and Tony Savino, were ex-cops like me, working for the Feds like everyone else these days. One of the wives, Ann Burke, was an MOS – Member of the Service – and still on the job, working in the 103rd Precinct. The other lady, Marie Savino, was a stay-at-home mom with two crumb snatchers under five and one in the oven.

Which gave me an idea. If Kate were to get pregnant – like about four hours from now – then the Yemen thing was off. I reached under the table and ran my hand over her thigh. She smiled.

Anyway, we tend not to talk business when we're out, but tonight I said, 'Kate and I have been asked to apply for a posting to Yemen.'

Ed Burke, a former NYPD detective with the Intelligence Unit, advised, 'Just say no.'

Tony Savino said, 'I know two guys who were there.'

I inquired, 'What do they say about it?'

'I don't know. No one has ever heard from them again.'

This got a big laugh. Cops have a sick sense of humor.

I informed everyone, 'I was actually there for a month in August 2001. The beaches are topless. You get your head blown off.'

Good laughs.

'John.'

'In Yemen, the men are men and the camels are nervous.'

'Enough, please,' said Kate.

So I dropped the subject.

But Tony said, 'Seriously, the two guys I knew who were there said there's no place safe outside the American Embassy.' He added, 'They know who you are when you get off the plane, and you have a target on your back every time you move.'

I already knew that. And now Kate had heard it from someone else — but she did not waver. In fact, she's stubborn. She said, 'If we don't go, someone else will have to go.'

Hard to argue with that. But the problem, as I saw it when I was there, was that we had a very small American presence in a very hostile environment. A recipe for disaster. Ask General Custer about that.

We dropped the subject completely, or so I thought until Ed Burke said to the waiter, 'I'll have the camel dick on a stick.'

Everyone's a comedian. Sunday morning we got up late and I offered to make breakfast. I asked Kate, 'Do you feel like pickles and ice cream?'

'What?'

'You should make sure you're not pregnant before we see Walsh tomorrow.'

'John, I'm on the pill.'

'Right. How about scrambled eggs?'

We had breakfast, read the *New York Times*, and watched a few morning news shows. The BBC is really the best source of world news that Americans don't give a shit about, and we tuned in just in time to discover that there was yet another civil war going on in Yemen.

Apparently some tribal leader in the north named Hussein al-Houthi was trying to topple the government in Sana'a and restore the Imam to power and create an Islamic fundamentalist state. Hussein, according to the reporter with the British accent, wanted to kick out all the foreigners and infidels in the country and return Yemen to Sharia law. Not a bad idea. Kicking foreigners out, I mean. Me first. Hussein also wanted to cut off the head of

41

Yemen's longtime dictator president, a guy named Ali Abdullah Saleh. Hussein sounded like a guy who took the fun out of fundamentalist.

Kate hit the mute button and said to me, 'I didn't realize there was a war going on there.'

'There's always a war going on there.' I inquired, 'Did you know that Yemen has the highest ratio of guns to people in the whole world?' I explained, 'They have to do *something* with those guns.'

She didn't reply, but I could sense she was rethinking her year abroad. We belong to a health club on East 39th Street, and we spent a few hours there, burning off the beef fat from Michael Jordan's and sweating out the red wine.

Kate and I stay in pretty good shape, and we also spend time at the pistol range. If we were FBI accountants, we probably wouldn't bother with any of this.

I needed a drink after the health club, so we walked up to Dresner's, a neighborhood pub where they know my name too well.

We took a table near the window and ordered two beers to rehydrate.

Kate asked, 'Do you want to talk about Yemen now?'

I replied, 'I thought that was a done deal.'

'Well . . . I'm still leaning toward it, but I want you to go with me.'

What she actually wanted was for me to talk her out of it. My role – if I choose to accept it – is that of bad guy. But I didn't want to play that role or that game. I said, 'If you're going, I'm going.'

'I don't want you to do something you don't want to do.'

'I want to do whatever you want to do, darling.'

'Well ... maybe we should weigh the pros and cons.'

I couldn't think of a single pro, but in the spirit of weighing all the issues, I said, 'Maybe your parents could come for a long visit.'

She seemed a little annoyed and said to me, 'If you're going to be flippant about this, then I say we should just go.'

'Okay with me.'

End of discussion. Right? Well, no. It doesn't work that way. She said, 'I don't think you mean that.'

Obviously Ms. Mayfield was wavering, and I was elected to give her the push one way or the other. I could have killed this thing right then and there, but I was taking some perverse pleasure in this. I mean, she was gung-ho for Yemen on Friday, but now some reality had set in.

Oddly enough, I was starting to think of some reasons why we *should* go. Not good reasons, but reasons — the biggest being that like most husbands, I sometimes let my wife do something I've advised against, which gives me the pleasure of saying, 'I *told* you so!' I was actually looking forward to that moment. I pictured us in the desert with an overheated vehicle — maybe with bullet holes in the radiator and all the tires shot out — surrounded by Bedouin tribesmen with AK-47s. As I was slamming a magazine into my Glock, I'd look at her and say, 'I *told* you so!'

'What are you smiling at?'

'Oh ... I was just thinking about ... how beautiful the desert is at night. Lots of stars.'

The waitress came by and I ordered a bacon cheeseburger with fries and another beer. Kate did the same. Hey, life is short. I informed Kate, 'Not much beer or pork in Yemen.'

'If we go, I don't want to hear you complaining for a year.'

'I'm not a complainer.'

'That's a joke – right?'

'Complaining is a New York thing. It's an art.'

'It's annoying.'

'Okay. I won't complain in Yemen. No one there gives a shit anyway.' I added, 'Or they just kill you. End of complaint.'

She suppressed a smile.

I said, 'There's actually an off-Broadway theater in Sana'a, and they've got a long-running musical called "Guys and Goats".' I broke into a show tune: 'I got the goat right here, the name is al-Amir—'

She reminded me, 'You're an idiot.' Back in our expensive apartment, we had coffee and watched some TV. The History Channel had yet another documentary about the end of the world, this one about the End of Days, as predicted by the Mayan calendar. December 21, 2012, to be exact. But they weren't saying what *time* this was going to happen. I mean, you wouldn't want to be sleeping and miss it.

Anyway, I felt like a cigar, so I went out to the balcony, lit up, and looked out over the city. It was a clear, cold night and I had great views to the south, and from here on the 34th floor I could see where I worked. We used to be able to see the Twin Towers, and after they were gone we could see the smoke rising for weeks, and then a few weeks later twin light beams rose high into the sky to symbolize the Towers. And now there was nothing.

Kate came out wearing a coat and carrying one for me. 'Put this on.'

Real men don't wear coats while they're smoking a cigar on their balcony — but I put it on.

We didn't speak for a while, and we watched the moon rising over the magical lights of Manhattan Island.

Finally, Kate said, 'I'm actually going to miss New York.'

'You'll appreciate it even more when you get back.'

She said, 'This is obviously not a routine foreign assignment. This is something important. And Tom is showing confidence in us by asking us to take the job.'

'It's very flattering,' I agreed.

'Which is why it's hard to say no.'

'I thought we were saying yes. But if you want to say no, that's easy.' I reminded her, 'I signed on for domestic anti-terrorist work. So I have no legal or moral obligation to go to Yemen or anywhere else outside the US. You're in a different position. So if you feel you need to go, I'll go with you.'

She thought about that, then replied, 'Thank you.' She said, 'This may be a chance for us to make a difference. To actually apprehend the mastermind of the Cole attack.'

'Right.'

I looked toward the skyline where the Towers once stood. We'd both lost some good friends that day. And tens of thousands of other people lost friends, family, and neighbors. We were all heartbroken. Now we're pissed.

Kate stayed quiet awhile, then said, 'I really wouldn't have gone without you.'

'You would have. But you're not.'

We went inside and I settled into my soft leather La-Z-Boy recliner. I was really going to miss this chair.

Kate was curled up on the couch with her laptop, and she said to me, 'You were right — Yemen has the highest ratio of guns to people in the world.'

'It's a typical baby shower gift.'

She also informed me, 'It's the most impoverished, backward, and isolated country in the Mideast.'

'And that's from the Ministry of Tourism. Wait until you read what the critics say.'

'Over a hundred Westerners — tourists, scholars, and businesspeople — have been kidnapped in the last ten years and held for ransom. Some were killed.'

I didn't respond.

She continued, 'Did you know that Yemen is the ancestral homeland of Osama bin Laden?'

'I did. It's also the homeland of Nabeel al-Samad.'

'Who?'

'My breakfast date.'

'He was Yemeni? Did you talk to him about Yemen?'

'Yeah. He said don't drink the water.'

She went back to her computer and informed me, 'Yemen is known as the Land That Time Forgot.'

'Sounds romantic.'

'In ancient times, it was the Kingdom of Sheba — where the Queen of Sheba came from.'

'Where's she living now?'

'She's biblical. King Solomon's lover.'

'Right. As long as you're up, can you get me a beer?'

'I'm not up.' She read her screen silently for a minute or two, then said, 'This place is a shithole.'

'What was your first clue?'

'You never said much about it when you got back.'

'I don't like to complain.'

I launched myself out of my chair and got two beers from the refrigerator. I handed one to Kate and said, 'You understand that if we tell Tom we're going, and he tells us more about this, then there's no turning back.'

'Tom thinks this is right for us and I trust him.'

'I don't. Tom only knows part of this. We get the real deal after we land.' I added, 'It's like quicksand.'

'I'm still in. As long as you promise that after we get there, you won't say, "I told you so".'

'That's the only reason I'm going.'

'No, we're going there to apprehend the man who master-minded the murder of seventeen American servicemen.'

'Correct.' We clinked bottles and drank.

CHAPTER SIX

Monday morning.

Kate and I got to 26 Federal Plaza at 8 A.M.

The lobby elevators are surrounded by thick Plexiglas walls and a Plexiglas door with a security pad. I punched us in and greeted the three armed and uniformed security guards, who are actually FBI Police. I gave the senior guy, Larry, my card, on the back of which I'd written Nabeel's info, and told him, 'Arab gent to see me. He's supposed to show in the A.M. If he's late or he doesn't have his passport, beat the shit out of him until I get down.'

Larry thought that was funny. Kate, Ms. FBI poster girl, pretended she didn't hear that. But on the way up in the elevator, she said to me, 'Tom's right. You'll do better overseas.'

'I do just fine here.'

'Every Islamic civil rights group in the city has a wanted poster of you hanging in their office.'

I assured her, 'I just joke around.'

'Like when you punched that Iranian U.N. diplomat in the groin?'

'He slammed his nuts into my fist.'

Anyway, we got to our office on the 26th floor and separated. Kate is in the FBI cube farm, I'm on the NYPD side. The FBI gets more sunlight, but the cops are closer to the elevators.

I gave ICE a call. Immigration and Customs Enforcement is in the same building and they work closely with us. I explained to a woman I know there, Betty Alvarez, that I had a possible informant and he had a work visa problem. I gave her the info from my notebook, and she said she'd try to check him out in her data bank. She asked, 'Do you have his passport info?'

'No. But if he shows, I will.'

'Okay. Call me later.'

'Right.' I asked her, 'Are you here legally?'

'John, fuck off.'

'Okay. Thanks.'

I was feeling a little nuts this morning, a result no doubt of the liberating effect of my pending departure to Siberia.

I used my landline phone to call Alim Rasul. Alim is NYPD, working for the Task Force. He was born in Iraq, but now lives in Brooklyn and calls himself Al.

He answered, and I said, 'Are you around this morning?'

There was a second of silence, then he asked, 'Is this Corey?'

'Yeah. Are you around?'

'John, I'm sitting right next to you.'

'Good. Do you speak Arabic?'

'Why are you calling me on the phone?'

'This is a secure landline.'

'You're a fucking idiot.'

'*Me?* You're the one still talking on the phone.'

He hung up and came around to my cube. 'What can I do for you?'

I explained about Nabeel and said, 'I need you to be in the interview room.'

'To translate?'

'No, Al. I just need you to hold him while I headbutt him.'

Al smiled politely.

I said, 'I have to see Walsh at nine. If Nabeel shows while I'm with El Cid, maybe you can go down and get him.'

'Sure.'

I also informed him, 'I may be out of town for a while. Maybe you want to handle this guy.'

'Okay.' He asked, 'Where you going?'

'Sandland.'

'That's a derogatory term.'

'Sorry. I'm going to the shithole of Yemen.'

'You screw up?'

'Not recently.' I let him know, 'This is a promotion.'

He thought that was funny. He asked me, 'Kate?'

'She's coming.'

'Good. It's b.y.o.b. in Yemen.'

'Yeah? I thought the babes were hot.'

'No, it's the guys who will make you lose your head.'

So, with all the cultural jokes and slurs out of the way, I thanked Al for sitting in on the interview – formerly known as the interrogation – and I promised to bring him back a crucifix from Yemen.

I spent the next half hour on my computer, reviewing and updating my cases for whoever was going to get them.

Kate came over to my desk and said it was time to go see Tom.

On the way up the elevator to Tom's office, she asked me, 'Are we still okay with this?'

'I've always wanted to go to Sweden.'

'It's Yemen, John.'

'Oh ... well, that's different.'

We got off at the 28th floor – housewares, supervisors, aggro, and bullshit – and walked to Tom's door.

I was about to knock and enter, but Kate said, 'Last chance.'

I knocked on the door and said to her, 'You make the decision. Surprise me.' I added, 'Remember the Cole.'

I opened the door and we entered.

CHAPTER SEVEN

T om stood and greeted us at his desk. He asked, 'How was your weekend?'

I informed him, 'We saw the Monet exhibit at the Met.' And I got laid Saturday night. How about you?

All the pleasantries aside, he asked us, 'So have you reached a decision?'

Kate, without even a glance at me, said to Tom, 'We'll take the assignment.'

He smiled. 'Good. Have a seat.'

There's a grouping of armchairs and a couch around a coffee table that Tom uses for important people, or people he needs to screw nicely, and Kate and I took the chairs facing the window. Tom sat on the couch and began, 'First, I want to say that I appreciate your willingness to accept this overseas assignment.'

And so on. We got a short speech that he probably gives to everyone who's going off to some craphole or another.

I interrupted Tom's good-bye, good-luck speech and asked, 'Are you going to tell us what this is about?'

He feigned surprise at the question and replied, 'It's pretty much what I said Friday.' He elaborated, 'One of the three masterminds who were behind the Cole attack is in Yemen. He has been indicted in absentia. You will be part of a team that is looking for him.'

I asked, 'What do we do with him when we find him?'

'You arrest him.'

'And?'

'And, we will extradite him to the US. Or maybe to Guantanamo.'

'Right. But as I was told when I was there, and as you probably know, Tom, the Yemeni constitution specifically forbids extradition of any Yemeni citizen for any reason – including terrorism and murder.'

'Yes ... that's true. But they make exceptions. And that's what Kate will be working on as our legal attaché.'

'They haven't made an exception yet, but okay.' I asked him, just to set the record straight, 'Are you sure we're not supposed to terminate this guy?'

He informed me, 'We don't assassinate people.'

'We don't assassinate people,' I agreed. 'But we have used Predator drones with Hellfire missiles in Yemen and elsewhere to ... let's say ... vaporize about fifty or a hundred people.'

'That's different.'

'I'm sure the vaporized guys understood that.'

Tom seemed a little impatient with me and said, 'I'll give you both a piece of information that you will get in Yemen. This suspect holds an American passport. He claims dual citizenship – Yemen and US. So yes, we have a good case with the Yemeni government for extradition.' He also reminded us, 'We don't kill US citizens.'

'Actually we do if they're enemy combatants. Also, as you know, if we do apprehend him and turn him over to the Yemenis, we may never see him again.' I reminded him, 'Some of the Cole plotters were captured, put in Yemeni jails, and miraculously escaped.'

Tom nodded, then said, 'Let's not get too far ahead of ourselves. First things first. First, we need to apprehend this man.'

'Right. So to recap, we find this Yemeni with US citizenship, turn him over to the Yemeni government, and hope they give him back to us.'

'Correct.'

'Can we at least torture him? Just a little?'

Tom asked, 'Any other questions?'

Kate asked, 'What is this man's name?'

'You'll be given his name when you get there. But he goes by the nom de guerre of al-Numair. Means The Panther.'

It seems to be my fate to get mixed up with Arabs who name themselves after big cats. The last guy was Asad – The Lion. Now I've got a panther to deal with. Hopefully, the next one will call himself Kitty.

Anyway, it seemed to me that Tom wanted to say as little as possible at this end. Or he didn't know much.

In fact, he said to us, 'To be honest with you, I don't have a need-to-know, and what I know is what you now know. You'll be fully briefed when you get there.'

Since Kate and I were about to depart on a dangerous mission into a hostile country, I felt I could be a little disrespectful of Tom with no consequences, so I reminded him, 'You indicated Friday that what you were going to tell us was classified, and that once we heard it, we were committed to the assignment. Correct?'

He nodded.

I continued, 'What we've heard is nothing. We could get up, go back to work, and forget about Yemen.'

'I suppose you could. But that wouldn't make me happy. Or you happy.'

'Okay, let's try a different approach. On a scale of one to ten, how dangerous is this mission?'

He thought about a reply, then said, 'Capturing a top-ranking Al Qaeda leader is dangerous.'

'One to ten.'

'Ten.'

'Because?'

'Should be obvious.' He explained the obvious, 'He'll be guarded, he'll be in hostile territory, he's aware that he's a target, and our resources and assets in Yemen are scarce.'

'Right. And we're not going to vaporize him with a Hellfire missile because . . . ?'

'I suppose because we want him alive. To interrogate him.'

'So we're not really turning him over to the Yemeni government. Our job is to kill his bodyguards, take him alive, and sneak him out of the country for interrogation.'

'You'll be briefed over there.' He added, 'As I said, you'll be part of a team.'

Kate asked, 'Who is on this team?'

'I have no idea.'

Kate had an important question. 'If we're detained by the Yemeni government, who comes to our aid?'

'The embassy. You'll both have diplomatic immunity, of course.'

Love that diplomatic immunity. It works about half the time

when you get caught breaking the local laws. The other half of the time, the embassy can't seem to remember your name.

I thought I understood one reason why Kate and I were chosen to participate in what amounted to a Black Ops mission. It had to do with my cover and Kate's cover. Officially, the US was there only to aid the Yemeni security forces in investigating the *Cole* bombing, and our FBI personnel, people like me, rotated into and out of the country on a regular basis. As long as we kept the numbers small and didn't stay too long, the Yemeni government was okay with Americans operating on their soil.

Most of the Americans doing anti-terrorist work were attached to the embassy for cover – as Kate would be – so that the Yemeni government could take the public position that their country hadn't become an American ally or outpost. In fact, if the USS *Cole* hadn't been bombed in Aden Harbor, we wouldn't have anyone in Yemen except a small embassy staff. But now we had our foot in the door – or in this case, the Yemenis had let the camel get his nose under the tent. But they didn't want the whole camel sleeping inside.

And for all those reasons, the CIA was not welcome, but a few CIA officers were tolerated.

I asked Tom, 'Is the CIA involved in this operation?'

'I'm sure you'll find out when you get there.'

'I'm sure we will.' I reminded him, 'You said this guy was Al Qaeda.'

'Did I?' Tom 'fessed up, 'He's actually the head of the Yemen branch of a newly formed group called Al Qaeda in the Arabian Peninsula – AQAP.'

'Thanks for sharing.'

He reminded me, 'You have no need to know this now, and you didn't hear it from me. When you get there, you'll know more than I know. But I will tell you that this guy is wanted for other crimes aside from the Cole bombing.'

'Such as?'

'The usual. Murder, kidnapping, conspiracy, and so forth.' Tom added, 'He's killed a lot of people – Yemenis, Europeans, and Saudis – before and after the Cole.' He let us know, 'Most terrorist activities in Yemen can be traced to The Panther.'

'Bad dude,' I observed.

'One of the worst,' Tom agreed. He added, 'And a traitor to his country.'

'He's an asshole.' I asked, 'Is there a bounty on this guy's head?'

'The Justice Department is offering five million.'

'Not bad. Dead or alive?'

'Either.'

'How much do we get to keep?'

'None of it.' He reminded us, 'You get a paycheck every two weeks.'

'Will the Justice Department use the reward money to spring us if we wind up kidnapped or in a Yemeni jail?'

He replied, 'I'll make sure of that for Kate.' He smiled. 'You're on your own.'

I smiled in return. Tom *can* be funny. Especially when the joke is on me. I asked him, 'Are you going to miss me?'

'No.'

He stood, and we stood. He said to us, 'Make sure you go to

the Medical Office today, and call the Travel Office. I've asked Legal Affairs to assist you with whatever you need. Also, I'll set up a meeting for you with the Office of International Affairs – for a cultural awareness briefing.'

Oh, God. Not that. Before my last trip to Yemen, I'd managed to avoid this four-hour State Department lecture, but I'd heard about it from other guys who'd had to sit through it. I said, 'That's cruel, Tom.'

'It's mandatory for Kate,' he informed me, 'but I know you'll both benefit from it.' He concluded, 'You have until Thursday to put your personal affairs in order. I'll see you here Friday, ten A.M., for a final briefing and contact info in Sana'a. You leave Friday night. Any questions?'

Neither Kate nor I had any further questions, so we all shook hands and we left.

On the way to the elevator, Kate said, 'I can't believe we're going to Yemen to capture one of the masterminds of the Cole bombing – the head of Al Qaeda in Yemen.'

She sounded excited, but maybe a little apprehensive. Indeed, this was a big deal with a big upside for us professionally, and a big victory for the home team if we got our man. The downside was also big – like, we could get killed or captured. I've come to terms a long time ago with getting killed. But getting captured by terrorists in a foreign country was, as they say, a fate worse than death.

'John? Are you still good with this?'

I didn't recall ever being good with this. But I do like a challenge. And I was still pissed about how I and the other FBI agents in Yemen had been jerked around by the Yemeni police and their political security force when I was there. They were playing both sides in the *Cole* investigation, not letting us do our job and also tipping off the bad guys. Great allies. Actually, assholes. So this was a chance for me to shove it up their butts.

'John?'

'There is an old Arabic saying — "It is easier to kick a camel in the balls than it is to capture a black panther who's eating your ass".'

'Do you have more of those?'

'I'm afraid so.'

'Can you keep them to yourself?'

'Maybe they sound better in Arabic.'

'This is going to be a long year.'

'Be optimistic. We'll be dead before then.'

CHAPTER EIGHT

I got back to my desk, and Al Rasul informed me that he'd called downstairs, but Nabeel hadn't shown up yet.

It was still early, so there was no reason to send a cop car to get him. I did call Nabeel's cell phone, and it went to voicemail — Arabic and English. I left a message in English, then gave the phone to Al, who left the same message in Arabic — except Al's tone was very sharp. He explained to me, 'That's how the police talk to citizens in Sandland.'

'Right.' Anyway, Nabeel al-Samad was the least of my priorities today, but you have to follow up on everything because sure as hell the thing you didn't follow up on is what comes back to bite you in the ass. The people who dropped the ball on the pre-9/11 clues can verify that.

I gave Al a pencil and said, 'Transliterate the Arabic word for "panther" into real letters.'

'"Panther"?'

'Yeah. Big black cat.'

He took a scrap of paper from my desk and said, 'There are a few ways to transliterate . . .' He wrote, *Nimr — Nimar — Numair*, and said, 'The last is maybe the most standard transliteration.' He pronounced the word for me.

'You need a tissue?'

He asked me, 'What's with panther?'

'If I tell you, I have to kill you.'

'Anything else I can do for you today?'

'Yeah, if Nabeel shows up.' I added, 'Thanks.'

Al's a good guy and he takes a lot of crap well. But he also knows how to dish it out. If you're an Arab and you work here, you have to have a sense of humor — and very thick skin. I wondered why Al Rasul wasn't asked to go to Yemen. Right?

I checked my email and found a note from Tom to me and Kate telling us that we were expected at Legal Affairs and the Medical Office before noon. I've never seen government workers move this fast. Tom really wanted us out of here, which compelled me into some paranoid thought processes, and the word 'expendable' kept popping into my mind.

I had an email from Betty Alvarez informing me that she had

no info on a Yemeni male named Nabeel al-Samad. She asked for his passport info and visa, if any. I replied: *Still waiting for subject to show.*

I used my ATTF password to access the internal files on ACS – the Automated Case Support system. I didn't have a case name, but I typed in 'USS *Cole*,' which got me hundreds of hits, though probably nothing I didn't already know. I typed in 'Panther,' which got me nothing, then 'Numair' – thank you, Al – which got me a file that said 'Restricted,' followed by rows of Xs. Usually you get something, even on the restricted files, like when the file was opened, what the classification level was, and who to see about getting access to the file. But apparently all this was above my pay grade, and all I saw was 'Numair' and Xs. Well, at least Walsh didn't make that up.

I emailed Walsh and asked him about getting access to the Numair file, based on my recent need-to-know.

A few minutes later, he replied: *Your need-to-know begins when you're in Yemen. P.S. Stop snooping.* He didn't actually write that, but that was the message.

Kate came over to my desk and asked, 'Where to first? Legal or Medical?'

'Medical. We need our heads examined.'

'That could take all day. Legal first.'

The FBI Legal Affairs Office here normally deals with cases, warrants, wiretaps, documents, and so forth, and not with employees' problems or work assignments. But this was a special case, and it needed to be done on an expedited basis.

We had a few papers to sign, including a new confidentiality statement, and also a statement having to do with 'interrogation under duress.' As I signed it, I said, 'As a married man, I am an expert on interrogation under duress.'

No laughs.

Our wills were on file and we checked them over, then we were given powers of attorney to fill out and sign. Jennifer, a young lawyer I'd seen before my first trip to Yemen, explained, 'This is in case you're abducted or go missing.'

I asked, 'So we just show this to our kidnappers?'

'No. You—'

Kate interrupted and explained to me, 'If we're dead, the executors of our wills handle our affairs. But if we're missing or unlawfully imprisoned, then someone has to act on our behalf — someone to write checks, pay our bills, and so forth. It doesn't have to be an actual attorney.' She inquired, 'Didn't you do this last time?'

'Right. I named you as my attorney-in-fact.'

'Good. We'll name each other. But ... if we share the same fate, we'll need an alternate.'

This was getting a little heavy.

Kate said, 'It should be a family member.' She suggested, 'How about my father?'

Am I related to him? I mean, what if we both wound up kidnapped or missing, then got free and found out that her father had spent all our money on his collection of J. Edgar Hoover memorabilia?

'John?'

'Yeah. Fine.' They'll never take me alive anyway.

We filled out the forms, signed them, and Jennifer notarized them.

Finally, Jennifer produced our black diplomatic passports, which had been kept in a safe since our last make-believe diplomatic assignments to Tanzania and Yemen.

Jennifer also informed us that the State Department had called the Yemeni consulate office and our visas should be ready after 1 P.M. for us to pick up.

There aren't many Americans who go to Yemen, so by now our Yemeni allies were aware that John Corey and Kate Mayfield would be arriving soon. Maybe they'd have someone at the airport to greet us.

Another thought popped into my head — a thought about the speed of all this paperwork — and I asked Jennifer, 'When did State call the Yemeni consulate about our visas?'

She replied, 'Thursday.'

Kate and I glanced at each other. *Thursday?*

Anyway, we finished up with Jennifer, who said, 'You get to do exciting things. I wish I was going.'

I wish you were, too, Jennifer.

As we walked down the hallway, Kate said, '*Thursday?*'

'The Friday meeting was just a formality. Yemen is our fate. It is written in the sands of time.'

No reply. Clearly she was not happy with her friend Tom. Good.

I said to Kate, 'By the way, I went into ACS and there's a file called Numair, which is Arabic for "panther", and it's restricted.'

'Who do we see about getting access?'

'Didn't say.'

'Odd.' She suggested, 'We'll ask Tom.'

'Did that. He said go to Yemen.'

We took the elevator down to the nurse's office, where a young lady named Annie was expecting us.

Because Kate and I were scheduled for departure within five days, we couldn't get the shots spaced over the recommended seven days, and sweet Annie stuck us like we were voodoo dolls.

We got eight shots – diphtheria, dysentery, typhoid, anthrax, scarlet fever, and three diseases I've never heard of. I especially enjoyed the two shots in the butt. Annie gave us each a starter vial of malaria pills and said, 'Start taking these now.' She added, 'Come back Friday morning for the rest of the shots.'

'How many more diseases could there be?'

'Leprosy, for one.'

Jeez.

She advised us, 'You have a lot of vaccines in you, so you may not feel well later.'

'Can I have alcohol?'

'Sure. Just be close to a toilet.'

We went to Kate's desk, and she called the FBI Travel Office at Headquarters in DC.

Kate put it on speaker phone, and a woman answered, 'Travel Office. Mrs Barrett speaking. How may I help you?'

Kate said we were calling from the New York office, and she gave our names and our travel authorization numbers.

Mrs Barrett replied, 'Hold on ... yes, here you are. Sana'a.'

'Santa Ana,' I corrected. 'California.'

'No ... Sana'a. Yemen.'

Kate picked up the phone and disengaged the speaker, saying, 'Ready to copy.'

She listened to Mrs Barrett, made some notes, then said,

'Thank you,' and hung up. She said to me, 'American Airlines to London, British Airways to Cairo, Egyptair to Sana'a. First class.'

'Hard to believe there are no direct flights to Sana'a.'

'There are. From Cairo.'

'How do the deli guys get back and forth from Brooklyn?'

'I'm sure I don't know.' She informed me, 'If you really want to go direct, there is a military flight twice a week from Dover Air Force Base in Delaware. One to Sana'a, one to Aden.'

That was interesting. Sounded like we were getting our noses a little farther under the tent.

Kate said, 'If we want to go that way, Mrs Barrett will check it out. Departure times and days vary.'

'Yeah. Let's check it out. Might be interesting to see who and what is going to Yemen.' Also, this was probably the way we'd sneak The Panther out of Yemen. Direct US Air Force flight from Yemen to Guantanamo. The shithole to hellhole express.

I went back to my desk, and Al informed me that Nabeel had not shown. It was 12:15.

Al called Nabeel's cell phone, but got his voicemail again and left a loud message. I phoned the deli, a place named George's in Bay Ridge, and spoke to some guy with an accent who wasn't helpful. Al took the phone and spoke sharply in Arabic, then discovered that the guy was Mexican. Funny. What a great country.

Al volunteered to drive us to George's Deli, but I had lots to do and Brooklyn was not on that list. I suggested, 'Find one of our guys in the area and ask him to check out the deli and Nabeel's home address.'

'No, I'll go. I could use a break here. What's this guy look like?'

'Green teeth.' I described Nabeel's other features and related a

64

little of my short conversation with him in Ben's Deli. I suggested, 'See if this deli is under the eye for any reason. Maybe we have surveillance photos.'

'I did that. Nothing.'

'Okay. Thanks, Al. I owe you one.'

My next task was to go to a separate stand-alone computer where I could access the internet. We can't do that from our desk computers, or we'd be playing video games all day. I did a Google search on Al Qaeda in Yemen, and got a few hits on al-Numair, The Panther, and I actually got his real name from Wikipedia – Bulus ibn al-Darwish. No wonder he changed it.

Apparently some of this info was not as classified as Tom thought. In fact, there is little that is not available online if you know what you're looking for.

I checked out the Wikipedia entry. Bulus ibn al-Darwish, a.k.a. The Panther, was born in Perth Amboy, New Jersey, on May 8, 1965, making him thirty-nine years old in May, if he lived that long. So he was not a naturalized citizen – he was actually born here. Interesting.

His parents were both Yemenis who'd immigrated to America, but there was no further info on them. Dead? Alive? Living where?

Little Bulus attended public schools in New Jersey, then graduated from Columbia University in 1987 with a degree in economics – making him an Ivy League terrorist. He should have gone to Wall Street – same work, better pay.

At some point, according to the entry, Mr al-Darwish became radicalized and went to Yemen in the early 1990s.

The remainder of the entry was a mix of facts and speculation about his activities in Yemen, Saudi Arabia, and perhaps Iraq. He was identified as one of the planners of the attack on the USS *Cole* and also the 2002 attack on the French oil tanker *Limburg* in the Gulf of Aden.

Additionally, the subject asshole had been implicated in two or three armed attacks on Westerners in Sana'a, Aden, and the surrounding areas, resulting in a number of deaths and kidnappings. Plus, while he was at it, he'd planned two rocket attacks – one on the American Embassy in Sana'a, one on the Sheraton Hotel in Aden. Both attacks had been thwarted. The planned attack on the Sheraton interested me, because that's where I stayed with the other American personnel in Aden. We called the place Fort Apache.

And last but not least, Mr al-Darwish and some friends had been involved in a shoot-out at the Saudi Arabian border last year, resulting in the deaths of six Saudi soldiers.

Bottom line, this was a bad guy. Maybe fearless, maybe nuts, and definitely angry about something. Maybe he got teased in school.

Also, I'd never heard of this guy. And I knew the names of lots of terrorists. So this guy was being kept under wraps. Why? Probably because this was strictly a CIA case, and they were not sharing the info with the FBI. Until now. The Agency only talks to you when they need you.

I clicked next onto the website of the US Embassy in Sana'a and checked out Citizen Services and what's called Warden Messages. The Department of State, I saw, was concerned about Al Qaeda in the Arabian Peninsula and had issued a Travel Warning for Yemen regarding 'possible attacks by extremist individuals or groups against US citizens, facilities, businesses, and perceived interests.'

I guess that included the embassy itself, not to mention everyone working or visiting there.

The embassy website further informed me that 'travel on roads between cities throughout Yemen can be dangerous.' Really? 'Travel outside Sana'a is restricted.' Right. That's where those roads are. 'Travel in tribal areas north and east of Sana'a is particularly dangerous, and kidnappings are common.' Best to avoid the whole country.

There was also a mention of the ongoing civil war that Kate and I had seen reported on the BBC. This rebel leader, al-Houthi, was taking control of bigger parts of North Yemen. And that led me to wonder why anyone wanted to rule this fucked-up place.

So to recap, Yemen was ruled by a corrupt dictator, and the country was half overrun by a rebel leader, and the rest of the place was run by tribal warlords, except the areas that were infiltrated by Al Qaeda. Plus, the Red Sea and the Gulf of Aden were infested with pirates. The good news was that everyone was stoned on khat and didn't give a shit.

I read a last entry on the embassy website, which advised, 'From time to time, the US Embassy in Sana'a may temporarily close or suspend public services as necessary to review its security posture and its adequacy.'

With luck, they'd shut down before I got there.

Anyway, I could have spent a week surfing the internet, getting background on Yemen and Al Qaeda in the Arabian Peninsula and The Panther, but why bother? By Saturday or Sunday I'd be in the belly of the beast.

I logged off the computer and went back to my desk.

CHAPTER NINE

Kate and I decided to have lunch at Fraunces Tavern, the place where Washington gave his farewell address to his officers, and where I would now give my farewell address to Washington.

We exited 26 Federal Plaza onto Duane Street, which since 9/11 has been blocked to vehicles between Broadway and Lafayette on the theory that someone might want to detonate a car bomb under my window.

In fact, all of Lower Manhattan has become a security zone since that day, and though it's not too intrusive, it's annoying. More to the point, it's a constant reminder that these bastards have made America the front lines. So maybe taking the war to them is good quid pro quo.

We got to Fraunces Tavern, in business since about 1762, which is a lot of grog.

A hostess showed us to a table in the crowded main dining room. The clientele was mostly out-of-towners who wanted to tell the folks back in Peoria that they had lunch at the very table where George Washington dug his wooden choppers into a mutton chop.

Mindful of Nurse Annie's warning about mixing alcohol and

vaccine, I ordered club soda with a shot of scotch on the side. Does that work? Kate had a Coke, and we looked at the menus. Mostly traditional American fare. I said, 'I think I'll have the Yankee noodles.'

'Dandy.'

We ordered – sliced steak for me, a sissy salad for Kate.

There's another piece of history here that you won't find in most tour guides, but you will find on the Automated Case Support system – back in January 1975, a group of Puerto Rican separatists exploded a bomb here during lunch hour, killing four people and injuring more than fifty. I'm not sure what kind of statement they were trying to make, but the attack shocked the city and the nation, which was not then used to terrorism on American soil.

It was this attack, along with some other Puerto Rican separatist activities and the activities of the Irish Republican Army and the Black Panthers, that led to the formation of the Anti-Terrorist Task Force in New York in 1980.

Now the focus has shifted, and The Panther I was looking for was an Arab. But he wasn't here – he was in Yemen, by way of New Jersey and Columbia University. Hard to figure that out. I mean, I can figure out the foreign-born terrorists, but I can't figure out the increasing number of American-born Muslims who have defected to Islamic countries that they've never even seen, and who have taken up arms against America. What was *that* all about?

Kate asked me, 'What are you thinking about?'

'About when this place was bombed by the FALN. And I was also thinking about The Panther. Did you know he was born and educated in the US?'

'I did. I went on the internet after you did.'

'So why would a man who grew up in relative comfort, in a free society, and who went to one of the best universities in the country, choose to go to the backward and dangerous country that his parents had left, to engage in terrorist activities against the country of his birth?'

'When you find out, let me know.'

'But we need to find out why the melting pot is not working. There's something wrong in our thinking – or their thinking.'

'Maybe both.' She added, 'It's about jihad, but that doesn't fully explain it.' She observed, 'Even scarier is that John Corey is thinking about all this. What happened to the guy who used to say, "Nuke 'em all"?'

'Well … I guess because we're going to Yemen to find this American-born Islamic terrorist, I'd like to get into his head a little.' I added, 'It might help us.'

'It would, if we could do that.'

I thought a moment and said, 'When I worked Homicide, we did a lot of psychological profiling on murder cases, especially serial killers, and it was helpful. But this is different. The common criminal is usually stupid, though they're smart enough not to want to be killed or captured. These people don't care if they die. They blow themselves up. They fly airplanes into buildings. Then they go to Paradise. That's where the wine and virgins are. For us, it's the opposite. We get our wine and women here, then we go to hell and get more.'

'Theology may not be your strong point.'

Our food came as my cell phone rang, and it was Al, who said, 'Our guy Nabeel is not working today, and the twenty Yemenis living at his address haven't seen him since Saturday, and he's not answering his cell phone. I'm checking out the local hookah bars, the storefront mosques, other delis, and so forth.'

'Check the jiggle joints.'

'Is that an order?' Al went on, 'Nabeel worked in that deli for only a week and no one knows anything about him, or his family, or friends.' He speculated, 'Maybe he just got here, he got spooked by his conversation with you, and he bolted.'

I replied, 'He said he was a regular guest worker.'

'Well, maybe he worked someplace else. No one at George's knows him.'

'Maybe people are lying to you, Al.'

'They don't lie to *me*, John. They lie, they die.'

'Right.' We need more guys like Al Rasul. I'm too easy on the usually uncooperative Mideastern community. Well ... maybe 'easy' is not the right word.

Al said, 'I've asked for a surveillance team on his apartment and his place of business, and a trace on his cell phone. Meanwhile, I'll keep checking out the neighborhood.'

'Okay.'

'There's something not right about this.'

'Could be,' I agreed.

'See you back at the fort.'

I hung up and Kate asked, 'What's happening?'

'My Yemeni disappeared.'

'Not to worry. I know where to find lots of them.'

After lunch, we took a taxi to the Yemeni consulate on East 51st near the U.N.

The offices of the Yemeni Mission to the United Nations

71

wouldn't win any design awards, though the walls of the consulate section were decorated with very nice tourist posters showing spectacular scenery and happy people, not a single one of whom was carrying an AK-47.

We seemed to be the only customers today, though I'm sure this place is usually mobbed with people who want to travel to Yemen.

The receptionist was a middle-aged man, reminding me that women in Yemen didn't get out of the house much. I stated our business, and the man took our passports and disappeared for a few minutes – long enough to photostat them – then returned with another middle-aged man who introduced himself as Habib, who asked me, 'When and by what means do you plan to arrive in Yemen?'

This was none of his business, and he knew he shouldn't be asking that of Americans with diplomatic passports.

I replied, 'We're awaiting our travel orders.'

'Yes? But you requested your visas for not later than Wednesday.'

I informed him, 'We're here to pick up our visas – not answer questions.'

He didn't like that, but he ignored it and flipped through our passports, checking our photos against our faces. He said to me, 'I see you have been to Yemen.'

I didn't reply.

He glanced at Kate, but did not speak to her. Then he asked me, 'Do you plan to arrive in Sana'a or Aden?'

'I plan to leave here with our visas in two minutes.'

He didn't respond, but said something to the receptionist, who put two completed visa forms on the desk. I looked them over. My visa was for forty-five days, and Kate's was for an indefinite stay. Both listed us as American Embassy staff with diplomatic status. The purpose of our visit was government business. No mention of Panther hunting.

I did notice that, as per security procedures, the State Department had falsified our home address by giving it as 26 Federal Plaza. Also, our US contact information was the State Department Foreign Office in Washington. Fine, except that falsifying the required info on the visa app could get your diplomatic immunity nullified, or at least compromised if you got into some trouble in the host country. Well, I'd worry about that if and when there was a problem in Yemen. Or I'd let our friends at the State Department worry about it. I was on a diplomatic mission. Right?

Everything else looked in order, and Kate and I signed the visas along with two copies. The receptionist stamped the forms, then stamped our passports, and Habib said to me, 'There is no charge. A diplomatic courtesy.'

They should pay *me* to go to Yemen.

We left the consulate, hailed a cab, and went back to 26 Fed, my home away from home. By five we'd posted updates on our computers for all our cases and sent emails to friends and colleagues announcing our imminent departure to Yemen.

Most return messages wished us luck; some suggested we were crazy.

Al returned and reported that he'd had no luck locating Nabeel al-Samad, and that Nabeel's cell phone was not sending a signal according to CAU – the Communications Analysis Unit. Al said he'd make a report and see what the bosses wanted to do, and I said I'd do the same.

Bottom line here, Nabeel al-Samad was not high on anyone's list of people to find. Informants, Mideast or otherwise, are notoriously fickle and usually liars. And sometimes these guys are playing a double game, so I had the interesting thought that Mr al-Samad had another job outside the deli, and he just wanted to get a look at me. Maybe he took a picture.

As Annie predicted, Kate and I were not feeling well, so Typhoid Kate and Anthrax John went home.

Back in the apartment, Kate got into her pjs and went on the internet. I channel surfed. The History Channel had a special on Adolf Hitler's dog.

Kate informed me, 'According to the website of the Yemen Tourism Promotion Board, Yemen is, quote, "Arabia's undiscovered gem, and so little is known about the real Yemen, that when visitors travel across the country, it is almost always a beautiful voyage of discovery".'

'Watch that "almost".'

She continued reading: '"Camel racing is one of the old favorite sports of Arabs and of course Yemen, as Yemen is the origin of Arabs".'

'I thought they came from Brooklyn.'

'"Paragliding",' she went on, '"like in the legend of Suleiman and his bird, who cross the Yemen to see the Queen of Sheba, have fun and discover our country by flying above mountains and seas".'

'Like Predator drones.'

'I don't see anything about that.'

'Al Qaeda ambushes?'

'That might be under trekking and hiking.'

'Right. What's for dinner?'

'A malaria pill.'

We took our malaria pills and watched a rerun of *I Love Lucy*. Could the world have been that simple?

CHAPTER TEN

Tom Walsh, as promised, arranged an appointment for Kate and me with the State Department Office of International Affairs for our cultural awareness course. The OIA is right here at 26 Fed, which is convenient, but still sucks.

On Tuesday morning at 8 A.M., we met Mr Buckminster Harris — where do WASPs get these names? — in a small, windowless conference room. Mr Harris asked us to call him Buck, and he invited us to sit.

Buckminster Harris was a well-dressed gent of about sixty, and I guessed he'd seen some of the world during his long and I'm sure distinguished career with the State Department. This was probably his last posting before he retired to some genteel WASP enclave in the Northeast where he'd write his memoirs for Yale University Press. Meanwhile, he was stuck with me for the morning, and I with him.

There were apparently only two people going to Yemen this

week – Kate and me – so the class was small and intimate. Kate had a notepad, of course, so I didn't need the one I forgot.

There was a colored map of Yemen on the wall, and on the table were State Department handouts, which I'd be sure not to forget.

Mr Harris took a seat at the head of the table and began, 'So you're going to Yemen?'

Why else would I be here?

He informed us, 'I was there during the civil wars.'

I inquired, 'How many were there?'

'A few.'

'Right. Who won?'

'The north,' he said.

'Good. Right?'

'The south was Marxist.'

'Karl or Groucho?'

He chuckled and continued, 'The north is tribal, backward, and fundamentalist.'

'Glad the good guys won.'

I thought Buck was going to take me out in the hallway for a scolding, but he smiled and said, 'They told me about you.'

Really?

'I understand you've been to Yemen.'

'Correct. Short assignment. Back in '01.'

'Well, nothing there ever changes, except for the worse.'

'Looking forward to seeing that progress.'

He smiled again, then said, 'It's a country you can love and hate at the same time.'

Actually, it's a country you love to hate. But this was Buck's class and I wasn't going to be like those dopey students who spent a month someplace and tried to impress their teachers with their half-assed observations.

Buck continued in his very prep school accent, 'The capital of Yemen is Sana'a. South Yemen, also known as Adan, with an A, had its capital in the city of Aden, with an E.'

Also known as the Shithole, with a capital S.

He also let us know, 'The country was unified in 1990 after another war that the north won, but there is still a separatist movement in the south, and also a movement to restore the Imam as ruler in Sana'a.'

Kate stopped taking notes and said, 'Led by the warlord Hussein al-Houthi.'

Buck was happy to have at least one bright student in the class and smiled. 'Yes, very good. I see you've done some homework.'

I mean, who gives a rat's ass? I wasn't going to Yemen to make friends or discuss politics. I was going there to probably whack some asshole who needed whacking. Sorry – to capture a prime suspect in the *Cole* bombing and return him to American justice. Maybe, though, I could learn something here that might help me. But probably not.

Buck said a few words about the al-Houthi rebels and the tribal warlords. I sort of listened. Warlords are interesting. I'd like to be a warlord.

Buck said, 'There are dozens of Bedouin tribes that hold power in their respective regions. And now, to add to the political and social divisions, we have Al Qaeda, who have gained influence in some of the towns and villages.' He concluded, 'Yemen is a failed state.'

Right. Not even worth nuking.

Buck recapped the history of Yemen, which was mostly a history of civil wars, revolutions, and invasions. Also, there was a period of British colonial rule in Adan until the 1960s when the British left after another war. Buck said, 'You'll see some vestiges of British rule in the south. Like a statue of Queen Victoria in Aden, which the Yemenis have left standing for some reason.' He added, 'She is often veiled by fundamentalists.'

I actually saw that when I was there. I thought it was a statue of Elton John in drag.

Buck continued, 'When the British left, South Yemen became Marxist – the only Communist Arab country in the world.' He added, 'You'll also see some vestiges of the Soviet presence in Aden during this period, such as ugly architecture, black market vodka, and a Russian nightclub that features Russian strippers and prostitutes.'

Address?

Buck continued, 'During this period, there were a series of wars between the north and south, alternating with reunification talks. With the collapse of the Soviet Union, the Russians left and unification was achieved, but then the south changed its mind and waged a new war of secession, which failed and led to the present reunification.'

Who's on first?

Buck further informed us, 'I was in Sana'a and Aden during this period. It was a very bloody time and the scars remain.' He added, 'Yemenis have become used to war, which has led to a sort of national psychosis, and which is why Yemen is an armed camp.'

I glanced at Kate, who seemed to be getting that Yemen wasn't the Switzerland of the Mideast.

Buck continued, 'During the first Gulf War, Yemen sided with Saddam Hussein, which annoyed their large and powerful neighbor of Saudi Arabia. The Saudis retaliated by expelling a few hundred thousand Yemeni guest workers.'

Who are now in Brooklyn.

Buck continued, 'The Saudis and Yemenis are currently engaged in a border dispute.' He explained, 'They share a long border including the area of Ar Rub` al Khali, what is called the Empty Quarter, an uninhabited expanse of scorching desert and shifting sands.' He added, 'This area includes the border province of the Hadramawt, which means "the Place Where Death Comes".'

The Yemen tourist board should really think about renaming that. I mean, the Empty Quarter is bad enough, but Death Comes is not a winner.

I asked Buck, 'And the loser of the border dispute has to keep this place?'

'There is oil there,' Buck answered, then continued. 'It is a porous, ill-defined border and a suspected crossing point of AQAP – Al Qaeda in the Arabian Peninsula.'

Right. Maybe that's where The Panther had a shoot-out with Saudi soldiers. I'm glad I didn't have to go there. Right?

Buck concluded, 'This brief history brings us to the Cole bombing in October 2000. Since then, as you well know, the US has gained a foothold in Yemen, but it is a very tenuous foothold and our mission there could end suddenly if the Yemenis have a change of heart or a change of government.'

That would be nice.

Buck took an ornate curved dagger out of his briefcase, which he unsheathed as he said, 'I can cut your throat with this.'

Not if I get to my gun first, Buck.

He smiled and said, 'But only if you fall asleep.' He informed us, 'This is called a jambiyah, and it's worn by most men in Yemen. You can buy a jambiyah at a souvenir stand for about three dollars, but the ones made by artisans can cost thousands of dollars. This one is an antique with semi-precious stones and a rhinoceros-horn handle, and is worth about five thousand dollars. According to the last owner, it has been used to kill at least six people.'

Buck advised us, 'Never ask to see a man's jambiyah.' He explained, 'A man only unsheathes his jambiyah if he is going to use it.'

He continued, 'There is an old Arab war song' – he didn't sing, but recited – '"Terrible he rode alone, with his Yemen sword for aid; ornament it carried none, but the notches on the blade".'

Right. I'd actually heard those words before, from a guy named Gabe Haytham, an Arab-American on the Task Force, when I was working the case of Asad, The Lion.

Buck was going on now about religion – ninety-eight percent of the country was Muslim, the rest were Christians, Jews, and Hindus. He said, 'Before the creation of Israel in 1948, the Sana'a government tolerated its Jews, who are part of their heritage from the days of King Solomon and the Queen of Sheba. In fact, many Yemenis were Jewish until the arrival of Islam.'

Maybe that explains the Yemeni delis in Brooklyn.

He informed us, 'Most of the Jews fled to Israel after 1948.'

He continued, 'The Yemeni constitution supposedly provides for religious freedom for minorities, but there are no churches or synagogues remaining where you can attend services.' He added, 'As in most Islamic countries, the conversion of a Muslim to another religion is prohibited, and punishable, usually by death.' He warned us, 'Do not proselytize. It's a capital offense. Though you may quote from the Old and New Testaments, which Muslims consider sacred texts. But try to learn a few passages from the Koran as well.'

'Which Korean?'

'The *Koran*, Mr Corey.'

'Right.'

Buck continued, 'Yemenis speak Arabic, including ancient dialects. Yemeni Arabic is considered the most pure form of the language — unchanged for thousands of years because of the isolation of the country. Many Arabic-language scholars, including Westerners, go to Yemen to study the language. Think of Yemeni Arabic as Shakespearean English, though it is much older.'

I asked Buck, 'Do you speak Arabic?'

He replied in Arabic, and I said, 'That's easy for *you* to say.'

Kate accidentally kicked me under the table.

Buck said, 'Sex.'

I sat up.

'Sex,' he repeated. 'We all know or think we know about the Muslims' attitude toward sex, so I won't repeat all that you've heard, but I'll recap. Sex outside of marriage is forbidden, and adultery is punishable by death.'

'Right. Screw the divorce lawyers. Get that jambiyah sharpened.'

Buck smiled and said, 'That shouldn't be a concern for a happily married couple.'

Correct, but I had to ask, 'Do guys get the death penalty for screwing around?'

'Not usually, but—'

Kate interrupted, 'They do with me.'

'Just asking.'

Buck also informed us, 'Homosexuality is often punished by death, but rape is usually settled with a cash payment to the victim's family. But if the rapist claims the sex was consensual, which they always do, then the victim, if she can't produce four witnesses to the contrary, is sometimes killed by her family. What they call honor killings.'

Okay, we knew all of this, but it was jarring to hear it.

Buck next discussed marriage and family. 'Polygamy is legal under Islamic law, and a man may have up to four wives, but polygamy is not common in Yemen.'

'Why not?' Kate asked.

Because what guy wants four women telling him to take out the garbage?

'Because,' said Buck, 'most men can't afford more than one wife.'

Most men, Buck, can't afford *one* wife.

Buck continued, 'Most marriages are arranged.'

I asked, 'Do they have Match.com?'

'Yes, but the women in the photos are all veiled and they have no hobbies, interests, jobs, or education.'

Funny. I liked Buck. Even Kate laughed.

Buck informed us, 'Custom regards the ideal marriage as a marriage between cousins.'

Like in Kentucky.

'Women are viewed as subordinate and must serve their fathers, husbands, brothers, and even their male children.'

This might be a good year.

Buck said, 'The Yemeni constitution states that women are equal to men, but then incorporates many aspects of Sharia law, which negates that equality. For instance, in a court of law, the testimony of one man equals that of two women.'

My lawyer wife asked, 'How can they call that equal?'

I volunteered, 'Buck just told you. One equals two. Do the math.'

I got another kick. Restless leg syndrome?

Buck also told us that the Yemenis had the highest birth rate of any Arab country – six to ten children were not uncommon – so something was happening when those veils came off.

Buck also said, 'There's a population explosion in progress, and there are now more than twenty million Yemenis, mostly young, in a small, impoverished country with few natural resources. This is a demographic time bomb waiting to go off, and most analysts predict social upheaval within ten years.' He added, 'We're seeing it already.'

Recalling Nabeel, I suggested, 'More Yemeni delis in Brooklyn.'

He replied, 'In fact, there is a high emigration rate to America, Western Europe, and the oil-rich countries of the Arabian Peninsula, which serves as a safety valve for Yemen and is a source of outside money. But millions of unemployed youths remain in the country.'

Right. I remembered hordes of young men hanging around the

streets and souks in Aden with nothing to do. A surefire recipe for trouble, and a fertile ground for Al Qaeda recruiters.

Buck finished up with love and marriage; divorce is easy for men – just say, 'I divorce thee' three times – but nearly impossible for women. Pre-nups – marriage contracts – exist and are enforceable, unless you get an asshole judge like I did.

Buck switched to the subject of clothing. 'Ninety percent of the population wears traditional Arab dress that probably hasn't changed much since biblical times.' He advised us, 'Buy a set of traditional clothing for yourselves.'

'Why?' I asked.

He replied, 'Just for fun. Or you might wear it when wandering around the streets and souks.' Buck confessed, 'I often dressed as a native when I left the embassy.'

I inquired, 'Do you have a picture you can show us?'

He smiled, then described to us the native Yemeni attire. The men wore headgear called a thob or shiwal, usually white, and in the north they dressed in a white fouteh, a robe, and in the south the men wore a white sarong. Underwear optional.

Sometimes, I recalled, they also wore a ratty Western-style sports jacket over their robe, the pockets stuffed with khat and magazines of the metal variety. They all wore sandals, and the whole country needed a pedicure.

Two things a man never left home without were his dagger and his rifle. The right to bear arms in Yemen seemed to be an obligation, and ninety percent of the males over the age of about fourteen toted an assault rifle, usually an AK-47, capable of taking out all his friends and neighbors in a few seconds of automatic fire. Oddly, though, there was little random gun violence or crime. I mean, everyone was packing, so you thought twice before you walked into a store and said, 'This is a stickup.' Everyone in the place would blow you away. Right?

Non-random gunplay was another matter. Most people who got whacked got whacked for a reason. Usually something to do with politics, or honor, or a business dispute that couldn't be settled over a khat chew. Also, Westerners were rarely robbed at gunpoint. If you got a gun stuck in your back, you were not likely to hear, 'Your money or your life.' Instead, you'd hear, 'Come with me.' The purpose of kidnapping Westerners was not only money, but also a way for the Bedouin tribes to embarrass the central government and/or extort favors or services from them, which was a common pastime of the tribes. These abductions were called 'guest kidnappings,' and kidnap victims often reported that nothing was taken from them, except maybe an admired watch or piece of jewelry that should be offered as a gift while you were waiting for the ransom money to arrive. Your food and upkeep isn't free, you know. And you were getting an authentic experience.

When I first got to Yemen, I was, I admit, a little taken aback by the sight of almost every male carrying an assault rifle. But after about a week I didn't even notice it – in fact, what caught my attention were men *without* rifles. Who were these wimps?

Anyway, Buck was done with menswear and we moved on to ladies' wear. Almost all the women wore the balto, like a burqua, an all-encompassing cloak that, like the first Model T Ford, came in any color you wanted as long as you wanted black.

Buck then moved on to the subject of veils. He said, 'Very few women show their faces in public, and those who do are often harassed by fundamentalists.'

'Because they're ugly?'

'No, Mr Corey, because it's *immodest*.'

'Right.' I wondered if I was going to get a cultural awareness certificate in my personnel file.

He continued, 'As for Western women' – he looked at Kate, who is from Minnesota – 'you are not required to wear a veil, but you may feel more comfortable on the street if you cover your face with a hijab, a head scarf that can also be wrapped around your face.'

Kate stated, 'I have no intention of covering my face.'

Buck nodded in solidarity with his compatriot, but advised her, 'It's best to wear a pantsuit with long sleeves, but it has to be loose-fitting.' He informed us, 'There have been reports of Western women traveling in the rural villages who have been jeered at and even had stones thrown at them for their seemingly immodest attire.'

I mean, what do you say about that? Nothing.

Buck looked at his watch and said, 'Fifteen-minute break.'

CHAPTER ELEVEN

Out in the hallway, Kate said to me, 'I am very impressed with your probing questions and your astute observations. I can tell, too, that Mr Harris is in awe of your insights and your instinctive grasp of the material.'

'Thank you.'

'Can you do me a favor when we go back in there and shut the fuck up?'

'I'm trying to make it fun.'

'This is serious. Pay attention.'

'I divorce thee.'

'Speak to my lawyer.' She looked at her watch and said, 'I need to freshen up.' She turned and headed toward the ladies' room.

I think Kate was annoyed with me. I mean, I'm not good in classroom situations, but I usually listen. Maybe it was the subject – Yemen, Islam, and cultural awareness, which meant cultural sensitivity. How many people from the Mideast take a cultural sensitivity class before they come to America? Why is it always us who have to be sensitive to other cultures? Works both ways. But maybe I could learn something useful. Like where to pull a guy's shiwal to spin him around like a top.

I went back into the classroom where Buck was sitting, looking over some notes. I said to him, 'Sorry if I was a little … inattentive.'

He looked up, smiled politely, and said, 'I'm enjoying your participation.'

See? *He* didn't think I was annoying. I was brightening his morning.

Kate returned and sat, and Buck picked up where he left off and said, 'The only absolute requirement of dress in Yemen is modesty. For men, therefore, shorts and short-sleeved shirts are not acceptable. For women, all that may show is their eyes, their hands, and their feet. The rest,' said Buck with a smile, 'is left to the imagination.' He glanced at me as though expecting a good joke, but I just gave him a studious nod.

Buck had some good news about bare skin and said, 'As Mr Corey will remember, there are a few resort hotels around Aden where parts of the beach are set aside for Westerners to wear modest bathing attire.' And bad news. 'But these beaches are sometimes visited by fundamentalists who cause a scene.'

Right. I recalled playing volleyball with the Marines on the beach behind the Sheraton in Aden where we were quartered, and we wore shorts and T-shirts, but there were no women on the beach except a few female FBI colleagues who wore similar outfits. This didn't seem to be a problem, but that's because we also had a few fully clothed and armed Marines at both ends of the beach. I recalled, too, that I felt naked and exposed without my gun on my hip, though our weapons were always nearby. Also, we weren't supposed to swim, because that would make us sitting ducks. I mean, between the terrorists and the fundamentalists, I wasn't having much fun at the beach.

Buck moved on from bare skin to balls. He said, 'As a warrior people, Yemenis hold courage in the highest esteem – higher than other virtues such as hospitality or honesty.'

In fact, in my experience there, honesty was very low on the list of virtues, and lying was elevated to an art, if not a virtue. The Yemenis were, however, brave, and I could relate to that and respect it. In fact, this was something to keep in mind when I met The Panther.

Buck continued, 'Conversely, cowardice is viewed with extreme contempt. If, for instance, the sight of armed strangers on a street corner makes you uncomfortable, you cannot show fear. If you appear fearful, then this invites an aggressive reaction from the men.'

'In other words,' I said, 'they don't like pussies.'

'Correct. Look a man in the eye and say, "As-salaam alaikum!" Peace be upon you. He will reply, "Wa alaikum as-salaam" — and upon you be peace.'

'Okay. How do you say, "Make my day, punk"?'

Buck continued, 'Women may appear fearful without inviting contempt. Also, women should never look a man in the eye and say anything. Women lower their heads and pass by a man quickly.'

I asked Kate, 'Got that?'

She had no reply. Clearly, Ms. Mayfield was having a little trouble processing this. But she'd be fine when she got there. She adapts easily.

'Hospitality,' said Buck, 'is very important to the Yemenis, and it must be accepted when offered. Even if you knock on a man's door to ask directions, he must offer you something to drink or eat, and you are obligated to accept it. Be aware not to give offense to a man who offers you something.'

Right. Especially if he's carrying an AK-47 and offers to blow your head off.

Buck informed us, 'Women are mostly exempt from the rules of hospitality.' He advised us, 'Read the handouts on these subjects.'

Buck continued, 'The Yemenis tend to be creative with the truth, which is a diplomat's way of saying they lie.'

Right. I remembered having to deal with the authorities in the central jail where the *Cole* suspects were imprisoned. I didn't mind the prisoners lying to me, but when the cops, jailers, and translators all lied to me, I had to wonder if the whole country wasn't pathological liars. I recalled, too, getting into screaming matches with the above assholes, and a few times I thought we were headed for a shoot-out.

Buck said, 'They lie to each other, so don't feel you're being singled out because you're a Westerner.' He added, 'The truth is hard to come by for someone trying to do a job there, and basically you should trust no one. Having said that, you *will* get the truth if the truth will serve the person you're speaking to. As an example, if someone wants to betray someone else, he'll tell you where you can find that person. The problem is, you have no way of knowing if you're being given good information, or if you're being set up for a kidnapping – or worse.'

This was true, and didn't even need to be said, but it's good to be reminded. Also, Buck apparently knew we had other duties in Yemen beyond evidence recovery and legal attaché.

Buck continued, 'Yemen is a land of distrust, which in a way removes any ambiguity. Trust no one and you won't be betrayed or misled. If a government official is assigned to assist you, he is not there to assist you. All informants lie, even the ones you pay. If an ordinary man begs you to get him a work visa to the States in exchange for information, he is working for the government or for Al Qaeda, and he just wants to get close to you and obtain your trust. Why? You'll find out the hard way. Any questions?'

I thought of Nabeel and said to Buck, 'Same with the Mideastern guys I talk to here.'

'Then you understand.' Buck continued, 'The tribes. They make up the majority of the population, and they live mostly in the highlands in the north, though there are also tribes in the south. Some tribes are nomadic Bedouin, but most live in small settlements. Some tribesmen have emigrated to the towns and cities, but the individual retains his loyalty to his tribe.'

Sounds like Kate's family.

Buck continued, 'The tribes are led by sheiks or chieftains who are usually elected, but sometimes inherit the title.' He added, 'We sometimes call these sheiks or chieftains warlords, though they may consider that a derogatory term.' He advised us, 'If you should happen to meet one, address him as sheik.'

I had the feeling that Buck was giving us a mission briefing and that a sheik was in my future.

Buck went on, 'The tribes distrust the central government, and they distrust one another, though they will form alliances of convenience, even with the government, but these are shifting alliances and it's hard to keep score on who is allied with whom on any given day.'

Sounds like 26 Federal Plaza.

'The tribes have a primitive, pre-Islamic code of honor, and in many ways they are chivalrous. If you are their guest, whether by invitation, chance, or kidnapping, they will show you extreme hospitality. They have no particular animosity toward the West, but they're not presently happy with the American officials in Yemen, who they see as propping up their government, which they hate.' He reminded us, 'The friend of my enemy is my enemy. That said, if you should somehow wind up as guests of a tribe, you aren't automatically dead. But don't try to pass as innocent tourists. Be upfront about who you are. But be sure to criticize the government in Sana'a.'

'That's easy.'

'And it may save your life.'

'That's good.' I reminded him, however, 'We'll be working in Sana'a and Aden. No tribal lands on the agenda.'

He didn't reply to that and said, 'You'll be briefed more fully on these subjects when you arrive.'

Kate asked, 'What is the tribal attitude toward Al Qaeda?'

'Mostly negative,' replied Buck. 'Al Qaeda doesn't fit into the social or political matrix of tribal society. Neither did Marxism, obviously. The tribes are distrustful of all foreign ideologies, urban dwellers, intellectuals, politicians, and even Muslims who are not Yemeni. They like things the way they were two thousand years ago.'

'But they were all Jews then,' I reminded him.

He smiled and replied, 'Don't remind them.' He added, 'Another thing to remember about the tribes is that they tend to be monarchists. They actually owe allegiance to and take orders from the exiled princes, sheiks, and sultans who live mostly in Saudi Arabia and who command the loyalty of different tribes. We, meaning the Foreign Office, are in contact with many of these Saudi princes and sultans and through them we can gain the assistance of certain tribal chieftains. In fact, if you do go into the tribal lands, you may be provided with letters from these exiled princes, sultans, and sheiks asking the tribal chieftain to give you safe passage or assistance.'

We seemed to have returned to this subject of us going into Indian Territory.

Kate asked, 'Do these letters actually work?'

'Sometimes.'

And sometimes not. Like, hey, chief, I got a letter here from Sultan Salami asking you to help me out. Oh ... that's the next tribe? You don't like Sultan Salami? He did *what* to your brother? Sorry. Which way to the next tribe?

This was moot anyway, because we weren't going into the tribal regions. Or did Tom mention that we might do that?

Buck said, 'The social and political situation in Yemen is complex beyond understanding – part feudal, part Islamic, and part modern dictatorship – and the Yemenis themselves are confused by shifting alliances and a central government that sends mixed signals to friends and foes alike. Their president, Ali Abdullah Saleh, has said, "Governing Yemen is like dancing with snakes", and I couldn't have said it better. So you have some challenges ahead of you.'

'We love challenges,' I assured Buck.

'Good,' he said. 'You're going to the right place.'

I thought maybe the class was over, but Buck continued. 'Khat. It's cheap and plentiful. About ninety percent of the males chew khat. And almost eighty percent of the arable land is used for growing it, which has caused food shortages, water shortages, and widespread malnourishment – not to mention a population that is under the influence from about noon to bedtime.' Buck also said, 'Part of the malnourishment is a result of khat being an appetite suppressant, which works well in a country with food shortages.'

Right. Not like pot, which gives you the munchies.

Buck continued, 'Khat is an amphetamine-like stimulant that causes excitement and euphoria. Individuals become very talkative and may appear to be emotionally unstable.'

My last girlfriend must have been a khat chewer. Also, I hope that the ninety percent of the men who chew khat are not the same ninety percent who carry assault rifles. On the plus side, they probably couldn't shoot straight. Right?

Buck said, 'Khat can also induce manic behavior and hyperactivity.'

Maybe Tom Walsh chews khat. But I was thinking about khat as an appetite suppressant. I saw an opportunity here to make a fortune in lard-ass America. Amber waves of khat.

Kate asked, 'Do women chew khat?'

Buck replied, 'About half the women do. The other half get the work done.'

I was really getting excited about this. Lose thirty pounds in thirty days. Also good for alcoholics. Dry out, stay blitzed.

Buck continued, 'Some people say khat is a mild aphrodisiac, or at least it makes people uninhibited, which may account for the high birthrate.'

Triple wow. Lose weight, get high, get laid. Does it get any better than this?

'Mr Corey? I seem to have lost you.' He brandished his dagger playfully.

'Oh ... sorry. I was just thinking about ... any downside to khat?'

'I just told you. Loss of appetite, erratic behavior, plus it turns your teeth green.'

'How green?'

'Long-term use can cause male impotence.'

'Viagra.'

'And the withdrawal symptoms are very unpleasant.'

Why stop? Anyway, every drug has a few side effects, and that never stopped Big Pharma. Let's focus on appetite suppressant. Thirty days, thirty pounds. America can be thin again.

Buck broke into my reverie and said to me, 'I don't know if you tried khat when you were there, but I warn both of you, khat has been the downfall of many a Westerner in Yemen.'

I observed, 'But if you're thinner, you make less of a target.'

He smiled, then got serious and said, 'Khat will get you through a bad day in Yemen, but it will not get you through the year.'

'Day at a time.'

I had the thought that Buck must have been a good American diplomat — Arabic speaker, cross-dresser, khat chewer, culturally sensitive. I asked him, 'What was your job with the embassy?'

He replied, 'Cultural Affairs.'

Right. And I'm going there to gather evidence on the *Cole* bombing, and Kate is there to issue visas. We all lie like Yemenis.

The khat chat was finished, and Buck moved on to climate — sucks. Geography and topography — empty beaches, lethal deserts, dangerous tribal highlands. Health concerns — every disease known to man, plus some. Medical facilities — get evacuated to someplace else. Relations with neighboring Oman and Saudi Arabia — pretty bad. Boating on the Gulf of Aden or the Red Sea — pirates. Food — tastes good, but you might get sick. Local water — tastes bad and you will get sick. Security concerns — not much petty crime; just kidnapping and getting whacked. Tourist attractions — lots of good ones, but that's where you'll get kidnapped or whacked. Agriculture — eighty percent khat, twenty percent wasted on food. Manufacturing — incense, perfume, and

AK-47 knockoffs. Entertainment – khat and kidnapping. Sports – soccer and shooting. Tourism – down slightly from none. Leisure activities – khat. Arts and crafts – daggers. Government – dysfunctional and oppressive, except where non-existent.

There were a few other areas that Buck covered, and basically I was getting the impression of a country that had lots of problems and no solutions.

Buck, in fact, had painted a picture of the land and the people that didn't look like the tourism website. And yet I had the impression that Yemen historically had once been part of the world, an important center of trade and commerce between East and West, a center of learning, and a happier land than it was in the twentieth and twenty-first centuries. It had, unfortunately, devolved into a hell on earth. Shit happens, but in Yemen it happened hard.

Buck was finished with the required tutorial, and he said to us, 'I'm aware that your mission to Yemen is not entirely diplomatic, and I hope you learned something this morning that could be useful to you – though you may not recognize it at this time.'

Neither Kate nor I replied to that leading statement, and Buck concluded with what was probably his standard wrap-up. 'Yemen is an ancient land where time has stood still, and where you can see glimpses of an almost biblical civilization. It is where the Arabs are thought to have originated, where the people practice customs and rituals that are rooted in a forgotten, pre-Islamic past. Whatever you know or think you know about the Mideast is not necessarily true in Yemen. So keep an open mind, and think of your time there as a unique and incomparable experience. And good luck.'

Eleven A.M. Not bad.

We stood and shook hands with Buck, who gave Kate his card and said to her, 'If you think of any questions, don't hesitate to call or email me, even after you've arrived in country.'

To me, he said, 'I would strongly advise you, Detective, not to underestimate these people. They may be backward, but they're not stupid, and they will use your Western arrogance and disdain to play you like a lute.'

'I've figured that out.'

'Good. You're intelligent.' He said to both of us, but really to Kate, 'And don't go the other way, as some Western people do, and patronize them, or try to find excuses for their sometimes unacceptable customs and practices.' He advised us, 'Remember who you are, why you're there, and what you believe in, and they will respect that.'

'Good advice,' Kate agreed.

He concluded, 'You will have no natural allies there, but neither will you have natural enemies — except Al Qaeda. With everyone else, it's very situational. Learn to read the situation. And above all, learn how to make a good deal. It's all about the deal. But don't promise what you can't deliver. And keep in mind, the Yemenis can't always be bought with money. As with the Italian Mafia, it's often about favors. If you can help a group or an individual in a vendetta against another group or individual, they will help you in your mission.' He looked at us and said, 'For instance, the Sana'a government helps us locate Al Qaeda targets for our Predator drones and Hellfire missiles. In exchange, the government tells us which tribal chieftain or political opposition leader they'd like to see dealt with in a similar manner.' He added, 'It's all about quid pro quo.'

Neither Kate nor I responded to that, and Buck told us, 'You didn't hear that from me.'

The post-class chat seemed to be finished, so we thanked him, said our good-byes, and Kate remembered to take the hand-outs.

CHAPTER TWELVE

Out in the hallway, Kate remarked, 'An interesting man.'

'Especially at the end.'

'CIA?'

'No. He was too nice. Maybe State Department Intelligence.'

She nodded. 'That would fit.'

'Right. Hey, do we get a certificate for this course?'

'Just a note in our file so we don't have to take it again when we do another tour in Yemen.'

Not funny. We got on the elevator and rode up to the 26th floor. I said, 'I think we just got a mission briefing – a glimpse of how we're going to find and eliminate The Panther.'

She nodded.

And did I have a problem with that? 'That' being a promise to the corrupt and nasty Yemeni government to vaporize some poor tribal leader or political opponent if the government gave us the location of Al Qaeda targets, including, hopefully, The Panther.

And how did Kate and I fit into this? Maybe we were on the team that would coordinate this with the Yemeni government, and/or we would be on the waste collection team, i.e., going out to the hills or desert where a Hellfire missile just turned some guys into hamburger, then collecting fingers for a print match or a DNA analysis to make sure we got The Panther.

Well, no use speculating. We'd know when we got there.

We got off on the 26th floor and Kate said to me, 'I'm feeling a little more prepared for the country, but still not sure about the job.'

'Cultural awareness is ninety percent of the job.'

We returned to our desks and got some work done. I love reading memos and electronically checking that I've seen them. Plus, some emails needed a response. It occurred to me that none of this had anything to do with me anymore. I was going to the front. I was free.

Before I knew it, it was noon, and the sacred lunch hour had begun. Short of a national emergency, you cleared the building at noon. To have lunch at your desk was unpatriotic or suspicious, and you might be questioned by the Office of Professional Responsibility.

I grabbed my topcoat and met Kate at her desk, and we left the building with no plan other than to get some air and clear our heads.

Before we'd left on our last overseas assignments, Kate and I had gone for cocktails to the Windows on the World in the North Tower of the World Trade Center. That was no longer possible, so we walked to the observation deck at the WTC site.

It was a cold day, but there were dozens of people on the deck, mostly tourists, but also some office workers, construction guys, and a group of elementary school kids.

We don't come here often – we don't need to – but today seemed like a good day to reconnect with this place, to remember, as Buck said, who we are, why we're here, and what we believe in.

We walked down to Battery Park, got a coffee and hot dog at a food cart, and sat on a bench, looking out at the harbor.

There was a time when everyone coming to New York from overseas – tourists, immigrants, and Americans returning home – had to sail past the Statue of Liberty. Now, ninety percent of overseas travelers came in through the airports, and they were definitely missing something. Almost everyone arriving here – immigrants, tourists, people on work or student visas, and businesspeople – was here for legitimate reasons. The ones who weren't, like the bastards who took down the Towers, became my problem.

But now I was going to one of the breeding grounds of this sickness – to find one diseased sonofabitch. A guy who helped kill seventeen American sailors as well as other innocent people. Tom Walsh keeps telling me it's not about revenge; it's about justice. I keep telling him to get real.

Kate asked me, 'Any other thoughts on what Buck said?'

'No, not about what he said. But about what he didn't say.'

'Meaning?'

'Why us?'

'I'm sure he has no knowledge of that. And you can keep asking that all week and you'll never get the answer. The answer is in Yemen.'

'Right.' But I think I already knew the answer.

CHAPTER THIRTEEN

O n Tuesday night, some of our civilian friends gave us a going-away dinner in what used to be the basement speakeasy of the 21 Club. We celebrated the end of Prohibition in America, and drank enough to get us through a year of Prohibition in Yemen.

I invited everyone to come to Yemen and promised an exciting visit, including a civil war re-enactment, except, I confessed, they weren't acting.

We used Wednesday and Thursday to settle our personal affairs, including the usual of having our mail forwarded – in this case to a State Department address in Washington where it would be sent on to the US Embassy in Sana'a in a diplomatic pouch. Can't wait to get those Victoria's Secret catalogues.

Our travel orders instructed us to take only a week or two's worth of clothes and necessities, and to arrange with the State Department Travel and Relocation Office for a hundred pounds each of additional personal items to be shipped at government expense to an address in Yemen, which was not yet known. I wondered if I could sneak my La-Z-Boy recliner into the shipping container.

We arranged with Alfred, our excellent doorman, to let the shippers in and to have someone look after our apartment. I gave Alfred a nice tip and promised him a jambiyah when we got home.

We also saw our lawyer and gave him power of attorney for certain legal matters, including the shipment of our mortal remains – but only if we were dead. He asked for the name of a local funeral director, so I said, 'Walsh Funeral Home,' and gave him Tom's home address.

Kate wanted to shop for modest clothing that would be appropriate for wear both in the embassy and on the streets of Sana'a or Aden. I suggested, 'A black balto is good for day or night wear, as well as the beach, and you can accessorize with different-colored veils.'

Kate had managed to get us a direct military flight from Dover Air Force Base to Sana'a, but later we got an email from DOD – Department of Defense – informing us that the flight was full. I suppose a big C-17 could be full, but the question was, what was it full of? Military equipment? Troops? Hellfire missiles? Or maybe people we weren't supposed to see or talk to. The email further advised us that we were authorized to use a commercial air carrier, which we knew.

On Thursday night, a number of our Task Force colleagues – NYPD and FBI – gathered at Walker's, a neighborhood pub on North Moore, a few blocks from the office. The supervisors, including our pal Tom Walsh, made an early appearance before the gathering got out of hand and before the owner had to call the police – most of whom were already there.

The FBI and NYPD don't usually socialize, but this was a

going-away party for two extremely popular colleagues, one of whom was FBI, and the other NYPD.

There were a few NYPD guys there who'd been to Yemen with the Evidence Response Team, and one female FBI agent who'd spent half a year there. They all had some useful advice, like sleep with your gun, never travel alone, and don't chew the khat. The FBI lady, however, said to Kate, 'Without alcohol, the only way your marriage is going to survive with this guy is to chew khat.'

Al Rasul was there, of course, and he got behind the bar and did a funny impersonation of a Yemeni bartender telling his customers it was ladies' night and the women could drink for half price, but no women were allowed, and neither was alcohol. Al also accused the Christians of turning his water into wine.

Later, Al told me, 'Still nothing on Nabeel.'

On Friday at 10 A.M., after getting our final shots in the nurse's office, we were sitting in Mr Walsh's office.

Tom asked us how the rest of the evening went and apologized for not staying longer.

I assured him, 'The party died when you left.'

We were again sitting in the preferred seating section, and Tom had thoughtfully ordered coffee, which I needed.

Tom Walsh is not really a bad guy — well, he is, but he's not much different than any NYPD boss I've ever dealt with. It comes with the job — or it comes with ambition.

Tom, however, had been a little deceitful in the past, lying mostly by omission, then telling me after I'd found out the truth that I had no need to know what he hadn't told me. When I was a cop, the bosses told you all they knew because you had a need to know everything about a criminal case. But this was a different game. Lots of classified information, compartmentalization, firewalls, and outright lies. Some of this was necessary; most of it was not. It's gotten better since we lost three thousand people on 9/11, but old habits die hard.

With all this in mind, I listened to Tom Walsh's final briefing. Basically, he had nothing new to add, but he did say, 'You will be part of a five-person team. Two are already in place, and one will join you later.'

He put a manila envelope on the coffee table and said, 'These are your travel documents, including your airline tickets. Also included is your contact info for when you arrive at Sana'a Airport.' He continued, 'The Travel Office did the best they could, but you'll be arriving in Sana'a at about two-thirty A.M. on Sunday morning. You'll be met, of course, but in the event you're not, you have instructions that will tell you what to do.'

I asked, hopefully, 'Take the next flight home?'

'No.'

Kate inquired, 'Why would we not be met?'

Walsh replied, 'Things can go wrong.'

'So,' I inquired, 'if four guys in white robes ask us to get into a black van, we should say no?'

'You should definitely say no.' He added encouragingly, 'We've never lost anyone at the airport.'

I inquired, 'Anyone ever *delayed* at the airport?'

'Now and then.' He reminded us, 'But you're traveling on diplomatic passports, so you're not required to answer any questions, except for your destination, which is the American Embassy.' He added, 'Demand a phone call to the embassy. The night duty officer is alerted to your arrival.'

'If he doesn't answer, can I call you?'

'No.' Tom continued, 'You will be met before you go through passport control. You will not have to go through customs, but if someone demands that you open your bags, then open them. And make sure there is nothing in your luggage that is offensive, compromising, or contraband.'

'Like soap?'

'Like weapons, alcohol, or certain magazines. Or anything made in Israel.'

'So no Uzi submachine guns?'

He informed us, 'There's a list in the envelope.' He continued, 'Assuming all goes right at the airport, there will be a three-car convoy to take you to the embassy.'

I asked, 'Do our guns travel in the dip pouch?'

'No. You will leave your handguns here. When you get in your vehicle in Sana'a, you'll be issued handguns which you are authorized to carry at all times.'

Kate asked, 'Who's our contact person at the airport?'

Tom replied, 'His name is Paul Brenner. There's a photo of him in your envelope. I understand he's former Army CID – Criminal Investigation Division. He's now working for the Diplomatic Security Service.'

Kate asked, 'Does he know why we're in Yemen?'

'I don't know.' Tom stood and said, 'I want to thank you again for taking on this assignment. And I want to wish you both the best of luck.' He looked at me and said, 'I know you have some reservations about this, John, but I also know that you will become more enthused about this assignment when you learn how important it is to the country.'

'I can feel it already, Tom.'

'Good.' He said to Kate, 'You'll have a more difficult time as a woman – and as the member of the team who has to keep John in line.'

They both got a chuckle out of that. Really funny.

Tom and I did a good, firm handshake, and Kate got a hug, which in a Federal building is sexual assault.

We promised to stay in touch by email and send cards on the holidays.

Out in the hallway, Kate said, 'I can't believe we're getting on a plane tonight to go to Yemen for a year.'

'Did you unplug the toaster?'

'Well ... maybe it won't be a full year.'

'Probably not.'

She asked me, 'Are you excited?'

'I keep pinching myself to make sure I'm not dreaming.'

She stayed silent as we walked to the elevators, then said to me, 'I feel better that we're together and we can look out for each other.'

'Right.' I remembered an old Arab saying. 'When walking through a minefield, make one of your wives walk fifty paces in front of you and your camel.' I didn't say that, of course. I said, 'If I had three more wives, we'd have a whole five-person team looking out for each other.' Actually, I didn't say that either. I said, 'We always look out for each other.'

She kissed me as we waited for the elevator, and we held hands on the way down.

CHAPTER FOURTEEN

Al Rasul said he wanted to see me before I left, so I went to his desk and he suggested a cup of coffee in the break room.

We sat at a table with our coffees, and I said to Al, 'Tom has agreed to send you to Yemen with us.'

He smiled, then said, 'You know, I've never actually been to a Muslim country.'

'Except Brooklyn.'

He smiled again and said, 'I don't think I'd like it. I know my wife wouldn't.'

'She Muslim?'

'Yeah. But born here. She sees the new immigrant women with the scarves and veils and it makes her crazy.'

Which reminded me of the question that had been bugging me, and I asked him, 'Maybe you can tell me why some American-born Muslims have gone to Sandland to fight for the bad guys?'

Al Rasul replied, 'The short answer is jihad. The long answer is God, history, Sharia law, and lots of hate. And here's a secret — they hate the West only slightly more than they hate their own corrupt governments, and a little more than they hate themselves.'

I thought about that, and I guess I understood what he was

saying. But it didn't really answer the question of how all this had translated into a growing jihad.

Al had part of an answer and said, 'Islam began with military conquest, forced conversions, religious fundamentalism, and an intolerant theocratic state. And then there was a period of enlightenment. But what you're seeing now is a return to the good old days. The Dark Ages.'

'Right. But don't forget those seventy-two virgins in Paradise.'

He smiled, then got serious and said, 'The fundamentalists take that literally. If you kill innocent non-believers, you don't go to hell where you belong – you go to Paradise.' He added, 'Their goal on earth is Sharia law and world domination. Their spiritual goal is to ascend into Paradise.' He advised me, 'Don't try to make sense of it. And don't think that what these homegrown radicals need is a good dose of Western civilization and a few beers. They've had that – here and in Europe – and they reject it.'

'*You* don't reject it.'

'I'm a bad Muslim. At least by their standards. I'm also a marked man.'

'Right. Don't sit so close to me.'

I looked at the Department of Justice wanted posters on the wall. Mostly bearded guys with dark, dead eyes. Almost all the captions said *Wanted for Murder*, some said *Suspected Murder*, and some said *Conspiracy to Commit Murder*. Murder used to be my game, but this wasn't murder. It was something else, and it wasn't war; it was sick and it was evil.

Happily, a lot of the posters had big red Xs on them, and notations: *Killed, Captured, Convicted*.

There was no wanted poster for Bulus ibn al-Darwish, a.k.a.

The Panther, and I wondered why not. I guess for the same reason that al-Numair came up empty on the automated case system; The Panther had gone from wanted by the Department of Justice to the CIA kill list.

Anyway, assuming that Al Rasul wasn't Al Qaeda, I confided in him, 'I'm going to Yemen to look for an Al Qaeda guy who was born here.'

'I know that. The Panther. Al-Numair.'

'How do you know that?'

'If I tell you, I have to kill you.'

'Right. Any advice?'

'Yeah. Watch your ass.'

'That's it? That's the total wisdom of the East?'

'That's the total wisdom of East Flatbush, where I grew up, and the Lower East Side, where you grew up. But here's another tip — this guy is not some rural desert hick like your last big cat, The Lion. You may or may not be able to get into The Panther's head, but he's multicultural so he's already in *your* head.'

'Right. I know that.'

'Good. So don't try to guess what he's going to do as an Arab. Try to guess what his conflicts are. His strength as a Westernized Arab is also his weakness. His head is on Channel One some days, and Channel Two other days, and sometimes both channels, and that's when he gets static. He would tell you that he has no sympathy and no admiration for the West, and that the West is not in his heart or soul. But it *is* in his head, and if he were honest with himself, he'd understand that his hate was, in fact, a form of respect. You don't bother to hate what you think is contemptible.'

'Right.' And Al Rasul knew all of this because … ? I asked him, 'How do I actually find this guy?'

'You know very well that he will find you.'

I was afraid he was going to say that.

'Make sure you let *everyone* know you're looking for him. The word will reach him – if it hasn't already.' He reminded me, 'You understand that you have somewhat of a reputation after The Lion. Asad Khalil was not Al Qaeda, but as you well know, he worked with Al Qaeda on his last mission here. And he was a respected jihadist, and because you sent Khalil to Paradise, you are not unknown to Al Qaeda.' And then the kicker. 'In fact, Al Qaeda would like to see you in Yemen to even the score.'

Actually, that thought had occurred to me. In fact, it kept occurring to me, but I'd put it into my denial file. Now good old Al had pulled it out for me. Also, I think Tom Walsh forgot to mention that I was actually going to Yemen to be red meat for The Panther. See what I mean about Tom?

I asked Al, 'Did someone tell you to brief me?'

He hesitated, then replied, 'Not officially. And not Tom Walsh.' He confided to me, 'I'm working this end of the case. Mommy Panther and Daddy Panther in New Jersey.' He let me know, 'They're clean. Good citizens. Very upset. But they're not giving up their son … Still, we might get some leads through them.'

'Let me know.'

'Will do.' He also let me know, 'Bulus ibn al-Darwish is on the CIA's kill or capture list, and Mom and Dad have actually brought suit in Federal court to get their son removed from the kill list. Their reasoning is that their son is an American citizen and therefore can't be assassinated by the American government.'

'Okay. But did anyone explain to them that their son has killed American citizens? Like seventeen US sailors.'

'In fact, that's why they may get their son removed from the CIA kill list.' He explained, 'His parents have also made the legal argument that what their son did, did not constitute an act of terrorism, but was an act of war.' He further explained, 'This legal theory is backed by some past decisions in American courts and the International Court. So if attacking an American military target – as opposed to attacking civilians – is ruled an act of war, then The Panther has committed no crime and he will not be brought to trial. He will be detained as a prisoner of war, and under the Geneva Convention he is not obligated to give any information other than his name, rank, and service number.'

That sucked. I mean, not only couldn't I kill him, I couldn't even torture him. I said to Al, 'Sounds to me like Mom and Dad are playing it both ways. First, their son is an American citizen with Constitutional rights. Next, he's a soldier in a foreign army and he has protections under the Geneva Convention.'

'Right. Whatever works.'

I said, 'What he actually is, is a traitor to his country, and that's a hanging offense.'

Al agreed, but reminded me, 'We don't assassinate traitors. We put them on trial. Bottom line, Mom and Dad may get Junior removed from the CIA terrorist kill list.'

I didn't reply, but I wondered now what the goal of the mission was. It's a lot easier to whack someone than it is to capture them and return them to US soil. Therefore, someone – like the CIA – had perhaps decided that Bulus ibn al-Darwish needed to be killed quickly, before some Federal judge got him removed from the kill list. After The Panther was dead, the lawsuit became moot. Strange war. I mean, judges, lawsuits, and all that.

Al advised me, 'You didn't hear any of this from me.' He stood, we shook, and he said, 'Good luck.'

'Thanks. See you next year.'

'Maybe sooner.'

I found Kate strolling around, saying a few goodbyes to colleagues, but I hate long and repetitive goodbyes, and I got us out of there in five minutes.

We began the six-mile walk back to our apartment – her idea, not mine – and we took in the sights and sounds of New York City, my hometown. Could be the last time, but with luck, we'd be back.

I thought about telling Kate of my conversation with Al Rasul, and how I'd just discovered the real reason I was being sent to Yemen. *Bait.* But ... well, did she have a need to know that? Actually, yes. But she wanted to think that her pal Tom chose us for this mission because we were the best of the best. And we were. So Tom only half lied to us.

Also, Tom knew I wouldn't go alone, so he told the bosses in Washington that they had to include Kate, who he knew would want to go. Plus, Kate had worked the Asad Khalil case with me, so for all I or Washington knew, Kate was also on The Panther's menu.

A sane man would have pulled the plug on this. But ... did it make any real difference? If Tom had told us we were bait, would we have said no? And if I confronted Tom with this, he'd say, as he always did, 'I didn't know that. Nobody told me that. Where did you hear that?'

In any case, I now understood what had happened behind the scenes. Actually, I always understood.

We spent our last afternoon in our apartment, taking care of some final details and calling our parents. Hers were in Minnesota, as I said, and mine were retired in Florida. Thank God none of them would visit us in Yemen. The place sucked enough.

I'd already convinced my parents that Yemen was the Switzerland of the Mideast, so they weren't too concerned, though my mother warned me about getting too much sun. 'You know how you burn, John.'

Kate's parents were a little more hip to the situation, and they expressed a mixture of pride and concern for their little girl. And some advice for me. 'Take care of our daughter.'

How about me? Maybe they were in on this with Tom.

Funny, though, that when all is said and done, the last thing you do is call Mom and Dad. I wondered if The Panther ever called home.

At 5 P.M., we phoned Alfred, our doorman, and told him we needed a porter with a luggage cart and a taxi to JFK.

As the porter was loading our luggage into the taxi, Alfred, who knew what we did for a living, and knew we were going to someplace in Sandland, said to us, 'Thank you for your service to our country.'

Kate and I shook hands with Alfred, then got into the taxi. Kate, I saw, was wiping a tear from her eye.

I took her hand and squeezed it.

At least, I thought, I was going into the jaws of the beast

armed, finally, with the truth, as revealed by Al Rasul. The truth is good, except when it's bad.

And there was another truth that had occurred to me — another reason we were being asked to go to Yemen, and it also had to do with the past — but not The Lion — something else that happened years ago, that involved Kate and the CIA.

I put that thought in the back of my mind, but not too far back. The answers to Why me, why Kate, and why Yemen, were in Yemen.

PART III

Marib, Yemen

CHAPTER FIFTEEN

Bulus ibn al-Darwish, al-Numair, The Panther, wearing the white robes and shiwal of a Bedouin, stood before a gathering of his fighters; forty-two jihadists, armed with AK-47 assault rifles and shoulder-fired rocket launchers.

It was past the midnight hour, but he could see his men sitting cross-legged in the bright light of a waxing half moon, and he could see, too, the flat, desolate landscape of rock and powdery soil, stretching to the star-filled horizon.

The Panther said to his men in a loud, clear voice, 'This night, you will achieve a great victory for Islam!'

The men cheered and raised their rifles in the air.

'You will kill the infidel and cleanse the sacred soil of Islam with their blood!'

Another cheer.

The Panther looked out at his soldiers. They were mostly new recruits, hastily trained in the mountain camp. But among them were four hardened jihadists from Afghanistan, and two officers of the defeated Army of Iraq.

These two former officers had met the Americans in battle and had fled their homeland after the defeat, and they were now here in Yemen to avenge that humiliation. What they lacked in the spirit of holy war, they more than compensated for in hate.

One of the officers, Behaddin Zuhair, a former captain of the elite Iraqi Guard, would lead the attack on the American-owned Hunt Oil installation. The other Iraqi, Sayid al-Rashid, would be his second in command.

The Panther had great faith in these combat-proven soldiers, and he knew they would give courage to the young recruits. With these two Iraqi officers, and with the four battle-hardened jihadists from Afghanistan within the ranks, The Panther saw no reason to lead this attack against the American oil facility himself.

The Panther reminded his men, 'The security forces of this foreign compound are all paid mercenaries – men who have no loyalty to the Americans, only to the American dollar. They will surrender and beg for mercy, or they will run – or they will die at your hands!'

The men cheered more loudly.

The Panther knew, as did his officers and men, that the Americans had also hired a hundred men of the Yemeni National Security Bureau to provide additional protection for the oil installation – the housing units, the offices, the trucks, the machinery, and the pipelines and pumping equipment. These one hundred paramilitary policemen were well paid by the Americans but poorly trained by the government in Sana'a, poorly equipped, and poorly motivated. And, as The Panther recalled from his dealings with these men at the Bilqis ruins, they were easily intimidated and more easily bought.

He reminded his fighters, 'The police camp is outside the

perimeter of the oil company, on the north side, and you will attack from the south.' He also assured his men, 'The police will not engage you. And you will not provoke them.' He smiled and said, 'They will be sleeping like lambs and will hear nothing.'

The men laughed, but Bulus ibn al-Darwish could sense that it was forced, nervous laughter.

Men on the edge of battle, he knew, were fearful. This was understandable. But faith overcame fear. Leadership overcame inexperience. And that was his job – to foster faith and show leadership.

He said to his fighters, 'You have been shown the plans of the defenses of this American colony on the soil of Islam. You know that this place is weak, and you know the secrets of these defenses. And you know that the mercenaries who guard this place for the Americans are infidels without heart or soul. And the Yemeni laborers who are with them have sold themselves to the Americans and are unworthy of God. They are all sheep to be slaughtered this night!'

The men stood and cheered wildly.

Captain Behaddin Zuhair stood to the side and watched his men, then looked at his chief, Bulus ibn al-Darwish, who called himself The Panther, though some called him al-Amriki – the American, which al-Darwish did not like.

Behaddin Zuhair thought that al-Darwish had great presence and spoke well. The Panther had become a legend since he planned the successful attack on the American warship in Aden Harbor, so the men listened to him, trusted him, and revered him. Al-Darwish, thought Zuhair, was a great inspirer of men, a smart planner, and perhaps a great thinker. But he was not a great military strategist. In fact, he knew nothing about war. If the truth be known, this attack on a fortified compound, executed with poorly trained troops, had all the ingredients of disaster. But no one would tell that to Bulus ibn al-Darwish.

The men were still cheering, and The Panther motioned them to sit.

He let the silence fall over the desert, and he looked out at the star-filled night. A soft, hot wind came from the north, from Ar Rub` al Khali, the Empty Quarter, the desert of the blazing sun and the massive, shifting dunes of scorching sand where even scorpions died.

It was here where God put the oil, and here where the Americans came to drain it from the soil of Islam. And The Panther was moved to say, 'It is here where the Americans and their paid servants will die. And the dunes will march south and cover their bones and cover every trace of them, and all evidence that they were here and have polluted the sacred soil of Yemen and Islam.'

The men raised their voices in agreement.

The Panther shouted, 'You will be victorious!'

The men stood again and shouted, 'Victory!'

'You will show no mercy!'

'No mercy!'

'You will kill the infidels and their servants! No one escapes alive!'

The men cheered and continued cheering.

Captain Zuhair, too, cheered, as did his lieutenant, Sayid al-Rashid. But they exchanged glances with each other. These officers, who had seen battle against the Americans, against the

Kurds and the Iranians, and against the Iraqi rebels who fought against the great leader Saddam Hussein – these two men knew victory and defeat, and they knew fear, cowardice, bravery, and death. The Panther knew none of this.

Zuhair looked at his men. Too young – not in their years, but in their hearts and their heads. Too many idealists and religious scholars who came from comfort. Too many Saudis who had seen battle only on television.

Well, thought Zuhair, what they lacked in hardness, perhaps they made up for in faith and zeal.

Zuhair looked again at Bulus ibn al-Darwish. The Amriki, too, must have had these thoughts and doubts. Which perhaps was why al-Darwish was not leading the attack tonight.

The Panther called out to his men, 'You have gathered here from many nations of Islam to engage in jihad. Tonight will be the first victory, followed by many more, until the Americans are driven from Yemen. And then we will turn to Sana'a and annihilate the corrupt government men who have invited the Americans into holy Yemen.' The Panther raised his voice and said, 'We will hang the ministers and the generals from the lampposts of Sana'a and celebrate our victory in the palace of the puppet president, Ali Abdullah Saleh!'

The men stood again and shouted, 'Death to Saleh!'

The Panther smiled and raised his arms, but his thoughts were elsewhere. He himself would not be leading this attack, though some among his jihadists might question why he was not joining them. In fact, Captain Zuhair had raised this issue.

Bulus ibn al-Darwish did not fear death, but he did fear capture, especially at the hands of the Americans, his former compatriots. He feared prison, he feared torture, he feared the humiliation of having his family in America — his father, his mother, his sister — seeing him kept like an animal in an American prison.

Death was far better, and to die during jihad would assure his immediate ascension into Paradise. But there was no guarantee of death in battle.

If he were taken prisoner, the entire jihadist movement in Yemen would suffer or collapse. So for that reason, and because God willed him to stay alive and free to fight the Crusaders, he could not join the attack.

But he did intend to be there to join in the victory, and to oversee the execution of the survivors.

He motioned for his men to be silent, and he said to them, 'I will be with you at the moment of victory.' He drew his jambiyah from its sheath — still stained with the blood of the Belgians — and raised it high. 'I will join you in cutting the throats of all who fall into our hands. No mercy! No prisoners!'

The men cheered wildly.

Captain Zuhair tilted his head toward Lieutenant al-Rashid and whispered, 'He *does* know how to cut throats.'

Al-Rashid nodded.

Bulus ibn al-Darwish turned and faced toward the Kaaba in Mecca, raised his arms, and called out, 'God is great!'

'God is great!'

'Let us now pray.'

It was not the time of the dawn salat, though the dua — the prayers for supplication in times of crisis or danger — could be said at any time, so Bulus ibn al-Darwish sat cross-legged facing

122

Mecca, as did his men, and he recited from the Koran, '"When the heavens are stripped away, the stars are strewn, the seas boil over, the tombs burst open, then shall each soul know what it has given and what it has held back"'.

The Panther then said, 'Let each man now pray silently to God for strength, for courage, and for victory in battle.'

Again the desert went silent, except for the wind from the Empty Quarter.

Bulus ibn al-Darwish prayed silently, beseeching God to give his men courage. He prayed, too, for himself and said, 'Let me cut many American throats this night.'

But as often happened when he prayed for American deaths – such as before the *Cole* attack – other thoughts intruded into his prayers and his mind; thoughts of his childhood and school years in America. Thoughts of his family, and his former home.

These were troubling thoughts, confused memories, and they weighed heavily on his soul.

He had not been happy in America, but he was happy now in the land of his ancestors. Yemen was ancient and once pure, and he would make it pure again.

He looked up at the wondrous desert sky, a sky that had not changed since the days of his forefathers – since the day of Creation. He vowed, 'The land of Yemen shall be as clean and pure as the sky above it.'

And God spoke to him: 'You, Bulus ibn al-Darwish, will be the savior of Yemen and Islam.'

He felt a light touch on his shoulder and looked up to see Captain Zuhair, who said softly, 'If you have a moment, sir, before I move the men to battle.'

The Panther stood and followed Captain Zuhair into a mud hut.

Inside the small hut, lit by a single candle, was Lieutenant al-Rashid.

Captain Zuhair began, 'I am confident, sir, in total victory tonight.' He paused, then said, 'But I must report to you, sir, that I have just received, by cell phone, some information from our friend who is inside the American compound.' Zuhair continued, 'This man reports that the Americans and their security forces, who number perhaps thirty, are arming themselves and their laborers, including our friend, and they are preparing themselves for an attack.'

The Panther stood quietly in the dark and did not reply. Could this be true? Or could it be that Captain Zuhair was losing his courage?

Captain Zuhair suggested, 'Perhaps, sir, we should delay this attack until another night. Perhaps a week. The men can train further. Also, sir, we should consider adding more fighters to the force.'

Again The Panther stayed silent, but then he said, 'We attack tonight. And we cannot add any men to this force.' He reminded Captain Zuhair, 'Forty men are as of this moment making their way to Aden to attack the Sheraton Hotel, and to kill the American soldiers and spies who live there. Another forty will soon be on their way to Sana'a to attack the American Embassy. And that, Captain, is all the fighters we have in the camp.'

'This is true, sir. But perhaps we should not divide our forces. Perhaps we should concentrate our forces on the American oil installation to ensure a complete and rapid victory.'

The Panther had already discussed this with Captain Zuhair, and now the man was speaking of it again – on the eve of battle.

The Panther said with some annoyance and authority, 'I have made the decision to attack on three fronts. This will cause the government to react with fear and confusion. They will not know when or where to expect another attack, and they will become paralyzed with indecision, and they will begin arguing with the Americans, who always want action and decision.'

Captain Zuhair had no reply.

The Panther reminded Captain Zuhair, 'I have told you this before.' Then he reminded the captain, 'The Americans are arrogant and the government is cowardly. You will see both when these attacks are successful.'

'Yes, sir.'

'If you had been here after the attack on the Cole, you would understand what I am saying and doing.'

Like all bad generals, Zuhair thought, this one is reliving his victories and forgetting his defeats. But Zuhair said, 'Yes, sir.'

The Panther turned to Lieutenant al-Rashid and commanded, 'Speak. What do you say?'

Sayid al-Rashid said nothing, but then drew a deep breath and said, 'I can certainly see the concerns of Captain Zuhair, but ...' He glanced at Zuhair, then said to The Panther, 'But I can also see that what you say, sir, is true.'

The Panther nodded.

Al-Rashid continued cautiously, 'We ... Captain Zuhair and I are simple soldiers, sir, and we think of tactics. But you, sir, know of strategy. And it is an excellent strategy. To throw fear into the government and cause strife within the government—'

'And between the government and the Americans.'

'Yes, sir. And of course, our victory tonight will be all the greater because of your leadership and planning.'

The Panther nodded curtly, then said, 'If there is nothing further, I suggest you speak to each man now to be certain they understand the plan of attack.' He also said, 'You will say nothing of what you have just said to me.'

'Yes, sir.'

He reminded them, 'It is six kilometers to the oil installation, and if you start now, you will be there in less than two hours.' He ordered, 'The attack must be completed at least two hours before dawn so that we may withdraw into the hill camp under the cover of night.'

Both men replied, 'Yes, sir,' then Captain Zuhair said, 'Nabeel would like a word with you.'

'Now?'

'He says it is important.'

'All right. Tell him to come in.' He also ordered, 'You stay.'

Lieutenant al-Rashid ducked out of the hut and returned seconds later with Nabeel al-Samad, a junior aide to The Panther.

The Panther looked at his aide in the dim light of the candle. Nabeel, like himself, had lived in America, though Nabeel was an occasional visitor who went there only for business — Al Qaeda business. And also to deliver a verbal message now and then to the family of Bulus ibn al-Darwish, and to bring a message in return from his father, mother, and sister. Nabeel had already done this three days before, so what now did he want?

The Panther asked his aide, 'What is it, Nabeel?'

Nabeel al-Samad made proper greetings, then said, 'Sir, I have just heard from our friend at El Rahaba.'

'Yes? And what do you hear from our friend at the airport?'

Nabeel reported, 'There is an Egyptair flight arriving in Sana'a at two forty-five this morning. The manifest for this flight lists two Americans from New York City who are traveling on diplomatic passports.' Nabeel also said, 'We knew of these people perhaps two weeks ago when the American State Department applied for visas in their names.'

'Yes? And?'

'One of these Americans is a man named John Corey, and the other is a woman called Katherine Mayfield, who is his wife.'

'And they are diplomats?'

'No, sir, they are both agents of the Federal Bureau of Investigation.'

The Panther nodded and said, 'Continue.'

Nabeel further reported, 'Our friend in the New York consulate office informed me when I was in New York that these agents had arrived to pick up their visas, and our friend gave me copies of the visas and their passports. Both of these agents had listed their home address as the government building in which they work. Further inquiries revealed to me that they both are employed in the office of what is called the Anti-Terrorist Task Force.'

Again, The Panther nodded and motioned Nabeel to continue.

'This, as you may know, sir, is an internal American security agency, but the agents are sometimes sent to various places in the world—'

'Yes, I know that. They are *here*.'

'Yes, sir.' Nabeel continued, 'The man, Corey, was in fact in Aden approximately three years ago. Now he is back.'

The Panther stayed silent awhile, then asked, 'And how is this man and this woman different from the other American agents who come here?'

Nabeel informed The Panther, 'These two agents have been specifically placed by name on the assassination list of the Supreme Council.'

'Yes? And why?'

'This man, sir, is the American agent who killed Asad Khalil, The Lion, in New York.'

The Panther nodded. He certainly remembered that. Was it a year ago? Perhaps less.

Nabeel reminded The Panther, 'Asad Khalil had traveled to New York to kill this man, Corey, and his wife, Mayfield.'

'Yes, I recall.' But it had not gone well. Khalil was a Libyan, and he had gone to America on an earlier mission to avenge the bombing of his homeland by the Americans. He had exacted a degree of revenge, but not all that he wished. So he returned. And this time, they killed him.

Khalil was not within Al Qaeda, but he worked *with* Al Qaeda. And thus the Supreme Council had sought to avenge his death by calling for the assassination of this man Corey, who had killed the great jihadist, Asad Khalil, The Lion.

The Panther inquired, 'Why do you think this man has come to Yemen again?'

Nabeel replied, 'Perhaps, sir, to kill *you*.'

That came as no surprise to Bulus ibn al-Darwish. The

Americans had a special hatred of Muslims who had been born or achieved citizenship in America and then joined the jihad.

The Americans, he understood from his more than twenty years in that country, were so arrogant as to believe that anyone who lived among them would come to love them and love their corrupt and licentious country. And when you did not love them, they hated you for your lack of appreciation of them and their wonderful nation. True arrogance and true vanity. *Pride goeth before destruction,* as it is written in the Hebrew Book of Proverbs.

And of course, the Americans in Yemen were here to avenge the killing of seventeen seamen on the American warship. And Bulus ibn al-Darwish knew from his parents and other sources that his name had been placed on what was called the CIA kill list. And this list, according to custom, or perhaps law, had to be approved by the President of the United States. That was interesting. Interesting, too, that this man Corey, who was perhaps here to kill him, was himself — along with his wife — on a similar assassination list that was approved by the Supreme Council of Al Qaeda. So the hunter and the hunted were listed for death. The question was, Who is the hunter, and who is the hunted? The answer for now is, Both are both.

Also, he knew, his mother and father had engaged an American attorney to have his name removed from the CIA list. Corey's name would be removed from the list of the Supreme Council when he, Bulus ibn al-Darwish, killed him.

The Panther thought about all this. To him, it was an honor to have his name placed on that American list. But his mother and father — and probably his sister, who was an American — would rather see him rotting his life away in an American prison. They did not understand him because they had been too long in America. They did not understand martyrdom, and perhaps they had even ceased to believe that martyrdom in jihad earned a man his rapid ascension into Paradise. His parents, he thought, would someday go to hell.

'Sir?'

The Panther returned to the present problem and said, 'So if this man and this woman are in Yemen to kill me, then they have made it convenient for me to kill them.'

Nabeel nodded, but said nothing.

It was possible, thought The Panther, that these two Americans were not here specifically to kill him, but in any case the man Corey had killed The Lion, and for that reason the Supreme Council had ordered a death sentence for him. So if he, Bulus ibn al-Darwish, could kill this American agent, he would gain great honor with the Supreme Council.

He said to Nabeel, 'Kill them both.'

Nabeel nodded, then asked, 'When? Where?'

'Whenever you can, wherever you can.' He added, 'In Sana'a. Or in Aden if they should go there.' He thought a moment, then said, 'Or in Marib, if they should come here seeking me. Take as many men as you need and kill them at the first opportunity.'

'I will see to it, sir.'

The Panther was about to dismiss Nabeel, but then Nabeel said, 'I have actually met this man.'

'Yes? Where? How?'

'In New York, sir. Just last week.' Nabeel had been waiting for this moment to impress his chief with his knowledge of the enemy, and to show his usefulness in America. Nabeel enjoyed his visits to New York, and he wanted those visits to continue. He explained, 'After I received this man's name and office address from our consulate in New York, I telephoned the number on his visa application and asked to speak to John Corey with the claim that I had important information for him about terrorist activity.'

The Panther smiled and said, 'Well, that is a true claim.'

Nabeel and the two Iraqis, seeing that The Panther was smiling, laughed.

Nabeel continued, 'Corey came to the telephone and I explained that I had gotten his name from a man who did not wish to be identified. We spoke briefly and arranged to meet.'

The Panther asked, 'At the government office?'

'No, sir. That is not the procedure for the first meeting.' Nabeel thought this could be amusing, so he had rehearsed his English and replied in that language, 'The agent Corey and I arranged to meet at a Jewish delicatessen.'

The Panther smiled again, but the Iraqis spoke no English and they did not understand.

Nabeel, emboldened by his chief's smile, continued in English, 'Ben's Jewish deli – on West three-eight.' He asked, 'Do you know it, sir?'

The Panther said in English, 'West Thirty-eighth Street.' He seemed no longer amused and said abruptly, in Arabic, 'Tell me of this man.'

Nabeel did not want to say that the meeting was brief, or that his poor English inhibited the talk, but he did say, 'The man was arrogant.'

'They are all arrogant.'

'This man more so.' Nabeel thought back to his brief meeting with the American agent and said, 'He was abrupt, and his manner was that of a man who had little respect for me or those of our faith who live in America.' Nabeel wasn't certain if that was completely true or accurate, but this is what his chief wanted to hear.

The Panther nodded and said, 'Arrogant.'

Nabeel continued, 'He seemed anxious to leave – it was Saturday last, and the agents do not want to work on Saturday or Sunday. So I arranged with him for me to come to this government building for a new meeting – on Monday, in the morning.' Nabeel did not mention the need for an Arabic translator.

The Panther asked, 'And did you go to this meeting?'

'No, sir. That would be dangerous.'

The Panther smiled and joked, 'So perhaps it is *you*, Nabeel, who this man is looking for in Yemen, and you who he wishes to kill.'

'No, sir, it is you. But I will kill him first.'

'You will. And his wife.' He asked, 'Is that all?'

Nabeel replied, 'That is all, sir. But I wish you to have this—' He reached into his fouteh, and the Iraqi officers became alert.

Nabeel produced a small white card and handed it respectfully to The Panther, saying, 'This is the business card of the agent, John Corey. He gave it to me to present at the government building when I called on him.'

The Panther took the card and held it near the flame of the candle. He read:

John Corey, Detective
N.Y.P.D./FBI
Anti-Terrorist Task Force
26 Federal Plaza
New York, N.Y. 10278

There was the office telephone number for contact, but not the man's cell phone.

Also on the card were two seals — one of the Federal Bureau of Investigation and one of the New York Police Department.

Bulus ibn al-Darwish stared at the card for longer than it took to read it, then he turned it over and read, *Nabeel al-Samad to see Det. Corey.*

Nabeel was aware that some men who worked for and with Al Qaeda in America at times exaggerated their deeds and accomplishments, so this card was good proof to have of his work — and his truthfulness.

The Panther handed the card back to Nabeel, who said, 'It is yours, sir. I have no use for it.'

'Neither do I. And neither will Corey after you kill him, so keep it, Nabeel, to remind yourself of your task.'

Nabeel took the card and said, 'Yes, sir.'

Nabeel made to leave, but The Panther said, 'Wait.' He thought a moment, then said, 'There will be a good reward for you, Nabeel, if you are able to capture this man instead of killing him. Capture him and bring him to me. And also his wife.'

'Yes, sir.'

'But do not allow this reward to blind you to the task of killing them if that is the only way.'

Nabeel vowed, 'This man and his wife will be captured and brought to you, or they will be killed.' He further vowed, 'They will not return to America.'

'And neither will you if they escape.'

'Yes, sir.'

Nabeel again made to leave, but The Panther again said, 'Wait.' He said to Captain Zuhair and Lieutenant al-Rashid, 'Begin the preparations for the march.'

Both officers saluted and left the hut quickly.

Bulus ibn al-Darwish, alone now with Nabeel al-Samad, recently arrived from America, inquired of his aide, 'So they looked well to you?'

Nabeel knew who 'they' were and replied, 'As I said, sir, they looked well, and they send you their greetings and their blessings.' He added, because his chief wanted more, 'Your father is prospering in his business and your mother has become closer to her faith.'

The Panther nodded and asked, 'And Hana?'

'She, too, has become more devout, and as I have said, she is very content in her work at the office of your father.'

None of this was true, of course — at least about the sister and the mother. The father *was* prospering, but he had aged badly in the three years since Nabeel had begun visiting them after the *Cole* attack. The mother, too, looked drawn and sad. Hana, however, was more angry than sad, and she had told Nabeel, 'I have no brother,' but Nabeel would never tell that to his chief.

The parents of al-Darwish had given Nabeel photographs and letters for their son, but he could never allow these things to remain on his person, and he had burned everything at the first opportunity after he left these meetings, which were always arranged for a public place in Manhattan or Brooklyn — a park or a museum, or sometimes a department store. The authorities, he was certain, did not know of him, though of course they knew of the al-Darwish family. The authorities sometimes watched their house, and their mosque, and the father's place of business. But the family was not under constant surveillance, and they traveled often to the city for shopping and entertainment. Also, Nabeel knew, they had a sense, after all these years, of knowing if they were being watched.

Still, it was a danger to meet them, and Nabeel was glad that he had to do this only once or twice in a year. But it was also a good thing for him to do this, because it raised his status with his chief.

Bulus ibn al-Darwish said, 'You did not say if my sister was still betrothed.'

'She is, sir.'

'And is there a date set for the wedding?'

'Not yet, sir.' He added, 'But soon.' Or perhaps not. In truth, Nabeel had not asked the family about any of this, and Hana had said nothing to him on this subject.

Nabeel always found himself in a difficult situation on these occasions — in New York, and in Yemen. He needed to be careful. A lie was not good, but sometimes necessary. And the truth was not always good.

The Panther stayed silent with his thoughts. He did not want to ask a question that Nabeel had answered three days before, and he did not want to seem overly concerned about any of this. So he said nothing.

He knew that one day he would again see his mother, his father, and his sister, and it would be here in Yemen. And that day would be soon after his total victory. He would see them in Sana'a — in the palace of the president. On the day he became Supreme Leader of Yemen. On that day, his family would be with him to share in his triumph. And they would never again return to America.

The Panther looked at Nabeel and said, 'That will be all.'

Nabeel bowed and left the hut.

The Panther remained standing in the light of the flickering candle, then blew it out and went into the night.

Zuhair and al-Rashid were preparing the soldiers for their movement, and The Panther motioned them to him.

He said to his two commanders, 'Well, you have heard Nabeel. The Americans are sending more agents here, and soon they will be sending soldiers unless we kill the small numbers who are already here.' He added, 'More reason to attack the embassy and the Sheraton Hotel in Aden.'

Captain Zuhair thought that the opposite might be true; every attack on the Americans in Yemen increased the number of Americans in Yemen. The jihadists, he thought, should be attacking the Yemeni Army and security forces, but Bulus ibn al-Darwish, the Amriki, had a hard hate in his heart for his former countrymen. Nevertheless, Captain Zuhair said, 'Yes, sir.'

The Panther said to his two officers, 'Let us go now and begin the march.'

The three men moved closer to the soldiers, and Captain Zuhair called out to them, 'It is time!'

The men cheered.

The Panther, too, called out a last time to his jihadists, 'We will meet again, amid the inferno of the oil camp, and among the corpses of the Americans – or we will meet in Paradise!'

The men let out a long, loud shout: 'Victory!'

Captain Zuhair and Lieutenant al-Rashid paid their final respects to their leader, who blessed them and blessed the jihadists. Then the officers took charge of their men and began the march toward the American oil compound.

The Panther watched them disappear into the dark, then he turned and walked toward five waiting vehicles, filled with his personal bodyguards. He would remove himself from this place and await the outcome of the attack in a nearby Bedouin camp. It was necessary, he knew, to keep moving, to not stay in one place too long, and to take shelter under a roof or in a cave away from the probing eyes of the American Predator drones. And it was for this reason that he wore the robes and long beard of a Bedouin.

He glanced up at the desert sky. It *looked* the same as it did since the beginning of time – but there was something new up there, something that had already killed too many of his fellow jihadists. And they were looking for him. And now, perhaps, the Americans had sent a man – and maybe a woman – to look for him also. Well, he thought, the Predators would not find him, and the man Corey would not find him. He could not kill the Predators, but he could kill the man. And kill the man's wife. And kill any American who came to the sacred soil of Yemen to find him.

The Americans may rule the air, but he, Bulus ibn al-Darwish, The Panther, ruled the land.

PART IV

Sana'a, Yemen

CHAPTER SIXTEEN

I t was 2:35 in the morning and the Egyptair flight from Cairo was approaching Sana'a International Airport. The airport had a name — El Rahaba — which according to my Arabic dictionary means, 'I'd like the fruit salad.' No. That can't be right.

Anyway, it had been almost three hours since we'd left Cairo, and this leg of the flight was unexpectedly full; mostly young men, probably all Yemeni guest workers bringing home a few bucks so their families could eat. It was a sad country.

Kate and I were sitting in first class and the other gentlemen in first class were dressed Western, but looked Mideastern; maybe Yemeni and Egyptian businessmen or government officials. A few of them had their wives with them, and the women were dressed in traditional clothing. Most of the ladies had been unveiled in flight, but now that the aircraft was landing, they all had scarves and veils in the full upright position.

Kate, FYI, was wearing loose blue pants and a matching high-collared blouse with long sleeves. Buck would have approved, except that Kate had no head covering and her medium-length blonde hair was completely exposed for every man to see, as was her pretty face. Also, FYI, she'd gone light on the make-up.

As for me, I had on my usual tan slacks, navy sports jacket, and a blue shirt, which was a Christian Dior. Christian — get it?

The big Airbus continued its descent, and I leaned over and peered through the window. It was a clear night and I could see hills in the distance, and below was an expanse of arid landscape washed in blue moonlight. In the near distance I saw a few scattered lights that must be Sana'a.

As we crossed over the airport boundary, I could see the military end of the airport: two jet fighters with Yemeni markings, a few helicopters whose markings I couldn't make out, and a huge United States Air Force C-17 cargo plane. The outpost of Empire.

We touched down and the aircraft rolled to a halt, then taxied to a hardstand a hundred yards from the terminal. The engines shut down and Kate said, 'He's not taxiing to the gate.'

'We walk.'

'I'm assuming that's a joke and it's not funny.'

Clearly Kate was a bit anxious, not to mention tired and cranky after a nearly thirty-hour journey. I said to her, 'This whole country is a joke. Learn to laugh or you'll go crazy.'

No reply.

Everyone was standing, and I stood and moved to the exit door and looked through the porthole at the terminal, which I remembered from last time; a low building not much longer than a strip mall, badly lit by three stanchion lights. I could see the headlights of the mobile staircase, followed by a bus, heading toward the first-class exit door, which reassured me that the peasants in the rear wouldn't be on my bus.

I returned to my seat, and Kate and I collected our things and moved into the aisle.

The staircase pulled up without smashing the aircraft, the door opened, and I could smell the fresh, cool morning air rushing into the cabin. Yemen.

So down the stairs and across the tarmac to the waiting bus. Our fellow passengers from first class were all seated, but Kate and I stood in the rear. Kate was the only unveiled woman on board, and the men, who had not taken much notice of her on the aircraft, now looked at her, as did the women. It was as if we'd all been on a nude beach, then got dressed and boarded a bus, except that one of the women was still naked.

There are two gates in Sana'a Airport, and we stopped at the one called two. We let everyone get off first, then followed. So far, so good.

Inside the terminal, our cabin mates moved toward the passport control booths. Only two booths were manned at this hour, and the booth marked for VIPs, diplomats, and crew was closed. Also, there was no one around who looked like us, and Kate said, 'Maybe we have to go through passport control.'

'We're supposed to be met here.'

So we waited. The buses that were filled with coach peasants started arriving and the passport lines got longer. Two Yemeni soldiers carrying AK-47s were giving us the eye.

Kate said, 'Let's call the embassy number.'

'The payphones are on the other side of passport control, and I'm not standing in line with the peasants.'

'We can't stand here.'

'Okay, let's cut the line.'

I went to the head of the line at one of the booths and Kate followed. No one objected and I recalled that the Yemenis, for all their faults, were exceedingly polite and tolerant of Westerners, whom they expected to be arrogant assholes.

Kate and I went to the passport guy and presented our diplomatic passports. The guy checked our visas, then our faces against the passport photos, and he stared at Kate. I mean, every woman in line was veiled, so this guy must be good at eyes. Right?

He stamped our visas, then motioned us to pass through. For some reason — instinct — I glanced back and saw he was on the phone.

Before we got to the double doors marked EXIT, a tall guy with a two-day beard, wearing a crumpled suit but no tie, approached and without identifying himself said, 'Come this way,' and motioned us to follow him to a side corridor. I said to him, 'We're meeting someone here from the American Embassy.'

He seemed to understand and said impatiently, 'Yes, yes. Embassy man is this way. We must discuss your visa.'

Sounded like bullshit to me, and I didn't want to leave the public area — not that it mattered a whole lot where you were when you got arrested. But if we stayed here, we might see our embassy guy. I said, 'We are traveling on American diplomatic passports, as you know, and we have been instructed to wait here, and we're not moving from here.' I suggested, 'Go get the embassy man.'

He seemed very annoyed, and at this point he should have IDed himself and asked for our passports, but instead he said, 'Wait,' and walked toward the corridor.

The two soldiers with the AK-47s moved closer to keep us company. Meanwhile, the Yemenis from the flight were giving us furtive looks as they hurried toward customs.

I said to Kate, 'See what happens when you cut the line?'

'John, what's going on?'

'I don't know.' And I wasn't waiting around to find out. I eyed the double exit doors that led to baggage and customs, and thinking our contact guy might be there, or in the terminal, I said to Kate, 'Let's go.'

'He said wait—'

I took her arm and we moved toward the exit doors. 'Walk like an Egyptian.'

We got within ten feet of the doors before I heard a shout, and the two soldiers suddenly rushed ahead of us and we found ourselves looking into the muzzles of two AK-47s.

Our Yemeni friend reappeared and shouted, 'I say to you wait here!'

'Yeah, you also said the embassy man was with you.'

'Yes. Now he is here.'

'Mr and Mrs Corey, I presume.'

I turned, and walking toward us was a guy wearing jeans and a windbreaker. He was, in fact, the guy in our photograph. Paul Brenner.

He said to Kate and me, 'Sorry I couldn't meet you. I was speaking to this gentleman about your visas.'

I told him, 'The Yemeni consulate in New York assured me there was no charge.'

He smiled, put out his hand to Kate, and said, 'Paul Brenner. Nice to meet you, Mrs Corey. Welcome to Paradise. I hope you had a good flight.'

'Yes . . . thank you.'

He extended his hand to me and said, 'Your reputation precedes you.'

'Apparently it does.' I asked, 'Who is this joker?'

Brenner introduced the joker as Colonel Hakim of the Political Security Organization – the Yemeni secret police. Colonel Hakim didn't shake hands, but said to Brenner, 'I will now wish to speak to your colleagues in private.'

Brenner replied, 'I told you – not happening, Colonel.'

'Do you say no to me?'

'I say you must either arrest all of us or let us leave.'

Colonel Hakim seemed to be considering his two choices, then said to Brenner, 'You may join us.'

'That's not one of your choices.'

It was my turn to be alpha and I said to Colonel Hakim, 'Tell these guys' – I pointed to the soldiers – 'to lower their rifles.'

He hesitated, then barked something in Arabic and the soldiers lowered their rifles. Hakim said to me, 'There is a problem with your visa, and that of your wife. A discrepancy of address. So I may ask you both to leave Yemen.'

Who said there's no God?

Brenner said to Hakim, 'That's not a decision for you to make, Colonel.'

Sure it is. Shut up.

Colonel Hakim had no reply.

Brenner said to him, 'The embassy will lodge a formal pro-test with your foreign minister tomorrow. Good evening, Colonel.'

Colonel Hakim again had no reply, but then Brenner unexpectedly stuck his hand out and Hakim hesitated, then took it. Brenner said to Hakim, 'We must remain allies in the war against Al Qaeda. So cut this crap out.' He added, 'As-salaam alaikum.'

Colonel Hakim, given the chance to save face in front of the soldiers, replied, 'Wa alaikum as-salaam.'

I said to Colonel Hakim, 'Let me know if you're ever in New York.'

And off we went into the second ring of hell, the baggage and customs area.

As we walked, I asked Brenner, 'What was that all about?'

He replied, 'Just the Yemeni government trying to assert its authority.' He added, 'They think they run the place.'

Kate inquired, 'Don't they?'

Brenner replied, 'No one runs this place. That's why we're here.'

Right. Nature abhors a vacuum. Or, to be more positive, we're here to help.

I said to Brenner, 'Actually, our visas list our home address as 26 Federal Plaza.'

'These clowns don't need your home address.'

'Right. We practically live in the office anyway.'

Brenner muscled his way through the maze of carts and people, saying something in Arabic, like maybe, 'Excuse me, we're Americans and we need to get out of this shithole. Thank you.'

Brenner said something to a porter, who nodded.

The carousel showed no signs of life, and Brenner said to us, 'This could take a while.' He added, 'Sometimes the carousel doesn't work. Then they carry the bags in, and pandemonium breaks loose. It's fun to watch.'

I asked Mr Brenner, 'How long have you been here?'

'Too long.'

'Me, too.'

He smiled.

Mr Paul Brenner looked to be in his early fifties, tall – but an inch shorter than me – not bad-looking, well built, full head of black hair, and very tanned. Under his blue windbreaker he wore a gray T-shirt that I now saw said 'Federal Prisoner.' Funny. Not so funny was the collar of a Kevlar vest that I could see above his T-shirt. Also under his windbreaker was a bulge on his right hip.

He informed us, 'We have a three-car convoy that will take us to the embassy.'

'Guns?' I asked.

'Guns? You want guns, too?'

Paul Brenner seemed to have a sense of humor. I know someone with a similar sarcastic wit. This was not going to make us buds; there's room for only one top banana in the show. I didn't think Mr Brenner was part of our team, but to find out I asked him, 'Will we be working together?'

He replied, 'I'm with DSS – Diplomatic Security Service. I work for the State Department to provide security to American Embassy personnel and official visitors.'

That didn't answer the question, but I left it alone, and said, 'Sounds interesting.'

He let us know, 'I was Army CID. A homicide investigator. Like you were, Mr Corey. I was a chief warrant officer. You were a detective second grade, NYPD. Now we are both civilians, pursuing second careers.'

'Right. Except I'm not exactly pursuing my second career.'

'I hear you.'

Kate commented, 'This is the only career I've got.'

Brenner smiled, then looked at her and said, 'You've got a lot of guts to come here.'

She didn't reply, but to set the record straight, I told Brenner, 'It was her idea.'

He let us know, 'It's a tough assignment, but you'll get through it, and you'll be able to write your own ticket when you get back.'

I replied, 'We're hoping for Afghanistan next.'

He laughed, then said to me, 'So you were here in August '01?'

'Yeah. Forty days altogether. Mostly in Aden.'

'Right. Well, things have heated up a bit since then.' He explained, 'Al Qaeda is here.'

I informed him, 'They were here when I was here. They blew up the Cole.'

'Right. Well, now they're all over.' He went on, 'If possible, this place has become more dangerous.'

Typical war-hardened vet trying to scare the newbies. I said, 'In my day, when we walked down the street in Aden, we had to throw grenades just to go get a newspaper.'

He laughed again and said, 'Well, in Sana'a we fire so many rounds from the embassy that we wade knee-deep through the shell casings.'

Kate said, 'Please.'

It's a guy thing, sweetheart.

Anyway, we chatted awhile as we waited for our luggage, and Brenner said to Kate, 'Take what I'm about to say as a professional observation — you're very good-looking, and you have a face that, once seen, is not forgotten. That may be a liability.'

Kate smiled nicely and replied, 'That's never been a liability before.'

'Let me make a suggestion,' said Mr Brenner. 'You should always wear a long head scarf that you can wrap or hold over your face. The Western ladies here find this is a good compromise to the veil.'

'Thank you,' replied Kate a bit coolly.

The carousel jerked to a start and the baggage began dropping out of a hole in the wall.

I've never actually seen so much stuff on a baggage carousel – boxes, crates, weird shapes wrapped in plastic, and some of the worst luggage I've seen since my aunt Agnes visited from Buffalo. I said, 'I hope our chickens made it.'

The Yemenis picked the carousel bare like piranha stripping a carcass.

Our first-class bags were among the last, and Brenner asked, 'Is that all you've got?'

I informed him, 'There is a large cargo ship sailing out of New York with the rest of my wife's luggage.'

Kate smiled. She loves sexist jokes.

The porter had our suitcases and overnight bags on his cart and we moved toward the customs counters, but Brenner led us directly toward the doors. A customs guy in uniform hurried toward Brenner, and Brenner held out his passport from which protruded an official document called a thousand-rial bank note – about five bucks – that the guy snatched as he waved us through.

Brenner commented, 'This is one of the worst airports in the world in terms of security and screening. There's no watch list, so

Al Qaeda guys and other bad actors can come and go. Also, you could ship a bomb out of here addressed to someplace in America.'

I said to Kate, 'We should have given them Tom Walsh's home address.'

We went out into the badly lit and nearly deserted concourse, which was as run-down as I remembered it. The few shops were closed, as was the only car rental and the Yemenia airline counter. I saw a big sign that said, in English and Arabic, NO KHAT CHEWING. I'm not making that up. But smoking was okay, because a soldier had a butt in his mouth.

We went through the exit doors, and at the curb were three black Toyota Land Cruisers with dark-tinted windows. Standing close to each SUV were two guys toting M4 carbines, who were obviously also DSS, and they were eyeing everything around – especially the six Yemeni soldiers with AK-47s. How come everyone else gets a gun?

Brenner said, 'We're in the middle.'

As Kate and I moved to the middle vehicle, two DSS guys opened the rear doors and we slid in. Brenner got in the passenger seat, and the other DSS guys grabbed our luggage and jumped in the front and rear vehicles. Brenner said to the driver, who was Yemeni, 'Yalla nimshee,' which I remembered means, 'Let's go,' and off we went.

Brenner informed us, 'These are FAVs – fully armored vehicles – and the glass is bullet-resistant.' He added, 'Resistant as in duck. There are two flak jackets in the rear. I suggest you put them on.'

I turned and retrieved the two heavy military-issue flak jackets, which could stop anything from a bullet to anti-aircraft fire. I helped Kate into one and put on the other.

This all seemed a little like overkill, but I recalled being met this way the last time, and it was considered standard operating procedure; also known as the embassy covering its ass if something went wrong.

We cleared Sana'a International Airport in less time than it takes to say 'Sana'a International Airport,' and we were on the surprisingly decent four-lane road toward Sana'a. This was the way I'd come to Yemen last time, and it was a bit of déjà vu – except for being met by Colonel Hakim. More to the point, this was a good introduction to Yemen for Kate, who by now must be thinking, 'I should listen to my husband.'

Brenner broke into my thoughts and said, 'Half the fun is getting there.'

No, half the fun is *me* making wisecracks – not you.

Anyway, a rival wiseass was the least of my problems. I asked Brenner, 'How long you got left here?'

He replied, 'As long as you've got left. We're all leaving together.'

Well, maybe that answered part of the question of who else was on the Panther team.

I suggested, 'Let's wrap it up in thirty days.'

He replied, 'Now that you're both here, that's very possible.'

I hadn't yet given Kate the good news that we were here to be Panther bait, and she was missing some of the nuances, so she said, 'That's very flattering, Mr Brenner.'

He said, 'Please call me Paul.'

And call me red meat.

CHAPTER SEVENTEEN

There wasn't much traffic at this hour — it was now 3:55 A.M. — and we clipped along at 120 KPH. The Yemeni driver yawned loudly. The khat must have worn off.

Brenner said to Kate and me, 'This is Mohammed. We pay him a dollar an hour to drive for us. Two dollars to stay awake.'

Mohammed laughed, so he understood English, or he'd heard the joke so many times he knew he was supposed to laugh.

I asked, 'Why the Yemeni driver?'

Brenner explained, 'The Yemeni government now insists that we have at least one Yemeni driver in a convoy at night for our enhanced security.' He further explained, 'Partly it's so we have an Arabic speaker who can talk to the idiots at the checkpoints, or call for police or army backup if we get into a situation.'

I said, 'That sounds almost plausible.'

'Right. But it's bull.' Brenner let us know, 'We actually don't know who Mohammed works for, do we, Mohammed?'

He replied, 'I am just a simple driver, sir.'

'Right. And I'm the cultural affairs attaché.'

'You are, sir.'

That out of the way, Brenner turned and said to us, 'The only incident we've ever had happened at this hour.'

Kate said, 'Thanks for sharing.'

I asked, 'Guns?'

'Oh, right. You want guns.' He passed us a black canvas bag and said, 'You'll carry the M1911 Colt .45 automatic, A1 model.'

I opened the bag and saw the two military-issue automatics, a dozen magazines, two boxes of ammo, two hip holsters, and a cleaning kit.

Brenner asked, 'You familiar with these?'

Kate replied, 'I'm qualified on this.'

Right. Very qualified. In fact, she killed someone once with a Colt .45 automatic. I assured Mr Brenner, 'I've been shot at with this gun.'

'Good. Kate can give you a quick lesson on how to shoot back.'

Wise guy.

I made sure both guns had a loaded magazine in place, and checked that there was a round in each chamber and the safety was on. I left the guns in the bag, but kept it open between us.

I asked Brenner, 'Do we get automatic rifles?'

'If you should need to leave Sana'a or Aden.'

'Right.' I asked, 'How's the civil war going here?'

'I don't know.' He asked Mohammed, 'How's the civil war going?'

'Oh, I do not know, sir. I only know what I read in the news-paper.'

Brenner informed us, 'The government is downplaying it, and it seems to be contained to the north of here, but for all I know we could wake up one morning and find rebel troops outside the embassy.'

'They could be there now,' I suggested.

'I think someone in the embassy would have called me.'

Mindful of Mohammed, we didn't speak much on the drive into the city, but Brenner spent some time texting on his cell phone. He let us know, 'I'm making a report.'

'Spell my name right.'

He looked at a text message and said to us, 'We'll stop at the embassy before going to your apartment.'

I didn't ask him for any details. In fact, there wasn't too much we could talk about with Mohammed listening, and anything Brenner said was probably disinformation for Mohammed's consumption.

I'd noticed about five military checkpoints so far, though no one had stopped us, but I wouldn't be surprised if they reported our position.

The lead vehicle and the trail vehicle were keeping fifty-foot intervals, and now and then Brenner would speak to the American drivers on his hand-held radio.

Mohammed said he had to make a cell phone call – 'a security requirement,' he assured Brenner. I didn't know how much Arabic Brenner understood, but apparently not enough to let Mohammed call his buds and say something like, 'Hey, Abdul, where's that ambush supposed to be? Did I miss it?'

Brenner said to Mohammed, 'La,' which means no.

Mohammed shrugged.

The good road had ended and we were in an unpleasant slum now. There weren't many vehicles or people on the dark and unmarked streets, some of which were dirt, making them excellent places to bury an explosive device.

Brenner, feeling an urge to be a good host and guide, said,

'We're close to the center of Sana'a, the old walled city, which is a World Heritage Site with buildings over a thousand years old and still standing.' He informed us, 'The city, however, has spread out and the population has grown to nearly two million people, most of whom live in squalid shanty towns like this one, without indoor plumbing or sewers.'

In fact, I noticed an aroma strong enough to penetrate the bulletproof SUV, which I guess wasn't gas-proof. The good news was that we could all fart freely and no one would notice.

Brenner said, 'I'll show you around old Sana'a tomorrow if we have time.'

Kate said, 'That would be nice.'

I had missed seeing old Sana'a last time I was here, and I wouldn't mind missing it again, so I didn't second that. But I'm sure Mohammed made a mental note of it, which was maybe why Brenner said it. Bait has to advertise.

We made a few turns that I could tell were solely for the purpose of varying the route to the embassy. In fact, Brenner said, 'We never go the same way twice.' Brenner also let us know, 'If we get hit, my first shot goes through Mohammed's head. Right, Mohammed?'

Mohammed did not reply.

I glanced at Kate and saw she was handling this well. So maybe this wasn't the right time to say, 'I told you so.' I'd know the right moment when it arrived.

We were now in the hilly eastern suburbs, a better part of the city, and Brenner said, 'Five minutes to the embassy unless we run into an ambush. Then you have to add ten minutes.'

Mohammed thought that was funny. It occurred to me that

everyone here was crazy. Maybe I was in the right place after all.

We approached the illuminated walls of the American Embassy compound, and I could see Yemeni soldiers sitting on the concrete barricades or lounging in white plastic chairs.

Brenner commented, 'These guys are members of an elite unit called Sleepy Company, part of the Slacker Brigade.'

I inquired, 'Is this their day off?'

'Every day.'

The lead vehicle stopped, and one of the soldiers stood and ambled over to the driver.

The embassy walls were about fifteen feet high, except around the gates where an ornate section rose about thirty feet. Embedded in the wall over the gates was the Great Seal of the United States. A welcome sight.

Brenner informed us, 'If this place got hit, I'm confident these fine Yemeni soldiers would give their lives to protect the American Embassy.'

'They look half dead already.'

He laughed.

The electric gates slid open, and two United States Marines with M-16 rifles, wearing body armor and battle dress uniforms, stepped outside as the lead vehicle entered the embassy compound into what's called a sally port – a walled-in pen with another steel gate that opened as the first gate closed.

It was our turn, and as we passed through the gates, two more Marines stood at attention and saluted. Kate, I thought, looked a little more relaxed. In fact, we both removed our flak jackets and threw them in the rear.

We passed through the second checkpoint, and I could see the main embassy building – the chancery – about fifty yards ahead at the end of a wide driveway.

The chancery building was of recent construction, and in the spirit of cultural sensitivity, it looked like a theme park sultan's palace, with big arches, a white stone façade, and lots of fretwork.

The embassy compound, I recalled, was about five or six acres, surrounded by high walls. On the grounds were several ancillary buildings, including the ambassador's residence, Marine guard quarters, housing for embassy staff who lived inside the walled compound, and other structures that housed everything you'd need if you were suddenly cut off from the world, including an electric generator and a water tank. For fun, there was a small movie theater, a swimming pool, and two tennis courts that doubled as a helipad. Also, alcohol was served.

The first time I saw this place, I recalled thinking, 'Not bad if you had to live and work here.' I also recalled, however, that there had been a few terrorist plots to launch rockets into the embassy, which I recently learned were planned by The Panther himself. No Mideast assignment is perfect. In fact, none of them are. I remarked to Brenner, 'I don't see any shell casings.'

'The incoming rockets blow them into little pieces.'

Kate giggled. I think she found this guy funny. But if *I* had said that, she'd roll her eyes. What's with wives?

We stopped at the big front doors of the palace-like chancery building, and Brenner opened his door and said, 'You can leave your luggage in the car.'

I opened my door and said to Kate, 'Take the guns, leave the cannolis.'

Kate got out with the gun bag, which she gave to me to carry, and we followed Brenner up the steps of an arched portico. The three SUVs pulled away, and I saw that our luggage had been deposited at the curb.

Brenner informed us, 'You're actually staying here tonight. Just in case Colonel Hakim is on the prowl. Later today, you go to the Sheraton Hotel.'

Kate asked, 'Why not our apartment?'

Brenner informed us, 'There is no apartment.' He let us know, 'You may not be here long.'

Kate asked, 'Why not?'

'We need to discuss a few things later.'

Right. Like, do we want to be Panther bait? Or do we want to go home?

Kate and I followed Brenner past a Marine guard who saluted. Former Chief Warrant Officer Brenner returned the salute.

The big atrium lobby looked as impressive as it did two and a half years ago, assuring me again that our tax money was well spent.

There was a huge American flag on the wall, and also some photos of the chain of command, starting with the president down to the current ambassador, Edmund James Hull, who had a big smile on his face like he just got the word he was leaving this hellhole. In fact, according to the embassy website, his posting had come to an end. Lucky Eddie. I should be so lucky.

As we passed through the empty lobby, Brenner said to us, 'FYI, Mohammed probably works for Colonel Hakim's Political Security Organization. Or maybe an outfit called the National Security Bureau, which was formed in 2002, after John was here, to patrol the main roads, protect tourists at historical sites, and protect oil fields and foreign oil workers in Yemen.' He added, 'Sounds good, but they're just a branch of the PSO.'

I speculated, 'So maybe Mohammed wasn't his real name.'

Mr Brenner further informed us, 'The PSO and the NSB have been infiltrated by Al Qaeda from other Arab countries. The Yemeni government knows this and doesn't seem to care.' He concluded, 'With allies like this, we don't need enemies.'

Nuke 'em all.

Brenner stopped and said, 'I know you're tired, but before I show you to your room, I thought we'd have a nightcap and meet someone.'

'Nightcap is good,' I agreed. Meeting someone maybe not so good.

Brenner got on his cell phone and texted. He explained to us, 'I can use my regular cell phone in Sana'a, because we have a secure cell station and tower on the embassy roof. But away from here, we have to use satellite phones, which I'll give you later.'

I replied, 'Same as last time.'

'Right. I keep forgetting you were here.'

'I don't.'

While we waited in the lobby to meet someone, Kate asked Brenner, 'Is my office here in the chancery building?'

Brenner replied, 'Yes. Most working offices are on the second and third floors. The legal attaché office in Yemen has just been authorized by a strategic framework agreement, but will not officially open for a week or two.'

I said to Kate, 'You won't be the first government employee with nothing to do.'

Brenner said to Kate, 'Your boss will be a man named Howard

Fensterman, who arrived a few days ago. He is the chief legal attaché, and you are his assistant.' He added, 'Mr Fensterman, like you, is FBI.'

Right. Everyone here has two hats, but they keep one in the closet.

Brenner went on, 'As you may have heard or read, the ambassador, Edmund James Hull, has just left Yemen and will not be returning.'

'Right.' And the official reason for his departure was given as personal, which could mean anything from diarrhea to his wife packing up and leaving this shithole.

When you're assigned to a small diplomatic mission in a small, backwater country, you actually get to meet the higher-ups, who are happy to speak to anyone from the States. Even me. So when I was here last time, I got to meet the former ambassador, Her Excellency Barbara Bodine, who had been in Yemen when the *Cole* was bombed. I'd spoken to her here in the embassy on two occasions, and once down in Aden when she'd visited the *Cole* investigators in the Sheraton Hotel and played volleyball with us on the beach — wearing knee-length shorts and a T-shirt. She was an attractive woman, and not a bad person, but I came to share the opinion of the FBI and others here that she had … let's say, not handled the *Cole* crisis well. She, too, must have come to that conclusion, and she left in August 2001, about the same time I did. This place can make you or break you.

Brenner said, 'I don't know when we can expect the new ambassador, and to be honest, things run better — for us — when the ambassador is on home leave, or quits.' He confided, 'We have different agendas.'

Right. The dips are here to make nice; we are not.

Also, I was getting the impression that Paul Brenner's job went beyond meeting people at the airport. He may actually be DSS, but as I said, everyone here has a second job. Brenner's second job, which I'm sure he volunteered for, was panther hunting. Hey, anything to get out of the embassy. The real issue was, could I work with this guy? Did I have a choice?

Brenner got a text and said to us, 'This way.'

We followed him to a set of glass doors that I remembered led out to a small covered terrace overlooking a patch of greenery.

Brenner opened one of the doors and said, 'We can sit out here. It's a nice evening.'

It was actually about five in the morning, and there was nothing nice about it so far, but for a drink I'd sit anywhere.

There was wicker furniture on the terrace, and a man was sitting with his back to us. As we approached, he stood, turned, and said, 'Welcome.'

It was dark, but I recognized that preppy voice. It was, in fact, Mr Buckminster Harris.

CHAPTER EIGHTEEN

Bucky!' Kate and I did a group hug with Buck and we all spoke excitedly.

Actually I said, 'What the hell are *you* doing here?'

He walked over to us, and I could see him smiling as he said, 'I thought I'd continue my class here.'

I replied, 'I thought we were done.'

'You're never done learning, Mr Corey.'

He took Kate's hand and said, 'Welcome. I hope you had a pleasant journey.'

Kate replied, 'We did until we met Colonel Hakim.'

'Ah, yes,' said Buck. 'Colonel Hakim is like goat droppings – he's everywhere.'

Kind of funny. Anyway, Buck was wearing one of those white linen jackets that you see in 1930s British colonial movies, and for some reason I had an urge for Kentucky Fried Chicken. I asked him, 'Did you take the C-17 direct to Sana'a?'

'I did. Awful flight. Uncomfortable, and the meals come out of a box. And no alcohol.' He asked, rhetorically, 'Have we become Muslims?' He assured us, 'You did better taking the slow route.'

'Well,' I said, 'we're taking the fast route out of here when the time comes.'

'You will.'

And then I had a mental image of a human remains box in the back of a C-17. Be careful what you wish for.

Buck returned to the subject of Colonel Hakim and said to Kate and me, 'Paul texted me about your delay at the airport, and it's nothing to worry about.' He added, 'We will file a formal complaint.'

'Good,' I replied, not giving a damn. I said, 'Thank you, a scotch and soda would be fine.' I thought you'd never ask.

Buck invited us to sit, and he played host and moved to a rolling bar, asking, 'And what would Mrs Corey like?'

'Just water, please.'

Brenner, too, wanted water. Wimp.

Buck seemed to be drinking what looked like a gin and tonic with lime, but no little paper umbrella.

So we sat around a cocktail table, lit with a few bug candles, and Buck raised his glass and said, 'To a successful mission.' We all clinked.

Buck informed us, 'I'll be joining you on this assignment, as will Paul.'

Mr Buckminster Harris didn't look like the killer type, but I've been surprised before. And as I suspected, Mr Brenner was on the team.

Buck reminded us, 'I speak fluent Arabic and you'll need that.' He informed us, 'Paul speaks a little, but it's not conversational. It's giving orders, such as, "Get out of my way, you son of a goat"'.

Brenner and Harris both got a chuckle out of that, as though they'd shared this joke before. So obviously they knew each other, and obviously Buck worked here, or maybe he shuttled back and forth to DC and/or New York. He had me fooled back at 26 Fed, and I was sure it wasn't the last time I'd be fooled here, but it was the last time I'd take it so well.

Buck continued, 'There is a fifth person on our team, but he's not here tonight.'

Kate asked, 'Where is he, who is he, and when can we expect him?'

Buck looked at her and replied, 'I can't answer that now.'

I said to Buck, 'Maybe you can tell us now who the boss is.'

'I am,' said Buck.

'And may I ask who you work for?'

'The United States government, Mr Corey, the same as you do.'

There's always a CIA guy when it's an overseas whack or snatch job, but as I'd concluded in New York, Buck didn't look or act like any CIA guy I ever had the pleasure of knowing or working with, including the late Mr Ted Nash. More on Mr Nash later. Nevertheless, for the record, I asked Buck, 'Company man?'

'No.'

I looked at Brenner, who shook his head. Well, I wasn't CIA, and I didn't think Kate was, so if everyone was telling the truth then the fifth person was the guy.

I like to know who I'm trusting my life with, so I asked Buck, 'SDI?'

He nodded. State Department Intelligence was sort of a gentlemen's game, so that fit.

I looked at Brenner, who said, 'DSS, as I said.' He added, 'But this job sounded interesting, so I volunteered.'

Buck leaned forward and said in a soft voice, 'I'm enjoying the cool morning, but we'll need to go inside to speak more freely.'

Right. The embassy walls could have electronic ears, though that was unlikely here in Yemen. I mean, this wasn't the Cold War, the Arabs weren't the Russians, and the PSO weren't the KGB. Still, you had to follow security procedures, and not make the common mistake of underestimating these people.

Buck said to us, but really for anyone listening, 'We have a number of very good leads on the location of six of the Cole plotters.' He winked and continued, 'We have good sources inside the Political Security Organization.' Then for fun he said, 'This

Colonel Hakim that you met at the airport is actually on our pay-roll.'

We all got a smile out of that. And if the PSO *was* listening, then poor Colonel Hakim would have electrodes clipped to his nuts in about an hour. Payback's a bitch, Colonel.

Buck, on a roll now, continued, 'We've also been able to plant listening devices inside PSO Headquarters.'

Okay, Buck, don't push your credibility.

Clearly he was enjoying this game, and you'd never expect Buck Harris to be so delightfully devious, or such a con artist. I had the thought, based on Buck's age and my instincts, that Mr Ivy League of State Department Intelligence had been an old Cold Warrior, and maybe this new war on terrorism was just a way to occupy his time and his mind at the end of his career. Or, like me, Brenner, and thousands of other men and women since 9/11, he was retired and called back as a contract employee to fill the ranks in the new war.

He asked me, 'What are you thinking about, Mr Corey?'

'You.' I inquired, 'Do you also speak Russian?'

He replied in Russian.

I didn't know what he said, but I told him, 'I'm impressed.'

'And well you should be.' He informed me, 'When the Russians were the foreign power in South Yemen, I spent many years there keeping an eye on them.'

'Then you must have spent a lot of time drinking vodka in that Russian brothel.'

'Nightclub,' he corrected. He smiled at me and said, 'You're not as simple-minded or unsophisticated as you pretend to be. In fact, you're very bright and perceptive.'

'That's very perceptive of you.'

'But stupid people think you're like them, and they lower their guard and say things they shouldn't say.'

I replied, 'There are probably a hundred people still in jail who made that mistake.' I added for Mr Brenner's benefit, 'And a few dead people.'

'I'm sure.' Buck let me know, 'When the idea of asking you to go to Yemen came up, there was some thought that you might not be right for the job. My job, then, was to make an evaluation of your fitness for this assignment, and thus our time together in New York had a dual purpose.'

I admitted, 'I didn't know I was on a job interview.'

Buck smiled again and continued, 'I assured the people in Washington who are running this mission that you were not only qualified for this assignment, but that I was certain you would be an invaluable addition to the team, and that I looked forward to working with you.'

'Thank you, sir. I will be forever grateful for this opportunity.'

I think Buck was tired of smiling at my wit, and he said, 'Prove me right.' He added, 'Our lives now depend on each other.'

'Indeed they do.' And by the way, when are you going to tell me why I'm *really* here? That my strongest qualification for this job is that The Panther would like to eat my ass?

He turned to Kate and said to her, 'You are career FBI and you would be here if ordered, but it's my understanding that you wanted this assignment, and there's no substitute for enthusiasm and spirit.'

That's true if you're a cheerleader, but this was a little more complex and dangerous than yelling, 'Go, team!'

Buck, understanding that, continued, 'Your record speaks for itself, including your excellent work on the embassy bombing in Dar es Salaam, and I also know that you've exhibited a high degree of courage and composure under fire and against great odds.'

Kate, to her credit, said nothing, not even mentioning the guy she whacked with the Colt .45. But I was certain Buck already knew about that.

Buck turned his attention back to me and said, 'You're a very lucky man.'

Then why am I here?

He got his smile on again and said to me, 'By the way, you had me thinking about some possible medicinal uses for khat.' He added conspiratorially, 'Perhaps when we're done with this business, we can explore that further.'

Brenner laughed, so I guessed that Buck had shared some of my classroom wit with him.

Buck said to me, 'You enlivened my class, Mr Corey.'

I replied, 'Your class, Buck, was like waterboarding without the water.'

Everyone got a good laugh out of that.

Buck looked at Kate and said, 'You've chosen your clothing well, but you need a head scarf.' And he had one for her. He presented Kate with a paper-wrapped package that she opened, revealing a long black scarf.

Kate said, 'Oh, this is beautiful. Thank you.'

Buck said, 'It's called a hijab. It's made from a very fine mohair, and it comes from a shop here in Sana'a called Hope in Their Hands.' He explained, 'It's a non-profit co-op that sells handcrafts made by women throughout the country, and all the proceeds go directly to these women to help them improve their lives and the lives of their children.'

'That's very nice,' Kate said.

Buck further informed us, 'Most of the embassies, expats, and tourists shop there as often as possible.' He added, 'Good quality, good prices, and a good deed.'

Indeed. I asked him, 'What did you get for me?'

'Nothing. But I'll give you the name of the best jambiyah shop in Sana'a.'

'Thanks. I left mine at home.'

Kate draped the scarf over her head, and Buck leaned toward her and showed her how to wrap it with a long tail, saying, 'Use your left hand to hold it over your face.'

'Is that custom?' she asked.

'No, it frees your right hand to draw your gun.'

Joke? No.

He assured us, 'Sana'a is actually quite safe compared to most of the country. There is very little crime in the city and very few political or religious attacks directed against Westerners. However, it does happen, and there have been a number of plots against the American and British embassies, so you need to be vigilant while you're here.'

I asked, 'How long will we be in Sana'a?'

'I'm not sure.'

Brenner said, 'I know you're exhausted, but we'd like to finish this conversation inside.'

It was still my turn to carry the gun bag, and we went back into the lobby and up the elevator to where I knew that the

SCIF – the Sensitive Compartmented Information Facility – was located.

It was in that room, I was sure, where Buck would mention the small and apparently forgotten fact that Kate and I were here not to find The Panther, but for The Panther to find us.

CHAPTER NINETEEN

The SCIF was on the third and top floor, a windowless and soundproof room, lined with lead and kryptonite or something, impervious to directional listening devices and other types of electronic buggery.

Half of the big, dimly lit room was filled with commo and crypto, and the other half, partitioned with thick glass, was taken up with work stations and a round conference table.

A young woman was attending to the electronics, and when we entered she stood and greeted Brenner and Buck, said hello to Kate and me, then closed the glass door between us.

We'd had a similarly purposed room in the Sheraton Hotel in Aden, but that had been an emptied bedroom in which a lead-lined tent was pitched. The world of spying has come a long way since the days when gentlemen did not read each other's mail, or when it was bad manners to listen at the keyhole or stand outside a building and literally eavesdrop. Today, even pissant countries like Yemen had access to off-the-shelf electronic listening devices and decoding equipment, and the world of secure communication had become a game. The Americans had the best equipment, but you never knew who just developed something better.

Buck Harris broke into my thoughts and assured us, 'We can speak freely here.'

Right. Except, of course, every word was being recorded.

Brenner got on the intercom and made contact with the Yemenis in the kitchen, and ordered in Arabic.

Buck got down to business and said to me and Kate, 'There is something else about this mission that you may not have been told.'

I didn't reply.

'Or maybe you *were* told.'

Again I didn't reply. He was fishing to see what we knew, and I was waiting to see if he'd actually tell us why we were in Yemen.

Buck glanced at Brenner, then said to Kate and me, 'Well, then, I'll fill you in.' He hesitated a second, then said, 'One of the reasons you were both picked for this assignment is because the CIA has knowledge or belief that Bulus ibn al-Darwish, The Panther, would likely make you a target if he knew you were in Yemen.'

'Actually,' I replied, 'it is the *only* reason we were picked.' I said to Kate, 'The Panther is looking for payback for The Lion.' To be sure she understood, I added, 'We are Panther bait.'

Kate looked at me, then Buck, then Brenner, and said, 'I see.'

'Good,' I said, 'and that makes us the best-qualified people for this job. Just as Tom told us.'

She thought about that, then instead of saying, 'That bastard,' she asked, 'Do you think Tom knew that?'

Jeez. Sweetheart, your buddy is a deceitful prick. I said, 'Uh ... let me think—'

Buck interrupted my sarcasm and said, 'None of us knows if he did or not, and it's really a moot point.'

Not for me, so I said to Buck and to Brenner, 'It would have been nice if Tom Walsh or anybody had given us that information in New York so we could have made an informed decision about whether or not we'd like to be bait for a homicidal terrorist.' I asked, 'Agreed?'

'Agreed,' agreed Buck. 'But you're here, you've heard *why* you're here, and now all you have to decide is if you want to stay here or get on that Air Force plane and go home.'

Brenner, to help us decide, pointed out, 'Does it really matter who is the hunter and who is the hunted? It doesn't change the tactical approach that much.'

Actually, it does if you happen to be the hunted. But I understood his point and said, 'Right. But we're talking about truth in job advertising here. We're off on the wrong foot.'

Brenner replied, 'I never lied to you. And I never will.'

We looked at each other and my instincts said to believe him.

I looked at Kate, who I knew was annoyed that she was the last to know. As for me, I've gotten used to being lied to by the Feds, but Kate was still capable of being upset by all the bullshit and need-to-know crap.

She said to me, 'Apparently you knew about all this, and yet you didn't tell me.'

I knew that was coming and I replied, 'I wanted you to hear it here. And not from me.'

She nodded, but said nothing.

Buck suggested, 'We can leave you alone to discuss this.'

I reminded him, 'Every word is being recorded. You may as well hear it live and not have to play the tape.'

Brenner said impatiently, 'Just give us your decision, please. You already know in your guts what you want to do. So let us know.'

Well, this shouldn't be that tough of a decision. Do we stay in this dangerous shithole and dangle ourselves from a meathook to attract The Panther? Or do we go home and have dinner in a nice restaurant?

There *were* career considerations, but that wasn't too important to me, though it was for Kate.

The bottom line was really about the *Cole* victims, the war on terrorism, this asshole called The Panther, and maybe a little payback for 9/11. When it's only about you, you do what's best for you. But when it's about something bigger than you, you do what's right, not what's best.

I knew why I was here, so I said, 'I'm in.'

Kate said, without hesitation, 'Me, too.'

'Good,' said Buck. 'You won't regret ... Well, you might, but with luck and good teamwork, it will be The Panther who regrets your decision, as well as his own bad decisions.'

Brenner added, 'As I said, now that you're here, we have a good chance of wrapping this up quickly and successfully.' He smiled. 'And I can get the hell out of here.'

Buck seconded that, then looked at us and said, 'I was Yale, Class of '65, and in those days, before Vietnam got ugly, and before we lost confidence in ourselves and lost our innocence, we believed in the school motto — "For God, for Country, for

Yale"'. He smiled and said, 'Well, Yale doesn't give a damn, and I'm not sure about God, but we do this for our country. Not for the government, but for the people, and for the innocent victims of terrorism. There's no other reason to be here.'

Can't argue with that. I mean, the pay is okay, but not good enough to put your life on the line. The ego needs feeding once in a while, but my ego was already stuffed. Adventure and danger are interesting, but I did that every day. So what was left to motivate people like me? Maybe Buck had the simple but rarely spoken answer: patriotism. But also something else that is usually not said in polite American society, and I said to Buck, 'Don't forget revenge.'

He nodded and said, 'With the Soviets, I never thought of revenge. But now I think about it often.'

Brenner agreed, 'Revenge is good.'

Kate said, 'I'll stick to God and country.'

There was a buzz on the intercom, and Brenner said, 'Breakfast. Then we can go over the plan.'

It was good to hear that there was a plan. I was sure I wasn't going to like the plan, but the bait never does.

CHAPTER TWENTY

The SCIF was off-limits to Yemenis, so Brenner left to meet the kitchen guy in the hallway.

I took the opportunity to ask Buck, 'What are *his* qualifications for this job?'

Buck replied, 'Paul is a Vietnam vet — two tours, one as a combat infantryman, one as a military policeman. He's been decorated for bravery, and he has a B.S. in criminal justice. He's also been to post-war Vietnam on a clandestine mission.' He added, 'Forget that.'

'And how does all that qualify him for *this* mission?'

Buck seemed a little impatient with me and replied, 'He understands police work, as you do, and what we're doing here is basically looking for a fugitive from justice.' He added, 'Also, Paul has been shot at, so if that happens here, he knows how to shoot back.'

'All right.' Basically, Paul Brenner was no more qualified for a Black Ops job than I was — but they weren't bad qualifications. And I had one up on him — I had a target on my back. Who the hell put this together?

Kate said, 'I think we have a good team so far.'

Buck replied to her, 'I know we do. And when we apprehend this suspect, then you, as an FBI agent with arrest powers, and as a legal attaché, will make the formal arrest in the name of the people and the government of the United States.'

Kate said, 'I'm looking forward to that.'

Me, too. Then I'll put a bullet in his head and save everyone a lot of trouble.

Brenner returned pushing a cart on which was tea, coffee, and fresh-baked muffins.

We helped ourselves, and Buck informed us, 'Yemen is where mocha coffee originated.' He asked me, 'How is that?'

'It was probably good last week.'

We were sitting again and Buck said, 'I'll outline some of what we're thinking, but our fifth team member has a more detailed plan.'

Well, if this was a CIA plan – which it was – then it was probably over-planned, over-thought, and over-complicated. But I'd keep an open mind. My concern was that this plan might rely too much on Mr and Mrs Corey's roles as red meat.

Buck began, 'First, we're positive that Bulus ibn al-Darwish is somewhere in Yemen. That's why we're here. What we don't know is if he knows that John Corey and Kate Mayfield of Lion fame are also here. And third, we can't be certain that The Panther would make an attempt on your lives if he knew that.' He added, 'But we'll make those assumptions, based on CIA information.'

Brenner said, 'As for The Panther knowing you're in Yemen, the names of all Americans coming through a port of entry are considered a saleable commodity – especially Americans traveling on a diplomatic passport. Those names go to the government, of course, and to the local police and the PSO. And as I told you, the PSO is infiltrated with Al Qaeda members and sympathizers, so Al Qaeda knowing you're here is not a problem.'

Sounded like a problem to me. But I guess that was the whole idea.

Buck picked up the ball and continued, 'We're hoping and assuming that AQAP – Al Qaeda in the Arabian Peninsula – is competent enough to identify the arriving John Corey and Katherine Mayfield Corey as people whom they'd like to kill.'

'God, I hope so.'

Even Kate laughed. I mean, as I said, you have to laugh.

Kate had a good question and asked, 'Don't you think Al Qaeda will suspect that this is a setup to lure The Panther into a trap?'

Buck reminded us, 'You both have good cover and plausible reasons to be here. John has returned to continue with the Cole investigation. Kate has been assigned to our new Legal Affairs Office.' He added, 'It's not unusual to assign a husband and wife together when possible. Hopefully, Al Qaeda will not think much beyond that.'

Kate wasn't sure and said, 'It seems too pat.'

Buck got philosophical, or maybe metaphorical, and asked, 'Does the panther or the lion know that the meat is a trap?' He answered his own rhetorical question and said, 'I think he does on some instinctive level. Have you seen those wildlife documentaries where the big cat approaches the live bait – the tethered goat or lamb? He doesn't charge at the animal. He stalks it and approaches with caution. But the important thing is that he goes for it. Every time. Why? Because he's hungry and because he's at the top of the food chain and he's strong and confident.' Buck paused then said, 'And then he's trapped. Or dead.'

I asked, 'What happened to the goat?'

Buck replied, 'Who cares? Goats are expendable. But people are not.' He assured us, 'You'll always be covered. More importantly, you can both think for yourselves and defend yourselves. Goats and lambs can't.'

I looked at my watch and asked, 'Can we still make that flight?'

Buck took this as a joke, smiled, and didn't reply.

Brenner said to Kate and me, 'You're both free to modify any final plan if you think it's too risky.'

Goes without saying. Also, I had the thought that the CIA would in fact be okay with The Panther eating the goat if it meant getting The Panther. Paranoid? Maybe. But we'd already been lied to, and lies are like cockroaches – if you see one, there are more.

Buck continued, 'Al Qaeda in Yemen, like us in Yemen, are small in numbers. They have perhaps four or five hundred hard-core members. But they also have thousands of sympathizers and active supporters, including, as I said, inside the PSO, and also inside the army, the police, and probably the government.'

I inquired, 'How many sympathizers and supporters do we have in Yemen?'

'Two,' replied Buck. 'The lady who runs the craft shop and the man who cuts my hair – and I'm not sure about him.'

Good one, Buck.

He continued, 'But as I told you in New York, among the general population there is not an attitudinal animosity here against the West or Americans. But neither can we expect any help from the average citizen, except maybe from a Jew or Christian. Also, some tribes can be rented on a short-term lease with an unknown expiration date.'

Brenner said to us, 'The sheiks who are tribal chieftains are mostly clients of the Saudi government, and our arrangements and payments to the tribes go through the Saudi royal family. The Saudis are our allies and they've been helpful – except when they're not.'

Buck reminded us, 'As I said in New York in answer to Kate's question, the tribes do not like Al Qaeda, and the feeling is mutual. However, a few tribes have now and then accepted Al

Qaeda money — or Al Qaeda favors — so we can't always trust them.'

I observed, 'It sounds like the tribes are part of the plan.'

Buck replied, 'They have to be. They control most of the countryside.'

Kate asked, 'Does that mean we're going into the tribal lands?'

Brenner replied, 'That's the plan.' He explained, 'The cities and towns are where the government security forces are strongest, and we don't want any interference from them, and we don't want to get into a shooting match with Al Qaeda in a complicated urban setting.' He further explained, 'In the hinterlands we have the advantage of tribal help, or at least tribal neutrality. Also we have the big advantage of Predator drones armed with Hellfire missiles.'

Right. I always knew this would play out in Indian Territory, but I asked, 'How do we know The Panther will meet us on that turf?'

'We don't,' Brenner replied, 'but if he wants you, he'll go where you are.'

'We're in Sana'a,' I reminded him.

Brenner replied, 'As I indicated, we're not staying here.' He further informed us, 'In a day or so, we're traveling by road to Aden, and with luck we'll run into trouble on the way.'

It seemed to me that Paul Brenner's idea of good luck and my idea of good luck were not the same.

Buck let us know, 'I'm not certain that The Panther himself would lead a frontal attack on our convoy, but it's possible he would, and also possible that we can capture someone who knows where he is.'

Right. You bring the water, I'll bring the board.

Buck continued, 'Also, we don't know if The Panther would like to kill you or capture you.' He said, unnecessarily, 'Killing is easier, but capturing both of you would be a real coup for Al Qaeda and The Panther. A major humiliation for the US.'

'Not to mention a major inconvenience for me and Kate.' I observed, 'I see you've thought this out, but I'm not hearing an operational plan that's based on concrete information.'

Buck replied, 'As I said, our fifth team member will provide that.'

'Okay.'

Buck also said, 'It's my understanding, Mr Corey, that you're not plan-oriented. That you shoot from the hip and make it up as you go. So you shouldn't be too concerned about a detailed plan.' He added, 'In fact, that's one of the reasons you were invited to be here.'

'Right.' The other reason was the same reason that the turkey is invited to Thanksgiving dinner. I said, 'I'm flexible.'

Kate, in a rare instance of agreeing with her husband, said, 'John is very good at reading a situation and changing tactics on a dime.' She added, 'But sometimes he bends the rules.'

That's my girl.

Brenner and Buck made a mental note of that, and then Brenner continued, 'We don't want to run this operation from the embassy, which can cause problems. So Aden will be our operational base. From there, we'll go where we think we have to go. Also, Aden is where Al Qaeda has many eyes and ears.' He looked at me and said, 'You remember that, and it hasn't changed much. Point is, if we're at the Sheraton in Aden, The Panther will know it. Also, Aden is where you're supposed to be for the Cole investigation.'

'Got it.'

So we spent the next ten minutes talking this out, and I was alert despite the lack of sleep. Maybe it was the mocha coffee. Maybe the subject matter. War and talk of war focuses your mind and body like nothing else can, except maybe sex.

It occurred to me that Buck and Brenner, via the CIA, knew something I didn't know – like hard information from a radio or satellite phone intercept, or a paid informant, or a vigorously interrogated detainee – that indeed Al Qaeda already knew Kate and I were here, and that The Panther would strike.

It also occurred to me that the State Department's application for our visa – before we even knew we were coming to Yemen – was the trigger that set Al Qaeda in motion, long before we landed at Sana'a Airport. In any case, whatever information the CIA had was not necessarily going to be shared with Mr and Mrs Corey at this time. And whatever information The Panther had would be shared with us at a time and place of his choosing.

Buck and Brenner wrapped it up and Buck said, 'You must be exhausted. So I thank you for your attention.' He smiled and said, 'I hope this was more interesting than my class in New York.'

I assured him it was, except for the info on khat.

Before we retired to our rooms, I said, 'One thing that's bugging me – Bulus ibn al-Darwish. We haven't focused on him, and I'm trying to figure out why an American-born Muslim would defect *from* America. I mean, most defectors defect *to* America. Right? What's motivating this guy? What's his problem?'

Brenner replied, 'I don't know, and I'm not sure I care. But when we get him into an interrogation room, you can ask him.'

I replied, 'At that point I don't care either. But if we knew *now* why he turned against his country, and if we could get into his head a little, it might help us predict what he'll do and what his strengths and weaknesses are.'

Buck informed us, 'In fact, the CIA has a psychological profile on him that we'll see shortly, and that might be helpful.'

'Good.' It takes crazy to know crazy. Not that I meant the CIA was crazy. Or did I?

Buck asked me, 'Are you aware that the suspect's parents are bringing suit in Federal court to have their son removed from the CIA kill list?'

'I am.'

Mr Brenner said, 'That's one reason why we need to make every effort to take him alive.'

Actually, it was a good reason to whack him quickly, before some Federal judge intervened.

I looked at Brenner, who motioned toward the ceiling to remind me that we were being recorded. Then Paul Brenner made a cutting motion across his throat.

Great minds think alike. I was starting to like this guy.

CHAPTER TWENTY-ONE

B renner said the guest house in the embassy was full, but we could get a few hours' sleep in the chancery building before going to the Sheraton, and he showed us to a bedroom on the second floor where our luggage had been delivered.

He informed us, 'We had to convert a few offices here in the chancery into sleeping quarters.' He explained, 'If the threat level goes up, embassy personnel who live outside the compound are required to move into the compound, so it gets crowded inside the fort until it blows over.'

I asked him, 'Is that why the guest house is full?'

'It is.'

Well, I was glad we were getting out of Sana'a. Unfortunately, we were going to Aden.

Anyway, the room looked comfortable enough for an embassy staffer on the lam from psychotic jihadists. Two stars.

Brenner informed us, 'The bathroom is down the hall.'

One star.

Brenner told us, 'You'll check in at the Sana'a Sheraton this afternoon.' He assured us, 'It's heavily guarded, and more comfortable than here.'

'Also,' I added, 'you'd like us out there to see if we come to the attention of the person we're looking for.'

'That is correct.' He also told us, 'I'll have satellite phones for you later, but meanwhile feel free to use the room phone, though as I remind everyone, we record everything for security purposes, and the PSO records for their own purposes. And in answer to your next question, there are no electronic bugs in your room — only real bugs.' He smiled.

I believed him, because if Kate and I found a listening device in our bedroom, we all knew that would be the end of our Yemen visit.

Kate asked him, 'Do you live in the embassy?'

'No. I have an apartment not far from here.'

'And are you staying there even though the alert level is elevated?'

He smiled. 'I'd rather take my chances with terrorists than living with State Department people.'

Me, too.

Kate also asked him, 'Are you alone here?'

He looked at her and replied, 'I am.'

'Sorry ... I didn't mean to ask a personal question.'

He assured her, 'Over the next few weeks or months we'll learn a lot about each other.' He let us know, 'There's someone back in the States.'

He changed the subject and said, 'I'd like us to meet in the lobby at, let's say, eleven A.M. Is that good?'

Kate and I said it was.

He informed us, 'There is a non-denominational church service at eleven in the parlor if you'd like to attend.'

Kate thought that would be nice, and I was trying to think of a reason why it wasn't.

Brenner said, 'You can decide when you come down.' He advised us, 'Bring your luggage down and we'll go over to the Sheraton, then if you'd like we'll take a walk around town.' He smiled. 'Hopefully someone will try to kill or kidnap us.'

Especially if Mohammed dropped a dime on us. Maybe we should go to church instead.

He reminded us, 'Sana'a is relatively safe. But bring your guns.'

Goes without saying.

He also advised us, 'If you hear a siren, move immediately to the basement.'

'Wine tasting?' I asked.

He thought that was funny. I think I was one up on him.

He said, 'There is a safe room down there. Blastproof. Use the stairs, not the elevator, and come as you are.' He reminded us, 'Take your guns with you.'

He gave us instructions on how to find the safe room – follow everyone else – and he wished us a good sleep and left.

Kate said, 'I didn't know what to expect here, but I wasn't expecting this.'

'Meaning?'

'I don't know . . . I guess I didn't understand the security situation.'

'Sure you did.'

'I guess . . . also, I thought we'd have an apartment, then I'd spend some time in my office . . .'

I reminded her, 'You're not really the legal attaché.'

She nodded and said, 'I was surprised to see Buck here and surprised to discover that we were bait for The Panther.'

'Were you?'

'Maybe not.' She asked me, 'How did you know about that?'

I was almost certain the room wasn't bugged, but I didn't want to say 'Al Rasul,' so I said, 'I figured it out,' which was partly true. I told her, 'So did you.'

She nodded again, then asked me, 'What do you think of Paul?'

'I feel the beginning of a beautiful friendship.'

She said, 'I like him and I trust him.'

'Let's see how he and Buck handle the CIA guy. That could be the game changer.'

She advised me, 'Don't let your past experiences with the Agency prejudice you.'

'Of course not. My mind is open to a miracle.'

I took both Colt .45s out of the bag and asked Kate, 'Which one would you like?'

'They're the same, John.'

'The serial numbers are different.'

She didn't reply so I threw both guns on the bed.

Kate looked around the room, then out the window. The sky was getting light, and she said, 'I can see the city from here. We're on a hill.'

'Right.' And in the surrounding hills were guys with mortars and rocket launchers who could target this big compound with their eyes closed.

As though reading my mind, Kate asked me, 'If I hear the siren, would you like me to wake you, or let you sleep?'

Do we need a third wiseass? I said, 'The explosions will wake me.'

I went to the phone on the nightstand and picked up the receiver.

Kate asked, 'Who are you calling?'

'Tom.'

'It's' — she looked at her watch — 'past eleven P.M. there.'

'The FBI never sleeps.' I dialed zero and got the embassy operator. I gave him Walsh's cell phone number and he said to me, 'This is not a secure—'

'Right.'

He put the call through, and I got Tom Walsh's voice mail. I said, 'Tom, John here. I thought you'd be waiting up for my call. Well, as you may have already heard, we're here. And guess what we just found out? I can't say because it's not a secure phone, but you know what I'm talking about. Cat food, Tom. This is exciting and I wanted to thank you for this opportunity.' To mess with his head, I added, 'We may take the next flight out and thank you in person. Don't give away our desks.' I hung up.

Kate asked rhetorically, 'Was that necessary?'

'Tom wanted to hear from us.'

She reminded me, 'We have no business with Tom anymore and vice versa.'

'That was a personal call.'

She had no further thoughts on that subject, and she began to undress, so I did, too. There didn't seem to be a closet in the room, so we threw our clothes on a chair, and I put a gun on each nightstand.

Kate collapsed on the bed, naked, and said, 'We need to burn those clothes. And I need a shower.'

'Down the hall.' I reminded her, 'If we hear the siren, it's come as you are to the safe room.'

She smiled and said, 'That could be fun.'

I asked, 'Is the bed hard?'

'No.'

'Well, I am.'

'Oh ... my goodness. How can you think about sex now?'

'That's a silly question from a naked lady.'

She smiled again, then motioned me to hop aboard.

CHAPTER TWENTY-TWO

Kate and I came down to the atrium lobby with our luggage, dressed in our Sunday best – Kate in a tan pantsuit, and me in fresh khaki trousers, black blazer, and another Dior shirt. Onward Christian Dior.

For footwear, we both had black running shoes; the mark of the urban guerrilla. To accessorize, we carried our Colt .45s – Kate's under her loose top, and mine discreetly strapped to my pants belt. Kate was also wearing her new scarf draped over her shoulders, and my outfit would be complete when I bought a jambiyah.

Paul Brenner, wearing his blue windbreaker, black pants, and a sports shirt, was waiting for us in the lobby, and he had another man with him – a guy in his early forties, sporting a mustache and wearing a dark suit, who I thought might be our CIA guy. But Brenner said, 'This is Howard Fensterman, the new legal attaché.'

Kate and I shook hands with Mr Fensterman, who said to Kate, 'I'm looking forward to working with you.'

Kate replied, 'I'm excited about opening the new office.'

So maybe Kate really was the assistant legat, and I was going down to Aden to join the *Cole* investigation. Great. Better than Panther bait.

But Mr Fensterman cleared that up by saying, 'I'll be providing any legal assistance you might need for your mission in Yemen. Feel free to call me when you leave Sana'a if you have any questions or need any clarifications regarding procedures.'

'Thank you,' said Kate.

I mean, did George Patton have a lawyer on his staff? Hey, Counselor, can the Third Army cross the Rhine yet? Are we still waiting for a legal opinion?

Mr Fensterman asked us to call him Howard and continued, 'I'm working closely with State and Justice regarding extradition procedures, and I'm being kept up-to-date by Justice regarding the Federal lawsuit brought by the suspect's parents.'

I said, 'I hope you're also working on covering our asses if by chance the suspect should meet an untimely end during his apprehension.'

Howard replied, 'I'll address that if and when it occurs.' He added, 'It's all a little complicated because, as you know, the suspect is an American citizen.' He reminded us, 'He has Constitutional rights.'

'Of course.' And I had the answer to all those pesky rights on my hip.

Howard informed us, 'I'm about to attend the church service in the parlor. Would you like to join me?'

'No,' I replied. 'We're carrying guns, and we're pagans.'

'That's all right,' Howard assured us. 'I'm Jewish.'

Huh?

Howard told us, 'Friday night I went to one of the mosques that allows non-believers to enter. Saturday, I went to services in the home of a Yemeni Jew. So today I'm going to the Christian service here in the embassy.'

I asked him, 'Are you very spiritual?' Or confused? Or maybe covering all your bases?

He replied, 'The three religions have much in common.' He also said, 'I'm bored.'

Try khat.

Howard really wanted company, and he also wanted to show Kate her office after the service. Kate didn't want to disappoint her new boss, and Brenner was in no hurry to get to the hotel, so Kate, I, and Brenner accompanied Howard to the parlor.

The big, sunlit room was filled with about fifty people – embassy staffers and spouses and about ten uniformed Marines. Everyone was sitting on the upholstered furniture or in folding chairs, and they were all dressed nicely. The American tax-payers, who were there in spirit, had provided vases of cut flowers.

The preacher, or whoever he was, was standing at a lectern wearing a celestial blue suit, and he greeted us and introduced himself as Ed Peters, adding, 'It's always good to see new faces, and I'm happy to see Mr Brenner.'

As we searched for empty seats, I saw Buck sitting comfortably in an armchair, still wearing his white jacket. I found a folding chair in the rear on which was a photocopied program of only four pages. Thank God.

Mr Peters began, 'Welcome to all who slept late and missed the service in the British Embassy.'

A few chuckles.

It occurred to me that maybe half of these people never went to church back home, but when you're in weird-land you get religion, or maybe you just want to accentuate the difference between you and the people on the other side of the embassy walls. How's that for insightful analysis?

Mr Peters asked us to rise to sing 'Rock of Ages,' the words to which were in the program. There was a baby grand in the parlor, and a nice lady in a floral dress tickled the ivories.

I could see Kate standing near the window and she seemed angelic singing in the sunlight with a post-coital glow.

Buck was singing without looking at his program, and Howard was belting out the hymn like he was auditioning for the church choir. Brenner was two seats away from me and he was moving his lips like he was reading an eye chart. As for me, I hummed along.

Anyway, we got through that, sat, and Mr Peters read from the Old Testament, the First Book of Kings: *When the Queen of Sheba heard of the fame of Solomon . . . she came to test him with hard questions.* And my favorite: *King Solomon loved many strange women.* And from the New Testament, Matthew: *Ye shall hear of wars and rumors of wars.*

We sang two more hymns and recited two prayers, then Mr Peters gave a talk or homily about the sacrifices we were all making here in the service of the American people, and about the difficult times we lived in.

He also urged us to see this time as a growing and learning experience, and he predicted that when we looked back on our service in Yemen, we would all come to appreciate our days in this shithole. But he used another word.

Mr Peters went on a bit about reaching out to the Yemeni people, about being guests here, and about tolerance of the host country even though it was fucked up beyond all understanding. Or words to that effect.

According to my program there was no Holy Communion, so

we were basically finished as soon as this guy wrapped it up. Is that a siren I hear?

But then Mr Peters asked for a minute of silent prayer for our military and civilian personnel who were serving in Iraq, Afghanistan, and all over the world, including this hellhole. Amen to that.

After the minute of silence, Mr Peters invited us all to join him in the lobby for refreshments and fellowship. He concluded, 'Go in peace.'

That's not why I was here, but I needed a cup of coffee, so Kate and I, along with Brenner and Howard Fensterman, went to the lobby and mingled.

There was an employee cafeteria off the lobby that provided what looked like good approximations of American cookies and cakes. They even had bagels, which made me homesick.

The congregants of the First and Only Church of Jesus Christ in Sana'a seemed like nice people. Among them were not only embassy staffers and a few spouses, but also expats and others who were seeking company, God, or a small piece of America. Probably all three.

I noticed there were no children – a sure sign that this was a dangerous place.

Life in the Foreign Service was unlike any other overseas experience, except maybe the military or being a missionary. How do people do this? But then I started thinking about Paul Brenner and the Diplomatic Security Service. Maybe that's the job I should ask for if we got our man. A few years in Paris, London, or Rome. Kate would be a legat. Something to think about.

I chatted with a few of the Marines and they were all very professional and called me 'sir', and they seemed gung-ho and mission-oriented. They assured me that if the embassy were attacked, the twenty Marines and ten DSS guys could hold the fort until the Yemeni Army arrived. One guy explained, 'Then we'd have new targets — the Yemeni Army.' Everyone laughed. Everyone here was nuts.

I moved over to Buck, who was in his element here, mingling with his Foreign Service brothers and sisters, most of whom I'm sure shared his background and some of whom also had funny first names, like Livingston, Kelvin, and Winthrop — a.k.a. Livie, Kel, and Winnie. You can't make this up.

Buck said to me, sotto voce, 'There was an Al Qaeda attack near Marib early this morning.'

I wasn't sure where Marib was, but I hoped it wasn't too close to the embassy lobby.

Buck continued, 'The target was an oil installation partly owned by Hunt — an American company.' He let me know, 'Security forces killed six of the attackers and took one wounded prisoner who said he was Al Qaeda.' He added, 'The Company is questioning the prisoner about our man.'

The oil company? No, the CIA. I asked, 'Where is Marib?'

'About two hundred kilometers east of here.' Buck speculated, 'This could be a sign that Al Qaeda is beginning attacks against American and Western interests in Yemen.' He added, 'Al Qaeda attacks are rarely isolated.'

'Right.'

He also informed me, 'The al-Houthi rebels have ambushed a military convoy north of here.'

'Any good news this morning?'

'Yes. I flew in with a fresh shipment of Boodles and dry vermouth. Martinis tonight.'

Make mine a double, hold the vermouth.

Anyway, I finally got my coffee and a bagel with cream cheese, and as I was munching, Mr Peters came up to me and said, 'Welcome to Sana'a.'

'Thanks. Good service, Padre.' Short.

He informed me, 'I'm a lay preacher. Non-denominational.'

'Me, too.'

He thought that was funny and continued, 'My weekday job is chief of DSS here.'

'Yeah? How do I get a DSS job?'

'Apply. We're short-staffed all over the Mideast. No one wants the job. Everyone wants Paris, London, and Rome.'

'Wimps.'

He informed me, 'Paul is my second-in-command. He's a good man.'

'Right.'

'Hate to lose him.'

'Where's he going?'

'With you. Then home.'

I didn't know how much Peters knew, so I didn't respond.

Mr Peters said he wanted me to meet someone, and he led me over to a big guy who looked like a weightlifter wearing his First Holy Communion suit.

Peters said to me, 'This is John Zamoiski, DSS. You might remember him from the airport.'

'Right.' One of the guys in the lead car.

We shook and the guy gripped my hand like it was the last cold beer in hell.

John Zamoiski said, 'Call me Zamo.'

'Okay. Call me John.' Later we'll switch.

Mr Peters said to me, 'Zamo will be with you when you drive to Aden.'

'Good.'

'He'll also be with you if you go into the Badlands.'

'The more the merrier.'

Mr Peters continued, 'Zamo was an Army sniper in Afghanistan.'

I looked at Zamo. He still had a military haircut — you don't want hair blocking your crosshairs — and a face that didn't move much. He wasn't more than thirty, and I noticed that his dark eyes never blinked. He seemed to be a man of few words, but he had Mr Peters to speak for him, and Peters said, 'Zamo is also a martial arts expert.'

'You draw soldiers?' I asked.

His mouth turned up in a smile. He liked me. Good boy, Zamo. *Sit!*

Brenner joined us and suggested that we get moving. He said to Zamo, 'You'll accompany us to the Sheraton.'

Zamo finished eating his coffee cup and nodded.

I guess Zamo was the team sniper. It's good to have a trained killer on the team. And a churchgoer at that.

Thinking back on our time since we landed, I had the same feeling that I'd had the last time I was here; I'd stepped through the looking glass and everyone on this side was crazy, and they'd been crazy for so long that they made sense to one another, but not to anyone who just arrived from Earth.

Anyway, Brenner and I found Kate, who was with a group that included Howard, and I said to her, 'Time to go.'

Howard reminded us, 'I wanted to show Kate her office.'

Brenner suggested, 'Tomorrow would be good.'

I wasn't sure of the pecking order here, but in places like this, security guys had some weight, so Howard said, 'Fine. See you at nine.' He added, 'I need to give you a copy of the arrest warrant for the suspect.'

I asked Howard, 'Can I have a copy of the CIA kill order?'

Howard didn't reply.

Anyway, Kate and I collected our luggage, and we met Brenner out front where a single Land Cruiser was waiting for us. It was a bright, sunny day, but already getting hot.

Kate said, 'What a beautiful day.' She asked me, 'Isn't this better than New York in February?'

'No.'

Zamo loaded our luggage in the rear, then slid behind the wheel. Brenner got in the front and Kate and I sat in the back.

I asked, 'Where's Mohammed?'

Brenner replied, 'Getting fitted for a suicide belt.'

Funny. I was really getting into this place.

So off we went, and I commented that there was no lead or trail vehicle. Brenner said, 'It's only about six hundred yards to the Sheraton and we don't want to attract undue attention on the street or at the hotel.'

Right. So only one armored Land Cruiser, two armed security men, and two armed passengers. No one will notice.

We got to the outer gates, which slid open, and we were on the street. The Yemeni soldiers were still sitting around, at the top of their game.

Brenner and Zamo had their guns in their laps, so Kate and I did the same.

Across the way from the embassy I saw another walled and guarded compound that I remembered from last time, called Tourist City for some reason, though it was actually a complex of apartment houses and shops for resident and transient Westerners, some of whom were staff from the various embassies. Also living in Tourist City were aid workers and a few poor bastards who were transferred here for business, mostly the oil. This was probably where Kate and I would have lived if we were staying in Sana'a.

Yemenis, I recalled, were not allowed in Tourist City, except as trusted servants, though it was rumored that a few of these servants were Al Qaeda, which you'd expect. In my opinion, it was the least safe place in Sana'a; a terrorist attack waiting to happen.

The best thing about Tourist City was the Russia Club, owned and operated by two entrepreneurial gentlemen from Moscow whose personal mission it was to bring alcohol, drugs, and hookers to Yemen, thereby spreading the benefits of European civilization to this benighted nation. The Russia Club had a second location in Aden, as Buck mentioned in his class, and I'd been invited to both clubs on my last trip to Yemen, but I'd declined. Honest.

We turned right onto a narrow, tree-shaded road, and I asked, 'If I roll down my window, will someone lob a grenade in?'

'Probably,' replied Brenner. 'Just throw it back.'

We all got a laugh at that.

This was going to be a fun assignment.

CHAPTER TWENTY-THREE

Brenner passed us a nylon bag, saying, 'Two satellite phones with chargers, and two hand-held radios. The sat-phones are programmed with the speed dial numbers you'll need. The radios have a selection dial for twenty frequencies, but we are using only two — zone one and zone two. There's also a list of radio call signs in the bag.' He informed us, 'The radios have a short distance — basically point to point — because we don't have antennas or repeaters here.'

I asked him, 'Is our absent team member programmed?'

'Not yet.' He instructed us, 'If death or capture seems imminent, destroy the phones and radios.' He suggested, 'A bullet will do it.'

If I have a bullet left, I'm not shooting my phone.

Brenner also informed us, 'Our radio call sign is Clean Sweep.' He added, 'This has some significance regarding the USS Cole.' He explained, 'Warships returning to port after an engagement often tied a broom to their mast which signaled "Clean Sweep".' In other words, "We got the bastards".' Brenner further informed us, 'The name of this operation is also Clean Sweep.'

Every operation needs a code name, something that doesn't give the enemy any info. Clean Sweep was good. Avenge the *Cole*.

Paul Brenner, man of many bags, passed us another bag, a big blue one, and said, 'Two Kevlar vests. Size should be okay.'

I asked, 'Is that it for the bags?'

'I was going to give you a bag of cookies, but now I'm not.'

Kate laughed.

As we continued on, Brenner informed us, 'This neighborhood is where the US and UK embassy people live who don't live in the embassy compound, or in Tourist City.'

Kate inquired, 'Is this where you live?'

'No, I live near the khat souk. Not too far from here.'

Kate processed that for a second and said, 'Khat souk . . . ?'

'Biggest open-air drug market in the world.' He assured us, 'They sell other things – chickens, cows, firewood, and guns.'

'So,' I speculated, 'you can get high, buy a cow, shoot it, and cook it, all right there.'

'That's what I do most Saturday nights.'

We pulled into a circular drive and headed toward the portico of the Sheraton, which had a mock Mideastern façade, sort of like the embassy.

I'd spent two nights in this Sheraton on my last visit to Sana'a, which I had thought was my last visit to Sana'a.

Zamo stayed with the vehicle, and Brenner, Kate, and I got out and moved toward the front doors where two men in blue camouflage fatigues and blue berets stood with AK-47s. Brenner said, 'They're NSB guys – National Security Bureau.' He added, 'Tonight they could be Al Qaeda.'

'Should we tip them?'

We entered the air-conditioned lobby, and Kate and I went to the front desk, while Brenner stood near the doors. The check-in clerk said, 'Welcome, sir and lady.'

'Thank you, man.'

We gave him our passports, and he looked us up on the computer, then assured us, 'You have beautiful mountain view room. See sunrise.'

'Great.' And at night we can see the mortar flashes before the incoming rounds hit the building.

He also said, 'You stay with us four nights.'

News to me.

The hotel charges were pre-paid, though the clerk didn't know by whom. And neither did I. There's an old saying in this business — 'It's not important to know who fired the bullet; it's important to know who paid for it.'

If I had to guess, I'd say it was the Agency, a.k.a. the Company, not the embassy or the FBI who was paying for all this. Which brought me to the Golden Rule — whoever has the gold makes the rules.

As the clerk photocopied our passports and visas, he told us about the hotel's amenities — fitness center, safe deposit boxes for our guns, medical services if we got wounded, pool, tennis courts, cocktail lounge, and so forth.

'Can I chew khat by the pool?'

'Yes. But please not to spit.'

Sounded reasonable.

Brenner came over to us and said, 'You can stay here, or as I mentioned last night, we can take a walk in the Old City.'

'Thanks, but—'

Kate piped in, 'I'd love to see the Old City.'

'Good. I'll meet you here in the lobby. How about half an hour?'

How about never? Does that work for you?

Kate said, 'See you then.'

Brenner suggested, 'Guns and Kevlar.' He also said to Kate, 'And your scarf, and a camera if you have one.'

We followed the bellhop to the elevators, where an NSB guy with an AK-47 sat in a white plastic chair contemplating his navel. We rode up to the fifth floor of the six-story building, which put a floor between us and incoming.

Our room was nice, and it did indeed have a mountain view and a minibar, and even a bathroom. Three stars. Four if the window was bulletproof.

I tipped the bellhop two bucks, and as Kate and I unpacked, I said to her, 'We could get into a contact situation with Al Qaeda, but not with The Panther.' I added, 'This is not like The Lion, who personally wanted to kill us.'

She said, 'I'm assuming, as Buck and Paul mentioned, that the CIA knows something we don't know.'

'They always do,' I agreed.

Well, now that I was here, I was looking forward to the job. But something was bothering me, something I'd thought about back in New York, and it had to do with the CIA. They were devious, not team players, and they had their own agenda. And those were their good points.

More importantly, they had long memories, and they were into payback. Their official company motto was, 'And ye shall know the truth and the truth shall set you free.' And their unofficial mission statement, also biblical, was, 'An eye for an eye, a tooth for a tooth.' I'm all for that, except if it's my eye or tooth that they want.

And why, you ask, would the CIA want to get even with me or with Kate? Well, once upon a time, Kate and I had inadvertently screwed up a major CIA plan – Operation Wild Fire – that, if it had been successful, would have turned Sana'a and other Islamic cities into nuclear ash. The plan was clever, diabolical, illegal, and very dangerous to human life on earth. Other than that, it was a good plan. Actually, it wasn't.

But it didn't matter what I thought – as I said, Kate and I got caught in the middle of it, and without going into details, Kate and I found ourselves looking down the barrel of a Glock held by the previously mentioned Mr Ted Nash, CIA officer, and I think Kate's one-time lover, which may or may not be relevant to what happened next. Bottom line, Kate was a half-second quicker than Ted, and Ted was dead. Self-defense. Except for the next seven shots. But the police and FBI cleared her of excessive target practice. The CIA, however, did not, and they were not happy.

I didn't worry too much about Kate or me being on a CIA kill list – I mean, I *thought* about it, but it had been a year and a half since the incident, and officially it was over, and the CIA had been advised that they should forget it. But there's only one way to get off a CIA kill list.

Back in the States, it would be unlikely that Kate or I would meet with an unfortunate accident. But overseas, especially in a place like this where the CIA is its own law, it was quite possible that John Corey and Kate Mayfield could have that unfortunate accident. That is, if The Panther didn't get us first. A win-win for the Agency would be dead Panther, dead John, and dead Kate — and all these deaths obscured by the fog of war.

Crazy, I know. I shouldn't even be *thinking* like this. I mean, yeah, this was a CIA operation, and yes, the Agency wanted me and Kate in Yemen — but not to settle an old score. No, they wanted us in Yemen to lure The Panther into a trap; not us into a trap. Right?

Anyway, I didn't think I should share these thoughts with Kate at this time. Maybe I'd wait until we met our CIA guy and see if I picked up on anything that didn't smell right.

Kate asked me, 'What are you thinking about?'

'The CIA wants to kill us.' No, I didn't say that. I said, 'The CIA has been taken to task for failing to predict, suspect, or warn of the attack on the USS Cole. It was a total intelligence failure.'

Kate replied, 'There's enough blame to go around. Naval Intelligence, Defense Intelligence, and the Navy itself for not instituting better security procedures when entering a hostile port.'

'Right. But the CIA always catches the flak. So I think they're motivated and anxious to even the score.' I added, 'They never forget a failure, especially if their failure leads to American deaths.' How's that for planting a thought in her head?

Kate didn't reply for a second, then said, 'The FBI is no different.' She asked me, 'What point are you trying to make?'

'I'm not sure. Just thinking.'

We put on our vests, put a few things in the room safe, then spent the next fifteen minutes getting familiar with our satellite phones and hand-held radios.

The problem with satellite phones was that you needed a clear view of the sky, and the antenna needed to be clear of obstructions, so the sat-phone didn't work well in the woods or work at all indoors. That, plus the line-of-sight limitations on the hand-held radios could make for some interesting situations if the feces hit the fan.

As Brenner said, the satellite phones had about a dozen speed dial numbers, all identified by initials in case the phones fell into the wrong hands. I scrolled through the directory: B.H. – Buck Harris; J.C. – Jesus Christ or John Corey; K.C. – Kate Corey; P.B. – Paul Brenner; and M.D., which could be the closest McDonald's or a doctor. Last time I was here, we usually had a medical doctor with us when we traveled. Not a bad idea.

The embassy number was also on speed dial, plus about six other initials, including H.F., who was probably Howard Fensterman. It's always good to have your lawyer on speed dial when you're out and about trying to whack someone.

I pretended to call and said, 'Hello, Howard? Look, these guys are firing submachine guns at us. Can we return fire? What? You'll call Washington and get back to us? Okay. I'll hold.'

Kate laughed, then said, 'Be nice to Howard.'

Anyway, I didn't recognize the other initials, but I guessed they were our DSS drivers and shotgun riders. None of them, according to Brenner, were our CIA guy, who wished to remain anonymous until he revealed himself. The Agency loves secrecy and drama.

I next looked at our list of radio call signs. On Frequency One were most of the same people as on our satellite phone speed dial. Buck was Clean Sweep One, Brenner Clean Sweep Two, I was Three, Kate was Four, and so forth.

The second radio frequency was to be used by and for Command and Control — the US Embassy in Sana'a, and the Sheraton Hotel in Aden, i.e., the bosses. But as Brenner said, the transmitting and receiving distances were short, so as soon as we were out of Sana'a, we were out of radio contact with the embassy, and same for the Sheraton in Aden. This could be good in regards to upper-echelon meddling. But it could be bad if we needed help.

Next, Kate showed me how to field-strip the Colt .45, then gave me a few tips on aiming and firing.

I'm sure this gun brought back bad memories of when she capped Ted. In fact, as we rode down the elevator, she said to me, 'We haven't worked with the CIA since that last time.'

'Right. How did that work out?'

She didn't reply, then said, 'I just had a troubling thought.'

'Keep that thought.'

She nodded.

CHAPTER TWENTY-FOUR

We met Brenner in the lobby and went out to the Land Cruiser where Zamo was still behind the wheel. I said I wanted to ride shotgun, so Kate and Brenner got in the rear, and off we went.

Brenner said to us, 'We won't be in Sana'a long, but it's good if you have a general sense of the city in case something comes up and we're told to stay here awhile.'

'Also,' I reminded him, 'we want to see if anyone tries to kill us.'

'Right. That too.' He reminded me, 'We want to advertise your presence in Sana'a.'

'How about a billboard?'

Zamo laughed.

'Also, that's why you mentioned in front of Mohammed about us seeing the Old City today.'

'Correct.'

So, tell me how sharp I am. But he didn't, so I moved on and said, 'We're checked into the hotel for four days.'

Brenner informed me, 'That usually means one or two days.' He explained, 'We don't give out information to Yemenis.'

'Right.' And not much to me either.

As we drove downhill toward the Old City, Brenner announced, 'Sana'a was founded by Shem, the son of Noah, after the Flood subsided.'

Maybe it was waterfront property then.

Brenner continued, 'Sana'a claims to be the oldest inhabited city in the world.'

Kate, sitting next to our guide, said, 'That's amazing.'

I inquired, 'How about lunch?'

Brenner replied, 'We'll have lunch in the Old City.'

He pointed to another walled compound on the left and informed us, 'That's the new British Embassy.' He let us know, 'If you're in a tight situation and can't make it to the American Embassy, or if our embassy is under attack, the Brits will let you in.'

'What if they're also under attack?'

'Go to Plan B.'

'Right.' Plan B was bend over and kiss your ass goodbye.

Brenner continued, 'Coming up on the right is the Mövenpick Hotel, where you also have a reservation.' He explained, 'Confuses the enemy.'

Not as much as it confuses me.

Brenner also let us know, 'The hills to the east of here, that you can see from your room, are good places to launch rocket and mortar attacks toward the US and UK embassies, as well as Tourist City and the hotels.'

'That was mentioned in the hotel brochure.'

Zamo laughed again. I liked Zamo.

Brenner continued, 'About six Al Qaeda plots have been foiled in the last year, including one plot to ambush the British ambassador when his convoy left the embassy, and another plot to drive a truck bomb through the US Embassy gates.'

'I thought you said this was a safe neighborhood.'

'I think I said heavily guarded.'

'Got it.' I had a realtor like him once.

Mr Brenner informed us, 'The farther east you go, toward Marib, the more you're in tribal territory and Al Qaeda territory.' He pointed to a road sign and informed us, 'That road to Marib city has become very dangerous, and Marib province seems to be the center of Al Qaeda activity in Yemen.'

I asked Brenner, 'Did you hear about the Al Qaeda attack in Marib on the Hunt Oil installation?'

'I did.'

I said to Kate, 'Early this morning. Buck mentioned it.'

Brenner had nothing to say on that subject, and we continued in silence. I wondered if we'd be going to Marib. In fact, we probably were.

Brenner continued his country orientation and said, 'As you travel south toward Aden, which we'll do in a few days, you're in the tribal lands for a while. Then as you get toward the Gulf of Aden, you're in Al Qaeda territory again, and you're also in the territory of the South Yemen separatist groups who are still trying to secede from North Yemen.' He completed his briefing by saying, 'To the west, as you get to the Red Sea coast, there are also Al Qaeda operatives who are in cahoots with the Somali pirates.'

So, to recap, al-Houthi rebels to the north, Al Qaeda to the south and east, Al Qaeda and pirates to the west, separatist rebels to the south, and tribal warlords in between. Not much room left for camping, hiking, and boating.

Kate asked, 'What does the government control?'

Brenner replied, 'Mostly main roads and towns. But that changes and you have to check with the military, who lie.'

'Then why bother to check?' she asked.

'Protocol.'

Zamo pulled over at a wide bend in the road, and Brenner suggested we get out and look down into the city.

So we got out and stood on an overlook, though Zamo stayed close to the SUV.

We used the opportunity to do a commo check with our sat-phones and hand-held radios. You need to check government-issued equipment.

The old walled city of Sana'a was about half a mile to the

west, and the newer parts of the city spread across the high plateau, as far as the surrounding hills and mountains.

Brenner said, 'Old Sana'a is famous for the tower houses which you can see rising up to ten stories above the walls. There are thousands of them, some going back to the eleventh century, and they are said to be the world's first skyscrapers.'

Kate took a few photos from the overlook, then insisted that Brenner and I pose, which we did without putting our arms around each other's shoulders. Then Kate gave me the camera, and I took a shot of her and Brenner, who did put their arms around each other.

The photo ops were finished, and Brenner returned to his narrative, saying, 'Up until the early 1960s, the old walled city was the entire city of Sana'a, with a population of only about sixty thousand. Now there are about two million.' He added, 'The water table is dropping quickly, and food is becoming a problem.' He informed us, 'Sana'a has become politically and socially unstable, and the city is full of troops and security forces to keep the population in line.'

'More khat.'

'Khat,' replied Mr Brenner, 'is not the solution. It's part of the problem.'

It's actually both, but I didn't want to argue with my tour guide. I asked, 'Does Al Qaeda do khat?'

'Good question. The answer is no. Most Al Qaeda members in Yemen are not Yemenis, and those who are, are prohibited from using khat. So Al Qaeda is sober all day, and everyone else here is spaced out after lunch.' He added, 'That's one reason why I think Al Qaeda is going to win here. Unless we can stop them.'

Right. Like in Vietnam, Paul. How did that work out for you?

Mr Brenner put on his tour guide hat again and said, 'If you look to the west, beyond the tower houses, you'll see what used to be the Jewish and Turkish quarters of the city.' He informed us, 'The Turks are long gone, the Jews mostly gone, and the few remaining Christians live up here now where it's safer.'

'I think you said heavily guarded.'

'Right.' Brenner continued, 'In 1948, during some civil war, tribes from the north laid siege to the walled city and broke in. They looted, pillaged, and burned for days, and a lot of the Old City still remains damaged.' He added, 'That's when the new state of Israel organized what they called Operation Magic Carpet and airlifted about fifty thousand Yemeni Jews to Israel.'

Kate said, 'That's fascinating.'

Lunch?

Brenner continued, 'Sana'a has a long history of being conquered and looted by foreigners, but the main threats have always come from the tribes, who see the city as a piggy bank, a place full of gold, spices, art, and other things they don't have.' He added, 'The population of Sana'a still fears the tribes, who most recently besieged the city in 1968. And now there are the al-Houthi tribesmen, who have come as close as sixty kilometers to the city.'

Kate commented, 'Sounds almost medieval.'

Actually, it sounded like fun. I want to be a warlord.

Brenner switched topics and said, 'Down there, you can see ath-Thawra Hospital – Revolution Hospital – and on the other side of the city is the Kuwait Hospital. If you can't get to the embassy, it's good to know where the hospitals are if you're sick, injured, or nursing a gunshot wound.'

I asked, 'Do they take Blue Cross?'

'No, but they'll take your watch.'

Good one.

Brenner further informed us, 'There are also a number of traditional healers and folk remedies available.' He smiled and said, 'If, for instance, you get malaria, you can sell your disease to the ants.'

'Excuse me?'

'You lie down on an ant mound and proclaim your intent to sell them your malaria.'

I wasn't sure I'd heard him correctly, but I asked, 'Why would the ants want to buy your malaria?'

'I'm not sure,' Brenner confessed, 'but there have been a number of cures reported.' He speculated, 'Maybe it has something to do with the ant venom.'

I asked, 'Who do I sell my hemorrhoids to?'

'Another asshole.' He didn't say that, but I know he was *thinking* it.

Anyway, Brenner pointed out a few other sights and landmarks, including the khat souk, near where he lived, and a place called Ghumdan Fortress, which was built into the eastern wall of the city. He informed us, 'This is the site of the famed Ghumdan Palace, built almost two thousand years ago. The palace was said to be twenty stories high, and the roof was made of alabaster that was so thin and transparent you could see birds flying overhead.'

Kate asked, 'How did they clean the bird shit off the alabaster?'

Actually, I asked that. Kate said, 'John, please.'

She always says that. Meanwhile, we've been standing here too long, twenty feet from the armored vehicle, and at least a dozen vehicles had passed by and slowed down. Zamo was standing with the Land Cruiser between him and the road with his M4 carbine at his side.

Brenner, oblivious to my concern, continued, 'Ghumdan Palace was destroyed in the seventh century by the Islamic armies that were sweeping across the Arabian Peninsula. The stones were used to build the Great Mosque, which you can see over there.' He added, 'The Qalis Cathedral was also destroyed, as were the synagogues.' He paused, then said, 'Islam had arrived.'

Right. And as Al Rasul said, what we were seeing now was a return to a dark and bloody past.

Brenner continued, 'Ghumdan Fortress was built on the palace site by the Turks during the Ottoman Empire, and it now houses Yemeni military barracks and a political prison.' He let us know, 'Later, we have an appointment to speak to a prisoner.'

I asked, 'You mean the Al Qaeda guy captured in the Hunt Oil attack?'

'Correct.'

'Good.' I like interrogating starving prisoners after I've had a big lunch.

We got back in the SUV and continued down toward the city along a winding road.

Kate, sitting next to Brenner, said to him, 'Thank you for an interesting history lesson.'

Brenner replied, 'This is a fascinating place. It grows on you.'

Not on me, Paul.

Today being Sunday, and thinking about Noah, Shem, Sana'a, and all that, I asked, 'After God sent the Flood to cleanse the earth of the sinful and the wicked, do you think he was pissed off that the people who repopulated the earth got it so wrong again?'

No one replied to my profound question, and no one bothered to defend the earth's inhabitants. Amen.

CHAPTER TWENTY-FIVE

We came down onto the plateau and into a drab neighborhood of modern concrete buildings that sat between the hills and the east wall of the Old City.

Brenner pointed across the road and said, 'That's where I live,' indicating a three-story concrete slab structure that looked like it had seen better days. He informed us, 'Built in the late sixties when the city first started spreading outside the walls. It has hot water and a manageable vermin population.' He added, 'Ten bucks a month for Yemenis, forty for me.'

I asked, 'Does that include parking?'

'It does. I keep my motorcycle in the foyer.'

So Mr Cool has a motorcycle. Figures.

He informed us, 'That's the best way to get around this city, and I can go where assassins in cars can't go.' He added, 'I can be in the embassy in five minutes if I push it.'

I had the thought that Mr Brenner was showing off a little for Mrs Corey. Guys are assholes.

Anyway, Zamo pulled over beside a concrete wall, and Brenner said, 'We'll walk through the khat souk, then into the Old City.' He told Zamo, 'I'll call you every half hour, or call me.'

So we left Zamo in the nice air-conditioned armored Land Cruiser and walked toward a gate in the concrete wall where a guy sat cradling his AK-47.

Brenner said, 'This is a fairly new souk, built I think in the seventies outside the Old City wall, but the mentality was still walls, so this souk is walled, as you can see.'

Right. Walls are good. Moats, too. Keeps the riff-raff out. Especially riff-raff with guns.

Brenner suggested to Kate, 'You might want to wrap that scarf over your face.'

Kate did that and I asked her, 'Would you like a cigarette?'

She mumbled something through the scarf that sounded like, 'Fook-yo.' Arabic?

Anyway, we passed through a gate into the khat souk, which was sort of like a farmers market, filled with jerry-built stalls in the open plaza and surrounded by permanent buildings along the perimeter walls.

The place was bustling and crowded with white-robed men wearing jambiyahs, who shared the space with donkeys, cows, and camels. Some of the cows had been disassembled and their parts were hanging from crossbeams, covered with flies. And did I mention that the ground was covered with shit?

Brenner said, 'It's relatively safe here, but let's stick close.'

We were the only Western people I saw, except for some young guys in jeans and T-shirts who were snapping pictures of piles of green leaves that I assumed were not spinach. I mean, this was junkie heaven. I had a sudden urge to make a bust.

I didn't see any women in the souk, except for Kate, and oddly no one seemed to be paying much attention to us. But now and then, when I looked back over my shoulder, I caught people watching us.

Brenner stopped at a khat stall and said something in Arabic to the proprietor, who looked very happy with his career choice. Brenner said to us, 'There are dozens of varieties of khat. This gentleman claims he has the best khat in all of Yemen, grown in Wadi Dhahr, and picked fresh daily.' He also informed us, 'This man claims he is the purveyor to the president.'

'George Bush chews khat?'

That got a laugh.

Anyway, we did a walk around the souk, avoiding the cow pies and donkey bombs. Brenner took Kate's camera to shoot pictures for her, and he paid a kid about ten cents to take a great shot of the three of us standing in front of a shoulder-high pile of wacky weed. I couldn't wait to send the picture to Kate's parents with a nickel bag of khat and a note: *Chewing khat with Kate. Love, John.*

After admiring the cow pens and the piles of firewood, we stopped in the sporting goods department, where there were tables of fully automatic assault rifles sitting along a wall.

Brenner said, 'Most of these AK-47s are cheap knockoffs, some are better-made Chicoms – Chinese Communist – but a few are the real deal, made in Mother Russia. Those go for about five hundred bucks – a year's pay for a working man.'

But a good investment for the future.

Brenner informed us, 'I have one in my apartment.' He added, 'It's a good gun.' He picked up an AK-47 and stared at it a long time, then said, as if to himself, 'A very good gun.'

Right. And obviously it brought back some memories for Paul Brenner of another hellhole.

He put the gun back on the table, and the proprietor said in English, 'Five hundred for you. And I give a hundred rounds for free.'

I said to him, 'Throw in a cow and you got a deal.'

We left sporting goods and headed through a gate that led toward the high wall of the Old City.

Brenner speed-dialed his satellite phone and said, 'Leaving the khat souk, entering the Old City.' He listened, then said, 'Okay. Four-thirty at the al-Mahdi Mosque.' He hung up and said to us, 'Our appointment at Ghumdan prison is for five P.M. We'll meet Zamo at the mosque on the other side of the Old City, then drive to Ghumdan.' He also informed us, 'Kate has to stay in the vehicle.'

Girls miss all the fun around here.

We passed through an opening in the city wall, and it was literally like stepping back in time. Huge tower houses with ornate façades blocked the sun from the narrow, alley-like streets, and the sound level went from loud internal combustion engines to the hushed murmur of people and animal-drawn carts.

Brenner said to us, 'This is the largest and most pristine walled city in the Mideast, covering an area of over one square kilometer. The old Jewish and Turkish quarters on the west side of the city cover another square kilometer.' He further informed us, 'The east and west halves of the city are divided by Wadi as Sa'ila. When the wadi is dry, as it is now, it's used for vehicle traffic.'

'And when it's wet, how do they paint the white line?'

He smiled politely, then continued, 'The Mahdi Mosque is near the wadi. If we get separated, our rendezvous point is there.'

'Okay. Mahdi at the wadi.' My appetite had recovered from the shit souk, and I asked, 'Where is lunch?'

'Up ahead in a tower house converted into a guest house.'

So we continued on through a maze of alleys and narrow, twisting streets, some of which led into souks that were crowded with people, animals, and motor scooters.

We noticed the buildings that had been damaged or destroyed by the 1968 storming of the Old City by the tribes, and Brenner said, 'The tribes could come again. Or maybe Al Qaeda this time. And that could be soon.'

Right. But first, lunch.

Anyway, I was sure we didn't have a tail, and the place seemed safe enough, but I was happy to be packing heat and wearing a vest.

Brenner motioned to the tower houses and said, 'The first few floors as you can see are made of stone, and the upper floors are mud brick. The ground floor is used for animals and to collect human excrement from the upper floors.'

'Sounds like 26 Federal Plaza.'

Brenner continued, 'Each tower house has a shaft for excrement, and another shaft that's used to haul up well water.' He informed us, 'This presents a sanitation problem.'

'You think?' I asked Brenner, 'Is this restaurant on the ground floor with the animals and excrement?'

'No. Two floors up.' He explained, 'That's called the diwan, where guests are received.'

And no one would know if you farted.

He continued, 'Above the diwan are the floors where the

extended family lives, sharing a single kitchen.' He concluded, 'The top floor is called the mafraj, literally, a room with a view — sort of the penthouse, and this is where honored male guests gather to chew khat and watch the sunset.'

I need a room like that. Hey, guys, let's go up to the mafraj and stare into the sun and get wasted. Then we can bungee jump down the excrement shaft.

Anyway, Kate seemed overwhelmed by the experience, and she took lots of photos and asked Brenner lots of questions, and he was happy to share his knowledge with her, or make up answers. If he was a peacock, his tail feathers would be fully fanned out by now.

We continued our walk without seeing much evidence of the twenty-first century. There were a few other Westerners wandering around on some of the streets, so we didn't stop traffic. But these annoying kids kept following us asking for 'baksheesh, baksheesh,' which I remembered from Aden meant either alms or get-the-fuck-out-of-here money. Brenner said to ignore them, but Kate wanted to engage them in playful conversation, or take their pictures, which cost five cents.

Brenner also said, 'If the kids suddenly disappear, we may be having a problem.'

Gotcha. 'Hey, Abdul, you want a piggyback ride?'

Anyway, as a detective, I noticed what was missing. Women. I'd seen fewer women on the streets than I'd seen dead rats.

I asked Brenner about that and he replied, 'The women do their errands in the morning, usually with male escorts, then they stay indoors to cook, clean, and take care of the kids.'

'Sounds grim,' said FBI Special Agent Kate Mayfield.

Brenner had a joke and said, 'But Thursday is wet burqua night at the wadi.' He added, 'Bring your laundry.'

Funny. But Kate didn't laugh, so I didn't either. You gotta be careful, even here.

Sunday wasn't the Sabbath around here so everyone who had a job was at work. But what I noticed, as I'd noticed last time in Aden, were hundreds, really thousands, of young men on the streets and in the souks, obviously unemployed and killing time. Their futures would probably take one of three paths: petty crime, emigration, or Al Qaeda. Or maybe someday they'd just revolt against the government, hoping that anything that came after would be better than this. Indeed, they were a demographic time bomb waiting to explode.

Brenner said, 'Here's the restaurant.'

Kate said, 'That was fascinating.'

Brenner offered, 'If we don't go to Aden tomorrow, I can show you the rest of the city.'

I thought we'd already pushed our luck. But this was the guy who did a second tour in Vietnam. But hey, you gotta die somewhere.

CHAPTER TWENTY-SIX

The restaurant was called, appropriately, 'Old Sana'a,' and so was the tower guest house in which it was located.

I assumed Brenner had been here and he hadn't died of *E. coli* or a gunshot wound, so we followed him through an open arch into a large, high-ceilinged space, lit only by sunlight coming through narrow windows in the stone walls. I was relieved to see that the space had been cleared of livestock and excrement, though a hint of all that remained in the air.

We climbed a spiral staircase to the diwan level, where a white-robed man sat behind a table, on which was a stack of assault rifles. I guess you had to check your guns here. The man smiled, decided we were probably English speakers, and said, 'Welcome. For lunch or room?'

Brenner replied, 'Restaurant, please.'

The desk clerk/maître d'armaments stood, grabbed three menus, and we followed him through one of those Casablanca-type archways with hanging beads into a large, sunlit dining room that took up the whole floor of the tower house. He escorted us to a low round table with beanbag chairs near an open window and said, 'Good looking.'

I wasn't sure if he meant the view, or if he meant me or Brenner. Kate was scarfed, so he didn't mean her. I replied politely, 'Thank you. This is a Christian Dior shirt.'

'Yes?'

So we sat cross-legged on these horrid stuffed cushions, and I looked around. It was a pleasant enough place, with ceiling fans, oil lamps on the tables, and carpets on the floor – sort of a cross between Rick's Place and the den of Ali Baba and the Forty Thieves.

I asked Brenner, 'Come here often?'

'Now and then.' He explained, 'It's not a good idea for a Westerner to be a regular anywhere in Sana'a.'

'Right.' Except maybe the Russia Club.

I looked out the window into the backyards of several tower houses. The yards were crowded with vegetable gardens, goats, and chickens. There were no play swings or slides, but a few barefoot kids were having fun chasing the poultry. A woman in a full black balto and veil was scrubbing clothes in a copper tub. In some weird way, this scene reminded me of the tenement I grew up in — sans goats. It was such an ordinary, peaceful scene that it was hard to believe the rest of the country was descending into violence and chaos.

Brenner said, 'That's our emergency exit if we need one.'

'Right.' About a twenty-foot drop into a pile of manure. How would I phrase that in my incident report?

There was a weird, smoky smell in the air, which I commented on, and Brenner informed me, 'That's frankincense.'

'Where's he sitting?'

'It's an Arabic gum resin. Used in perfume or incense.'

'Yeah? How about frankin-khat chewing gum? Yes?'

Kate interjected, 'Stop.'

Brenner further informed us, 'The Yemenis believe it was a Yemeni wise man who brought the gift of frankincense to the baby Jesus.'

Better than fruitcake. Right?

Anyway, the place was about half full on this Sunday afternoon, mostly young Westerners, male and female, but also some weird-looking dudes wearing daggers and white robes, with dark beards and black eyes, who were glancing at us. There were no Yemeni ladies lunching.

Kate still had her scarf over her face, which limited her choices on the menu, but Brenner said to her, 'You can uncover your face here, but I'd advise you to keep your hair covered.'

Kate did that, and I said to her, 'I forgot how beautiful you were.'

Brenner also said to Kate, 'It might be best if John or I gave your order to the waiter.' He explained, unnecessarily, 'Men don't take orders from women.'

'Incredible,' Kate said.

Brenner was right — this place could grow on you. But to show my sensitivity to women's issues, I said, 'Unbelievable.'

Brenner agreed and said, 'The male guest workers who return from Europe and America have seen the twenty-first century, and they've been subtly influenced by what they've seen in the West.'

I thought about Nabeel, and also The Panther, and I wondered if this was true. Or, if they *had* been influenced by the West, it wasn't in a positive way. Bottom line, the winds of change that were sweeping Islam were blowing backwards. They were happily miserable and rigid, and we should leave them alone — except for knocking off a few of them who fucked with us. Like Osama bin Laden. And The Panther.

A waiter dressed in theme costume came over, and Brenner suggested the local fruit drink or the shai, a spiced tea. Kate said to Brenner, 'Shai,' and Brenner repeated it to the guy and ordered one for himself. The menu was written in Arabic and bad English, and I saw that they had non-alcoholic beer, which possibly had fermented in the bottle, so I said to Kate, 'Tell Paul to tell the waiter I want a beer.' Did I get that right?

Anyway, we made small talk, and Kate asked Brenner, 'Where are you from?'

'South Boston.'

'Do you miss it?'

'I don't get there much. I live in Virginia now. Falls Church.' He added, 'That's where CID Headquarters is, and it was my last duty station before I left the Army.'

Kate seemed to want to know more about Paul Brenner, and with some prodding, he gave her his history — drafted into the Army at eighteen, infantryman in Vietnam, decided to make the Army a career, went to military police school, second tour in Vietnam as an MP, then transferred to the US Army Criminal Investigation Division, and served in various Army posts around the world. He had apparently been in a special CID unit that handled high-profile and/or sensitive cases, and his last case involved the murder of a female US Army captain who was also the daughter of an Army general who had been highly decorated in the first Gulf War.

I thought I remembered this case, because it had made the news at the time, a year or so after the Gulf War, and I had the impression that this case had somehow led to the early retirement of Chief Warrant Officer Paul Brenner.

Brenner didn't mention his clandestine mission to post-war Vietnam, either out of modesty or because he still wasn't allowed to talk about it. This mission, though, must have redeemed his reputation or something, and maybe the Army's equivalent of Tom Walsh asked him to name a job, and Brenner picked the Diplomatic Security Service. Fun and travel. In fact, Brenner told us that he'd served with the DSS in London, then Athens. I wonder what he did wrong to get sent here.

Brenner concluded his edited history, and I noticed it was all professional, lacking any personal details, with no mention of marriage or divorce, kids, or the current lady back in the States.

Kate didn't prod him on that subject, and I certainly didn't. All I wanted to know about Mr Paul Brenner was if I could trust him, and whether or not he had a set of balls. He seemed okay in both categories. He also seemed bright, which was good, but I couldn't determine if he had good or bad professional judgment, which was crucial. I myself display impressively bad judgment on occasion, but I always temper that with acts of irrational risk taking. Ask my wife. Brenner, I suspected, was a little like me in those respects, which is the sign of the alpha male. Most of us are dead by now, of course, or incarcerated, or permanently disabled, but some of us are lucky. I'm lucky. And smart.

Anyway, I thought I could work with this guy, and I didn't think he was going to get me killed – I could do that on my own, thank you.

Kate, too, seemed impressed with Paul Brenner, though I doubt she'd analyzed why. Women's intuition.

Our cocktails arrived, and the waiter asked if we had made a choice for lunch. We hadn't, but a quick scan of the menu showed me that my choices were limited to animals that I could see from the window.

Kate said to Brenner, 'Why don't you order for us?'

Brenner had to order for Kate anyway, so I agreed but warned him, 'No organs.'

Brenner ordered in Arabic, then asked us, 'Do you want utensils? Or do you want to use your fingers?'

We didn't know one another that well, so we agreed on utensils, and when the waiter left I took the opportunity to speak to

Brenner without Buck present. I asked, 'Why do we need a CIA guy on the team?'

'It's their show. Also, they have all the information we need.'

'Let's get the information and leave the CIA guy in Aden.'

Brenner asked me, 'Why wouldn't you want a CIA officer on the team?'

Because the CIA wants to kill me and my wife. But that would sound silly if I said it out loud, so I replied, 'They tend to complicate things. And they're not team players.'

'Neither are you from what I hear.'

'If I'm on the team, I play with the team.'

Kate said, 'That's true.' She remembered to add, 'But John sometimes makes up his own rules.'

You see why I love my wife.

Brenner stayed quiet a moment, then said, 'To further answer your question, it's my understanding that Predator drones with video surveillance cameras are an important part of this operation. And as you may know, in Yemen only the CIA has operational control of the Predators. So that's why we need a CIA officer with us when we go into the Badlands – to control the Predator drones on aerial reconnaissance missions.' He explained, 'We can have real-time video surveillance transmitted directly to a video monitor on the ground.'

'And then the Predator launches a Hellfire missile against the target.'

He didn't reply for a second, then said, 'I suppose that's an option.' He added, 'That has been very effective here and in Afghanistan. We've killed dozens of important Al Qaeda leaders that way.'

'Right.' They leave their cave or mud hut to go take a leak, and next thing they know, they're holding their dick in Paradise.

I asked Brenner, 'What about taking this suspect alive?'

Brenner shrugged and replied, 'I don't know. I'm not sure what the actual goal is.'

'That makes three of us.'

He continued, 'The way I see it, Washington would like to take this guy alive, but it's easier to kill him. So maybe if the opportunity to capture him presents itself, then that's what we'll try to do. But if that seems impossible – or too dangerous – then we fix his location and call in the drones and Hellfires.'

I nodded, and added, 'Then we Ziploc some pieces for ID.'

'Right. We have the suspect's prints on file – and also DNA from his family.'

Kate commented, 'Maybe I don't need my arrest warrant.'

Brenner assured her, 'We need you and your arrest warrant in case we have the opportunity to apprehend the suspect.'

Kate nodded tentatively. Actually, Kate and her arrest warrant were cover for what was most likely the assassination of an American citizen. I had no problem with that, and I was happy to have the cover in case this thing came back to bite us in the ass vis-à-vis Mr and Mrs al-Darwish's lawsuit, or some other silly legality. Fucked-up war.

Kate also asked, 'If we do apprehend the suspect, do we turn him over to the Yemeni authorities, then ask for extradition, or do we attempt to get the suspect out of the country?' She added, 'In other words, extradition or rendition?'

Brenner shrugged again and replied, 'This is all beyond my pay grade.'

'Why,' I asked, 'is State Department Intelligence involved?'

Brenner replied, 'First, keep in mind that Buck Harris is officially a diplomat, attached to the economic assistance mission, which is why he travels around the country. Forget SDI. Second, we want a diplomatic component to our operation.' He stressed, 'We want to involve the State Department.'

'Right.' Meaning that if things went wrong — or even if things went right — the State Department could do what they do best: apologize to the host government for violating their sovereignty and offer them a few million bucks to forget it. That's what diplomats are for.

Brenner reminded me, 'Buck is an invaluable asset. He knows the country, the people, and the language.'

'Right. We love Buck. But he knows more than he's sharing.'

Brenner said, 'Let's take it a step at a time and see how it plays out.' He also suggested, 'We'll get some clarification from our Agency guy.'

Paul Brenner had apparently not worked with the CIA before.

Our food came and it was served family style in big bowls, and everyone around us was eating directly out of the bowls with their fingers. We, however, had plates, serving spoons, and utensils. The food actually tasted good, whatever it was. Did I take my Cipro this morning?

I said to Brenner, 'Tell me about this wounded Al Qaeda guy that we're seeing in the slammer.'

Brenner told us, 'We got this appointment because we told the PSO that we think this attack could have been planned by one of the Cole plotters. Therefore, Mr John Corey of the FBI Evidence Response Team would like to speak to the prisoner.' He added,

'We have an understanding with the Yemeni government, based on cash and other good and valuable considerations, that they will cooperate in anything having to do with the Cole.' He concluded, 'I have no idea if this prisoner knows anything about the Cole or The Panther, but we'll certainly ask.'

'Can we torture him?'

'I'm sure that's been done.' He added, 'But the PSO was probably focusing more on the oil installation attack than on The Panther.'

'Right. But when we ask this guy about The Panther, the PSO guys who are present will know what our focus is.'

Brenner replied, 'That's okay.' He explained, 'Assuming someone in the prison is reporting to Al Qaeda, then this is one way of getting the message to The Panther that John Corey is in town looking for him.' He reminded me, 'That's the point.'

'Right. Why do I keep forgetting I'm bait?'

'Not bait,' Brenner corrected. 'That's such a negative word. I like to think of you as a lure.'

Funny? Maybe not.

Kate asked, 'Will Colonel Hakim be at the prison?'

Brenner replied, 'Probably.' He explained, 'He seems to be the PSO guy who is assigned to keep an eye on the American Embassy.'

I asked, 'Whose side is he on?'

Brenner replied, 'The CIA thinks he's loyal to the Yemeni government – but what does that mean? It doesn't mean he's pro-American, or anti-Al Qaeda. Like most people here, his first loyalty is to himself, then to his faith – or vice versa. His next loyalty is to his ancestral tribe, his clan, and his family, followed by a loose loyalty to the concept of being a Yemeni. His last loyalty, if it exists at all, is to the government.'

I could see why this country wasn't working. I said to Brenner, 'The question is, Does Colonel Hakim have ties to Al Qaeda?'

Brenner replied, 'He may have contacts. Most high-ranking people do. But in this country, that doesn't make him a traitor. It makes him smart.' He added, 'People with money or power are covering all their bets until they see who looks like the winner here.' He further explained, 'The Americans are putting their money on a bad government, but it's the only play we have.'

I suggested, 'Let's whack who we have to whack to avenge the Cole, and get the hell out of here before we get in deeper.'

Brenner thought a minute and said, 'It sort of reminds me of Vietnam ... a corrupt, double-dealing government, backed by the US out of necessity, fighting a tough, single-minded enemy who terrorized a population that didn't care who won as long as they could live in peace ... Even the hill tribes here remind me of the hill tribes in Vietnam who hated and fought both the government and the Viet Cong. And we were right in the middle of it. The quagmire. And we keep doing the same thing, expecting different results.'

No argument there.

Kate said, 'It's the same situation in Iraq and Afghanistan.'

Brenner seemed to have returned from the jungles of Southeast Asia to the sands of the Middle East, and he said to me, 'I understand you've had some experience with interrogating Cole suspects in Aden.'

'Right. But not too successfully.' I explained, 'Everyone had fun lying to the Americans – the police, the PSO guys, the prisoners, and even the translators. And after we left the prison, they probably all had a khat chew together and yucked it up.' I added, 'Assholes.'

Brenner assured me, 'The Yemeni government is a little more worried now, and they've been more cooperative.'

'You mean like Colonel Hakim at the airport?'

Brenner didn't reply, and asked me, 'When you were interrogating the Cole suspects in Aden, did the name Bulus ibn al-Darwish or al-Numair – The Panther – ever come up?'

'No. I don't think the FBI or CIA knew about him at that time.' I thought a moment, then added, 'But I remember now there was some suspicion, or a rumor, that an American-born Muslim may have been involved.'

Brenner nodded, then said, 'It was apparently The Panther's idea to attack an American warship that was on a regularly scheduled refueling stop in Aden Harbor.' He informed us, 'This was different from most Al Qaeda attacks in Europe or the Mideast, which are directed against soft targets. This was a rare attack against the American military.' He added, 'Very bold, with a high risk of failure. And yet they succeeded in crippling a high-tech American warship and killing seventeen American sailors.'

Right. But in a way, The Panther miscalculated. This attack got the Americans into Yemen, and now Al Qaeda in the Arabian Peninsula was under pressure. I said, 'As with 9/11, Al Qaeda got more than they bargained for.'

'Agreed. And that's what we have to show them. There is a price to pay.'

Kate said, 'They know that. But it hasn't stopped them from escalating the attacks. In fact, they're stronger in Yemen than they were at the time of the Cole attack.'

Brenner replied, 'That's partly due to a dysfunctional government.'

I asked, 'Ours or theirs?'

Anyway, we called for the check, which was written on a scrap of paper — eight million rials or something, which came to about three bucks, drinks included, and Brenner treated. I could live like a sultan in Yemen.

I would have asked for a doggie bag, but the waiter might misunderstand and I'd wind up eating Fido later.

I asked, 'Does anyone have to use the excrement shaft?'

On the way out, I said to the guy at the front desk, 'Everything was terrific. We'll be back tomorrow for lunch. One P.M. John Corey.' Tell The Panther.

'Good. Tomorrow.'

'Is one of these guns mine?'

'No, you don't bring gun.'

'Okay. I think I left it on my donkey—'

'John.'

'Ciao.'

Kate wrapped her scarf over her face, and Brenner checked in with Zamo, then we went down to the street into the bright sunlight where it had gotten hotter.

Without any discussion, we checked out the crowded street, then crossed to the other side and watched the door to the restaurant.

You always need to go through the drill, even when things look and feel safe. In fact, that's when you most need to keep your head out of your ass. And you needed to keep reminding yourself that the hunter is also the hunted.

CHAPTER TWENTY-SEVEN

B renner knew his way around the narrow, twisting streets of the Old City, and he said we had time to stop at Hope in Their Hands before we met Zamo.

I'm usually good at spotting a tail, but half the men here looked alike, with the same white robes, headgear, and beards. And we three had the opposite problem; there weren't many Westerners in Sana'a, and we stuck out like pigs in a mosque.

We reached Hope in Their Hands and entered. The clientele were all Western — male and female backpackers, a European tour group, and some ladies who could have been aid workers or Western embassy people.

Brenner said to Kate, 'You can remove your scarf here.'

I suggested, 'Wrap it around your eyes while you shop.'

'Maybe I'll wrap it around your neck.'

I saw that coming.

Kate unwrapped, revealing herself as the best-looking woman in the shop, except maybe for a twenty-something backpacker with an Australian accent and long red hair. But I digress.

As Kate looked around the shop, and Brenner looked at the

door, I got into a conversation with a young guy, an American named Matt Longo from New York. Young Mr Longo was living in Sana'a in a tower guest house, though not the one where we had lunch. He was a Yale grad with a degree in Mideast studies, spoke passable Arabic, and he was here to learn the more pure and ancient Arabic in the Land That Time Forgot. He'd been in Yemen a month, and he had another month to go.

I asked him, 'Has anyone tried to kidnap you yet?'

He thought that was funny and replied, 'No. These are really nice people.'

'Right. But the State Department keeps issuing travelers' warnings about the not so nice people here.'

He shrugged and said, 'They overreact. I've been all over the Middle East. Never had a problem.'

'Good. But watch yourself.'

He confessed to me, 'I'm half Jewish, so I get it.'

'Keep that to yourself.'

'Yeah.' He asked me, 'Have you seen the Jewish Quarter yet?'

'It's on my list.'

'It's worth seeing. Still mostly deserted. Like, houses with Stars of David on them that haven't been lived in for fifty, sixty years. It's weird. Like, why don't the Yemenis tear them down? Or move in? It's like they're waiting for the Jews to come back.'

'That might be a long wait.'

'Yeah. But you never know.'

'Maybe after the next flood.'

He told me, 'Next week, I'm going to Marib with a few people.' He explained, 'The pre-Islamic ruins. Temples to the sun

233

and moon gods. Queen of Sheba's palace. You should check it out.'

'You should check out the security situation first.'

'Yeah. I know.' He informed me, 'There's like a police force here – the National Security Bureau. They protect tourists. For a price. They're giving us, like, twenty armed guys for the trip for two hundred bucks. Includes transportation.'

I reminded him, 'You get what you pay for.' I gave him some recent intel. 'There was an attack in that area last night. American oil installation. Looks like Al Qaeda.'

Mr Longo, who was twenty-something and immortal, did not seem concerned.

He asked me, 'Why are you here?'

'I thought the travel agent said Sweden.'

He laughed, then assured me, 'You'll get more out of this.'

'I plan to.' I asked, 'You alone?'

'My girlfriend's coming in a few days.'

I advised him, 'Register your names and local address with the consulate at the embassy.'

'Okay.'

'You know where the American Embassy is?'

'No.'

'Find out.'

'Okay.'

'Do I sound like your parents?'

'Sorta.'

I told him where I was staying, and I said, 'If I'm still in town when your girlfriend gets here, come on over to the hotel and my wife and I will buy you dinner and a real drink.'

'Thanks.' He said, 'If you want to go on that Marib trip, we have room.' He added, 'About twenty bucks a head.'

That's about what Al Qaeda pays for a head.

I took his satellite phone number, wished him good luck, and joined Kate in the veil and balto department.

It occurred to me that Sana'a was a deceptively serene city; not dangerous enough to keep you off the streets, but not safe enough for a Westerner to be wandering around alone. I think it all depended on who you were and what the situation was at the moment. For us – American Embassy people – Sana'a was always an adventure. For Matt Longo, it was one stop on a long journey.

Anyway, the Yemeni ladies who ran the shop were nice, spoke English, and seemed to be of the educated class. One of them, Anisa, insisted on taking us upstairs where Yemeni women – mostly widows and divorced ladies, Anisa said – were cutting fabrics and sewing garments by hand or on old treadle sewing machines.

It's rare for women in this country to work outside of the home, but this shop and factory seemed to be tolerated because of its charitable purpose. Brenner informed us, 'The Koran exhorts Muslims to be charitable and help the poor.'

'What Korean?'

'Koran.'

'Oh, right.' How many more times could I use that one?

Anyway, Kate helped the poor to the tune of three shopping bags full of clothes, reminding me that her clothes were still in New York awaiting a Yemen mailing address. She also bought a black balto, which, as Buck suggested, is not a bad garment to own if you should need to blend in. They didn't sell men's dresses, or whatever they call those things, so I was off the hook on that.

Kate's stuff came to about twenty bucks, so I couldn't complain, and I was moved to donate another twenty to the charity, partly in gratitude for the third-world factory outlet prices.

We left the shop, and Kate wrapped her pretty face in the scarf. We crossed the street to the jambiyah souk, a small square that looked like it had been there since the Year of the Flood. Literally.

Brenner steered me toward a tiny shop that Buck had recommended, and where the proprietor, Mr Hassan, seemed to remember Mr Brenner. I wouldn't be surprised if Brenner and Buck got a kickback. Or if Mr Hassan made a call to someone after we left.

Brenner seemed happy to share with me his knowledge of curved daggers, and within fifteen minutes I found myself the about-to-be proud owner of a mean-looking jambiyah with a sheep-horn handle. A hundred bucks, marked down from three hundred because we were Americans. Or marked up from twenty bucks because we were Americans. Arguing price with an Arab in a souk is not one of my many strengths, so I gave Mr Hassan the hundred bucks, and he threw in a hand-tooled leather belt and a silver-tipped sheath.

I asked Mr Hassan, a wizened old man with a long white beard, 'Anyone ever killed with this?'

He understood enough English to smile, and he was honest enough to reply, 'No. For you to make first kill.'

I had this sudden fantasy image of me in Tom Walsh's office, saying to him, 'I have something for you from Yemen. Close your eyes.'

The transaction completed, we left the knife shop with me

wearing my belt and sheathed dagger, which, if you're interested, is worn not at your side, but in front, with the curved tip pointing to the right. Left if you're gay. I made that up.

Kate said to me, 'That knife cost five times more than all the clothes I bought.'

'Boys' toys are expensive,' I reminded her.

We didn't have time to visit the nearby donkey market, which was a disappointment, but something to look forward to another day. We headed west until we came to the wide wadi that separates the Old City into east side and west side, sort of like Fifth Avenue does in Manhattan. And there the comparison ends. The wadi was dry, as Brenner had said, and the streambed was partially paved and heavy with traffic. We crossed at what looked like the only bridge and headed south toward the al-Mahdi Mosque.

If Al Qaeda was following, this was their last chance to make a move before we got in the armored vehicle – and I would have welcomed an early opportunity to use my new gun. The only thing I really worried about was someone with a car filled with explosives or someone wearing a suicide belt who wanted to be in Paradise before dinner. Everything else, I and my companions could handle.

Brenner called Zamo on the radio, and we stayed in contact until we spotted one another.

Zamo pulled up as we were walking, and we jumped into the Land Cruiser and continued south along the wadi, with me riding shotgun again.

Brenner asked Zamo, 'Anything interesting?'

'Nope. Just some guy giving me a crate of mangos.' He added, 'It's in the back.'

Brenner said, 'The mangos are ticking.'

They laughed.

Obviously these two had developed a gift for frontline humor. I guess this kept them sane. Or they were past that point.

CHAPTER TWENTY-EIGHT

As we headed toward Ghumdan Fortress, I pulled out my jambiyah and showed it to Zamo, who glanced at it and said politely, 'Nice.' He advised me, 'No one should ever get close enough that you have to use a knife.'

'Agreed.' I remembered my last meeting with The Lion and said, 'But it happens.'

'Yeah. But it should only happen if you want it to happen.'

'Right.' I changed the subject and asked him, 'So, how many kills you got?'

He replied matter-of-factly, 'Eleven confirmed, two possible, one miss.' He added, 'The asshole bent over for some reason.' He laughed and said, 'Maybe he saw a nickel on the ground.'

'His lucky day.' I again changed the subject and asked, 'What do you do here for fun?'

'I'm doing it.'

Within five minutes, we were approaching the walls and watch-towers of Ghumdan Fortress, a forbidding-looking place of dark brick that dominated the landscape.

Brenner said to us, 'The Turks built this place in the nineteenth century, on the site of the ancient Ghumdan Palace as I mentioned.' He added, 'The Turkish occupation was brutal, and it was said that no Yemeni who entered Ghumdan Fortress ever came out.'

Right. Most old cities have a place like this, an iconic fortress-prison with a bad history whose very name strikes fear into the city's inhabitants – especially the kids. Like, 'Clean your room, Amir, or you're going to Ghumdan.' Most of these places in the civilized world are now museums and tourist attractions, like the Tower of London. But here, it was still in the same old business, under new management.

As we pulled up to the gates of the fortress, I advised, 'Veils for those who need them.'

Brenner lowered his window and said something in Arabic to the soldier, and I heard the names Corey and Brenner. That's us. The soldier stared at Kate, then said, 'Wait,' and went back into the guardhouse.

I asked Brenner, 'Been here before?'

'Once.' He explained, 'Some idiot from DC on an official visit to the embassy was speaking to a Yemeni woman on the street. She was upscale, unveiled, and smiling too much.' He added, 'They both got busted.'

I pointed out, 'It was all her fault. If she was wearing her veil, none of that would have happened – not the chatting up, and not the smiling.'

Brenner had no comment on that and said, 'Anyway, I sprung him and got him on a plane home.'

Kate asked from behind her scarf, 'What happened to her?'

Brenner replied, 'Don't know. Probably got slapped around and got a warning.'

Definitely hard to get laid here.

An officer came over to our vehicle, and he was quite pleasant, saying, 'Please to park car near flagpole and await a person.' He added, 'Lady not go from car.'

Brenner said something in Arabic, including 'As-salaam alaikum,' and off we went.

The center of the fortress was a large, open field of dirt and gravel, probably once a parade ground and muster area, now used mostly for military equipment. A few soldiers sat around in white plastic chairs, chewing something. What could it be?

Brenner pointed out some old Soviet tanks and self-propelled howitzers, plus newer American Humvees and trucks. He said, 'We're supplying them with as much equipment as we can spare from Iraq and Afghanistan. But we don't want to give them too much because this place could become Al Qaeda nation in a year or two.' He further explained, 'Also, half this stuff sits here needing parts or repairs, and they don't have trained mechanics or a parts inventory system, which they don't really need anyway because most of the parts get stolen. And the equipment that works is used to fight the tribes instead of Al Qaeda.'

Who cares? Not me. I just need to whack one guy and get the hell out of here. Brenner has been here too long.

He also told us, 'The Yemeni government doesn't want American military advisors who could straighten out their logistical and training problems, but they want American money and equipment, neither of which they can handle responsibly.'

Same at 26 Fed.

'It's like Vietnam,' said Brenner, who understandably saw a lot of the world through that prism. 'Incompetent and weak-willed allies fighting an enemy who are motivated by something higher than saving their own worthless asses.' He added, 'But we could turn it around with a few Special Forces units, maybe a Ranger battalion, and a Military Advisory Team.'

I pointed out, 'I think that's what the Pentagon said about Vietnam.'

'Right ... but ...' He said to Zamo, 'Park here.'

Zamo pulled into a space near the flagpole between two American-made trucks.

Brenner said, 'Okay, Kate and Zamo will stay in the vehicle, and John and I will get out and await a person.' He added, 'If we're not back by Wednesday, call the embassy.'

That got a chuckle, and Zamo added, 'It's easy to get in here, but not so easy to get out.'

Not so funny.

Brenner said to Zamo, 'Call in a sit-rep.'

I asked Kate, 'You okay with this?'

'I'm fine. I have Zamo and a Colt .45.'

Brenner advised her, 'Keep the scarf on.'

In the spirit of cultural outreach, I kept my jambiyah on, and Brenner and I got out and walked away from the parked vehicles where we could be seen by the person, whoever he was. Actually, I was pretty sure I knew who was meeting us.

I looked at the surrounding stone and brick buildings. Some old forts are romantic; some are sinister and depressing. This place would get the Midnight Express award for Creepiest Turkish-Built Prison.

Brenner reminded me, 'You are here as the interrogator for the FBI Evidence Response Team investigating the Cole attack. But if you don't mind, I'd like to take a shot at the prisoner.'

'Sure. You go first. Then I'll show you how it's done.'

He took that well, but also reminded me, 'I was a criminal investigator.'

'Right. But if this is like the Central Prison in Aden, don't expect too much.'

A Humvee came across the dusty field and stopped a few feet from us. The rear door opened and out came Colonel Hakim of the Political Security Organization. He was dressed in a uniform this time, but that didn't make him any more attractive than the last time I saw him.

He glanced at my jambiyah and smiled – or was that a sneer? – and motioned us to the vehicle. I got in the front with the driver, who had spent the day with livestock, and Brenner kept Colonel Hakim company in the rear.

Colonel Hakim said something to the driver and off we went.

Brenner, sticking to protocol, said to Hakim, 'Thank you, Colonel, for meeting us.'

Colonel Hakim replied, 'I am not for this arrangement, but I follow my orders.'

What a gracious man. Hey, shithead, you're riding in a Humvee that I helped pay for.

Brenner reminded the colonel, 'We have the same enemy, and the US is here to offer assistance.'

No reply.

To confirm what Buck said about the CIA, I asked Mr Happy, 'Have any other Americans come to speak to the prisoner?'

He didn't reply at first, then asked, 'Do you not know?'

'I just got here.'

'Yes? So you ask your friends.'

Asshole.

We stopped at a particularly grim-looking four-story building, and even without the bars on the windows, I would have known this was the prison.

I've seen too many prisons in my life. And too many prisoners. And each visit to a prison took something out of me, and left something with me.

Colonel Hakim said, 'You have half hour. No more.'

But I'm sure Colonel Hakim was hoping that the next time he brought us here, it would be for more than half an hour. Like maybe twenty years. Meanwhile, we were just visiting.

CHAPTER TWENTY-NINE

We entered the prison through a rusty iron door into a dark stone vestibule where a guard stood and snapped to attention.

We followed Colonel Hakim down a quiet corridor whose walls were covered with rotting stucco. This building may have a mold problem.

My mind went back to the Central Prison in Aden, which had been built by the Brits when they ran South Yemen. That, too, was a grim and creepy place, but this place made the Aden prison look like a health spa.

Colonel Hakim led us into another quiet corridor of closed wooden doors. I guess it was past quitting time, but when we passed a narrow staircase that led to the second level, I heard a man scream, followed by a man shouting, then another scream. Glad to hear someone was still at work.

Colonel Hakim opened a door, and we followed him into a room where two men sat in plastic chairs at a small table. Along one wall were file cabinets, and on the far wall was a barred window without glass that let in sunlight and whatever else wanted to fly in. A floor fan moved the bad air around.

On one wall was a large picture of Yemen's President for Life, Ali Abdullah Saleh, a mustachioed Saddam Hussein look-alike, who was desperately trying to avoid the same fate as his Iraqi idol.

On another wall were signs and posters in Arabic that I guessed were not the prisoners' bill of rights, though one of them may have said EMPLOYEES MUST WASH HANDS AFTER BEATING PRISONERS.

Anyway, the two men were standing now and neither of them looked like a prisoner. In fact, Hakim introduced one as the interpreter, and the other as a doctor. Hakim explained, 'Prisoner speaks no English and prisoner is sick.' Makes sense.

The interpreter, a young guy in Western clothing, asked us to call him Sammy, and the doctor, an older gent in a ratty suit without a tie, introduced himself as Dr Fahd. Brenner introduced himself using his former military rank, so I introduced myself as Commander Corey. Why not?

The interpreter invited us to sit, which we did, though Hakim remained standing, and Dr Fahd sat with a newspaper and lit a cigarette. Sammy had a dossier in front of him and he flipped through it, then said to Brenner and me, 'The prisoner's name is Rahim ibn Hayyam—'

Brenner interrupted and said, 'Can we have a copy of that?'

Hakim, standing near the window, asked Brenner, 'Do you read Arabic, Mr Brenner?'

Brenner replied, too politely I thought, 'No, but I can have it translated.'

Hakim informed him, 'That is a classified dossier and may not leave this room.'

I took out my pen and my detective's notebook, which I never leave home without, and said to Sammy, 'Can you spell that name?'

Hakim said, 'No. No notes. I tell you to listen.'

Brenner said to me, 'We'll put in a request through channels.'

Sammy continued, 'The prisoner says he is twenty-two years of age, and that he is a Saudi citizen by birth. His passport was taken from him by Al Qaeda, so all this is his word. He tells us he is from a good family of the upper middle class who live in Medina. He has two years of university in Riyadh. He further states that he is a good Muslim, he answers the daily calls to prayer, and he has made the Hajj.'

That's good. I guess. Sammy went on a bit about the prisoner's religious background – he was a Sunni Muslim – and his devotion to the teaching of the Koran and so forth.

I mean, did I need to know this? But I guess around here this was important stuff. Why? I have no idea. Maybe a good Muslim got better food or one less kick in the balls. Meanwhile, the clock was ticking, and I give Brenner credit for saying, 'Can we move on to other information?'

Sammy glanced at Hakim, who knew he had wasted as much time as he was going to get away with, and Hakim nodded.

Sammy flipped a page of the dossier and continued, 'The prisoner says he was recruited by Al Qaeda in Medina four months ago. He does not know the family names of his recruiters, only their given names, and that they, too, were Saudis. Shortly thereafter, he was flown on Yemenia airlines to Sana'a on his own passport with a tourist visa. He was met at the airport by two unnamed men, then taken to a house in an outlying district, the location of which he does not know. He stayed in the house for five days, with two other recruits from Saudi Arabia, and they passed their time fasting and praying.'

Some guys have all the fun. No wonder they wanted to join Al Qaeda. Travel, adventure, meet new people, fast, pray, get shot, and go to jail where you get tortured. Sign me up. I mean, what the hell are these people thinking? That is the question.

Sammy continued, 'On the fifth day, at dawn, the prisoner and the two others were put into a Toyota Hilux with a driver and traveled east on the Marib road. They were stopped at three military checkpoints, but upon showing their Saudi passports and saying they were tourists and students on their way to the Marib ruins, they were allowed to pass. The driver, a Yemeni, told the soldiers he was a paid guide.' Sammy commented, 'This is a place of ancient temples from the times of Sheba, and the place where the Ark of Noah is said to have come to rest, so it is interesting to Jews, Christians, and Muslims.'

Right. And American oil companies and Al Qaeda. Lots going

on around Marib. Maybe Matt Longo was right – this was someplace I should see.

Sammy continued, 'This was a five-hour journey on the Marib road, and then another half hour into the mountains. The prisoner claims that he cannot tell us or show us where he was traveling in the mountains or where he ended because the three men were asked to bind cloths over their eyes.'

I hope the driver wasn't blindfolded. But seeing how these people drove, it wouldn't matter much.

Sammy said, 'The prisoner, with his two compatriots, arrived in a mountain camp, which he describes as primitive. Mud houses and caves, and also some Bedouin tents. Perhaps it was once a Bedouin camp. This, he says, was the Al Qaeda training camp, populated by perhaps a hundred recruits from various countries, including Oman, Iraq, Egypt, and Kuwait. And also ten or twelve others who were officers, military trainers, and spiritual guides.'

Spiritual guides? Maybe that's what I needed instead of a supervisor. There was no spiritual element to the Anti-Terrorist Task Force. How could we be Crusaders without spiritual guides? Anyway, it seemed to me that Islamic jihadists, including Al Qaeda, had medieval heads and twenty-first-century weapons. And that, I thought, made this war very different. I missed the godless Communists.

Sammy flipped a page and said, 'The training in the camp lasted for three months – training with rifles, explosives, maps, and communication equipment. The prisoner described the training as very tiring and very hard, and the food was of poor quality.'

This was sounding like more fun every minute. But, I mean,

you gotta give these bastards credit. My teenage nephew won't clean his room, but Al Qaeda gets these mostly middle-class kids to leave their air-conditioning, televisions, and indoor plumbing and go out to the boondocks to live in mud huts and eat goats and learn how to be fighters. Sort of like the Peace Corps, except for the guns. And then there was The Panther from Perth Amboy, New Jersey. What's going on here?

Sammy continued, 'The prisoner says there was a medical person in the camp, but this person lacked skills and supplies. He says one recruit died of a fever, and one of injuries received in a fall from a mountain path. He says there was much sickness in the camp.'

Right. They didn't have a nurse sticking needles in their ass before they got to Yemen. Bottom line, Al Qaeda in Yemen was in stage one or two of development; they had arrived, they were setting up camps, they had recruits and a training cadre, but they weren't strong enough yet to make a major move toward toppling the government. Meanwhile, Al Qaeda was gaining confidence and respect by mounting attacks against foreign interests and individuals – tourists, embassies, and businesses – and not taking on the Yemeni military, which would make even a lazy and incompetent army retaliate. And then there was the USS *Cole*, the first and so far most spectacular and successful Al Qaeda attack in Yemen. That got them noticed.

Sammy continued, 'When this training was complete, the prisoner and forty others traveled by vehicle to the region north of Marib town. There they lived in the huts of sheep herders who were not present. And there they planned and prepared for the attack on the American oil facility, which is nearby.'

Sammy looked up from the transcript and said to us, 'That is as far as the interrogators got before the prisoner became ill and had to be taken to the prison hospital.'

Right. It's always a delicate balance between vigorous interrogation and putting the prisoner in the hospital. Or the morgue.

Sammy assured us, however, 'The prisoner is somewhat better now and you may speak to him.' He also editorialized, 'This is a misguided young man who is frightened, and he cries for his parents and his good life in Saudi Arabia.'

No shit. This kid was looking at ten or twenty years in a Yemeni slammer, which was a death sentence. Unless, of course, Al Qaeda sprung him. Or if Al Qaeda took over here. Then he'd be a hero. Meanwhile, he needed to survive, and the best way to do that was to talk, which he sounded happy to do if these idiots didn't kill him first.

Brenner asked Sammy, 'Did the prisoner say who his leaders were?'

Sammy replied, 'As I have said, he has stated that he knows his companions only by their given names.'

Okay, but how about a description of the leaders? Their nationality? Like did one of them have a New Jersey accent and a Jersey Shore T-shirt? I mean, if I had this prisoner alone for two hours, I'd wring him dry. But these interrogators, as I saw in Aden, were inept sadists. All they wanted, ultimately, were more names and a full confession. I wanted to know what the prisoner had for breakfast and what his favorite TV show was, and we took it from there.

Brenner asked Sammy, 'What did the prisoner say about the relationship between his camp and the local tribes?'

Sammy replied, 'He says nothing about that.'

Brenner then asked, 'Why wasn't he asked? How could this camp exist without the permission of the tribal chieftains?'

Sammy shrugged, then speculated, 'Perhaps they had an arrangement. Or this camp was too strong for the local tribe. Or—'

Hakim interrupted, 'Do not interrogate the translator, Mr Brenner. He is here only to say what the prisoner has said.'

True. But as long as Sammy seemed chatty and helpful to the Americans, I asked him, 'Was the prisoner cooperative with the other Americans who were here this morning?'

Sammy replied, 'Yes, but the prisoner was sick, in the hospital, so it was a short talk.'

I asked Colonel Hakim, 'Were you here this morning when the CIA was here?'

'You should ask them, not me.' Colonel Hakim had become impatient with us and said, 'Let us see now the prisoner.'

Dr Fahd grabbed his medical bag, and we all stood and followed Hakim out of the room and down the corridor.

I wasn't sure if all this was bringing us any closer to The Panther, but it was at least interesting. A small insight into Al Qaeda's modus operandi, though not their heads. Probably I'd never get into their heads — we weren't even on the same planet. But I thought I understood a little about Rahim ibn Hayyam, though I hadn't yet met him. He was a scared kid, and he was happy to talk. He might not think he knew much about the bigger picture, but he probably knew more than he thought he did.

With any luck, Rahim had met The Panther, and with any more luck, The Panther was still in the Marib hills. And if he stayed there, he'd have John Corey up his ass.

CHAPTER THIRTY

We came to an iron door where a guard was taking a khat-nap in a white plastic chair. Hakim kicked the man's leg, and the guard stood quickly and opened the door.

Hakim entered first, followed by Sammy, Dr Fahd, Brenner, and me.

The cell, probably an interrogation room, was about ten feet square, lit only by a high, barred window and a single hanging lightbulb. The walls were whitewashed brick with some interesting reddish stains around the perimeter, including a few red handprints.

A filthy mattress lay on the stone floor, and on the mattress was a young man with a wispy beard, wearing dirty white prison pajamas that were bloody around his left leg where his wound had bled through the bandages. I noticed, too, that his right eye was swollen shut. Also, his lower lip was split, and his hooked nose was crooked. I also saw that his arms and legs were shackled, and the leg chain was bolted to the floor.

Hakim explained to his American guests, 'He is chained to prevent him harming himself.'

Right. He has lots of people to do that for him.

Hakim snapped at the prisoner, who sat up slowly and moved his back against the wall.

Hakim also explained, 'As you can see, this man has been injured when he resisted capture by the security forces at the American oil company.'

I recalled the same bullshit in the Aden prison. Interesting that the Yemenis thought they had to lie to the Americans about beating prisoners. My jokes to the contrary, I'm not a big fan of torture. It's messy, risky, not productive, and not right. What you want from a prisoner is in his head, so you have to beat up his brain, not his body. Takes longer, but you get better results.

Dr Fahd moved a chair beside the prisoner to check out his vitals.

There were four other white plastic chairs in the room, and Colonel Hakim invited me, Brenner, and Sammy to sit facing the prisoner. Hakim moved a chair against a wall between us and the prisoner and sat.

As my eyes adjusted to the dim light, I saw an empty plastic water bottle near the prisoner, and a full basin of what looked and smelled like urine. There were old cigarette butts on the floor, and what appeared to be well-masticated khat leaves. The whole room reeked of a hundred years of misery.

Dr Fahd looked in the prisoner's eyes with a light, took his temperature, listened to his heart and lungs, then took his blood pressure.

The good doctor stood and said, 'The prisoner is well.'

Actually, the prisoner looked like he'd just gone ten rounds with Mike Tyson. But maybe his vitals were good.

Dr Fahd sat in a corner and lit a cigarette. I guess it's all right for doctors to smoke here.

Colonel Hakim spoke to the prisoner, obviously introducing his visitors, and I heard the word 'Amrika.'

The prisoner closed his good eye and nodded.

Hakim said to us, 'You may begin.'

I nodded to Brenner, who looked at Rahim ibn Hayyam and asked, 'How are you feeling?'

Sammy translated, Rahim replied, and Sammy, who apparently forgot or wasn't told that Brenner understood some Arabic, said to us, 'He is feeling well.'

Brenner corrected, '*Not* well. And he says he needs food and water.'

Sammy glanced at Colonel Hakim, and Hakim said to Brenner, 'If your Arabic is so good, I will send the translator away.'

Brenner replied, 'My Arabic is good enough to know when I hear a false translation.'

Hakim ignored him and looked at me. 'And you, Mr Corey? How is your Arabic?'

'Better than your English.'

Hakim didn't like that, but he said something to the guard, who left. Hakim said to Brenner, 'Continue.'

So having established that we couldn't be totally conned, Brenner, with the clock ticking, got right to the point and asked, 'What is the name of your commander?'

Sammy asked, Rahim replied, and Sammy said to us, 'As he has stated, he knows only given names.'

'Okay. What was the given name of his commander?'

Sammy asked and Rahim replied, 'Sayid.' Rahim said something else, and Sammy told us, 'This was one of the men who died in the attack.'

Well, I guess that's a dead end.

Brenner asked, 'What was Sayid's nationality?'

The answer was Iraqi.

The guard returned with a bottle of water that he threw on the mattress, and Rahim opened it and finished it in one long gulp.

Brenner asked a few more questions about Rahim's comrades in arms. Bottom line, this platoon-sized unit of fighters really didn't know each other's full names, which was good security in the event one of them, such as Rahim, was captured. They did, however, know nationalities and some hometowns, and Brenner established that about half of them were Saudis – our good allies – and some were from Kuwait, the country that we liberated from Iraq in the first Gulf War. There were also a few recruits from neighboring Oman, a few from Egypt, and only five Yemenis – probably recovering khat chewers. Interestingly, most of the spiritual guides were from Saudi Arabia, and most of the military trainers and commanders were Iraqis, former members of the now-defunct Iraqi Army, who were currently employed by the group called Al Qaeda in Mesopotamia. Hey, you got a kill skill, you gotta sell it somewhere.

Anyway, Brenner, ex-soldier, then asked Military Intelligence-type questions about command structure, equipment, morale, and so forth, and he got some interesting information to pass on to the embassy military attaché. But we weren't any closer to The Panther.

In fact, this interrogation, as we both knew, had some problems. Not only was time short, but Colonel Hakim of the Political Security Organization was listening to every word, so he'd know what we were looking for, and he could figure out what we already knew or didn't know.

If these people were real allies, it wouldn't matter much. But they weren't. In fact, for all I knew, Colonel Hakim, and maybe the interpreter and the doctor, had a brother-in-law in Al Qaeda. I remember having the same problems with interrogations in Aden.

Considering all that, Brenner and I had to do a balancing act. This was probably our only shot at the prisoner, and we had to maximize the opportunity without giving away too much to our allies. Or our enemies. On the other hand, we did want Al Qaeda to know one thing – John Corey was looking for The Panther from Perth Amboy.

Brenner now put on his cop hat and said to Sammy, 'Tell Rahim that if he continues to answer truthfully, the Americans will assist in returning him to his home.'

Sammy glanced at Hakim, who nodded, and Sammy passed on Brenner's kind bullshit. I mean, Rahim was an Al Qaeda jihadist who just attacked an American-owned oil facility, so he had a better chance of being repatriated by the Yemenis than by Americans – and if Rahim ever wound up on American soil, the place would be called Guantanamo. But the offer must have sounded sincere to the desperate Rahim, and he nodded vigorously.

Brenner then asked, 'Did any of your companions or commanders ever live in America?'

Sammy asked the question, and Rahim seemed to hesitate, then replied. Sammy said to us, 'He says one of his companions, Anwar, the Egyptian, lived for a time in America. He also says he had heard that a high commander once lived in America.'

Brenner was smart enough not to ask a quick follow-up question and changed the subject. He asked, 'Did you receive any assistance or information from any of the tribes in the Marib area?'

Rahim listened to the translation, then said something that Sammy translated as, 'He says a sheik of the Yafi tribe – a local chieftain of that tribe – took money from Al Qaeda for safe passage and for the use of this Bedouin camp.'

It was interesting that Al Qaeda was able to make a deal with the local chief. All differences aside, money talks. Or, as Buck said in New York, favors were exchanged.

Brenner followed up with, 'What else did this sheik provide?'

Sammy asked Rahim, then said to us, 'He says the sheik provided food, guides, and information concerning the security of the American oil installation. He also says he and his comrades were told by their commanders that with this information, their attack would be successful.'

Rahim volunteered something else, which is always a good sign, and Sammy told us, 'He says the American oil company security forces appeared to be expecting them, and he now believes that someone betrayed them to the Americans or to the Yemeni security forces.'

Hey, welcome to Yemen, Rahim. Only here we don't call it betrayal, we call it business as usual. And it was probably the local sheik who was playing both ends of that business.

Brenner asked, 'What is the name of this sheik?'

Sammy asked, but Rahim said he didn't know.

Brenner said to me, 'The Yafi are a large tribe around Marib, but like all tribes, they're broken into many clans that sometimes take their name from their ancestral sheiks. So if we had this sheik's name, we could identify the local tribe and maybe get a fix on this Al Qaeda camp.' Brenner then said to Colonel Hakim, 'You should look into this.'

Hakim replied curtly, 'Do not tell me what I should do.'

Ally or asshole?

Brenner thought asshole and explained to me, 'The PSO doesn't like to leave the safety of the cities.'

I thought Hakim was going to blow a gasket, but he controlled himself and said to us, 'Five minutes.' He added, for the record, 'The prisoner is sick and must rest.'

I pointed out, 'The doctor said he was doing great.'

'Five minutes.'

Brenner said to me, 'Your turn.'

Okay. As I said, I like to soften up the prisoner with personal questions and sports talk, but we had a big cultural divide here, and I had about four minutes, so I went right for the big enchilada and asked a typical leading question. 'When was the last time you saw Bulus ibn al-Darwish – al-Numair?'

Rahim's puffy eyes opened wide even before the translation.

Sammy translated, and I could see that Rahim was struggling with his response. Finally, he replied.

Colonel Hakim sat stone-faced as he listened to Rahim, and Brenner was nodding as though he understood every word – or at least every third word.

Finally Sammy translated, 'He says ... al-Numair – The Panther – was present on the evening of the attack. Last night. Al-Numair spoke to the fighters and assured them they would be victorious. They prayed together ... then al-Numair entered a vehicle and drove away.'

I exchanged glances with Brenner, then I asked a standard police question. 'What kind of vehicle? What color?'

Sammy asked, then told us, 'He says it appeared to be a Toyota Hilux. White.'

Brenner informed me, 'A very common SUV in Yemen. And ninety percent of the vehicles in this country are white.'

'I noticed.' So The Panther was tooling around in a commonly used vehicle, which was no surprise. But what was surprising was that he seemed to have safe passage in this tribal area.

I asked, 'How many vehicles were with him?'

The answer was five, and Sammy said they were all white SUVs, though Rahim couldn't be certain of their makes or models.

I asked another standard police question. 'What was al-Numair wearing?'

The answer was traditional North Yemen clothing – a white fouteh, and a shiwal on his head. No Jersey Shore T-shirt. The Panther, it seemed, was returning to his roots.

I tapped my dagger and asked, 'Jambiyah?'

Sammy didn't have to translate, and Rahim nodded and said, 'Jambiyah.'

'Facial hair?'

Yes. A long black beard.

'What was his general appearance? Sick? Healthy? Heavy, thin?'

Sammy asked and said to me, 'Rahim believes this man looked healthy. But very thin.'

I asked, 'Does Rahim know that Bulus ibn al-Darwish is an American citizen?'

Sammy seemed surprised at that, though Rahim did not. Sammy said to me, 'He has heard this. But did not know if it was true.'

In a normal interrogation, I'd now mention the big reward and ask, 'Where is he hiding?' But I was sure that Rahim didn't know. Not even for five million bucks. And if he did know, and if he told us, it wouldn't be the Americans who got there first. In fact, it would probably be someone telling The Panther to beat feet. Or if the Yemeni Army gave it a try, they wouldn't necessarily ask us to help, and left to their own proven incompetence, The Panther would get away.

So instead of 'Where is he hiding?' I asked, 'Where and when is the next attack?'

Sammy translated and Rahim replied. Sammy said to me, 'There was talk in the camp of attacks on the oil pipeline between Marib and As-Salif, attacks on oil engineers, aid workers, and Western tourists.' He added, 'And talk of an attack on the American Embassy.'

This was hardly hot news, and I doubted if a low-level jihadist had any specific times or places for these attacks. I thought of young Mr Longo and his planned excursion to see the temples of Marib. Maybe he should just visit the website of the Yemeni Tourist Board, click onto Marib, and call it a day.

Remembering that The Panther got his big start in Yemen with the *Cole* attack in Aden Harbor, and knowing that criminals sometimes return to the scene of their crimes, I asked another leading question. 'What is al-Numair's target in Aden?'

Rahim seemed to understand the question before it was translated and replied in Arabic to Sammy.

I heard the word 'Sheraton,' which was not the word I wanted to hear.

Sammy said to me, 'The Sheraton Hotel. He says he was told there are many American soldiers and police in the hotel ... infidels on sacred Islamic soil ... He says his companions who did not participate in the attack on the American oil installation are now traveling to Aden. But he has no further knowledge of this.'

I said to Brenner, 'That might be interesting information to anyone planning to stay at the Sheraton in Aden.'

Brenner did not respond.

Colonel Hakim said, 'Your time is finished.'

I ignored him and said directly to Rahim, 'Thank you for your cooperation. If you continue to cooperate with the Americans, we will do everything possible to help you return to your home.'

Sammy didn't translate, and Hakim stood and said, 'It is finished.'

As I suspected, Rahim, like most educated Saudis, actually understood a little English, and he probably enjoyed contraband American DVDs – maybe The Sopranos or Sex and the City, and he said to me, 'Please, sir. Help me. I help you.'

I looked at Rahim sitting against the wall, his eyes on me. If he got sprung, I wondered if he'd go home and get his life together, or if he'd rejoin the fight. About twenty-five percent of the jihadists released from Guantanamo had turned up again on the battlefields of Afghanistan. And others had been rearrested for terrorist activities in Saudi Arabia, Iraq, and Europe. I wasn't sure about Rahim, but from experience I know that all prisoners are sorry for what they've done. Once freed, however, they're only sorry they got caught.

Maybe Rahim was different. But even if he was, he didn't join Al Qaeda to promote world peace. And he didn't go to the American oil installation looking for a job; he went there knowing he was going to kill people. And if his jihadists had overrun the facility, they'd have killed everyone in it — American and European civilians, security people, Yemeni workers, and anyone else who lived or worked there. It didn't turn out that way, but it could have. And now Rahim was sorry.

'Please to help me. I help you.'

I turned and left.

CHAPTER THIRTY-ONE

In the better air outside the prison, Brenner said to Colonel Hakim, 'Thank you for your time and assistance.'

Hakim didn't reply to Brenner, but he did say to me, 'Your visa, and that of your wife, remains a problem.'

'Sorry. Hey, maybe I need a tourist visa like all the Al Qaeda guys have who come through Sana'a Airport.'

Colonel Hakim didn't have much to say about that, but he did advise both of us, 'Be very careful here.'

If Ghumdan had a soundtrack, this is when I'd hear an ominous organ chord.

Brenner said to Hakim, 'We can find our way back to our vehicle.' Then Brenner did a nice thing and saluted, and Colonel Hakim returned the salute. Military guys do that, even when they hate each other. Good bonding.

As Brenner and I walked back to the Land Cruiser, he said to me, 'You shouldn't piss him off.'

'Me? How about you?'

'He's got some power, and we may need him at some point.'

'He and his government actually need us more than we need them.'

'True. But they don't get that yet.'

'They will.'

It was good to be out of that prison. The place was rotting, and everyone in it was rotting. In fact, this whole country was rotting.

Brenner asked me, 'What did you think of all that?'

'Let me speak to my spiritual advisor and I'll get back to you. Meanwhile, I did get some insight into Al Qaeda in the Arabian Peninsula.'

'Right. The Yemenis don't know what they're in for, or that they have a small window to snuff out Al Qaeda before these guys get their game on.'

'Well,' I pointed out, 'if the Yemenis don't know what's coming, it's no one's fault but their own.'

'Correct. But the Yemeni Army and government are obsessed with their tribal problems, and their ongoing fight with South Yemen.' He added, 'They think Al Qaeda is an American obsession.'

'Well, it is. But with good reason.'

'Correct.' Brenner said to me, 'Good question about Aden.'

Actually, all my questions were good, but I replied, 'I'm surprised the Sheraton in Aden hasn't been attacked yet.' I pointed out, 'Aside from the embassy, that's where to find the most Americans in one place. And it's not that secure.'

He nodded. 'I've been there.'

'Me, too, and we're going there again.'

We made our way through a cluster of decrepit buildings that looked like barracks. I could smell food cooking somewhere, and at the end of the barracks I saw the minarets of a small mosque. Soldiers lounged around, smoking and chewing whatever, and giving us the eye. Garrison life is no treat, but I'm sure the Yemeni Army liked it better than mounting field operations against a tough and motivated enemy. Same with the National Security police, who apparently sat out the attack on the Hunt Oil installation.

Brenner asked me, 'Do you think The Panther is still in the Marib area?'

'I think he's found a tribal sheik who's giving him a secure base — a sanctuary.'

'Sounds that way.' He added, 'But Marib may get hot for him after that attack.'

I motioned toward the crack troops sitting around and asked, 'Will it?'

'Well, maybe not.'

On another subject, Brenner said to me, 'The PSO always knew we were looking for The Panther. Now they know that a guy named John Corey has arrived to join the search.' He reminded me, 'Assuming this information gets to Al Qaeda, then we have to hope that the name John Corey has some meaning to The Panther.'

Right. Like, 'Hey, isn't John Corey the guy who killed Asad Khalil? Let's kill John Corey.' I said, as I'd already said, 'God, I hope so.'

We were now crossing the dusty parade ground and I could see the Land Cruiser where we'd left it. I thought I saw Kate's head in the rear seat. I really didn't think there'd be a problem, but anything was possible in Yemen.

I asked Brenner, 'So what's with this tribal sheik who helped Al Qaeda?'

'Don't know. But it happens. Either for money, or because a sheik wants to poke the government in the eye.' He assured me, 'Next week, this sheik could be helping us.'

'Maybe he already did.'

'Right – Rahim thinks someone betrayed them. But that was Rahim's first introduction to the battlefield, and what looked to him like a setup could just have been Hunt's hired mercenaries doing what they get paid for.' He also informed me, 'Our military attaché and the CIA are doing an analysis and report of the attack.'

'Can't wait to read it.' I reminded him, 'The CIA was here before us.'

'Correct. They're looking at the bigger picture. We're looking for The Panther.'

'That *is* the bigger picture.'

'Good point.'

I returned to the subject of this tribal sheik and said, 'If we go out to the Badlands, are we supposed to trust the sheiks of Araby?'

Brenner assured me, 'They're good for their word – until some-one makes them a better offer.'

'You can't buy that kind of loyalty.'

Brenner said, 'At least the Montagnards – the hill tribes – stayed loyal to the Americans right until the end.'

'That'll teach them.'

'Well, we projected great power. No one bets on a loser. Right now in Yemen, no one can say who has the power, and who the winner is going to be. But if Al Qaeda starts to look like a winner, they'll be able to recruit young Yemenis in great numbers. Then we have a problem, and we either have to cut and run, or get involved in a third land war.'

'Nuke 'em. It's cheaper.'

He ignored my suggestion and said to me, 'We can buy some time if we kill or capture Bulus ibn al-Darwish. He's the driving force behind recruiting, training, and motivating this small but growing movement. Also, he apparently has some access to big money and he's a hero to the jihadists because of the Cole attack. So if we get him, that will be a strategic and psychological blow to Al Qaeda here and around the world.'

'Right. And don't forget that The Panther is an American. So maybe he thinks more clearly and logically than most of these whacked-out jihadists.'

'Maybe.'

We were closer to the Land Cruiser now, and I could definitely see Kate in the rear. Sometimes I forget how much I love my wife, and maybe I don't always say it or show it, but then when a situation becomes dangerous, I realize I could lose her. I try to picture a life without her, living alone in New York in a big apartment on the fashionable Upper East Side, surrounded by trendy bars and restaurants bursting with single women ... Is this coming out right?

I asked Brenner, 'Any chance of us getting Rahim alone, with an embassy interpreter?'

'Not a chance.'

'Right.' Same as when I was questioning the *Cole* suspects in Aden. The PSO was the five-hundred-pound gorilla in the room. 'Any chance of another chaperoned interview?'

'We'll put in a request. But to be honest, the Agency has first dibs on Rahim.' He added, 'You got your FBI Evidence Response Team shot.'

'Right.' I also asked him, 'Are we going to Marib?'

'Maybe. But we're going to Aden first to set up a command post in the Sheraton.'

'When?'

'Could be tomorrow.'

We got to the Land Cruiser, and I wanted to sit with Kate, so Brenner sat up front. Zamo started the SUV and off we went.

Kate unwrapped her scarf and asked, 'How did it go?'

I replied, 'Not bad, but not great. Hakim was in the room, and we had only half an hour, and the prisoner wasn't feeling his very best.'

Brenner said, 'We'll bring you up to speed when we see Buck.'

Zamo was heading toward the watchtowers, and we sailed through the open gates into the city.

Brenner said, 'I'll drop you off at the Sheraton, and Zamo will pick you up at seven.' He informed us, 'Martini night at the embassy.'

Kate, of course, asked, 'What is the dress?'

Brenner replied, 'People dress a bit.'

I suggested, 'Wear your new balto.'

She suggested, 'Why don't you wear it?'

That got a laugh. We were really having a good time.

Brenner reminded us, 'Guns will be worn. Vests optional.'

We pulled up to the Sheraton, and Zamo got Kate's shopping bags out of the rear. I didn't see the exploding mangos.

Brenner also reminded us, 'We may be leaving for Aden tomorrow, so think about packing.'

He and Zamo pulled away, and we walked past the National Security Bureau guards and into the lobby.

I stopped at the front desk to see if there were any messages for us, and the desk clerk handed me an envelope, which I opened on the way to the elevator.

It was a fax from Tom Walsh, sent not from the ATTF office, of course, but from a Kinko's near 26 Federal Plaza. I read the fax aloud. 'Dear John and Kate, Thanks for your call. Hope you're enjoying the sights and the good weather. Snow here today. You're lucky to be in Yemen. Have a wonderful trip. See you soon.'

I commented, 'Asshole.'

Kate reminded me, 'You started it.'

There was a P.S., and I read, 'You knew what this was about before you got on the plane.'

Double asshole. But he was right. And yet here I was. What was I thinking? Not much.

The NSB guy at the elevator didn't ask to see our key or anything, and we took the elevator up.

We ran a bit long in the shower, and by the time we got dressed it was a little after seven.

I had a tie and jacket on, and Kate was wearing a nice black dress. She had her gun in her purse, and I had mine in my holster. She talked me out of wearing my jambiyah, and neither of us had our Kevlar vests, but Kate had her scarf on to walk through the lobby.

Down in the lobby, I noticed a lot of Mideastern-looking men in sunglasses, dressed in Western clothing, heading for the bar. Guilty pleasures aren't the same for everyone, everywhere. Here, narcotic leaves were guilt-free, a martini was not.

Kate commented, 'They go out without their wives.'

'What's the fun in that?'

Anyway, Zamo was waiting in the Land Cruiser, and we hopped in, me riding up front.

He said to us, 'Looks like we're heading to Aden tomorrow.'

I asked him, 'Have they improved the road?'

'No. But we've improved our armor and firepower.' He laughed.

I love being the straight man for a comedian doing sicko humor.

As we headed up the road toward the embassy, I said to him, 'The prisoner we spoke to today said Al Qaeda was planning an attack on the Sheraton in Aden.' I added, before he could, 'But no problem. We'll probably never make it to Aden.'

He laughed, then confided to me, 'I like you.'

Kate said, 'I need a drink.'

CHAPTER THIRTY-TWO

Cocktails were in the embassy's atrium lobby, and this was for staff only, not an embassy reception, which would be held in the more formal parlor.

The unstated reason for this free alcohol was that the new ambassador had not yet arrived, and this was everyone's last chance to get snockered before he showed up.

And if we needed another reason for the taxpayers to buy us a drink, this was a welcome party for the two new legal attachés, FBI Special Agent Howard Fensterman and FBI Special Agent Kate Mayfield, a.k.a. Mrs Corey. And, I guess, it was a hello party for me, too, though I wasn't on staff here, and I'd be saying good-bye shortly.

I suspected that there were not many social demands on the American Embassy staff in Sana'a, nor were there more interesting things for them to do in Yemen on a weekend, so I was sure most of them were here tonight.

The size of an embassy staff is classified, but I'll say we had three bartenders, and six Yemeni men passing hors d'oeuvres. Hopefully, the Marines or the Diplomatic Security Service had checked them all out for suicide belts.

None of the Marines were in attendance, except for the two

officers, a captain, and a young lieutenant who told me he'd served in Afghanistan. I asked him, 'Would you rather be here or Afghanistan?'

He replied without hesitation, 'Afghanistan,' explaining, 'There you know you're in a combat zone, and so does everyone around you. Here, everyone around you – the civilians – pretend there's no war, and that's dangerous.'

'Right.' Which was probably not much different than the mindset in the presidential palace and the government ministries. Except now and then, reality intruded into the deep bunkers of denial.

I looked around at the embassy people, who were nicely dressed, sipping cocktails and chatting. This could have been anywhere in the civilized world, including New York. But outside the guarded walls was another world that had absolutely nothing in common with this world. Except, to be optimistic, a shared humanity, a love of children and family, a hope for peace, prosperity, health, and happiness, and a belief in a higher being who was loving and kind – except when he got pissed off and sent plagues and floods to get rid of everyone.

Kate was making the rounds, getting to know her new colleagues, who actually would never see her again. I chatted with people who came up to me and welcomed me to Yemen. Everyone seemed to know I was going to Aden with the FBI Evidence Response Team, and that my stay in Sana'a would be short. Interestingly, no one wanted to know anything about the *Cole* investigation. I think the dips put a distance between themselves and those men and women who used the cover of the embassy for other kinds of work.

Among those who did that kind of work was the military attaché, a.k.a. the Military Intelligence officer, who introduced himself to me as Colonel Drew Kent, US Army, a tall, middle-aged man in mufti. His job here, he informed me, was challenging, but fulfilling. A few minutes later he modified that a bit and said, 'The Yemeni Army is a friggin' joke. The unwilling led by the incompetent. Ill-paid, ill-equipped, ill-trained, and unmotivated.'

'But are they good?'

He thought that was funny and advised me, 'If you need to depend on them to provide security for your work – whatever it is – make sure you watch your back and sleep with your boots on and your gun handy. Better yet, stay awake.'

I asked him, 'How about the National Security Bureau?'

'You mean the blue clowns? Half police force, half tourist pro-tection service, and all corrupt. They don't have a clear mission or a clear chain of command. They're used and abused by the politicians to further their own agendas. If you need to rely on them for security, make sure you pay them well – half up front, half if you get back alive.'

I hoped Matt Longo knew all that. I inquired, 'How much is well?'

'About two dollars per man, per day. Extra if they have to fire their rifles.'

'Sounds reasonable.'

He informed me, 'The blue clowns did a disappearing act on a bunch of Belgian tourists last August. At the Marib ruins.'

'Really? What happened to the tourists?'

'They disappeared, too. Maybe kidnapped, but no one has heard from them.'

'I hope they're all right.'

'Don't bet on it. Their Yemeni guide and their bus driver were found with their throats slit.'

Ouch. I didn't remember hearing about this, but bad news out of Yemen wasn't big news in the States unless it had to do with Americans. I mean, I'd been surprised to discover there were over a hundred Westerners kidnapped in the last ten years, mostly Europeans. Now and then you'd hear about tourists being killed, sometimes in a crossfire between Yemeni security forces and tribal kidnappers. But what Colonel Kent was describing didn't sound like a tribal kidnapping.

I asked him, 'Could that have been an Al Qaeda attack?'

'That seems to be the consensus. But the Yemeni government plays down these incidents.' He let me know, 'They like the tourism. In fact, tours still go to the Marib ruins.'

'How many come back?'

On the subject of Marib as an exciting place, Colonel Kent said, 'There was an Al Qaeda attack last night on the Hunt Oil installation north of Marib.'

'I heard.'

'Did you?' He continued, 'Hunt hires its own security force – mostly American and European mercenary types. Unfortunately, the NSB insists on being in on the arrangement – for money, of course. But as I said, you can't trust them, so when the excrement starts to fly, you don't know if the NSB has your back, or if they ran away, or if they joined the other team.' He concluded, 'Tactically, it's a damned nightmare.'

'Right. But the Al Qaeda guys were routed.'

'Luck. Or maybe the Hunt guys knew they were coming.

Information is cheaper than a barrel of oil around here.' He added, 'Maybe the Al Qaeda force was inept.'

I thought of Rahim and partly agreed. But I was also sure that the Al Qaeda guys were going to get better.

Colonel Kent said to me, 'They got an Al Qaeda prisoner from the attack.'

I didn't respond, so he asked me, 'You know about that?'

'You know I do and that's all I can say.'

He accepted that and advised me, 'The Agency always knows more than they're saying. If you're FBI, which I guess you are, you'll get more help from my office – Military Intelligence – than you'll get from our Comrades In Arms.'

'Right.'

'And be aware that State Department Intelligence cozies up to the CIA more than they should.' He opined, 'SDI should be working more with MI.'

Who's on first? Anyway, Colonel Kent seemed to be a man of opinions, so I asked him, 'What's your opinion of the Political Security Organization?'

He replied, 'Like any internal political security force, they can be nasty. In most countries in the Mideast, they're called the Mukhabarat, which they were once called here. But that name has a lot of negatives attached to it – like the old KGB or the Gestapo – so they changed the name here. But it's the same bunch of thugs. And as in every other dictatorship, people are frightened of them and people think they're everywhere. Truth is, they're not, but they promote fear and distrust.' He advised me, 'Steer clear of them if you can. They answer to no one except the president and his inner circle.'

I wondered if they were hiring – or did I really want to be a warlord? Anyway, I asked Colonel Kent, 'Do you know this PSO guy, Colonel Hakim?'

'Sure. Nasty thug. But not stupid.'

'Whose side is he on?'

'He's on his side. He wants to keep his job and his high status no matter who wins. He'll shoot an Al Qaeda captive one day, then let another one escape another day. He does the same with the tribal rebels. But someday he's going to get a bullet in the head from one side or the other.'

I wouldn't mind doing that myself. I asked him, 'Who's going to win here? The government, the al-Houthi rebels, the South Yemen separatists, or Al Qaeda?'

'Well ... in the end, the tribes always win – if they can agree on a leader. This al-Houthi guy may be the one. There's another one – a Bedouin sheik – in Marib who could unite the tribes. If not, I'd put my money on Al Qaeda.'

'Why?'

'Because they're organized, disciplined, and they believe they are the future.'

'They're the past.'

'That is the future.'

'Right.'

Then he said to me, sotto voce, 'If you're here to find The Panther, I wish you luck. But I'll also tell you that it might be best in the long run if Al Qaeda won in Yemen.'

'Why?'

He explained, 'This regime is broken. They're the walking dead. If Al Qaeda wins, they control Sana'a, and the Saudis will find that intolerable, and the Saudis, with American military help, will unite the tribes and get rid of Al Qaeda in Yemen.' He informed me, 'The Saudis have united the tribes before when they didn't like the government in Sana'a, and also when the Communists took over in Aden. But first, Al Qaeda needs to be out in the open – in the presidential palace. In other words, the quickest way to win this war is to lose it. Follow?'

Maybe I needed another martini to follow this. But I think I got Colonel Machiavelli's line of reasoning. I suggested, 'So we get to fight a real land war with Al Qaeda as soon as they win here.'

'That's it. Same as with the Taliban in Afghanistan.' He let me know, 'Al Qaeda should be careful what they wish for.'

So should we.

Colonel Kent asked me, 'What's your clearance?'

'About six foot two inches.'

He smiled politely at the old joke and said, 'I'll tell you an open secret. Our goal here is to force the Yemeni government to sign a treaty giving us a ninety-nine-year lease on a big chunk of water-front property near Aden. We need to do this before the government collapses. We need to build a land, sea, and air base for operations and refueling. An American Gibraltar. From there, we can control the Red Sea and the Gulf of Aden, and we'll do it with a friendly government that we help install later, like the British did two hundred years ago when they grabbed Aden. We can mount operations against Al Qaeda in the Arabian Peninsula and the Horn of Africa. And we can also wipe out the Somali pirates who are in league with Al Qaeda. Plus, we'd have a place other than Guantanamo and closer to the battlefields to warehouse and interrogate enemy combatants.' He got a dreamy look in his eyes and said, 'Sweet.'

'Beautiful,' I agreed. Grand strategies and geo-politics always give me a little headache, but to be polite I said, 'I like multi-purpose land use.' Maybe I could put my khat spa there.

Colonel Kent continued, 'And while we're at it, we can tell the Saudis to go fuck themselves, and we can shut down our bases in Saudi Arabia before they tell us to get out.' He asked me, 'Understand?'

'Sounds like a plan.'

'And here's the kicker. The biggest construction company in this part of the world is bin Laden Construction. Owned by that asshole's family. So we contract them to do some of the work.' He asked me, 'See the irony?'

'I do. But watch the cost overruns.'

'Right.' He looked at me and said, 'You didn't hear any of that from me.'

'Correct.' I needed another drink, so I excused myself and headed for the bar.

On the way, I was intercepted by Brenner's boss, the sometimes reverend Ed Peters, who asked me how my day went, and I told him I was disappointed about not seeing the donkey market.

He assured me it wasn't that interesting, then asked me, 'What did Colonel Kent have to say?'

Well, Colonel Kent reminded me a little of the general in Dr Strangelove, but I didn't want to share this thought with Ed Peters. I mean, I had no idea what the interpersonal relationships were here, or who thought who was a loon, or who was jockeying for position. As I said, everyone here seemed a little nuts to me, and my short-term goal was to get out of this embassy, find The Panther, whack him, and go home. In fact, Tom Walsh was looking very good to me right now.

I said to Ed Peters, 'The colonel gave me a briefing about the Yemeni Army.'

'That's always good for a laugh.'

'Right. We need more serious allies.'

'You won't find any in this part of the world.' He shifted into diplomatic mode and said, 'The irony is that the Yemenis are good people, and they could be good allies if they – or we – got rid of their government.'

'Let's hope the people choose a better government in the next election.'

'This country is three thousand years old. There hasn't been an election yet.' He changed the subject and said, 'We're using a five-vehicle convoy tomorrow. That should be all right.'

'I'm sure we can get away with three.'

'Five is better.'

How about twenty? I asked him, 'Why don't we fly?'

'We don't trust Yemenia air. And we don't have any of our own air assets here. I wish we did, but these idiots won't let us bring in helicopters.'

'How about Spook Air?' Meaning the CIA air assets.

He replied, 'I don't know if anyone asked.'

'How about the C-17?'

'We like to have one sitting at Sana'a Airport in case we have to move the whole embassy out of here.'

'Good thinking.'

He explained, 'When one C-17 comes in, the other leaves

for the States, and the one that came in waits for another to arrive.'

'Got it.' I asked him, 'Why don't we charter an aircraft to take us to Aden?'

'We do that sometimes. But not this time.'

'Why not?'

'I don't know.'

Well, I did. We were driving to Aden because someone wanted to see if Al Qaeda snapped at the bait. Which reminded me, if I needed reminding, that Al Qaeda fighters were on the way to Aden, and I asked Peters, 'How would you evacuate the American personnel at the Sheraton in Aden?'

'By ship.'

'Whose ship? And how do we get to it?'

'I'd try the backstroke.'

Why do I think he's used this joke before? But it *was* funny, so I gave him a chuckle. But seriously.

He said, seriously, 'My DSS counterpart in Aden, Doug Reynolds, will brief you.' He asked me, 'What was your evacuation plan when you were in Aden last time?'

'I think it was the breaststroke.'

While I was wondering if I should mention that I'd just discovered that the Sheraton in Aden was in imminent danger of attack, Howard Fensterman came over to me, and Ed Peters excused himself. There seemed to be an unwritten rule here that conversations needed to be compartmentalized, so it was like a Shakespeare play where the actors entered, delivered their lines, then exited, making way for new actors who didn't know what the last ones said, which usually led to some misunderstanding or troublemaking, which in turn led to someone getting whacked. That's what happens when people don't communicate. Right?

Anyway, Howard said to me, 'You and Kate went into Sana'a today with Paul.'

'We did.'

'I would have joined you.'

'We thought you were attending the Catholic Mass at the Italian Embassy.'

He smiled, but he wasn't amused. He said to me, 'I have your satellite phone numbers and we'll stay in touch when you're on the road.'

'Why don't you come to Aden with us?'

'I would, but I have a lot to do here to get this office up and running.' He informed me, 'There was an attack last night on an American oil installation in a place called Marib.'

'I heard.'

'One suspect was captured. I'm trying to get permission from the Ministry of Justice to interview him.'

So do I tell him — been there, done that? He was the FBI legat, Kate's supposed boss, but no one had told him that we'd been to Ghumdan. Who the hell was in charge here? And what was going on behind the scenes? For some reason I pictured Buck as the guy with all the strings in his hands, manipulating the whole puppet show.

I said to Howard, 'You need to speak to Buck Harris about that.'

'I do? Why him?'

'Why not?'

Howard asked me, 'What is his actual job here?'

'I don't know. Protocol officer?'

Howard changed the subject and said to me, 'I told Kate she needed to see me first thing tomorrow. I have the arrest warrant, a copy of the indictment, and instructions on how to effect a lawful arrest on a suspect in a foreign country who claims dual citizenship.' He also let me know, 'You need to read him his Miranda rights, but you first need to establish that he understands English.'

'When can I kick him in the balls?'

He ignored me and said, 'I also have all this in Arabic – the warrant, the indictment, and his Miranda warning for him to read and sign.'

'Howard, is this a joke?'

'No, it is not. This arrest will be made lawfully and properly, and it will stand up in an American court of law.'

Well, if I had any second thoughts about whacking The Panther, Howard just put them all to rest.

I said to him, 'Brief Kate on all this.'

'I will. But I want you, as one of the likely arresting agents, to understand this.'

'Okay.'

He assured me, 'I'm just trying to keep you from making a mistake that could jeopardize a Federal prosecution, and get you or us in trouble.'

'Thank you.'

'That's what I'm here for.'

'Right.' I actually liked Howard, and I could see that he was bright enough to learn how the world really worked. After a few months in this place, he'd lose his idealism and his fine legal scruples and he'd be helping the PSO torture suspects in Ghumdan Prison. Well, maybe not. But like all of us who've been on the front lines too long, and all of us who lived through 9/11, Howard Fensterman would become a little more like the people we were fighting. Of that, I was sure.

Buck came over to us, and instead of Howard asking him about the captured terrorist – sorry, the suspect – Howard asked him, 'What time are you leaving tomorrow?'

Buck replied, 'Before eight A.M.' He explained to Howard and to me, 'It's about four hundred kilometers to Aden, and it can take anywhere from four to six hours. So we want to get there in time for the convoy to turn around and get back to Sana'a not too long after dark.' He further explained to us, 'We'd rather the DSS agents not stay overnight in Aden, because we need those resources here.'

I thought we might need them more at the Sheraton.

I again suggested to Howard, 'Come along for the ride. If we get ambushed, you can tell us when we can legally return fire.'

Even Howard laughed at that.

Buck said to Howard, 'We have room, and we can always use another gun. We gather in the chancery parking lot at seven.'

Howard acknowledged that and exited stage left.

Buck asked me, 'Were you giving him a hard time?'

'Not me.'

'He's doing his job,' Buck assured me. 'Unfortunately his job makes our job more difficult.'

'Not for me.'

Buck changed the subject and said, 'Paul told me you learned a few things at Ghumdan.'

'We did. Our allies are assholes.'

'Did you learn anything you didn't already know?'

'Maybe.' I informed Buck, 'Howard didn't know we were at Ghumdan.'

'Is that so? Did you tell him?'

'No. I told him to see you.'

'I'll speak to him.' He added, 'We're not sure how the legat fits into this.'

'Let me know when you know.'

'I will.' He asked me, 'What did you speak to Colonel Kent about?'

'The Yemeni Army.'

He let that go and asked, 'What did you learn at Ghumdan?'

I never liked it when an NYPD boss wanted to debrief me without my partner present. There could be a misunderstanding. So I replied, 'I think Paul wanted the four of us to discuss that.'

'Of course.' He asked me, 'So how did you like Ghumdan?'

'It has a way to go to become a model penal institution.'

'I thought so, too.'

I asked him, 'Were you there this morning?'

'No, but I've been there many times in the past.'

'When will we see the CIA report on their interrogation of the prisoner?'

'After it's been seen by the station chief.'

I had not yet been introduced to the CIA station chief in Yemen, so I asked, 'And who is that?'

'You don't need to know.' Buck added, 'And he doesn't need to know you.'

I asked, 'How many games are in town?'

'Several. But ours is the main game at the moment.' He added, 'You ask good questions.'

That's not what he meant, but I said, 'Thank you.'

'Paul said Colonel Hakim was his charming self.'

'He was obstructing American justice.'

'That's his job.'

I told him, 'The fact is, if we had two or three hours alone with the prisoner, with an embassy interpreter, we'd know a lot more about Al Qaeda in Yemen than we do now.'

Buck replied, 'If the situation were reversed — if it was *your* prisoner in New York, Detective Corey — would you allow a foreign policeman or intelligence officer to question him alone?'

Spoken like a true diplomat. But not a rhetorical question, so I replied, 'You're assuming some sort of equality, and there is none. We're here to save the ass of a weak and corrupt government. The least they can do is get out of our way.'

Buck nodded, then informed me, 'Sometimes they do. But as we say in the world of diplomacy, it's about quid pro quo. We give them something, then they give us something.' He informed me, 'I think it's our turn to give them something. Aside from money.'

'Like what?'

'Well, as I told you in New York, they want our help to ... neutralize some particularly aggressive and dangerous tribal leaders.'

'And?'

'And we're reluctant to do that.'

'Why?'

'We want to keep the goodwill of the tribes.'

'I didn't know we had their goodwill.'

'We do, but not directly. As I also explained to you, the tribes are culturally and historically closer to the monarchy in Saudi Arabia than they are to the republican government in Sana'a. And the Saudis are our allies, and our link to the tribes.'

'So we don't want to vaporize tribal chieftains with our Hellfire missiles and piss off the Saudis.'

'Correct. But we might ... neutralize a few sheiks and chieftains in exchange for the Sana'a government giving us more help in locating and eliminating Al Qaeda leaders.'

'Right. But they should do that anyway. It's good for them, too.'

'That's what we're trying to explain to them, and believe me they know it, but they're using our fixation with Al Qaeda to force us to use our Predator drones and Hellfire missiles against these tribal chieftains as well as the South Yemen separatists.'

'Got it. And round and round it goes.'

'Indeed it does.' He further explained to me, 'It's a delicate balancing act, and it all comes back to quid pro quo.'

'Got it.'

He returned to my complaint and said, 'Regarding our interrogation of their prisoners, the PSO really doesn't want us getting free information. They want to sell it to us. So if they give us some good information on The Panther, for instance, then they want us to give them a bucket of guts that used to be an annoying tribal sheik.'

The graphic imagery sort of surprised me, but it made me remember that Buck Harris was only ten percent diplomat, and ninety percent intelligence officer. In fact, in the good old Cold

War days, Buck and his pals would have a cocktail and talk about the nuclear obliteration of hundreds of millions of people. Now the potential body count could be measured in terms of a bucket of guts. That's progress.

On a more immediate subject, I said to him, 'I assume Paul told you that the prisoner told us there are about forty jihadists on their way to Aden to attack the Sheraton.'

'Yes, Paul did mention that, and we've alerted our people there.'

'Good. Especially since we are going to be some of those people.' I suggested, 'Maybe the Yemeni Army can intercept them.'

He informed me, 'The Yemeni Army seems to have little luck in intercepting Al Qaeda fighters when they come out of the mountains.' He added, 'We believe that Al Qaeda travels in small groups or individually, in civilian clothing, and they may even take public transportation. Buses, planes, hired vehicles.' He reminded me, 'Men in Yemen with AK-47 rifles aren't stopped and questioned because of the rifles. That would be like stopping men with umbrellas in London.'

Buck was getting three-martini clever, and I smiled.

He glanced at his watch and said to me, 'We're actually meeting Paul at eight upstairs. It's that time.'

'I'll get Kate.'

'I think she's already there.'

'All right.' So we ditched our drinks, went to the elevator, rode up to the third floor, and made our way to the secure communications room.

Interesting cocktail party.

CHAPTER THIRTY-THREE

M rs Corey and Mr Brenner were sitting at the table chatting, and two commo people were manning the electronics on the other side of the glass wall. I was sure there was a lot of traffic today between here and Washington.

We sat, and Brenner told us, 'The recording devices are off.'

Now I'd never know what Paul and Kate were talking about. Actually, I'd never know anyway.

Buck asked us, 'So did you all have a good day in Sana'a?'

I replied, 'How could anyone have a bad day in Sana'a?'

Buck smiled, then urged us to tell him about our day.

So we did, and Buck listened without comment, except to ask us how the food was at Old Sana'a, and to ask Brenner if he was sure he'd gotten me the best jambiyah for the best price. He also asked Kate if she'd been successful at Hope in Their Hands.

This was Buck's schtick, of course, putting life-and-death topics on the back burner and asking us about lunch and shopping. This is a good interrogation technique, but an annoying debriefing technique.

Buck moved on, asking us, 'And you're sure you weren't followed?'

I'd already said we weren't, so I got a little pissy and said, 'Buck, I'm a cop. I know if I'm being followed.'

Buck pointed out, 'This is not New York.'

'Assholes are the same everywhere.'

Buck smiled, then said, 'Well, I'm sure that someone, some-where today saw you and made a phone call, which is actually what we want.' He added, 'It's good, though, that no one acted on that information while you were in an exposed situation.' He said to Brenner, 'Maybe you should have had DSS backup.'

Brenner replied, a bit testily, 'I felt it was safe enough to go out without backup.'

Well, it wasn't. But safety wasn't the point. Backup is easily spotted and scares off the bad guys, and that's not what Paul Brenner or John Corey wanted to do.

Buck said, 'All right. All's well that ends well. So ... oh, by the way, Mr Corey, that was good of you to give the lady in the shop an extra twenty dollars. We like to support them.'

Had I mentioned that? No, I had not. So probably one of those Westerners in the shop was his snitch, or more likely he'd just called the shop and chatted in Arabic with the manager. In any case, in the world of spooks and spies, it's all illusion, and nothing is as it seems. Old Buck had been at this game a lot longer than anyone in this room, and he wanted everyone to know it.

Point made, Buck said to me and Brenner, 'Tell me and Kate what happened at Ghumdan.'

So we did. And as former cops, we got right into sync and gave Buck and Kate a clear, concise, and accurate report of our Ghumdan experience.

Buck listened intently, as did Kate, and neither of them interrupted.

When we were finished, Buck stayed silent awhile, then said, 'You seem to have gotten more information than we usually do at these interrogations.' He said to me, 'I suppose your past experience in Aden was helpful.'

I replied, 'To the extent that I knew what to expect.' I informed him, 'The prisoner was more cooperative than our ally, Colonel Hakim.'

Buck said to us, 'I'll ask Howard to put in a formal request with the Ministry of Justice to get the transcript of this prisoner's interrogation by the PSO.' He let us know, 'They won't honor that request, but then we have something new to complain about.'

I asked Buck, 'Is the PSO more cooperative with the CIA?'

He looked at me and said, 'Good question. The short answer is yes.' He smiled. 'Birds of a feather.' Then he added quickly, 'I'm not suggesting the PSO and the CIA have anything in common.'

I thought he just said birds of a feather.

Buck informed us, 'They have their own understanding between themselves. Very much quid pro quo.'

That was a little scary.

Kate, who I was certain was the only person here who had once slept with and shot a CIA officer, said, 'I'm assuming our fifth team member can fill in some of our information gaps.'

Buck replied, 'That is our expectation.'

Right. The CIA is happy to fill you in. Unfortunately, they lie.

Mr Brenner had no comment on this topic, and he returned to the subject by reminding us, 'The Panther could know from his fighters that one of them was taken prisoner – but he might also think Rahim was killed. So we don't know if The Panther is worried about a prisoner talking about his location.' He added, 'I hope this prisoner wasn't mentioned in the government press release.'

Buck assured us, 'The Sana'a government is not that stupid. They are, in fact, crafty, which is why they're not all hanging from a noose. So they will report the attack, but claim four killed. Or twenty. Or whatever number they like. There will be no mention of a prisoner.'

True. But I reminded everyone, 'Someone at Ghumdan could tell Al Qaeda that there's a talking prisoner who said he saw The Panther at Marib.'

Buck replied, 'That's very possible, but let's hope it doesn't send The Panther running.' He reminded us again, 'If there is a leak from Ghumdan to Al Qaeda, they will also mention the name of John Corey.'

Right. That's why I was at Ghumdan.

Buck asked Kate, 'Any questions for John or Paul?'

Kate asked me, 'Is it possible that this prisoner was rehearsed? That what you heard was not the whole truth?'

I really don't like being interrogated by my wife, but it was a good question and I replied, 'It's possible. But the prisoner had the appearance of truthfulness.' I looked at Brenner, who seconded that and added, 'This guy was scared, hurting, and desperate.'

Kate asked Brenner, 'What was Colonel Hakim's demeanor during the interrogation?'

Brenner replied, 'Not a happy guy. He really wanted us out of there, which is why I think this wasn't rehearsed and wasn't disinformation.'

Kate and Buck both nodded. So we kicked this around awhile,

and after about ten minutes Buck said, 'All right. It appears we've been handed an opportunity. So in the absence of any new or contradictory information, I think our first excursion into the countryside from Aden will be to Marib.'

Obviously.

He continued, 'If The Panther is not there, we can at least see those magnificent pre-Islamic ruins.'

Who gives a shit? You wanna see ruins? Go to Newark. I pointed out, 'We really won't know if The Panther is still there, but if we stay there looking for him, I'm sure he *will* know that. Also we now know that The Panther has assets around Marib, including a tribal sheik, so even if he moved because of this attack, he'll return to meet us on his turf.'

'Precisely,' agreed Buck. 'And we can see the ruins while we're waiting for him.'

'There you go.'

Brenner commented, 'Now we know where to set and bait the trap.'

Bait? What happened to lure?

Buck said, 'Assuming Colonel Hakim is thinking along the same lines, don't be surprised if we see him there.'

Right. Could get crowded at Marib. And we could scare off The Panther. But I was betting that John Corey on The Panther's turf would be irresistible to him.

Buck next brought up the subject of the possible Al Qaeda attack on the Sheraton in Aden and assured us, 'The FBI SWAT Team, the DSS men, and the Marines at the Sheraton are on full alert, as are all American personnel in the hotel. Also, we are officially notifying the Yemeni government at the highest level about this possible attack, so they have no choice but to increase their security around the hotel.'

I, of course, remarked, 'That will make us sleep better.'

Brenner assured us, 'You'll never sleep as well as the Yemeni Army.'

Funny. But not.

'The last time the Sheraton in Aden was attacked,' Buck said, 'was before the Americans were there. During one of the civil wars in the eighties. A rebel group lobbed a few mortar rounds into the hotel.' He added, 'The Communists ran South Yemen in those days, and they allowed alcohol – which is the best thing I can say about them. In any case, this rebel group was fundamentalist, and the cocktail lounge offended them.'

I reminisced, 'When I was at the Sheraton, we made up fun names for the cocktails.' All right, I'll tell you. 'High Explosive Mojito. Martini Mortars. My favorite was the Incoming Cosmo.'

No one thought that was funny. I guess you had to be there.

Anyway, Kate asked Buck, 'Is there any other place for us to stay in Aden?'

'No. The Yemeni government has given us two floors of the Sheraton, and that's our operational base in Aden.' He assured us, 'I wouldn't worry about this too much.' He added, 'Unless you start to see Arab guests checking out.'

Funny? Maybe.

Kate also asked, 'Do we have an evacuation plan?'

Yes, the breaststroke.

Buck replied, 'We'll ask Doug Reynolds, who is Ed Peters's DSS counterpart in Aden.'

Buck then said to us, 'Final subject. The road trip to Aden. We haven't notified the Yemeni authorities of our movement, so, theoretically, Al Qaeda will not be tipped off that we are taking a convoy to Aden tomorrow morning. In that respect, we aren't advertising this trip in advance with the hope of making contact with Al Qaeda – but as soon as we leave the compound, cell phones will be ringing all over Sana'a and along our route, so our movement will then be known.'

Brenner continued Buck's thought and said, 'The longer we're on the road, the more chance that Al Qaeda will try to set up an ambush or roadside bomb along our route.' He added, 'It will be obvious that we're headed to Aden. But if we maintain good speed, and maybe vary the route, we should be able to stay ahead of anything they try to plan.'

Buck reiterated, 'It's not as though we're *trying* to get into a fight with them, but it may happen, and we are prepared – and we may be able to kill or capture a key Al Qaeda leader.'

That sounded a bit optimistic, but since we were driving to Aden anyway, I guess we might as well kill some bad guys on the way. Right?

Buck had some good news and said, 'We may be crazy, but we're not stupid. So we've arranged to have two Predator surveillance drones on station along our route.' He informed me and Kate, 'They have infrared video cameras that can see through cloud cover if necessary, and the high-resolution cameras can operate from as high as twenty thousand feet and still see a man with a rifle.' He concluded, 'We should know about an ambush long before we reach it.'

Well, that *was* good news. The bad news, of course, was that the surveillance drones might still miss fifty jihadists sitting in a mud hut waiting for us to come by. Or miss a roadside bomb. I asked, 'And what do we do if we get this aerial surveillance information?'

Brenner, ex–combat vet, replied, 'I will make the decision about how we react to an ambush warning.'

'Give me a call,' I suggested.

Kate asked a good question. 'How about Hellfire missiles?'

Buck replied, 'We are not authorized to use Hellfire missiles without the explicit permission of the Yemeni government.'

Kate, the lawyer, asked, 'Not even as a purely defensive means to save lives?'

Buck informed us, 'Unfortunately not.' He also let us know, 'It takes a very long time to get this permission from the Yemeni authorities, so we can't count on Hellfire missiles in a rapidly developing situation.'

I thought about that and said, 'I assume that the Predator sur- veillance drones *will* be armed with Hellfire missiles, and that we will in fact use them if we're ducking AK-47 rounds.'

Buck didn't reply directly, but said, 'To ask permission is to invite rejection. We do what we have to do, then apologize.'

'Right. And give the Yemenis another million.'

'Maybe two.' He smiled and said, 'In Yemen, we pay to play.'

Right. Even wars have rules, but the rules here in Yemen did not favor the Americans. The good news was that we broke the rules. The better news was that the punishment was a small fine. Two million. Hell, give the Yemenis ten million and carpet bomb the whole country. Better yet, nuke 'em. Check's in the mail for that.

Bottom line on this trip to Aden was that it was more than a method of getting from Point A to Point B; it was also trolling for sharks — fishing for Al Qaeda.

Buck announced, 'That's all I have. And if no one has anything further, this meeting is adjourned.'

Wonderful.

But Buck said, 'Let me buy you all dinner at the Mövenpick. They have a new French chef.'

I said, 'I'd love to, but—'

Kate interrupted, 'That would be very nice.'

'Good,' said Buck. 'Afterwards, if you're game for it, we can go to the Russia Club.'

I reminded everyone, 'We need to get up early.'

Buck told us, 'We can sleep on the way to Aden.' He smiled and assured us, 'The roadside bombs will wake us up for the ambush.'

I felt like a guy who thought he'd joined an ace fighter squadron and found out it was a kamikaze group. I mean, bravery is one thing; war psychosis is something else. I said to Buck, 'You've been here too long.'

'I know. But we're all going home.' He added, 'One way or the other.'

CHAPTER THIRTY-FOUR

So we left the embassy and squeezed into the armored Land Cruiser with Zamo driving and Buck up front for the short drive to the Mövenpick Hotel.

It was a nice hotel, and I was glad I was checked in there, though I was staying elsewhere.

I'm not a big fan of Continental cuisine, except French fries, preferring instead pigs-in-a-blanket, but the restaurant was good, and if you let your mind wander, you could be anywhere but here. I'm sure the new French chef felt the same way.

We had a nice, wine-fueled, getting-to-know-you dinner, and talked a bit about ourselves.

Buck Harris, it turned out, was married, with a wife in Silver Spring, Maryland, outside of DC. I got the impression he had some family money, and he didn't rely on his State Department salary to buy five-thousand-dollar jambiyahs. So for Buck, maybe the Cold War had been a gentleman's hobby, something to keep him busy. What, then, was the war on terrorism? Probably the same thing, but with the added incentive of revenge, as he said. I could imagine him being buddies with his former Soviet enemies, but I couldn't imagine a day when he, or any of us, would be having drinks with former jihadists. For one thing, they didn't drink. More to the point, this was a war without end, and there would be no forgiving or forgetting.

Buck had a grown son and daughter who he said did not share his ideology or his enthusiasm for fucking America's enemies. Buck told us, 'They believe we should try to understand Islam.' He speculated, 'If they'd been old enough during the Cold War, they would have told me I should try to understand Communism.' He assured us, 'I understand both.'

Right. Hey, it sucks when your own kids think you're part of the problem.

But Buck said philosophically, 'The important thing is that I know I've spent my life doing what I thought was right — not just for me, but for my country, and for civilization — and also for my children and their children.'

Kate assured him, 'You don't need to justify your life or your work to anyone.'

Buck agreed, but said, 'In this business, however, you are sometimes forced to compromise your own beliefs in the interest of the greater good — national security, global strategy, and so forth.' He confided to us, 'During the Cold War, there were a few occasions when I had to betray or abandon an ally as part of a complex plan.'

No one commented on that, but I did wonder if he was hinting that the past was prologue to the future. Hopefully not.

Kate, too, spoke a bit about her background, including her wonderful FBI father, now retired, and her loony mother who was a gun nut, though Kate mentioned that only in the context of growing up around guns and learning at a young age how to hunt and shoot.

This was a great opening for her to tell everyone about how she whacked Ted Nash, but she didn't go there. Maybe she was saving this interesting story for when we met our CIA teammate, thinking that the retelling of it would be even more interesting to a CIA officer. But I'm sure everyone in the CIA already knew this story.

I used our bonding occasion to tell some funny cop stories, which made everyone laugh. But to show it wasn't all fun and games on the NYPD, I mentioned getting shot on the job, and my medical retirement, and my rocky transition from NYPD to the Federal Anti-Terrorist Task Force, and of course, my first case, where I met Kate Mayfield, the love of my life.

Paul Brenner seemed to have had an interesting and adventurous life in the military, but like most combat veterans, he downplayed his war experiences, and again he didn't mention his clandestine mission to post-war Vietnam. But he did say he'd had a brief wartime marriage, though he didn't say anything about his current lady in the States, and I didn't expect he would; he seemed to be a private person. Also — how do I put this? — he was smitten with Kate Mayfield. Hey, no big deal. I think Tom Walsh has the same problem. And it wasn't my problem.

Anyway, four-fifths of the A-team got to know one another a little better, which might or might not make us work better together. And with luck, we'd all get home and have a few stories to tell. Or, in this business, not tell.

I suggested a reunion. 'We'll meet at seven under the clock at Grand Central Station, just like in the movies, and we'll go to Michael Jordan's Steak House.'

Everyone liked that happy ending and we agreed to be there, date to be determined by fate. I wondered who, if anyone, would make it.

Buck paid for dinner as promised — sixty bucks, including tip, wine, and drinks. That's a month's pay for a Yemeni, and about four drinks in a New York bar. Maybe I should buy a retirement house here.

Anyway, showing the poor judgment of the intoxicated, we thought it was a great idea to go to the Russia Club.

Zamo drove us the few hundred meters up the road to Tourist City. The half dozen guards at the gate appeared to be Eastern European, and they looked tough and menacing with their flak jackets and AK-47s. But they recognized the American Embassy

Land Cruiser, and probably recognized Zamo, and waved us through.

I said to Brenner, 'They seemed to know you.'

No response.

Tourist City was a collection of five- and six-story concrete slab buildings, not unlike an urban housing project for the poor. But here, in Sana'a, it was the height of luxury, and more importantly, it was guarded. Not safe. Guarded.

I could see why Paul Brenner might choose not to live here; it was sort of depressing, but also an admission that you felt unsafe on the outside. And macho men would never admit that. They'd rather die. And often did.

There were a few low-rise buildings on the grounds, including a few shops, and in one of the buildings was the Russia Club.

Zamo pulled up and we piled out.

There were two more armed guys in front of the place, and they definitely recognized Mr Buckminster Harris. In fact, they greeted him in Russian, and Buck replied in Russian with what must have been a joke, because the two guys laughed.

Ironic, I thought, that Buck Harris, who'd spent most of his professional life trying to screw the Russians, was now yucking it up with them in Yemen, where he'd spent part of the Cold War spying on the now-defunct Evil Empire. If you live long enough, you see things you could never have imagined.

We entered the Russia Club, and the maitre d' saw me and shouted, 'Ivan! It is you! Excellent. Tatiana is here tonight. She will be delirious with joy!'

Just kidding.

But the maitre d', Sergei by name, did know Buck, though not Paul Brenner, which disappointed me. I would have liked to discover that Mr Cool dropped his paycheck here every month, boozing and whoring. Kate, too, would find that interesting.

Anyway, the place looked a bit sleazy, which it was. There was a long bar to the right, a raised stage, and a ceramic-tile dance floor surrounded by tables, half of which were empty. A DJ was playing some god-awful seventies hard rock, and a few couples were on the dance floor, looking like they were having seizures.

The bar was crowded with casually dressed men and barely dressed women. I mean, I haven't seen so much deep cleavage since I drove through the Grand Canyon. The men looked Western – Europeans and Americans – and most of the ladies appeared to be from Eastern Europe and Russia, though there were a few black ladies who, I'd once been told, were from Djibouti, Ethiopia, Somalia, and Eritrea, which is not far from here if you cross the pirate-infested Red Sea. Also at the tables were a few Western-looking women accompanied by their gentlemen friends or husbands. I recognized two men and women from the embassy, but they didn't wave.

If there were any Yemeni customers or service staff in the Russia Club, I didn't see them. In fact, I'm sure one selling point of this place was the promise that you didn't have to see a single Yemeni, unless you stayed until closing time and watched them mop the floor under the eye of armed Russians.

Kate broke into my thoughts and asked me, 'Been here before?'

'They've named a cocktail after me.'

Anyway, Sergei escorted us to a table, though I'd have preferred the bar.

Buck ordered a bottle of Stolichnaya on ice, a plate of citrus fruit, and zakuskie — snacks.

My last case, involving The Lion, had taken me to a Russian nightclub in Brighton Beach, Brooklyn, which is home to many Russian-Americans. The club, Svetlana by name, was a lot more opulent than this place, and the clientele were mostly immigrants from the motherland on a nostalgia trip. This place, named simply the Russia Club, was the Village of the Damned in the Country of the Lost.

Anyway, the vodka came quickly and we toasted, 'Na Zdorovie.'

Kate seemed comfortable enough in the proximity of horny guys and hookers, and her only complaint was the volume of the bad music.

Mr Brenner asked her to dance, of course, and she accepted and walked unsteadily onto the slippery dance floor with Brenner holding her arm.

Buck said to me, 'She's a delightful woman.'

'She is,' I agreed. More so when she's had a few. However, if it was me who'd suggested coming here, she might not be such delightful company.

Kate slipped on the tile floor, but Brenner caught her, and Kate kicked off her shoes and they danced to some horrid disco tune.

An attractive, scantily clad lady came over to the table carrying a tray suspended from a strap around her neck, and in the tray were two huge hooters and a selection of cigars and cigarettes. Take your pick.

Buck found three Cubans hiding under the lady's left humidor, and gave her a twenty-dollar bill, which included tax, tip, and a light.

The lady said to Buck, in a heavy Russian accent, 'I don't see you for many weeks.'

Buck replied in Russian, and the lady laughed and tousled his thinning hair. Buck was apparently still fucking the Russians.

The lady checked me out and asked, 'You are new in Sana'a?'

'I feel I've been here all my life.'

'Yes?' She further inquired, 'Is that your wife or girlfriend? Or his?'

'My wife, his girlfriend.'

She thought that was really funny, then said to me, 'Maybe I see you again.'

'Tomorrow night.'

So Buck and I sat there, smoking Cuban cigars, drinking Russian vodka, listening to American disco, and watching the human comedy.

I was sure that if you stayed in Yemen long enough – like more than a month – you'd develop a deep fatalism, which led to strange and risky behavior. I'm not being judgmental – just expressing an awareness that the people I needed to work with and trust had gone a little around the bend.

Anyway, the DJ switched to American big band, and an instrumental of 'I'm in the Mood for Love' filled the room while a Russian chanteuse on the stage did her best to sing along.

'Ahminda moot fa loov, zimply becus yerneermee . . .'

Brenner and Kate were getting to know each other.

On the subject of fatalism, I imagined that every dangerous mission from the dawn of time through World War Two and the Cold War to the war on terrorism began with an alcohol binge. Or should begin that way. Hey, eat, drink, and be merry. Nothing puts things into perspective like the thought that you might die tomorrow.

I said to Buck, 'This was a good idea.'

'It's the thing to do on the eve of battle.' He added, 'War is a good excuse for any type of behavior.'

Indeed.

The DJ was now playing 'Moonlight Serenade' and Kate, observing the one slow dance rule, came over to the table, took Buck's hand, and led him to the dance floor, leaving Mr Brenner and me to dance if we chose to.

Before I could ask, Brenner sat and said, 'Oh, good. Cigars.' He busied himself with pouring a vodka while getting the attention of the cigarette lady, who came over and clipped his Cuban, then lit it for him.

We didn't have much to say to each other, but he did say, 'Good cigar.'

Mr Brenner, I thought, was becoming less funny and less interesting as he became more distracted by Ms. Mayfield. I'll write this off to too much alcohol and too much time in the land of limited dating opportunities. Not that you had to be drunk or horny to find Kate Mayfield attractive.

Anyway, I watched Buck and Kate sharing the dance floor with Western European and American men, and Eastern European and African hookers. It was great that so many diverse cultures could get along so well. It would have been even greater if we could get the Arabs out there in their robes and veils, all liquored up, doing the Bristol Stomp.

A few ladies came by to ask if they could sit or have a dance, and Mr Brenner and I politely declined.

To make conversation, I said to Brenner, 'Someday a rocket is going to come through this roof.'

He informed me, 'They have steel planking and sandbags on the roof.'

'It should say that on the menu.'

'Moonlight Serenade' ended, and it was my turn to dance with my wife.

The DJ was still spinning big band and the smoky air filled with trombones and saxophones playing Tommy Dorsey's 'I'll Never Smile Again.'

Kate and I danced, and I didn't spin her much because I could tell the room was already spinning in her head.

She didn't have much to say, and I walked her back to our table.

It was past midnight now and the Russia Club was in full swing. Buck suggested cognac, which was not a good suggestion.

Kate said, 'I'm ready to go home.'

Me, too. Let's go to the airport.

Brenner picked up the tab — about forty bucks, which he paid in American dollars.

Sergei showed us to the door and said to us, 'Tomorrow is belly dancing show. You come.'

Buck said we'd be back. We left, and Zamo pulled up to the door. I put Kate in the front seat and the boys squeezed in the rear.

As we passed through the gates of Tourist City, Zamo suggested we have our guns handy, which was a good idea considering we were so drunk it would take five minutes to find them.

Zamo also suggested that he drop Kate and me off first at the Sheraton, then double back to the embassy. His final suggestion was that Brenner should stay in the embassy tonight since Zamo had no intention of driving him to his apartment after midnight.

So just another night out in wild and crazy Sana'a.

Kate and I got dropped off at the Sheraton, and Zamo said he'd pick us up at 6:45. Buck told us not to check out, and Brenner said to wear the Kevlar. I said, 'Good night and good luck.'

I stuck my gun in my belt and steered Kate into the lobby, which was empty and quiet, though I could hear music from the cocktail lounge.

We went to the elevators, where there should have been a security person, but the chair was empty. We drew our guns and rode up to our floor, where I told Kate to keep an eye on the corridor while I cleared the room.

There were no terrorists under the bed or in the closet so I motioned Kate in, and I closed and bolted the door. The drapes were open and I drew them shut.

Kate, not feeling her very best, collapsed on the bed.

I looked around the room to see if anything struck me as wrong — like a stuffed black panther on my pillow. Everything looked kosher — or I should say halal — and I lowered myself into the stuffed chair.

All in all, this was not a bad day in the Land That Time Forgot. I mean, we learned a lot, and we could make good use of what we learned, and by now, maybe The Panther knew that John Corey, who'd killed The Lion, was now here to kill him. There ain't room in this country for both of us, asshole.

My teammates seemed more than competent, and I trusted Brenner. Professionally, I mean. Not so much with Kate. Buck seemed trustworthy, though he had a self-admitted history of throwing friends under the bus — but only for patriotic reasons.

Our CIA person was as yet unknown, but not for long. That could change the team balance.

Kate was still gung-ho, and she was a fast learner. I was honestly glad she was with me and I looked forward to that moment when I could say, 'I told you we should have stayed home.'

So, tomorrow the road to Aden, which I'd traveled round-trip last time. This time, there would be no round trip. It would be one-way to Aden, then to Marib. And that, too, could be one-way. But to be optimistic, let's say Marib was the last stop before home. And the last stop for The Panther.

PART V

Death Highway, Yemen

CHAPTER THIRTY-FIVE

At 7 A.M., everyone who was going to Aden had assembled with weapons and baggage in the small parking lot at the side of the chancery building.

It was a nice morning, dry and cool, with a clear sky for the Predator drones.

Standing around the five black Land Cruisers were about fifteen people, all men, except for Kate and a woman in tan cargo pants and a white T-shirt. She was, according to Buck, our doctor, and her name was Clare Nolan. She looked very young, and I asked Buck, 'Is she old enough to use alcohol swabs?'

'She's very competent,' Buck assured me. 'She worked in an inner-city hospital trauma unit for six months. Gunshot wounds and all that.'

'Can she treat a hangover?'

'You look fine, my boy.' His satellite phone rang and he excused himself and went off to speak to someone in private.

I was actually feeling not too bad, considering I'd had a few glasses of wine with dinner, after the martinis and before the bottle of vodka.

Kate also looked good, but that may have been the make-up. I hoped she remembered that she'd saved the last dance for me.

On that subject, Mrs Corey and Mr Brenner seemed to have little to say to each other this morning. Ah, yes. Been there myself.

Anyway, Kate and I had chosen desert boots and jeans for Death Highway and she wore a black pullover, under which was her Kevlar vest. Over my vest I wore a khaki shirt that I'd worn last time I was in Yemen — my good-luck shirt. And since we were going through Indian Territory, we had our .45s unconcealed, strapped on our hips.

The uniform of the day for the DSS guys was cargo pants and sleeveless bush jackets over black T-shirts, and that's what Mr Brenner was wearing along with his heart on his sleeve.

Howard Fensterman had decided to show up, and he looked ready for adventure in his bush shirt with his Glock slung low at his side. All FBI Special Agents are trained and qualified on a variety of weapons, but some are more qualified than others. Still, I'd been surprised before by who was a good gunslinger. It's all in the head.

Howard also carried the most lethal of lawyers' weapons: his briefcase. In the briefcase, he informed Kate and me, was all the paperwork we needed to make a lawful arrest of one Bulus ibn al-Darwish, a.k.a. al-Numair, a.k.a. The Panther.

Mr Fensterman also informed us, 'I have copies of everything for both of you and for Buck.'

I was tired of giving Howard a hard time so I said, 'Thank you.'

'I also have copies of the suspect's fingerprints, and three color snapshots of him taken in the US about twelve years ago, plus his last driver's license and US passport photo.'

'Good.' If you look like your passport photo, you're already dead.

Anyway, I thought we'd get all this in Aden, but it was good to have it now in case we ran into the suspect on the road.

Mr Fensterman continued, 'He's clean-shaven in these photos, but we know from various sources that he's grown a beard.'

That's what Rahim said at Ghumdan.

Howard further informed us, 'He's also wanted by a number of foreign governments for attacks against their citizens.'

'Right. The Saudis want him for killing some of their border guards.'

'Correct. And the Belgians for a possible kidnapping and suspected murder.'

I'd just heard about this from Colonel Kent, but I hadn't mentioned it to Kate, who asked, 'What was that about?'

Howard replied, 'Back last August, nine Belgian tourists disappeared at the ruins near Marib.'

Kate said, 'I remember reading something about that in the Times.'

She may have read it in the *Post*, but she always cites the *Times*. I do the opposite.

Howard continued, 'It looked like a tribal kidnapping, but there was no ransom demand, and there was blood found at the ruins.' He added, 'The Yemeni tour guide and bus driver were found ... dead.' He added, 'Throats slit.'

Didn't sound good for those tourists. I asked, 'Why does the Belgian government think it was The Panther?'

Howard replied, 'The Belgians arrested an Al Qaeda suspect in Brussels on an unrelated charge, and apparently this information came out during the interrogation.'

Right. That's how we get half our information; bad guys know lots of bad things.

Howard said to us, 'So, aside from the Yemenis, other governments, including the Saudis, will want to be notified if we make an arrest, and they may ask for extradition. So we need to make a strong case for our Cole-related charge.'

'Right.' The Saudis could be a problem if we did snatch The Panther and had to beat feet with him across the Saudi border. Therefore, we were probably not taking The Panther to Saudi Arabia, and certainly not handing him over to the Yemenis. It occurred to me that there was more going on here than I knew. I'm shocked.

Bottom line here: A bullet in the brain settles all extradition requests, jurisdictional disputes, and silly lawsuits.

Howard also informed us, 'I'm going to stay on with you in Aden.'

Shit. But I said, 'Great.' I felt obligated, however, to advise him, 'We have intel that the Sheraton in Aden might be the subject of an Al Qaeda attack.'

'Really?'

'With luck, this will happen before we get there and the cocktail lounge won't be damaged.'

Kate suggested to Howard, 'You might want to return to Sana'a today.'

Howard thought about that – Death Highway back to Sana'a this afternoon, or Ground Zero in Aden tonight? Personally, I'd head inside for a muffin. But Howard said, 'No, I'll stay in Aden until a convoy heads north again.' He added, 'I want to be close to this.'

'Your call.'

Zamo came over and asked us to join him at his Land Cruiser for a quick course on the M4 carbine.

He handed each of us a weapon and said, 'This is the Model A1, a shorter and lighter version of the standard military M-16 assault rifle, which I'm sure you're all familiar with.'

I hefted the carbine in my hands. It felt good. It felt *bad*.

Zamo, warming to his favorite subject, said, 'It has a telescoping stock, and this model fires fully automatic.' He continued, 'It takes the standard 5.56mm cartridge, and has a thirty-round magazine. The cyclic rate of fire is seven hundred to nine hundred and fifty rounds a minute.'

Kate asked, 'Effective range?'

'You'll get good accuracy at three hundred yards.' He further explained, 'The short barrel reduces the effective range, but we have day and night scopes that I'll give you.'

I inquired, 'Do you have your sniper rifle with you?'

'Does the Pope leave home without his cross?' Zamo continued, 'This gun is built for close-in defense and medium-range offensive use. So if we get into a situation where the bad guys are firing from a distance with AK-47s, then you have to compensate by laying down full automatic suppressing fire to keep their heads down.' He assured us, 'What the M4 lacks in long-range capability, it more than makes up for in its high cyclic rate of fire.'

Howard asked a good question. 'Any jamming problems when it gets hot?'

Zamo replied, 'Theoretically yes, but no one has reported a combat jam.'

Maybe because they were dead.

Zamo continued, 'The small size makes it easy to transport and conceal. Easy to carry it in and out of tight and confined spaces like vehicles or caves.'

Caves?

Zamo looked at Kate and said to her, 'Its size, weight, and low recoil makes it popular with the ladies.'

I asked Zamo, 'Will it chip her nails?'

Zamo laughed and Kate said, 'Fuck you.' Which made Zamo laugh even more. This was fun.

So Zamo went on a bit about the M4, using more words than I'd heard him use all day yesterday.

All in all, the M4 seemed like an excellent weapon. I hoped I never had to use it, but if I did, I knew I'd have a blast.

On that subject, Zamo said, 'I'm sorry we never got a chance to test fire, but we'll go out in the Badlands tomorrow and give it a rip.' He added, 'We might even find live targets.'

I reminded him, 'We might find those on the road this morning.'

'Right.' Zamo asked, 'Any questions?'

Howard asked, 'Which thing is the trigger?'

Funny.

Okay, so deadly force course completed, Kate and I and Howard slung our M4s over our shoulders, and Zamo gave us each a black satchel stuffed with loaded magazines and telescopic sights. He said to us, 'Good luck and good hunting.'

Mr Brenner, the caravan master, had gathered the DSS drivers, and he was now speaking to them, reading from a sheet of paper that outlined the route and the order of march. I wondered if by chance Mr Brenner and Mrs Corey were riding in the same vehicle. Would he do something so stupidly obvious? Why not? I would.

Ed Peters had come out of the chancery building, though I didn't think he was going to Aden with us. Maybe he was here to bless the caravan.

Kate and I were standing with Buck now, and Peters came over to us and said to Buck, 'I've got only two fully armored vehicles left, and I have to pick up the new ambassador next week, so don't get ambushed.'

Buck assured him, 'You can get five new vehicles on a C-17.'

Peters replied, 'That can take over a week.' He said to me, 'I hate these trips to Aden.'

'You're not going,' I reminded him.

'My vehicles are.'

'Sorry. Is there a bus I can take?'

Clearly Mr Peters was worried about his vehicles. And, of course, his DSS agents. As for his passengers, they were the cause of his worries. A larger issue was the lack of American helicopters in this dangerous and inaccessible country. Without them, we had to drive through Indian Territory, and basically we were no more mobile than Al Qaeda in their Toyotas.

On the plus side, we had Predator drone surveillance – and maybe Hellfire missiles – but I didn't know if Peters knew that, or if he knew we were taking his men and vehicles on the road to see if we could get into a fight with Al Qaeda.

Mr Peters thought he might be causing the newbies some anxiety, so he said to me and Kate, 'We've never gotten hit on the Sana'a–Aden road.'

Buck, too, assured us, 'The most dangerous thing about the trip is the Yemeni truck drivers.'

Kate asked Buck and Peters, 'Aren't the National Security police supposed to provide road security?'

Peters replied, 'Sometimes the police themselves are the problem.'

Right. In Yemen, even the good guys are bad. This place sucked. Did I already say that?

Bottom line here was three possible outcomes of this trip: a nice drive in the country, a successful encounter with the enemy, or headlines in tomorrow's newspapers. *American Convoy Wiped Out in Yemen; Thirteen Dead.*

Public reaction would be total bewilderment – Where's Yemen? Good question.

CHAPTER THIRTY-SIX

Buck got another sat-phone call, and he moved off to speak. Maybe it was his wife in Maryland questioning him about all the Russia Club bills on his Amex.

Anyway, Buck returned and we chatted awhile, though he didn't mention the phone call.

Brenner came over to us and said, 'We're ready to roll in five minutes.' Mr Brenner glanced at Mrs Corey, but asked me, 'You all squared away on the M4?'

'We are.'

Brenner summoned everyone to draw near and said, 'Listen up, please.'

As everyone gathered around, Brenner began, 'First, let me introduce you to Dr Nolan, who some of you may already know.'

The young doctor raised her hand and waved. She wasn't bad-looking if you like the looks of, say, Scarlett Johansson. But I digress. What was I saying? She looked competent. Right.

Brenner informed everyone, 'Dr Nolan is fully equipped to treat carsickness, and gunshot wounds smaller than nine millimeters.'

That got a good laugh. Even Howard laughed on his way back inside the embassy. Just kidding.

Dr Nolan said, 'I make house calls.'

Brenner then introduced 'our very important passengers, Mr John Corey of the FBI Evidence Response Team, and Ms. Kate Mayfield, our new legal affairs attaché.'

I held up my hand and said, 'I'm John. That's Kate.'

That got a few laughs. I mean, we were the reason for this risky trip to Aden, so I thought I should show everyone we were just nice, silly people.

Brenner also introduced Howard Fensterman, then said to everyone, 'Okay, the order of march.' He read from his paper, naming the five DSS drivers and their assigned vehicles, and informed everyone, 'I will be in the lead vehicle.'

Or as they say in the military, on point – theoretically the most dangerous position in a convoy, so if Mr Point Man thought Kate was riding with him, I'd have to correct that.

Brenner, however, moved on, saying, 'Mr Harris will be riding shotgun in Vehicle Two.'

Buck raised his hand and informed everyone, 'I am second in command if Mr Brenner is not able to perform his duties.'

Right. Like dead.

Moving right along, Brenner announced, 'Mr Corey will be riding in Vehicle Three.'

The middle vehicle was usually the safest one in a convoy, sometimes reserved for the commander. But Mr Brenner had assigned me the place of honor. Why? Because he liked me? No, because I was actually the goat that needed to be delivered as safely as possible to the trap.

Brenner then announced, 'Also in the middle vehicle will be Dr Nolan.'

Well, how about *that*? Actually, it was standard procedure to put the medical person in the middle, so that's how that happened. Nothing to do with my prayers. But where was Kate riding?

Brenner answered my question. 'Ms. Mayfield will be riding in Vehicle Four.'

I was really disappointed that Kate wasn't riding with me and Clare.

Brenner continued, 'Also in V-4 will be our other new legal affairs attaché, Mr Fensterman.'

Poor Kate. Just kidding. I really liked Howard. But if I had to spend five or six hours with him in a car, only one of us would walk out alive.

Howard, perhaps reading my and everyone's mind, said, 'Kate and I are available by sat-phone if anyone has any legal questions about returning fire.'

That got a big laugh of recognition from everyone who had to deal with this nuttiness. Even Howard laughed at himself, bringing him another step closer to reality.

Brenner went on, 'The trail vehicle is our enhanced security unit.' He named the two DSS agents, one of whom was Zamo, who'd be riding with the DSS driver. He added for the newbies, 'This vehicle has specialized armaments and security devices.' He quipped, 'This is our Bondmobile.' He also told us, 'The Bondmobile may change positions and may drop back or move out front to scout.'

This all sounded like standard convoy security procedure with maybe some variations based on past experience. Bottom line here, Paul Brenner was responsible for five expensive vehicles, lots of pricey commo and weapons, some sensitive paperwork, and thirteen American lives.

This was not the kind of job you trained for; it was the kind of job you were born or not born to do.

I wasn't sure if Paul Brenner was enjoying this, but it was obvious to me that he was at home here. Back in the States, he'd be looking for another job, and in London, Paris, or Rome he'd be just another cog in the big embassy wheel; here, he was one of the wheels. I had a feeling he was staying in Yemen, though he himself didn't know that.

Brenner said, 'Commo. The hand-held radios should work well when we stay in line of sight, but remember there are some mountain curves and dips in the road. If necessary, we can relay radio messages. Also, please keep the radio chatter to a minimum for security and tactical reasons. I will initiate most calls.' He continued, 'Each vehicle is equipped with a sat-phone antenna jack. If attempting a call, please don't forget to plug in your phone.'

This got a few laughs, and it was obvious that some lunkhead had forgotten to do that once. These guys had a history together, and Kate and I were just a new chapter. And hopefully not the final chapter. It was also obvious that the DSS agents liked the boss, and that told me a lot about Paul Brenner. Actually, I liked him, too. He had good taste in women.

He continued, 'As for other calls, specifically calls of nature, we may not be able to stop, so there are male and female bottles in each vehicle.' He advised, 'If you don't know which to use, call me.'

Good laughs, though they'd heard this one before.

He also informed everyone, 'We have brown-bag lunches in each vehicle, compliments of the cafeteria.' He added, 'Dr Nolan can treat food poisoning.'

There was really a lot of good material in Yemen. A joke a minute. I couldn't wait to get to Ecco's and try out some of this stuff. 'So, this camel walks into a bar in Sana'a, and the bartender says, "Hey, why the long face?".'

Brenner continued, 'Because these Land Cruisers are FAVs — fully armored vehicles — they are heavy, and we will have to make a refueling stop.'

He glanced at the paper in his hand, then said, 'The route. We are taking the main road to Yarim. There we will decide if we'll take the Ta'iz road, or the new road to Aden, depending on the security situation.'

He concluded, 'I'll be in sat-phone contact with the embassy and also with the Sheraton in Aden to see if they have any info for us en route.' He then announced, 'We have been promised Predator drone surveillance, but I can't promise that it will be extensive or effective.'

I noticed that Brenner didn't mention that those surveillance Predators might be armed with Hellfire missiles, or if they were, that the Hellfires would be used. Bottom line for any commander is don't promise more than you know you can deliver. The men know the risks, and they appreciate honesty. Bullshit is not part of the pre-mission briefing.

Brenner also informed everyone, 'The Yemeni authorities have not been advised of our movement, but as always, we'll encounter National Security Bureau police on the road as well as local police and military checkpoints. If we're asked to stop, Mr Harris will deal diplomatically with the situation.'

Buck said something in Arabic, then translated, 'Get out of my way, you stupid sons of diseased camels.'

Big laugh from the boys. It was obvious that no one here had a very high regard for the host country or its citizens. I could certainly see why this was so — but American arrogance led to over-confidence, and that led to mistakes.

Brenner also reminded everyone, 'Flak jackets will be worn even though you're wearing Kevlar vests. We will maintain the top speed possible, and I will set the speed. Vehicle intervals are determined by speed or terrain.'

He then got down to the tough stuff and said, 'As per our training, we will not deploy or return fire if fired on — we will trust our armor, and we will drive through the ambush, even if our so-called puncture-proof tires are flat. If a vehicle is disabled by an explosive device, we will encircle the disabled vehicle, take up defensive positions, and return fire if fired upon. If we are engaged by a moving vehicle while we are moving, you may at that time lower your windows and blow him the fuck off the road.'

That got a big cheer. Even Howard let out a whoop. I'm starting to worry about him.

I watched Mr Paul Brenner, combat veteran, and I could see, as I said, that he was very much in his element here, getting the troops psyched up, showing a mixture of professional confidence and personal aggressiveness. This was a competent leader, and a man everyone could trust – except maybe if you happened to have your wife with you. But, hey, no one is perfect. I just hoped he was focusing more on the mission than on his lonely dick.

I glanced at Kate while Brenner was speaking, and I could see she was somewhat taken with Mr Macho. She had that admiring look in her eye that she usually reserves for me and Bon Jovi.

Anyway, Brenner wrapped it up with, 'We have no reason to expect any problems on the road, but if we do have an encounter, we're more than equipped and ready to handle anything. I wish us all a safe journey and a nice ride in the country.'

Everyone applauded. Bravo. Encore. Well, maybe it was time to go.

Ed Peters, part-time preacher, called out, 'Godspeed, and safe home.'

And bring those Land Cruisers back in one piece.

Brenner shouted, 'Mount up! Let's roll!'

Everyone gathered their gear and made their way to their assigned vehicles, but I, of course, walked Kate to Vehicle Four. Howard was already sitting in the passenger seat with his M4, talking to the driver, and I loaded Kate's luggage in the rear compartment beside Howard's.

I closed the hatch and said to Kate, 'Sounds like a milk run.'

She didn't respond to that, but advised me, 'Behave yourself.'

I put on that confused look that I do so well and asked, 'What are you talking about?'

'You sit up front.'

'Of course. Shotgun.'

'Give me a kiss.'

We did a hug and kiss, and she said, 'See you at the refueling stop.'

Or sooner.

So I threw my bags in the rear of the middle vehicle, where Dr Nolan's CPR unit and oxygen were stowed. I got in the front seat and said hello to the driver, whose name was Mike Cassidy.

Dr Nolan was already in the rear seat with a big medical bag, wearing her flak jacket, and I turned to her and said, 'Hello, Doctor.'

'Call me Clare,' said Scarlett.

The big engines of the five Land Cruisers all fired up, we buckled up, and off we went.

Both gates of the sally port were open, and the convoy passed quickly out of the American Embassy compound and into Yemen.

CHAPTER THIRTY-SEVEN

Across the road was Tourist City, the scene of last night's Russian adventure. Thinking back, I was certain that Buck knew of Mr Brenner's interest in Mrs Corey, and I wondered what the wise old diplomat would advise his friend. I'm sure Buck would tell Brenner to cool it. Mission first.

'John?'

I turned in my seat. 'Yes, Clare?'

'Have you driven to Aden?'

'Actually, I have. About two and a half years ago.' I asked, 'How about you?'

'First time.' She told me, 'I just got here three weeks ago.' She asked me, 'How long will you and your wife be here?'

Who? Oh, my wife. I replied, 'Hopefully not long. How about you?'

'I signed on for a year.' She told me, 'The State Department is helping me repay my student loan.'

'Right. Me, too.'

She laughed.

I asked, 'How do you like Yemen?'

'Sucks.'

'Give it time.'

Mike Cassidy, our DSS driver, assured her, 'It doesn't get better.'

We continued south, past the British Embassy and the Mövenpick Hotel, then turned onto the Marib road, which was not well traveled, making it easier to see if anyone was following. Then we doubled back to intersect with the main road heading south again.

The Bondmobile reported on the radio, 'We're alone.'

There was some truck, bus, and SUV traffic going both ways, as well as motorcycles and scooters. The more traffic the better. Not that we were blending in – I mean, five big black Land Cruisers caravanning in the land of little white vehicles were attracting some attention, and it was obvious to even the densest Yemeni that this wasn't a tour group. Probably, I thought, everyone in Sana'a knew these SUVs, and it wouldn't be long before Abdul called his cousin Abdullah who was a fink for Al Qaeda. Cell phones. Everybody had one. Even here.

We passed through the ramshackle outskirts of Sana'a, and the traffic started to thin out.

Mike Cassidy announced to his passengers, 'I have three weeks to go here.'

I asked him, 'Where you heading?'

'Home. Daytona Beach, Florida. Then I got a great gig in Madrid.'

'You deserve it,' I assured him. I asked, 'Ex-military?'

'Yeah. Six years in the Army. One deployment in Afghanistan with the Tenth Mountain Division, one in Iraq with the First Cav.'

Clare said, 'Thank you for your service.'

'Still serving,' Mike said. 'But the pay is better.'

I thought about Mike Cassidy, John Zamoiski, a.k.a. Zamo, and the other DSS agents, and even Paul Brenner. We'd built this extensive and expensive intelligence and security apparatus, of which I was a part, to fight what amounted to a pissant war. But this war could turn very deadly in a heartbeat, as we saw on 9/11, and on other occasions such as the *Cole* bombing. And when you put nukes into the equation, or biological and chemical weapons, you were talking nightmare time. Day to day, however, no one in the States gave much of a rat's ass about any of this since 9/11, but 9/11 would come again, and this time we couldn't say we were surprised or unprepared. Meanwhile, we followed leads, guarded embassies, chased shadows, and now and then whacked a major asshole, which made the homeland just a little safer. That's why I was here.

Mike asked me, 'How long are you signed on for?'

'I have a forty-five-day visa with the ERT, subject to extensions.'

'You should think about those extensions.'

'Right. But my wife is here with the embassy for at least a year.'

'That can be tough.'

'Right.' Especially if I *did* get sent home after my visa expired, and Kate stayed on in the embassy with Paul Brenner. Definitely gotta get that Panther.

Mike asked me, 'We got any new leads on the Cole bombing?'

'I'll find out in Aden.'

Clare asked, 'Are you investigating the Cole bombing?'

'I am.'

'That was awful.'

'Right.' It was murder.

So the three of us got to know each other a little. Dr Clare Nolan was from someplace called Iowa and this was her first trip outside of America – except for the week she spent in Washington, DC, before coming here.

Mike said to me, 'The guys in Aden are very good. You'll enjoy working with them.'

I wasn't going to be working with them, but I said, 'Looking forward to it.'

He did a quick rundown of his fellow DSS agents in Aden, who numbered only six. Like last time, there was also an FBI SWAT Team in the Sheraton, numbering ten, and also, like last time, an FBI doctor. My FBI Evidence Response Team, Mike said, numbered five at the moment, but that varied. There was also a Marine FAST Team of twenty men out of Dubai, for hotel security. So, give or take, there were about forty Americans in the Sheraton — pretty much the same as last time I was here. Enough people to do the job, but maybe not enough to defend Fort Apache if the Indians attacked — which seemed to be a real possibility.

Also in the Sheraton, but not officially counted as warm bodies, were CIA officers and Military Intelligence officers. When I was there, I counted three of each, but they kept to themselves. They didn't even play beach volleyball with us.

Clare said, 'Someone told me the Sheraton was okay. Pool, gym, beach.'

'And a bar,' I assured her. I asked, 'Are you staying?'

'I am.'

Ah. 'I didn't know that.'

She informed me, 'If you need to go into the Badlands, I may go with you.'

'You sure you want to do that?'

'No. But if you need me, I'll go.'

I couldn't think of why we would need a doctor in Indian Territory. Well ... maybe if I thought really hard, I could imagine a situation where people were firing automatic weapons at us.

Clare also said, 'I wouldn't mind seeing some of the country.'

Mike suggested, 'You're seeing all you need to see now.'

Clare didn't respond.

I opened the manila envelope that Howard had given me and slid out the photos of Bulus ibn al-Darwish.

The first photo, in black and white, was of a young man in a cap and gown. The caption read: *Bulus ibn al-Darwish, Columbia University graduation, 1987.*

Young Bulus was not bad-looking in an exotic sort of way, with a hooked nose, dark eyes, and high cheekbones. His long hair was swept back, and I was surprised to see that his thin lips were smiling. He was happy to be graduating. He had the whole world in front of him.

The next two photos were color blow-ups of what were captioned *Driver's License photo, 1982,* and *Passport photo, 1990.* In the passport photo, he was still clean-shaven, but his demeanor had changed. He looked serious, or maybe he was thinking about returning to his ancestral home. By this time, he'd gotten his head full of radical thoughts, probably through the internet, and maybe from some local spiritual guides who had a different view of Islam than most Muslims had, and who preyed on young men such as Bulus ibn al-Darwish.

The last three photos were color snapshots, and one of them showed a big Victorian house in the background, and it was captioned *Perth Amboy, home, May 1991. Last known photo.*

Bulus, twenty-six years old in this picture, looked older, and without reading too much into the snapshot – but with the knowledge that he'd gone to Yemen a year or so after this photo – I had the impression of a young man who was about to sever his ties to home and family; a man who had seen his future and was anxious to make his mark in the world.

Who, I wondered, took the photo? Probably Mom. Taken in May, so maybe a birthday photo. And did Mom and Dad know that their boy was about to leave the nest and fly east? Probably.

I wondered, too, if Bulus had a girlfriend. Was he getting laid? Did he have only Muslim friends? Or did he also pal around with Christians and Jews? Did he watch American sitcoms on TV? Maybe he did all that in college and afterwards. But somewhere along the line, young Bulus started slipping away into an alternate universe. And now he was here, killing people – American sailors, Europeans, Saudi co-religionists, and his own countrymen.

What happened? Maybe I'd never know. Maybe he himself didn't know what happened, or how it happened. But at some point he'd come to a fork in the road, and he'd taken the wrong one. And I was on a collision course with this guy. If I had a moment with him, I'd ask him about all this. But more likely, there would be no moment of discovery; there would be a quick death. Mine or his.

Mike asked, 'Is that the subject asshole?'

'It is.'

Mike glanced at the birthday photo and said, 'Looks normal.'

Right. Some monsters look normal.

Clare leaned forward and asked, 'Who is that?'

'That,' I replied, 'is Bulus ibn al-Darwish. He is a mass murderer.'

She didn't reply for a few seconds, then asked, 'Are you here to find him?'

'I am.'

'Good luck.'

I took a last look at the subject, then put the photos in the envelope.

If he knew I was here, maybe he had a photo of me.

CHAPTER THIRTY-EIGHT

Brenner was maintaining a good speed, and we were passing slow-moving vehicles, which is always interesting on a two-lane road with large trucks coming at you.

After a particularly close encounter, Mike remarked, 'These armored SUVs don't respond well to the gas pedal.'

'You're doing great,' I assured him. I asked Clare, 'You carrying anything aside from that medical bag?'

'You mean ... like a gun?'

'Yeah. Like that.'

'No. Well ... yes.' She informed us, 'It's in my medical bag.'

'What is it?'

'A gun.'

'Right. Can I see it?'

She opened her medical bag and produced an unholstered 9mm Glock.

I unfastened my seat belt, leaned between the seats, and took the gun from her. I checked it out – full magazine, no round in the chamber. I gave her a one-minute lesson on how to chamber a round, how to change magazines, and reminded her that the Glock had no safety.

She said, 'Paul Brenner showed me all this.'

'Good. Did he also tell you how to aim and fire?'

'He said to hold it with both hands, arms outstretched, look down the barrel, and squeeze the trigger.'

'That's about it.' I reminded her, 'Aim for the center mass of the target. Heart is on the right.'

'Left.'

'His left, your right, Doctor.'

She nodded.

I turned and refastened my seat belt.

The traffic had gotten lighter, and we were picking up speed. Winter is the dry season here, and the high rolling plateau was brown. I saw fields of what looked like newly planted grain, and scattered fruit trees. But mostly I saw what I knew was the cash crop – khat shrubs with dark green leaves and pretty white flowers. The goats seemed to like the khat. Happy goats.

I mentioned the khat cultivation to my driving companions, and Dr Nolan gave us a medical analysis of *Catha edulis*, a.k.a. khat. She made no moral judgment, but her medical opinion was that you shouldn't operate machinery under the influence. Probably you shouldn't fire a submachine gun, either.

Our radios crackled to life now and then, mostly negative sitreps from our leader, and from our trail vehicle. Indeed, this looked like a milk run, but it could turn on a dime.

I noticed that when there was no oncoming traffic, Brenner moved the convoy into the left lane. He was either practicing for an assignment in the UK, or he was keeping away from possible roadside bombs whenever he could. Good thinking.

About fifty miles south of Sana'a, Mike pointed out an oil pipeline that he said came from Marib and went to the Red Sea port city of As-Salif. He informed us, 'The hill tribes to the east of here blow up the pipeline about once a month.'

'For fun?'

'Fun and profit. They make the government and the American oil company pay them protection money.'

'Protection money is supposed to stop them from blowing up the pipeline,' I pointed out.

'Yeah, but this is Yemen.'

Right. Case closed.

The radio said, 'Ma'bar, two K.'

Mike and the other drivers acknowledged, and we started to slow down. Mike said to us, 'Small town.'

I was remembering this road a little, and I recalled that there weren't many towns along the way, and Ma'bar, about sixty miles from Sana'a, was the first.

What I also remembered about my trip between Sana'a and Aden was that the road wasn't considered too dangerous two and a half years ago. I mean, it wasn't totally safe, but it wasn't ambush alley either. Things, however, had changed, and not for the better, as Buck mentioned in New York, and the embassy website said.

The convoy slowed down, and Mike said, 'Expect a checkpoint.'

We entered the small town of Ma'bar, which I sort of remembered, a collection of two-story mud brick buildings, goats, children, and chickens.

There was indeed an army checkpoint in the center of town, and we stopped. I saw Buck get out of the second vehicle and walk up to the soldiers. He shook hands with the honcho, said something that made the soldiers laugh, then got face-to-face with the boss, Arab style, and had a serious conversation with him.

And while he was at it, he slipped the guy some baksheesh, which made everyone happy.

Buck got back in the Land Cruiser. Piece of cake.

As we passed the checkpoint, the Yemeni soldiers looked into the dark-tinted windows, and though they couldn't see inside, Mike flipped them the bird anyway, saying, 'They should be paying *us*.'

Brenner's voice on the radio said, 'Dhamar, thirty K. Expect another stop.'

Within twenty minutes we were in the larger town of Dhamar. I recalled that an earthquake had pretty much leveled this place back in the eighties, and it was still half in ruins. This country can't catch a break.

Clare asked, 'What happened here?'

'It wasn't a battle,' I assured her. 'Every two years the residents smash up the town with sledgehammers. It's called the Festival of Al-Smash.'

Silence from the rear. But Mike laughed.

Clare said, 'This is going to be a long day.'

My wife says that. Every day.

Anyway, we were stopped again in the center of town, and Buck again got out, but this time Brenner accompanied him and they had a conversation with the soldiers.

Mike said to us, 'They're talking about road security.'

'And why do we trust these clowns to give us good information?'

'We don't, but if you talk to all of them, like Brenner is doing, you can get a feel for the situation. Like, if they're bullshitting.'

'Right.' The other thing to consider, of course, was what the surveillance drones had seen — or not seen — and what to make of those video images that were being transmitted to some ground control station somewhere. I mean, in a country where everyone carries an AK-47, how does an analyst determine who's up to no good? Right?

I looked out the rear, and I could see that Zamo and another DSS agent had lowered the windows of the Bondmobile and were covering our rear with their M4s.

Buck and Brenner were now heading toward their SUVs. The radio crackled, and Brenner's voice said, 'Continue on the main road to Yarim.'

And off we went, through the ruined town of Dhamar.

The road from Dhamar to Yarim was mostly uphill and I saw that the plateau was rising. There was a map in the glove compartment and I looked at it.

Mike said, 'When we get to Yarim, we can pick up the new road that goes to Aden, or we can stay on this road — the old caravan road — to Ta'iz, then to Aden.'

I wasn't sure I wanted to share the road with camels, so I asked, 'What's the difference?'

Mike replied, 'The new road is good, and more traveled, but there are more mountains, and better places for ambushes and IEDs.'

'Okay. And the camel road?'

He replied, 'Less traveled, so it's easier to avoid suicide trucks. Also, it's mostly low hills, except for about sixty miles of mountain.'

Clare asked, 'Which is the *safest* road?'

The answer, of course, was neither, but Mike said, 'Depends.'

Anyway, we got to the small decrepit town of Yarim, which

Mike informed us was a hot springs resort town with old Turkish bathhouses — sort of like Saratoga Springs, except this place sucked. I mean, I wouldn't wash my socks here.

Anyway, we stopped again at a military checkpoint, and Buck and Brenner got out to talk to the soldiers.

Mike said, 'Whichever road we take will be radioed in by the military to some headquarters, and that info can get to the wrong people.' He added, 'In either case, we're passing through territory where Al Qaeda has a presence.' He further informed us, 'That territory starts here in Yarim.'

I suggested, 'They should have a road sign: Al Qaeda, Next 100 Kilometers.' But seriously, this sucks.

I watched Brenner and Buck talking to the soldiers, and I imagined the conversation. 'So, guys, which road should we take to avoid ambushes and roadside bombs?'

And the soldiers laughed and replied, 'You should take the Long Island Expressway.'

Anyway, Buck and Brenner got back in their SUVs. The radios came alive and Brenner said, 'We will head toward the new highway, but then double back around this checkpoint and take the old road to Ta'iz.'

Everyone acknowledged and we moved past the checkpoint.

Buck came on the radio with some good news. 'Predator reports no suspicious activity on the Ta'iz road.'

That's because the bad guys didn't know yet what road we were taking.

In fact, Mike had the same thought and said, 'There are a thousand eyes and five hundred cell phones along either route. So it really doesn't matter what road we take.'

'Right.'

He further added, 'We just need to be fast and try to keep ahead of anything that Al Qaeda tries to put together for us.'

Clare said, 'This is scary.'

What was your first clue?

Anyway, we did the old, 'I'm going this way, fellas,' then the switcheroo and the double-back, and within ten minutes we were south of Yarim on the old caravan road to Ta'iz.

Mike said, 'I think this is a smart move.'

That depended on whether or not we actually wanted to make contact with Al Qaeda.

Clare asked, 'Is this really Al Qaeda territory?'

Mike replied, 'According to what's called the CIA Areas of Influence map.' He added, 'But you can't always go by the map.' He assured her, 'The CIA likes to overstate the danger. Keeps them in business.'

Overstating the danger is also called covering your ass, as in, 'Hey, we *said* the roads were dangerous. Sorry about what happened to that convoy.'

CHAPTER THIRTY-NINE

The old caravan road wasn't bad, and it was lightly traveled so we were making good time, about 120 K per hour, and within half an hour I could see the mountains on the horizon.

As we came over a hill, I saw the brake lights of the two lead vehicles, and on the road ahead I saw a convoy of five military trucks. I took the binoculars from the console and focused on them. There were about twenty men in each open truck, wearing the berets and blue camouflage fatigues of the National Security police.

The radio crackled, and Brenner said, 'We'll pass one at a time.'

The drivers acknowledged, and Brenner's lead vehicle pulled out into the oncoming lane and accelerated. But suddenly, the last police truck swerved in front of him, and the Land Cruiser had to brake hard, drop back, and get back into the right lane.

Mike said, 'Assholes.'

Clare asked, 'What's happening?'

Mike replied, 'Probably a shakedown.' He informed us, 'The military has some discipline, but the police are banditos in uni--form.'

The police convoy slowed, then one of the trucks moved into the oncoming lane, and all the trucks came to a stop. Roadblock.

The five Land Cruisers also came to a halt, but we kept thirty-foot intervals between us. This was a lonely stretch of road, and the only vehicles around were us and them.

Brenner said on the radio, 'Everyone stay in their vehicles, but be prepared to make a show of force.'

Brenner and Buck were out of their vehicles, and unarmed; they stood where we could see them and waited. Brenner was carrying his hand-held radio, and Buck was talking on his satellite phone, probably in contact with the embassy. Or maybe the Predator drone ground station. Good. Or at least it looked good.

Mike said, 'These clowns want Brenner to walk to them. Not going to happen.'

Clare asked, 'Should I be frightened?'

Mike replied, 'I think pissed off is better.'

This seemed to be a standoff, and it could go on for a while. I wasn't sure of the protocol here, but male egos I understood.

The tailgates of the trucks started dropping and the police began jumping out, carrying their AK-47s. Their blue cammies were covered with dust, and I saw that most of them had dust bandanas covering their mouths and noses, making them look, indeed, like banditos. They didn't make any moves toward the Land Cruisers; they just milled around, and some of them used the opportunity to take a leak.

I saw Brenner raise his radio, and he said, 'Everyone just sit tight.'

I saw that Buck was now conversing with a few of the National Security police guys, probably telling them to go get the boss, but it didn't seem to be working.

Patience is not one of my many virtues, and it was about time I made Buck and Brenner understand I wasn't just along for the ride, so I opened my door and got out with my M4 slung over my shoulder.

Mike said, 'Brenner is going to be pissed.'

Clare said, 'Be careful.'

I walked past the two Land Cruisers in front of us, and Brenner saw me and said, 'Get back in your vehicle.'

I didn't respond. I took Buck's arm and said, 'Let's go find the boss.'

Buck resisted for a moment, then came along with me, and we

walked up the road through the mob of police. Brenner stayed behind so he could be in sight of us and keep point-to-point radio contact with the convoy.

I said to Buck, 'Find out what these idiots want, and let's get moving.'

Buck replied, 'All they want is to show us who's the boss here, and a few hundred dollars.'

'They're not going to get either.'

Before we got to the lead vehicle, a tall guy with important-looking insignia on his uniform walked up to us and said something in Arabic.

Buck replied in Arabic, and the guy didn't seem surprised that Buck spoke the language — I guess he'd been briefed by radio — and he and Buck started jabbering.

I interrupted, 'What is this clown saying?'

Buck said to me, 'This is Captain Dammaj of the National Security Bureau, and he wants to know who we are and where we're going.'

'He knows damn well who we are and where we're going. Tell him to go fuck himself.'

Buck said something to the guy, but probably not what I suggested.

The guy replied, and Buck said to me, 'He says this road is closed for security reasons, and we must go back to Yarim and take the new road.'

'Yeah, well, here's your chance to say, "Get out my way, you stupid son of a diseased camel".'

Buck said something to the guy, but I didn't hear the Arabic word 'gamal,' which I knew.

Buck listened to the guy, then said to me, 'He says he will provide security for us through these mountains to Ta'iz.' Buck added, 'Five hundred dollars.'

'Tell him we'll provide security for him. Six hundred dollars.'

'John—'

The guy said something, and Buck said to me, 'He senses you are angry, and he believes you are insulting him.'

'Me?' I smiled at Captain Dammaj and said in a pleasant tone, 'I'll give you two minutes to get the hell out of our way.'

Buck, ever the diplomat, also smiled and said something to Captain Dammaj.

They chatted, maybe negotiating the deal.

Anyway, I'd really gotten myself worked up, maybe for no reason, and maybe I was being overly aggressive and making an annoying situation into a bad situation. But thinking back to what Buck had said in New York, the Yemenis didn't like pussies. No girly men here. So I was just following Buck's advice, though Buck didn't seem happy with me.

Anyway, I could hear someone on my hand-held and I put it to my ear, and Buck did the same.

It was Brenner, who said, 'What is going on there? John, I want you back here.'

Buck replied, 'The officer in charge says this road is closed for security reasons. We're trying to work out a deal. Over.'

Brenner said to me, 'John, let Buck handle this.'

I replied, 'Negative. Out.'

I could see that Kate had gotten out of her SUV and she was in a serious discussion with her friend Paul about something, maybe saying, 'I told you John wasn't a team player.' Or maybe she thought I was just trying to show her I was much cooler than Paul Brenner. That was totally not true. Well . . . maybe a little true.

Buck and Captain Dickhead exchanged a few more words, then Buck said to me, 'He'll take four hundred dollars—'

'Highway robbery. I know they get two bucks a man.'

Buck was looking a bit unsettled now, and he said to me sharply, 'John, please calm down.' He told me, 'The money is in the budget. It's not your money, and you're making this more difficult than it needs to be.'

'It's not about the money, Buck. It's about balls.' I reminded him, 'You told me to be aggressive with these people.'

'No. I told you that if you look fearful, it invites aggression on their part.'

'Oh . . . did I get that wrong? Sorry about that.' I let Buck know, 'We're playing good cop, bad cop. I'm the bad cop. So you talk nice to this asshole and tell him I'm the boss and I'm being a prick, but I'll agree to a hundred bucks.'

Buck seemed a bit frustrated with me, but he forced a smile and said something to Captain What's-his-name.

As he spoke, I prompted him by saying, 'Tell this clown the Yemeni government should be kissing our asses for being here.'

Buck interrupted his conversation with the captain and said to me, 'John, shut up.'

'Okay.' I don't think I'd make a good diplomat.

Finally, Buck turned to me and said, 'Two hundred. That's as low as he'll go.' He reminded me, 'In Yemen, it's all about the deal. This man needs to save face now. And we're not exactly bargaining from strength, and we don't want to go back to Yarim, so I'm giving him two hundred dollars and we'll be on our way.'

'Until the next shakedown.'

Buck said something to Captain Dammaj, who replied, and Buck said to me, 'He'll give us ... let's call it a laissez-passer, in diplomatic language. A written pass to Aden.'

Sounded like bullshit to me, but Buck was getting stressed, and the police were finished urinating in public, and they were getting restless, plus Brenner was totally pissed off, and Kate looked worried. Or pissed at me. Also, she was unveiled, and these clowns were giving her the eye. So ... I said to Buck, 'All right.'

Buck said something to Captain Dammaj, who nodded and smiled at me.

I asked Buck, 'Do I hug him?'

'Just shake hands.'

So I extended my hand to Captain Dammaj, we shook, and I smiled and said to him, 'You're a thief.'

He smiled in return and said something that Buck translated as, 'You are a brave man and a hard negotiator.'

I don't know if Dammaj really said that – maybe he said, 'You're a total asshole and you eat goat shit' – but Buck was intent on smoothing things over.

Buck got on his radio and said, 'We'll be on our way in a few minutes.'

Captain Dammaj walked to one of the trucks, I guess to write a pass or something.

Buck said to me, 'I could have handled this without your help.'

'I made it fun.'

Captain Dammaj returned with a piece of paper, and he and Buck exchanged the pass and the money. As Buck was reading the pass, I asked him, 'Did he sign it Ali Baba and the Forty Thieves?'

Captain Dammaj smiled and said to me, in English, 'You are not so funny.'

Whoops.

Buck almost dropped his laissez-passer.

Captain Dammaj said to both of us, 'Be very careful on the road. And have a pleasant stay at the Sheraton.'

'And you have a nice day,' I said.

Before he turned to walk off, he said to me, 'Go fuck yourself.'

Buck looked at me, but he seemed at a loss for words.

On the walk back to the Land Cruisers, I asked Buck, 'Do you think there really is a security problem ahead?'

Buck replied, 'We'll find out soon enough.'

We got to the lead Land Cruiser where Brenner and Kate were standing. Brenner, showing a lot of restraint, said to me, 'I appreciate your initiative, but it's Buck's job to handle these situations.'

I didn't respond to that and kept walking.

Kate caught up to me and asked, 'What is wrong with you?'

Sounded like a rhetorical question, so I didn't answer, but I said, 'You were told to stay in the vehicle. Follow orders.'

'Me? How about you?'

'I don't take orders from Paul Brenner.'

She didn't reply to that, but said, 'I'll see you later,' and kept walking.

I got in my Land Cruiser, and Mike asked, 'How much?'

'Two hundred.'

'That's about right.'

Clare asked, 'Is everything okay?'

'We're good to go.'

The police truck that was blocking the left lane moved over,

343

and Brenner's lead vehicle pulled out and led the way for the Land Cruisers to pass the stopped trucks.

I looked in my sideview mirror and saw that the police trucks were doing a U-turn. We were on our own.

Within a few minutes we were clipping along and the police convoy was out of sight.

About twenty minutes later, we were on a steep upgrade, and the road narrowed and turned through a mountain pass.

Brenner got on the radio and said, 'Niner-niner' — meaning all personnel — 'it gets interesting here. Spread out, but keep the vehicle in front of you in sight.' He added, 'Stay alert.'

Goes without saying, Paul. But I wasn't worried. We had a pass from Captain Dammaj.

There was no oncoming traffic on the mountain road, and Mike informed me, 'That's not a good sign.'

'Right.'

Mike asked me, 'Did the police say anything about the security situation?'

'I think the chief did say something about the road being closed for security reasons.'

'Yeah? And?'

'Just a sales pitch. He wanted five hundred bucks to escort us.'

Mike didn't say anything for a while, then suggested, 'He may have been telling the truth.'

'We'll see.'

'Yeah ... anyway, you can't trust the police to provide protection — even if you pay for it.'

'Right.' I thought about those Belgian tourists at Marib. They didn't get much for their money.

Clare said, 'Maybe we should turn around.'

Mike replied, 'That's for the boss to decide, and he's already decided.'

Right. Paul Brenner wasn't turning around. In fact, we'd gotten ourselves into a dicey situation. But I think that was the goal.

Mike said, 'Well, we got the road all to ourselves.'

'I hope so.'

The road skirted a town high up on a hill, and Mike said, 'That's Ibb. Last town we'll see in these hills.' He added, 'Almost no government presence here.'

'Good. We're almost out of shakedown money, so that works.'

He continued, 'The tribes rule here, but they won't take on this convoy.' He reminded me, however, 'Al Qaeda is the new boy on the block here.'

Right. And they don't want your money. They want your head.

CHAPTER FORTY

The mountains were parched, and there were herds of goats nibbling at the brown vegetation. I could see mud huts on the slopes and in the alpine meadows. People lived here, but I hadn't seen anyone for a while. Khat time?

White clouds had developed around the peaks, but the Predator infrared cameras should be able to see through them.

The narrow road was paved, but clouds of dust partly obscured the two Land Cruisers ahead of us. We were driving mostly on the left to lessen the damage from a roadside bomb planted on the right. But a bomb could also be planted on the left.

We were maintaining a speed of about a hundred KPH – about sixty miles an hour – which was pushing the limit here.

The radios were quiet, and so were my companions.

Finally, Mike said, 'In about thirty minutes we'll be coming down onto the plateau.'

I could tell by Mike's tone of voice that he seemed to have a mountain phobia, and probably with good reason.

Every now and then I scanned the terrain with the binoculars, but I didn't see anything suspicious. Not that I'd know what suspicious looked like around here. But I'm sure if I saw it, I'd know it.

I asked Clare, 'How you doing?'

No reply.

I turned and saw she was sleeping. I guess that's the best way to get through a terrifying ride through enemy territory. I said to Mike, 'You should try to catch some sleep, too.'

I thought that was funny, but he didn't laugh. I hoped he wasn't flashing back to Afghanistan.

The radio crackled, and Brenner's voice, cool and calm, said, 'Predator reports ambush ahead.'

That got my attention.

Mike said, 'Shit!'

Clare, awake now, asked, 'What did he say?'

I said to her, 'Get down below the windows. Now. Quick.'

She unfastened her seat belt and got flat on the seat.

Brenner said, 'Maintain max speed.'

I focused my binoculars on the road ahead, and about three hundred yards in front of Brenner's lead vehicle I saw three things: a mud hut close to the right side of the road, then fifty yards farther a white Toyota SUV on the narrow shoulder with its hood up, and finally at a bend in the road a donkey cart and driver coming toward us.

Mike said, 'There's the ambush – maybe IEDs . . .' He said to me, 'Get below the windows.'

I kept looking through the binoculars.

Brenner's lead vehicle was literally seconds from the mud hut, and I saw his brake lights come on, and he swerved to the far left on a collision course with the donkey cart. Then all of a sudden I saw a streak of smoke coming out of the sky, and a second later the mud hut exploded, then erupted again in a secondary explosion whose shockwave rocked the SUV.

Clare screamed.

Holy shit.

Two more streaks of smoke came out of the sky, and in quick succession the Toyota and the donkey cart erupted in deafening explosions.

Debris was falling out of the sky, the brown grass was burning, and black smoke billowed from what remained of the Toyota.

Brenner's vehicle hit a chunk of donkey as it shot through the devastated area, followed by Buck's vehicle, then ours. Something hit the windshield and left a thick red smear on the glass.

Mamma mia.

I looked in the sideview mirror and saw Kate's vehicle coming through the smoke and the debris field, followed by the Bond-mobile.

Then something else hit our SUV, and it took me a second to realize we were taking rounds.

Mike hit the gas and we two-wheeled it around the S-curve as we got hit again. A loud noise filled the SUV and I turned to see a big dimple in the back windshield where it had taken a bullet. I could also see green tracer rounds coming from the hills around us, streaking toward the speeding convoy.

I really wanted to lower my window and return fire, but Brenner had said not to do that, and maybe it wasn't a good idea with bullets coming at us. But when I looked again through the back windshield, I saw that someone in the Bondmobile, wearing a flak jacket and Kevlar helmet – maybe Zamo – was leaning out of the rear driver's side window gangster-style, firing back at the streaks of tracer rounds. The other DSS guy riding shotgun was doing the same, and the Bondmobile was drawing most of the fire now.

The Land Cruiser took another hit, and Clare shouted, 'Stop!'

Mike yelled, 'Look!'

I turned, and on the road coming toward us was another Toyota SUV traveling at top speed, quickly closing the distance between him and Brenner's lead vehicle. Bad guy? I'd never know, because a white smoke trail angled down out of the blue and the Toyota erupted in a ball of flames, followed by a loud explosion.

Brenner's and Buck's SUVs swerved and shot past the burning wreckage, and by the time we reached it, pieces of burning junk started falling on us, and something bounced off the hood. Mike was temporarily blinded by the black, billowing smoke, and we were going off the pavement, but he jerked the wheel back in time to avoid an off-road trip into a ravine.

I unfastened my seat belt and looked out the back windshield. Kate's SUV was right behind us, and the Bondmobile was coming up fast. We seemed to be out of the killing zone and I didn't see any red tracers following us. I took a deep breath and looked down at Clare, who was now on the floor, her face and chest covered by the big medical bag. I said to her, 'It's okay. It's over.'

She didn't respond and I reached down and lifted the medical bag. She stared up at me, but said nothing. I asked, 'You okay?'

She nodded.

I turned back toward the front and Mike said, 'Three fucking weeks.'

'Right.' In fact, time is relative. The ambush seemed to last forever, but it was probably less than two minutes since the first Hellfire hit.

Mike had the windshield washers on now, and the wiper blades were smearing a red goo across the glass.

The hand-helds crackled and Brenner's voice, still calm and cool, came over the radios. 'Sit-rep. Vehicle One okay.'

Buck said, 'Two is ... fine.' He sounded surprised.

Mike had a death grip on the steering wheel, so I transmitted, 'Three okay.'

I waited for V-4 to transmit, and I was getting concerned, but then Kate's voice, almost upbeat, said, 'Four okay.'

The Bondmobile reported, 'Trail okay ... but Z has a graze wound.'

I said to Clare, 'One customer for you.'

The mountains were receding off to the left and right now, and the terrain started to flatten on both sides of the road. Brenner increased the speed and we were flying down the middle of the crumbling blacktop. The color had returned to Mike's face, but his knuckles were still white.

Brenner transmitted, 'Predators see nothing ahead.'

Everyone acknowledged the good news.

Mike found his voice and said, 'Predators usually operate in pairs ... two Hellfires each ... so we're out of missiles.'

'Right. But the bad guys don't know that.'

'Yeah ... and they don't want to find out.'

I hope.

Clare was sitting low in the rear seat, and she had her radio in her hand. She transmitted, 'V-5, M.D. here. How's Z?'

Z himself replied, 'Don't need you.'

Then the other DSS agent transmitted, 'Bullet passed through his brain. No damage.'

Everyone was on an adrenaline high now, happy to be alive and very happy to joke about death.

Someone else transmitted, 'I feel bad about the donkey.'

Another guy said, 'Legat, legat. Permission to return fire.'

Howard replied, 'I'm checking.'

Brenner said, 'Can the chatter.'

So we continued on in radio silence.

Clare confessed, 'I've never been so frightened in my life.'

Mike replied, 'Welcome to the club.'

I focused my binoculars on Buck's SUV, then Brenner's. I could see some raw metal where they'd taken hits. Also, Brenner's back windshield had been hit. I wondered what the new ambassador would say when he was picked up at Sana'a Airport with these vehicles.

The road was straightening out, and we were definitely on the downslope. I began seeing more mud and stone huts, livestock, and people, plus a few motor scooters raising dust on the mountain trails.

We increased our speed, and as we crested a hill I could see flatlands in the distance.

Mike's knuckles were pink again.

Mike had his sat-phone plugged into the antenna jack, and I speed-dialed the DSS driver in Vehicle Four. The driver answered, 'Steve.'

'Is Ms. Mayfield awake?'

'Yeah ... hold on.'

Kate's voice came on the line. 'Who is this?'

'Just called to see how you're doing.'

'I'm doing fine. How about you?'

'Good.' I asked, 'How's Howard?'

'Fine ... a little concerned that there may have been ICs back there.'

'Only the donkey was an IC.' I added, 'And by the way, I *told* you this place was dangerous.' *Finally*, I got to say it.

Kate replied, 'You may be right for a change.'

'See you later.'

I hung up and Mike said to me, 'As we used to say in Iraq and Afghanistan, we can't tell the ICs from the jihadists, so kill them all and let Saint Peter sort them out.'

'They're Muslims,' I pointed out.

'Right. So the innocent Muslims get the seventy-two virgins, and the jihadists get to jerk off for eternity.'

Interesting theology. More importantly, Mike Cassidy, who seemed like a regular guy from Daytona Beach, had apparently become a little callous, maybe numbed by years of this stuff. Well ... maybe it was happening to all of us, by small degrees, and we didn't see it.

We were onto the plateau now, and there were farms, people, and vehicles around. I'd say we were back in civilization, but that would be stretching the definition of civilization.

The radio crackled and Brenner said, 'Fuel status.'

Mike looked at the computer display: 96 kilometers left to empty.

Everyone reported about the same, and Brenner said, 'Refuel in Ta'iz. Details to follow.'

Mike let us know, 'Ta'iz is a big town – maybe three hundred thousand people, and a dozen gas stations. But sometimes they're out of gas.'

I thought they produced oil here. The only thing this place was never out of was ammunition.

The radios crackled and Brenner said, 'We're not out of the woods yet, so stay alert.' He added, 'Everyone did a good job back there.'

Thanks, Paul. The drivers actually did a great job, and so did Zamo and the other DSS guy who literally stuck their necks out to return fire. The rest of us didn't do much except keep our sphincters tight and our bladders full.

The best job was done by the Predator ground pilots, and if I ever met them, I'd give them a big hug. But I'd never meet them. I didn't even know what continent they were on.

I said to Mike, 'Good driving.'

'Thanks.'

Clare seconded that and added, 'I thought we were dead.'

Mike admitted, 'It was a little close.'

Clare offered brown-bag lunches, but all anyone wanted was water.

We continued toward Ta'iz, then Aden, then maybe Marib. The Panther, apparently, had found us. And now we had to find *him*. And kill him, before he killed us. This was simple. I like simple.

CHAPTER FORTY-ONE

We didn't want to go into Ta'iz with shot-up vehicles, and Mike also explained that Ta'iz was a hotbed of Al Qaeda and anti-government activity, and that the Commies were still strong there.

Sounded like the San Francisco of Yemen.

The good news was that the Predators had spotted an open gas station outside of town. The Predators are better than GPS — they shoot missiles.

Anyway, we followed Brenner's vehicle and up ahead we saw the gas station.

Brenner got on the radio and said, 'Vehicles One and Five, fill up. Everyone else take up positions.'

Mike parked on the side of the road with the engine running, as did Buck's and Kate's SUVs, while the lead and trail vehicles pulled up to the two pumps.

Brenner, carrying his M4, got out of the SUV and went to the trail vehicle to check on Zamo.

Buck, also armed, got out, and Clare said, 'I need to make a house call,' and exited with her medical bag.

I got out, too, carrying my M4, and checked out my surroundings as I walked. The gas pumps were modern, but the parking area was dirt, and the building was a small concrete-block hut, from which emerged six Yemenis in ratty white robes, all carrying their Yemeni walking sticks, a.k.a. AK-47s. I haven't seen this much firepower at a gas station since my road trip through Alabama.

Two of the Yemenis were the gas attendants — no self-service here — and the other four were nosy. They checked out the shot-up Land Cruisers, and Buck was conversing with them. I had no idea what he was saying, but he should tell them we were just shooting at each other for laughs. They'd totally believe it.

Clare had gotten into Zamo's SUV, and Brenner had his head stuck in the window. He made room for me and I poked my head in. Zamo was sitting in the rear seat, and Clare was unwrapping a bloody first-aid pressure bandage from his left forearm.

I asked him, 'How you doing?'

'I'd be doing better if people stopped asking me.'

Clare got the bandage off and said, 'This is not bad.'

'I know that,' said Zamo.

'I'll clean and dress it, and maybe suture it when we get to the hotel.' She handed Zamo a vial of antibiotics and asked him, 'You want a painkiller?'

'No.'

354

Brenner asked the doctor, 'Is he okay for duty?'

Zamo himself answered, 'Good to go.'

Everything seemed under control here, so I walked into the station hut looking for the restroom, and thinking maybe I could buy a few Slim Jims and a Dr Pepper. But there was nothing in the hut except some white plastic chairs and a prayer rug. Which way is Mecca?

Buck joined me and said, 'The restrooms are out back.'

We went through an open doorway where there was a slit trench, and we held our noses and dicks and did our business, joined by a few of the DSS guys, in shifts, then Brenner, then Kate, who asked, 'Who left the toilet seat up?'

We stood watch with our backs to Kate as she used the unisex trench. This was a great bonding experience, and I was sure there'd be more of them in the Badlands.

Anyway, the A-team was all assembled, so we used the opportunity for a quick meeting before we got back on the road.

Buck informed us, 'I've reported the incident to the embassy by sat-phone, and they have relayed my report to Washington.' He added, 'The State Department will notify the Yemeni government. But we are not admitting to any unauthorized use of Hellfire missiles.'

I pointed out, 'I don't think rifle fire can cause that kind of damage, Buck.'

It was Mr Brenner who replied. 'Small-arms fire can detonate roadside bombs and fuel tanks.' He added, 'The Yemenis don't have the sophisticated forensics to determine otherwise.'

Right. Whatever.

Kate then said, 'Howard may want to report this as it happened.'

Buck said to Kate, 'Tell him I'd like a word with him.'

Kate nodded and left.

Buck explained to me and Brenner, 'It's important that there are no conflicting accounts of what happened.'

'Right,' I agreed. 'Especially true accounts.'

Buck further explained, 'We were the victims of an apparent Al Qaeda attack. We don't want to be seen as aggressors or provocateurs.' Buck also informed us, 'There are certain groups in the States who are not in favor of our Hellfire assassination program.' He added, 'This incident, if it became public, could be misinterpreted as offensive rather than defensive.'

Right. We don't want to upset human rights groups in the States with our HAPPY program – Hellfire Assassination Program to Pacify Yemen. I made that up.

Buck also said, 'It is important that we four are not declared persona non grata and asked to leave Yemen.'

I agreed, but pointed out, 'If it wasn't for the Hellfires, we'd all be declared persona non breathing.'

Buck ignored that and continued, 'This attack, along with the Hunt Oil attack, will cause Washington to re-evaluate our military mission in Yemen.' He added, 'Just as the Cole did.'

Right. So, bottom line here, you sometimes need an attack to get things going your way. The Alamo, the *Maine*, Pearl Harbor, the Gulf of Tonkin, the USS *Cole*, and so forth. Sometimes the attack is an unprovoked surprise, and sometimes it isn't.

Howard appeared from the hut, spotted the trench, and used it. He then said to me, 'I don't know how I can ever repay you for inviting me along.'

'I'll think of something.'

Buck had already thought of something and said to Howard, 'This is a national security matter, Howard, and a sensitive diplomatic matter at the highest level.' He added, 'Please do not say anything to anyone that would jeopardize this mission.'

Or we'll kill you.

Howard, practicing not saying anything to anyone, just nodded, then left.

We all assembled in front of the station. The Land Cruisers were topped off, the windshields were cleaned of mortal remains, and we got in our vehicles. Gentlemen, start your engines. And off we went, southeast toward Aden.

Brenner transmitted, 'Predators still on station until we reach our destination.' He added, 'Two new Predators with Hellfires on the way.'

Great. So, what did we learn from our drive in the country? Well, we learned that Al Qaeda knew of our trip to Aden — but that was almost a given. We learned, too, that Al Qaeda was willing and able to attack an armored American convoy. They were getting their act together. What Al Qaeda didn't know, however, or didn't expect, was Hellfire missiles — and that was because the Yemeni government idiots usually said no to Hellfires. But we solved that problem by not asking. This was a new game.

What *we* didn't know was if Al Qaeda knew that Mr John Corey was in the convoy. But we could assume they did. In fact, Al Qaeda knew that John Corey and Kate Mayfield would be in Yemen before we knew we were going. What we didn't know was if The Panther was now in Paradise, or in Marib, or someplace else. Wherever he was, he was pissed.

Good. I was pissed, too.

CHAPTER FORTY-TWO

The convoy continued on toward Aden.

Mike informed Clare and me, 'The farther south we go, the less Al Qaeda is present.'

'Good.'

'But Al Qaeda is strong again around Aden.'

'Bad.'

'Also, when we cross into what used to be South Yemen, you have secessionist rebels.'

Clare asked Mike, 'Is there any part of this country that's ... like, safe?'

'Not one square inch.'

You're safe with me, sweetheart.

She said, 'At least we can feel safe in the hotel.'

Uh ... about that hotel, Clare ...

We were on the downslope from the central highlands and making good time toward the coastal plains despite the traffic on the well-traveled Ta'iz–Aden road.

Mike said, 'About a hundred K to Aden.'

Brenner's voice came over the radio. 'New Predators with Hellfires on station. No suspicious roadside activity ahead. But stay alert for suicide vehicles.'

The fun never stops.

Mike informed us, 'The Predators can keep flying for up to twenty-four hours without refueling.'

Correct. And the pilot was on the ground, and he could hand off the controls every few hours. The Predator drone with Hellfire missiles was an awesome weapon system. This was probably how we'd bag The Panther, if we hadn't already vaporized him back in the hills. American military technology is a beautiful thing — unless you're on the receiving end.

I asked Mike, 'Where are the Predators stationed? And where are the ground control units?'

He replied, 'No one knows. But I'd guess Oman, or Saudi Arabia. Or maybe Djibouti across the strait.'

'So not here?'

'Not in this screwed-up country.'

'Right.'

It was almost 1 P.M., and we'd made okay time considering we took the old caravan route, though I hadn't seen a single camel. The ambush hadn't actually delayed us — in fact, it sort of moved things along. Nothing like getting shot at to get your ass moving.

We intersected the new highway that came from Sana'a and headed due south toward Aden. It was a good road, and if we'd taken it, I wonder if we'd have had the same exciting experience we had on the caravan route. I was fairly sure that it was the Predator controller who advised us to take that route. In the end, the CIA — who had operational control of the Predators — got what they wanted: a show of American force, dead bad guys, and an incident.

359

I asked Mike, 'Will you guys be able to get back to Sana'a before dark?'

'Maybe . . . We'll see what Brenner wants us to do.'

I used that opening to fish. 'He seems like a good guy.'

Mike replied, 'He's good.' Silence. 'But he pushes his luck sometimes.'

Which meant pushing everyone else's luck. Maybe he had nothing to live for. But maybe he'd just found a new interest in life. I said to Mike, 'He told me he had a lady in the States.'

'Yeah. She was here once.' He let me know, 'A real knockout.'

'So no embassy romance?'

Mike realized he was saying too much about his boss and replied, 'Not that I know of.' He added, 'Slim pickings here.'

Clare piped in, 'I beg your pardon.'

That got a laugh.

Clare also offered, 'I think he's cute.' She added, 'But a little old for me.'

What? He couldn't be five years older than me. I'm crushed. I wish I had died in the Al Qaeda ambush.

We were on the coastal plain now, and up ahead I spotted a road sign, one of the few I'd seen in the last four hundred kilometers, and I focused the binoculars on it. It said something in Arabic, but beneath that it said ADAN – with an A – GOVERNATE.

Mike said, 'We are crossing into the former South Yemen, also once known as Adan.' He added, 'It's almost like another country in some ways.'

Actually, it was once. But I said, 'Looks like the same crap hole to me.'

'Different attitudes here. A little more modern, maybe because of the British influence, then the Soviets, and all the ships coming into Aden Harbor from around the world.'

'Right. Like the Cole.'

Mike replied, 'Al Qaeda is new in Aden.' He added, 'South Yemen is regressing.'

Actually, the whole Middle East was regressing.

A half hour later, we were in the outskirts of Aden. I looked to the southeast, where I knew the Sheraton was located, and I didn't see any smoke rising into the air, so that was a good sign.

The Sheraton Hotel is located away from the city, on a peninsula that juts into the Gulf of Aden. The landscape was formed by a hopefully extinct volcano, and there are high hills and bluffs overlooking the beaches, which is very scenic, but not good for security.

There was a construction project up ahead, and a big sign in English said: BIN LADEN CONSTRUCTION COMPANY, which reminded me of what Colonel Kent said in Sana'a. I'm sure most of the Yemeni-based bin Laden family were good citizens, but it was sort of jarring to see that — like if I saw in Germany ADOLF HITLER VOLKSWAGEN DEALER. Right? They might want to change that company name.

We passed the airport and began an uphill climb into the high ground above the beaches.

I could now see the Sheraton below, a white six-story contemporary-style building, sitting peacefully in the sunlight. Behind the hotel was a stretch of white sand and palm trees, and the calm blue waters of the Gulf of Aden. Paradise. Not.

Clare said, 'Looks nice.'

Looks like a target.

Mike asked me, 'Bring back memories?'

'Lots.'

We came down a narrow road on the downside of the high bluffs, and right in front of us was the Sheraton Hotel. Brenner radioed, 'Niner, niner. We have arrived. Good job, everyone.'

Mike and the other drivers blasted their horns as we pulled into the hotel driveway.

I have returned.

— PART VI —

Marib, Yemen

CHAPTER FORTY-THREE

Bulus ibn al-Darwish, al-Numair, The Panther, wearing the white robes and shiwal of a Bedouin, sat on the dirt floor of a goat herder's hut situated in a narrow gorge in the highlands south and west of Marib town. The sun was low over the mountains and the hut was in shadow, though a shaft of sunlight came through the doorway.

Sitting around the walls of the stone hut were ten men – his inner council of advisors, and also his most senior aide, Altair, an older man, from the province of Ta'iz where the al-Darwish family originated. In fact, Altair was a distant kinsman, and the old man had known the father of Bulus's father, and had also known Bulus's own father as a young man, before he emigrated to America.

Nearby was the camp of The Panther's jihadists, but he could not go there for this meeting because of the American Predator drones. The drones may have seen the camp – though from the air it appeared to be a Bedouin village of tents and also stone and mud huts. And in fact it once was a Bedouin village, but not any longer, thanks to Sheik Musa, who had given – for a price – this village to the jihadists of Al Qaeda. The Panther did not know if the Americans had become suspicious of the camp, but in any case he had called for a gathering here, in the narrow gorge, which was also not far from The Panther's maghara, his cave, where he lived alone – except for a woman – and which was known to only a few of his most trusted aides, including Altair.

The Panther addressed his council of advisors, saying, 'God is testing us.'

The men nodded.

The Panther had just recently received the news that the ambush on the American convoy had failed – because of the Predator drones firing Hellfire missiles – and many jihadists had been killed and wounded.

He said to his council, 'The Americans are operating freely on the sacred soil of Yemen. And they are doing this with the blessing of the government in Sana'a – the corrupt lackeys of the Americans who sell their souls for the American dollar.'

Some of the men made sounds of agreement. But not all.

The Panther continued, 'We will avenge these deaths.'

Again, there were only a few signs of agreement among his ten advisors.

Bulus ibn al-Darwish knew that some of these men had been against the attack on the Hunt Oil installation. And for that reason, he had not consulted with them about mounting an ambush on the American Embassy convoy. This was the first they were hearing of it, and they were not pleased.

He had suffered two defeats at the hands of the Americans within days, and he needed someone to blame for these defeats. He also needed a victory.

He reminded his advisors, 'Forty of our jihadists are as of this moment on their way to Aden. They will attack the Sheraton Hotel and kill all the Americans there – the spies and the soldiers who are using the hotel as a base on the holy soil of Yemen – and also the Americans from the embassy who have arrived from Sana'a. All of them will die within the next few days.'

A few in his council of advisors nodded, but The Panther was aware that some of them were beginning to doubt him – to doubt that he was blessed by God.

He continued, 'And forty jihadists have journeyed to Sana'a and will mount an attack on the American Embassy compound.'

A senior advisor, Jawad, reminded his chief, 'This council must approve of the embassy attack and it must also be approved by the Supreme Council.'

The Panther did not reply.

Jawad also reminded his chief, 'If the embassy attack is successful, and if our jihadists enter the embassy compound and kill all the Americans – perhaps a hundred who live and work there – this act will have consequences which go beyond these borders.' Jawad also told his chief and the others, 'I fear an invasion of American soldiers in our country if these attacks on the embassy and on the hotel in Aden are successful – or even if they are not.' He also reminded his chief, 'You recall what happened after the successful attack on the American warship.'

The Panther replied, 'Yes, Jawad, I recall.' He told Jawad and everyone, 'Men and money flowed to us in abundance.'

'And so did the Americans flow into Yemen in abundance.'

The Panther again did not respond.

Another man on the council said, 'We are not ready yet to attack. We must build our forces. We need another year, perhaps.'

The Panther replied, 'The more we attack, the more men and money will come to us.'

Altair, sitting at the right hand of The Panther, looked at the advisors in the dim light and he could see their doubt. His young friend, Bulus, he thought, was still glowing in the victory of his bold and successful attack on the American warship, the *Cole*. But that was over three years ago, and since then Bulus ibn al-Darwish had only small victories against the Sana'a government and no victories against the Americans. The council was willing to wait, but The Panther was not.

Altair knew also that the killing of the nine Belgians and the two Yemenis at the Bilqis ruins had not been celebrated by all jihadists, or by all sympathizers to the cause. True, the Supreme Council of Al Qaeda had approved the attack, but the population of Marib province, including the Bedouin tribes, were not happy that the foreigners had been killed, and many saw it as an act of cowardice, and many in the province had suffered financial loss because the tourists had ceased to come to the ruins.

Altair knew also that if the attacks on the Sheraton Hotel in Aden and on the American Embassy in Sana'a did not result in victory, then his young friend's leadership would be in jeopardy. Also, perhaps, his life.

The Panther was still addressing his council of advisors, and Altair thought he was saying too much. What more was there to say? What had already happened – the two defeats – spoke for themselves. If his jihadists were successful with their attacks in Aden and Sana'a, that, too, would speak for itself.

In any case, Altair did not believe in The Panther's strategy of attacking the Americans. The jihadists should be attacking the government forces. If al-Darwish wished to someday live in the presidential palace, as he said, then he needed to defeat the hated government — not the Americans, who were here in small numbers.

He knew also that if the government was not defeated, the corrupt men in Sana'a would give in to American pressure to let the Americans build a military base in Aden, as the British and then the Russians had done. And if that happened, then the Yemeni people would have the Americans with them for a very long time. But al-Darwish could not see that far into the future. He was blinded by the sight of a small number of Americans, and did not see the ones waiting for an excuse to do what they had done in Iraq and Afghanistan. That would be a disaster for Yemen.

Altair leaned toward al-Darwish and whispered, 'We have much to do.'

The Panther paused in his address to his council, then said to them, 'We will meet again in perhaps one week — after our victories in Aden and Sana'a.'

The Panther stood and his advisors stood also. The advisors left the hut silently, and only a few took their leave with proper expressions of respect.

The Panther and Altair stood alone, and Altair said, 'Perhaps you should reconsider these attacks.'

The Panther replied with a question. 'How can you live as a Muslim and as a Yemeni while the Americans are on the sacred soil of Yemen?'

Altair replied, 'They are here because the government invited them. And they are here because you attack them here.' He advised, 'Destroy the government and the Americans will leave.'

'They will not leave unless we kill them here.'

Altair had already had this discussion with al-Darwish, and he had concluded that his young friend was more interested in killing his former countrymen than in a wise strategy to free their country from the corrupt men in Sana'a.

Altair did not want to argue with this man – and if the attacks in Aden and Sana'a failed, he would not need to argue with him. But he advised, 'Hate blinds us to the truth.'

The Panther had no reply.

The Panther's junior aide Nabeel al-Samad was standing a respectable distance from the open door, and Altair motioned him to enter. Nabeel entered quickly and made proper greetings, kissing the hands of both men.

The Panther remained standing and said to Nabeel, 'Tell me and tell Altair what happened with this ambush, and also about your mission in Sana'a to kill the American agents.'

'Yes, sir.'

Nabeel did not wish to make this report, but if he was truthful and direct, it would go better. As he began to describe the ambush, The Panther interrupted and said, 'Tell us first about your failed mission in Sana'a.'

Nabeel licked his dry lips, then said, 'Yes, sir ...' He related his journey by vehicle to Sana'a after The Panther had given him the mission to kill the two Americans who had landed at the airport.

Altair interrupted, 'I did not know that. Who are these Americans?'

It was The Panther who explained to Altair about John Corey and his wife, and that these two American agents were on the assassination list of the Supreme Council of Al Qaeda. The Panther explained also that the Americans were marked for death because the man Corey had killed Asad Khalil, The Lion.

Altair nodded and said to Nabeel, 'Continue.'

Nabeel was surprised that The Panther had not consulted his most senior and trusted aide on this matter, but he knew why that was so; Altair did not want to provoke the Americans, thinking correctly, perhaps, that the Americans were seeking an excuse to send more forces into Yemen – as happened after the *Cole* attack. The Panther, however, wanted to kill more Americans.

Nabeel continued, 'Friends at the airport informed me that Corey and his wife had left that location in a convoy of three armored vehicles which took them to the American Embassy, where they spent the remainder of the evening.'

Nabeel continued his report, saying that embassy watchers as well as friends in the Sheraton Hotel confirmed that the two Americans had been transported to the hotel in the late morning by a single armored vehicle, and that they had registered there and gone to their rooms.

Nabeel also said, 'I arranged for our watchers in Sana'a to keep them under observation, and I also called together four jihadists with myself to assassinate the Americans at the first opportunity.'

The Panther commented, 'That opportunity apparently did not present itself.'

Nabeel took a long breath and replied, 'It is difficult in Sana'a—'

'Continue.'

'Yes, sir.' Nabeel related what he had heard from the watchers. 'The two Americans were later met at the Sheraton Hotel by two American security men from the embassy, with an armored Land Cruiser, and they drove into the city.'

Nabeel then told The Panther and Altair of the movements of these four Americans in Sana'a – the khat souk, the Old City, lunch at Old Sana'a, the shop called Hope in Their Hands, the jambiyah shop, then the drive to Ghumdan Fortress.

The Panther already knew from his sources in the Ghumdan prison that Corey and the security man called Brenner had come to the prison and had spoken to Rahim ibn Hayyam, his jihadist, who had been taken prisoner at the Hunt Oil installation. This was troubling, because if Rahim ibn Hayyam had given information to the Americans, or to the Political Security Organization, then perhaps Rahim ibn Hayyam had revealed that The Panther was in Marib province on the night of the attack. If that were the case, then he, The Panther, could expect more Predator drones and perhaps more government activity, or even the presence of Americans who might come here to find him.

Altair also understood this and said to al-Darwish, 'Perhaps you should leave Marib province before the government forces – or the Americans with their drones – come here to find you.'

The Panther did not think Altair should have said that with Nabeel present. In any case, he replied, 'It is acceptable for men in our situation to hide, but it is not acceptable to run.' He vowed, 'I will remain here.'

Altair responded, 'As you wish.' He thought Bulus ibn al-Darwish would be wise to remove himself from this province, but al-Darwish was not wise; he had acquired in his youth the arrogance of the Americans whom he so hated.

Altair also understood that if the prisoner, Rahim ibn Hayyam, had revealed the location of The Panther, he may also have revealed the plans to attack the Sheraton Hotel in Aden –

if he knew of these plans. And Hayyam *might* know from talk in the camp. And Bulus knew this, and yet he had said nothing to the council, and he had not halted the plan to attack the hotel. Truly this attack could end in disaster if the Americans were alerted.

Altair took al-Darwish aside and asked him about this.

The Panther replied, 'Even if Hayyam is speaking under torture, he would not know of this plan to attack the Americans in Aden.'

Altair disagreed. 'Soldiers in camp talk, my friend.'

The Panther told Altair, 'We have many watchers at the Aden hotel, and they report no increase in the security there. No army troops have been dispatched to the hotel.'

Altair thought about this, then said, 'The Americans may have chosen not to ask for additional soldiers.' He explained to al-Darwish, 'They may be waiting for the attack, and they may welcome it. Just as they did at the Hunt Oil installation – and as they may have also done with the ambush.'

The Panther did not reply.

Altair said to him, 'Do you not see? This is how they conduct war. You think you are surprising them, but they are surprising *you*, Bulus.'

The Panther replied, 'That is not true. You will see.'

Altair looked at Bulus ibn al-Darwish. Clearly this man did not have the wisdom or patience of his forefathers. In Yemen, war is a slow thing, a never-ending struggle against the invaders and also against whoever sits in the palace in Sana'a. But al-Darwish, al-Amriki, did not understand how war was done in Yemen. And Altair was not going to tell him again how it was done. He would discover that for himself — and become either a great leader, or a dead man.

Also, Altair knew, this man was dangerous. He killed those who disagreed with him and those who proved him wrong. Altair did not fear The Panther, but perhaps he should.

Altair returned to Nabeel and asked him questions about what he had related, and Nabeel stressed that his watchers had been thorough, and that they kept in contact by cell phone with friends who watched outside the embassy, and friends in the Sheraton Hotel. Even the proprietor at the Old Sana'a restaurant had called an assigned telephone number to report the presence of the Americans.

The Panther nodded in approval. He had gone to great lengths to build a telephone network of friends in each town and city in Yemen. These friends, who asked only a few rials for their trouble, numbered in the hundreds, and most of them, he thought, did not know or care whom they were reporting to when they called the telephone number assigned to them. Some of them would be surprised to learn it was Al Qaeda who wanted this information about the movements of the Americans and British, and also other Westerners — but most understood who was paying them. There were so few Westerners in this small country that they could be tracked by only a few hundred friends. The Panther believed that his network of informants was even larger than that of the PSO, who in any case were more interested in Yemeni political opponents than in Westerners.

Also, The Panther knew, the number of Westerners who came to Yemen for tourism, business, and aid work was smaller each year as the security situation became worse for them. And this was the purpose of his attack on the Belgians. Soon, he thought, the number of Westerners in Yemen would be reduced to the embassy staffs – and also the American spies and military men in Aden.

Nabeel was now speaking of the embassy party on the Sunday night. Two of the Yemenis working in the embassy kitchen were friends. Nabeel continued, 'Four Americans then left the embassy with a security man who drove the armored vehicle to the Mövenpick Hotel, where the Americans had dinner.' Nabeel informed his chief and Altair, 'Two of our watchers entered the hotel and confirmed to me that two of the Americans were Corey and his wife, and one was the security man, Brenner, and one was a diplomat called Harris.'

The Panther nodded again. This would have been a good place for Nabeel and the jihadists to visit and kill all four Americans at dinner as they drank alcohol. The Mövenpick employed National Security police and private guards on the premises, but these were of no consequence. What *was* of consequence was the money paid by the Mövenpick and other Western hotels to Al Qaeda in return for peace. But if The Panther had known of the four Americans in the hotel – if Nabeel had telephoned him – he would have ordered the assassination in this case.

Nabeel continued, 'The Americans then drove in their vehicle to the Russia Club.' He reminded his chief, 'The security in this compound is very strong, and we have no friends in this place.'

The Panther responded, 'Soon, when our jihadists enter Sana'a, there will be no one alive in that filthy place.'

'Yes, sir.' Nabeel completed his report, which on balance, he thought, showed that he had done a very fine job of knowing where the Americans were throughout the day and evening.

The Panther, however, said, 'So, it was good that you knew every movement of the Americans. But I believe you were supposed to kill them.'

Nabeel explained, 'As you know, sir, these are trained men and they take precautions.' Nabeel reminded The Panther of the armored vehicles, the weapons, the bulletproof vests, and the possibility that other American security men were watching their compatriots. Nabeel also said, 'And, of course, sir, the PSO also watches the Americans.'

The Panther stared at Nabeel for a long moment, then asked him, 'Were you frightened, Nabeel?'

Nabeel replied quickly, 'No, sir. We were waiting for the moment when we could be certain the Americans could not escape our bullets – when they could be shot in the head, to ensure—'

'But that moment never arrived.'

'Not on that day, sir. But for the next day, we set forth a plan to—'

'Or were you waiting for the opportunity to kill only the security men, then kidnap Corey and his wife and claim your reward?'

Nabeel hesitated, then replied, 'No, sir. A kidnapping was not possible in Sana'a with the police, the PSO—'

'Enough!' The Panther said to Nabeel sharply, 'So on the following day, your two fortunate Americans again escaped death. Correct?'

Nabeel took another breath and replied, 'They were taken from the Sheraton Hotel in an armored vehicle in the early morning and delivered to the American Embassy. Sometime later, the embassy watchers observed a convoy of five vehicles leaving the embassy.' Nabeel reminded his chief, 'The armored vehicles have black glass, so neither the watchers nor a soldier who is a friend could say for certain if Corey or his wife were in any of the vehicles, but—'

'But you made the assumption that they were.'

'Yes, sir.' He explained, 'Corey and his wife had arrived at the embassy at an early hour, then perhaps half an hour later the convoy passed through the gates, so—'

'I understand, Nabeel. So it was at this time that you decided to ambush the convoy.'

Nabeel had made no such decision. He had, in fact, called The Panther, who agreed that Corey and his wife were most probably in the convoy, and that an ambush should be set for the convoy. But this was not what The Panther wished him to say with Altair present.

Altair asked Nabeel, 'Are you saying that you took it upon yourself to authorize an attack on the American Embassy convoy?'

Nabeel lowered his head and replied to Altair, 'I did attempt, sir, three times to call al-Numair on the cell phone and satellite phone.'

The Panther said to Nabeel, 'You should have attempted calls to others around me.'

'Yes, sir.' Nabeel knew that if the ambush had been successful, then this conversation would not be taking place in this way. He remembered something from the Hebrew Book of Leviticus: *Let him go for a scapegoat into the wilderness.*

The Panther said to Nabeel, 'Now tell us what you know of this ambush.'

'Yes, sir.' Nabeel could take no blame for the failure of the ambush – that blame went to Faris, the local Al Qaeda leader who had organized the ambush – but by taking the blame for ordering it, Nabeel knew he had perhaps condemned himself to death.

'Nabeel? Speak.'

'Yes, sir.' He stood straight and addressed The Panther and Altair. 'When I received word of the American convoy leaving the embassy, I immediately contacted our provincial leaders along the expected route.'

It was actually The Panther who had told him to do this, and it seemed a good strategy. Nabeel continued, 'The route, as usual, was south, toward Aden, which is where the Americans go by convoy.'

The Panther said, 'That was a good thought, Nabeel. I would have approved – if you had contacted me.'

'Yes, sir.' He continued, 'Many friends along the route reported on the location of the convoy, and within hours, Faris had assembled fighters for an ambush in the hills south of Ibb.'

'Excellent,' said The Panther. 'So is the convoy destroyed? Are all the Americans dead?'

Nabeel had been witness to his chief's unusual manner of speaking to men who displeased him. He wondered if Bulus ibn al-Darwish had learned that way of speaking in America.

'Nabeel? Am I not speaking loudly enough for you?'

Nabeel drew a deep breath and replied, 'I apologize, sir, for my slowness in responding—'

Altair interrupted, 'Continue, Nabeel. What happened with this ambush?'

Nabeel continued, 'Faris has told me that the ambush was well planned, with twenty jihadists, a car bomb, a roadside bomb, and a bomb in a donkey cart, whose driver was prepared to become a martyr, but—'

'Enough.' The Panther had already been told that the American Predator drones had seen the ambush and launched Hellfire missiles at the jihadists, so he said to Nabeel, 'I have heard enough from you.'

'Yes, sir.'

He said to Nabeel, 'I wish to see Faris. He is to travel to Marib town and await further instructions.'

'Yes, sir.'

'Or perhaps I should have someone else call him. Perhaps you will not be able to contact him with your troublesome cell phone.'

Nabeel did not reply.

The Panther commented, 'You seem frightened, Nabeel. What is frightening you?'

Nabeel again lowered his head and replied, 'My own inadequacy frightens me, sir.' He looked directly at The Panther and said, 'I have failed you, and I have failed our great cause.'

'I agree with you, Nabeel. I agree that you failed to kill the two Americans as I ordered, and I agree that you ordered an ambush that ended in disaster. And what do you think your punishment should be?'

'Whatever you wish, sir.'

'Even death?'

'If it pleases you, sir.'

The Panther drew his jambiyah from its sheath and held the razor-sharp blade against Nabeel's throat.

Nabeel felt his body and legs begin to tremble, and felt himself losing control of his bladder.

Altair said, 'That is not necessary, Bulus.'

Perhaps, hoped Nabeel, the old man suspected that The Panther was lying and that it was The Panther who had ordered the ambush. Altair knew Bulus ibn al-Darwish well — perhaps too well. Nabeel prayed that Altair would save his life.

The Panther pressed the blade harder against Nabeel's jugular vein, but did not draw the dagger across his throat. 'Look at me. Look into my eyes.'

Nabeel looked into the eyes of The Panther and saw hate, but not of him, he thought. The hate was always there when the talk was of the Americans.

The Panther said to Nabeel, 'So the Americans are now at the Sheraton in Aden, Nabeel. They are perhaps swimming in the pool. Or on the beach. Or perhaps they are having alcoholic drinks in the bar room. And how many jihadists lie dead in the hills and on the road because of your stupid decision to attack this convoy? How many, Nabeel?'

Nabeel swallowed and felt the blade press deeper into his flesh. 'Ten, sir . . .'

'I think more.'

Altair said, 'Bulus, we have been here too long.' He reminded him, 'If the drones and the missiles trouble you, then we need to leave before they visit us.'

'Yes, but first I need to cut a throat.'

'Yes, but not this man's throat. Another throat awaits you.'

The Panther did not reply to Altair, but he said to Nabeel, 'Perhaps your throat can wait for another time.'

Nabeel felt a flood of relief passing through him and he closed his eyes, which filled with tears, and he nodded.

Still holding his curved dagger to Nabeel's throat, The Panther said to his aide, 'You are to travel to Sana'a with all speed, and board an aircraft to Aden. You are to take a room in the Sheraton Hotel and complete the task I have given you.'

Though he knew this was a suicide mission, Nabeel managed to say, 'I will, sir.'

'And if you do not, or if you should leave Yemen out of fear, I assure you I will find you. And if I do not find you, I will find your family.' He asked, 'Do you understand?'

'Yes, sir. I will kill—'

The Panther drew his blade across the left side of Nabeel's neck and cut into his flesh.

Nabeel let out a sharp sound of surprise and pain, staggered backwards and grasped his neck with his right hand. Blood ran between his fingers as he probed the wound and satisfied himself that it was not fatal.

The Panther slipped his bloody jambiyah back into its sheath and said to Nabeel, 'Come outside. I want you to see that I do know how to cut a throat.'

The Panther and Altair left the hut, and Nabeel hesitated, then, pressing his hand against his wound, he followed.

Outside, sitting on the rocks of the narrow gorge, were the survivors of the failed Hunt Oil attack. Kneeling on the ground facing the men was their commander, Captain Behaddin Zuhair. His wrists were bound behind his back and his head was bowed so he did not have to look at his men, who had passed the time in conversation while waiting for The Panther.

The men grew silent as their chief and the old man, Altair, stepped out of the hut.

The Panther walked directly to Captain Zuhair, but he did not address him. Instead, he addressed his jihadists and his council of advisors and his aides, and called out, 'This man, Behaddin Zuhair, showed cowardice and stupidity as he led his brave jihadists against the American oil facility. He ignored the advice of our council and of his own lieutenant, Sayid al-Rashid, who died a hero's death while his captain cowered behind a rock.' The Panther continued, 'When Zuhair should have pressed the attack to total victory, he hid, then fled like a woman as the Americans and their mercenaries fired their weapons.'

The jihadists and the council of advisors sat silently.

The Panther continued, 'I share in the blame for this defeat, because it was I who failed to see that Zuhair was not a true leader of men.'

The Panther's council of advisors remained silent, but one of his personal aides called out, 'No! No! It is Zuhair who is to blame!' Another aide shouted, 'Zuhair spoke bravely, but hid his cowardice!'

The Panther motioned for silence. He noticed, as did Altair, that no man in the council of advisors had spoken for their leader as they were expected to do when the leader publicly confessed to a lapse of judgment or a wrong decision.

But he also noticed that the jihadists who were with Zuhair in the attack did not say anything in defense of Zuhair. They sat quietly, avoiding the eyes of their captain, and of The Panther.

The Panther knew he had to end this quickly, so he moved closer to Zuhair's side and shouted at him, 'Confess your cowardice and your incompetence and I promise you a quick and merciful death.'

Zuhair turned his head toward The Panther and spoke in a loud, clear voice, 'I have nothing to confess. I have done my duty on the field of battle—'

'Quiet! I have asked you for a confession. Not excuses.'

'I make no excuses.' Captain Zuhair faced his men and, still kneeling with his wrists bound, he exhorted them to come to his defense. 'Tell what you know! Tell what you saw! Speak truthfully of my actions—'

'Quiet!'

Zuhair suddenly stood and shouted, 'Have I not led you well? Have I not done my duty . . . ?' He looked out at the men who had trusted him with their lives – his men who themselves had faltered under the intense fire from the American compound. Did they not remember that he had rallied them and shouted words of encouragement and comfort as they lay on the ground, paralyzed with fear?

But no one spoke for him.

He called to them, 'I do not fear death in battle, but I do not deserve this death. I do not deserve to have my reputation and honor—'

A shot rang out, and Zuhair fell forward on his face.

Everyone looked at the old man, at Altair, who had fired the shot from a pistol.

They then looked at Captain Zuhair, who was still alive, and those who were closest saw that Zuhair had been shot in the left buttock, where blood was spreading across his white fouteh.

The Panther looked at Altair, who was now standing close to

383

him, and Altair said softly, 'You let him speak too long, Bulus. Now finish it your way.'

The Panther nodded, then ordered two fighters to lift Zuhair into a kneeling position.

The Panther drew his jambiyah and came up behind Zuhair as the two men held him up. The Panther said to Zuhair, 'You have chosen this death.'

Zuhair summoned all his energy to shout, 'You will burn in hell!'

The Panther had heard too much already from this man, so instead of cutting his jugular and his arteries, he sliced deep into Zuhair's throat where his larynx sat, and said, 'Satan will be pleased not to hear you speak.'

The two men held Zuhair in the kneeling position as the man began choking and spitting up blood.

The minutes passed as Zuhair continued to drown in his own blood.

The Panther took this opportunity to mock Zuhair, saying to him, 'You were too cowardly even to confess your cowardice. A man of honor, a soldier, would have said he had lost his courage and begged for a quick death. But instead, you dishonored your-self further by lying. You—'

Another shot rang out and the front of Zuhair's head exploded with bone, brain, and blood.

Altair holstered his pistol and said to the jihadists, 'Bury him quickly and deep so the animals do not find him.'

To Bulus ibn al-Darwish he said quietly, 'You may show no mercy, Bulus, but you may not show such disrespect.' He reminded The Panther, 'We are civilized.'

— PART VII —

Aden, Yemen

CHAPTER FORTY-FOUR

The Land Cruiser's outside temperature gauge read 102 degrees Fahrenheit, so I wasn't too shocked when I opened my door and got hit by a blast furnace.

Clare and I left our flak jackets in the SUV and I told Clare to go ahead inside.

I took the binoculars and looked up at the hills that rose above the hotel. Last time I was here, there was no Yemeni Army security up there, and I didn't see any now.

The perimeter security seemed to consist of the dozen Yemeni soldiers I saw along the entrance road, sitting on their asses in their white plastic chairs under sun umbrellas, chatting on their cell phones. Ice coolers completed the picture of intense vigilance. Did anyone tell these guys that Al Qaeda was heading this way?

Also, as I recalled, there was a white tent pitched on a ridge that ran down to the beach on the south side of the hotel, which the Yemenis said was an army observation post. But our commo people said it was a PSO listening post to intercept our radio and sat-phone communications — which was one reason we had the lead-lined tent on the fourth floor. The other reason was Al Qaeda, who also had some commo intercept capabilities.

I focused the binoculars on Elephant Rock on the north side

of the hotel. There was still a Yemeni Army pickup truck on the rock, and on the flatbed of the truck was a .50 caliber machine gun manned by four Yemeni Army assholes who liked to keep the gun pointed at the hotel instead of at the surrounding hills. They probably thought this was funny; we did not.

The National Security Bureau, whose job it was to guard hotels, didn't exist when I was here last time, and I was happy not to see their blue cammies here this time, even though I'd developed a special relationship with Captain Dammaj.

As for our own security, we had the Marines and FBI SWAT Team, and I recalled that there were always four Marine snipers on the roof, and four or five Marines with M-16s on the beach. At night, that figure doubled.

I shifted my attention to the convoy. Everyone was out of the Land Cruisers — all thirteen of us — and one of the DSS agents was overseeing the transfer of luggage and equipment into the hotel lobby, while the others were keeping an eye on things out here.

A few Arab guests, who looked like rich Saudis, in full robes and headgear, exited the lobby doors and spoke to the doorman about the shot-up vehicles.

It's not often that you have armed military and paramilitary groups staying in a hotel where civilian guests are also staying. But this was Yemen, and the guests didn't seem to mind our presence as much as we minded theirs. In a way, though, we provided protection for each other — Al Qaeda probably wouldn't shoot up a hotel full of their co-religionists. Right? I recalled Buck saying not to worry unless the Arabs started checking out.

I also recalled that this Sheraton franchise was owned by a

Saudi prince, but I wasn't sure if that was a good thing or a bad thing in regard to the hotel getting blown up by Al Qaeda. Probably depended on who the prince was paying off or pissing off.

Anyway, all the luggage was inside, so I slung my M4 and moved into the cool lobby.

A few DSS agents, including Mike and Zamo, were keeping an eye on the luggage cart, and Brenner was at the front desk checking us in without showing passports or giving names, which was none of the hotel's business. The Americans owned floors three and four, forever, and the Saudi prince had a great cash cow going here, compliments of the American taxpayers.

The lobby had just been remodeled when I was last here, and it wasn't bad – lots of mahogany woodwork and wicker furniture; sort of British tropical colonial, like hotels I'd been to in the Caribbean. And there the similarities ended.

I noticed the ubiquitous photo of Ali Abdullah Saleh, President for Life – until someone killed him – hanging on a wall. Big Ali is watching you.

I also noticed a few Western guests, probably clueless Europeans who got a good deal on a winter getaway. American tourists had the big advantage of never having heard of Yemen or Aden, and neither had their travel agents, and if they had, they didn't want to go anyplace where Americans were not welcome – which was just about everywhere these days. Europeans thought they were welcome all over, which was another kind of ignorance or arrogance.

Also in the lobby were two Yemeni soldiers with AK-47s, and two US Marines with M-16s. What must those European tourists be thinking by now? Great beach, cheap rates — but what's with all these people carrying assault rifles? They must be shooting a movie.

I saw that a welcome committee of our colleagues had arrived, and Buck was speaking to three men and one woman in the sitting area of the lobby. Buck seemed to know them, and none of them looked like they could be our CIA guy, who I was sure would reveal himself in a more dramatic way — like maybe paragliding onto the beach. Or a more clandestine way, like if that potted palm over there started whispering to me. 'Psst. Corey. Over here. The palm tree. Don't look at me. Just listen.'

My wife, who'd gone off to freshen up, came up to me and said, 'This isn't a bad place.' She asked, 'Did you have a good time here?'

That question was more loaded than a sailor on shore leave, and I replied, 'Without you, darling, there are no good times.'

She seemed to doubt my sincerity, then moved on to, 'How did Dr Nolan handle the problem back there?'

That wasn't the real question, but I replied, 'Shook her up a bit.'

'Were you able to calm her down?'

'I was too busy fighting her for her tranquilizers.'

Kate suppressed a smile, then informed me, for the record, 'I'm still annoyed at you for that police stop.'

'Well, try to get over it.' I reminded her, 'Life is short.'

She softened and said, 'You're a brave man, John, but reckless and arrogant.'

'Thank you. Hey, the bar here is not bad. Can I buy you a drink?'

'Paul says drinking alcohol is on hold until further notice.'

'Yeah? Then how about a beer?'

Howard, who had also gone off to freshen up, came up to us and said, 'Not a bad place. But is it safe?'

'No,' I assured him. I suggested, 'You may want to return to Sana'a.'

'I think I've had enough car travel for one day.'

'I'd hate to see you miss the return-trip ambush.'

He actually laughed. Howard was now a combat vet who laughed at death.

He informed us, 'I live on Long Island. I love the beach and I'm a competitive swimmer.'

'Good. The sharks love competitive swimmers.'

Clare, too, joined us and said to Kate, 'Your husband is a very brave man.'

Kate replied, 'He's my hero.' Actually, she said ... well, nothing.

Clare continued, 'I've never been so frightened in my life. But John – and Mike – were totally cool and calm, and John made sure I stayed below the windows.'

'And,' I added, 'I covered her with my body.' No, I didn't say that. I'm not *that* brave.

Kate had no comment.

Brenner was finished at the front desk, and he came up to us and handed out key cards in envelopes with our room numbers on them. Brenner had remembered to put me in the same room as my wife, so I think he was over Kate.

Brenner suggested, 'Let's meet our Aden colleagues.'

I asked him, 'Where is our Company man?'

'I don't know.'

Okay. But if I had to guess, I'd say our missing teammate was in the commo room speaking by radio to his station chief in Sana'a, asking if there was any intel about the Hellfires vaporizing The Panther. Wouldn't that be nice? Or did I really want to whack this guy myself? It's been a while since anyone from the New York Task Force personally whacked a bad guy, and I think I had the last kill. The Lion. Which was why I was here for an encore performance. Also, maybe Kate whacking a CIA guy was the other reason we were here.

In any case, I was on a roll with killing big cats, and I hoped to continue my winning streak.

CHAPTER FORTY-FIVE

We moved to where Buck was chatting with the welcome committee, and Buck did the honors and said to the four people, 'You all know Paul Brenner. And this is FBI Special Agent Kate Mayfield, our new assistant legal attaché in Sana'a, just arrived from the ATTF in New York. And this is Kate's husband, also known as Detective John Corey of the FBI Evidence Response Team, also from the New York ATTF.' Buck added, 'John, as I told you, has been here before and he was homesick for Aden.'

That got a laugh, but not from me.

Buck also introduced Dr Clare Nolan, and FBI Agent Howard

Fensterman, the new legat, adding, 'Howard volunteered to come along for the ride.'

Did I hear someone say, 'Schmuck'?

We shook hands all around, and each person introduced himself and herself.

The lady was Betsy Collins, Supervisory Special Agent and Team Leader of the five-person FBI Evidence Response Team. She seemed pleasant and welcoming, and assuming my reputation had preceded me, she was probably thrilled to have learned from Buck that she didn't actually have to work with me.

Brenner's Aden counterpart in the Diplomatic Security Service was Doug Reynolds, whose title was Regional Security Officer, and who looked like ex-military.

I took the opportunity to tell him, 'The DSS did a hell of a job getting us here.'

He nodded and said, of course, 'That's what they get paid for.'

The second guy was Lyle Manning, Supervisory Special Agent of the ten-man FBI SWAT Team. He was a young guy, obviously in great physical shape, and like most FBI Special Agents, he wasn't sure if an ex-cop was his peer. He was okay with Kate and Howard, though, who were in the club. FBI, by the way, means Fabulously Boring Individual. Just kidding.

The third guy was easy to identify – he wore desert cammies, a Marine cap with globe-and-anchor insignia, captain bars on his collar, and a name tag that said 'McAndrews,' though he said, 'Call me Mac.'

We all pulled up wicker chairs, and we stacked our rifles neatly against the cocktail table. A hovering waiter put menus on the table and said, 'Welcome, new sirs and new ladies, and already

393

honored guests to the Sheraton Aden. I am Masud. Please to inform me of your wishes.'

'Water for me and a scotch for my rifle.'

Anyway, we all ordered soft drinks, and Masud floated off to the lobby lounge.

Captain McAndrews said to the Sana'a contingent, 'So you had a little excitement on the road.'

Brenner replied, 'Five hours of boredom, two minutes of pure terror.' He added, 'Predators did a great job.' He further added, 'Road security is going downhill fast.'

Doug Reynolds, the DSS guy, said to Brenner, 'I spoke to Ed Peters and he's okay with your men staying here overnight – not happy, but okay. Meanwhile, I've put in a request through channels for a Yemeni Army escort back to Sana'a.'

Brenner replied, 'Normally I wouldn't want that, but I'll take it if we can get it.' He added, 'If we get offered a National Security police escort – for hire or for free – the answer is no.'

I interjected, 'Especially if it's Captain Dammaj.'

Buck and Brenner both laughed. See? *They* weren't pissed at me.

Doug asked, 'Who's Captain Dammaj?'

Buck replied, 'An NSB officer we met on the road. I sat-phoned that in.' He further explained, 'John told him to go fuck himself.' Buck apologized to the three ladies for my language and added, 'Unfortunately, we didn't know that Captain Dammaj spoke English.'

Everyone got a good laugh at that.

Buck told our colleagues, in case they didn't know, 'This country is close to dysfunctional.'

Betsy Collins said, 'Dysfunctional would be an improvement.'

As I said, and as I saw the last time I was here, our relations with our Yemeni allies were not good. The Americans saw the Yemenis as corrupt, devious, and inept, and the Yemenis knew what we thought of them. I had no idea what they thought of us, but it was easy to guess.

And to make matters worse, we were stretched so thin here that we were barely able to accomplish our mission, and barely able to protect ourselves from our enemies, not to mention our Yemeni allies.

The soft drinks came, and Doug proposed a toast. 'Welcome to our guests, and here's to much success on your mission.' He added, 'Whatever it is.'

That got a few conspiratorial chuckles. Plausible deniability is important with Black Ops jobs.

I didn't think we'd have much to do with these Aden people once we left here to find The Panther, and as with most Black Ops missions, we'd be mostly on our own. Also, though we might never see them again, they might see us if they were assigned to a body identification and recovery detail. But think happy thoughts.

Doug asked Clare, 'How's your patient?'

Clare replied, 'He'll be fine. But I'll have to see if he needs sutures, and he needs to keep it clean.'

Captain Mac offered, 'Infections are rampant here.' He added, 'This whole place is a petri dish.'

Shithole.

Lyle Manning, the FBI SWAT Team Leader, changed the subject and said, 'We're a little concerned about this reported threat of an Al Qaeda attack on this installation.'

Actually, it wasn't an installation; it was a hotel with plate glass windows. I reported, 'Paul and I heard this firsthand from an Al Qaeda prisoner at Ghumdan, and the prisoner seemed credible.'

My buddy Paul agreed and added, 'Al Qaeda has lost the element of surprise, so I'm sure we can deal with anything Al Qaeda tries here.'

Captain Mac added, 'If, as reported, it's only forty or so enemy combatants, it won't be a problem. In fact, it's an opportunity.'

Why was I not seeing these Al Qaeda attacks as opportunities? What is wrong with me?

I glanced at Clare, who looked like she wasn't hearing this correctly. *This hotel is an Al Qaeda target? Did I miss that memo?*

More importantly, Howard, as an attorney and an employee of the Department of Justice and an honest man, did not need to be hearing things he didn't need to hear. We hadn't gone there yet, but we would, so I suggested, 'If it's all the same to Mr Fensterman and Dr Nolan, and the rest of us, I think Howard and Clare might want to recon the hotel and the beach.' I said that nice. Right?

Howard and Clare got it, stood, and excused themselves.

Brenner inquired of one and all, 'What are the Yemenis providing or promising in the way of extra security?'

Lyle Manning replied, 'To be honest, we haven't requested anything.'

Say again?

Lyle looked at Buck, who informed us, 'It was I who suggested that we not ask the Yemeni government for a large show of force.'

What were you thinking, Buck? I reminded him, 'You said back at the embassy that you were going to notify the Yemeni government at the highest levels that we needed extra security here.'

'Yes, I did say that.' He explained, however, 'If I asked the

Yemenis for extra security, that would alert Al Qaeda that we knew this hotel is a target.' Buck continued his reasoning. 'If Al Qaeda thought we had information about an attack on the Sheraton, they would also think that we had information from the same source – the prisoner in Ghumdan – about the last known location of The Panther.'

No one had anything to say about that, and I had the feeling that the Aden contingent agreed with the old Cold Warrior's crafty thinking – though they were sitting in the bull's-eye.

More interesting, Buck seemed to have the power of life-and-death decisions. Buck was a big man.

Captain Mac also reminded us, 'The fewer Yemeni Army people we have around here, the better I like it.' He smiled and confided to us, 'The first targets we take out are the Yemeni Army's .50 caliber along with the Yemeni commo tent.'

Don't forget the guys under the sun umbrellas.

On the subject of tipping off Al Qaeda, no one was suggesting that we evacuate the European or Arab guests. I guess the attitude was 'Fuck them.' There's a reason for cheap high-season rates. If you don't know the reason, that's your problem. Indeed, we had become a bit callous. Except when it came to American lives. Everyone else was expendable. Well, maybe our European and Arab allies needed a deeper appreciation of what the Americans were up against. They could stand on the sidelines if they wanted, but they could get killed there, too.

Lyle Manning let us know, 'The entire SWAT Team will be pulling all-nighters until further notice.'

Doug Reynolds added, 'We also now have the DSS men from Sana'a.'

Brenner reminded him, 'Only for tonight, Doug.' He let us know, 'There's a new and credible threat to the embassy, and they need to get back.'

The safest place in Yemen might be swimming in the gulf with the sharks.

My other thought was that any attack on Americans would trigger the *Cole* response. Within two weeks of the *Cole* attack, there were close to two hundred American military, intelligence, and anti-terrorist people in this hotel and on ships out in the harbor. The Yemenis had made us scale down since then, but there were people in Washington who wanted to ratchet it up. All we needed was an excuse. And a few more dead Americans.

Kate, who hadn't said anything so far, now said, 'I understand the decision not to increase security here. But I also don't want to risk any of our team being . . . becoming casualties here.' She added, 'We need to depart this location as soon as possible and go to where we think we will make contact with the suspect.'

Buck replied to Kate, 'We understand that.' He let our colleagues know, 'We hope to be out of here — and out of your hair — as soon as we get the intel we need.'

This brought us to the subject of our missing team member, but I wasn't sure any of the Aden people had any info on that, so I didn't bring it up. That was up to Buck, and he wasn't saying anything about the CIA.

But I did want to know about the evacuation plan, though I think I already knew the answer to that. Nevertheless, I said to Doug Reynolds, 'Ed Peters said you'd brief us on an evacuation plan.'

Doug smiled, which was not what I wanted to see. He said, 'Ed tells everyone coming here to ask me about that.' He confided to us, 'It's called the Alamo plan.' He asked me, 'Any questions?'

I guess not.

Betsy Collins did say, however, 'If we have advance warning from our sources, and if we could get to the airport, we have air resources in the area that could evacuate us.' She added, 'Or, if we could get to the harbor, we can rendezvous with or commandeer a ship.'

I pointed out, 'I think we actually have advance warning of an impending attack.' Remember?

Captain Mac ignored my sarcasm and cautioned, 'The worst thing we could do would be to destroy all our equipment here, then evacuate and find out there was no imminent attack.' He added, 'That would make us look bad.'

Looking bad is not as bad as looking dead, but to be a team player, I responded, 'Sounds good.'

Betsy Collins asked me, 'What was the evacuation plan when you were here, John?'

'The backstroke.'

Good laughs. I was being accepted by the inmates.

I did ask, however, 'What about the civilian guests here? And the hotel staff?'

After a long silence, Captain Mac replied, 'You should ask Al Qaeda that question.'

Right.

Buck did have some good news and informed us, 'We now have two Predators on station twenty-four-seven, reconning the area.'

I asked, 'With Hellfires?'

Buck nodded.

Good. I had recently become a big fan of Hellfire missiles.

We also spoke about the ongoing *Cole* investigation – slow progress – then we discussed recent developments in Aden and the surrounding area. The big concern was that Al Qaeda was becoming politically stronger around Aden, though not yet a military threat – notwithstanding the forty jihadists on their way from Marib. The CIA and Defense Intelligence were closely monitoring the situation and keeping everyone here informed. Glad to hear that.

We seemed to have covered all topics and Buck said, 'We'll let you all get back to your jobs, and we can meet again tonight in the cocktail lounge if you don't have other plans.'

Betsy Collins said, 'We do have a full social calendar here, but if we're not in a firefight with Al Qaeda, we'll be in the bar.'

Funny.

We all stood, shook hands, and set the time for cocktails at 7 P.M. At least something important had been decided here.

CHAPTER FORTY-SIX

Buck, Brenner, Kate, and I walked back to our luggage, which was still under the watchful eyes of Mike and Zamo.

Brenner informed Mike, 'You're all staying here tonight on full alert. Secure the vehicles, then get some sleep.' To Zamo he said, 'You can return to Sana'a with the convoy tomorrow. We'll ask for a SWAT sniper for the team.'

Zamo, of course, replied, 'I'm staying.'

'Okay. But see Dr Nolan ASAP.'

Bellhops were not permitted on the American floors, so we gathered our bags and walked toward the elevators.

Buck said to us, 'Everyone is free until seven. I'm going to the pool in an hour.'

I'm going to get laid in ten minutes. Getting shot at makes me horny.

But Kate said to Buck, 'We'll see you there.'

Sitting at a desk near the elevators was a Marine with an M-16 rifle and a hand-held radio. He stood and we made the acquaintance of Lance Corporal Brad Schiller, who asked to see our passports and creds. Schiller checked our names against his list, then handed each of us a red-and-white plastic ID card on a chain that said, 'American Embassy – Sana'a Yemen.' On the other side of the card was a bull's-eye. Just kidding.

Corporal Schiller said, 'I'll call upstairs.' He added, 'Welcome to Paradise.'

Everyone's a comedian.

We rode up to the third floor, which I recalled was reserved for the FBI Evidence Response Team, the FBI SWAT Team, the Diplomatic Security Service, the FBI doctor, and transient guests, mostly from the embassy, and rarely from Washington. There was also a common room on the floor where we used to sit, drink, play cards, and complain.

On the fourth floor were the twenty Marines, two to a room, plus our offices and our equipment and supply rooms. At the end of the fourth-floor corridor were rooms for our CIA colleagues and Defense Intelligence Agency officers, who mostly kept to themselves, which made everyone happy. Also on the fourth floor was the CIA's lead-lined SCIF in a cleared bedroom.

These two floors constituted the American outpost in Aden. The camel's nose under the tent. But if people like Colonel Kent had their way, we'd soon be building an Arabian Guantanamo down the coast. Call bin Laden Construction.

We stopped at the third floor, and Buck said, 'I'm on four. See you at the pool.'

Kate, Brenner, and I got off, and there was a Marine in the hallway standing behind his desk, on which was his M-16 rifle and radio.

We introduced ourselves to Lance Corporal Wayne Peeples. He directed us to the right, and as we walked I checked my room number again to be sure Kate and Paul weren't sharing a room.

Actually, Brenner's room was next to ours, and we all said, 'See you later,' and entered our rooms.

We had a room overlooking the Gulf of Aden, as I'd had last time. Same room? Are those my socks on the floor?

Kate said, 'This is nice.'

'Nothing is too good for Christian Crusaders.'

We threw our luggage and weapons on one of the two king-size beds, and I suggested we throw ourselves on the other.

Kate thought that was a swell idea. Afterwards, we stood on the balcony and looked out at the turquoise water. This was the view I'd had for forty days of living in this hotel, and it brought back some memories.

The bay, called Gold Mohur Bay, was formed by two ridges of bare volcanic rock that ran down into the water.

Kate spotted the lonely white tent on the south ridge and asked, 'What's that?'

'That's the tent that Captain Mac was referring to.' I explained, 'It's either a Yemeni Army observation post, or a PSO eavesdropping facility. In either case, the men inside the tent are not there to help us.'

Kate nodded, then looked to the right at Elephant Rock, which indeed looked almost exactly like the head of an elephant, complete with a long trunk which formed a stone arch that ended on the rocks below.

At the risk of stating the obvious, I said, 'That's Elephant Rock.'

'I wonder why they call it that.'

Kate noticed the pickup truck farther down the elephant's back with the .50 caliber machine gun pointed our way. 'What's that?'

'That's our Yemeni Army security.'

'Why is the gun pointed at the hotel?'

'They're sending us a subtle message.'

She had no comment on that, and she looked down at the stone terrace below, where we used to have barbecues at night and pretend we were in Hawaii waiting for the hula dancers.

Beyond the terrace was the pool where about a dozen tourists were sitting or swimming, and beyond the pool was a white-sand beach where the volleyball net was still strung, but there was no game at the moment.

There was also no one sunning on the beach or swimming in the bay, but I did see four Marines in full gear at either end of the beach.

The hotel had planted small palm trees all over, but the climate here was so hot that even the palms had trouble staying alive.

Kate said, 'Now I can picture where you were.'

'Right.' I hadn't taken many photos, and the ones I'd taken were designed to show the port city of Aden as the shithole it was — mostly dilapidated buildings, barefoot urchins, women in black baltos, and men with guns. I mean, I didn't want anyone thinking I was having a good time here.

Kate said to me, 'My forty days in Dar es Salaam were no treat, but it wasn't Yemen.'

'There is only one Yemen,' I assured her.

I pointed toward Elephant Rock and said, 'On the other side of that peninsula is Aden Harbor, where the Cole was anchored on October 12, 2000.'

Kate nodded.

Seventeen American dead and thirty-nine wounded, some disabled for life. And that suicide boat should never have gotten anywhere near an American warship.

So, what have we learned from the Cole and from 9/11 and from all the terrorist attacks before and since? Two things that we'd forgotten over the years: Kill them before they kill you, and if they kill you, hunt them down and deliver lethal justice. That's why I was here.

CHAPTER FORTY-SEVEN

Kate wanted to go down to the pool, so, good husband that I am, I said I'd keep her company. Also, Clare was in the pool, but that had nothing to do with my decision.

Our rooms here are considered secure, so we were able to leave our rifles in the room, but we locked our papers in the safe, as per regulations. We did need to take our sat-phones, radios, and handguns, which we stuffed in the pockets of our bathrobes, and we took the elevator to the lobby and went out to the pool.

Buck and Brenner were also there, as was Howard, and they got out of the pool, along with Clare.

I should mention here that pool attire for gentlemen was long bathing trunks or shorts, and a T-shirt. For women it was long shorts and a long, loose T-shirt. And that's about as risqué as it got at any of the hotels or beaches in Yemen. So if I was looking forward to seeing Clare in a bikini — and why would I be? — I would be disappointed.

Clare, however, still looked good in a wet T-shirt. In fact ...

'John.'

'Yes, dear?'

'We're sitting over there.'

'Right.'

We all sat around a table under an umbrella and ordered a pitcher of iced tea. There was no sea breeze from the gulf, and it was *hot*.

A few Western tourists swam in the pool or lay on chaises, but there weren't any Mideastern guests at the pool, and there never would be. Not that I was dying to see Abdul or Afiya in shorts and T-shirts, but it might do them some good to get a little sun on their skin – vitamin D – and learn how to swim. Or am I being culturally insensitive again?

Anyway, we all chatted awhile and drank iced tea, which is as bad a drink as anyone ever invented.

Buck, holding court, said, 'Local legend says that the graves of Cain and Abel are located here in the Ma'alla quarter of the city.'

I had an old homicide sergeant who claimed he worked that case.

Buck further informed us, 'The Yemenis also believe that this is where Noah's Ark sailed from.'

Lucky for life on earth that suicide bombers didn't blow a hole in its side.

Buck concluded, 'The Yemenis like to appropriate history from the Old and New Testaments and move it here.' He added, 'The American Mormons have also speculated that some of their history began here.'

Yeah? Why *here*? Maybe because the great truth about Yemen was that it was the land of lies and half-truths. As I was discovering.

'I never thought I'd say this,' Buck confided to us, 'but this place was better under the Yemeni Communists.' He explained, 'They were secular, and they kept the fundamentalist Muslims in line – with Russian help.' He added, 'Now that South Yemen is dominated by the north, it is slipping back into fundamentalism.'

On a more important topic, Clare had put on her bathrobe. Which has nothing to do with anything. Why did I even mention that?

Buck informed us, 'I was here in January 1986, when the thirty-day civil war devastated Aden. Thousands were killed, and I was almost one of them.'

He got a faraway look in his eyes, then continued, 'The war of 1994 was particularly devastating. This city was under siege for two months and the water pumping facilities were destroyed and people were dying of thirst.'

Kate asked him, 'Did you stay in the city?'

'I did, and I sent radio reports to the State Department . . .' He let us know, however, 'I had several months' supply of Seera beer put away for such a situation.' He informed us, 'The Seera brewery was built by the British, and it supplied the whole country with beer. But when the North Yemenis took the city, they blew up the brewery.' He added, 'Bastards.'

That got a chuckle. But it was also a hint of what went on here not too long ago. And also a hint of what Buck Harris had experienced here over the years. I had no doubt that this man was a dedicated professional. What troubled me, though, was his profession. I have a thing about intelligence officers, no matter what alphabet agency they work for. I mean, they do a necessary job, and I respect what they do, but if you're not one of them, you can wind up on their expendable list, as Buck himself had confessed in vino veritas.

On that subject, I was still waiting for our CIA guy to show himself, and my instincts said it would be soon.

We were all baking in the heat, so we unrobed and dove into the pool, which was warm as bathwater.

Everyone, I assumed, had a gun and extra magazines in their bathrobes, and the staff knew that and stayed away from our table. Also, as per my last visit here, there was a Marine sniper on the roof keeping an eye on the pool and beach. Every resort hotel should have a sniper on the roof. Helps you relax.

Anyway, after about a half hour of pool frolics, I suggested a beach volleyball game, admitting, 'I got very good at this when I was here.'

We carried our bathrobes down to the beach and hung them on the net pole, then chose up sides: Buck, Clare, and me against Brenner, Kate, and Howard.

We played best out of five, and I seemed to be the only one who knew how to play the game. My team swept the first three, with me as the high scorer, of course. Hey, I played this stupid game for forty days. That's why I suggested it.

Brenner, I noticed, was a competitive player, and not a very good loser. Neither am I, which is why I play games I can win.

Buck suggested a walk on the beach, so we asked one of the Marines to watch our backs and watch our robes and guns, and we all went down to the water. As I said, naked on the beach in Yemen means you don't have your gun.

Howard announced, 'I want to take a swim. Who's coming in with me?'

How could I resist saying, 'Do you know why sharks don't eat lawyers? Professional courtesy.'

Okay, old joke, but it got a laugh because of the immediate proximity of the lawyer and the sharks.

Brenner, of course, took the challenge, and I did, too, but Kate said, 'John, I don't want you — any of you — to go in.'

Buck informed us, 'It's very dangerous.'

Well, that settled it. Howard, Brenner, and I ran into the surf and dove in. The gulf was calm, the salt water was buoyant, and the tide was running out, so it was an easy swim, even with the weight of our heavy shorts and T-shirts.

We got about a hundred yards out when I spotted two gray dorsal fins about twenty feet away. Holy shit.

Howard said hopefully, 'Could be dolphins.'

I suggested, 'Tell them the lawyer joke and when they laugh we can see if they have sharp teeth.'

Anyway, we headed for shore and made it back to the shallow water, where Buck, Kate, and Clare stood waist-deep in the surf watching us set a swim speed record.

Buck asked, 'Sharks?'

I replied, 'I didn't ask.'

We all waded ashore, and Kate said to me sharply, 'We didn't come all the way here and survive an ambush so you could get eaten by a shark.'

'Yes, dear.'

Brenner was probably rethinking his infatuation with Kate Mayfield. My rule is, if you're thinking of having an affair with a married woman, first see how she treats her husband.

Anyway, we all decided that the pool was safer, but before we began our walk up the beach, I saw Buck looking at a guy who was standing about thirty feet away at the water's edge, smoking a cigarette and staring out at the sea.

I had the impression that Buck knew this guy and knew he would be there.

Buck said to Clare and Howard, 'You go ahead. We'll join you later.'

So we were about to meet our last teammate.

CHAPTER FORTY-EIGHT

T he guy flicked his cigarette into the surf, then began walking toward us.

He looked to be in his mid-thirties, medium height and very lean, though I had the impression he'd once carried more weight. He was barefoot, wearing white cotton pants and a green flowered tropical shirt, which was unbuttoned.

His hair was long and straight, and it was bleached almost white by the same Saudi sun that had burned his skin almost black. His eyebrows, too, were sun-bleached, and as he got closer I saw that his eyes were a weird, almost unnatural blue.

At first glance, you'd say beach bum or surfer dude. But if you looked closer, you'd see a man who'd been here too long; a Westerner who had not gone native, but had gone somewhere else.

Buck met him halfway and they shook hands. I heard the guy say, 'Good to see you again.' His voice was flat as was his whole affect, but he did force a smile.

Brenner, Kate, and I joined Buck, who introduced us to Chet Morgan. He knew who we were, of course, and now we knew our CIA guy, though Buck hadn't mentioned Mr Morgan's affiliation.

He shook hands with Kate first, saying, 'Glad you could come,' then with Brenner, saying, 'Good job on the road.'

Brenner responded, 'Thanks for the Hellfires.'

He didn't acknowledge that, and as I shook his hand, he said, 'Thank you for coming here.'

Weird. And for the record, his handshake was more of a jerk than a shake, and his skin was cold. Maybe he was dead.

Chet, as he wanted to be called, suggested a walk on the beach, so we walked toward Elephant Rock.

Chet hadn't said walk and talk, so we walked in silence, like we were old buds just enjoying the moment together.

I glanced at Buck, who seemed subdued, which is not like Buck.

Chet lit another cigarette.

I didn't give a shit if this guy never said another word, but Brenner broke the silence and asked Chet the standard question, 'How long have you been here?'

Chet replied, 'Since the Cole.'

So that was about three and a half years. No wonder the guy was buggy. But Buck had been in Yemen on and off for a lot longer, and he was okay. Maybe if I stayed here another six months I'd think Chet was okay, too.

As a cop, I can spot someone who is indulging in a controlled substance, and I had the thought that Chet was on something, maybe khat. So maybe the A-team had a junkie on board. Terrific. Takes the pressure off me.

Brenner, a man of few words himself, was apparently uncomfortable with a man of no words, and he asked Chet, 'Any chance our target was KIA in the ambush?'

Chet drew on his cigarette and replied, 'I don't think so.' He added, 'Chatter puts him in Marib.'

Well, I guess we were going to Marib to end the chatter.

Buck asked Chet, 'Do you or your people think that this attack on our convoy in any way compromises our mission?'

Chet replied, 'I'm not hearing anything. But it's a good question.' He added, 'I think we need to move fast before somebody in Washington starts asking the same question.'

Right. As always, it came down to the age-old clash between the hawks and the doves – the ballsy and the ball-less – just like during the Cold War. The Pentagon, the State Department, the intelligence establishment, and the White House all had different agendas. The only people who had a clear agenda were the terrorists.

Kate asked, 'Why would anyone in Washington not want to go ahead with apprehending The Panther?'

'There are legal issues,' Chet replied, 'and diplomatic issues.'

Right. The Yemenis had this silly idea that their soil was sovereign. Plus there was Mommy and Daddy's lawsuit. Also, there was a chance we'd be kicked out of Yemen for using the Hellfires today. I asked Chet, 'How fast do we need to move?'

'Maybe tonight.' He added, 'It may not be safe here.'

When was it safe here?

We continued our walk along the beach, past a Marine patrol, and reached Elephant Rock, which jutted into the gulf.

There were about a dozen fishing boats moored or anchored in the shallows, and Chet waded into the water toward one of them, so I guess we were supposed to follow.

He pulled himself into an open twenty-foot wooden boat with an outboard engine, and Buck followed. Kate and I and Brenner glanced at one another, then climbed aboard.

Chet unfastened the mooring line, put a key in the ignition, set the throttle, and pulled on the starter cord. The engine caught, and off we went. But where were we going?

The only seat in the open boat was in the stern near the engine, and that's where Chet sat and steered. The rest of us sat on overturned white plastic buckets. The boat smelled fishy, and our bare feet were submerged in about four inches of nasty bilgewater.

Also, not to complain, but the sun was starting to burn my exposed skin, and I could see that Buck, Kate, and Brenner were getting a little lobsterish as well. A more immediate concern was that our guns and commo were back on the beach.

Chet Morgan, I concluded, was crazy. And we were following him. That didn't make us crazy; it made us stupid.

There were a few rocks sticking out of the water, and on one of the rocks stood a large black-and-white bird. As we got within fifty feet of the rock, Chet reached under his shirt into the small of his back, pulled a .40 caliber Glock, took aim, and popped off a round at the big bird. Kate, who hadn't seen Chet pull his gun, was startled; the rest of us were astonished, and Chet was annoyed because he missed. The bird flew away.

To make him feel better, I said, 'To be sure of hitting the target, shoot first and call whatever you hit the target.'

Chet ignored that and informed us, 'That was a masked booby.' He assured us, 'Not endangered.'

I remarked, 'And never will be with shooting like that.'

I thought Chet was going to shoot me, but he laughed – a real laugh, which almost made me think he wasn't nuts. He said, 'I'd never shoot a white-eyed gull. They're endangered. And they bring good luck.'

Whatever you say, Chet. Now put the gun away.

But he put it on the seat beside him. Well, at least one of us had a gun. Unfortunately, it was the crazy guy.

Chet glanced up at Elephant Rock, and I followed his gaze. The Yemeni Army guys in the pickup truck had swung their heavy machine gun toward us, and one of the soldiers was looking at us with binoculars.

Chet commented, 'They get jumpy when they hear gunfire.'

Me, too.

He said to us, 'If we have time, I'll take you shark fishing. I have good luck nearly every time I go out.' He smiled and said to me and Brenner, 'The sharks almost got lucky when you went out.' He laughed.

So, here we were on a small boat with an armed psychopath. How do I get myself in these situations? I need to check my contract.

I glanced at Brenner, who I knew was thinking what I was thinking. Kate, too, seemed a bit unsure about Mr Morgan, but she has a history of giving CIA nut jobs the benefit of the doubt. Up to a point. Then she shoots them. Well ... only one so far.

Buck had a dopey smile on his face, and I knew he had a lot of tolerance for screwy behavior as long as the screwball was a colleague and a peer. I mean, I had the feeling, based partly on their preppy accents, that Buck and Chet had gone to the same schools or similar schools and came from the same social stratum. Chet was the bad-boy frat brother who was always on double-secret probation, and everyone loved him as long as he didn't actually get anyone killed. Later in life, however, what had been funny and zany behavior progressed into something less entertaining.

Also, with these CIA guys, they all cultivated eccentric behavior, which became part of their self-created legend. They wanted their peers to tell stories about them and to spread the word of their unique flamboyance.

Kate's aforementioned pal, Ted Nash, was a good example of all this. Plus Ted was an arrogant prick. But now he was dead, and you shouldn't speak ill of the dead. Even if they were assholes. Which brought me to another thought: Did Chet Morgan know Ted Nash? Probably. But this wasn't the time to ask.

Anyway, Chet Morgan had set the stage for his entry into the show, and as they say in the theater world, if you show a gun in the first act, you need to use it in the final act.

We rounded the peninsula and Chet set a course for the middle of Aden Harbor. I knew where we were going.

We sailed into the setting sun for about ten minutes, then Chet killed the engine but didn't drop anchor, and the boat drifted out with the tide.

Chet said, 'This is where the Cole was moored.'

I informed him, 'I've been here.'

He nodded.

In fact, nearly everyone who worked this case had been taken out to this spot where seventeen American sailors had been murdered.

Chet lit another cigarette and stared into the blue water. He said, 'The USS Cole, a Navy destroyer, under the command of Commander Kirk Lippold, sailed into Aden Harbor for a routine refueling. The mooring was completed at nine-thirty A.M., and refueling started at ten-thirty.'

Everyone knew this, but this is the way you begin – at the beginning.

Chet continued, 'At around eleven-twenty, a small craft, like this one, with two men aboard – two suicide bombers – approached the port side of the destroyer. A minute or two later, the small craft exploded, putting a forty-by-forty-foot hole in the side of the armored hull.' He added, 'It's estimated that four to seven hundred pounds of TNT and RDX were used.' He asked rhetorically, 'Where the hell did they get that much high-grade explosive?'

The answer was, just about anywhere these days. The real question had to do with the two Al Qaeda guys who woke up that morning knowing they were going to die. They worked hard to load the boat with the explosives that were going to kill them, then sailed the boat into the sunny harbor. I sort of pictured them watching the gulls flying overhead, and I wondered what they said to each other or what they were thinking in the last few minutes of their lives.

'Asymmetric warfare,' Chet said. 'A small boat like this one, worth maybe a few hundred dollars, two guys who probably had no military training, and they crippled a billion-dollar, sixty-eight-hundred-ton state-of-the-art warship, built to take on any enemy warship in the world. Except the boat that attacked them.' He flipped his cigarette over the side and said, 'Fucking amazing. Fucking ridiculous.'

Fucking right.

'And how were they able to do this?' asked Chet, and answered his own question. 'Because the Navy's Rules of Engagement were rewritten by some committee of politically correct, ball-less wonders in the bowels of the Pentagon.'

Right. Worse yet, the *Cole*'s crew and commander actually followed the new Rules of Engagement. I wouldn't have. But I'm not military.

Chet informed us, 'For hundreds of years, naval rules called for challenging an approaching ship by voice or signal to identify itself. If the ship keeps coming, you sound the alarm for battle stations and fire a shot across its bow. And if it still keeps coming, you blow it the hell out of the water.' He reminded us, 'The Cole did none of that, even though this is known as a potentially hostile port. They let an unidentified ship come alongside, right here, and blow them up.' He added, 'Because internationally recognized rules of the sea had been changed, for no reason except political correctness.'

The only good news is that the Navy has re-evaluated its new, sensitive Rules of Engagement after seventeen sailors died on the *Cole*, and we've all re-evaluated the rules of war after 9/11. As for poor Commander Lippold, he was officially exonerated of any fault – he was just following stupid rules – but unofficially his career was finished and he was passed over for promotion and retired. I'll bet he wished he had that ten minutes to live over again.

Chet continued, 'To make this attack even more incomprehensible, Al Qaeda had tried the very same thing nine months earlier in January of 2000 as part of the millennium attack plots.' He reminded us, 'The USS The Sullivans, right here in Aden Harbor. A refueling stop, just like the Cole. A boat approached The Sullivans, but it was so overloaded with explosives that it sank before it reached the ship.'

Right. In my former business, that's a clue that somebody wants to kill you, and you know they'll try again. Same with the February 1993 truck bombing at the World Trade Center. A cop on the street can see the pattern, but the geniuses in Washington were whistling in the dark through the graveyard with their heads up their asses. Well, we all woke up after we lost three thousand people on 9/11. But that wasn't going to bring back the dead.

Chet continued, 'The enemy are not the brightest bulbs in the room, but they only have to get it right once. We have to get it right every time.'

Chet lit another cigarette and looked toward Aden. 'See that brown apartment building on the hill? Five Al Qaeda operatives were in there on the morning of the attack and they were supposed to get over to the Al-Tawahi clock tower and videotape the explosion.'

I looked at the clock tower, a tall Victorian structure built by the British over a hundred years ago. I'd been in the top of the tower, and from there you had a good view of the harbor. But the videotape guys never saw that view.

Chet continued, 'Unfortunately, the idiots were asleep in the apartment and missed the whole show.' He commented, 'Total fuckups. But even fuckups get lucky once in a while.'

I'd also been in that apartment, which had been sealed off as a crime scene when I was here and maybe it still was. Hard to believe that five jihadists had slept through the big moment. I mean, total assholes. They were probably sleeping off a big khat chew. But as Chet said, even fuckups get lucky, and the two guys in the boat got very lucky that day — if lucky is the right word for blowing yourself up — helped a bit by the Pentagon.

We were drifting with the outgoing tide and a small land breeze had come up and was pushing us farther out into the open gulf. Around us were a few dozen fishing boats, and like most men in Yemen, including fishermen, the guys on board were probably packing AK-47s. I mean, I wasn't concerned per se, but I don't like to get myself in exposed situations for no good reason. Chet, however, seemed unconcerned or unaware, so maybe he had some backup out here on the water. Or he was, as I suspected, crazy. Maybe arrogant, too.

Chet said to us, 'The place on the hull where the jihadists detonated the explosives was the ship's galley where crew members were lining up for lunch, which is why there were seventeen dead and thirty-nine injured.' He thought a moment and continued, 'So it would seem that Al Qaeda knew the location of the galley and knew it was the first lunch shift.'

I thought about that. A hundred or more crew members clustered in the galley for lunch. And right on the other side of the armored hull was a boat filled with maybe seven hundred pounds of explosives. The question was, Did Al Qaeda know — or did The Panther know — where and when to detonate those explosives? Or, like most of their successes, was it just dumb luck?

Chet concluded his briefing, 'The crew fought the flooding and had the damage under control by nightfall. Divers on board inspected the hull and reported that the keel was not damaged, so the billion-dollar ship was salvageable.' He continued, 'Because we have no military base in this part of the world, the Cole was on its own for a while. But there was a Royal Navy frigate in the area, the HMS Marlborough, that proceeded at top speed and provided medical and other assistance. Eleven of the most injured sailors were flown by medevac to the French military hospital in Djibouti for surgery before being flown to the US military hospital in Landstuhl, Germany. The rest of the injured – and the dead – were flown to Landstuhl.' He added, 'Fortunately, none of the thirty-nine injured died, but many are disabled for life.'

No one had anything to say, but then Chet surprised us by suggesting, 'Let's say a silent prayer for the dead and injured.' He bowed his head, so we all did the same and said a silent prayer.

I'm not good at this, but I did pray that the two suicide bombers were burning in hell with their dicks blown off and not getting any wine or sex in Paradise. Amen.

'Amen,' said Chet, then he started the engine and we headed back.

I looked at Chet Morgan, who was staring off into space with those glassy blue eyes. This guy was either very good at what he did, or very nuts. Maybe both. In any case, he needed close watching.

CHAPTER FORTY-NINE

C het opened the throttle, and we were making good time around the peninsula and back toward Elephant Rock.

There were a lot of big dorsal fins gliding around close to the boat, and if Kate and I had been alone now with Chet and his Glock, I might have been a little concerned. But then I remembered that we were here to be Panther bait, not shark bait.

Chet said to his captive audience, 'If you recall, we weren't certain that Al Qaeda was responsible for the Cole attack. This was pre-9/11 and Al Qaeda was only one of many terrorist groups that were causing us problems.'

Right. And Al Qaeda never claimed responsibility for the attack. But on the Arab street, the word was out that Al Qaeda was behind the *Cole* attack, and Al Qaeda recruitment went way up, just as it did after 9/11.

Chet continued, 'By August 2001, right before 9/11 — about the time Mr Corey was here — we identified Bulus ibn al-Darwish, al-Numair, The Panther, as one of the three main plotters. That's when a lot of this started to make sense.' He asked rhetorically, 'Who else could have thought of this, organized it, and executed it so perfectly? It had to be an American.' He reminded us, 'Most of these so-called jihadists are too stupid to even *think* of something like this, and too inept to pull it off.'

I partly agreed, but I said to him, 'Some of the top guys are very smart and very sophisticated.'

'True,' replied Chet, 'but I see a Western-educated head behind this attack. Not someone like bin Laden who's really a country bumpkin and a clueless fundamentalist and two-bit philosopher who has his head in the clouds when it's not up his ass.'

Interesting, and maybe true. At least the CIA thought so.

Chet continued, 'No, it was someone who understood us. Someone who had knowledge about our idiotic Rules of Engagement, and someone who may have had some knowledge of the Cole's layout and the time and date that the Cole would put into Aden Harbor, and the time of the refueling and the first lunch shift. Also someone who understood the psychological impact of an attack on an American warship that caused the death of so many American sailors.' He added, 'This bastard, Bulus ibn al-Darwish, has a big hate toward America and this attack was a manifestation of that hate – a humiliating kick in our balls.'

No argument there, and I'd add that Chet Morgan had a big hate, too. I guess we all did, but Chet seemed to be taking it more personally than most of us. I mean, we're not supposed to get into the hate game, which can screw up your judgment and your performance. You need to be cool, and most people in this business are cool to the point of cold-blooded. Hot is not cool.

But Chet had been here a long time, and he was probably frustrated and under pressure to get results. Plus he had more info than we did about The Panther, including the asshole's psychological profile. As sometimes happens in a long investigation, the case officer starts to obsess on the fugitive and begins to see him as the cause of all his problems. It's kind of complex, but I've been there. The other thing that struck me was that Chet, who had initially come across as a bit burned out, was now very animated, like a switch had been turned on. Or maybe the khat had kicked in. Or the hate.

Chet continued, 'This attack has not been fully avenged. But it will be. These bastards, including Mr al-Darwish, have to learn that there is a price to pay.'

'They know that,' Kate assured him, 'and they are ready to pay it.'

'And we're ready to make them keep paying.'

Chet was into revenge, which was good regarding terrorists, but maybe not so good regarding Ms. Mayfield whacking Chet's colleague. But that was another subject, and probably not on today's agenda.

I wasn't sure I had a good take on this guy, but I was certain that Buck knew about him, though Buck doesn't always share.

Chet had said he'd been here since the *Cole* was bombed, but I didn't remember him. On the other hand, the spooks were in and out, flying off to Sana'a, Djibouti, Oman, Qatar, Bahrain, and Saudi Arabia. And even when they were in the Sheraton in Aden, they were nearly invisible. Part of their mystique.

It must be a lonely job, and I often compared CIA officers to vampires who only hung out with other vampires and had no human friends. That's not nice. Maybe I have CIA envy.

Chet continued his history of the *Cole* incident and said, 'The first FBI agents sent to Yemen in response to the Cole attack worked in a very hostile environment. They were met at Aden Airport by Yemeni soldiers pointing AK-47s at them when they got off the plane.' He confided to us, 'I was with the FBI that day, and I can tell you, we thought we were going to get into a firefight right there on the tarmac.' He added, 'Assholes.'

So, another ugly American who didn't like the Yemenis. How are we going to win this war on terrorism if we don't win the hearts, minds, and confidence of our Islamic allies? Right? I mean, true, they were assholes. But they were *our* assholes.

Also, I was sure that Chet had been very frightened that day when he was threatened by Yemeni Army guys with lots of firepower. And when you let something or someone frighten you, you get very angry later. And you want to redeem your manhood – by killing someone. Same as on the mean streets of New York. Maybe that's what some of this was about.

Chet continued, 'Speakers in the Yemeni Parliament were calling for jihad against America, like it was *us* who did something wrong, and this was broadcast live on radio and TV every day.' He added, 'Most of the Americans here – tourists, oil workers, and businesspeople – left the country quickly.'

Buck informed us, 'The embassy was in lockdown and we sent all non-essential staff to Oman or Riyadh.'

Chet nodded, then went on, 'The Yemeni government was sending us mixed signals. They said it was okay to bring our people in, but when we got here, we were threatened.'

Buck explained, 'There was a lot of confusion and panic within the government.'

Ours or theirs?

Chet then related another scary story, one I'd heard when I was here. 'The American response team was given the two floors of the Sheraton, but one night the hotel was surrounded by a few hundred men wearing traditional dress, though they had military jeeps and were armed with military weapons, so we knew they were Yemeni soldiers and maybe PSO men in disguise.' He stayed silent a moment, undoubtedly recalling that night, then said, 'We organized defensive positions on the roof and on the ground floor, and we wouldn't let any of the Arab guests leave the hotel.' He added, 'There were still a few Western tourists in the hotel, and they were afraid to leave, so we gave them handguns for self-defense.' He let us know, 'We all thought we were going to die that night ... The officer in charge of the Marine unit issued a single order — "Take a few of them with you".'

Right. No surrender. No American hostages. And when I was here in the Sheraton, that order still stood. *Take a few of them with you.*

No one spoke for a while and the boat continued on toward the Sheraton beach. I looked at Kate, who appeared to have acquired a new appreciation of the situation here, and maybe a new appreciation of her husband who'd spent a month in this dangerous place. It wasn't all beach volleyball, sweetheart.

To Buck and Brenner, Chet's stories were nothing new, but it probably reinforced their resolve to get the job done and get the hell out of here. There comes a time in every hazardous tour of duty when you realize you've used up your quota of luck. Buck, Brenner, and Chet were past that time, but the goal was finally in sight; just a few hundred kilometers from here, in Marib.

Chet continued, 'By dawn, all these assholes surrounding the hotel had disappeared. But we were ordered to get out of the hotel, and we were ferried by boat to US naval vessels in the harbor. Two days later, the Yemeni government said it was safe to return to the Sheraton, so we took Navy helicopters back to the beach. But on the way in, the helicopters got radar lock-ons from SA-7 ground-to-air missiles, the pilots had to drop down to sea level, and we came in over the water ready for a shoot-out.' He looked out at the water and the approaching beach as though this scene brought back that memory, and continued, 'But there weren't any hostile forces on the beach — I think the Yemeni military probably thought we'd turn around when the choppers got the missile lock-ons, and when we kept coming they beat it out of there. So we retook our two shitty floors in the Sheraton and we've been there ever since.'

Right. And Mr Chet Morgan, a privileged child of a superpower country, had had a lot of time since then to reflect on the poor reception he'd received in Yemen. He came here to help — well, not really, but officially — and the Yemenis treated him like a piece of crap, and threatened to kill him, and he wasn't leaving here until he evened the score. Of course by now he was nuts, so even M-16 therapy wasn't going to make him a happy man — but it would help.

Chet wrapped up his background briefing. 'The weeks after the Cole was bombed had a surreal quality to them ... maybe more like slapstick comedy with the Yemeni government and military running off in different directions like the clowns they are, saying, "Welcome Americans", then "Yankee go home".' He concluded, 'Totally dysfunctional country.'

Dysfunctional, as Betsy Collins said, would be an improvement.

We were about a hundred meters from the beach now, and Chet backed off on the throttle as he steered around some sandbars toward the shallows near Elephant Rock.

There were a lot of gulls on the rocks, but Chet left them alone, and instead he flipped the bird at the Yemeni Army guys manning the machine gun. Chet needs some anger management classes.

As he maneuvered the boat, he said, 'In the old days of gunboat diplomacy, if some pisspot country attacked Westerners, a naval fleet would assemble and bombard the port city until it burned to the ground. Now ... well, the primitive little assholes of the world get away with too much. But there will be a day of reckoning.' Chet thought a moment, then said, 'In fact, every day since 9/11 has been a day of reckoning.' He nodded to himself and added, 'And for Mr Bulus ibn al-Darwish, a traitor to his country and a mass murderer, his day is close at hand.'

I hoped so. What I knew for sure was that there would, indeed, be a day of reckoning here in Yemen, but I wasn't sure who would be reckoned with.

CHAPTER FIFTY

The cocktail hour had arrived, and Kate and I joined our colleagues in the hotel bar. Chet Morgan did not make an appearance, but he had asked us to meet him in the SCIF at 10 P.M. to discuss the operational plan.

Chet had stayed with his boat after dropping us off in four feet of water, and we had returned to the hotel pool where Howard and Clare were watching our things and apparently getting to know each other better.

Howard and Clare knew not to ask us about our new friend on the beach, but Clare did say she was worried when we were gone so long. Clare really cares about me.

Kate and I had gone back to our room to shower and dress for dinner and/or a trip to Marib later that night, as per Chet. Once things start to roll, they roll fast, and you have to keep one step ahead of the terrorists and two steps ahead of Washington.

Kate and I discussed Mr Chet Morgan of the Central Intelligence Agency, and I confided to her my suspicion that Chet was a chewer. She thought about that, but wasn't sure, so I dropped it.

I didn't share with Kate my other thoughts about Chet in regard to his nuttiness or what was driving him, but I did say, 'He seems a bit intense. When he's not spacey.'

Kate replied, 'You have a built-in prejudice against the Agency.' Me?

Anyway, Kate was reserving judgment on Chet. Unfortunately, we needed to make a quick decision about going up to Marib with this loon to find The Panther.

I also broached the delicate subject of her complicated relationship with Ted Nash and said, 'I think we should ask Chet if he knew Ted, and how he's feeling about your last encounter with the deceased.' How's that for subtle?

Kate didn't reply for a few seconds, then said, 'I'll take care of that.'

Actually I would take care of that, but I said, 'Okay.'

Well, we were now down at the bar for drinks with our colleagues, including our DSS guys from Sana'a and most of the Aden team, except for the twenty Marines, who were on guard duty.

Unfortunately, because of the high alert, and our possible trip into Indian Territory tonight, alcohol was still off the menu. The bartender was whipping up fruit drinks in the blender, and I had a mango slushie. It sucked.

But the conversation was good, and we talked about home, family, and everything but the war on terrorism, and no one mentioned the forty Al Qaeda guys heading our way. I noticed, though, that everyone was wearing Kevlar vests and sidearms and had automatic rifles with them, which is not SOP in the bar. The bartender, waiters, and the civilian clientele noticed, too, and they were looking a bit concerned. I wondered which one of them had a suicide belt. Maybe the fat Saudi guy in robes sitting by himself drinking scotch. This was a lot more exciting than Ecco's.

At 8 P.M., Captain Mac, thinking maybe we'd pushed our luck a bit, and that we needed to get serious about security, asked all American personnel to leave the bar and return to their rooms or their posts.

A few of us, however, had a dinner meeting scheduled, and we went out to the back patio where the grill was blazing.

We sat at a round table — me, Kate, Buck, Brenner, Betsy Collins, Doug Reynolds, Lyle Manning, and Captain Mac.

It was still hot, but the sky was clear and the stars were out, and a half moon was rising in the east. Out on the water I could see the lights of big cargo ships and oil tankers. A few Western tourists were cavorting in the pool, and the really dumb ones were strolling on the beach, probably wearing T-shirts that said, 'Kidnap Me.' This place was a headline waiting to happen.

The barbecue was good, as I recalled from last time, though I passed on the goat kebobs. We all drank non-alcoholic beer and chatted about how wonderful it was to be living the dream and working for the government — foreign travel, great pay, appreciative bosses in Washington, and a chance to make a difference by killing some assholes who wanted to die anyway.

We got around to security concerns, and Doug Reynolds told us he'd sent a message to Washington requesting a standby ship in the harbor for possible evacuation, and an unmarked charter aircraft – meaning CIA – at Aden Airport. So far, he said, no response. It occurred to me that Washington might be looking for an excuse to land a thousand Marines on the beach.

Captain Mac, who preferred a fight instead of a flight, said, 'I can't kill them if I'm not here.'

Right. You stay here. Good balls, though.

Buck announced, 'We may be leaving tonight.'

No one, of course, asked where we were going, but everyone wished us good luck.

I said, 'And good luck here.' And don't pay for the rooms if you have to check out under fire.

Captain Mac assured me, 'We don't need luck. We've got twenty Marines.'

No one asked us how we were getting to wherever it was we were going, but Betsy Collins did say, 'Travel at night is risky.'

Buck informed her, 'We're flying.'

Really? How did he know that?

It was understood that this was probably a CIA operation, so no one had any further comments or advice. But I sensed that the Aden team might open up if asked a direct question, so I asked directly, 'What do you think of Chet Morgan?'

Silence.

Okay, so that answered that question. I said, 'For the record, I think he's been in the sun too long.'

Buck interjected, 'John, we don't need to—'

I continued, 'We could be going up to Marib with him tonight – I guess by plane – and I'm concerned that Mr Morgan may be suffering from in-country stress and fatigue.'

No one argued with that, but they'd have to report my statement in the event some of us didn't return from Marib alive.

The dinner and the conversation seemed to be finished, and Buck said, 'If you'll excuse us, we have a meeting in the SCIF.'

Buck stood and we all stood and did handshakes, goodbyes, and good luck.

Lyle Manning, who didn't seem to like me, surprised me by saying, 'You've made a good evaluation of the situation.'

This was one time I wouldn't have minded being wrong.

So we went into the hotel, and Kate, Brenner, Buck, and I rode the elevator up to the fourth floor. On the way up, Buck said to me, 'You have permission to leave anytime, but you do not have permission to discuss this operation with anyone at any time.'

'The subject, Buck, was Chet Morgan.'

Buck assured me, 'I've known Chet for three years. He's a good man.'

'Right. I could tell by what everyone said about him.'

Kate interjected, 'John, let's discuss this after our meeting with him.'

Brenner said, 'I'm more interested in the plan than in Chet Morgan.'

Well, you're wrong. The reason the best-laid plans of mice and men often go astray is not the plan; it's the mice and men. And Chet was about ten rials short of a Happy Meal. But to be a team player, I said, 'Fair enough.'

We got off the elevator, greeted the Marine guard, and walked down the corridor to the Sensitive Compartmented Information Facility.

Bottom line here, The Panther was only one of my problems.

My teammates were another. But hopefully the plan wasn't as crazy as Chet.

CHAPTER FIFTY-ONE

B uck had a key for the locked door and we entered.

A black tent filled most of the emptied guest room, and we ducked inside through a flap. The dim interior of the SCIF tent was about fifteen feet by twenty, crammed with electronic equipment, desks, and file cabinets, lit only by a few desk lamps and the glow from the computer screens.

Sitting at the shortwave radio was a young man in a T-shirt and shorts, wearing headphones. He noticed us and said, 'Chet's on the balcony.'

Good. I hope he jumped. But probably he was smoking; a slower form of suicide.

We left the tent and went around to the balcony, where, sure enough, Chet stood at the rail with a butt in his mouth, contemplating the moonlit sea. He was still wearing his white ducks and silly Hawaiian shirt, and he was still barefoot. Time for home leave, Chet.

Without turning around, he said to us, 'Yemen was known to the Romans as Arabia Felix – Happy Arabia.' He added, 'No one has called it that since then.'

Right. Now it's called Shithole.

Chet continued, 'If Afghanistan is the graveyard of empires, then Yemen is the slaughterhouse of imperial ambitions.'

God save me from a nutcase with an Ivy League education. Right?

Chet informed us, 'Alexander the Great sent a colony of Greeks to Socotra, an island off the coast here, but it didn't last long, and the Romans invaded from the north and got as far as Marib before their army was decimated by battle, hardship, and disease.'

Marib? Isn't that where we're going? Don't forget the Cipro.

Chet continued, 'Yemen has seen a succession of conquerors and would-be conquerors — Egyptians, Persians, Romans, Ethiopians, Turks, the British, and the recently departed Russians. But no one has ever controlled all of Yemen. Not even the Yemenis.' Chet concluded, 'I wouldn't want to see us in a land war here, which is why these surgical operations need to succeed.'

I suggested, 'Nuke 'em.'

Chet assured me, 'I have no problem with that.'

Maybe he really wasn't crazy after all. I mean, he agreed with me. And I'm not crazy. Right?

Anyway, Chet dropped his cigarette into a pail of water that had been put there for that purpose — and maybe as a khat spittoon — and he turned toward us.

The light was bad, so it was hard for me to tell if he had been chewing, or where he was in the rising and falling arc of a khat trip. But if I had to guess, I'd say he was on the upgrade of the roller coaster, about twenty feet from the top. Coming down is a bitch.

Chet said, 'I'm sorry I couldn't join you tonight, but I heard you had an interesting conversation at dinner.' He looked at me.

Well, first off, you weren't invited, and second, I guess someone told him I'd commented on his mental health. But I didn't think that Betsy, Doug, Lyle, or Captain Mac would give Chet Morgan a call about that. And Buck didn't have the opportunity to speak to Chet. Probably Chet just assumed, from past experience, that someone called him a nut job, and he further assumed it was me. Good deduction, Chet. Or ... he had a directional listening device and he heard us down on the patio. That's really not nice. But I guess that's why they're called spies.

Anyway, Chet led the way into the tent.

There was a small map table in the corner, and Chet invited us to sit.

As my eyes adjusted to the dim light, I saw taped to a wall the official photo of President Ali Abdullah Saleh, but this one was captioned *Asshole of Arabia*. Funny.

I also noticed a few steel-cut axes, burn boxes, and paper shredders, all necessary office equipment in a sensitive facility that was located in hostile territory. I pictured Chet high on khat, swinging an ax at the computers, and someone shouting to him, 'I said there were *tourists* in the hallway – not terrorists.' Whoops.

Anyway, the young man at the radio couldn't hear us with his headphones on, and Chet said, 'There are no recording devices activated for this discussion.' He added, 'Operation Clean Sweep is top secret, of course, and you will never divulge or reveal what was said here, or what happens here.'

Right. Just like a bachelor party in Vegas. What annoys me is that the CIA thinks they have to re-pledge you to secrecy. Like no one but them gets the concept of keeping your mouth shut.

Bottom line, the CIA doesn't like joint operations, and they see them as babysitting jobs. On the plus side, if something went wrong, they had someone else to blame.

To get something straight, I asked Chet, 'Who is running this operation?'

Chet replied, 'Buck is the team leader.'

'I mean, who in Washington is running this? Who do *you* report to?'

'You don't want to know.'

Then why did I ask? But obviously this was a CIA operation, directed from the highest level. If it was FBI, they'd make everyone wear blue windbreakers with big white letters that said 'FBI.' They like to advertise. The CIA does not.

I asked Chet, 'What is your job on this team?'

He reminded us, 'I have operational control of the Predators.'

'Right. So we're going to vaporize this guy?'

He also reminded us, 'Predators are used primarily for aerial observation.'

Then why are they called Predators? Why not Doves with good eyesight?

Chet added, 'I'll get to the goal of this mission later.'

You usually start with the goal, then outline the plan. But Black Ops jobs were a little different, mostly because the goal — like whacking someone — was not always legal and therefore not spelled out; it was understood.

Chet began, 'First, our intelligence sources — human and electronic — put The Panther in the vicinity of Marib.'

Brenner informed him, 'This is what John and I heard from the prisoner in Ghumdan.'

'Right.'

I added, 'And your colleagues in Sana'a also questioned the prisoner — or you did.'

No reply.

I asked, 'Do you have a transcript of that interrogation?'

'Not yet.' He added, 'Translation problems.' He inquired, 'May I move on?'

'Sure.'

He continued, 'Second, I have to tell you that we'll be leaving here about midnight and flying to Marib, and we may not be coming back.'

Brenner asked, 'Can you phrase that a bit differently?'

Chet actually smiled, then clarified, 'If the mission is a success, we will not return here.' He advised us, 'Pack only what you absolutely need, and leave everything else in your rooms, to be forwarded on.'

To *where*? Next of kin?

Brenner inquired, 'And if the mission is not a success?'

'Then we may return here to continue the operation.' He added, 'Unless we're dead.'

Got it.

I informed Chet, 'Just to let you know, Kate and I need to hear and approve of the operational plan before we go anywhere. That was the deal.'

Chet didn't seem to know there was a deal and said, 'I think you've passed the point of no return on that, Mr Corey.'

Buck interjected, 'John and Kate have volunteered to be bait, so they can suggest some changes to the plan as it relates to their roles.' He then said to Kate and me, 'But I must tell you, this may be our only chance to apprehend The Panther before he disappears again.'

Kate replied, 'We understand that.'

Chet continued, 'We are flying out of Aden Airport on a DHC-6 Twin Otter.' He explained, 'This is a two-engine short takeoff and landing plane, with reinforced fixed landing gear, capable of putting down on a road, which we will do.'

Say again?

He also informed us, 'The Otter is registered in Kuwait as a regional charter craft, but it will be flown by two American pilots.'

Thank God. The Otter, of course, was actually owned by a CIA front company, and the pilots were CIA employees, though both those facts would be difficult for anyone to prove. The Company has excellent air resources all over the world, known in the trade as Spook Air. If anyone was ever able to count all the aircraft owned by the CIA, Spook Air would probably be bigger than American Airlines.

'Flight time,' said Chet, 'will be under three hours.'

On that subject, Spook Air could have gotten us safely from Sana'a to Aden in under three hours without an ambush. But some idiot had decided to see what Al Qaeda knew, and what they could do. And also to see what the Hellfire missiles could do to Al Qaeda. I don't remember volunteering for that, but if we'd blown up The Panther, I'd be patting Chet on the back now and getting ready to fly to New York instead of Marib.

Brenner asked, 'Will there be a pathfinder on the ground?' Meaning a guy with a flashlight or at least a cigarette lighter.

Chet replied, 'Yes, a trusted local.'

Brenner informed him, 'No such thing.' He flashed back to

some jungle clearing in Southeast Asia and said, 'It has to be an American.'

'That's not possible here.' Chet assured Brenner and the rest of us, 'We've used this man before. He is well paid.' Chet added, 'And he has family in the States whom he'd like to see again.'

Me, too. Well ... not my in-laws.

Chet continued, 'This man, who is code-named Tariq – which means "night visitor" – has a hand-held radio that will work on the frequency that the Twin Otter will monitor.' He said, 'To mark the runway portion of the road, Tariq has a backpack full of small, self-contained electronic transponders that he'll place as instructed along the road, and also at the beginning and end of the runway portion of the road to mark the thresholds.' He further explained, 'The pilots will be able to see the signals from these transponders on the GPS flight panel display in the cockpit.' Chet assured us, 'Tariq has done this dozens of times and so have the pilots.'

'And you?'

'Many times.' Chet continued, 'All the transponders will be turned on when Tariq sets them on the road, but just before our arrival, Tariq will consider wind conditions and other factors, then turn off the threshold transponders at one end of the runway – the end he doesn't want us to approach from. The pilots will now know the direction of their landing, but more importantly, if all the transponders are still on at both ends of the road – or if none of them are on – that would mean that Tariq, for some reason, is out of action.'

'Or sleeping like those schmucks who were supposed to video-tape the Cole explosion.'

Chet forced a polite smile and continued, 'That will be our first indication that we need to pull up and keep going.' He went on, 'If the transponders are all set properly, then the pilot will ask Tariq by radio a single question — "Any dust?" Tariq will say "Yes" if there are unfriendlies in the area, or if he has a gun pressed to his head. If Tariq says, "No dust tonight," then it's all clear. And he will double verify that he is not under duress by also saying "Safe landing" as we approach the runway.' Chet added, unnecessarily, 'If he doesn't say those words, or if the threshold transponders are not properly set, then we fly directly back to Aden.'

I saw this in a World War II movie once, but the pathfinder got captured by the Nazis, who tortured him and made him give them the sign and countersign for all clear. Everyone on the incoming aircraft was captured or killed. War is hell.

Buck told us, 'I've made a few night landings around the country under similar circumstances, and it's always gone well.'

Obviously, or you wouldn't be here to say that.

Chet added, 'Al Qaeda is too stupid to have identified Tariq as working for us, but even if they did, they're too stupid to follow him, and too stupid to turn him around. They'd just kill him.' He added, 'They're not Germans.'

He must have seen that movie. But Al Qaeda was not *that* stupid.

Chet also assured us, 'Predators will be watching our approach and landing.'

Kate said, 'I'm okay with this. Let's move on.'

Chet continued, 'After we land, we will be met by a local sheik. Sheik Musa.' He explained, 'No operation in the tribal lands can succeed without the cooperation and armed security of at least one local sheik. Musa's tribesmen will take us by car to a remote safe house and his men will provide security for us.'

Really? What are you chewing, Chet? I mean, letting Tariq in on this was risky enough – but letting a whole tribe of crazy Bedouin in on it was suicidal.

No one had anything positive to say about the travel arrangements, and I sensed that Chet was losing the confidence of the team. Chet understood that, too, and continued matter-of-factly, 'Sheik Musa has provided us with assistance in the past, and he is well compensated for his help.'

Silence.

So Chet further informed us, 'Musa's tribal lands encompass the ancient ruins of Marib, and he provides security and protection to tour groups, scholars, archaeologists, and others who visit the ruins. This is a very lucrative arrangement for him,' he assured us, 'and on that basis alone he can be trusted to do what he's paid to do and what's best for him, which is to keep the peace.'

I guess. Money talks. But didn't I just hear that nine Belgian tourists disappeared at the Marib ruins? And weren't their guide and driver found with their throats cut? Maybe that was another Marib.

I waited for Chet to mention this, but he went on, 'Sheik Musa is not happy with Al Qaeda, most of whom are not Yemenis and not royalists as he is—'

'Excuse me,' I interrupted. 'I seem to remember that nine Belgian tourists went missing at the Marib ruins last summer.'

Chet looked at me and I could see his icy blue eyes narrowing in the dim light. Finally, he said, 'I was about to get to that.'

'Sorry. I thought you forgot about that.'

He informed us, 'No one knows who was involved in that incident, but it certainly wasn't Sheik Musa.'

'Right. But Sheik Musa, protector of Western tourists and scholars, fell down on the job. No?'

I could see that Chet was annoyed, Kate was concerned, and Brenner, who had to know about this incident, was quiet.

Buck, who'd forgotten to mention this to me and Kate, explained, 'Sheik Musa took full responsibility for his failure to protect these tourists, and he's provided Yemeni and Western authorities with some leads.' He added, 'The sheik was embarrassed and angry, and he has vowed to avenge this insult to his honor and his reputation.' Reminding me and Kate of his classroom lecture, Buck said, 'When a Yemeni extends his hospitality, and someone else violates that hospitality, that violator becomes the subject of a blood feud.'

Chet added, 'And for that reason, Sheik Musa can be trusted.'

Right. Lots of reasons to trust Sheik Musa. And for all I know, he's looking for a visa to open a deli in Brooklyn. Still, I had some doubts. Also, it seemed to me that Buck, who had denied detailed knowledge of the operational plan, knew more than he'd let on. But I already knew that.

Chet said, 'Al Qaeda are the primary suspects in this incident, but it could also have been a tribal kidnapping that went badly.' He added, 'Not Musa's tribe, obviously.'

I informed Chet, 'The Belgian authorities were told by a captured Al Qaeda operative in Brussels that it *was* Al Qaeda, and that the Belgians are probably dead.'

Chet wanted to ask me where I got my information, but he

didn't. He said, 'Point is, Sheik Musa works for us. Not Al Qaeda, and not the Yemeni government.'

Buck also informed us, 'The sheik owes his loyalty to the Saudi royal family, who have him on retainer.' He further advised us, 'A Saudi prince has had a letter delivered to Sheik Musa, a copy of which I have, asking him to provide us with hospitality, safe passage, and any assistance we may need.' Buck let us know, 'That letter to the sheik from the Saudi prince is worth more than all the gold, money, or weapons we could give him.'

I inquired, 'Is there anyone you forgot to tell that we're going to Marib?'

Buck did not reply, but Chet said, 'We have no choice but to reach out to people who are ... situational allies.'

I asked, 'Do our Yemeni government allies know we are going to Marib?'

Chet replied, 'Not from me.'

'Can they guess?'

'Maybe.'

I thought of Colonel Hakim, but I didn't ask.

Chet inquired, 'Can we move on?'

Everyone nodded and Chet continued, 'Sheik Musa will have two SUVs at the safe house for us to use. We will stay in the safe house overnight, then at about one or two P.M. we'll drive to Marib town, as though we've just arrived from Sana'a, and we'll check into the Bilqis Hotel where we have reservations under our own names. Then we drive to the ruins, to see and be seen. We're trying to pass as tourists, but virtually no one will believe that. The word will be out that we're on an Al Qaeda hunt – a Panther hunt.' He continued, 'Sheik Musa will provide protection for this trip, though it's only about ten kilometers between the safe house, the town, and the ruins. At the ruins, there may also be National Security police for protection.'

Brenner said, 'I hope we're not there on the day they're working for Al Qaeda.'

Funny. Unless you were going there.

Brenner inquired, 'Can we carry our M4s at the ruins?'

'No,' replied Chet. 'As I said, we're going as tourists.'

I thought tourists carried automatic rifles in Yemen. If they didn't, they should. There'd be fewer dead tourists and more dead terrorists.

Chet assured us, however, 'We will wear Kevlar and carry our handguns, concealed.'

Brenner asked, 'How about Zamo?'

'He will stay with our vehicles close to the ruins with his sniper rifle. Also, our M4s will be in the vehicles.'

Brenner didn't seem keen on this, but he said nothing.

I really wanted to ask if Dr Clare was going with us, but Kate might misconstrue my question. Maybe I should cough, then ask.

As if reading my mind, Kate asked, 'Is Dr Nolan coming with us?'

'No,' replied Chet.

Why not?

Chet told us, 'It's too dangerous.'

That's why we need a doctor, Chet.

Well, no one had anything to say about that, but Chet's statement certainly put things into perspective.

I said, 'I hope we're taking Howard along to advise us if we're doing anything illegal.'

Chet replied, 'If this was an FBI operation, we'd need six lawyers.'

Touché.

Chet continued, 'On our way back from the ruins to the Bilqis Hotel, about dusk, our two vehicles will be stopped by tribesmen in vehicles, and we will offer no resistance as we're kidnapped.'

Huh?

Chet continued, 'We will be taken back to the safe house to await developments.'

Developments? Like what? Having our throats cut?

But Buck assured us, 'It's all a sham, of course. The kidnappers are Sheik Musa's men. We'll have our weapons, and we'll be under the watchful eye of Predator drones armed with Hellfire missiles.'

Great. And who controls the Predators? Chet. And he's been kidnapped.

Chet clarified that and said, 'At the safe house is a van, which is a mobile Predator ground monitoring station, so I won't actually be with you when you check into the Bilqis Hotel, or at the Marib ruins, or when you're kidnapped. I'll be at the safe house, watching the live camera feeds from the drone that is watching you, and the other drone that is watching the safe house.' He added assuringly, 'If something happened to me, or to the ground monitoring station at the safe house, then the Predators will pass under the control of the distant ground control station where the pilots maintain satellite radio control of the drones.' He added, 'They will, if necessary, use the Hellfires.' He asked us, 'Understand? Any questions?'

Lots of questions, but Chet was on a roll so we shook our heads.

Chet continued, 'Once we're all assembled back at the safe house, ostensibly as the kidnapped guests of Sheik Musa, the sheik will get the word to the Al Qaeda operatives in the area that the sheik has a present for them — a team of American intelligence operatives, including Mr John Corey and Ms. Kate Mayfield, both of whom work for the Anti-Terrorist Task Force, and who are both on Al Qaeda's kill list.' He added, 'Buckminster Harris is also known to Al Qaeda, and they would like to question him. Mr Brenner, I'm sorry to say, is not that important to them, though they'd like to question and kill him as well. And your sniper, Zamo, would make a nice trophy, and they'd like to have his sniper rifle.' He paused, smiled, then said, 'As for me, Al Qaeda has never killed a CIA officer, so cutting my head off will make them look good.'

And it might make the rest of us feel good. Sorry. That was not nice. Actually, I was developing some real respect for Chet Morgan. He had balls. He was also crazy, and probably a liar. But very cool, very smart, and apparently fearless.

Chet added, however, 'Since I won't be with you when you all check into the Bilqis Hotel, or go to the ruins and get kidnapped, then I'm not known to be in Marib, and I won't be offered to Al Qaeda.' He further explained, 'Al Qaeda in Yemen equates CIA officers with Predators and Hellfire missiles, and we don't want to put that into their heads.'

Right. That's why they're called spooks. They're there, but no one can see them. But I was okay with this, and Kate and Brenner seemed to be, too. Buck, of course, already knew this plan.

Regarding the plan, I had a few problems with it, and I asked, 'Why would The Panther or Al Qaeda think that Sheik Musa would kidnap Americans if he's paid to protect Westerners and if he wants Marib to remain a must-see tourist destination?'

'Good question,' replied Chet. He explained, 'The sheik has promised Al Qaeda that his tribal lands will be neutral. Tourists and scholars are welcome, but American intelligence operatives are not. They — we — are fair game.'

'Okay. Sounds plausible. But why would Sheik Musa go to Al Qaeda with the six — sorry, five — kidnapped Americans if the sheik is not on good terms with Al Qaeda?'

Chet nodded as though he expected the question and replied, 'Money.' He expanded on that. 'Al Qaeda believes they have established an accommodation with Sheik Musa, based on money.' He informed us, 'Al Qaeda and the sheik negotiated a deal for Al Qaeda to set up their training camp in one of the sheik's Bedouin camps, so while Al Qaeda doesn't trust Sheik Musa, they think he can be bought.'

I pointed out, 'Sounds like he *was* bought.'

Chet shook his head and explained to me patiently, 'That was our idea, Mr Corey. Now we know where the training camp is.'

Right. Clever. If true. I asked, 'Why don't we take out the camp?'

'It's better to watch it.' Chet also let us know, 'It appears from Predator observation and from local sources that The Panther never goes to the camp, but if he did, and if we could establish that, we'd have put a Hellfire up his ass a long time ago.'

'Got it.'

'As part of Musa's neutrality deal with Al Qaeda,' Chet continued, 'Al Qaeda is not allowed to carry out any armed operations within Sheik Musa's tribal territory. But when Al Qaeda kidnapped – and murdered – the Belgians, and made it look like a tribal kidnapping, Musa told Al Qaeda he was pissed off. Al Qaeda denied any involvement in the disappearance of the Belgians, but they gave Musa some money and weapons and smoothed it over. But Musa didn't believe them, so when he got word of the planned Al Qaeda attack on the Hunt Oil installation, he tipped us off – for ten thousand dollars – and we sent observation drones into the area and relayed the info to the Hunt security forces, who, as you know, were ready for the attack. But Al Qaeda can never be sure who, if anyone, ratted them out – though Sheik Musa told Al Qaeda he was looking into it.'

It was hard to follow the lies and the liars without a scorecard. In the world I lived in, a lie was a deal-breaker – or got you some jail time. In this world, getting caught in a lie meant you needed a bigger and better lie, or at least a nice gift for the guy who caught you in a lie.

Chet said to me, 'So to answer your question, Al Qaeda believes that Sheik Musa will make a deal with them, when it is in the sheik's best interest to do so.' He also added, 'The sheik has not canceled the lease on the Al Qaeda training camp – at our request – and Al Qaeda sees that as a positive sign that the sheik is in business to make money.' On that subject, he informed us, 'For five kidnapped American intelligence operatives, Al Qaeda will pay the sheik ... maybe a hundred thousand dollars.'

'Each?' I inquired.

'No. Together.' He smiled. 'Don't overestimate your worth.'

Right. Life here is cheap.

Chet also told us, 'The National Security police were paid

about four hundred dollars to do a disappearing act on the Belgians.'

Very cheap.

So, to recap, Sheik Musa was a double-dealing, double-crossing rat fink who was collecting bribes, rent, and retainers all over the place. He'd make a good New York City landlord. And was I supposed to believe that the Al Qaeda attack on the Belgian tourists was a complete surprise to him? Chet believed that. Or said he did. Buck, too. Sheik Musa's stated goal to make his tribal lands the Switzerland of Yemen – or Arabia Felix – seemed to have some inconsistencies and problems of the sheik's own making. But this was the Mideast, where nothing made any sense.

Chet, who could guess what I and everyone was thinking, said, 'In the end, Sheik Musa knows that he's staying alive only as long as we don't let the Hellfires loose on him. He can play a lucrative double game now and then, but we control the endgame.' He looked at us and said, 'Hellfire missiles. The deus ex machina of this war. God shooting thunderbolts out of the sky. If you fuck with God, you're dead.'

Okay. A little Latin is very convincing. But Chet wouldn't be the first Westerner who was hustled by the East.

I spent twenty years as a cop dealing with snitches, rat finks, stoolpigeons, and scam artists. And I always made sure they understood that if they double-crossed me, they'd be dead. Or wish they were. When you're dealing with people who have no moral center, no loyalty to anyone but themselves, you don't always get the logical results you expect, or the truth that you paid for.

And on that subject, I wondered about Chet's moral center and his devotion to the truth. Yemen was indeed the land of lies, a place where bullshit was a commodity and deception was the norm. In that respect, Yemeni culture and the CIA culture were not too far apart, despite the CIA's motto that the truth will set you free. And Chet, I suspected, had himself been corrupted by this culture of lying, and he thought he was better at it than the Yemenis, who he thought were stupid. I don't know if they're stupid, but I know they're cunning. That's how they've survived for three thousand years. And they'll be here long after we're gone, which could be soon.

'Mr Corey?'

I looked at Chet.

'Don't overthink this.'

I didn't reply.

Chet continued, 'Musa will invite three or four Al Qaeda representatives to come to the safe house, under guard and, of course, blindfolded, to view the kidnapped Americans and to verify who they are.' He reminded us, 'Bring your passports. Then Musa will insist, as a matter of honor, respect, and trust, that The Panther himself negotiate the deal to buy the five Americans. Both sides will be allowed a fixed number of armed men, which the sheik will suggest should be ten or twelve, and that meeting will take place outside a goat herder's hut a few kilometers from the safe house. The sheik assures us that he knows what The Panther looks like, and to be doubly sure, we've shown him photos of Bulus ibn al-Darwish, with and without a beard.'

Buck, who as I said knew a thing or two about this plan and this place, informed us, 'This type of meeting between equal warlords is traditional in this culture, and a certain amount of good faith is expected on both sides. Nevertheless, both sides are armed, to ensure good behavior, but also to ensure that a third party does not take advantage of the meeting of the important leaders.' He added, 'It's a very medieval protocol, but in this case, the third party, the Americans, are not waiting in ambush behind rocks. We're watching from five thousand feet, and we can put a missile into The Panther's teacup.'

Chet said, 'If this meeting is to take place, I will call in two more Predators to be on station.' Chet also assured us, 'You will not actually be inside the goat herder's hut, of course. That's too close to what's going to happen. You'll still be in the safe house where I'll be in the Predator control van, talking to the four Predator pilots and watching what's going on at the hut, and what's going on around the safe house.' Chet continued, 'Back at the goat herder's hut, when Sheik Musa recognizes The Panther, he will greet him cordially and give him the traditional embrace and hand kiss.'

Also known as the Kiss of Death.

But to be doubly sure I understood this, I said, 'So we're not going to make an attempt to apprehend the suspect.'

Chet replied, 'No, we're going to kill the terrorist with a Hellfire missile.'

'So I don't have to read him his rights?'

'He has no rights.'

That's what I've been saying. But it sounded a little harsh coming from Chet. On the other hand ... it was a breath of fresh air.

Also, I was a little disappointed that I wasn't going to whack

The Panther myself – or at least be there when a Hellfire turned him into protoplasm. I love the smell of high explosives and burning flesh. But modern war is impersonal. At least I could watch the action on the video monitor from the Predator van at the safe house. Would it be in color?

Chet went on, 'After everyone greets everyone, Sheik Musa, as host, will invite The Panther and a few of his lieutenants to sit on a carpet for tea. But before the negotiations begin for the Americans, Musa and his close lieutenants will excuse themselves for a moment and go into the stone goat herder's hut – maybe on the pretense of retrieving the Americans. When I see this on the monitor at the safe house, I will direct the Predator pilots to fire their Hellfires – two at al-Darwish and his nearby retinue on the carpet, and two at the other Al Qaeda men and their vehicles.' He assured us, 'The surviving Al Qaeda guys will be totally stunned, and Musa's tribesmen will finish them off.' He also let us know, 'About the time this is happening, American Air Force fighter-bombers, operating out of a base in Saudi Arabia, will level the Al Qaeda training camp.'

There was a silence in the tent while we all formed a mental picture of what Chet had just outlined. It sounded good ... but there were some potential problems with the scenario. Like, people don't always do what you want them to do, or sit or stand where you want them to sit or stand. Right?

I asked, 'What if it's raining on the outdoor tea party?'

Chet assured me, 'It hasn't rained in Marib in two hundred years.'

That might be an exaggeration, but it sounded like zero per-cent chance of precipitation.

Chet also informed us, 'The second pair of Predators is our security at the safe house, and they will cover us as we drive to the scene to collect some bits and pieces of Mr al-Darwish and the men around him for DNA and fingerprint ID.' He added, 'Some photos, too, though I don't think there will be any recognizable faces.'

Chet was enjoying this. Hey, you earned it, Chet. Now you can go home and get your head tuned up.

Brenner had a thought and asked, 'Won't this assassination and massacre put a little strain on Sheik Musa's relationship with Al Qaeda?'

Chet replied, 'Sheik Musa, of course, will say he had no clue that the Americans were watching him, and he'll claim casualties of his own.' He added, 'There won't be any Al Qaeda witnesses alive to contradict his version of the attack. Also, after this, Al Qaeda won't be much of a problem in Marib province.'

I asked Chet, 'Does Musa get the five-million-dollar reward?'

'I think he earned it.'

Right. Better than a hundred thousand from Al Qaeda. I inquired, 'How much do we get?'

'The satisfaction of a job well done and the thanks of a grateful government.'

'Same as last time.'

Kate had a good question: 'How do we get out of there?'

Chet replied, 'As I said, we'll be covered by two Predators on our way to the scene. The Twin Otter will land on a nearby road and take us across the border into Saudi Arabia to a secret forward base in the Arabian Desert. We turn over the goo bags, the cameras, and our weapons, then the Otter will fly us to Riyadh

Airport, where we will hop commercial airliners and fly home, wherever that is.'

No one spoke as we all sat there in the dim, quiet tent, thinking about the plan, or about flying home first class or flying home in a box.

Well, I thought, this plan was based on a lot of past history, some of it true, some of it made up, and some of it not fully evaluated. The plan also depended on a lot of assumptions. The CIA, as usual, had come up with an operational plan that seemed clever, but was actually too clever by half. Keep it simple, stupid. But it might work.

Chet let the silence drag on, then asked, 'Questions?'

Kate asked, 'Don't you think The Panther will smell a trap?'

Chet replied, 'The Panther, as a devout Muslim, would not believe that the sheik, also a devout Muslim, would betray him to the Americans, who are, of course, infidels.'

I commented, 'That's a good assumption, making me wonder why Musa *would* set up a fellow Muslim to be whacked by the infidels.'

Chet replied, 'The short answer is the five million bucks. But also Musa and al-Darwish don't have much else in common beyond their religion. Musa is a royalist and Al Qaeda is anti-royalist. Musa is a Bedouin, and the non-Bedouin Arabs, like al-Darwish, look down on the tribesmen. Plus, most of the tribes in Yemen want Al Qaeda out of their tribal lands.' Chet added, 'Also, I think Sheik Musa may not consider Mr al-Darwish a true Yemeni. In fact, he probably thinks of him as an American intruder.'

Everyone in this room is an American intruder.

Brenner observed, 'You're making a good case for why Musa would betray The Panther, but not a good case for why The Panther would trust Musa and come to this meeting.'

Chet nodded, then said, 'The Panther needs a win after the Hunt Oil fiasco, and the recent failed ambush of our convoy, so the opportunity to get five Americans – not tourists, but intelligence operatives, including Mr and Mrs Corey, who are on Al Qaeda's kill list – will be so tempting that he'll talk himself into taking the risk.' Chet added, 'The Panther may not trust Musa, but he won't want to appear fearful and not go to the meeting.' He also told us, 'We have a psychological profile on al-Darwish that I'll show you on the way to Marib. Bottom line on Bulus ibn al-Darwish is that he's a megalomaniac.' He looked at us and said, 'Delusions of grandeur. Extreme egotism and narcissism.'

Like everyone else in this room. Well ... the guys. Kate was mostly normal.

Chet continued, 'We can discuss this analysis on the plane. But to answer Mr Brenner's question and Ms. Mayfield's concern, the worst-case scenario would be that The Panther just refuses to show up at the meeting to negotiate, buy, pay for, and take custody of the Americans.'

Actually, I could think of a few even worse scenarios, but I saw Chet's point. If The Panther didn't show, then we'd just fly back to Aden and try another approach.

Brenner said to Chet, 'The plan sounds okay in theory, and I see it's been well thought out and that you've done a lot of groundwork with Sheik Musa. But I don't trust the Yemenis, and this plan depends entirely on the assumption that everyone from Tariq to Musa is on our side.' He added, 'Our lives and this mission are in their hands, and not in our own hands.' Brenner continued, 'The only operations that really work are those that are completely run and executed by Americans – or by trusted Western allies. Not paid allies.'

Spoken like a true soldier. And he was right.

Chet replied, 'I agree, but that's not possible in Yemen.' He added, 'Ironically, this plan should work precisely because it depends on including some Yemenis in the operation. We've never done that before, so The Panther will not think we're now trusting a Yemeni to help us kill him.'

Chet seemed to have an answer for everything. And they were good answers. And to give Chet some credit, he was putting his own ass out there on the front line. So I guess he believed in this plan.

Buck spoke up. 'The plan is not foolproof, but it's not as dangerous as it sounds.'

'Sure it is,' I assured him.

Buck explained, 'The downside for Sheik Musa if he betrays us is so severe – Hellfires and the wrath of the Saudi royal family – that I'm very confident of his loyalty.' He added, 'The sheik may switch loyalties next week or next year, but for now the deal is made and he will live up to his end of the bargain.'

Chet agreed and added, 'If Musa has changed his mind, he will just tell Tariq to wave us off, and we return to Aden.'

I observed, 'Musa may be trustworthy, but all it would take to get us killed is for one of his tribesmen to be working for Al Qaeda.'

Neither Chet nor Buck responded to that, and Chet seemed a bit impatient and got down to the question of our participation in this plan. He looked at me, then at Kate and asked, 'Are you all right with this?'

I glanced at Kate, who nodded. I said to Chet, 'If you like it, Chet, then we love it.'

'I love it,' Chet assured us. 'In fact, I conceived of it.'

Wonderful. It takes an egotist to catch an egotist.

Chet looked at Brenner.

Brenner had probably been betrayed by the natives here and in Southeast Asia one time too many. Nevertheless, he was going to give it another shot and he said, 'I'm in.'

'Good,' said Chet. 'The A-team is ready to kill The Panther.' He added, 'And about a dozen of his jihadists.'

As I said, the bait never likes the plan, but at least Kate and I weren't the only ones with skin in the game.

Chet, to further incentivize us, said, 'I believe, based on what we know of the structure of Al Qaeda in Yemen, that if we kill The Panther and his top lieutenants, and destroy their training camp, then the Al Qaeda attack on the Sheraton won't happen.'

Buck seconded that and said, 'If the Marib operation is successful, Al Qaeda in Yemen will be in disarray and they won't risk an attack on the Sheraton, which could end in another failure.' He added, 'And that is also true for the suspected attack on the embassy.'

Okay. I got it. Captain Mac would be disappointed if he couldn't kill jihadists attacking the hotel. Same for the Marines in the embassy. But for everyone else in the embassy and the hotel, they would be happy if the attacks didn't happen – or were at least postponed.

Chet said to us, 'We'll meet in the lobby at midnight. Two DSS vehicles will take us to the airport, where the Otter will be waiting to fly us to Marib.'

This is where the coach gives the team the pep talk, and Buck, our leader and life coach, said to us, 'I believe we have assembled an excellent team for this mission, and I thank you for volunteering. There may not be any public glory in this, but somewhere your names will be recorded and known to future generations. You are risking your lives for a cause greater than yourselves, knowing that the success of this mission will make America safer and bring us closer to victory over those who wish us harm.'

Sounds good. Buck had lived long enough to see the end of the Cold War – but none of us would live long enough to see the end of this war.

Chet Morgan got down to specifics and said, 'Bulus ibn al-Darwish, al-Numair, The Panther, head of Al Qaeda in Yemen, is a traitor to his country of birth, a mass murderer of innocent civilians and seventeen American seamen, and a sworn enemy of America.' He assured us, 'We should have no moral qualms about ending his life and the lives of his jihadists on the field of battle.'

That's much better than me trying to read him his rights in Arabic.

Chet concluded, 'I know someone is watching over us to ensure our success and our safe return home.'

Correct. The Predator drones.

We all stood, shook hands, and left the SCIF tent. Chet went to the balcony to fuel up on whatever, and the rest of us went into the bright light of the hallway.

Buck, obviously not wanting to engage in a post-coital chat, said, 'See you later in the lobby,' and walked toward his room.

Kate, Brenner, and I went to the elevator and rode down to our rooms on the third floor.

As I was taught, and as I'd learned over the years, if the goal is simple – like whacking someone – the plan should be simple. When the plan is complex, then something else is going on.

CHAPTER FIFTY-TWO

Zamo called our room at 11:30 and said he'd be around to pick up our bags and rifles, explaining, 'The CIA guy doesn't want people in the lobby to see that you're going on a trip.'

Okay. That's the problem with conducting anti-terrorist operations from a hotel in Sandland; there could be Al Qaeda snitches watching what you do. Chet had good tradecraft. Also, he probably watches too many spy movies.

Zamo also said, 'Mr Harris wants Ms. Mayfield to pack her balto.'

'Wonderful.' I hung up and said to Kate, 'Great news. You have an occasion to wear your balto.'

A little after midnight, Kate and I, wearing cargo pants, desert boots, black T-shirts, sleeveless bush jackets, Kevlar, and concealed Colt .45 automatics, walked into the hotel lobby.

The lobby was nearly deserted, and I didn't see any of our teammates. I said to Kate, 'I'll look outside.'

'No. Chet said to meet in the lobby.'

Kate, who is usually cool before departing on a dangerous assignment, seemed a bit subdued, maybe uneasy. And who could blame her? I mean, just getting to the airport at this hour had some risks.

Anyway, we took a seat in the lobby and waited for our team-mates.

After our meeting with Chet, Brenner had called our room and asked to come by to talk. Not a bad idea.

I was ninety-nine percent sure there were no listening devices in our room, but recalling Chet's possible eavesdropping, and because of the PSO tent on the nearby ridge, I turned on the TV. Some guy in a beard and robe was literally screaming about something, and I kept hearing the words, 'Amrika,' 'jihad,' and 'mawt,' which means 'death.'

I asked Brenner, 'Is he a stand-up comic?'

'He's a mullah,' Brenner replied.

Actually, he was an asshole.

Anyway, we moved three chairs together and leaned close. Brenner got to the point and told us, 'I'm not sure about the plan.'

Kate agreed and added, 'If I was The Panther, I'd see a setup and smell a trap.'

Thinking about panthers, lions, and other predators, and remembering what Buck said back in Sana'a, I reminded them, 'The Panther is always going to be cautious and on his guard. But he wants to eat.' And recalling what Chet said, I added, 'If he does smell a trap, he'll just not show up.' I concluded, 'He's either in the trap or he's a no-show. I don't see the danger to us.'

Of course I certainly *did* see the danger to us. But I wanted to see if Kate or Brenner saw it.

In fact, Brenner said, 'The immediate danger isn't from The Panther. It's from this guy Sheik Musa. Musa is holding all the cards. Not us, not the CIA, and not even The Panther.'

Kate agreed with Mr Brenner and said, 'We have no idea what the politics are here, or who owes who what, or who is ready to betray whom.'

I agreed with that, but to continue to play devil's advocate, I said, 'Chet and Buck made a good case for why Sheik Musa could be trusted, and I don't see any holes in that logic. I mean, what's in it for Musa to betray us to Al Qaeda? Hellfire missiles. There's much more in it for him to take our five million bucks to get rid of Al Qaeda and The Panther.' I explained, 'That would not only make the Americans happy, but also make the Saudi royal family happy as well as the idiots in Sana'a. It's a win-win-win for Sheik Musa.'

Kate and Brenner thought about that, and they both nodded, though reluctantly.

Of course there were other parts and pieces to this plan and to the bigger picture. For one thing, Brenner might or might not know that his new friend Kate had whacked a CIA officer. But was that relevant to what was going to happen in Marib? Possibly.

And then there was the Political Security Organization. Yemen's CIA. Birds of a feather, as Buck said in an unguarded moment. Why did Chet not address the question of his Yemeni counter-parts?

Kate, thinking along the same lines, said, 'Chet never mentioned the PSO, the National Security Bureau, or the Yemeni Army. That's like totally discounting the fact that even this place has a security apparatus.' She added, 'Colonel Hakim knows from the prisoner where The Panther was last seen, and he can guess that we're going there.'

Brenner agreed. 'This is true. We could wind up in a confrontation with the army, the NSB, or the PSO.'

The devil's advocate replied, 'The tribes and Al Qaeda rule in Marib province, and the security forces are scarce there. So maybe that's why Chet didn't address that.' I added, 'Or Operation Clean Sweep has been cleared with the Yemeni government at the highest levels, but neither Chet nor Buck is authorized to share political information.'

Again, Kate and Brenner nodded reluctantly.

I'm smart enough not to believe my own bullshit, and I certainly didn't believe Chet's bullshit or Buck's bullshit. In fact, there *was* something else going on here, and I was beginning to get a picture of what it was. But not so clear that I could put it into words and share it with Kate or Brenner, or confront Chet or Buck with my suspicions.

Brenner was worried about Sheik Musa, and Kate was worried that The Panther would smell a trap, and they were both worried about the Yemeni authorities. My worry was the CIA. I mean, it was *their* plan. And there seemed to be something wrong with the plan. And the CIA, for all its faults, is not stupid. So if the plan seemed flawed, it really wasn't. The fact was, there was actually another plan.

But to calm the troops, I said, 'Bottom line, Chet and Buck are putting their asses on the line with us.' I said to Brenner, 'In the Army, you would never send your men on a mission that you yourself wouldn't go on or didn't believe in. Correct?'

He nodded.

461

So we kicked this around for a few minutes while the mullah was working himself into a frenzy about Amrika or whatever. I mean, the whole Mideast was fucked up long before we got here, and it would be fucked up long after we left. And with all the Jews gone, who are they going to blame for all their problems? Amrika. Truth is, as Al Rasul told me, they really hated themselves. Nevertheless, we were about to give them another reason to hate *us* – a whack job perpetrated by the infidels on the sacred soil of Islam.

Brenner said, 'Well, we have to make a decision.'

I informed him, 'The decision has already been made. Unless you two can come up with a fatal flaw in this plan – something other than it sounds dangerous – then we're getting on that plane tonight and flying to Marib.' I reminded everyone, 'We all volunteered for this. And what did we think we were volunteering for?'

Brenner looked at me and said, 'I've volunteered for missions in Vietnam and other places that were more dangerous than this. But I always had guys I could trust to watch my back. We don't have that here.'

'Sure we do,' I replied. 'Buck and Chet. And Zamo. And don't forget the Predators.'

Kate, who knows me too well, said, 'John, you feel the same as we do about this mission.'

'Maybe. But forewarned is forearmed. We'll keep an eye out for one another, keep an eye on Chet and Buck, keep Zamo close, and be ready to take charge if things start to smell bad. Agreed?'

Kate and Brenner nodded, and Brenner asked me, 'What's motivating you? Aside from the Cole?'

'That's enough motivation. But aside from that, all of us are in this business, and this is not a safe business. Never was, never will be. Look at Buck. He's put his balls on the line for over thirty years. And even Chet, living in this shithole for three years to avenge the Cole. And you, Paul, you've been in harm's way for a good part of your life. And so has Kate. This is not a career, it's a calling. It's not a paycheck, it's a life.' I concluded, 'We're making the homeland just a little safer.' Plus, I have a big ego, but I didn't mention that.

Brenner nodded and said, 'I'm still in. I just wanted to see if you two understood the problems with this plan and this mission.'

Kate said, 'We all understand. And I'm glad we spoke about it.' She added, 'We'll keep alert for problems.' She looked at me, then at Brenner, and said to him, 'John actually likes bad plans from higher-ups. He can't wait to change the plan, rescue the mission from disaster, and show everyone how smart he is.'

Totally not true. That's just the way it happens. Anyway, I said, 'First things first. First we have to get to the airport without getting kidnapped.'

We all stood, and I said, 'See you downstairs,' and Brenner left.

The guy on the TV was still going nuts and I thought he was going to pass out like that TV newscaster in Network. I wondered if the Evening News with the Mad Mullah had a big market share.

'John?'

I shut off the TV. 'Yes, dear.'

'I know you know what you're doing.'

'Absolutely.' Not a clue.

'And I'll trust you on this.'

463

'Smart move.'

She let me know, 'I think Paul still has some valid misgivings, but not enough to pull out.'

'We actually don't need him even if he does.' To be provocative and snotty, I added, 'And I know you won't think any less of him if he hightails it back to the safety of the embassy.'

'You're an asshole.'

'I am an alpha male on the A-team. We will kill The Panther, then go to Washington and get a handshake. Maybe we'll take a week and go to a nude beach in St Maarten. No Muslims on a nude beach to worry about. And if there were, where would they hide a gun or a suicide belt?'

She didn't reply to that, but she did give me a kiss.

So we stuffed some things in our overnight bags, and Zamo called to say he'd come for our bags and rifles, and now here we were in the lobby, waiting for the rest of the A-team.

CHAPTER FIFTY-THREE

My cell phone, which worked near the hotel SCIF, chimed and I looked at the text message: *Parking lot.*

Kate and I went outside and walked to the unlit parking area in front of the hotel, where I saw one of the Marines with a bomb-sniffing dog. As the Marine approached our five Land Cruisers, he commanded, 'Cummins, search!' Good doggie. A journey of a thousand miles can end quickly if your car blows up when you turn the key.

Cummins seemed happy with all the Land Cruisers, but he growled at Chet, sensing a CIA man. Or maybe Cummins smelled the khat. Also, FYI, Chet had changed into dark clothing and he'd found his shoes. This was getting serious.

Two of our DSS drivers from Sana'a, including Mike Cassidy, loaded the bags in the back of the two vehicles and handed us our rifles.

Brenner said to everyone, 'Top speed, we stop for nothing, keep your rifles at the ready.'

Right. Just in case we run into the forty Al Qaeda guys heading for the hotel.

Brenner, Buck, and Chet got in one vehicle with the driver, and Kate and I got in the rear of the other with Zamo up front and Mike behind the wheel.

Mike said, 'I thought I was done for the day.'

'Me, too.'

Brenner's Land Cruiser pulled out of the parking area, and we followed, past the Yemeni Army lawn chair brigade.

I asked Zamo, 'Did you see Dr Clare?'

'Yeah . . .'

Bullshit. Some guys look for the million-dollar wound that will keep them out of action, and some guys who get the wound, like Zamo, are afraid it will keep them out of the action. I wondered what motivated Zamo. Probably he liked to kill jihadists with his sniper rifle. That simple.

We accelerated uphill on the narrow, winding road that cut through the hills and bluffs above the beach. There were no other vehicles on the road, and we stayed in the middle of the blacktop, hitting 120 KPH. As we crested the bluff and got into the flatlands, Brenner's driver gunned it, and Mike followed.

This was the road we'd come in on, and it skirted around the city, then ran along the Gulf of Aden. In less than five minutes, I could see the lights of the airport, but I didn't see any aircraft flying at this hour.

We followed the lead vehicle into the airport and shot past a manned guard booth without stopping, then veered off the road that led to the terminal and headed across a dusty field toward the runway.

At the end of the runway, I saw a high-winged twin-engine prop aircraft that must be the Otter. The paint job was a monotone gray, the official color of Spook Air, and the small tail markings were almost unreadable, another indication that this was a Company aircraft. Also, the cockpit and cabin windows were dark, and as we got closer I saw that the cabin shades were pulled and the boarding door was closed.

As we approached the aircraft, the cockpit lights went on, both engines fired up, and the props began spinning.

The two SUVs stopped near the rear boarding door, and everyone piled out. Mike said, 'Good luck. Look me up in Daytona or Madrid.'

'Will do.'

We quickly retrieved our bags from the rear, including Zamo's sniper rifle case, some backpacks, and a heavy duffel bag that I hoped held junk food and extra ammo. As we got to the left rear boarding door, it opened and one of the pilots dropped a short ladder down, and up we went. At the top of the ladder I glanced back and saw that our two DSS drivers were covering the situation with automatic rifles.

The co-pilot was making his way up the aisle back to the cockpit, and I saw that the dimly lit cabin had rows of double seats on the right and single seats on the left that would hold about fifteen people. Here near the tail were two facing bench seats along the wall, I guess for napping. Chet pointed out an open baggage area to the right of the door where we threw our bags and weapons as Chet pulled up the ladder, closed the boarding door, and then directed everyone to take seats toward the front. Chet went up to the cockpit and spoke to the pilots for a few seconds, then returned to the cabin and took a single seat across from Buck in the row ahead of Kate and me. Brenner and Zamo had slid into single seats across the aisle, so the aircraft seemed balanced for takeoff.

The dim cabin light went out, then the PA speaker crackled and one of the pilots made a boarding announcement, 'Welcome aboard,' and a safety announcement, 'Get ready for takeoff.'

And thank you for flying Spook Air. I noticed, too, that neither pilot introduced himself by name. Not even a first name. Company policy.

The engines revved and we buckled in as the aircraft began rolling fast down the runway. In less than ten seconds, the Otter abruptly pitched up and we were airborne. The aircraft seemed to strain as it continued to climb at a very steep angle.

I reached across Kate and opened the window shade and looked down at the lights of Aden and the harbor where all this began. I mean, had Commander Kirk Lippold challenged the approaching boat and fired a shot across its bow, I wouldn't have been here two and a half years ago, and I wouldn't be here now. But for sure, I'd be someplace else. There was no end to this.

The ground was falling away at a fast rate as we continued our steep, full-throttle climb, and I turned my attention to my seat mate. 'How you doing?'

'Can we go back and get my stomach?'

I knew she'd start to see the funny side of anti-terrorist operations in dangerous, fucked-up places.

I said, 'This is nothing. Wait until you see the landing.'

'Not funny.'

'Just trying to lighten the moment.'

'Try jumping out.'

Anyway, a few minutes after our thrilling short takeoff maneuver, the pilot, still climbing at a steep angle, banked hard right, which caused the aircraft to shudder and caused Kate to grip her armrests. A voice on the PA said, 'Sorry, folks. There was some traffic ahead.'

I hate it when planes collide in mid-air.

The pilot or co-pilot also announced, 'We're flying dark – no exterior lights, and please keep all the shades down if you turn on your overhead light.'

I lowered my shade.

A few minutes later, we came out of our gravity-defying climb and leveled off. I turned on my overhead light and scanned the aisle for the beverage cart.

The pilot came back on the PA and said, 'Marib is almost due north of here, but unfortunately I forgot to file a flight plan with the authorities.' He chuckled. A little CIA pilot humor. He also told us, 'To confuse anyone watching us on radar, we'll take a northwesterly heading towards Sana'a, then as we approach Sana'a we'll drop below radar coverage and head east into Marib.' He informed us, 'Marib has an airstrip, so if someone thinks we're going there, they'll think we're heading for the airstrip.'

Right. Because no one would think we were stupid enough to land on a road in the dark.

The pilot also assured us, 'Weather is good en route, and we have some moonlight to fly by and we have night vision goggles for the landing.'

Do we have parachutes?

'Flight time is about two and a half hours.'

Well, we had reached the point of no return regarding Operation Clean Sweep.

Actually, Kate and I had reached that point when we walked into Tom Walsh's office to talk about Yemen.

And here I was.

And here we all were, all six of us, with not much in common except one goal — to kill someone. I'd be lying if I said I didn't have some misgivings about this, but I'd be lying more if I said I wasn't looking forward to the kill. That's the reason I came here. Well, one of the reasons.

PART VIII

Marib, Yemen

CHAPTER FIFTY-FOUR

The pilot announced that we'd reached our cruising altitude of thirteen thousand feet, and we were free to help ourselves to refreshments from an ice chest in the rear.

So we all got up and fished soft drinks and bottled water out of the chest, and Chet invited us to sit on the facing bench seats. Zamo had no need or desire to know what Chet was going to say, so he returned to his seat with a Dr Pepper. Was it my imagination, or did his left arm seem not to be moving normally? I mean, if you take a hit like that, with soft tissue trauma, it's going to stiffen up, and maybe it was also infected. Great. A sniper with a bum arm.

Anyway, Kate, Brenner, and I sat together, and Buck and Chet sat facing us. Chet turned on an overhead light and I saw that he had a file folder in his hand — what the CIA calls a dossier, just to be très cooler than the FBI.

Chet spoke over the steady din of the twin engines. 'This is our psychological profile and background analysis of Bulus ibn al-Darwish. It was put together by a team of FBI and CIA psychologists and investigators over the last three years since we identified Mr al-Darwish as a prime suspect in the Cole bombing.' Chet also informed us, 'This report is based on interviews with the suspect's parents, a younger sister, childhood and college classmates, teachers, school counselors, Muslim clerics, and others who knew the bastard in the States.'

I asked, 'Any girlfriends?'

'Only one that we know of.'

'There's the problem. He wasn't getting laid enough.'

'John, please.'

Who said that?

Chet agreed, 'Young men without women are a problem in this culture, and that often leads to male aggressiveness and other abnormal behavior.'

'Right.' When I get horny, I get mean.

Chet continued, 'It may not seem necessary to know all of this, considering that we're going to terminate the subject. But I thought you'd find this interesting, maybe for future assignments. And maybe you'd also just like to know what's inside the head we're going to blow off.'

I would. And I'd also like to know what's going on in Chet's head.

Chet continued, 'Also, if you know how al-Darwish got to where he is, and who he is, you'll see why I think he's going to walk into that meeting with Sheik Musa and get himself killed.'

Chet, as I said, was a small breath of fresh air after my four years with the FBI, which, as part of the Department of Justice, needed to at least *sound* legalistic. Ergo Howard. And Kate, too. But I was working on Kate. The CIA, on the other hand, made few public statements, and therefore they had not developed a politically correct vocabulary for public consumption. Maybe I should consider asking Chet for a job. I was sure I could explain about my wife killing one of his colleagues.

Chet informed us, 'The subject, as he is called in this report, was born in New Jersey to Yemeni-born parents. As I said, he has a younger sister, Hana. His father, Jurji, was and is a successful importer and wholesaler of Mideastern goods, and he commutes to his office in Newark. He uses the name George, which is Jurji in Arabic. The mother, Sabria, is a stay-at-home housewife. They live in a large Victorian house in the waterfront section of Perth Amboy, which is more affluent than most of the working-class city.'

Right. The house I'd seen in that photo.

Chet said, 'FYI, Bulus means Paul, but the subject never used Paul to identify himself to non–Arabic speakers.' He added, 'We shouldn't make too much of that, but it's interesting that his father calls himself George, and mother's and sister's names are nondescriptive – Western-sounding.'

Right. A shrink would have a field day with that. More importantly, in a few days Bulus would be known as Mayit – Dead.

Chet also told us, 'The al-Darwish family and the wife's family in Yemen are city dwellers – Ta'iz – and they remain there. We have asked the PSO to keep these families under surveillance, but nothing has come of that.' He added, 'I'm sure the suspect doesn't go to Ta'iz for family visits. The senior Mr al-Darwish, George, sends money to his and his wife's relatives, and he used to visit now and then on business, but since the Cole, George hasn't set foot in Yemen.'

Right. War separates families and divides loyalties, and for the emigrant, the fatherland can become a dangerous place. As for jihadists like Bulus, who do come home, they discover they can't pop in on Uncle Abdul for a cup of tea. They are alone. Except for their new friends with AK-47s.

Chet continued, 'The family in Perth Amboy kept a halal home, read the Koran, and attended a storefront mosque in the downtown section of the city. The mosque has not come to the attention of the authorities and neither has the al-Darwish family.' He added, 'Mr and Mrs al-Darwish have been known to have a cocktail or two with Christian friends.'

I hoped they reciprocated with a khat chew.

Chet flipped a page and continued, 'The subject terrorist attended the public schools and had few friends in grade school or high school, possibly because he lived in a non-Muslim community. The people we interviewed claim, however, that the subject's social isolation was his choice and not a result of any prejudices in the community. As possible proof of this, most of those interviewed confirmed that the subject's parents and sister had friends and social contacts in the non-Muslim community.' Chet speculated, 'If we believe that, then maybe the subject wrongly perceived prejudice and animosity, and reacted accordingly, and that reinforced his social isolation.'

Right. Little Bulus was an angry, unhappy, and weird kid, and this made him a prime target for other kids. And that's why he wanted to be a terrorist when he grew up.

Chet continued, 'The subject seems to have ignored the fact that his parents and sister were integrating well into the community, and the analysts believe that this shows the subject's tendency to exclude any realities that don't fit his preconceived beliefs.'

Kate suggested, 'That describes half the world's population.'

Chet nodded, but said, 'The subject takes it to an extreme.' He also said, 'But to be objective, we need to concede that the subject, being a Muslim, may have experienced some degree of prejudice.'

Right. But it's how you handle it that determines if you're going to move on and live the American dream or if you're going to become the American nightmare.

Chet went on, 'Bottom line on this is that the subject could never see himself as anything but an outsider in American society, and he had no attitudinal loyalty to the country of his birth. His alienation and anger were, of course, reinforced by the daily news, which gives extensive coverage to foreign and domestic acts of terrorism, the wars in Iraq and Afghanistan, our strained relations with Islamic countries, and so forth.'

Unless you listen to NPR.

Chet reminded us, 'Young people are impressionable and sensitive and there is a whole generation of American-born Muslims who are growing up in what some of them perceive as a hostile environment, especially after 9/11.' He added, 'Ironically, their foreign-born parents are better adjusted because they have voluntarily made the decision to become Americans. Most of them are happy with that decision, and if they're not, they can move back to wherever they came from. Children don't have that option, and the children of Muslim immigrants sometimes feel trapped and blame their parents for bringing them to America or for having been born in America. In contrast to earlier immigrants, these children sometimes romanticize their ancestral land and think they would have been happier if they'd never left there.' Chet concluded, 'We think this is what happened to Bulus ibn al-Darwish, based on statements he's made, letters and emails he's written, and long, rambling audiotapes that he's recorded and distributed.'

'So,' I said, 'this is all Daddy and Mommy's fault.'

'For starters.' Chet added, 'He became completely alienated from his parents in college, which is very unusual in this family-oriented culture.'

Brenner commented, 'But al-Darwish must know that his parents are trying to save his butt.'

Chet replied, 'Doesn't matter. He doesn't thank them for the opportunity of a better life in America – he blames them for coming to Christendom and living among the infidels.' Chet also informed us, 'The parents actually did screw him up, but not in the way he thinks.' He told us, 'As their only son – a rarity in traditional Muslim homes – they spoiled and indulged the little bastard the way most Western parents do with their children. Possibly the parents felt guilty about their decision to live in America, and they overcompensated by not pushing the kid to go play baseball or something.'

Kate commented, 'We see a lot of that in our work – young Muslims who are caught between two worlds.' She added, 'American culture does not fit them as well as it fits other immigrants, and their response is alienation, which eventually leads to radical websites and then radical friends.'

Right. Plus, America is *the* superpower, and America makes war on Islam, so Muslim Americans think of themselves as the neighborhood face of the enemy. And sometimes they're right.

The aircraft droned on as Chet flipped through the dossier and also droned on a bit about little Bulus's boyhood and adolescence. Chet concluded, 'The subject was treated like a prince at home, an outsider in school, and a target on the streets of Perth Amboy. He was headed for trouble, but not the kind of trouble we usually associate with an angry, alienated male.' He added, 'You can take this analysis for what it's worth. If the subject was ever brought to trial, you'd hear the same crap in the courtroom, and the media would dutifully report it. Therefore, no one will ever hear how and why the defendant got his head messed up by a cruel, uncaring, and prejudiced society.'

I agreed that it was probably better to terminate the subject rather than apprehend and prosecute him – for sure it was the easier thing to do. But I asked, for the record, 'Doesn't he have info we can use?'

Chet replied, 'Lots. But his legal status as a US citizen puts him and us in an awkward situation.' He explained, 'We would probably have to inform him of his right to remain silent, and that's exactly what he'd do. Plus, of course, his parents are all lawyered up. So . . .'

Right. Mr al-Darwish as an American citizen with the right not to be taken to a secret location and waterboarded was a problem. Therefore, as I'd guessed from the beginning, Bulus ibn al-Darwish had to be terminated. End of problem.

Chet moved on to the subject's college years and said, 'Despite the bastard's problems in public school, he did well academically and got accepted to Columbia University, which as you know is one of the best schools in the country.'

I asked Chet, 'Where did you go to school?'

'Yale.'

I pointed out, 'So you and the subject terrorist have something in common. You both went to Ivy League schools.'

Chet ignored that and informed us, 'He actually has a genius IQ – top two percent of the population – and he could have joined Mensa, but he didn't join anything in college except a campus Muslim group and a mosque.'

I wondered if the subject asshole was smarter than me. I don't think I've ever met or killed anyone smarter than me. This could be interesting.

Chet continued, 'Being a genius doesn't make you smart, happy, or successful. In fact, sometimes the opposite. Studies have shown that people with genius-level IQs are often unhappy, alienated from the society around them, impatient with people of lesser intelligence, angry at how stupid and ignorant the world is, and generally self-absorbed and untrusting. In fact, they only trust themselves and they rarely take the advice of others.'

Why is everyone looking at me?

Chet went on, 'As this relates to what may or may not happen in the next few days, we believe that Bulus ibn al-Darwish will ignore any advice or warnings he gets from his aides or advisors about the meeting with Sheik Musa. He is driven first by hate and what he sees as revenge against America for our attacks on Islam, and by the American military presence on the sacred soil of his country and other Islamic countries. And somewhere deep in his subconscious he's remembering all the shit he got from his schoolmates in Perth Amboy, and this is payback time.' Chet added, 'The Cole was payback, too, but that was impersonal. He wasn't even there to see the Americans die – and as you know, he didn't even get to see a videotape.' Chet let us know, 'But this time ... Well, this is his chance to get his hands on five live Americans — his former compatriots — people who remind him of all those years of misery and loneliness.' He let us know, 'If you — we — ever did fall into his hands, don't expect a quick death.'

I already knew that. In fact, what we could expect was months or years of brutal captivity, until The Panther got tired of playing with his captured mice, then he'd saw our heads off. I glanced at Kate, Buck, Brenner, and Chet, and thought about spending years with them as a prisoner. I mean, The Panther wouldn't even have to torture me; a few weeks with Chet and Buck would be torture enough.

Chet continued, 'The subject's college years were unremarkable, but this is the period when he seems to have become radicalized.' Chet informed us, 'As you may know, Columbia has a large Jewish student body, and it's generally understood that these Jewish students, and in fact most of the students at Columbia are, let's say, overly tolerant and empathetic toward the relatively small Muslim student body.' He speculated, 'You'd think that this would have opened al-Darwish's eyes and mind to the idea that not everyone was against him or against Muslims. He could have fit in very well in college, and gotten happier and made non-Muslim friends. Instead, he ignored the generally open and liberal atmosphere on campus and withdrew into a narrow world of like-minded Muslim friends on and off campus.' Chet also informed us, 'Interestingly, to appease his father, he majored in economics, but he minored in Middle Eastern studies.'

Ironic that he learned about his culture at an American university.

'He also took Arabic-language classes to improve his proficiency in the language,' Chet went on, 'and he lived off campus in an apartment with other Muslim students, American and foreign-born, who were observant of the calls to prayer, the dietary laws, and other strictures of the religion.' Chet added, 'He studied the Koran ... I guess you'd say religiously ... and did well in class.'

Young Bulus wasn't exactly Joe College. I mean, every American knows that you go to college to get drunk, get laid, and give your parents heartburn. But this idiot actually studied. I'm surprised he didn't come to the attention of the FBI as a possible subversive. But maybe he did. I asked, 'Any problems with the law?'

'Just once. The girlfriend.' Chet explained, 'He was dating a European Muslim lady from Bosnia, who had become Americanized. She was secular, liked a drink now and then, dressed Western, and apparently had sex outside of marriage. This was interesting, because in every other way Mr al-Darwish was a strictly observant Muslim. But he became involved with this lady who was not exactly the ideal Islamic woman by Mr al-Darwish's standards.'

I was happy to learn that even fundamentalist Muslim men think with their dicks. A ray of hope in the war on terrorism.

Chet informed us, 'We interviewed this lady where she lives in Manhattan, but she wouldn't say much except that her college boyfriend, Bulus, was not a barrel of laughs.' He added, 'They dated for two semesters, then she broke it off and began dating a non-Muslim. A Christian. Well, Mr al-Darwish became violent and he physically assaulted her in her apartment, someone called the police, and they came and arrested him.' Chet let us know, 'She refused to press charges and the case was dropped.'

Right. Before I was a homicide detective, I responded to dozens of domestic violence cases. Most of the guys involved would turn up again in one way or another, usually another violent crime. Mr al-Darwish, too, had turned up again – big-time.

Chet went on a little about the subject's college years, and truly there was nothing remarkable about his four years at Columbia. One instructor described him as 'brooding,' another as 'quiet.' One Muslim student, however, described him as 'seething.' Most of his classmates couldn't remember him at all. Not exactly big man on campus, and not a campus troublemaker. Interestingly, no one recalled him ever making anti-American remarks, or anti-Semitic statements. In fact, the impression I got was of a young man who was quiet in public, but filled inside with bad stuff. Like a ticking time bomb.

Chet also told us, 'This brush with the law – arrest, the booking procedure, which probably included a strip search, the night in jail – seemed to have a profound effect on him. A few college classmates said he became even more withdrawn and went into a deep depression.'

Right. For the average middle-class kid, this was a traumatic experience. The upside was that most of them got scared straight and kept their noses clean. But as I said, when you're frightened you later get angry, and you look for payback. If I fell into this guy's hands, I should probably not mention that I'm former NYPD. But I'm sure he already knew that.

Chet continued, 'Interestingly, although al-Darwish apparently visited a number of radical websites, he did not seem to be under the influence of any specific fundamentalist or radical religious mentor as many of these radicalized young people are. Our profilers and behavioral science people believe he saw himself as his own inspiration, and quite possibly he believed then, and believes now, that he's being guided from above.'

Right. Like, I hear voices. I've had a couple of those. Scary people.

Chet added, 'But we don't know if he's that kind of nut job. And we'll never know.'

'Well,' I pointed out, 'if he walks into the trap we'll know that no one from above warned him.'

Chet conceded, 'Good point.' He continued, 'If you study the lives of men who've gone on to become powerful dictators and mass murderers, you'll discover that many of them were like this bastard – angry, driven, obsessed, and sociopathic – but they were also quiet as boys and young men, as though they were biding their time until they could break away from the restraints of society and the law.' Chet continued, 'It was almost inevitable, in retrospect, that al-Darwish would go to Yemen, a country that shares many of his beliefs, and also a country that's dysfunctional enough for him to gain some power. In other words, he was a zero in America, but here in Yemen he filled the void in the power vacuum and blossomed into a feared and respected leader.' Chet added, 'Ironically, being an American – or as the Arabs say, al-Amriki – gave him some cachet and credibility. And some respect.'

Right. Everyone else here was born in this shithole and lived and died here. Bulus ibn al-Darwish came from Amrika to save and serve his people, and they thought that was pretty cool. It *was* ironic. Plus, the bastard knew America – Islam's number one enemy – first-hand. I recalled what Al Rasul told me about The

Panther being multicultural and the conflicts in his head. I wondered what language he dreamt in. Maybe it depended on the dream. Sex dreams in English, killing Americans in Arabic.

Chet let us know, 'There are a growing number of American-born or American-raised Muslims who have followed this path back to their ancestral countries and become leaders in the jihadist movement.' He added, 'To be fair, however, many Muslim Americans have returned to these countries to do good.'

I observed, 'That's what al-Darwish thinks he's doing.'

'Maybe. But he's not. He's a sick puppy.'

I agreed, 'He sucks.'

Chet continued, 'Under the category of megalomania and delusions of grandeur, Bulus ibn al-Darwish is not content to have become the leader of Al Qaeda in the Arabian Peninsula. According to an Al Qaeda defector who knew him, al-Darwish has bigger ambitions. He sees himself as the supreme leader of Yemen. The prodigal son returns and takes over. He wants to unify and purify Yemen, to kill or kick out all foreigners. And while he's at it, he wants to wipe out all political opposition, including the Westernized intelligentsia in the cities, and then he'll move on to the armed opposition, including the al-Houthi rebels, the tribal sheiks and warlords, and the South Yemen secessionists.'

Sounds like a lot of work. But maybe he'd enjoy it.

Chet continued, 'Al-Darwish wants to restore Sharia law in Yemen and make the country into a medieval theocracy.'

I asked, 'How can we help him?'

Chet nodded in understanding and maybe agreement. I think everyone in this business was a little tired of trying to save these people from themselves. It was a thankless task and usually counterproductive. If left to their own devices, they'd find a century they were comfortable with – maybe the tenth century – and go live in it.

The problem was assholes like bin Laden and al-Darwish who engaged in attacks on the West. If they were smart, they would cut this shit out and the West would ignore them – as long as the oil kept flowing.

On that subject, Chet told us, 'Yemeni oil is not important to us now, but geologists believe there are vast oil deposits in Ar Rub` al Khali, the Empty Quarter, which straddles the undefined border with Saudi Arabia.' Chet said, unnecessarily, 'We want to control that oil with the Saudis.'

Of course we do.

Chet continued, 'Aside from that consideration, if al-Darwish actually did gain power in Yemen, our political analysts are certain that Yemen would become a big Al Qaeda training camp, as Afghanistan was, and that Bulus ibn al-Darwish, the American, would surely export violence – not oil – to America.' Chet let us know, 'Aside from avenging the Cole, *that* is what is at stake here.'

Right. It always comes back to oil and to protecting the homeland against terrorism. The terrorist thing I get. The oil ... well, produce more corn alcohol. You can drink it, too.

Anyway, Chet changed the subject and continued, 'The Panther is also known within Al Qaeda as al-Amriki – the American. Oddly, this is not used in a pejorative sense. There are a number of men in Al Qaeda and other Islamic groups who are known as al-Amriki. But it is our understanding that Mr al-Darwish does not like this nickname. Possibly this reminds him that he is an outsider here – just as he was an outsider in America.'

His whole life might have been different if he'd just called himself Paul, or even Al.

Chet went on, 'Our sources tell us that al-Darwish often misses the nuances of Yemeni culture, society, and even the language, which is understandable for someone who spent their first twenty-five years or so in another culture. Al-Darwish tries to compensate for this by acting more Yemeni than the Yemenis, and more Islamic than the mullahs. But in the end, he has no tribal affiliation, he wasn't born in a mud hut, he never raised goats, he doesn't chew khat, and most importantly he was not imbued by his father and male relatives with the warrior ethos that is common here. And yet he's come a long way, mostly because he's been a successful jihadist, and because Al Qaeda has suffered from the loss of so many leaders, in battle and in assassinations – Israeli bombs, American Hellfires, and unfortunate accidents.' Chet smiled, gave himself a CIA pat on the back, and added, 'Also, maybe al-Darwish does sometimes think logically like an American, and therefore he's made some good career choices, plus he's had some luck in murdering people.'

Brenner said, 'I think it was more than luck. The Cole was an intelligence failure on our part.'

Chet, a member of the intelligence establishment, didn't like that and he stayed silent. Well, Chet was not here just to avenge the *Cole*, but also to redeem the reputation of his Company. Everyone is driven by something.

Chet picked up his train of thought and said, 'Think of an Italian-American from, say, New Jersey, who goes to his ancestral Sicily to join the Mafia. His accent and mannerisms are wrong, but his head and heart are in the right place. People such as this may be accepted and even trusted, but at the end of the day ... well, they are different.'

Right. You can take the boy out of New Jersey, but you can't take New Jersey out of the boy.

Chet added, 'Al-Darwish's American background might impress most Yemenis, but it does not impress the Bedouin, who would be distrustful of anyone born and raised outside of Islam.' He said, 'Sheik Musa is not impressed, and this is another reason why Musa would betray al-Darwish, al-Amriki.'

I guess. But the A-team are *real* Americans. Like, Christians and all that. Chet, I thought, was overanalyzing this. But that's what the CIA does.

Chet further informed us, 'Regarding the warrior thing, al-Darwish has gone out of his way to be a hands-on warlord. We're sure he was present when the Belgian tourists were killed, and he's led his jihadists in attacks against Saudi soldiers on the border. But for some reason he didn't lead his men in the failed attack on the Hunt Oil installation – maybe God told him to sit it out – and I'm sure that didn't look good to his close lieutenants or his jihadists. Plus, The Panther has just had another setback with the failed ambush on our convoy. So when Sheik Musa requests The Panther's presence at this meeting to negotiate the sale of the Americans, Bulus ibn al-Darwish, the weirdo from Perth Amboy, has little choice but to be there – to be The Panther, and to meet with the great tribal sheik on equal terms, man to man, Yemeni to Yemeni, warlord to warlord.' Chet concluded, 'That is my analysis.'

Either Chet had been here too long or I'd been here too long, because some of this made sense to me.

So we all sat there for a minute as the Otter continued toward Marib, sipping our drinks, thinking about Bulus ibn al-Darwish. Killing this guy would be good for everyone, including maybe Mr al-Darwish himself, who didn't seem to enjoy life. But when you kill these guys, they become martyrs, and they go on beyond death.

And yet maybe when all was said and done, that's where he belonged. Dead. Remember the *Cole*.

Chet asked, 'Any questions? Any comments?'

No one had either and we all returned to our seats.

Kate said to me, 'Chet is overconfident. This thing could easily go the other way.'

'We all know that.'

So, did I now have my question answered? Like, how could someone born in America, in a free and open society, raised in material comfort and educated in a liberal atmosphere, become a fucking terrorist? A murderer.

Maybe. But not completely. The answer wasn't in the externals of life. The answer was deep in Bulus ibn al-Darwish's head. The mind excludes external reality, or processes it differently, and justifies nearly anything.

No matter what kind of society we created, the terrorists, the murderers, the bullies and the wife-beaters and the sexual predators and all the rest would always be with us and among us.

So, no, I still didn't know how Bulus ibn al-Darwish got to where he is, and what happened on that long, strange journey from Perth Amboy to Marib. Only he knew that.

And in the end, it didn't matter. It only mattered that he died very soon.

The big, lumbering Otter flew on through the night, toward our rendezvous with Bulus ibn al-Darwish, who I imagined was sleeping now, unaware that his fate had been discussed and sealed. Or someone – maybe the voice in his head – had tipped him off and it was *our* fate that had been sealed. We would know soon enough.

The pilot said, 'Landing in about an hour.'

CHAPTER FIFTY-FIVE

The cabin was pitch dark, and I couldn't even see Kate sitting next to me, but we were holding hands. I wondered if Chet and Buck were holding hands in the dark.

I could feel our speed and altitude decreasing, and I reached across Kate and opened the shade. There were no lights on the ground, but the moon illuminated a silvery expanse of jagged hills. I estimated we were at about three thousand feet, traveling at less than 200 MPH. It was 2:45 A.M., so we must be close.

Kate glanced out the window, but didn't have anything to say. In fact, no one had much to say since Chet's briefing, and the cabin was quiet except for the drone of the prop engines.

The PA crackled and the pilot said, 'About ten minutes.'

It's times like this when you wonder what the hell you were thinking that got you in situations like this. I remembered what my father used to say to me when I got in trouble with my friends: 'An idiot will try anything. That's how you know he's an idiot.'

The pilot informed us, 'Transponders are set correctly. Our designated road runs east—west, and we'll come around and land from the east.' He added, 'Light winds, good visibility.'

The Otter began a tight left turn, then leveled out and continued at the same speed and altitude. We were now lined up with the electronic transponders that marked the road.

The pilot left the PA on so we could hear him transmitting on his radio. 'Night Visitor One, this is Night Visitor Two. Read?'

A few seconds of silence passed, then we could hear the faint response coming through the PA speaker. 'Night Visitor Two, this is Night Visitor One. Over.'

The voice had a distinct Arabic accent — nit veeseetor tow — and I thought of Brenner's objection to the Arab pathfinder. I could see his point.

The pilot transmitted, 'Any dust?'

Again, a long silence, then a response that I couldn't make out over the PA speaker.

Kate asked, 'What did he say?'

I hoped he said, 'Get the hell out of here,' but the pilot said to us, 'He reports no dust tonight.'

Chet got out of his seat and opened the cockpit door so we could have visual contact with the pilots in case things started to go downhill.

Chet then said, 'Shades down. Lights on so we can get our weapons.'

I pulled down my shade, and we all turned our overhead lights on and made our way to the rear.

Buck said to Kate, 'Please put your balto on over your clothes.' He explained, 'Sheik Musa and his men would be offended to see a woman dressed in men's clothing.'

I added helpfully, 'No cross-dressing here. This is not New York.'

Kate said something unladylike, but pulled her balto from her bag and slipped it on over her mannish attire.

We all retrieved our weapons and returned to our seats and buckled up.

I assured Kate, 'Sheik Musa won't give you a second glance.'

'Lights off,' said Chet. 'Shades up. Give a holler if you see anything that doesn't look right.'

Kate put her shade up and we both looked out at the terrain, coming up fast. It was much flatter here than it had been a few minutes ago when we passed over the hills. I thought I saw a light here and there, but mostly it was a dark landscape, though the moon was bright enough to reveal some isolated areas of cultivation.

The Otter was in its final approach and it was getting a little bumpier as we came in lower.

The pilot came on the PA and said, 'Night Visitor has wished us a safe landing.'

Well, that was the final okay, and we had truly reached the point of no return.

I had this mental image of Tariq with a gun to his head, surrounded by smiling jihadists while The Panther and Sheik Musa were having a good laugh as they sharpened their daggers. Or maybe Tariq was in on it, too, and he was high-fiving Musa. Right?

The aircraft suddenly decelerated, and the pilot said, 'Two minutes.'

Chet said, 'As soon as the aircraft comes to a halt, we jump out and take up defensive positions in the drainage ditch on the left side of the road.'

Is that an FAA-approved procedure?

But there was some good news, and the co-pilot called out, 'Predators report no negative indications.'

Great. But how can they tell? Good-guy and bad-guy white robes and AK-47s all look alike. Right?

The high-mounted wings gave us an unobstructed view below, and we were all focused on the terrain outside the windows.

I didn't see anyone or anything in the dim moonlit landscape below. No people, no vehicles, no buildings. Just rocks, dry flatlands, some scrub brush, and a few stunted trees. The roadside drainage ditches, however, had some vegetation, and this would give us good concealment – and also good concealment to anyone waiting for us.

Chet informed us, 'We're going to put down in the middle of our designated landing strip, then roll out past the end of the transponders.'

Right. Just in case the bad guys were waiting at the end of our expected rollout. But the bad guys knew this trick, too, and they'd be farther down the road.

The pilot said, 'About thirty seconds.'

Kate said to me softly, 'Well, we're not drawing fire.'

'That's good.' In fact, if there *were* bad guys down there, they wouldn't shoot the Otter out of the sky; they'd let us land and get out, then shoot up the Otter, then try to take us prisoner. Well, that wasn't going to happen.

Chet called out, 'Order of exit – me, Paul, Buck, John, Kate, and Zamo last.'

At about fifty feet above the narrow dirt road the Otter's engines suddenly got quieter and we dropped quickly. The reinforced fixed landing gear hit hard, and we began a jarring series of bounces over the rough road, throwing up a cloud of dust. The aircraft fishtailed, but the pilot kept it on the road.

The pilot was pressing hard on the brakes and the Otter was decelerating rapidly.

Chet said, 'Unbuckle, get ready to move.' He stood, slung his rifle, and moved quickly toward the rear door as the Otter was still rolling out. Before the aircraft stopped, Chet opened the door, letting in a cloud of dust.

Everyone stood, slung their rifles, and lined up in the aisle. I asked Buck, standing in front of me, 'How do you say in Arabic, "Don't shoot. I'm an American with diplomatic immunity"?'

Buck replied, 'I'll do the talking, you do the shooting.'

Buck's okay for an upper-class, Ivy League, State Department bullshitting twit.

Chet grabbed a few bags from the luggage bin as the aircraft lurched to a sudden halt. He called out, 'Let's go!' then threw the bags out and jumped after them. Brenner and Buck did the same, and as I got to the door, the co-pilot came up behind me to shut the exit door and said, 'Good luck. See you on the return.'

Is this a round trip? I threw my overnight bag out, said 'Geronimo,' and jumped the three or four feet to the ground.

Kate was right behind me, then Zamo, and we all scrambled into the drainage ditch with our baggage.

The Otter's door closed, and a second later the engines roared and the aircraft began accelerating rapidly down the road.

If this was an ambush, this was when the Otter would begin taking fire. I divided my attention between my surroundings and the big, lumbering aircraft, which was quickly disappearing in the dark. Within ten seconds, I saw the Otter pitch up and go airborne at a very steep angle. No tracer rounds followed it, and I knew we were okay — for the moment. In fact, we were alone in the middle of Al Qaeda territory.

CHAPTER FIFTY-SIX

Chet said to keep low and keep still.

But Brenner, ex-infantryman, said, 'You don't stay where you were seen taking cover. Follow me. Leave the equipment.'

So we ignored the CIA guy and followed the combat vet through the drainage ditch in a running crouch.

After about fifty yards, we stopped and Brenner and Zamo crawled out of the ditch and scanned the dark road and countryside through their rifle-mounted nightscopes.

Brenner, looking east toward the direction we'd flown in from, said, 'I see a vehicle on the road, moving this way, no lights.'

Chet was on his sat-phone and he said, 'Tariq. This is Mr Brown.'

I thought his name was Morgan.

Chet listened, then asked, 'Is that you in the vehicle near the touchdown spot?' Then, 'Okay, keep coming.'

We could hear the vehicle now and we all poked our heads above the brush and peered through our nightscopes at a small pickup truck that was approaching slowly.

As it got closer, I could see a man behind the wheel, but no one was in the passenger seat – and hopefully there were no jihadists crouched in the rear. The truck stopped where we'd jumped out of the Otter.

Chet said into the phone, 'Keep coming.'

The pickup truck continued on.

Chet said to us, 'Stay down, cover me,' then he stood and raised his hand toward the truck, which came to a stop next to him.

Tariq stayed in the vehicle and he and Chet shook hands through the window and exchanged a few words. Chet said to us, 'Pile in the rear.'

So we all stood and jumped in the rear of the small pickup. Chet hopped in beside Tariq, who did a U-turn and took us back to our baggage, which we quickly collected, and off we went, up the bumpy dirt road we'd landed on.

Following Brenner's lead, we were kneeling on one knee, scanning the terrain through our rifle scopes. All I could see through my scope were long stone fences that penned in a few sheep and goats. Zamo was standing, steadying his sniper rifle on the roof of the cab as he peered ahead through his nightscope. It seemed to me that his left arm was definitely hurting.

Aside from that, so far, so good. We were on the ground, six cowboys in the middle of Indian Territory. But where was the cavalry?

I reminded everyone, 'I thought Sheik Musa's guys were going to provide an armed escort.'

Buck replied, 'We can't see them, but Musa's tribesmen are all around us.'

If you say so. Did that goat just wave to me?

Buck also told us, 'Musa himself will meet us up the road.'

What else does he have to do at 3 A.M. in Marib province? I mean, for five million bucks, I'd even go to Brooklyn to meet Musa in his new deli.

Kate was looking a bit tense, so I patted her cheek and said, 'Don't forget your veil when you meet the sheik.'

Anyway, after about a half mile, Tariq turned off the road onto a goat path or something, and up ahead I could see six white SUVs parked around a stone hut. Tariq stopped, and Chet got out and said to us, 'Okay, let's go meet the sheik.'

So we threw our bags out, opened the tailgate, and jumped down.

Tariq did a U-turn and off he went, back to the road to collect the transponders for the next idiots who wanted to land on a road at night. Hopefully that would be the Otter coming back to pick us up.

The stone hut was another fifty meters up the goat trail, so Chet said to leave our stuff there, and he and Buck led the way toward the hut. Kate remembered to wrap her hijab over her hair and around her face, and Buck suggested we sling our rifles as a show of trust and respect. Hey, why don't we just drop our rifles and walk with our heads tilted back to make it easier for them to slit our throats? Is that culturally sensitive enough?

Anyway, we were long, long past the point of no return on this one, so we strode confidently and cheerfully toward the hut, humming, 'We're off to see the wizard.'

No one was coming to greet us, so we marched right up to the hut. I would have knocked, but there was no door.

Buck entered first and called out, 'As-salaam alaikum!'

No one shot him, and I heard several voices returning the greeting, 'Wa alaikum as-salaam!' Did someone say, 'It's jambiyah time'?

Buck invited us to enter, and we all squeezed through the short, narrow doorway into the small hut.

The hut was lit with two kerosene lamps that hung from the ceiling beams, and around the stone walls, sitting on nice carpets, were six bearded gentlemen in white robes, wearing jambiyahs. All of them had AK-47s leaning against the walls, and in front of them were little piles of green leaves, the breakfast of champions.

One guy was resplendent in his snow white robes and jeweled jambiyah, and his head was crowned with a shiwal that looked like it was embroidered in gold. Must be the sheik.

Buck said to us, 'It is customary that we all greet each man, individually, using your first name, beginning with the most senior. Follow my lead.' He informed us, 'They will not stand, but that is not a sign of disrespect.' He further advised, 'Kate, you just stand by the entrance. Eyes on the floor, please.'

I need a picture of this.

Anyway, Buck began by greeting Sheik Musa, the guy with the golden hat, and Sheik Musa made the intro to the guy next to him, whom Buck greeted in Arabic, as Chet greeted Sheik Musa in English, and Musa replied in Arabic, and Mr Brenner was now calling himself Bulus, and round we went, Bedouin by Bedouin. The Arabs don't generally shake hands, but we all nodded our heads in respect. Hi, I'm John. What's your name again? Another Abdul. At some point in the round-robin I got confused and greeted Zamo.

Anyway, that over, the American men were invited to sit, and Buck advised Kate to keep standing near the door. So we five gentlemen squeezed in between the six Bedouin, whose deodorant had quit a few weeks ago.

Sheik Musa said something and Buck said to us, 'The sheik offers us khat, but we will decline. It's all right to say no.'

I protested, 'Let's have some khat, Buck.'

Buck said something to the sheik and he nodded, then ordered one of his guys to pass around bottled water from a crate. Brenner, who was closest to Kate, passed a bottle to her. Then someone passed a pizza-sized piece of flatbread, and everyone broke off a piece. Pass the Cipro, please. Kate took a piece of bread from Brenner, though I didn't see how she could eat or drink without dropping her scarf and causing a ruckus. Not my problem. I was a man amongst men. Fuck Manhattan. Fuck 26 Federal Plaza. Hello Bedouin. Where's my camera?

So with cocktails and hors d'oeuvres served, Buck addressed Sheik Musa in Arabic, and the sheik was listening intently, or he was wasted on khat, and he nodded a few times. Some of the other Bedouin were speaking to Buck and to one another.

Chet knew a few words of Arabic, too, and he used them, but Bulus Brenner kept his Arabic to himself.

Recalling Captain Dammaj who hid his English from us, I asked Buck, 'What are these nice people saying?'

Buck replied, 'They are confirming our understanding.'

'Right. Five million bucks.'

'And they confirm that they've received the letter from Prince Imad of the Saudi royal family.'

'Wonderful.' I smiled at Sheik Musa and said, 'Prince Imad is tops.' I gave the prince a thumbs-up.

Buck suggested, 'Please be quiet.'

Right. I do the shooting.

On that subject, I looked at Zamo on the other side of the room. He'd been sitting very still the whole time, but his eyes were moving around from Bedouin to Bedouin, who undoubtedly reminded him of Afghan tribesmen. I had the impression he was committing these faces to memory in case he saw them again through his telescopic sight. Good boy, Zamo.

Anyway, Buck and the Bedouin jabbered away for a minute or so and Buck announced, 'The sheik confirms that the van with the Predator ground monitoring equipment is here and is now at the safe house, guarded by his men.'

Great. And speaking of Predators, the sheik had to know they were circling overhead and that he had to be nice to us or he'd be toast.

Buck, Musa, and the other Bedouin exchanged a few more words and I heard, 'al-Numair' and 'Al Qaeda' a few times. Also, the word 'Sana'a' came up, as did the word 'Mukhabarat,' the PSO. It's good to get briefed by the locals, except when the locals have their own agenda.

I looked at Sheik Musa in the dim, flickering light. The guy looked imposing, almost regal, and he had a terrific beak — one of those ice cutters like on the bow of a ship. His eyes were alert despite the hour and the green chew, and his skin looked like my leather La-Z-Boy, which, by the way, I missed. I don't like sitting cross-legged.

The sheik said something that caused his five guys to nod and make approving sounds.

Buck said to us, 'The sheik says we are brave men.'

Hey, Kate's got balls, too. And we're all idiots.

Buck continued, 'He says that we have a common enemy. Al Qaeda. And of course, he says, the enemy of my enemy is my friend.'

Right. Until that changes. Not to mention that the sheik was doing business with our common enemy.

The sheik stood and we all stood. He said something, and Buck translated, 'He says we all must be tired from our long journey, so he will have us driven to our house and he wishes us a pleasant sleep, and a safe stay in Marib.'

He probably said the same thing to the Belgian tourists. But they didn't have five million bucks and Predator drones, so maybe this time he meant it.

Buck thanked the sheik and his trusted lieutenants for their hospitality and their assistance. The sheik decided to shake and he offered his hand to Buck, who took it and shook it. Then we all sheiked. Except for Kate, who kept admiring the carpet.

There were a dozen armed guys outside now, all dressed in robes, and they indicated three of the big Toyota Land Cruisers, which already had our bags in the back. So Kate and I got into one of the SUVs with two Bedouin up front, Buck and Chet got in another, and Brenner and Zamo got in the third. And off we went, down the goat path and onto the road, heading west, toward the rugged hills in the distance.

I announced to Kate, who was still wearing her scarf over her face, 'I want to be a warlord.'

No reply.

'But I want to ride a white Arabian stallion. Not a Toyota.'

'The only leather that's ever come in contact with your ass is your La-Z-Boy.'

Wives bring you down to earth. Every day.

Anyway, it seemed to me that Sheik Musa could be trusted. If he was going to turn us over to The Panther, he'd have already done that.

On the other hand, this was the Middle East. The land of the mirage, the shimmering pond in the sand that drew you farther into the deadly desert, and when you arrived at the lifesaving water, it disappeared, and you discovered the bones of those who'd been there before you. You discovered death.

CHAPTER FIFTY-SEVEN

The three-vehicle convoy continued on the road that had been our landing strip, toward the hills we'd flown over. Buck and Chet were in the lead vehicle, Kate and I in the middle, and Brenner and Zamo were bringing up the rear.

The SUVs had their lights off, but there was still enough moonlight to see the straight road, which was also defined by the drainage ditch. I doubted if the Bedouin had valid driver's licenses, but they seemed to know how to drive in the dark. I mean, camels don't have headlights. Right?

Question: If the tribes rule here, why don't these guys have their headlights on? Answer: There are other tribes. One is called Al Qaeda.

The night was cool and dry, and the starry sky was crystal clear. The half moon was sinking into the western hills and it would soon be dark, except for the starlight. The desert at night has a stark beauty, an otherworldly feeling that somehow changes your mood and your perception of reality. Maybe this was what drew The Panther to Yemen.

All Arabs were once nomadic, and they originated here, in Yemen, so maybe the desert was in The Panther's genes, and in his blood. So it would be good for him to die here. Better than dying in New Jersey, which is redundant.

Our driver and shotgun guy were jabbering away to each other while also speaking on their cell phones. Maybe they were calling their wives. Hi sweetheart, yeah, gotta work late again. Don't wait up. I'll grab some roadkill.

Actually, neither of these guys spoke English, which limited our ability to gain some knowledge of their culture and their lives. That was the good news. On the downside, I had no idea what they were saying. Hopefully it was all good.

Within half an hour we were at the base of the jagged hills, which, as I saw from the air, were more like a series of eroded plateaus or mesas.

The road suddenly got narrow and twisty as we climbed up a ravine on the face of the plateau. The moonlight was almost gone, but the drivers continued on without their headlights. As we continued up the plateau, the road became a stone-strewn goat path. Then a chipmunk path.

Finally, we came to the top of the plateau, which was not flat like a real plateau, but was studded with huge rock formations. I mean, if the flatlands below were the middle of nowhere, then this place was the top of nowhere. Good place for a safe house, though.

There was still some moonlight up here, and as we drove a few hundred meters across the rocky plateau, I could see the outline of a large structure up ahead, silhouetted by the sinking moon.

The vehicles all stopped near the structure, and I saw Buck and Chet getting out of the SUV. This must be the place.

Kate and I got out and so did Brenner and Zamo, and we all stared at our new safe house away from home.

Rising in front of me was a square tower, like the tower houses in Sana'a. This one was about six stories high with randomly spaced windows beginning about twenty feet from the ground. The top floor of the tower was formed by open arches, and attached to the tower was what looked like a walled-in courtyard, probably the camel parking lot. The entire structure was built out of the only building material around here: rocks. And more rocks. Also, I noticed, the tower sat at the edge of what looked like an eroding cliff.

Buck was speaking to two Bedouin who'd come out of the courtyard to greet us, and we all walked over to them.

Buck said to us, 'This is called a nawba, a watchtower or fortress, and it's named Husin al-Ghurab – the Crow Fortress.'

Right. You'd have to be a crow to get here.

Buck, sounding like a realtor trying to dump a white elephant on clueless yuppies, said, 'It was the property of Sultan Ismail Izzuddin ibn al-Athir.'

I wouldn't want to have to sign autographs with that name.

Buck told us, 'The sultan was expelled with all the Yemeni sultans after the 1967 revolution and he lives in exile in Saudi Arabia. Sheik Musa, who is his nephew, keeps an eye on the fortress for his uncle until he returns someday.' Buck informed us, 'A floor of the tower has been cleaned for us, and bedding provided.'

I wasn't going to think about that bedding, but I did ask, 'Water? Electricity?'

'Neither,' Buck assured us. He continued, 'The top of the tower, the mafraj, is good for observation and sat-phone communication.'

Right. The room with a view. Pass the khat, and call home. Hello, Tom? You're not gonna believe where I am. Asshole.

I inquired, 'Is there an excrement shaft in the tower?'

'I'm sure there is.'

Great. Maybe I can get Chet to stand under it.

Anyway, Buck exchanged a few words with one of the Bedouin, who led us toward the small fortress. I didn't see a door in the tower, but there was a gated opening in the courtyard wall, and we passed through into the large walled-in area where two small SUVs were parked. Also parked in the courtyard was a thirty-foot box van. The van was white and on the side was something

505

written in Arabic and a picture of a red fish. On top of the van's roof was what appeared to be a refrigeration unit, though I knew this was the sealed dome of a satellite dish.

One of the Bedouin spoke to Buck, who said to us, 'The two Hiluxes are for our use. The truck, as you know, is our communication system and Predator monitoring station.' He also let us know, 'This truck came into Sana'a Airport with me on the C-17.'

Which was another reason why Kate and I couldn't get a ride on the C-17. I wondered what else or who else was on board.

Buck and Chet went over to the two rear doors and satisfied themselves that the doors were padlocked. Buck had a penlight and he confirmed, 'This is the same padlock from the aircraft, and the wax seal is intact.'

Good. Recalling the Trojan horse, I wouldn't want to discover that the van was now filled with jihadists. Or explosives.

Buck also informed us, 'I have the padlock key.' He added, 'We'll open it in the morning.'

It *is* morning, Buck.

Chet confirmed that he had the backup key, then he unlocked the cab and checked that the ignition key was in the ignition lock, and Buck and Chet confirmed that they both had backup keys. Also, one of the Bedouin turned over a set of keys to Buck.

So obviously a lot of this had been pre-planned back in the States, including getting Mr and Mrs Corey to come along. And now it was all coming together here, in Marib province, where apparently the planners knew The Panther would be. And they knew this before the attack on the Hunt Oil installation. It occurred to me, not for the first time, that what I was seeing was the tip of the iceberg. That in itself was not unusual – you only need to know what you need to know in this business. But I had the feeling that there were things I *did* need to know that I didn't know.

Brenner asked Buck, 'How did the truck get here?'

Buck replied, 'We turned it over to two of Sheik Musa's men at the airport, and they drove it directly here, without incident, accompanied by a discreet armed escort of SUVs, also provided by Sheik Musa.'

The sheik was earning his five million Yankee dollars. He was incentivized. Money talks. Loyalty is just a word.

Kate, who was still recalling the thrilling ride up to this plateau, asked, through her scarf, 'But how did they get this truck up *here?*'

Buck informed all of us, 'My driver, Amid, told me there is a better road coming up here from the north.' He also let us know, 'Amid says the sheik has that approach guarded.'

Great. So we were protected by men and terrain. Unfortunately, protected also means boxed in. But to be positive, like Buck, I had to admit that Sheik Musa seemed to be living up to his end of the deal. And yes, we couldn't have done any of this without the help and cooperation of a local sheik. In this case, Sheik Musa.

The three Toyota Land Cruisers that we'd arrived in pulled into the courtyard and the Bedouin began unloading our bags.

Two of the Bedouin led us across the courtyard to a narrow opening in the base of the stone tower, and as we entered the dark space, I immediately recognized it as the livestock level, complete with dirt floor and pungent smell. I looked up at the high ceiling for the opening of the excrement shaft, but I couldn't see much in the dark.

The two Bedouin had flashlights and they pointed the beams at a stone staircase, then led the way up.

The second floor of the six-story walk-up was the diwan level, the prime space in the tower, and the Bedouin stopped there and said something to Buck, who said to us, 'This is where we stay.'

Our hosts began lighting kerosene lamps, illuminating the large open space that was the entire floor of the tower, supported by stone pillars. A few window openings let in some moonlight, air, and birds. The floor was rough-hewn planks covered with bird shit, and the walls were unplastered stone. This whole place was basically a pile of rock, like a medieval castle, hardly fit for a sultan, let alone six finicky Americans. Well ... maybe not all of us were finicky. In any case, this was where we'd be returned to after our staged kidnapping to await the Al Qaeda guys who'd be taken here by Musa's men to see us. Hopefully that wouldn't be a long wait.

As my eyes adjusted to the light of about ten lanterns, I spotted our bedroom — six ratty blankets spread over a bed of straw. I also noticed a small wooden shed in the far corner, and if I had to guess I'd say that was the master bathroom, a.k.a. the excrement shaft. Other than a washbasin on a stand, there wasn't a single stick of furniture in the place, leaving lots of room for a La-Z-Boy recliner. Also, it goes without saying that the only items in the room from the twenty-first century were us.

Buck said, 'All the comforts of home.'

Right. If home was Dracula's castle.

Buck also said, 'Someday, when this country is at peace and tourism returns, this will be a quaint country inn.' And he named it for us: 'The Sultan's Crow Fortress. Fifty dollars a night.'

'Great view,' I agreed. But don't put the reception desk under the excrement shaft.

A few of the other Bedouin began arriving, carrying our bags, which they deposited near the straw and blankets. Nice chaps. I would have tipped them, but if things went right, they'd be sharing in Musa's five million bucks. Warlords and tribesmen can do okay if they get tight with the Americans and the Saudi princes. I need to look into a career change.

Buck exchanged a few more words with our Bedouin bellboys, who, said Buck, wished us good sleep. But why were they grinning and fingering their jambiyahs? Or was it just the light?

With all the Bedouin gone, Kate pulled off her scarf and balto and threw them on a blanket.

Brenner quipped, 'Hussy.'

That got a laugh — the first laugh in a long time. I think we were all relieved to have gotten this far.

We were one step closer to The Panther, and soon he'd know we were here, if he didn't already know. Let the hunt begin.

CHAPTER FIFTY-EIGHT

We spent a few minutes exploring our accommodation, discovering a crate of bottled water and a sack of flatbread.

Chet excused himself to go up to the mafraj to make a sat-phone call, probably to his station chief in Sana'a, or maybe mission control in Washington. Also, he'd want to speak to the Predator ground control station, which could be anywhere in the world. And while he was doing all that, he might as well have a little chew.

Zamo was in his sniper mode, going from window to window, sighting his rifle and nightscope at the surrounding terrain. He let us know, 'Great perch. But too many rocks down there for cover and concealment. But no concealment between the rocks.'

Zamo saw life through a telescopic sight. Someone else would see a nice view. Position determines perspective.

Kate and I looked out a window into the courtyard below. The six Bedouin who'd driven us here were apparently staying with the two Bedouin who'd been here watching the van, and I could see them all in the fading moonlight sitting in a circle on a carpet that they'd rolled out. They seemed to be brewing tea on a camp stove and chatting away.

Chet returned and informed us, 'Predators report no unusual or suspicious activity in the area.'

I guess Chet told them that the eight Bedouin they saw in the courtyard were on our side. The problem with aerial reconnaissance, no matter how sophisticated, was that it couldn't read minds or hearts and couldn't predict intentions. That's where human intelligence – HUMINT – came in. The problem with human intelligence, however, was that not all *Homo sapiens* were sapient.

Brenner, who was our security guy, said, 'It's only a few hours to first light. So I suggest we stay awake, and at first light we'll post two lookouts, and sleep in shifts.'

Everyone, I was sure, was sleep-deprived, but you gotta do what you gotta do to avoid the Big Sleep.

There was a carpet laid out near our sleeping area, which I guess was the living room, and Buck suggested we sit.

Kate and Brenner brought over some bottled water and the sack of bread.

So we sat cross-legged, drank water, and passed around the flatbread, which Buck said was called tawwa, which must mean 'fresh last week.'

Chet didn't seem particularly hungry or tired and I guessed he had a chew in the mafraj. Maybe there was something to this stuff. Chet asked if we minded if he smoked, reminding us half-jokingly, 'We could all be dead tomorrow anyway.' Well, if you put it like that, Chet . . .

Zamo chose to pull guard duty and he extinguished all the lanterns except one near the carpet, then he began walking from window to window with his nightscope, while also keeping an eye on the stairwell.

When Zamo was on the far side of the room, I said to Brenner, 'I think his arm is hurting.'

Brenner replied, 'He's taking Cipro.'

It's times like this when you realize you need a good-looking female doctor.

We chatted a minute about Sheik Musa and the Bedouin tribesmen, and Buck, the old Arabist, told us, 'The Yemeni Bedouin are the most romanticized of any people in the Mideast, and they are also the most feared and the least understood.'

Now you tell us.

Buck continued, 'In semi-desert regions like Marib province, the distinction between the traditional nomadic Bedouin, who herd goats and ride camels, and the Bedouin who are settled farmers is becoming blurred.' He explained, 'Decades of drought and centuries of war and climate change have caused the settled Bedouin to return to a nomadic way of life.' He further informed us, 'Marib is the cradle of Yemeni civilization, and in ancient times it was more green and more populated. Now that the desert has arrived, the population is regressing to a pre-agricultural nomadic survival mode.'

Chet, not a big fan of Arabs in general, said, 'On all levels of society, these people are clinging more to their Korans, their guns, and to Sharia law.'

Buck agreed, and said, 'South Yemen in the seventies was becoming an open and enlightened society. The British and the Russians had left their mark on the educated Yemenis, but that's all gone.'

Along with the brewery.

'There is oil here,' Buck also informed us, 'but the Bedouin see virtually no money from this oil, and they resent that. Tourism could bring in revenue, but some tribes are hostile to foreigners, and the security situation has been made worse by Al Qaeda.' He added, 'Marib is economically depressed, politically unstable, socially unraveling, and it's becoming an ecological disaster as the desert encroaches.'

I suggested, 'This would be a good time for you to buy this fort cheap.'

Buck smiled, then admitted, 'Those of us who dream of a better Yemen — and a better Mideast — are fooling ourselves.'

Chet said, 'The only thing keeping the Mideast alive is oil. When that runs out, it's back to the Middle Ages here. Forever.'

Buck advised, 'Be careful what you wish for. When the oil runs out here, it runs out at your local gas station. But in any case, you see what the situation is here in Marib, and we are trying to ... let's say manage this instability to further American interests.' He confessed, 'It's about the oil – and Al Qaeda is not good for oil exploration, oil recovery, and oil pipelines. The tribes would be more helpful with eliminating Al Qaeda if the Sana'a government was fair to them, but this idiot Ali Abdullah Saleh is stealing the oil from the tribal lands and keeping the money. Al Qaeda promises to share the wealth, which is why they're tolerated by the tribes. So we need to do a delicate balancing act between the government, the tribes, and the Saudis, who are in conflict with the Yemeni government over the oil and most other matters.'

Chet said, 'But first we have to wipe out Al Qaeda, who is a new player. And a new problem.'

Buck agreed, then informed us, 'Sheik Musa is a particular enemy of President Saleh and the government.'

'And why is that?' I asked.

'Because,' Buck replied, 'Musa is strongly allied with the Saudi royal family, Musa has blown up a few pipelines to the coast, Musa demands millions in oil revenue, and Musa has defied the central government on every issue and at all levels. Also, Musa is a rallying figure for the other sheiks who are looking for a strong leader to unite them against the central government.'

In other words, Sheik Musa was on President Saleh's hit list. And one of those thoughts in the back of my mind now became clear – Bulus ibn al-Darwish might not be the only chief who was going to die in that Hellfire attack. This was what Buck was talking about in New York.

Everyone else seemed to be thinking this too, but no one had any comment.

Chet, who also had to know about this – he had operational control of the Predator drones – said, 'Some things that we do may not seem right, but we do what is best for our country.' He added, 'There is a bigger picture.'

There always is in this game.

Buck expanded on that and said, 'We need the cooperation of the Yemeni government in our war against Al Qaeda, and President Saleh needs a favor.'

Got it. This was a two-fer. We get rid of Musa for the Yemeni government, and the Yemeni government lets the Americans mount an operation in Marib using Hellfire missiles to get rid of The Panther. The Panther deserved whatever he got from us, but Sheik Musa, even if he was a double-dealer, did not necessarily deserve to die in an American Hellfire attack.

I suggested, 'This might not be a nice way to repay Sheik Musa for his assistance and his hospitality.'

Buck shrugged, then said, 'Accidents happen – which we will explain to the Saudis.' He assured us, 'If we kill The Panther, the sheik's family and tribesmen will get the five million dollars.'

'The late sheik would have been happy to know that.'

Kate, who was processing all this, said to Buck and Chet, 'You owed us this information before we got here.'

Buck replied, 'You had the information in New York. You should have come to the conclusion.'

Brenner, the former soldier who'd probably killed more bad guys than all of us put together – except for Zamo – said, 'I've killed soldiers in ambushes who were just walking along and were not an immediate threat to me, but I've never killed anyone who was helping me.'

Chet replied, a bit sharply, '*You* are not killing anyone.' He added, however, 'This was not part of my plan, but it is now part of my orders.' Chet further reminded us, 'I don't need your cooperation or your approval. I just need your silence.'

Buck said nicely, 'We've given you this information as a courtesy. You, John, Kate, and Paul, are professionals and you're intelligent enough to see that we are playing the long game. The goal here is to wipe out Al Qaeda in Yemen, and to avenge the Cole, and also to avenge 9/11 and all the other Al Qaeda attacks on Americans and American interests — and other Western interests — and to keep Yemen from becoming a staging area for Al Qaeda attacks against our country.'

Don't forget the oil.

Buck continued, 'We may not like President Saleh, but he's all we've got between us and Al Qaeda in Yemen.'

Right. So what's one dead Bedouin sheik? I don't even know the guy. Still, it sucked.

Also, this new information explained why Chet was not concerned about a possible run-in with Colonel Hakim and his PSO. The fix was in, and the government in Sana'a was giving us a free hand to deal with The Panther if we would also deal with Sheik Musa while we were at it.

So every time I got a new piece of information, something that didn't make sense made sense. It was like peeling layers off an onion; you keep seeing more onion, and the onion gets smaller. And at the center is something you probably don't want to see. But I don't think I've gotten there yet.

I said to Chet, and to Buck, 'I'm assuming the sheik is not going to get vaporized at the same time as The Panther. Correct?'

Chet replied, 'Correct. But soon after we're safely out of here.'

Right. We can't be here in the van watching Sheik Musa getting blown up by a Hellfire while the sheik's Bedouin tribesmen are here watching us, and maybe speaking on their cell phones to their Bedouin buddies, who are with Musa at the scene of the attack. Like, 'Hello, Abdul, an American Hellfire just landed on our sheik.'

Also, the Bedouin at the scene of the attack needed to finish off the Al Qaeda guys. And we needed to drive from here to the scene of the carnage and collect bits and pieces of The Panther and his lieutenants before we jumped on the Otter.

I asked, 'How do you explain this terrible accident to the Saudis?'

Chet gave me a straightforward CIA answer. 'You have no need to know that.'

Buck assured us, 'I'm personally unhappy about having to ... sacrifice Sheik Musa, but Chet and I wanted you to understand why there will be no interference from the Yemeni security forces.'

Chet said, 'We're also telling you about this because you may be asked about this someday. John, you, Kate, and Paul don't know anything about what happened after you left Marib.'

I didn't reply. But it occurred to me that Chet, by telling us not to say anything after we got out of here, was also saying that if we didn't promise to keep our mouths shut, we might not get out of here. Or was I getting paranoid again?

Something didn't smell right here, and I needed to talk this over with Kate and Brenner as we'd agreed back in Aden. Meanwhile, I said to Chet, 'Okay. I understand.' I looked at Kate and she understood, too, and said, 'I'm all right with this.'

Brenner got the drift and said, 'Sorry, I wasn't paying attention.'

Chet nodded, then stood and went to his duffel bag and retrieved a bottle of Hennessy cognac. Good move, Chet.

He passed the bottle around and we all took a swig, then passed it again.

The sky outside the east-facing windows was starting to get light, and I could hear birds singing. A black crow perched on a windowsill, then flew in and walked cautiously toward us.

Chet broke off a piece of bread and threw it toward the bird, who went right for it. Don't shoot the bird, Chet.

More crows arrived and more bread was tossed, and the cognac kept making the rounds.

The dawn came, which was one of the few things you could rely on in Yemen, along with death.

Kate and I volunteered for the first guard shift and we relieved Zamo, who literally hit the hay and was quickly asleep with his boots on and his rifle across his chest.

Buck, Chet, and Brenner also lay down with their guns and boots on, and Buck said to everyone, 'We leave here for the Bilqis Hotel about one P.M. Then we go to the ruins.' He assured us, 'You'll enjoy the ruins.'

I'm sure the Belgians enjoyed them, too, except for that problem.

I went to an east-facing window and watched the flat, distant horizon growing lighter.

Somewhere out there was Bulus ibn al-Darwish. It was hard to believe that this weirdo loser from Perth Amboy had come all the way here to metamorphose into The Panther.

And harder to believe I'd come all the way here to find and kill him.

In a day or two we'd see whose life journey had come to an end.

CHAPTER FIFTY-NINE

The straw bed was predictably uncomfortable, and the wool blankets smelled like camels or something.

And now a few words about the excrement shaft; it was basically a six-story indoor outhouse, with a hole in each floor. A squatter. So you had to look up, and if you saw someone's ass above you . . . well, too much information. More importantly, the shit shaft could be a means of escape. Always look for an escape.

Buck was kind enough to share a roll of TP he'd thought to steal from the Sheraton. A man who thinks of TP is a man who thinks of everything.

We heard noises in the courtyard and I looked out the window. The eight Bedouin were kneeling and prostrating themselves on their rug, facing Mecca, which around here is northwest.

Buck informed us, 'They are performing the noonday salat – the call to prayer.'

I looked at my watch. Right on time.

Buck also informed us that we were invited for lunch with our Bedouin hosts, but unfortunately the invite did not extend to Ms. Mayfield, who though she dressed like a man was still a woman. Kate took that well — she didn't give a shit and she didn't want to wear her balto anyway — and she took some bread and water up to the mafraj to keep an eye on our surroundings. Good thinking.

So the men of the A-team went down to the courtyard, and the Bedouin, who pride themselves on their hospitality to travelers, had hot tea for us and bowls of hot oats or groats, or some weird glutinous cereal product.

They also gave us plastic spoons, and Buck commented, 'They eat almost everything with their fingers, but they've discovered spoons for certain foods.'

There's progress. Next, napkins.

So we sat cross-legged on the rug with our eight new Bedouin buddies and we ate this glop, which was at least hot. The tea was herbal and did nothing for my cognac headache.

It was a little cooler here in the highlands than it was in Aden at this time of year, and on that subject my calendar watch showed that we'd rolled into March. You lose track of time when you travel back a few centuries.

The stone wall around the courtyard was about ten feet high, and the wooden gate was closed, so no one could see us, but neither could we see anyone approaching. There were, however, a few stone platforms around the walls for observation and shooting. I glanced up at the mafraj and saw Kate standing in one of the open arches with her M4 slung across her chest, enjoying the view through a pair of binoculars.

The Bedouin seemed very interested in our M4s, and Buck,

against all regulations and common sense, allowed them to examine his weapon, which they passed around, fully loaded. They seemed amused by the compact size, small caliber, and light weight of the automatic carbine, and they passed around one of their AK-47s to show us what a real rifle felt and looked like. Yours may be bigger than mine, Abdul, but I can paint you red in a heartbeat with my little rapid-fire plastic toy.

The Bedouin also seemed interested in Zamo's sniper rifle, but Zamo wouldn't let them touch it and they seemed to respect him for that. But they did want to know about it, and Brenner said it was okay to let them know what this rifle could do.

So Zamo, through Buck, explained that he was carrying an M24 Sniper Weapon System, and it fired a 7.62mm NATO cartridge, which he said could blow their heads off at a thousand meters, though I don't think Buck translated all of that.

Zamo also said that the US supplied this rifle to the IDF – the Israel Defense Forces – and again I was sure Buck did not translate that provocative fact to these Muslim gentlemen.

They were fascinated by the telescopic sight, and Zamo explained that the magnification was adjustable from three-power to nine-power, meaning that at its highest power, an object that is nine hundred meters away looks like it's only a hundred meters away.

The Bedouin seemed impressed, and since I can't keep my mouth shut, I said to Buck, 'Tell them that Zamo has killed fifty men with this rifle.'

Buck hesitated, then translated, and the Bedouin all looked at Zamo like he was a rock star. That's worth another bowl of glop.

Anyway, I wasn't sure this was a good strategy. I mean, on the one hand, it was good for Musa's men to know that Zamo could put a bullet through someone's head from a kilometer away. On the other hand, why advertise what you can do? People should find out the hard way.

Bottom line, though, there was a warrior thing going on here, and the Bedouin wanted to make sure they weren't being overly nice to a bunch of girly men. You know, like guys who dragged a woman along to do a man's job.

I mean, we weren't even on the same planet with these people, but in some strange way I was getting to like them. I thought about bringing two or three of them back to 26 Federal Plaza to show some of the suits what real men looked like.

Maybe I was getting a little carried away with the moment.

Brenner, though, said to the team, 'They remind me of the Montagnard tribesmen in 'Nam — basic, no bullshit, brass balls, and ready to kill without hesitation.'

Zamo, who also fit that description, and who'd fought men like this in the mountains of Afghanistan, said, 'Guys like these are hard to the core. They live, eat, and breathe war.'

Right. This must be what the world looked like a thousand years ago. But the tribesmen did have modern weapons and vehicles and also cell phones. Things to make killing easier and more efficient. Nice to see, though, that they still carried their jambiyahs and dressed weird. Good for tourism.

Regarding the warrior thing, I'd worn my jambiyah for the occasion and the Bedouin thought that was funny. Unfortunately, by custom, none of us could draw our daggers to pass around — only to cut someone's throat — but the Bedouin next to me, a guy named Yasir, examined my sheathed jambiyah, and Buck told me,

'He says it seems of excellent quality,' making me feel better about the hundred bucks it cost me.

Our hosts insisted we have more tea and they pushed some khat on us that Buck took 'for later.' Chet, of course, had his own stash, but he said, 'Shuqran.' Thanks.

So I liked the Bedouin. Too bad we were going to whack their sheik. Hey, Abdul, it's nothing personal. Just business.

Or for all I knew, Chet intended to whack these guys, too, on our way out of here. It would be nice if Chet told us what the hell was going on. But he probably figured that unpleasant information should be rationed out, like shit in a spoon.

Anyway, the picnic lunch was finished and it was time to examine the van.

Buck thanked our hosts for the meal and conversation, and Brenner told Zamo to keep Kate company. I asked Zamo how his arm was and he said it was fine, but it wasn't. I also asked him to bring Kate some tea and gruel in case she was tired of tawwa bread. I am a great husband.

Chet, Buck, Brenner, and I moved across the courtyard to the twenty-first century.

The thirty-foot windowless box van sat on the chassis of a Mitsubishi truck, and the van didn't open into the driver's compartment.

I asked Buck, 'What does this say?'

Buck read the Arabic on the van. '"Musa" — which means Moses — "purveyor of fine fish".' He also translated, '"Fresh to market from the Red Sea".' Buck smiled and said, 'Someone in Washington had fun with this.'

Right. A real knee-slapper. Musa — Moses — Red Sea. Get it?

Anyway, Chet did the honors and unlocked the padlock, opened one of the rear doors, and jumped inside. We all followed.

The interior of the van was high enough for us to stand, and the walls, floor, and ceiling were lined with Kevlar and, I assumed, lead. Unsurprisingly, there was no fish inside. Instead there was a large electronic console in the front of the van, similar to a pilot's cockpit array. In front of the console and the twin monitors were two swivel chairs.

Chet took a seat in the left chair and he invited Buck, the oldest gentleman, to take the other seat. Brenner, ever vigilant, stood against a wall where he could divide his attention between the courtyard and the van.

There were a few more electronic devices mounted on the long walls of the van, and on the floor were metal boxes marked with the names of the replacement parts that they contained. More importantly, there were three cardboard boxes of canned food on the floor and I read the American brand labels – mixed fruit, mixed vegetables, and, maybe as a joke, canned tuna. Who's supposed to eat this shit? Where's the chili? Is this the best those bastards in Washington could do?

Chet said, 'The electronics are low-powered so that everything can be run from our onboard generator.' He hit a switch on the console, and a few seconds later I could feel the vibration and hear the steady hum of the generator from somewhere under the floor. Chet also informed us, 'There are electrical outlets in here so we can recharge our sat-phones, cell phones, and hand-held radios.'

Chet glanced up at a gauge on the panel. 'Voltage is steady,' he announced as he hit another switch and the dark console suddenly lit up. 'We're in business.'

Chet played with a few dials, then switched on the two monitors and we immediately saw moving images on the screens — aerial shots in full color of two different landscapes gliding by.

Chet read some electronic info on his screen and said, 'The right-hand monitor is the view from a Predator drone that is, at this moment, running autonomously — meaning without an active ground pilot. The drone is executing a reconnaissance flight over this area using a pre-programmed computer plan.'

The screen showed the rugged and unpopulated terrain west of here that we'd flown over last night. It was easy to see how guerrilla forces could disappear in those hills. And easy to imagine The Panther making those hills his home. It might not be so easy to draw him out of there. But with the right bait — Mr and Mrs Corey and company — The Panther might come out to eat his former American compatriots.

Chet said to us, 'The images from both these Predators are transmitted by Ku-Band satellite link to this van and also to a ground control station where one or two pilots and aerial image specialists are sitting at a console similar to this one — in a van or in a room.'

I asked, 'Where is the ground control station?'

Chet gave me a CIA reply. 'It doesn't matter. Could be in Saudi Arabia, could be an Air Force base in the States, and it could even be at Langley.' He also had a Zen reply. 'With satellites and advanced electronics, real time is more important than real place. The only real place that matters is the target.'

Whatever. Thanks. I also asked, 'Where are the Predator drones based?'

Chet replied, 'I really don't know or care to know.' He added, 'And neither do you.'

Actually, I do, asshole. But I let it go.

Chet continued, 'The pilots have a flight control stick like this one, but my stick is deactivated.'

Have you tried Viagra? Maybe less khat.

Chet confessed, 'I'm not a pilot. But I can speak directly to the pilots and instruct and guide them regarding what I want or need.' He reminded us, 'I am the one who has operational control of the Predator drones and the Hellfire missiles during the execution stage of the mission.' To make sure we understood, he also said, 'I, along with the aerial image specialists, identify who or what is the target and I give the order to the pilots to launch the Hellfires.'

Right. That's why it's called the execution stage.

Chet, on a little power high, also said, 'This is what we call SAA – stealthy aerial assassination.' He concluded, 'Awesome.'

Indeed. But not as awesome as me blowing The Panther's head off with my Colt .45.

And then there was our sometime friend Sheik Musa, who was a full-time enemy of our sometime friend President Saleh. Some genius in Washington had figured out how to make this plan work for everyone. The idiots in Sana'a feared the tribes more than they feared Al Qaeda, but the Americans were obsessed with wiping out Al Qaeda. So if we put those two obsessions together, then Washington and Sana'a, the so-called allies, could solve their different problems in the same way – a thunderbolt out of the blue. It actually *was* a smart idea, and even Sheik Musa, who knew a few things about double-dealing, would appreciate it. Probably The Panther would, too. They could both talk about it in Paradise.

Chet directed us to the screen in front of him and said, 'That's us.'

And sure enough, there was a nice overhead image of the Crow Fortress on the screen. The slow-flying Predator drone was flying a tight circle over the plateau and we could see a few hundred meters in all directions, including the road we'd taken here, and also the better road that came from Marib in the north.

Chet punched in a command on the keypad and the Predator's camera enlarged the view of the fortress. I could see the Bedouin in the courtyard, sitting around, chatting and chewing.

Chet said, 'The Predator is about ten thousand feet, but with the fifteen-hundred-millimeter computer-enhanced zoom lens, the view looks like it's from about fifty feet.'

In fact, one of the Bedouin was taking a leak against the stone wall and I could see he wasn't circumcised. Okay, maybe I assumed that.

Chet put his headphones on and made radio satellite contact with the ground control station. 'Clean Sweep zero-zero, this is Clean Sweep six-six. Commo check.'

A few seconds later, a voice with a nice Down South accent came over the speaker. 'Sweep six-six, loud and clear.'

Six-six said to zero-zero, 'I called in a sat-phone sit-rep at five hundred hours, and I repeat, all okay.'

'Roger, six-six.' Zero-zero inquired, 'Whacha'all have for lunch down there? Looked like grits.' Zero-zero laughed.

Hey, were we having fun or what?

Chet, a.k.a. six-six, and zero-zero, whoever and wherever he was, exchanged some technical information, then Chet said to

526

zero-zero, 'I'll give you a heads-up when Clean Sweep is mobile — two small white SUV Hiluxes that you see here, plus the three white larger SUV Land Cruisers containing local escorts. Destination, Bilqis Hotel, Marib. Details to follow.'

'Roger. Predator Two will follow. Predator One remains on station above you.' He added, 'Both heavy.' Meaning armed.

Chet also told him, 'I'll be away from this station until the team goes mobile, so if you see anything in the area that we should know about, call my sat-phone. If I'm not able to receive, you have the five other sat-phone numbers.'

'Roger.' Zero-zero asked, 'Anything further?'

'Negative.'

Zero-zero said, 'Good luck.'

Chet signed off and said to us, 'I wanted you to see and hear that everything is in place, and that we are covered by the Predators.'

Wonderful, Chet. But can the Predators predict if our Bedouin buddies are going to smell a double-cross and whack us? Or worse, turn us over to The Panther? No. We have to figure that out ourselves.

Chet explained a few other features of the Predator monitoring equipment and informed us, 'As I said in Aden, during the execution stage of the operation we'll have four Predators. Two over the target, and two over this location for security, each armed with two Hellfires.' He further explained, 'I can split these two screens and watch all four images.'

I asked Chet, 'How do we get this million-dollar van out of here?'

'We don't. We can't.'

'So the Predators take care of it?'

'Correct.'

That's why my taxes are so high. I said jokingly, 'I assume we will be out of the van when the Hellfire hits it.'

'That would be a good idea.'

The show-and-tell seemed to be finished, so Chet, Brenner, and I each took a case of canned food and we exited Moses' fish van and Buck locked it up.

Buck said we should share our bounty with our hosts, to reciprocate for their hospitality – thanks for the glop, here's a can of tuna – so we did that and made our way back to the second floor of the tower.

Chet seemed upbeat, and I imagined he saw the end in sight – the end of all his work and his frustration, and the end of his time here in Yemen.

All we had to do now was go check into the hotel, go see the stupid ruins, then get kidnapped.

And then wait for The Panther.

CHAPTER SIXTY

At 1:15 P.M., the A-team, minus Chet Morgan, piled into our two Toyota Hiluxes, compliments of Sheik Musa. We left most of our personal items in the Crow Fortress because we'd be coming back later today as kidnapped Americans, also compliments of Sheik Musa. But we did take our overnight bags with us for when we checked into the Bilqis Hotel for a few days of sightseeing fun, cut short, unfortunately, by the above-mentioned kidnapping.

The purpose here, according to Chet's complex plan, was to make it appear that we were tourists driving in from Sana'a. And at the same time, we were obviously not tourists, so therefore we were Americans on a mission. Hopefully our arrival would come to the attention of The Panther, who would conclude, correctly, that his former compatriots were here to kill or capture him. The Panther, in turn, would make plans of his own to kill or capture *us*. But before he could do that, a third player — Sheik Musa — would upset The Panther's plan by doing what the Bedouin do best: kidnapping foreigners for ransom. And the first person who was offered the chance to buy the Americans would be The Panther. The Panther, theoretically, would not smell a setup or a trap because it would appear that Sheik Musa just happened to get wind of the American presence and was taking advantage of an opportunity.

And that's the way the CIA thinks. It's not the way I think — I'm a bit more direct and a lot less into the smoke and mirrors that the CIA loves. But, hey, it's their show and Yemen is the stage, so maybe they've got this one right. We will see.

Anyway, in my overnight bag, if you're interested, I'd packed some bottled water, a can of tuna, and yesterday's boxer shorts. Also, Chet had provided each of us with a toilet kit to complete the appearance of overnight visitors from Sana'a.

We were carrying our concealed sidearms, we wore our Kevlar, and our M4s were across our laps. Kate also wore her black scarf so she could cover her hair and face when appropriate, like when she was kidnapped by Muslim gentlemen who would be offended to see her face.

The three Bedouin Land Cruisers that had taken us to the Crow Fortress would now provide a discreet escort for us to the town of Marib, to prevent a real kidnapping – or assassination – by someone else. Two of the Land Cruisers had gone ahead to check out the road, and the third would trail behind. And if anyone noticed the Bedouin's SUVs, they would or should appear to be stalking us, not protecting us.

The two Bedouin who'd been here watching the Predator fish van when we'd arrived were staying here to hold down the fort, literally, and to provide security for Chet. I hoped they didn't cut his throat. We needed Chet to talk to the Predator pilots.

As for CCC – Command, Control, and Communication – the Bedouin had provided Chet, Buck, and Brenner with local cell phones so the convoy could stay in touch if a security situation arose. Also, we had our hand-held radios for point-to-point contact with one another, and our sat-phones, though they'd work only if we had clear sky, meaning not in the vehicles, unless we had our heads out the window.

The order of march was: Hilux One, Buck driving and Zamo riding shotgun; Hilux Two, Brenner driving, me riding shotgun, and Kate in the rear.

We gave the two lead Bedouin Land Cruisers a five-minute head start, then Chet wished us a safe drive to Marib, a nice day at the ruins, and a pleasant kidnapping. Chet thought that was funny. He waved goodbye, then stepped into the van, where he could watch us getting abducted as he ate a can of tuna.

Buck and Zamo pulled out of the courtyard, and Brenner, Kate, and I followed.

Buck didn't head back to the steep ravine we'd come up, but headed north and west across the plateau, following the tire tracks of the two Land Cruisers ahead of us, whose raised dust we could see in the distance. Follow that Bedouin.

The gray, rocky plateau looked like the video images from the first moon walk. This place could use another forty days and forty nights of rain.

Brenner said to Kate and me, 'I've been thinking about this thing with Sheik Musa.'

I asked, 'You mean about us killing Sheik Musa?'

'Yes.' He admitted, 'I see the reason for it. But I don't like it.'

'Neither will Sheik Musa,' I assured him. But the sheik *would* know the reason for it.

'Aside from the ethical issues, there are practical issues,' said Mr Brenner.

'You mean like, how do we explain to the Saudis that we whacked their Bedouin ally?'

'Yes, not to mention that the Bedouin here in Marib and else-where may not want to do business with us in Yemen ever again.' He let us know, 'They have long memories and they hold grudges for about a thousand years.'

I said, 'Maybe Washington has figured out a way to make Sheik Musa's death look like an accident or that someone else did it.'

Brenner replied, 'Assuming we use a Hellfire missile on Musa, that reduces the possible murder suspects to one. Us.'

'Right. But it's not murder. It's termination with extreme prej-udice, in CIA lingo.' I added, 'Sounds better.'

Kate, who's been hanging around me too long, said wisely, 'When you see a double-cross, look for a triple-cross.'

Brenner agreed with Ms. Mayfield and added, 'As we said in Aden, let's keep an eye on this and talk to each other.'

Paul Brenner was a good guy, a former cop, and a straight shooter. True, he seemed to have Restless Dick Syndrome, but, hey, we all have a little of that. I wondered what Clare was doing now. Probably floating in the pool with Howard. How did I get from Paul Brenner to Clare Nolan? Could I have RDS?

Anyway, it was interesting that the three of us didn't completely trust the two intelligence officers. Comes with the territory, I guess, though we were all on the same team. Whatever lies we were told and whatever information Chet and Buck withheld was based on the strong principle of need-to-know. If we needed to know, we'd be told when the time came, and if we never needed to know, we'd never know. And what we didn't know couldn't be gotten out of us if we were captured – or worse, interrogated by a congressional committee. And what we don't know can't hurt us. Wait. Let's back up on that one.

Anyway, Kate, Brenner, and I were now on the same page, and we had our antennae up, to mix metaphors.

Brenner's Bedouin-issued cell phone rang and he answered and listened. Are you allowed to drive while talking on your phone in Yemen? I guess if you're allowed to fire assault rifles out your window, you can talk on your phone.

Brenner hung up and said, 'That was Buck seeing if these cell phones actually worked.'

'Good thinking,' I agreed. Not that we didn't trust Sheik Musa; it was the Yemen Telephone Company that could be the problem.

Especially here. Lots of dead zones. Also, I wondered how the Bedouin paid their phone bills.

Brenner informed us, 'Buck said he got a cell phone call from Chet saying Predators report no suspicious activity ahead.'

Didn't they say that on the road to Aden?

The north side of the plateau, as I saw on the Predator monitor, was a gradual slope, and Buck followed the rutted track as it descended into the flatlands. I could see a road in the distance, a few vehicles, houses, and cultivated areas.

Halfway down the slope, I spotted a white SUV parked behind a big rock formation, and as we got closer I saw four men with AK-47s sitting on the rocks. Obviously they were Sheik Musa's men, guarding this approach to the fortress as promised. Our two lead escort vehicles had apparently sailed right past these guys, so everyone was in the same tribe. Right? On the other hand, this was Yemen and nothing was as it appeared.

Buck slowed down, and so did we. It's times like this when you fully appreciate fully armored vehicles. Beats the hell out of a Kevlar vest.

I took my M4 off safety and told Kate to do the same. Brenner drew his Colt .45.

Buck stopped about fifty meters from the men and they waved their arms to continue on. Like, 'Come on, people. Haven't you ever seen four guys in robes with assault rifles?'

The cell phone wasn't ringing, so I guess Chet and the Predator pilot were okay with these guys — or the pilot was about to put a Hellfire on them.

Our trail vehicle caught up to us, then our hand-held radios all crackled and Buck's voice said, 'They're Musa's tribesmen.'

Buck continued on and we followed. I reminded Kate, 'Scarf. Don't make eye contact unless you're firing at them.'

Brenner thought that was funny.

As Buck drew abreast of the Bedouin, he lowered his window and did his peace greeting — As-salaam alaikum — which they returned. So I lowered my window and called out, 'Shalom aleichem!'

Kate said, 'That's Hebrew, John.'

'Sounds the same.'

We continued on, and our trail escort dropped back.

We came down into the flatlands and followed the rutted track north through a sparsely populated area of small irrigated fields and brown pastureland where skinny goats wandered around looking for something they might have missed. Life here is tough. And short.

Brenner, Kate, and I made small talk, because to keep talking about the mission sounds like you're a little jumpy. And that was not cool.

Brenner informed us, 'I once flew to the Marib airstrip from Sana'a — about a year ago, before things started to go downhill here.' He explained, 'Some VIPs from Capitol Hill wanted to see the ruins, and I led an advance team from the embassy to check out the security situation.'

'And?'

'And I strongly suggested they not come here.' He added, 'It was okay for tourists ... until the Belgians disappeared last summer. But I couldn't guarantee the safety of congressmen and their staffs.'

I said to him sternly, 'Are you telling me that you missed an opportunity to get rid of some congressmen?'

That got a laugh. I'm way funnier than Paul Brenner.

Anyway, we intersected a paved road, and Brenner followed Buck, who turned right – east toward Marib.

Brenner said, 'This is probably the Sana'a-Marib road. The one we saw the sign for in Sana'a.'

Right. And I thought Sana'a wasn't safe. Sana'a was looking like Geneva about now.

Bottom line about third-world travel is this – there's always someplace more dangerous and fucked up than where you are. In this case, however, we had reached the very pinnacle of Places You Don't Want to Visit.

We continued east, toward Marib. I was looking forward to a cold beer and a hot shower in the hotel before I got kidnapped.

CHAPTER SIXTY-ONE

As we approached Marib, Brenner suggested to Kate that she rewrap, and I assured her that the black scarf made her look more mysterious – and thinner.

We entered Marib, which was a ramshackle but bustling town – the provincial capital, according to Brenner, and the only market town for many miles.

The main street was a collection of open-front shops and stalls, government offices, and a few gas stations, but not a single saloon. But to make the town lively, nearly every male was carrying an automatic rifle. I also noticed there was nothing ancient about the place, and Brenner explained, 'This is New Marib. Old Marib is a few kilometers from here and it's mostly abandoned.'

'Why?'

'The Egyptian Air Force bombed it in 1967.'

'Why?'

'Marib was royalist during the civil wars, and the Egyptians were allied with the republican government in Sana'a.'

These people went to war the way kids choose up sides for a football game. And we're getting involved in Yemen, why? They don't need us to help them kill each other.

The town smelled of diesel exhaust and dung, but I also caught the aroma of the outdoor grills in front of the food shops and my stomach growled. Maybe I should eat that tuna.

I asked Brenner, 'Where exactly is the Hunt Oil installation?'

He replied, 'About sixty miles north and east of here. At the edge of Ar Rub` al Khali – the Empty Quarter.' He told us, 'It's a hundred twenty degrees Fahrenheit in the summer.'

'How come oil is always located in shitty places?'

'I don't know. But I do know that geologists think the oil fields are huge and extend into Saudi Arabia. We thought we could control this oil because Yemen is weak. But then Al Qaeda showed up.' He also told us, 'This installation is heavily fortified, but the oil wells can't be expanded until the threat from Al Qaeda is eliminated.'

'Right.' I asked, 'Who the hell would want to work there?'

'There are only about a dozen Americans there. The rest are foreign workers and Yemenis. And mercenaries for security.'

'How much do the mercenaries get?'

'I hear about two thousand a week.'

I said to Kate, 'Honey, I just found us a better job.'

'Send me a postcard,' said Mrs Corey through her scarf.

Anyway, we continued to move slowly along the dusty, vehicle-choked main drag, and I asked Brenner, 'Where is this hotel?'

'The Bilqis is just outside of town.'

'Did you stay there?'

'No. I was just here for the day. But I checked it out for the VIPs. It's not bad.'

'Is there a bar?'

'No. Strictly forbidden in Marib province.'

The cold beer in my head evaporated like a mirage. I hate this place.

Buck made a right turn and we followed.

Brenner informed us, 'The other guests at the Bilqis are foreign aid workers, oil company visitors, the occasional American intelligence officer, and other shady characters.' He thought that was funny, and added, 'The passports of arriving guests are faxed to the National Security Bureau and the Political Security Organization, and photocopies are also sold to Al Qaeda. Or maybe they get them for free.'

'Probably free.'

The town thinned out after a few hundred yards, and up ahead on the right I could see a long white wall with two open gates, which Brenner said was the Bilqis Hotel.

Buck pulled over before we got to the gates and so did Brenner.

We had to get our rifles out of sight, which was why we had Chet's duffel bag.

I noticed that the two Bedouin Land Cruisers in front of us

had continued on, and the trail SUV now passed us and kept going.

Buck and Zamo were out of the Hilux and we got out, leaving our M4s in the vehicle.

Zamo was carrying the duffel bag, which was long enough to hold his rifle and big enough to hold our four compact M4s.

Zamo threw the duffel in the backseat, then got in the Hilux and gathered up our weapons and magazines, putting them in the bag and wrapping them in what looked like Chet's underwear.

Buck asked us, 'Did you enjoy the ride?'

Why does he always say things like that?

No one replied, which was his answer. Buck briefed us, 'We check in, go to our rooms, and meet in the lobby in, say, thirty minutes.' He assured us, 'That's enough time to enjoy a quick shower.'

Buck had new passports for us — same names, same photos, but different passport numbers, and these passports had standard blue covers, i.e., not diplomatic. Now we were tourists.

I asked Buck, 'Where did our escort go?'

'I don't know, but I know we'll see them again later.'

'Will they be kidnapping us?'

'Correct.'

'Good.' I wouldn't want to be kidnapped by strangers.

Zamo had finished wrapping our hardware in Chet's underwear, and we all got back in our vehicles.

Buck drove up to the big double gates and we turned in.

At the end of a long drive was an unexpectedly large hotel of white stucco, consisting of two three-story wings that flanked a single-story entrance structure. The hotel grounds were landscaped and irrigated and it was almost jarring to see green.

Buck stopped in front of the lobby doors and we pulled up behind him.

We all got out and a bellboy appeared who put our overnight bags on a cart, then took the duffel, which was, of course, heavy. Buck, pretending he had only a few words of Arabic, said something to the bellboy, then to us he said, 'I told him to be careful. We have expensive cameras and photographic equipment in there.'

Right. I guess telescopic sights could be photographic equipment.

Anyway, we moved into the large, oval-shaped lobby, which was nearly empty.

Buck informed us, 'This hotel was constructed in the late seventies for tourism and archaeologists, and this entrance lobby is supposed to be built in the oval shape of the Mahram Bilqis Temple.'

Who gives a shit?

He further informed us, 'There was a lot of hope for Yemen after the civil wars and revolutions of the sixties and seventies.' He let us know, in case we didn't, 'It hasn't worked out.'

The desk clerk was all smiley, like we were the first guests he'd seen this year. We produced our new but worn passports, which he handed to another guy to photostat for the PSO, the National Security Bureau, and the hotel, with a fourth copy for Al Qaeda. Another guy looked up our reservations on the computer. On the check-in card, we gave our Yemen address as the Sana'a Sheraton, where I assumed we were all registered. The CIA has good tradecraft and lots of money to make it work.

Because no one had been shot or kidnapped in Marib since last August, the rooms were fifty bucks a night. I noticed we were booked for four nights.

The desk clerk, Mr Karim, asked in English, 'How was your drive from Sana'a?'

Well, we first drove to Aden and got ambushed by Al Qaeda, then we flew in on a spy plane and landed on a dirt road at night, and some Bedouin gave us a lift to Dracula's Castle, and here we are. I replied, 'We took the scenic route.'

He nodded, but advised us, 'It is good if you stay on the main roads.'

'Are there main roads here?'

Buck, in the role of tourist, asked Mr Karim, 'Are any of the ruins closed to visitors?'

The clerk replied sadly, 'Unfortunately the Mahram Bilqis remains closed.' But he brightened and said, 'I think, however, I can arrange a private visit for you.'

Of course you can.

Buck asked a few more tourist questions while Brenner and Zamo kept an eye on our bags, and Kate stayed modestly quiet, admiring the floor.

So did we look like American tourists, or did we look like Americans who were trying to look like tourists? One of the guys behind the desk was definitely checking us out, especially Zamo. I mean, innocent faces aside, we were all wearing Kevlar and sidearms, which though covered by our bush vests could still be spotted by someone who knew what they were looking for. I had the impression that one of these guys behind the desk would be on his cell phone in two minutes talking to someone about us.

PSO? Al Qaeda? Probably both. The good news was that the PSO was giving us a free hand — or said they were. The other good news was that Al Qaeda would soon know we were in town. Does it get much better than that?

Mr Karim returned our passports and gave us four key cards.

He then asked if we'd like a dinner reservation, as though there could be a problem getting seated. Buck asked the clerk to book us for 8 P.M. Buck told us quietly, 'This is where the Belgians had lunch before they went on to the ruins.'

Thanks for that.

We followed the bellboy to the south wing, third floor, where our adjoining rooms awaited us. The bellboy showed Kate and me to our room, which was sparsely furnished, but not bad. Nice green lizard on the wall.

I went out to the big balcony and Kate followed. Below was a swimming pool in the shape of two attached ovals, so I guess ovals were the theme here. There was absolutely no one out on the terrace or in the pool.

Kate said, 'This place is empty.'

Maybe it had something to do with tourists getting kidnapped and murdered. I mean, even Europeans on a budget might find that unacceptable.

Kate said, 'This all seems unreal.'

'It's real.'

'Do you hate me for getting you into this?'

'Ask me later.'

She stayed quiet as we stared out at the empty pool, then asked me, 'Is this going to be okay?'

'Why shouldn't it?'

She didn't reply.

So with Buck's time clock ticking, we went back in the room, undressed, and showered and shaved together to save time and water.

We got dressed and left our overnight bags and toilet articles in the room. What happens to the luggage of kidnapped tourists? We took the stairs down to the lobby. Never trust the elevator in a third-world country.

Buck and Brenner were looking at some tourist brochures, and Zamo had the duffel with our photographic equipment.

The desk clerk, Mr Karim, came over to us and said, 'It is not advisable for you to visit the ruins without an escort.' He assured us, 'I can obtain the services of three or four Bedouin within fifteen minutes.'

Buck replied, 'We're meeting some Bedouin at the ruins.'

Who are going to kidnap us.

The clerk shrugged and further advised us, 'Be careful.'

Better yet, we're armed.

Our Hiluxes arrived and I said to Mr Karim, 'If we're late, hold our table.'

We walked outside, and Buck said, 'We'll go first to Old Marib, then to the Bar'an Temple – the throne of the Queen of Sheba.'

'Will she be home?'

Buck smiled. 'She was kidnapped.' He said to Brenner, 'I know the way. Stay close.'

Goes without saying, Buck.

We got into the Hiluxes and off we went.

I said to Kate and to Brenner, 'Just to remind everyone, the difference between a staged kidnapping and a real kidnapping is not always so clear.'

Brenner replied, 'That's what I've been saying.'

I hear you.

CHAPTER SIXTY-TWO

We headed south on a paved but disintegrating road, and within ten minutes we turned off on a worse road, where up ahead, on a hill, I could see the dark tower houses of Old Marib.

We stopped near a crumbling wall at the edge of the city, and we all got out and looked around. We had clear views down the hill, and there was no one in sight.

Buck said to us, 'Paul will stay here with Zamo. John, Kate, and I will go into the city for about half an hour of sightseeing.'

I told Buck, 'I've seen the South Bronx. I'll stay.'

Kate said to me, 'I want to see this and I want you with me.'

I asked Buck, 'If we're not getting kidnapped here, why are we here?'

'We need to be seen.'

'There's no one around, Buck.'

He informed me, 'There are people around, and they notice everything and everyone in a place like this. Especially Westerners. And they all have cell phones and phone numbers to call.'

Sounds like Kate's hick town in Minnesota.

Buck further explained, 'We need to give any potential kidnappers enough time to discover we are here and call men together to kidnap us.' He added, 'Our kidnapping needs to appear to be real.'

I see a CIA brainstorming session at work; clever people thinking of stupid things. Or Buck just wants to see Old Marib.

Regarding our kidnapping having the appearance of being real, I asked Buck, 'Isn't it unusual for us not to have hired some Bedouin to be with us? Or National Security police?'

Buck replied, 'There was a time when you could come here on your own. But it's not advisable now, though adventurous travelers — or unknowing travelers — still come here without armed escorts.'

'Okay.' I asked, 'Are the Predators watching?'

'Of course.'

I pictured Chet in his van watching us right now. Should I flip him?

Buck also said, 'Our Bedouin escort is close by and we can call them if a situation arises.'

Or when we're ready for them to kidnap us.

Zamo put the duffel bag with the serious guns on the hood of his Hilux and he and Brenner stayed behind to cover our backs.

Buck led the way and Kate and I followed him into the city, carrying only our concealed sidearms and a camera.

The dirt streets of Old Marib appeared deserted, but I noticed fresh goat droppings and recent footprints in the dust.

The mud brick tower houses rose as high as eight stories, except the ones that had collapsed from age or were blown up by the Egyptian Air Force in Civil War Twenty-nine, or whatever. More than half the city was gone, but you could see the surviving foundations filled with drifting sand and rubble.

Buck said to us, 'Several thousand people once lived here. Now maybe a dozen families remain.'

'Well, parking's not a problem.'

The place was creepy, and the dark mud brick buildings looked like high-rise haunted houses. It was deathly still, except for a weird wind that whistled through the streets and through the shells of the buildings, and small dust devils that appeared and disappeared in the roads and rubble. The words 'post-apocalyptic' crossed my mind.

I mean, the place *smelled* dead – like old ashes and rotting ... something.

I glanced at Kate, who seemed fascinated, but also anxious.

Buck said to me, 'Be honest. Isn't this interesting?'

'No.'

Buck chuckled. He was having a grand time, and he spotted a huge foundation stone in one of the tower houses, which he examined, saying, 'This is from a Sabaean temple. See the Sabaean writing carved in the stone?'

Kate dutifully got closer and examined the whatever. I kept an eye on the street.

Buck also found a square stone column that had been incorporated into the doorway of the building, and he informed us, 'This, too, is Sabaean. It's probably three thousand years old.'

I asked, 'What does the writing say?'

'It says "Yankee go home".'

Funny. But not a bad idea.

Buck also let us know, 'This hill is actually the result of layer upon layer of civilization here. Someday, archaeologists will excavate this right down to the first human settlement on this spot.'

And find the world's first delicatessen.

Anyway, it was time for a sit-rep, and I used my sat-phone to call Brenner.

He answered and I asked, 'Anything happening there?'

'Negative.' He asked, 'Am I missing something good?'

'I see dead people.'

'Get a picture.'

'Roger.'

So we continued to wander around, and Buck was all over the place, looking for bits and pieces of broken stone with this weird writing carved in it, which to me looked Martian. He took lots of pictures, and I was starting to believe we *were* tourists.

Buck asked us, 'Do you want to go into one of the houses?'

'No.'

'We can climb up to the mafraj and get a wonderful view.'

'Buck,' I said sternly, 'these towers are on the verge of collapse. I don't even want to be in the *street* next to them.'

'Well ... all right. But if we see real kidnappers – or Al Qaeda – we'll have to duck into a tower house.'

'I'd rather shoot it out on the street.'

We continued on, and Buck, ever the instructor, informed us, 'Islam has an ambivalent attitude toward pre-Islamic culture and artifacts. Some Muslims see these ancient pagan cultures as visible evidence that the early Arabs were civilized and very advanced. But the fundamentalists reject anything that is pre-Islamic and pagan, and they often destroy these artifacts – the same as the early Christians destroyed and defaced the statues and temples of pagan Rome.'

'Right. They knocked the dicks off the statues.'

'Correct. The fundamentalists here do the same.'

Can we leave now?

But he continued, 'The Bedouin feel some affinity for these ruins. The Sabaeans are their direct ancestors. But people like Bulus ibn al-Darwish want to erase all evidence that a civilization existed anywhere in the Middle East before Islam.' He added, 'And that is why the Western archaeologists have been threatened here, and why so many attacks on Westerners have occurred in and around pagan archaeological sites here and elsewhere in the Middle East.'

I thought that Westerners were attacked at archaeological sites because that's where Westerners went. And also because these places were isolated. That's what happened to the Belgians. They should have stayed in Sana'a. Actually, they should have gone to Paris.

But I got Buck's point. Westerners coming here were like people going to an African game preserve; the visitors want to see the wild animals, and the wild animals see the visitors as a lunch that walked into their dining room.

In any case, we were in the right place. Or the wrong place.

Buck reminded us, 'The Romans besieged this city, and Marib has been besieged dozens of times and survived until the Egyptian Air Force destroyed it in 1967.'

Jet fighters with two-thousand-pound bombs are a bitch.

Buck looked around and said sadly, 'War is senseless.'

I think the old Cold Warrior was going soft. I mean, this was nothing compared to thermonuclear Armageddon.

We came into an open area that Buck said was once a souk. There were goats wandering around the square and also a few kids — meaning young children, not baby goats. Anyway, the kids — the children — spotted us and stared at us like they'd seen ghosts. I guess they don't get many tourists here.

Finally, they got their courage up and about ten of them ran toward us, yelling, 'Baksheesh! Baksheesh!'

I said to Buck, 'Tell them to walk with us and we'll pay them.'

Buck nodded and said something in Arabic, and the children left their kids behind and surrounded us as we doubled back to our vehicles.

I mean, I hate to use children as shields, but they were getting paid.

About half an hour after we'd entered Old Marib, we came back to where we'd started.

Buck asked us, 'Did you enjoy that?'

Kate said, 'It was fascinating. Incredible.'

Sucked.

We walked out of the ruins and I was happy to see Zamo and Brenner, who had not been kidnapped or murdered.

We paid off the urchins, and I advised them, 'When you grow up, relocate.' But stay away from Perth Amboy.

Brenner wanted to ride with Zamo awhile, so we switched and Buck got behind the wheel with me still riding shotgun and Kate in the back. Buck took the lead again and we drove down the hill, toward the next dead ruin, the throne of the Queen of Sheba.

I pictured the headline in the *New York Post*: *Five Yanks Yanked Seeing Sheba*. Or, *Bedouin Bad Boys Snatch Our Boys*.

Hey, it's all make-believe. Part of a clever CIA plan.

So how about this? *Panther Pulverized by Predator in Perfectly Planned Ploy.*

I like that.

But first, a friendly kidnapping.

CHAPTER SIXTY-THREE

We headed south from Old Marib and crossed a narrow bridge over a flowing stream, the first running water I'd seen in Yemen that didn't come out of a tap.

In fact, Kate said, 'Nice to see a river.'

Buck informed her, 'There are no rivers in Yemen. That is a seasonal wadi, usually dry at this time of year, but the gates of the new Marib dam must be open upstream.'

Right. Gotta water that spring khat.

Buck also informed us, 'The old Marib dam was built about two thousand years ago, which made the Sabaean civilization possible. The dam collapsed in 570 A.D., the year Mohammed was born, which Muslims take as an omen.' He explained, 'The end of paganism, and the beginning of a new world.'

That's how I felt after the collapse of my first marriage.

Buck also told us, 'The new dam was built in the 1980s — fourteen hundred years after the old dam collapsed.'

'Union problems?'

Buck also let us know, 'A bridge limits your ability to go off-road.'

Right. That's where I'd set up a kidnapping.

Anyway, within ten minutes we were approaching the archaeological site of Bar'an. I saw a white minibus parked on the dirt road, and a blue military truck, probably belonging to the National Security police.

Buck parked behind the truck, and Brenner and Zamo parked behind us.

We all got out and looked around. There were patches of scrawny trees here and there and date palms and also a few irrigated fields, but mostly it was brown dirt and dust.

Buck, too, was looking at the arid landscape and said, 'The desert, when it decides to come, is relentless. The dam and the irrigation pumps are fighting a losing battle.'

So are we. And ironically, so are the jihadists. There will be no winners here. Except the desert.

We weren't out of the vehicles two minutes before we were attacked by kids yelling for baksheesh, then souvenir vendors, then two young men who said they were guides for hire. And finally, an NSB officer butted in and offered protection for twenty dollars. He must be related to Captain Dammaj.

I hope there's an ATM around here.

But Buck was our ATM, and he gave the NSB officer some rials, then paid off the kids to beat it. He also gave the two guides a nice tip for doing nothing, and he spoke pleasantly to all of them in Arabic. Buck is a good American diplomat; he gives money to anyone and everyone.

The police officer was looking at us as though his instincts told him we weren't the clueless tourists we appeared to be. I wondered if he could tell we were wearing Kevlar, and if so, did he conclude we were carrying? Or did he think we were stupid enough to be here unarmed?

He said something to Buck, who translated for us. 'He says the police are leaving, and we should not stay here too long.'

As though these clowns could be of any help. But thanks for the tip. I said to everyone, 'I wonder if these are the same NSB guys who took a hike on the Belgians.'

No one replied.

Anyway, the Keystone cop left, but the souvenir guys, six of them, hadn't been paid off yet, and they were waving their wares at us — cheap jambiyahs, probably made in China; shiwals, one size fits all; sandals, ditto; and postcards.

Buck gave the souvenir vendors a few hundred rials, took a few postcards, and we were now free to approach the entrance to the ruin.

Zamo stayed behind to provide security, as per the plan, and the four of us walked to a stone arch that looked new, where four Bedouin sat, chewing, and they hit us up for an admission fee of about three bucks each. At the end of the day, it is the Bedouin who control all movement and all access here.

The ruin was elevated above the surrounding land, and we climbed up some stone steps and looked out across a few acres of excavations and broken walls surrounding a paved courtyard. Across the courtyard, at the top of a flight of steps, were tall square columns where a group of tourists stood listening to their guide. Nice ruins. Better than Marib, which was creepy. Time to go.

But Buck, our unpaid guide, said to us, 'This is the Bar'an Temple, also known as the Temple of the Moon, and also known as Arsh Bilqis, which means the throne of Bilqis, which is the Sabaean name for Sheba.' Buck continued, 'Not far from here is the Temple of the Sun.'

Makes sense.

'This temple was dedicated to the Sabaean god called Almaqah.'

Please, someone kidnap me.

Buck went on awhile, as he does, and Kate, of course, asked questions. She's always trying to improve her mind, and as long as she doesn't try to improve mine, I'm okay with that.

Meanwhile, the real tourists were assembling in the courtyard with their guide, and I counted fifteen of them. I looked for my Sana'a pal, Matt Longo, but these were mostly middle-aged people, probably Europeans by their pale winter skin and atrocious footwear.

The guide led his clients toward the exit, and as they approached, Buck said something to the guide in Arabic, and they chatted a minute, then the tour guide moved on toward the minibus.

Buck said to us, 'Half the tour group are German, the other half are Danes.'

Totaling one bunch of adventurous idiots. Clueless in Bilqis.

Buck told us, 'They're returning to Sana'a.' He added, 'No one stays here overnight anymore.'

I inquired, 'Why does anyone even *come* here?'

Buck replied with impatience, 'To learn, Mr Corey. To see history. To experience another culture.'

Okay. I guess the Belgians experienced another culture.

Buck reminded me, 'If you stay home, the terrorists win.'

That's what everyone in New York said after 9/11, so we all went out and filled the bars and restaurants. Fuck Al Qaeda. Make that a double, bartender. God bless America!

But this was different. This was the belly of the beast. And for all I knew, the tour guide, the NSB officer, and everyone else here was on their cell phone right now telling someone there were American turkeys here to pluck.

Buck glanced at his watch and said to us, 'This area will be deserted within half an hour. We'll wait until then, then we'll head back to the Bilqis Hotel.'

Kidnapped at the oasis. Waylaid at the wadi.

Buck, with time on his hands, informed us, 'The Western archaeologists won't return here, and the local authorities won't remove the drifting sand.' He concluded, 'In ten, maybe fifteen years, all this will be covered again, except for those columns.'

Kate said, 'That's sad.'

Maybe they can put an oil well here.

Buck turned, looked toward the west, and said, 'Those hills on the horizon are the ones we flew over, and where the Crow Fortress is.' He told us, 'The Yemenis believe that Noah's Ark came to rest in those hills after the Flood.' He also told us, 'About forty kilometers farther west of the Crow Fortress is where the Al Qaeda training camp is. Also somewhere in those hills is where we believe The Panther's personal hideout is located.'

Maybe he's hiding out in Noah's Ark. I suggested, 'The Predators should look for the Ark while they're looking for The Panther's hideout.'

Buck reminded me, 'The Panther is coming to us.'

'Right.' We had as much chance of finding The Panther as

we had of finding the Ark. The Panther, however, would find us.

The sun was starting to sink in the western sky and I shielded my eyes as I stared at the distant hills. So the Crow Fortress was not too far from the Al Qaeda training camp, which would soon be pulverized by American fighter-bombers if all went well. And also up there in those desolate hills was Bulus ibn al-Darwish, a long way from New Jersey. And maybe Noah's Ark was sitting up there, too. A profound thought was taking shape in my mind, a unifying thread, perhaps, that would link all this together, and I said, 'This place sucks.'

Buck turned impatiently and led us down into the sunken courtyard. I noticed we were hidden from the road, and there wasn't a soul in sight. I drew my .45 and slipped it in the pocket of my bush vest. Brenner did the same.

Buck, addressing Kate and Brenner but not me, said, 'This is the temple that some Mormon scholars believe is the place where their prophet Lehi came after he fled from Jerusalem in the sixth century B.C.' He added, 'It was here where Lehi is said to have buried the prophet Ishmael.'

I hope Ishmael was dead.

I was really looking forward to my kidnapping.

Buck also told us, 'The Mormons also believe that it was here that Lehi built a ship for himself and his family and sailed to America.'

Hold on. Did that ship have wheels?

But Buck clarified, 'There is strong evidence that there was a river here at that time which flowed to the sea.'

Got it.

Buck led us across the courtyard and up fourteen — count 'em — wide and steep stone steps. At the top were five square columns, rising about sixty feet high. There was a sixth column that was broken, and Buck related a story about the symbolism of the broken column — something to do with the five undisputed pillars of Islam, and the one disputed pillar of the faith. I think he makes this stuff up. In fact, he makes up a lot of things.

Buck finished the story, then stayed uncharacteristically silent for a few seconds before saying, 'This is where the Belgians were presumably killed.'

No one responded to that. But in fact that thought had crossed my mind. And Buck wanted to save this moment for now.

Buck looked down at the paving stones at the base of the columns and said, 'The Yemeni Army personnel who were first called to the scene said these stones were covered with blood.'

In fact, they were still stained, but if you didn't know what happened here, you wouldn't know it was blood.

Buck continued, 'There were two older couples, retirees from Brussels, and a young unmarried couple from Bruges who were touring the Middle East, as well as a married couple, also from Brussels, with their daughter, age sixteen.'

Again, no one responded.

Buck continued, 'They were all staying at the Sheraton in Sana'a as part of a larger tour group. Those nine people decided to sign up for this day excursion to Marib.'

Bad idea. *Very* bad idea.

Buck again stayed silent and I noticed that the ruins were completely deserted now, and the bus and police truck had left. There was no sound from the road or from the ruins around us. We were alone.

Buck said softly, 'These people weren't here to hurt anyone, and the only thing they did wrong in Yemen was to be Westerners. Europeans. Christians. And for that, they paid with their lives.'

Indeed.

Buck continued, 'The bodies of the Belgians were never found, but their tour guide and the bus driver, young men from Sana'a, were found in a drainage ditch a kilometer from here with their throats cut ... so they were able to receive a proper Muslim funeral.' He added, 'Their crime was associating with infidels, and the penalty was death.'

Kate said quietly, 'How awful ... senseless.'

Brenner said, 'This is not war.'

Buck agreed, 'It was a merciless, cold-blooded act of butchery.'

I asked, 'And we think The Panther was here when it happened?'

Buck nodded and replied, 'That is the information we received from the Al Qaeda prisoner in Brussels.'

Well, if anyone had any qualms about killing those bastards with Hellfire missiles, those thoughts were now gone. In fact, high-explosive oblivion was too good for Bulus ibn al-Darwish.

Buck's sat-phone rang and he answered. He listened, then said, 'All right,' and hung up. He said to us, 'That was Chet.' He informed us, 'It's time to leave here and return to the Bilqis Hotel.'

Which was another way of saying, 'It's kidnap time.'

CHAPTER SIXTY-FOUR

The kidnapping itself was sort of anticlimactic.

I was with Buck in the lead vehicle, sitting in the rear of the small Hilux, and Kate was up front so she didn't have to sit with the kidnapper. I am a gentleman.

Brenner and Zamo were about twenty meters behind us.

We had pulled over after we left the ruins and everyone had retrieved their M4s, which we now had on our laps, and Zamo had his sniper rifle. Most importantly, Kate was wearing her scarf for her kidnapping. All was right with the world – if your world was Yemen.

As we approached the narrow bridge over the wadi, a white Toyota Land Cruiser pulled onto the road from the shoulder and slowed down on the bridge. A second white SUV pulled onto the road behind us and in front of Brenner. A third SUV fell in behind Brenner. So we were boxed and sandwiched. This might be a staged kidnapping, but these guys had done this before, for real.

The SUV in front of us came to an angled stop at the far end of the bridge and Buck stopped about ten meters from him.

I turned to see the SUV behind us stopping close to our rear.

Brenner, too, came to a halt, then the last SUV stopped behind Brenner and bottled up the bridge. Nice job everyone.

Kate, who probably thinks all Bedouin look alike, asked, 'How do we know these are our ... people?'

I assured her, 'Our Bedouin were bearded and wearing white robes, and these guys in the SUVs are bearded and wearing white robes.'

Buck was a bit more reassuring and said, 'Those are Musa's three vehicles, and I'm sure those are the men who escorted us last night and today.'

I added, 'We had lunch with them.' And Musa is still working for us. Right?

My Colt automatic was still in the pocket of my bush jacket, and I took it off safety.

I noticed a number of women on the banks of the wadi washing clothes, and some boys were wading in the water, and some men were fishing. A few of these people glanced up at the five SUVs stopped on the bridge: two Hiluxes and three Land Cruisers. They must have figured out it was a guest kidnapping – happens all the time – so they looked away.

Up ahead, a big truck stopped at the approach to the bridge, but he wasn't blasting his horn the way they would in New York. Just be patient, Abdul. The Bedouin are kidnapping a few tourists. Takes a few minutes.

The rear door of the Land Cruiser in front of us opened and a Bedouin got out, carrying an AK-47. I looked behind me and saw another Bedouin approaching Brenner's Hilux.

I recognized the Bedouin coming toward us – it was Yasir, the guy who had fondled my jambiyah – and he was waving the business end of his AK-47 at us as he opened the rear door next to me. He slid in quickly, slammed the door, and rested his rifle across his chest with the muzzle a foot from my head.

He didn't have much to say, but there wasn't much that needed to be said.

The Land Cruiser in front of us began moving, and Yasir said to Buck, 'Yalla nimshi.' Let's go.

We drove past the stopped truck and I looked at the driver, who was literally covering his face with his hands. I mean, he didn't see *nuthin'*!

Anyway, the kidnap convoy continued north, toward Marib, but before we got to the Bilqis Hotel, the lead vehicle turned left on a dirt trail, west toward the hills, and we all followed.

Our passenger seemed to relax a bit and he said something to Buck, who replied.

Buck said to us, 'This gentleman, Yasir, says it is good to see us again.'

I asked Yasir, 'Have you done this before?'

Anyway, everything seemed cool so far, and I didn't pick up on anything wrong or suspicious. Bottom line, I had my Colt automatic in my pocket, my M4 on my lap, my Kevlar in place, and my antenna way up.

Regarding that, everyone's hand-held radio crackled and Zamo's voice said, 'Clean Sweep Five here. Read?'

I replied, 'Sweep Three, loud and clear.'

'Everything good?'

'So far.'

'Same.' He added, 'This sucks.'

Could be worse. Could be real. Or it could turn real.

There weren't many vehicles on this dirt trail, and not too many people in the scattered fields, but there were a number of goat herders sitting around on stone fences, and they seemed interested in the five-vehicle convoy kicking up dust.

Buck made small talk with Yasir, who still seemed a little jumpy. Probably, I thought, despite the fact that this was Bedouin territory, Yasir didn't want to run into an army patrol, or even the National Security police, though the NSB was bought and paid for. I doubted if Yasir and his friends were worried too much about the Mukhabarat, a.k.a. the PSO, a.k.a. the secret police, who operated mostly in the towns. In any case, the fix was in with the government, though Yasir didn't know that, and neither did he know why the fix was in — because the Americans were going to whack his sheik as a favor to President Saleh.

The other thing on Yasir's mind would be Al Qaeda. They were on my mind, too. It was possible that Al Qaeda had been tipped off by now about the Americans at the Bilqis Hotel and at the ruins, and maybe they had put together a snatch job of their own.

Bottom line, though, if Al Qaeda was around, they'd have to defer to the Bedouin, who'd been here for two thousand years. Right?

Anyway, I saw that we were going southwest, and I could see the hills ahead, meaning we were on our way back to the Crow Fortress, which was the plan. If, however, we were going some-place else — like the Al Qaeda training camp — I was ready to cut this trip short.

I said to Buck, 'No detours, no bullshit from Yasir.'

Buck replied, 'Relax, please.'

'I'll relax when I'm on that Otter.'

Kate said, 'I'm going to call Chet.'

'Good idea.'

She opened her window and leaned out to get clear sky and dialed Chet on her sat-phone, but he didn't answer.

Yasir didn't seem to care if we used our hand-held radios or sat-phones or that our automatic rifles were on our laps, so maybe I shouldn't be paranoid. We were on our way to the safe house, the Crow Fortress. However, if we found Chet there with his throat cut, that would not be a good sign. Or was I ambivalent about that?

I reminded Kate, 'The Predators are watching us.'

Kate reminded *me*, 'You have a Bedouin sitting next to you with an AK-47.'

'Right. I'm on top of that.'

Buck said, 'This is all going as planned.'

And it was. So I said to Yasir, 'Where did you go to college?'

Buck translated, and Yasir replied, and Buck said to me, 'He thanks you for your compliment.'

'What compliment?'

'I told him you said you admired his shiwal.' Buck added, 'He might give it to you. Then you have to wear it.'

'Thanks, Buck.'

'And if you keep making me translate silly remarks, you'll be wearing his underwear.'

Kate thought that was funny, and I was happy she was starting to relax.

Anyway, I gave up on trying to make conversation with Yasir, and I paid attention to where we were going.

Within ten minutes we intersected the wide dirt road that I recognized as our landing strip, and we turned right toward the plateau where the Crow Fortress stood.

Kate said to me, 'Try Chet.'

So I opened my window, leaned out, and dialed Chet.

He answered and I said, 'We've been kidnapped.'

He replied, 'I saw that.'

I reminded him, 'In case you forgot, we're in the two small Hiluxes. Tell the Predator pilots.'

'Thank you. Anything further?'

'Any dust?'

There was a short pause, then he replied, 'No dust tonight.' Chet let me know, 'You should be here in fifteen minutes.'

'Keep the beer cold.'

'Further?'

'Negative.'

So I sat back and relaxed.

Chet thought I was funny, but annoying. Maybe even a bit silly. And it was good that he should think that. There are a lot of felons in jail who thought that.

Brenner, however, ex-cop, recognized the act. Zamo, too, may have seen beyond the jokes, and Buck had also been perceptive enough to figure out my M.O.

Kate, of course, had seen me play dumb and funny with suspects, as well as supervisors. Playing dumb is smart. People let their guard down. And make mistakes.

Buck and Chet were my colleagues, my compatriots, and my teammates. But they were not my trusted friends. In fact, they were up to something.

We got to the ravine at the base of the plateau, and up we went. This was actually scarier in the daylight.

We made it to the top and headed toward the Crow Fortress.

I had no idea how long we were going to be here waiting for the Al Qaeda delegation to come check us out and confirm who we were. But if I had to spend more than a week with Chet and Buck, I'd surrender to the first jihadist who came through the door.

Meanwhile, I had to keep an eye on Chet and Buck. Especially Chet. I could wait to see if Chet was here to settle an old CIA score with Kate and me, or I could confront him with it. If I waited, it might be too late to tell him, 'I knew you were up to something.' So maybe I needed to make a pre-emptive strike. Before he did the same.

CHAPTER SIXTY-FIVE

The five-vehicle kidnap convoy drove through the open gates into the walled courtyard of the Crow Fortress and we all got out of the SUVs.

The two Bedouin hadn't cut Chet's throat, and he greeted us and said, 'It looked picture perfect on the video monitor.' He added, 'I hope enough locals saw it happening, and that by now the word has gotten back to Al Qaeda.'

I asked Chet, 'What if the locals or Al Qaeda know or suspect that we're in the Crow Fortress?'

Chet replied, 'That's possible. But Al Qaeda is not going to interfere with a Bedouin kidnapping or mount an operation against a fortress occupied by Sheik Musa.'

Probably not. But I wouldn't want to leave here again until The Panther and his jihadists were ready for the goo bags.

We thanked our Bedouin hosts for a pleasant kidnapping experience and climbed up to the second floor of the tower, where we would await further developments, as per Chet's briefing in Aden.

Chet had retrieved a sat-phone antenna from the van that he'd rigged up in one of the windows, and he plugged his phone into one of the antenna cable jacks, saying, 'Now we don't need clear sky to be in direct sat-phone contact with the Predator ground control station.'

That's good.

'Or with the embassy, Langley, 26 Fed, or Washington, or anyone who needs to call us.'

That sucks.

He advised us, however, 'Sat-phone reception is sometimes spotty and also the PSO could be listening. Maybe even Al Qaeda if they have the capability. So we'll keep our sat-phone calls to a bare minimum.' He assured us, however, 'The satellite radio signal from the van is very strong, and it's scrambled and encrypted, so that's secure.'

Bottom line, this was a well-thought-out mission, but the ability to operate in this environment was severely limited. Chet, though, wanted this to work, to show that the CIA could mount surgical strikes in hostile territory as they did so well at the beginning of the Afghan war. The US military and others, however, would like to see boots on the ground. Lots of them. I found myself rooting for the CIA on this one.

So now that we saw the new sat-phone antenna, what else do we do for fun? Maybe we could play Chutes and Ladders with the excrement shaft.

Before I could suggest that, Buck said, 'I brought along some magazines, paperback novels, and crossword puzzles to kill the time.'

I asked Chet, 'Any more cognac?'

'One bottle for a celebration.'

Let's celebrate.

Anyway, we all sat cross-legged on the carpet, except for Zamo, who went from window to window with his rifle and binoculars.

Kate asked Buck and Chet, 'How long do you think it will take for Sheik Musa to contact Al Qaeda?'

Chet replied, 'Could be a day or two.' He explained, 'Musa will make it appear that he's biding his time, maybe exploring his options, or maybe waiting to see if Al Qaeda contacts him to inquire if he knows anything about some kidnapped Amriki.' He added, 'It has to play itself out and we don't want to micromanage Musa.'

No, but we want Musa to get his ass in gear.

Chet also reminded us, 'The Panther could have felt the heat here after the Hunt Oil attack, and maybe he left the area. If so, when Musa offers him five kidnapped Americans, The Panther will have to make the decision about coming back here or not, because Musa is not going to leave his tribal lands and go to The Panther with the five Americans.' Chet concluded, 'So it could be a long wait. But I'm confident that one way or the other, Bulus ibn al-Darwish will show up in the crosshairs of a Predator drone video camera.'

Maybe. But the problem was the long wait, and I asked Chet, 'How long do we wait?'

'As long as it takes.'

Holy shit. I asked, 'What happens when the tuna runs out?' I prompted him, 'Come on, Chet. What's the max time we sit here doing crossword puzzles?'

Chet thought about that, then replied, 'I say we give it two weeks. After that we may have a security problem.'

Not to mention a mental health problem. I mean, *two weeks* in this dungeon? We could get a disease. Call Clare.

Chet also informed us, 'The decision is not wholly ours to make. I need to consult with Langley on a day-to-day basis.' He added, 'We'll play it by ear.'

I suggested, 'We should also stay in touch with Sheik Musa. He's the guy who's in touch with Al Qaeda.'

Chet replied, 'We don't call Musa. Musa calls us.'

Buck also informed us, 'The Arabs in general, and the Bedouin in particular, have a different sense of time than we do in the West.' He let us know, 'They can negotiate for months over even a simple matter. They're in no rush.'

But Chet was more reassuring and said, 'The Panther, having a half-American head, will probably come to a quick decision.' He added, 'He's impatient. And hungry.'

'Me, too.'

So we had a long wait. Or a short wait. In the end, the best-laid trap still depends on the guy you're trying to trap.

Kate had a good question. 'Will our disappearance – or kidnapping – be reported to the media?'

Buck replied to that. 'There is a news blackout at the embassy PIO office.' He smiled and said, 'Which is redundant since the PIO doesn't put out many news releases from Yemen anyway.' He added, 'As for snooping Western journalists, there are virtually no resident American news organizations in Yemen. Only the BBC has an office in Sana'a, and the lone reporter there is on extended home leave. As for Yemeni journalists, or government sources, they either know nothing or they've been told to know nothing.'

Right. This was truly the Land That Time Forgot, and the black hole of the Mideast, and you could be missing here for months before anyone outside of Yemen noticed.

Kate asked, 'What if our friends or family don't hear from us, or are trying to contact us?'

I said to Kate, 'If you mean your parents, consider this a vacation.' No, I didn't say that. I kept my mouth shut.

Buck replied, however, 'Each of us will write a note that will be delivered by our respective offices in the States to anyone on your list.' He advised us, 'Keep it general, and don't mention that you've been kidnapped.' He smiled.

Buck also advised us, 'Any inquiries to our offices coming from friends or families will be handled by the embassy in Sana'a.' He added, 'We should have no problem staying incommunicado for a week or two.'

Chet informed us, 'I stay out of touch with friends and family for weeks at a time.' He added, 'Comes with the job.'

Also, no one gives a shit if they don't hear from you. In fact, they welcome it. That's not nice. Someone somewhere loved Chet.

On that subject, we knew virtually nothing about Chet's personal life, and he never volunteered a word. But Kate took the opportunity to ask him, 'Are you married?'

Chet hesitated a second, then replied, 'I am estranged from my wife.'

Maybe that has to do with Chet being strange.

Kate said, as women do, 'I'm sorry.'

The wife is probably not.

Chet volunteered, 'This assignment and the separation has put a strain on the marriage.'

I'll say. And I did feel a little sorry for him. On the bright side, he could have four wives here ... or maybe only three. He's already got one. Right?

Buck, who had seemed to make his marriage work despite decades of foreign assignments — or maybe *because* of that — said, 'This business is difficult for family life. We sacrifice a great deal for our country and sometimes I'm not sure it's appreciated by the country.'

How about never? And why do we care? We do what we do for other reasons. Appreciation is not part of the plan.

Buck said, regarding the long or short wait here, 'Let's be optimistic and assume that we'll be on a plane heading home before anyone even knows we are missing.'

Okay. Let's be optimistic.

I opened one of the crossword books and said, 'An Arab who ran out of ammunition? Eight letters.'

Brenner, who knew the joke, replied, 'A moderate.'

CHAPTER SIXTY-SIX

It was dinner time and we feasted on canned tuna, cold mixed vegetables, and tawwa bread, all washed down with warm bottled water. Chet had a smoke.

The light was fading and we lit a few kerosene lanterns. Out in the courtyard it was prayer time again and the Bedouin were praying loudly, making me homesick for Brooklyn.

After the call to prayer, Chet announced that he had to do a sit-rep and he was going to use the secure radio in the van. I said I'd keep him company, and we both went down to the courtyard where he unlocked the van and we entered.

Chet checked his voice mail and text messages, then made his sit-rep – all okay – then signed off and swiveled his chair toward me. He asked, 'You wanted to talk to me?'

'I do.' I remained standing and said to him, 'About Ted Nash.'

He nodded.

'You knew him.'

He nodded again, then said, 'But not well.'

'Whatever. Here's the deal, Chet. My wife, before we were married, was involved with Nash.' I looked at his face in the dim light of the console. 'You know that?'

'I heard.'

'So what happened was maybe more personal than business.'

He didn't respond.

I continued, 'On the other hand, Nash, a few seconds before his death, had a gun pointed at us – at me and Kate – and that was business. Did you know that?'

'I don't know the details.'

'I'm giving you the details. Here's another detail. Nash was involved in a rogue operation that would have caused a nuclear attack by the US on the world of Islam.' I asked, 'Did you know *that*?'

'If I did, I wouldn't tell you that I did.' He added, however, 'I did not.'

'Now you know.' I further informed him, 'That might sound like a good idea to you – nuke 'em, as I said, and you agreed. But wiping out tens of millions of innocent people and leaving the Mideast a nuclear wasteland is not really a good idea.'

He smiled and replied, 'That's your opinion.'

'Yeah. And my opinion was the one that counted.' I also informed Chet, 'Kate and I were prisoners of a nut job who was going to kill us. And Nash knew this. In fact, after Kate and I whacked the nut job, Nash showed up and was going to finish the job for the psycho. Follow?'

'I guess.'

'So we're talking about self-defense, with maybe a little personal history between the parties.'

'Okay. But what does this have to do with me? Or this mission?'

'You tell me.'

'Okay. Nothing.'

'Try again.'

Chet stayed silent a moment, then said, 'I think I see how your paranoid mind is working. And to be honest, I can understand how you might reach some wild and erroneous conclusions. But—'

'No buts, Chet. Do you think I'm stupid enough to believe that Kate and I were asked to come here because we're perfect for this job?'

'You *are* perfect for this job, John. And so is Kate.'

'Right. Perfect in every way.'

He asked me a question that I'd asked myself. 'If you really believe what you're suggesting, why in the world did you come here?'

'Because, Chet, this is the belly of the beast. And you are the beast. And I am here to talk to the beast, and if I have to, to kill the beast.'

He had no reply to that.

I advised him, 'When I walk out of here, you will cable or speak to Langley, and you will let them know that you spoke to me, and that this problem better be finished.'

Again he stayed silent, then said, 'I'll pass on our conversation.' He added, 'But as far as I know, you and your wife being asked to come here has nothing to do with what happened to Ted Nash. It has to do with you and Kate being good Panther bait – because you killed The Lion. Nothing more, nothing less.' He further informed me, 'I don't like being threatened.'

'I'm not threatening you. I'm telling you that if I smell a rat, or if something happens to Kate, you're dead.'

He was getting a little pissed off and snapped, 'If something happened to Kate, you can be sure the same thing would happen to you.'

'Not if I blow your fucking head off first.'

He backed off a bit and said in a controlled voice, 'I understand how you might come to the conclusion you came to ... And you know what? You could be right. But I don't think you are. But if you are, it has nothing to do with me. I'm not here to settle a score with your wife, or with you. I'm here to kill Bulus ibn al-Darwish.' He assured me, 'I don't assassinate American citizens ... well, except for al-Darwish.'

'I'm happy to hear that, Chet. And if you leave here alive, it's because I didn't kill you. So that evens the score. Tell the boys back in Langley.'

He nodded, then said to me, 'I need to send some cables. Are we finished?'

I turned and left the van.

Well, that was out of the way. Now Chet knew that I knew, and he could think about it and report it to whoever had the bright idea of sending me and Kate here to become unfortunate casualties of war.

I mean, I always thought that there was a CIA contract out on us since Kate whacked Ted, and this seemed like a good time and place for the Agency to act on that. And nothing that Chet said made me believe I was wrong. So, to further answer Chet's question of why I was here if I thought that, the answer was, 'You can't run from the beast forever.' You have to meet the beast. And you meet him on his turf. And you kill him. Or, because we're civilized, and because the beast has friends, you might make a deal with him.

I hope Chet understood the deal. If not, the Otter wouldn't be carrying as many passengers on the return trip.

CHAPTER SIXTY-SEVEN

Without electricity — except in the van — there wasn't too much to do after the sun went down. Also, I'll never again take hot running water for granted. Or a chair to sit in, or a cold beer.

I mean, I'm not a softie or a sissy; I'm an urban fighter. Urban is good. Comes from the Latin for city. As in electri-city. Right?

Well, maybe this rustic experience will do me some good. I'll get in touch with my inner Bedouin. But maybe I should rethink the warlord thing.

Also, it could be worse; this could be a real kidnapping. I could be waiting to have my head sawed off.

Anyway, we were all sleep-deprived, so it was no problem hitting the hay early. We posted a two-person guard for three-hour shifts — Brenner and Zamo first, me and Kate second, Buck and Chet last. That should take us to dawn. And Paul Brenner, I should point out, was fulfilling his desire to sleep with Kate — though probably not the way he envisioned it.

Chet and I had not revisited our conversation at any point during the evening, which in any case was not really possible in a communal setting. But Chet did say to me, in a rare moment of privacy, at the door of the excrement shed, 'I sent a cable relating your concerns.' He added, 'No reply.'

Bullshit.

During my and Kate's guard shift, as we looked out a window at the black night, I said to her, 'I spoke to Chet about Ted Nash.'

She didn't reply for a few seconds, then reminded me, 'I was going to do that.'

'I handled it differently than you might have handled it.'

'Meaning?'

'Meaning I shared with him my suspicion that you and I were asked to come to Yemen so that the CIA could even the score. Meaning you whacking Ted Nash.'

She stayed silent for a while, then said, 'I don't necessarily agree with your suspicion.' She added, 'It's too ... crazy.'

'You think? Look, it's not only about you terminating Ted, and you being cleared of any wrongdoing. It's also about you and me screwing up the CIA's plan to nuke Islam. That was a biggie. And we *know* about it.'

'We've stayed silent — as per the deal.'

'Right. But that's not good enough for worried people in Langley. Dead is better.'

She didn't reply.

'So that's why we're here.'

Again, she didn't respond, but asked me, 'What else did you say to Chet?'

'Well, I told him if anything happened to you, or if I even *thought* you or I were being set up, I was going to blow his head off.'

'You shouldn't have said that.'

'All right. I'll tell him it's okay for him to kill us.'

'What I mean, John, is that you may be *wrong* about this.'

'If I'm wrong, I'm wrong, and there's no harm done.'

'You don't threaten someone's life without some harm done. Especially if that person has done nothing wrong — or knows nothing.'

'Okay. But Chet took it well. He was even pleasant to me after he returned from the van. Did you notice?'

'You may be as crazy as he is.'

'Crazier, I assure you.' I reminded her, '*You* said to look for the triple-cross.'

She didn't reply.

I continued, 'What's in a name? Why is this called Operation Clean Sweep? Why are you and I here?'

'All right. I get it. But . . . what did he say?'

'He neither confirmed nor denied my suspicions. Actually, he said he could understand how I might come to such an erroneous and paranoid conclusion, and that I might actually be right, but he has nothing to do with whatever it was that I was wrongly suggesting.' I asked, 'Follow?'

'No.'

'I guess you had to be there. Bottom line here, I let the cat out of the bag, and Chet cabled his people in Langley. Or maybe he actually spoke to them. So I think we now have less than a fifty-fifty chance of becoming victims of friendly fire — or winding up whacked by Musa or Al Qaeda.'

Kate nodded, then said, 'In this business, the past comes back to haunt you.'

I'm not haunted by anything. My problem is when the past comes back to *kill* you. Like The Lion. Like Ted Nash. This business is a cycle of vendetta, an ever-widening circle without end. Someday, maybe when I'm old, sitting in a rocker, someone from the past will get me. But not today. Not this week.

To make Kate feel better, I said, 'It was self-defense. You saved our lives. Don't replay it.'

She nodded.

So we finished our three hours of guard duty and woke Chet and Buck. Chet was actually already awake. Maybe he had a bad dream about someone cutting his throat while he slept. The five gentlemen of the A-team had breakfast with the eight gentlemen of the desert down in the courtyard, while Kate used the opportunity of privacy to wash up with bottled water.

Breakfast was the same glop, except the Bedouin had added tuna.

After breakfast, Chet, Buck, Brenner, and I went into the van and watched TV. Both screens had reruns of yesterday's show – beautiful Yemen from the air. I felt like I was soaring.

Chet did a commo check and a sit-rep, and ground control reported no unusual activity in the area. Just another routine day in the tribal lands, and a quiet day in Al Qaeda territory. But that could change quickly.

We walked around the courtyard for exercise, the way convicts walk around the prison yard. I counted fourteen lizards.

Later I suggested to Buck, 'Ask our Bedouin hosts if they can get us a soccer ball. Also some real food from Marib. I'll buy.'

Buck informed me, 'They've told me they're not allowed to leave here. And no one can come here unless the food and water runs out.' He explained, 'We're all in lockdown until further notice.'

'When do we start killing and eating the camels?'

'There are no camels. But there are goats outside the walls and our hosts seem to be killing one a day.'

'How many are left?'

'Enough for a long siege.'

On that subject, Kate, Brenner, and I bugged Buck and Chet about getting some info about how Sheik Musa was doing in his talks with Al Qaeda.

But Buck and Chet both agreed that it was premature to send a message to the sheik.

Buck said, 'It would be impolite to ask him now. Maybe in a few days.'

Chet agreed. 'Let it play out.' He added, 'We need to appear trusting, unworried, and cool.'

Who makes this shit up?

Anyway, we had lunch on the diwan level where we lived. Tuna again. Buck explained away the poor provisions from Washington by saying, 'We don't want to accentuate the differences between us and our Bedouin allies.'

'That's idiotic, Buck. We should *celebrate* our differences. Like with pork chops.'

Buck continued, 'Also, we don't want to look too good for the Al Qaeda men who come to see us. We're supposed to be subsisting on goats and oats.' He smiled and added, 'We can't be getting fat in captivity.'

I pictured another CIA committee discussing this. They really are into smoke and mirrors, and as I just discovered, they are believers in method acting. The A-team had to starve a little to look the part of kidnap victims. Not to mention we all needed a shower and shave.

Anyway, there wasn't a lot to talk about anymore, without saying stupid things, so we all sort of retreated into ourselves, and read, and did crossword puzzles. Kate exercised a lot, and Mr Brenner joined her a few times, twisting and bending. I should call the Bedouin in to see this.

We had a first-aid kit, and Brenner helped Zamo change his dressing, and later Brenner assured us that Zamo was okay. Maybe he was. But maybe we had to get him out of here.

We also wrote out in longhand our required notes of assurance to friends, family, bookies, and whomever. These notes would be emailed to the parties we indicated.

Buck had some suggested wording for the last paragraph, and it went something like this: *I'll be out of communication in a remote area for a week or two, but if you need to contact me, this is the US Embassy email address set up for this purpose. I may not be able to respond for a week or more, but be assured I will see your email and I will contact you shortly.*

I said to Kate, 'Tell your parents I miss them.'

Chet and Buck gathered up the handwritten notes from Kate, me, Brenner, and Zamo, then took them down to the van for encrypted transmission to the embassy, or to Washington – they weren't clear about that.

I said to Kate, Brenner, and Zamo, 'This is like the stupid post-cards you had to send to your parents from camp.' Except there was something creepy about this.

The day passed, the Bedouin answered all their calls to prayer, and all their cell phone calls. We walked around the courtyard, and we explored each floor of the six-story tower, which was all the same except for the open-arched mafraj level. Good view. Also, to break up the monotony, I took a leak from the mafraj down the excrement shaft — six stories to the ground floor, which was piled high with shit. Longest piss I ever took. TMI. The other highlight of my day was recharging my commo equipment in the van. It's fascinating to watch the charge levels rise.

The Bedouin, by the way, never seemed bored. They had an infinite capacity to sit around and bullshit. And when they weren't talking to one another, they were talking on their cell phones. They made tea all day, prayed, and slept when they felt like it. They had some kind of washing ritual associated with the call to prayer, but it seemed more symbolic than rub-a-dub-dub.

Now and then one of them would climb one of the stone platforms and peer out over the wall, but they didn't seem to take guard duty too seriously. Probably because they didn't take the Yemeni Army too seriously. And they didn't yet understand the new boys on the block — Al Qaeda.

Also, I don't think the Bedouin really understood about the Predator drones watching us, or that we could see, on our monitors in the fish van, what the Predators saw from five or ten thousand feet.

I asked Chet about this, and he said, 'If I showed them the monitors, they'd understand the capabilities without understanding the technology. Just like with their cell phones.' He added, 'They know it's not magic, but the less they know, the better.'

Right. But I'm sure Sheik Musa knew a little more about Predator drones carrying Hellfire missiles; he knew he didn't want to appear on the video monitor with an X between his eyes.

Anyway, I suppose I could wax poetic about the Bedouin, and

maybe romanticize them the way most Westerners did — but basically they were just simple, uncomplicated, and understimulated people who took small pleasures in a cup of tea. And these eight guys in the courtyard were happy to be sitting around here and not busting their butts herding camels or goats, or scratching out an existence in the dead fields.

As Chet said, they had their Korans to read — if they could read — their guns, and their faith. Also a little khat to help pass the time and elevate their mood.

Speaking of which, Chet took about three trips a day to the mafraj and always came down with a smile. I had this mental image of him stumbling into the excrement hole and dropping six stories into a pile of shit. That could happen.

On a completely different subject, getting laid is no big deal, but *not* getting laid is a *very* big deal. Capisce? Enough said.

Evening came, and we dined al fresco with the Bedouin to do something different. Oats, groats, goats, tawwa, tea, and tuna. Canned fruit for dessert. The Bedouin liked the syrupy canned fruit and ate up most of our stock.

Kate was allowed to join us if she wore her balto and hijab and sat by herself off to the side. Sounded reasonable to me, but Kate balked. Buck, however, urged her to have dinner with us at a distance. He explained, 'This is a big break with custom and we should take advantage of the opportunity to bridge the cultural divide.'

I agreed and suggested, 'About forty feet should do it.'

Kate agreed reluctantly, and it was good to have her at dinner.

Anyway, early to bed, three guard shifts, restless sleep, and dawn. I never before appreciated the dawn. I can see why ancient people worshipped the sun. The sun was life. The night was death.

On the third or maybe fourth day, as I was re-reading the mixed vegetables label, Kate asked me, 'How are you holding up?'

'Fine. I've named all the crows.' I asked, 'How are *you* doing?'

'Okay.' She added, 'Physically, fine. But I'm developing Stock-holm Syndrome.' She smiled. 'I'm beginning to identify with the Bedouin.'

'They're great guys,' I agreed. 'Even though they've never seen your face, they knew you'd make an attractive dinner companion.'

She smiled again and said to me, 'It's very reassuring that you're still an asshole.'

'Thank you.' In fact, I knew that Kate would appreciate me more here in this manly country.

Another thing I noticed is that I didn't miss the news. Or the sports scores. When you're cut off from the civilized world, you go through a few days of withdrawal, and then one day you realize it's all bullshit. What difference does it make what's going on in Washington, London, Moscow, New York, or Cairo? They don't care what *I'm* doing. I would, however, like to know how the Yankees were doing in spring training. But someone could fill me in if I ever got back. And if I didn't, it was sort of moot.

On the subject of getting back alive, neither Chet nor I men-tioned our conversation in the van. There was nothing more to say, and he wasn't going to tell me what his bosses in Langley said to him.

Look, I could be way off base on this, in which case there was nothing more to say or do. But if I was right, Chet and his people were now trying to figure out if Operation Clean Sweep should include John and Kate.

It would have occurred to them, too, that if John Corey knew or suspected a whack job way back in New York, then I would have left one of those 'To Be Opened Only in the Event of My Death' notes with someone.

Maybe I should have, but I didn't. Maybe because I didn't intend to get whacked here by the CIA. Or maybe because if Kate and I got killed by Al Qaeda or The Panther, I wouldn't want the CIA to be suspected of a crime they didn't commit. No matter how I felt about the Agency, in the end they are our first line of defense, and I am a dedicated and responsible professional.

Early the next afternoon, after salat and after the last can of tuna had been eaten, Chet's sat-phone rang. He went to the window where it was plugged into the antenna, and answered.

He listened, then said, 'Okay, thanks,' and informed us, 'Predator reports three white Land Cruisers approaching from the north and heading toward this plateau.'

Kate asked, 'Who do you think they are?'

Chet replied, 'Could be re-supply ... or it could be the men we've been waiting for.'

Brenner asked, 'Why didn't Musa give us a heads-up?'

Buck replied, 'He would give his men a heads-up — not us.'

And sure enough, we heard a commotion in the courtyard.

We all went to the window, and I saw that our eight Bedouin were on their feet, AK-47s in hand, and one of them was on his cell phone. Then four armed Bedouin ran toward the tower and we could hear them coming up the stone stairs.

Everyone grabbed their M4s and we spread ourselves strategically around the stairwell. Buck stood at the top of the stairs with his M4 slung.

The four Bedouin were on the staircase now, shouting loudly and excitedly as they ran up the stairs.

Buck said to us, 'Al Qaeda is coming to see the kidnapped Americans.'

Great. I mean, you know you're bored when you look forward to a visit from Al Qaeda.

CHAPTER SIXTY-EIGHT

Chet, looking very happy, said to us, 'The Panther has bitten.' Right. But The Panther wasn't biting Chet, who, being a spook, was not really here. So Chet excused himself, saying, 'I'll stay in contact with the Predators.' And off he went down the stairs and into the van.

So now we had to look like prisoners of the Bedouin, who fortunately treated their kidnapped guests well.

Kate wrapped her hair and face in her black scarf as the four Bedouin came up the stairs and quickly gathered up most of our things, including our sat-phone antenna from the window. It might be hard to explain to the Al Qaeda guys if we got a phone call, so we also shut off our hand-held radios, sat-phones, and cell phones.

The four Bedouin carried our baggage up one level, as well as our boxes of canned food and our reading material, leaving only our bread and water on the floor. Our friend Yasir and another Bedouin rolled up our carpet and also carried it up the stairs.

The Bedouin wanted our M4 carbines and Zamo's rifle, but Brenner flat-out refused, and we stowed them under our straw bedding. We also kept our Colt .45s concealed in our holsters, which we moved to the small of our backs, though we had to take off our Kevlar vests in case the Al Qaeda guys were sharp enough to notice. Kate took care of that, modestly, in the indoor outhouse.

We also gave the Bedouin our watches and the non-diplomatic passports that we'd used to check in at the Bilqis Hotel, but we kept our diplomatic passports in case we needed to make a dash for the Saudi border.

We'd thought this out over the last few days, and it seemed that we'd thought of everything. But then Kate said, 'Chet's blanket.'

Right.

Buck picked up the blanket and tossed it out the window. I would have tossed it down the shit shaft.

So, did we look like prisoners who'd been cooped up here for four days? We certainly *smelled* the part.

Last thing. We scuffed up the floor where our carpet had been and Buck impressed us with his tradecraft by saying, 'Perhaps we should put some bird droppings here.'

I told him, 'That's your job, Buck.' But he let it go.

We heard something in the courtyard and we all went to the window. The gates were open now, and a white Land Cruiser drove into the courtyard. Then another, and another.

Al Qaeda was here.

We continued to watch as the four Bedouin in the courtyard

opened the rear doors of the Land Cruisers and assisted the black-hooded occupants from the vehicles. There were five of them, dressed in white foutehs and sandals. Also, they had their AK-47s slung over their shoulders. I mean, even blindfolded negotiators carried guns here.

Brenner remarked, 'They've got to know they were driven up to the Crow Fortress.'

Buck assured us, 'There are a number of places like this in the hills.'

That's good. I hope the Bedouin drivers were smart enough to drive these assholes in circles for a few hours.

Anyway, we watched as the five hooded Al Qaeda guys were walked across the courtyard toward the tower. Don't bump into that Predator van.

So now it was time for us to look like five prized Amriki worth a hundred thousand bucks.

We all sat on the bare wooden floor. From left to right it was Brenner, Zamo, Buck, me, and Kate on the far right. The four Bedouin produced three chained ankle shackles and keys. We refused their kind offer to shackle us and did it ourselves — Brenner and Zamo shared a set of shackles, as did Buck and I. Kate, being a woman, had her own set of shackles. We kept the keys. Last thing, we pulled off our shoes and socks, and the Bedouin put them under the straw.

Buck reminded us, 'Scuff the soles of your feet on the floor.'

Right. Never underestimate the intelligence or the perceptive powers of the enemy. They're not as dumb as they look. In fact, these guys probably knew what prisoners were supposed to look like.

This could be a setup, of course, and we could be real prisoners in about five minutes, or real dead. But Musa and his Bedouin had other opportunities to double-cross us. And bottom line, our hands were free and our guns were ready to be drawn.

Someone called out in Arabic from the stairwell and our buddy, Yasir, called back.

I asked Kate, 'You okay?'

'I'm fine.'

Buck reminded her, 'Keep your head and eyes down.'

A few seconds later, the five hooded Al Qaeda guys with three Bedouin guiding them came up the stone stairs and into the tower room.

The Bedouin placed the five Al Qaeda guys in a line, shoulder to shoulder, about five feet in front of us, then one by one they pulled off the black hoods. And we were face-to-face with the enemy.

CHAPTER SIXTY-NINE

The Al Qaeda delegation looked like a firing squad, lined up with their rifles slung on their shoulders.

Also, five men were more than they needed to ID the Americans, so this was a power play or a show of force, and the Bedouin shouldn't have allowed it. But they did, so I expected the Al Qaeda guys to throw their weight around.

Four Bedouin remained in the diwan, including Yasir, who seemed to be hosting this occasion.

The Amriki were supposed to look frightened, nervous, tired, and dejected, which meant mostly just looking down and keeping our mouths shut, unless spoken to. On the other hand, Al Qaeda knew we were not tourists, so we could show a little defiance now and then.

I looked at the five Al Qaeda fighters standing in front of us. They were on the young side – maybe early to mid-twenties, though their faces appeared weather-beaten and old beyond their years. They were beardless, but not exactly clean-shaven, and they looked pretty grim, though they should have been enjoying this.

The guy on the far right, however, was smiling and looking at me, which seemed strange. And then I recognized him.

Nabeel al-Samad said to me, 'Hello. You remember me?'

My teammates all turned their heads toward me, and the four Bedouin, who spoke no English, seemed confused that the Al Qaeda guy was smiling and speaking to the American captive. Hey, we had bagels together.

I was supposed to just nod, but I said, so my teammates understood who this guy was, 'Nabeel and I had a breakfast meeting in New York.' I added, 'He had some important information for me.'

Nabeel thought that was funny and he translated for his compatriots, who also thought that was funny.

What wasn't so funny was Nabeel saying to me, 'Jewish deli for me not funny. You not funny. You not go home ever.'

Nabeel needed help with his verbs, but I got that I was

supposed to appreciate the moment and the message, which in better English was, 'So, Detective Corey, we meet again, and this time the situation is reversed, is it not, Detective Corey?' Hee-hee-hee. Fuck you.

Anyway, I played the game and looked down at the floor.

Bottom line here, soon after the State Department applied for my and Kate's visas, that information had gotten to Al Qaeda in Yemen. Happens all the time and it's not usually a problem for American tourists, businesspeople, or diplomats heading to Sana'a – unless their names happen to be on the Al Qaeda kill list.

Anyway, the fun part was over and it was time for business.

Nabeel said something to Yasir, who handed Nabeel our five non-diplomatic passports.

Nabeel had sheets of paper in his hand, which I was certain were the photostats of these passports gotten from the Bilqis Hotel. Nabeel passed the five passports and photostats around to his four buddies, who studied the passport photos and looked at us.

Nabeel, who had seemed to me like a pleasant putz in New York, had another side to him, and he said to the Amriki sharply, 'Look up! Look to me!'

We all looked at Nabeel as the other A.Q. assholes glanced between us, the photostats, and the passports.

Nabeel, of course, made a positive ID on Detective John Corey, and the other Al Qaeda geniuses seemed to agree that Buck, Brenner, and Zamo were the Amriki in the passport pictures. The problem was Kate, wrapped in her scarf, and Nabeel said to her, 'Take off hijab.'

So Kate pulled her scarf away from her face, and the five Al Qaeda assholes stared at her a long time. I mean, how many women's faces had they seen in their lives?

They all seemed to agree that Kate's photo matched her face, and Yasir collected the passports.

Nabeel said to Kate, 'Put on hijab!'

Nabeel then produced two more sheets of paper, which he showed to Yasir. Yasir nodded, then said something to Buck in Arabic. Buck replied in Arabic, and said to us, 'They also have copies of John and Kate's diplomatic passports – probably from the Yemeni consulate in New York. And they want to know where—'

'Shut up!' shouted Nabeel. Then to all of us he asked, 'Where diplomatic passports?'

Buck replied in English, 'At the embassy.'

'You lie.'

But Yasir jumped in and said something, maybe assuring Nabeel that the Bedouin had searched us and not found any diplomatic passports in the possession of the Americans.

So Yasir, Nabeel, and the other four Al Qaeda assholes got into an argument, and Buck, sotto voce, was translating snippets, saying, 'They want to search us ... and search the bedding ... and search the diwan.'

Right. These things never go the way you want or expect. I asked Buck, 'Who the hell is in charge here?'

Buck said to us, 'Yasir seems to be losing control.'

Great.

Nabeel interrupted his argument long enough to tell me and Buck to shut up.

But Buck, understanding these people, said something to Yasir in Arabic, and his voice was firm. I heard the word 'Musa.'

Yasir seemed to find his balls and backbone, and he shouted at Nabeel and at the other Al Qaeda shitheads, who shut up.

I mean, what's the pecking order here? You tell 'em, Yasir. Meanwhile, I glanced at my compatriots, and I could see they were a bit uneasy. While Nabeel and Yasir were talking, I said in a low voice to Brenner, Zamo, and Kate, 'If I say pull, on the count of three, you know what to do.'

They nodded.

As Kate likes to point out, I sometimes change the plan. But only when Plan A is not going well. I mean, bottom line here, The Panther's prize was right in front of his jihadists, and I wouldn't put it past them to get the drop on the Bedouin and re-kidnap us. Or just blow us away.

So if we had to, we would draw on these five bastards and waste them all before they even got their AK-47s unslung. And that would be the end of the negotiations and the end of Operation Clean Sweep, and unfortunately the end of any chance we had of vaporizing The Panther with a Hellfire. But sometimes you gotta think of yourself first, and you have to take what you can get — like five jihadists who were getting a little too aggressive.

Nabeel and Yasir seemed to have settled down a bit, and they were still jabbering away.

Meanwhile, I noticed that the other four Al Qaeda guys were eyeballing us as if trying to determine if we looked like real guests instead of kidnapped guests.

The Al Qaeda delegation was also eyeballing the big tower room, and they all glanced out the windows to try to figure out where they were. Crow Fortress? Or some other tower in the hills?

The tip-off would have been the window behind them that overlooked the courtyard, and more importantly overlooked the fish van. Hey, Abdul, what's that doing here?

The other three Bedouin were standing directly behind the Al Qaeda guys, to keep them literally in line, head and eyes straight ahead. But then one of the Al Qaeda assholes tried to sneak a look over his shoulder, and I was surprised and pleased to see one of the Bedouin smack his head with the barrel of his AK-47. Like, 'I said no peeking, asshole. Try that again and your brains will be on the floor.' Good. It's your show, boys, and your fort.

More importantly, I could see there was no love lost between these two groups. The Bedouin ruled and have ruled for two thousand years; Al Qaeda was tolerated, as long as they understood whose land this was. Nabeel, however, had spent a little time in Amrika and he'd forgotten his manners. Interestingly, it was Buck who had to remind Yasir that Al Qaeda was not top dog here. Not yet.

But back to business.

Nabeel shouted at me, 'What you do here? Why you here?'

It was Buck who replied – Buck does the talking, I do the shooting – 'We are embassy personnel on a visit to see the ruins.'

Nabeel, of course, said, 'You lie! Why you go to Aden?'

'Embassy business.'

'You lie! How you come to Marib?'

'By car.'

'You say to hotel you come from Sana'a.'

'You know we came from Aden.'

Nabeel, perhaps realizing his English was too limited to get at the essential truth, took advantage of Buck's Arabic and continued his questions in that language. I heard the words al-Numair, Al Qaeda, Amrika, Sana'a, Aden, and Marib, and even the word Ghumdan.

Obviously Nabeel strongly suspected that we were here to find al-Numair. And the answer was, Why else would we be here, stupid? But Buck wasn't going to give them anything. I couldn't understand what Buck was saying, of course, but I trusted the old Cold Warrior to just stick to the story, no matter how implausible it sounded.

Also, I was certain that Nabeel and his compatriots, as well as their boss, al-Numair, were very pissed off about the Hellfire attack that killed their buddies. Not to mention getting their asses kicked at the Hunt Oil installation. So obviously the Al Qaeda guys were not in a good mood. In fact, they'd like to kill us. But first they had to buy us.

Nabeel, on the instructions of his boss, I'm sure, was trying to determine if the Amriki knew or suspected that The Panther was in Marib – and maybe Nabeel was trying to figure out if this was a trap set by the Amriki with the help of Sheik Musa. And *that* was the real issue. But Nabeel was not going to get that information from the Amriki, unless we were prisoners of Al Qaeda, which we were not – yet.

It's not easy questioning someone else's prisoners, as I discovered last time I was here, and more recently at the Ghumdan prison, and Nabeel seemed frustrated with Buck's replies, so he ended the conversation, then said something to Yasir.

Buck said to us, 'Nabeel now wants to see whatever weapons we were carrying when we were kidnapped.'

That was my cue to say, 'One, two, three — pull!' and show them the weapons. But maybe I should see how Yasir handled it.

Yasir and Nabeel seemed to be getting heated again, and Buck took advantage of the shouting to say to us, 'Yasir refuses to show these gentlemen anything — except us.' He added, 'John's New York acquaintance may be smelling a rat.'

Right. Al Qaeda is not stupid. I wish Chet was here to see and hear all of this. He might learn something — like how unpredictable people are.

Yasir, too, was getting the impression that Nabeel was smelling a rat, so he did a smart thing and shouted at Buck, probably telling him to shut up. Then Yasir did a smarter thing and kicked Buck in the chest, knocking him on his back. It was all an act — I think. Buck didn't seem to be hurt by Yasir's half-hearted sandal kick to his chest, and he sat up again. I would have kicked Buck in the balls — just to make it look real, of course.

Nabeel, taking his cue from Yasir, took a step toward Buck as though he intended to kick or hit him, but Yasir went ballistic and shoved Nabeel back and shouted at him.

The other four Al Qaeda guys looked like they were ready to get into a fight, but the three Bedouin behind them stepped back and leveled their rifles. One of them shouted, probably saying, 'Make my day, suckers.'

Anyway, Yasir seemed to be tired of his visitors, and he shouted, 'Imshee!' Go away.

The Bedouin began slipping the black hoods over the Al Qaeda dickheads, but before Nabeel was hooded, he looked at me and said, 'In Yemen, you die.' Then to my compatriots, he also promised, 'You die. But maybe not die. Maybe wish to die.'

Well, Nabeel, *you're* not getting an American work visa.

Anyway, I wasn't sure now if we were going to lure The Panther into a meeting with Sheik Musa, so why shouldn't I yell 'Pull!' and bag these bastards? Right?

I glanced at Brenner, who was looking at me, and I could tell he was thinking the same thing. Zamo actually had his right hand behind his back, ready for the count.

But Buck, the voice of reason, who could sense that the A-team was on the verge of some messy business, said softly, 'Let it go.'

Did he say, 'Pull'?

The Al Qaeda delegation was all hooded now, and whacking them would be easy, but not fun or sporting. And maybe not a good idea. I mean, I didn't think the Bedouin would like that, and I suppose there was still a chance that The Panther would schedule the meeting with Musa — if Chet was right about Bulus ibn al-Darwish taking chances. But for now, it was Kate who'd been right about Al Qaeda smelling a rat. As for Brenner not trusting the Bedouin, he seemed to be wrong about that so far. But this deal hadn't played itself out yet.

The four Bedouin marched the five hooded Al Qaeda guys down the stairs, and we were alone.

Kate was the first to unlock her shackles, which she threw across the room, saying, 'Damn it!'

Then, showing her feminine side, she asked Buck, 'Are you all right?'

Buck assured us all that he was fine, saying, 'Yasir pulled his kick.'

Yasir has more self-control than I do.

Anyway, we all freed ourselves from our shackles and stood.

Okay, this had all been a sham, but the five Al Qaeda fighters standing in front of us were real, and their AK-47s were real, and I think all of us were a little tense for a while there. I'm sure there's a better way to earn a living.

Anyway, we all went to the window.

The Al Qaeda delegation was being walked across the courtyard, and within a minute they were inside the three Land Cruisers, which headed toward the gate. Arrivederci, assholes.

Buck said, 'It could have gone better.'

You think?

Zamo said, 'We shoulda fuckin' wasted them.'

And possibly that would have been the right thing to do.

But Kate, who'd grown up hunting game with her nutty parents, said, 'Sometimes you let the does go and wait for the buck.'

Agreed. Let's shoot Buck. Sorry.

Kate said, 'I assume that was the informant you were looking for in New York.'

'Yeah. Sorry I bought him a bagel.'

Buck said, 'Al Qaeda's organization in America is sometimes more extensive than we realize.'

Right. But with a few million Muslims in America, we shouldn't be too surprised. Still, it was creepy that Nabeel had set me up for a look-see. Next time I see him, I'll kill him.

Anyway, Chet was not getting out of his van, so he was probably watching his video monitors.

Brenner asked Buck the sixty-four-thousand-dollar question. 'Do you think they suspected a setup?'

'I don't know,' replied the wise man. 'But we will know soon enough.'

Brenner suggested, 'If they did suspect a setup, and if The

Panther still wants to meet with Sheik Musa, then it's possible that The Panther is going to kill Musa – and us.'

That was not a happy thought, but it was a possible outcome of what just happened. Another possibility was that The Panther and Sheik Musa would work out another deal between themselves. In Yemen, any deal is possible.

Anyway, if Chet Morgan was not coming to us, then we had to go to Chet Morgan. I suggested, 'Let's get some air.'

So we put on our shoes and Kevlar vests, and we took our M4s, which we always carried when we went down to the courtyard. But this time we took extra magazines. The situation had changed, and I don't think we fully understood how it had changed, or what the Bedouin were thinking now. Zamo stayed in the tower and covered the courtyard with his rifle.

So Buck would speak to Yasir, and we'd all speak to Chet, the mastermind of Operation Clean Sweep, and we'd decide on our next move. But I already knew what Chet was going to say: We wait. The next move belongs to The Panther.

CHAPTER SEVENTY

B uck, Kate, Brenner, and I stepped into the van.
Chet was sitting at his console, watching the three Land Cruisers on his monitors, and he glanced over his shoulder and asked, 'How did it go?'

Buck replied, 'Not very well.'

Chet pulled himself away from his screens, swiveled his chair, and asked, 'Why not?'

Buck explained, 'I think they're suspicious.'

Chet replied, 'Of course they are. They're not stupid.'

I reminded him, 'You said they were stupid.'

'Yes. But they're also cunning and paranoid.' Chet reassured us, 'If The Panther wasn't interested in getting his hands on you, he wouldn't have even sent that delegation.' He explained, 'You don't make an appointment to see a car you're not interested in buying.'

True, but sometimes you go look at the car because you want to steal it.

Anyway, Buck gave Chet a quick briefing of what happened and Chet listened carefully, then again assured us, 'Al Qaeda is just doing due diligence. They need to protect The Panther, and they always proceed on the assumption that a double-cross is possible.' He reminded us, 'This is the Middle East.'

Right. Not the Midwest. Definitely not Kansas.

Chet said to me, 'So you knew this guy, Nabeel?'

I replied, 'He knew me before I knew him.' I explained about the leak in the Yemeni consulate in New York, and I suggested, 'The State Department should declare the whole consulate staff persona non grata.'

Buck, Mr State Department Intelligence, said, 'The leak could be in the Foreign Ministry office in Sana'a.' He informed me, 'We like the Yemeni consulate staff in New York. They also sell information to us.'

Right. It's a game. Double-Dealing for Dollars.

On a more important topic than me being pissed off about

buying Nabeel a bagel in New York and him making me look silly, I said, 'I think these Al Qaeda guys knew where they were taken.'

Again, Chet didn't seem to care, and he asked rhetorically, 'What are they going to do about it?'

But the question wasn't rhetorical and I said, 'They're going to send a hundred jihadists to the Crow Fortress one night and kill everyone here.'

Chet replied, 'That would be war with Sheik Musa, and they do not want war with Sheik Musa.'

Buck agreed and added, 'It's not these walls or our weapons that protect us. It's the wrath of all the Bedouin tribes that protects us.'

Chet added, 'And the Predators.'

'Okay.' But I suggested, 'We could use another ten or twenty Bedouin here.'

Chet informed me and all of us, 'The last thing we want here are more armed Bedouin. If things go wrong, or turn around,' he explained, 'we can handle these eight guys. We can't handle any more.'

I reminded Chet, 'Sheik Musa is our trusted ally.'

'He is,' agreed Chet. 'But alliances shift.' He reassured us, however, 'All that I said in Aden about Sheik Musa remains true. Unfortunately, with the Bedouin, they change their minds a lot.'

Was that in the Aden briefing?

Buck, Mr Arabian guy, said, 'There are no constants in the lives of the nomadic Bedouin. Even the desert that they travel changes with the shifting dunes. Their only constant is the tribe, and they will always do what is best for the survival of the tribe.' He added,

'Fortunately, what's best for Sheik Musa's tribe at the moment is to ally themselves with the Americans. And it's important that he keeps believing that.'

Right up until the time we put a Hellfire up his golden shiwal.

Chet said, 'The critical time is now, when Musa's tribal council speaks to The Panther's council to determine if The Panther wants to buy the Americans, and if he will do the deal in person.' Chet added, 'That discussion could produce a variety of possibilities, not all of them favorable to us.'

'Did I miss that memo?'

Chet said to me, Kate, and Brenner, 'I'm being honest with you.'

Kate responded, 'Honesty that comes late is not honest or useful.'

Chet advised us, 'Keep an eye on the Bedouin here. They're simple people and if you see a change in their attitude or demeanor, let me or Buck know.'

Actually, I was more interested in a change in Chet's demeanor.

Chet changed the subject and turned back toward the monitors, saying, 'You can see the three Land Cruisers heading north, toward Marib. See them? What's going to happen is that the Bedouin drivers will drop off the five Al Qaeda men in Marib – where the Bedouin picked them up, and where, unfortunately, they will disappear in the crowds or the buildings. Then at some point they will leave Marib, individually, by truck, bus, or SUV, driven by an Al Qaeda operative or a sympathizer, or just somebody looking to make a few rials. They will be let off near the highlands here, and make their way on foot to the Al Qaeda camp –

which is actually one of Musa's Bedouin camps, located about forty kilometers from here.' He explained, 'That is an effective way to escape Predator surveillance, because the Predators will have lost them in Marib, and five men traveling individually will not look like a target of interest to the Predators because every male here carries a weapon.' He continued, 'Unfortunately for Al Qaeda, we know where their camp is, so they waste a lot of time and energy trying to elude aerial surveillance.' He looked at us and smiled.

Chet, I think, was in love with his Predator drones. That's what broke up his marriage.

Chet turned in his seat and punched in a command on his console, saying, 'I'm directing Predator One to go on station above the Al Qaeda camp.'

We watched the monitor as the terrain slid by, showing the dry, rocky plateau west of here. Then the Predator began a counter-clockwise turn, and on the monitor we could see tents, huts, and vehicles spread out across a flat expanse of the plateau that was surrounded by large rock formations.

Chet said, 'That's the Al Qaeda camp.'

We all moved closer to the monitor and I could now see people moving on the ground. There were also map grid coordinates on the screen, which I made a mental note of. Why? Because you never know what information you might need.

Chet twisted a dial and the image grew larger. He said, 'It was — and still looks like — a Bedouin camp. But there are clues that it's not.' He explained, 'First, most of the men in the camp are not dressed in traditional Bedouin robes. Second, they're *all* men. No women, as you'd find in a Bedouin camp, and no children. Third, the men don't sit around and chew khat or herd goats as the Bedouin do. In fact, they train with rifles. Also, we spotted a mortar and rocket launchers, which are not typical Bedouin armaments.'

Chet concluded with a smile, 'But the big clue is that Sheik Musa told us the location of this camp that he rented to Al Qaeda.'

Right. Aerial reconnaissance analysis is impressive, but nothing beats someone on the ground telling you what you're really seeing from the air.

Brenner asked, 'Why does Al Qaeda think we wouldn't figure this out?'

Chet shrugged, then said, 'I don't think they fully understand what we can see from the air, and that we can accurately analyze what we're seeing. Also, they don't know that we've dramatically increased the number of Predators in Yemen.'

I watched the image on the screen and saw a few men in white foutehs walking around. So this is where Rahim ibn Hayyam lived for a few months before he was sent to attack the Hunt Oil facility. Even from the air, the place looked like a shithole. He's better off in jail.

Chet further informed us, 'The camp once held about a hundred fifty men, but now we're counting about fifty. About a hundred jihadists have left the camp — half on their way to the embassy and half on their way to the Sheraton in Aden.'

Right. And maybe the other fifty were headed for the Crow Fortress. But Chet or the Predator pilots who were watching twenty-four hours a day would notice if more men started leaving the camp.

Chet said, 'It's not a large camp, and it will be much smaller after the fighter-bombers level it.' He added, 'There are about five more camps like this in Yemen, and this is when we need to start eliminating them – because if we don't, there will be fifty, then a hundred, and then we have a real problem.'

Right. Kill the beast in the cradle.

Chet reminded us, 'We still don't know where The Panther's personal hideout is, and as with bin Laden in Afghanistan – or maybe Pakistan – it's almost impossible to locate a few individuals who are most likely living and hiding in caves. So we have to get The Panther out of his cave and kill him in the open.' He added, 'They all come out in the open eventually, for one reason or another.' He looked at us and said, 'And you, who have just been eyeball to eyeball with Al Qaeda, are a very good reason for Bulus ibn al-Darwish to come out of his cave.'

No one had anything to add to that, but I confessed, 'We came close to wasting those assholes.'

'Not a smart move,' said Chet.

Brenner said, 'A bird in the hand.'

'Tempting, maybe. But we have a bigger animal to kill.'

I asked Chet, 'What's the plan now?'

'We wait.'

'We're out of tuna.'

Chet didn't even smile, and he said, 'I can almost assure you that Bulus ibn al-Darwish will have an answer for Sheik Musa within two or three days.'

Buck needed to speak to Yasir, Arab to Arab, so he left the van. Kate and Brenner volunteered to put our cozy quarters back together, so they, too, left. I said I'd be along shortly.

Alone now in the van with Chet, we looked at each other for a few seconds, then he said to me, apropos our last private discussion, 'There's no problem. Never was.'

Wonderful news. I really felt awful about being paranoid and threatening Chet's life and all that.

I said to him, however, 'There *was* a problem. And if there's *still* a problem, then I am still *your* problem.'

He didn't reply.

I left Chet to watch his monitors and think about his problem.

CHAPTER SEVENTY-ONE

The A-team of Operation Clean Sweep, including Chet, gathered in the mafraj, whose high, open arches gave us an unobstructed view of the terrain for miles around. These watchtowers were the Predators of the last millennium. Hey, Abdul, there's a bad guy — drop a rock on him.

We all had our M4s and Kevlar, and Zamo did his march around the perimeter of the mafraj. The rest of us stood on the carpet of bird crap.

Buck began, 'Yasir had little to offer regarding whether or not the Al Qaeda delegation seemed suspicious about this kidnapping. Yasir did say, however, that he didn't like these men, and especially didn't like Nabeel, al-Amriki.'

Well, if Nabeel al-Samad was an American, then I'm a Bedouin. But from the Bedouin's perspective, Nabeel could have come from Mars.

Buck also told us, 'Yasir says he thinks that only Nabeel was a Yemeni. The rest, he believes, are from someplace else.' Buck added, 'The Bedouin do not trust these people.'

And the feeling is mutual. Recalling Chet's newfound concerns regarding Sheik Musa, I asked, 'So do you think we can still trust Musa and his men?'

Buck replied, 'The Bedouin practice a primitive democracy. Which means that even if their sheik wants to switch sides and make common cause with Al Qaeda, the tribesmen won't necessarily go along with it.'

We could use some primitive democracy in the ATTF.

Anyway, it occurred to me that the Bedouin tribesmen might not actually know that The Panther and his retinue were going to be vaporized by Hellfire missiles, so I asked Buck and Chet about that.

Buck replied, 'Musa and his men who will be with him obviously know what's going to happen at this meeting. And if one Bedouin knows something, they all know it. Also, the Bedouin know this was a sham kidnapping, so they all understand that the Americans aren't really being offered to Al Qaeda.'

Brenner said, as he did back in Aden, 'That is a massive security breach. All it would take is one Bedouin to tip off Al Qaeda.'

Chet replied, 'We're trusting that whatever the Bedouin know stays with the Bedouin.' He reminded us, 'They are very clannish.'

Let's hope so. Otherwise we have a problem.

Buck also told us, 'From what I can gather from my conversations with them, the Bedouin think that one of the purposes of this meeting is to discuss important matters which need to be resolved between the tribes and Al Qaeda.' He added, 'Sheik Musa is wise to take that approach, and it's a compelling reason for The Panther to show up in person. The two warlords need to talk. And even if they can't agree about the Americans, they have other pressing issues to discuss, man to man, chief to chief.'

Right. Like the rent on the Al Qaeda camp. Musa is smart. Five million bucks makes you think.

On another subject, Buck said, 'As we also know, neither the Sheraton Hotel in Aden nor the embassy in Sana'a have been attacked, and I believe, as do my colleagues in the embassy, and Chet's colleagues as well, that The Panther has put those attacks on hold until he makes his decision.'

Good news for everyone in Aden and Sana'a, except people like Captain Mac who were looking for a fight.

Chet added, 'Those attacks could end in disaster for Al Qaeda, and they are signs of The Panther's desperation or recklessness. The Panther, however, now sees an easier way to score a win.'

Buck continued, 'And The Panther knows he can still order those attacks after the deal is done with Musa.' He reminded us, 'But of course he'll be dead if he shows up at the meeting, and those attacks, we believe, will probably not be ordered by his successor.'

Well, not right away. But someday.

I thought the mafraj meeting was over, but then Buck, who

saves the best for last as he did at the Bilqis ruins, said, 'Yasir gave me a sealed envelope that was given to him by Nabeel.' He pulled a long white envelope from his pocket, and I saw that the logo on it was from the Bilqis Hotel. Our bill?

Buck told us, 'Nabeel told Yasir it was for Detective Corey, but I took the liberty of opening it.' He explained, 'In case it contained anthrax, or a letter bomb.'

Do I thank him for risking his life to open my mail?

Buck slid a stack of photographs from the envelope and handed them to Chet, saying, 'I warn you, some of these are not easy to look at.'

Chet looked at the first photo, then passed it to me. It was a group shot, taken in front of the columns at the Bilqis ruins. It showed what I assumed were the Belgian tourists – two older couples, two younger couples, and a pretty young woman, maybe sixteen or seventeen years old, all smiling into the camera. In the center of the group was a tall, bearded Bedouin in robes wearing a shiwal, and also wearing a jambiyah. He, too, was smiling. And what was making this murderer smile?

I passed the photo to Kate as Chet passed a second photo to me. This one was of the young woman standing close to the Bedouin – Bulus ibn al-Darwish, The Panther – and they were both smiling, though neither had their arm around the other. I passed the photo to Kate, who said, 'That bastard.'

The next few photos showed other posed shots with the couples and the man they thought was a Bedouin.

I knew what was coming, of course, but even so, the next photograph was difficult to process immediately, but then I recognized a close-up of one of the older women lying on the brown paving stone, her throat cut from ear to ear, and a pool of red blood around her head and face.

I stared at it. The woman's eyes were open, and there was a look of terror on her face. She could have been alive.

Kate, who was looking at me, asked, 'What is it?'

I passed the photo to her, and she stared at it, then said softly, 'Oh my God ... oh ...'

Brenner took the photo from her, looked at it and said, 'Sick.'

Buck asked, 'Do you want to see the rest of them?'

Chet took the photos from Buck's hand, flipped through them quickly, then handed them to me.

I, too, went through them quickly, noting that some of the long shots showed all nine Belgians dead with their wrists bound behind their backs, and around them were men dressed as Bedouin who were actually Al Qaeda jihadists.

In one photograph I could see a man at the bottom of the steps who had been pushed or had tried to run. One close-up photograph was of a young man who looked Arabic – the guide, I assumed – who had probably taken the group photo of the Belgians with the tall Bedouin who turned out not to be a Bedouin.

The last photograph was a close-up of the young woman. Her eyes were wide open, and her parted lips looked very dark against her white, bloodless skin.

I passed the photos to Kate who passed them to Brenner without looking at them.

Zamo had come over to see what was going on, and Brenner gave him the stack of photographs.

Zamo slung his rifle, shuffled through the photos, and handed them back to Brenner without comment, then he walked to one of the arches and stared out into space.

Buck said, 'Obviously, we can identify the man in the posed shots dressed as a Bedouin.' He added, 'There was no note with these photographs, but there was this . . .'

He handed me a business card, and I saw it was my card, the one I'd given to Nabeel in Ben's Kosher Deli a million years ago. On the back I saw where I'd written, *Nabeel al-Samad to see Det. Corey.* And someone, obviously Mr al-Samad, had drawn a smiley face. Good cultural awareness, Nabeel. Asshole.

I gave the card to Kate, who looked at it, then she asked of no one in particular, 'Why did they give us these photographs?'

It was Buck who replied, in Latin, no less, 'Res ipsa loquitur.' He translated, 'The thing speaks for itself.'

Indeed it does. And I got the message.

I said, 'I think this answers our question about what The Panther is going to do. He is not showing us what he's capable of doing, or what he's done – he's showing us what he is *going* to do. To us.' I concluded, 'He's made his decision. He will meet with Sheik Musa.'

Everyone agreed, but I still wondered if The Panther would want to avoid that meeting and try the direct approach by storming this fortress.

Either way, Bulus ibn al-Darwish had a lot of murders to answer for. And he would not answer for them in an American court of law. He would answer for them here, in Yemen, in an appropriate act of violence. He may not have been born here, but he *was* going to die here.

CHAPTER SEVENTY-TWO

The eight Bedouin again invited us to dine with them, which was a good sign that we were still their honored guests, because Bedouin hospitality demands that you don't kill your guests. I mean, from their perspective this was all a big pain in the ass. Not only did the Bedouin have to share their daily goat with us, but they'd also had to deal with the five Al Qaeda assholes who, in some existential way, were a threat to their ancient way of life.

We dressed for dinner — Kevlar and guns for the gentlemen; balto, hijab, Kevlar, and guns for the lady.

Buck said he'd be along shortly, after he made a sat-phone call. I, too, excused myself, saying I needed to visit the excrement shaft, so Kate, Brenner, and Chet went down to the courtyard. Zamo ordered goat takeout and went up to the mafraj.

Before Buck made his call and before I hit the shaft, I asked him, out of curiosity, 'How many tribesmen live around here?'

Buck replied, 'There hasn't been a census since the Queen of Sheba, but I'd guess there are about thirty thousand Bedouin in and around Marib province, and they make up about ninety percent of the population.' He added, 'Musa's tribe — men, women, and children — number maybe ten thousand.'

I did the math and said, 'Five million dollars is about five hundred bucks for every man, woman, and child.' I added, 'That's about a year's pay.'

Buck informed me, 'Musa will actually take the lion's share, and he will also share some of that with the other tribal sheiks as a traditional courtesy.'

Actually, Musa will be dead, but I asked, 'How about bribes to government officials?'

'A few.' Buck asked me, 'Why does this interest you, John?'

'Because five million is a lot of money and it's a good motivator, but big bounties attract other people.'

'Who did you have in mind?'

'Well, Colonel Hakim comes to mind.'

Buck said, 'I doubt if the US government would pay Colonel Hakim if he killed The Panther.'

'If they'll pay Musa for The Panther's head, they'll pay anyone for that head.' Except us. We get a paycheck. I asked Buck, 'Is the Yemeni government offering a reward for the death or capture of The Panther?'

'Yes, but it's our money they're offering.' He reminded me, 'Al Qaeda is *our* problem.'

'How about a Yemeni government reward for the death or capture of Sheik Musa?'

'Definitely not.'

'Why not?'

'Because if the Yemeni government put a price on the head of *any* tribal sheik, no matter how much they wanted him dead, that would cause a tribal uprising all over the country.'

'So that's why the Americans are whacking Sheik Musa, as a

favor to the Yemeni government. Musa is President Saleh's problem, but our job.'

'Correct.' He looked at me and asked, 'What is it that you don't understand about this?'

'I don't understand how we can help a corrupt, brutal, and treacherous dictator and his government kill a tribal sheik who has done nothing to us, and who is helping us in a very important matter.'

'We've been through this, John.' He informed me, 'I've done worse during the Cold War.' He let me know, 'The ends justify the means.'

I didn't reply, but on a related subject of people getting whacked, I inquired, 'Did you know that Kate killed a CIA officer?'

He nodded.

I asked him, 'Do you think that's one of the reasons that Kate and I are here?'

'I'm not following you.'

'Of course you are.'

He didn't reply directly but said, 'I believe you and Chet have discussed that.'

'Correct. And he assured me there was no problem.'

'Then there is no problem.'

'I'm relieved.'

'Good.' He asked, 'Anything else on your mind?'

'Yes . . .' I confessed to him, 'I want to be a warlord.'

He forced a smile and informed me, 'The Panther is a type of warlord, but he can never be a sheik, and neither can you.'

'Warlord is okay.'

'Good. I have a class on that.'

I smiled. Buck was easy to like. But not easy to trust.

The smell of dinner wafted through the window and I said, 'Smells like Italian sausage at the Feast of San Gennaro in Little Italy.'

'Goat.'

'Again?'

I didn't really have to answer a call of nature, but Buck really did have to make a call in private, so I went down to the court-yard where a fresh, whole goat was roasting on a spit. Good. I hate leftover goat.

Buck joined us a bit later, and Kate said she'd dine in the van and monitor the electronics. I think she felt awkward at a stag dinner. Also, the van was running and the generator was powering the small air-conditioning unit, so Kate shut the doors, saying, 'It's hot in this balto. Enjoy the fresh air, gentlemen.'

Right. A dozen gamey guys and a roasting goat. Does life get any better?

Anyway, after a simple and simply awful dinner, we joined Kate in the van and watched a little TV – Channel One was showing a rerun of the infrared night view of the Crow Fortress, and Channel Two was showing our immediate area of concern, mean-ing a wider view of the plateaus and the surrounding flatlands. Nothing seemed to be moving out there, except a diminishing herd of goats.

Chet announced that he was going to sleep in the van – which could be locked from the inside – so he could be near the screens, and in case he got a radio or sat-phone call from the Predator pilots, who remained vigilant through the night. Sounded like a good idea. Sleep light, Chet.

The rest of us went up to the diwan and posted our guard – Kate and I took the first shift, Buck and Brenner the second, and Zamo pulled the last shift alone.

During our guard duty, Kate said to me, 'I have to be honest with you, John, those Al Qaeda men and those photos shook me up.'

'That's what they wanted. But you should also be angry.'

'I am ... but ... I want to get this over with.'

I told her, 'You can actually leave. If you think about it, we're not needed here anymore. Al Qaeda saw the bait, and they won't see us again. The next thing they and The Panther will see is Sheik Musa, followed by Hellfire missiles.'

She thought about that and nodded, but said, 'I'm not going anywhere without you, and I know you're staying, so I'm staying.' She looked at me. 'We need to see this through to the end.'

We actually didn't, but we did. I said, 'If you change your mind, I'm sure we can get you to the Marib airstrip, then to Sana'a Airport, or back to the embassy.'

'This subject is closed.'

'Okay.' We separated and looked out different windows – north and west for me, south and east for Kate.

Right. We could actually leave now. So could Buck, Brenner, and Zamo for that matter. Only Chet had to stay behind to direct the Predators and the Hellfire missiles, and then, if all went well, he could go alone to collect pieces of the garbage. And even that wasn't completely necessary for a successful mission.

But I, and the rest of us, couldn't leave Chet here by himself.

I mean, our differences and egos aside, we'd sort of bonded as a team. Right? We'd come a long way and all of us wanted to be here to see this through together. Also, I wanted to see what Chet was up to.

And to be honest, we all wanted to see the blasted corpses of The Panther and his jihadists – to smell the burnt flesh and bone – to see what we had done by remote control that we would have liked to have done up close and personal. And, like warriors since the beginning of time, we wanted to take mortal evidence of our victory back to our camp – in this case, a forensic lab. Warfare has changed, but the heart of the warrior remains the same; it remains primitive.

CHAPTER SEVENTY-THREE

The following day brought no word from Sheik Musa about Al Qaeda, and I was beginning to think we weren't worth a hundred thousand dollars, which was a big hit on my ego.

The real problem, of course, was the provision in the deal that it had to be negotiated by the principals. No underlings.

I had the thought that many chiefs from the beginning of time had also found themselves in this quandary. I mean, do you show up and take a chance that the other chief has a surprise for you? Or do you strap on your brass balls and take the meeting?

I guess that decision depends on how brave you are. Or how

stupid you are. Or how paranoid you are. Or, in the end, how hungry you are for what was being offered.

By the second day, the A-team was beginning to doubt my conclusion — and their hope — that The Panther would say yes to the meeting. But I kept thinking about those photographs — the message *was* clear: I hate the West, I hate America, and I will do anything I have to do to cut your throats.

At about half past three of the second day, we had our answer.

Chet got a radio message from a Predator pilot reporting that a single Toyota Land Cruiser was climbing the north slope of the plateau, on its way toward the Crow Fortress — code-named Point A, in case anyone was listening.

The A-team went up to the mafraj and watched the Land Cruiser coming from the direction of the rock pile where Musa's men guarded the northern approach to the plateau and the fortress.

The Bedouin in the courtyard, who'd been called by the Bedouin guarding the approach, opened the gates and the white Land Cruiser entered.

We watched from the mafraj as five armed Bedouin piled out of the SUV and began talking to the eight men in the courtyard.

Chet said to us, 'They're not delivering food or water, so I think they're delivering a message.'

Good CIA thinking. But I would have welcomed a few chickens.

Chet and Buck volunteered to go down to the courtyard to see what was going on, and Chet also said, 'I need to see what's happening in the van. Cover us.'

Well, I'll cover Buck. You're on your own, Chet.

Buck and Chet, armed and armored, moved quickly down the stairs to the courtyard.

Brenner said to Zamo, 'Cover, but don't aim at anyone.' To us he said, 'Same. But be ready. Don't misinterpret. Only I give the order to fire.'

I thought Brenner was overreacting to what seemed like a non-threatening situation. But something *was* happening – a transitional moment in the routine and rhythm of life in the Crow Fortress.

Buck and Chet appeared in the courtyard, and Buck walked directly toward the Bedouin, who now totaled thirteen. That's a lot of AK-47s. Chet unlocked the van and disappeared inside. No one stopped him, and that was a good sign.

Buck was now speaking to one of the newcomers who seemed to be the boss. Yasir was in on the conversation and the other Bedouin stood around listening. With the Bedouin, when the bosses speak, the rank and file stand around and listen. Just like at 26 Fed. Not.

Anyway, it appeared that Buck and the Bedouin were having a normal, though slightly excited, conversation.

Finally, Buck did his Go in Peace thing and entered the van to report to Chet. The Bedouin continued their conversation.

Brenner told Zamo to stay in the mafraj, and we went down to the diwan where we could be closer to the situation, whatever it was.

Finally, Buck appeared from the van and moved quickly toward the tower.

He came up the stairs, slightly out of breath, and announced, 'The Bedouin say that The Panther has sent a verbal message directly to Sheik Musa.' He smiled and told us, 'They will meet in about two hours' — he looked at his watch — 'at six P.M. to discuss various matters of mutual interest, and also to discuss the sheik's offer of the five Americans.' Buck added, 'The Panther just tacked that on as though it was of peripheral importance.' He further informed us, 'Typical Arab bargaining technique.'

And not a bad technique. Like, 'Hey Abdul, let's talk about camel grazing rights. And by the way, how much do you want for your wife?'

Anyway, this was good news indeed, and we all did high-fives — even Buck, who didn't know what a high-five was.

Buck also told us, 'The meeting will take place at the same goat herder's hut where we met Sheik Musa.'

That must be the sheik's Camp David. More importantly, it was near the road where the Otter had put us down, and would now pick us up after we filled the goo bags.

I glanced out the window and saw that the five Bedouin who'd arrived were still there, and I asked, 'Are they staying?'

Buck replied, 'Yes. For extra security and also to escort us to the scene of the attack.'

I reminded Buck, 'I thought we didn't want more Bedouin in the courtyard.'

'It's their property,' he reminded us. 'They are on our side.'

'Right,' I agreed, 'but maybe they could be on our side someplace else.'

Buck assured us, 'The Bedouin won't be here long, and neither will we. In fact, we are two hours away from a successful mission, and maybe another hour away from jumping on that Otter.'

Right, and we should take Sheik Musa with us. He has some

big bucks coming to him, and I know a deli in Brooklyn he can buy, and the Yemeni government would be just as happy to see him gone as see him dead. But happy endings are not always so neat and tidy in real life.

It also occurred to me that what was driving The Panther — hate, revenge, and too many frustrating defeats — was the same thing that was driving Chet. And that's when your judgment gets clouded.

But to be more positive — like Buck and Chet — and maybe to be less cynical than usual, it could be that what we were seeing was what we were getting: one dead Panther who put his instincts aside and went for the meat.

Buck, who doesn't like it when he sees me thinking, asked, 'What's on your mind, John?'

'Not much.' I asked him, 'What's Chet doing in the van?'

Buck replied, 'Coordinating all aspects of a stealthy assassination attack.' He let us know, 'Two more Predators are coming on station over the goat herder's hut. They'll be ready for the meeting.' He also told us, 'Two Predators remain on station here, over and around the Crow Fortress. They will cover us when we drive with Musa's men to the scene of the attack, and they will cover the landing and takeoff of the Otter.'

'Right.' I asked, 'Who has the goo bags and latex gloves?'

'Chet.'

'If The Panther's head is in one piece, can I take that home?'

Buck didn't reply at first, but then said, 'We're primarily interested in the fingers for the prints and DNA.'

'Right.' I like being a little nuts now and then, and I said, 'I hope that little shit Nabeel is there. I want his balls in a Ziploc.'

Kate finally said, 'John, that's enough.'

'Sorry. I'm excited.'

Brenner, who'd seen war first-hand, and who may have taken a head or an ear himself, said nothing. War is hell, ladies and gentlemen, and all the euphemisms are not going to change the nature of the act. Kill them before they kill you, then celebrate.

Brenner said to Buck, 'I'll leave Zamo in the mafraj for cover and we'll join Chet in the van.'

But Buck informed us, 'Chet needs an hour or so by himself.' He explained, 'What's happening now is top secret. He's actually speaking to people in Washington by radio, getting the necessary clearances and go-aheads.'

Kate asked the obvious question. 'What is he saying that we can't hear?'

Buck replied, 'Just about everything.' He explained, 'This is all verbal so there is no written record of anything, and there can be no witnesses to what Chet says and what is said to him.' He further explained, 'Chet is speaking through the secure telephone unit, so names of personnel in Washington are en clair, and we don't need to hear those names – or hear anything.'

I could almost hear Chet now. 'Hey Dick, hi Ralph, Chet here. So, we're ready to vaporize some asshole jihadists and burn The Panther's traitorous ass with a few top-secret Hellfire missiles. You guys still okay with that? Any problems at that end? Just nod ... Oh, sorry, I mean just say yea or nay.'

Sounded reasonable. But who knew why Chet wanted to be alone or what he was saying and hearing? Not us.

So we had some time to kill before we were allowed to go into the van and watch the drama taking shape – the arrival of

Sheik Musa and his merry Bedouin at the goat herder's hut, the arrival of The Panther and his retinue, the kiss of death, the tea party on the carpet, and finally the sheik ducking inside the hut on some pretext. And where, I wondered, would the sheik's men be? Hopefully not too close to The Panther and his men who were going to be hit by four laser-guided Hellfire missiles, each warhead packing twenty pounds of high explosives. Maybe all of the Bedouin would need to go off to take a piss at the same time.

There is an old saying among detectives: Never overlook the obvious.

And what was obvious to me was that Sheik Musa and his men, along with The Panther and his men, were actually going to share the same fate at that meeting. So obviously the A-team was not driving to the scene of the carnage, where some of these men – Bedouin and Al Qaeda – might still be alive and very pissed off.

If the obvious were true, then how do we, the Americans, get out of the Crow Fortress with thirteen Bedouin around us who would know soon enough from the survivors what happened to their sheik and their buddies? Right?

Well, we will see how it actually plays out. I could be wrong. Or I could be half right.

Buck said he was going down to speak to the Bedouin again and see if he could get a better sense of what they knew about the sheik-Panther meeting, and also what their instructions were.

It's good to have an Arabic speaker on the team. We couldn't have even attempted this mission without Buck. Next time I volunteer to go into Al Qaeda territory, I want Buck with me. Or maybe another Arabic speaker who wasn't so full of bullshit. Or better yet, maybe I'd take a pass on the next offer.

Buck left, and I brought up my concern of Hellfire missiles causing collateral damage to friendlies, meaning Sheik Musa and his men, and thereby putting us in a dangerous situation here at the Crow Fortress.

Brenner, who has seen a lot of high-explosive warheads ripping people apart, said, 'I was thinking about that myself.' He added, 'As accurate as these missiles are, they throw out a lot of shrapnel. You don't want to be anywhere near a hit.'

Kate said, 'Why didn't you — we — bring this up at the meeting in Aden?'

Brenner replied, 'I was thinking that Chet knew what he was talking about.'

Well, he does, but sometimes he forgets the details.

Brenner continued, 'I'm thinking that when Sheik Musa excuses himself to go into the stone hut, that's obviously the signal for Chet to order the Predators to fire the four Hellfires — but it's also the signal for the Bedouin to haul ass and dive for cover.' He added, 'They have about four, maybe five seconds to do that before eighty pounds of high explosives and shrapnel turn the area into a slaughterhouse.'

One, two, three, four ... I could be in the next province if I knew a Hellfire was on its way.

Brenner also surmised, 'It would take The Panther and his men a few seconds to realize what's happening, but before they could react, they'll be in Paradise.'

Probably true. Nevertheless, I did say, 'There could still be friendly casualties.'

Kate and Brenner thought about that, and Kate said, 'God, I hope not.' She asked, 'How would we get out of here?'

'Very quickly.'

On that note, we climbed up the stairs to the mafraj to talk to Zamo and give him a heads-up on some of this. Brenner also said he wanted to show us something up there. Maybe a new species of bird shit, and that wouldn't smell half as bad as the bullshit we were getting down here from Buck and Chet.

CHAPTER SEVENTY-FOUR

We told Zamo the good news about the Panther-sheik powwow, and Brenner also told him, 'We're going home today.'

Zamo, man of few words, just nodded.

Brenner then drew our attention to the excrement shaft and pointed out a square hole in the ceiling directly above the shaft, whose wooden walls rose about eight feet, only half the way to the high ceiling of the mafraj. Brenner said, 'That's a vent hole.'

Right. Shit flows downhill, but the smell rises.

Brenner said to me, 'Give me a boost.'

So we walked over to the half wall of the shaft and I boosted him up so that he was standing precariously on the top of the wall with his fingers barely touching the edge of the vent hole for balance.

The squatter hole on each floor below was large enough for a person to squeeze through and drop to the next floor, which I'd noted as a means of escape. But you wouldn't drop straight through each hole into the pile of excrement without some squeezing and twisting. Nevertheless, I warned Mr Brenner, 'Careful. It's about sixty feet down. But the pile of shit will soften your fall.'

'Thank you.' He stood on his toes and grabbed the edge of the vent hole with both hands, then pulled himself up through the opening onto the roof.

Good upper-body strength. Now what?

He knelt at the hole and said, 'We can do this.'

I saw his legs and body drop through the hole, and he dangled by his fingers at the edge of the rough-hewn roof plank, then he swung himself clear of the wall of the excrement shaft and landed on the floor, announcing, 'The roof has a four-foot-high parapet around it, which is good cover if we're in a firefight.' Brenner, whose last war, Vietnam, was all about helicopters, also informed us, 'The rooftop will easily hold a helicopter.'

That was really good news if we were trapped on the roof and taking fire, but I reminded him, 'We have no helicopters in Yemen.'

'Correct. But we're about one hundred seventy-five miles from Najran airfield, right across the Saudi border — about an hour flight time.' He further informed us, 'That's where the Predators come from, and probably also where the Otter is now.'

'Okay. And?'

'And, if we have to, we can get a US Army or Air Force chopper here to take us off this roof.'

'Why,' Kate asked, 'would we have to do that?'

'Because,' he replied, 'if the Al Qaeda delegation figured out where they were taken, they may try to save a hundred thousand dollars and also show Sheik Musa who's the boss, not to mention avoiding that meeting.'

'I hear you,' I said.

Brenner continued, 'I'm also not sure about our Bedouin allies, so we need to have a plan of escape.'

And I thought *I* was paranoid. But this wasn't paranoia; this was Plan B from Point A.

Kate said, 'It seems to me that a helicopter from Najran would be a better way of getting out of here and across the Saudi border than an Otter landing on a road.'

'It would be,' Brenner agreed, 'but the Otter is Company run and this is a Company operation. Also, the helicopter – with or without US Army or Air Force markings – can be easily identified as American, and that's not what the plan calls for. But if it's an emergency situation – here, or at the scene of the attack – then a chopper is what we'll need.'

'Right,' I agreed. 'But an hour is a long time to wait for the cavalry to arrive.'

Brenner agreed. 'It is, but it's better than waiting for nothing to arrive.'

Kate asked the obvious question. 'Can we contact whoever it is we need to contact to get this helicopter?'

Brenner replied, 'I made a sat-phone call to Ed Peters in the embassy, and he's trying to locate a contact number for the American installation at this Saudi airfield.' He told us, 'Officially, the US is assigned there as a training group to the Royal Saudi Air Force, but everyone knows we also have some CIA and NSA resources at Najran to keep an eye and ear on the Yemeni situation. That's where the F-15s will come from to pulverize the Al Qaeda base camp.'

Interesting. I asked, 'Are we sharing this information with Chet and Buck?'

Brenner replied, 'I would bet money that Chet and Buck already have a direct sat-phone number and radio frequency for the American chief of operations at Najran airfield. And if they don't, they can radio the CIA at Najran.' He also pointed out, 'They haven't said a word to us about Najran or about helicopters.'

Right. I mean, there was some crap going on here, but maybe not as much or as deep as my paranoid mind had imagined. There could be rational and logical national security explanations for everything that wasn't adding up. But if it keeps quacking like a duck, and keeps telling you it's an American eagle, you gotta be a little suspicious.

I asked Zamo, 'Can you pull yourself up there?'

'Why not?'

'Because your arm is fucked up.'

Brenner said, 'I'll go first, you second, and we can easily pull up Zamo and Kate.'

Did we forget old Buck? How about Chet?

Kate let us know, 'I'm sure I can pull myself up.'

I looked at the wall of the excrement shaft, which as I said was about eight feet high, and I pointed out, 'The last person won't have anyone to boost them up.'

Brenner replied, 'That washstand in the diwan will hold Zamo's weight, and he's the heaviest person here.'

I guess they already tried that. You can always count on military guys to show initiative and good skills in solving field problems.

I let Brenner and Zamo know, 'Good thinking and good job. But let's hope we never have to get to the roof.' On a related subject, I said, 'You may have noticed that the squatter hole on each floor is big enough for any of us – even Zamo – to squeeze through.'

Brenner, the expert on tower houses, said, 'They're made big so it's easier to dump kitchen garbage and chamber pots down the hole to the excrement level.' He also informed us, 'The excrement shaft is a primitive fire escape in the tower houses.'

You learn something new every day. Anyway, I pointed out, 'If we need to go down the shaft instead of up, we can also manage that.'

We all agreed that the excrement shaft had multiple uses, but before we adjourned the meeting, I brought up a perhaps moot subject and said to Brenner and Zamo, as I had said to Kate, 'After the Al Qaeda guys came here and saw the bait, all of us, except for Chet, could have gotten out of here.'

Brenner nodded and said, 'I thought about that back in Aden.'

And that would have been an excellent time to bring it up, Paul.

Brenner continued, 'But' – he looked at me, Kate, and Zamo – 'I don't think any of us ever intended to leave.'

'No,' I agreed, 'we never did, but for the record, and for later, no matter what happens in the next few hours, we should acknowledge that we stayed beyond the time we were needed. We stayed to see how it ended.'

No one had anything to add to that, except maybe the words, 'Brave but dumb.'

So the mafraj meeting was adjourned for probably the last

time, and Kate, Brenner, and I went down to the diwan, leaving Zamo to contemplate the abstract thought that excrement shafts go up and down and either way could get you out of deep shit.

This was all coming to a head, and we had lots to think about, but the bottom line was the mission: Kill The Panther. Then worry about how to get out of here alive.

CHAPTER SEVENTY-FIVE

It was time to join Chet and Buck in Moses' Red Sea Fish van so Kate, Brenner, and I went down into the courtyard.

The sinking sun cast a shadow along the west wall, and the thirteen Bedouin sat or squatted in the shade, drinking herbal tea and chatting. Little piles of green leaves sat on the ground between them. It was the happy hour.

Kate, Brenner, and I went into the van where Chet was sitting in the left-hand chair, staring intently at the video monitor. Buck was in the right-hand chair doing the same.

Chet's screen showed the aerial view of the sheik's goat herder's hut, with a very close resolution of maybe a few hundred feet.

Buck's screen had a higher and wider image of the area around the hut, showing a two- or three-kilometer radius. I saw five white Land Cruisers heading for the hut from the east. The Bedouin? Or Al Qaeda? Probably the sheik and his men, who as hosts needed to get there early to make tea.

As we all knew, each of the two Predator drones over the hut had, in addition to video cameras, two laser-guided Hellfire missiles, each with a high-explosive warhead, ready to launch, then seek and destroy whatever was in the crosshairs of the monitors. Awesome.

Chet came out of his electronic trance and said to us, 'Look. The sheik is arriving.'

We looked closely at his screen and saw the five Land Cruisers pulling up about thirty yards from the hut, which was farther away than they had been when we'd arrived from the Otter to meet the sheik. In fact, the vehicles were far enough away from the kill zone to avoid winding up in an auto body shop.

As we all watched, the Bedouin began piling out of the five Land Cruisers, and I counted a total of fifteen, all carrying AK-47s, except one – the sheik.

Sheik Musa was distinguishable in his clean white robes and his regal shiwal. I couldn't see his face, but from this computer-enhanced height of a few hundred feet, I could actually see his awesome proboscis. I mean, that thing cast a two-foot shadow, and probably had its own zip code.

The Bedouin were unloading the SUVs – three carpets, and what were probably crates of bottled water, plus burlap bags of what was maybe bread and tea. They were carrying other things that could have been camp stoves and pots to boil water – but no khat for their Al Qaeda guests. Other than that, they had everything they needed for a Yemeni picnic, even ants in case someone had malaria. And, of course, they had their AK-47s, because later, in a gross breach of Bedouin hospitality, they'd kill any of their guests who hadn't been killed by the American Hellfires.

Sheik Musa ducked into the hut with a few of his men, and the rest of the Bedouin began setting up for the powwow.

Chet said to us, 'The Panther and his men will arrive in about an hour or more. It's okay to be late, but never early.'

If they had a woman with them, they wouldn't have to worry about being early. Sorry. That just slipped out.

Chet hit a button on his console and said, 'The video is on record. So we can play the final few seconds of Mr al-Darwish's life over and over again.'

There was still the question of friendly fire casualties, and Brenner asked Chet about that.

Chet had a ready answer and replied, 'The two sides don't mix. Al Qaeda is on their carpet or around their own vehicles, and the Bedouin do the same. Only the sheik and The Panther sit together on their own carpet and speak privately, and when the sheik excuses himself to go into the stone hut with a few of his men to drag out the Americans, that's the signal for the Bedouin to take cover.' He added, 'I then give the order to fire, and about four seconds later, it's all over for Mr al-Darwish and maybe half his men. The Bedouin will finish off the survivors.' He reminded us, 'We discussed this in Aden.'

We did, but maybe Chet was still full of shit and everyone down there was going to die. Or at least lose a body part. And then we had to get out of here. Quickly.

Chet split his screen and the left half now showed a wide view of the Crow Fortress taken from one of the second pair of Predators on station over the plateau. Chet said, 'There's no one out there.'

Right. No Al Qaeda army ready to storm the Crow Fortress.

So that was one indication that things were going as planned and that The Panther was going to show up at the goat herder's hut.

Chet said to us, almost matter-of-factly, 'There's been a change of plans.'

A little buzzer went off in my head.

He swiveled his seat toward us, looked at me, Kate, and Brenner, and said, 'But a good change.'

The buzzer got louder. Also, I noticed, Buck had been uncharacteristically quiet since we'd entered the van. Was he thinking about something? Or worried about something?

Chet continued, 'It has been decided at the highest level that you three will leave here. Now.'

Neither I nor Kate nor Brenner asked why. That was coming.

Chet said to us, 'Your role in this mission is finished, and in fact it's been finished since the Al Qaeda delegation saw you.'

We all knew that, but this was the first time Chet had mentioned it.

He answered the unasked question. 'The thinking in Washington was that you would stay around for a few days after these Al Qaeda guys saw you, in case they figured out where they were taken, and in case Al Qaeda was watching the Crow Fortress to attack it or to see if anyone left.' He went on, 'But now that everything is in place and moving toward a conclusion, the mission planners want to split the team to ensure that we don't have all our eggs in one basket.'

Again, the three eggs who were going to be put into another basket didn't raise any questions. Best to let Chet talk.

And he did, saying, 'Buck and I will stay here until the Hellfires do their job. We'll keep Zamo here for security. And we will also have a Predator overhead for observation and security – the other Predator follows you.' He looked at us again and said, 'You will take one of these Land Cruisers and drive it down the north slope, pick up the Sana'a–Marib road, and drive to the Marib airstrip, where you will meet a chartered aircraft – a Company plane – that will take you to a location in Saudi Arabia, and then to Riyadh International Airport and home.' He informed us, 'If you push it, you can be at the airstrip in less than an hour.'

Thirty minutes, if *I* was driving. Wow. This sounded too good to be true.

Chet asked, 'Any questions? Any problems?'

It was Kate who said, 'We intend to stay here until it's over. We are going to the scene of the attack with you and we are flying out of there together on the Otter.'

Chet informed her, 'That's not going to happen, Kate.' He reminded us, 'These are orders from the top.' He added, nicely, 'But I appreciate your dedication.'

Brenner asked, 'What's the purpose of us leaving now? I'm not understanding *why* we're splitting up.'

Chet explained, 'Something could go wrong as we drive between here and the scene of the attack, or at the scene, or something could go wrong with our rendezvous with the Otter.' He further explained in a paternalistic tone of voice, 'There is no reason for all of us to take that risk, and there is every reason to split up so as to ensure that ... well, some of us get out of here.'

Right. But who?

Chet added, 'We don't want a situation where the mission is successful but the whole team is lost.'

Like, the operation was a success, but the patient died. Got it.

Kate asked Chet, 'Do you think it's safe for a single vehicle to drive from here to the Marib airstrip?'

Chet assured her and us, 'The roads are safe enough in the daylight, and you don't have to worry about a Bedouin guest kidnapping in Sheik Musa's territory, and you don't even have to worry about Al Qaeda, who rarely leave these highlands in the daylight.' He reminded us, 'If you move fast, you'll be at the airstrip before anyone even knows you're on the road, or even knows who you are. These Land Cruisers are generally recognized as Bedouin vehicles, and as you know, the windows are tinted, but Kate should wear her balto and sit in the rear.' He again assured us, 'You'll have a Predator covering you just in case, and we have sat-phone contact with each other. The drive to the airstrip should be a piece of cake.' He inquired, 'Any worries?'

I, like Buck, had remained uncharacteristically silent, but I now asked, 'Any reason we won't have a Bedouin escort?'

Chet replied, 'You don't need that, and quite frankly, if something goes wrong at the scene of the attack, the last thing you want is a carload of Bedouin near you talking to other Bedouin on their cell phones.'

Chet, it seemed, was concerned about our safety and our survival. And he and Buck would do the dangerous job of driving to the scene of the carnage, then they'd do the dirty work of collecting, bagging, and labeling the mortal remains of The Panther and his men, and maybe they'd also take some photos of the dead — as The Panther had done at the ruins. As for Sheik Musa, I was sure he and his Bedouin would be long gone from the scene, either in their Land Cruisers — or on their way to Paradise. So either way, Chet and Buck didn't have to deal with them. Check's in the mail, sheik.

And did Brenner, Kate, or I need to be here for any of that? Not really, but I was going to miss the blood and guts, and the smoking bones and flesh. That's not fair.

Chet asked us, 'Any other worries?'

'Worries' was a word designed to make us look and feel like nervous troops who needed to man up and follow orders. Chet, like most crazy people, thought he was the smartest man in the room – or in the fish van. Well, he wasn't. That would be me.

Anyway, I looked at Kate, then at Brenner, and we exchanged glances of, I guess, acceptance of the situation.

I said to Chet, 'Okay. No worries.'

Kate said, 'I'm not okay with this, but I understand.'

Brenner said, 'I also understand the reasoning. But Zamo will make his own decision about coming with us or staying here.'

Chet said, 'His orders are to stay here and provide security.'

Brenner replied, 'I don't care what his orders are. He's not under your control. He's under the control of the DSS and me.'

Chet didn't reply, and Buck didn't explain to Chet about embassy procedures and protocols.

Finally, Chet conceded, 'All right. It's his decision.'

But we – Kate, Brenner, and me – had no decision to make. We had been ordered to get out. Not by Chet, but by someone at the top. To be honest, I was more than a little ambivalent about this. Getting a head start on the trip home was good, and the road trip to Marib airstrip was a much smaller danger than sticking around here for the fireworks. Still, this was a big disappointment, and I'm sure Kate and Brenner felt the same. But Chet and the mission planners were right – if we split up, there was a better chance of someone getting back to make a full report, and Washington needed a few people alive to congratulate.

Chet said to us, 'Take only what you need and be on the road in ten minutes. When you land in Saudi Arabia, you'll turn in your weapons, Kevlar, and commo, and you'll be flying up to Riyadh Airport within fifteen minutes.' He further instructed us, 'Burn the passports that Buck gave you and take your dip passports for the international flight to the US.'

Chet kept mentioning that flight home as though us hearing it would make us believe it was going to happen. And maybe it was. And maybe it wasn't.

Chet also reminded us, 'Stick your head in here before you leave.'

I promised him, 'We wouldn't leave without saying goodbye, Chet.'

He smiled.

I said to Buck, 'See you later.'

He nodded, sort of smiled, and said to us, 'See you later.'

The now-unemployed members of the A-team left the fish van, mission completed.

CHAPTER SEVENTY-SIX

We returned to the tower, and Brenner called Zamo down from the mafraj and told him what was happening.

Brenner said, 'It's your decision if you want to stay here and cover Buck and Chet or come with us to Marib.'

Zamo didn't agonize much over his decision and replied, 'I work for you.' He also reminded Brenner, 'I don't get paid to make decisions.'

Brenner did get paid to make decisions, and he said to Zamo, 'You'll come with us.'

I suggested, 'Let's get moving.'

We gathered up what we needed, which all fit into our overnight bags, and we left everything else for the Bedouin, including my socks and underwear.

Kate slipped her balto over her clothes, and we went down to the livestock and excrement level and built a small bonfire of passports and crumpled magazine pages, which Zamo lit with a match from his field survival kit. We made sure everything burned, then we went out into the fading sunlight of the courtyard.

The Bedouin were still sitting and squatting along the wall, probably thinking about their approaching sundown prayers, and a new recipe for goat.

Kate covered her face with her hijab, and Brenner, in his limited Arabic, seemed to be thanking our hosts for their hospitality. The Bedouin remained sitting as they all said, 'As-salaam alaikum.'

Brenner responded with, 'Wa alaikum as-salaam.'

And arrivederci.

Brenner said something to Yasir, who stood and waved his arm toward the parked SUVs, and Brenner told us, 'He says take any one we want.'

'Which one has the bag of khat?'

Brenner didn't ask, but Yasir did give us three shiwals, one off his own head and two from his buddies, and Brenner said to us, 'This is a gift to remember them by.'

And they have my underwear to remember me.

Brenner told them that everything we'd left behind, which was mostly luggage, clothing, and one can of mixed vegetables, was theirs to keep. And, no, they couldn't have Zamo's sniper rifle.

I said to Yasir, 'See you in New York. Ben's Deli.' I also said, 'Shuqran,' which means 'thanks.'

We threw our overnight bags into the rear of one of the Land Cruisers, and carrying our weapons, we all walked to the fish van.

Chet and Buck were still watching the screens, and Chet was on the radio speaking to someone. As we entered, he said into the mic, 'I'll call you back. Out.'

He and Buck stood, and Chet said, 'So, you're taking Zamo.'

Brenner replied, without explanation, 'We are.'

It was Buck who said, 'The Bedouin in the courtyard are all the security we need, and some of them will accompany us to the scene.'

So we said our goodbyes without getting too teary-eyed, and we all agreed that the A-team had performed admirably.

Chet said to us, 'Thank you for your very professional performance.' He admitted, 'It hasn't always been easy to work together, but we've put our differences aside in the service of our country.' He looked at me and said, smiling, 'You have been a challenge, Mr Corey, but I'd rather work with a man like you than someone who never questions authority.'

'Thank you.' I think. Why do I always get singled out? This started in grade school.

Anyway, Buck added, 'You can all be proud of your work here.

Thank you for volunteering and for putting your lives at risk.' He reminded us, 'The homeland will be a little safer after Bulus ibn al-Darwish is dead.'

I reminded Buck, 'We have a rendezvous under the clock at Grand Central Station.'

'I'll be there,' Buck promised. 'We'll stay in touch.'

Chet said, 'I'll try to be there, too.'

You weren't invited, Chet. But, hey, anyone who's alive at the end of today is invited.

Buck, and even Chet, hugged Kate, we all shook hands, and we wished each other good luck and Godspeed.

Buck said, 'As-salaam alaikum.'

To relive our first meeting a million years ago, I smiled and said, 'That's easy for you to say.'

He smiled.

We left the van and piled into the Land Cruiser. Brenner was behind the wheel, Zamo was riding shotgun, and Kate and I were in the rear. The gentlemen had their shiwals with them, but no one saw any need to wear them at this time.

Yasir got off his butt and ran across the courtyard to open the gate as we approached it. We all waved to Yasir, who seemed delighted to see us go. But not as delighted as we were.

Brenner drove around the courtyard walls of the Crow Fortress, our home away from home, and we headed across the rocky plateau, toward the rock pile where the Bedouin guarded the northern approach to the fortress.

Brenner was following the dusty tracks of the other vehicles that had been to the Crow Fortress, and I asked him, 'Do you know where you're going?'

He hesitated, then replied, 'Down the north slope ... to pick up the Marib road.' He assured us, 'I've been to the airstrip and I can find it.'

'Good.' We continued on toward the north edge of the plateau. Kate said, 'I can't believe this is happening.'

Brenner assured her, 'It is, and within an hour we'll be on board a Company aircraft lifting off and heading for Saudi Arabia.' He added, 'Probably Najran airfield.'

Kate asked, 'Does anyone feel ... sorry or disappointed that we didn't stay until the end?'

Brenner and I, who are really in touch with our feelings, agreed that we would have liked to be there for the grand finale. Zamo, probably not into his feelings, said, 'Tactically, this makes sense.' He added, 'But it sucks.'

We continued on, and up ahead I could see the big rock formations and the SUV at the edge of the plateau where Musa's men sat in the shadows of the rocks.

I said to Brenner, 'Slow down.'

He reduced his speed and asked me, 'What's up?'

I replied, 'Here's what's up, Paul. Not too long ago, Kate killed a CIA officer — in self-defense.' I asked him, 'Did you know that?'

He hesitated, then replied, 'I heard.'

'Good.' And you still have the hots for her? Brave man. I sleep with one eye open. Just kidding. I continued, 'I think the Company is looking for some rough justice on that.'

Kate said, 'John, we are not supposed to discuss this—'

'This is really important, Kate. Do not interrupt.' I continued, 'As if Kate killing this guy wasn't bad enough, we had also inadvertently messed up a CIA plan to turn most of the Mideast into a nuclear wasteland.'

It was quiet in the Land Cruiser, and I continued, 'So, Kate and I know this big secret, and we're sworn to silence forever – in exchange for the Company giving Kate a pass on the firearm incident. But the CIA doesn't really work that way.'

Brenner, happily, agreed with me and said, 'No, they don't.'

'Right. They might let the gun incident go, but they are not comfortable with two witnesses walking around with that knowledge about the nuclear Armageddon that they'd planned for Sandland.'

Brenner was driving even slower now, and he seemed to be thinking. Finally, he realized I'd said my piece, and asked, 'So what . . . what are you saying?'

'I'm saying that Kate and I, and anyone who happens to be with us, are not getting out of Yemen alive.'

No one had a response to that, and I explained, 'That's why Kate and I are here – this is the perfect killing zone. No one answers to anyone for anything here. It's a black hole.' I added, 'And this is Operation Clean Sweep.'

Brenner stopped the Land Cruiser. He glanced in his rearview mirror and said, 'Kate? Do you believe this?'

My soul mate replied, 'No, I do not.'

Zamo, who usually has no opinion, said, 'I do.'

There you go. It's settled.

Brenner asked the obvious question. 'How do you think this . . . this is going to happen?'

'I'll get to that later, but I can say it will happen between right here and the Marib airstrip.'

No one had any response to that.

I asked, 'Why do you think we're in this SUV, out of the Crow Fortress and away from Chet and Buck?'

Brenner replied, 'What Chet said makes perfect tactical and operational sense.'

'Indeed, it does, which is why my paranoia wasn't supposed to kick in. And you know what? I'm only, let's say, seventy-three percent sure I'm right about Chet wanting to get me and Kate whacked.'

Kate said, 'If we sit here all day, we *could* get killed. We need to get to the airstrip.'

Brenner asked me the next logical question. 'What does this – if it's true – have to do with me, or with Zamo?'

I replied, 'You are just in the wrong place at the wrong time. It's logical that you would be ordered to leave with Kate and me, and if you weren't, that would look suspicious. As for Zamo, he was never going to stay behind. That was all bullshit to make this look like a tactically sound plan.' I informed Mr Brenner, 'Buck knew exactly what you were going to say about Zamo staying here, and one way or the other, Zamo was not going to stay with Buck and Chet.' I added, 'And if he did, Chet would kill him with an AK-47, take his sniper rifle, and make it look like the Bedouin did it.'

Both men remained silent, then Brenner said, 'I'm just not buying that Zamo and I are going to get wasted by our own people just because we happen to be with you.'

'You should believe it, but here's another reason you're not in a good place – for all Chet knows, I or Kate have confided in you about my suspicions, and you are therefore a person like us who knows too much.' I reminded him and everyone, 'And in this business, when you know what you're not supposed to know, you become a worry to the Company.' I added, 'The Company chose well when they chose Chet Morgan for this job.' I explained, in case no one noticed, 'He's crazy.'

Brenner, Kate, and Zamo thought about all that, and I could imagine them concluding that John didn't need a Kevlar vest as much as he needed a straitjacket.

But Brenner, either avoiding the topic of my paranoia, or maybe testing it, asked, 'So do you think Buck is in on this?'

That was a tough call. The answer was that Buckminster Harris had been in the deception business so long, he really didn't know what was real and what he was making up. Right and wrong was a little blurry, too. Plus, he just enjoyed the game. I was sure he liked me, Kate, and all of us, but if Chet presented him with a national security problem and a solution, then Buck would work with Chet on both. Nothing personal.

Finally, I replied, 'Buck has to be in on it.'

Well, by now, Paul Brenner was waiting for me to announce that I'd been abducted by space aliens. But he was smart enough to be concerned, and he was still enough of a cop to want all the info. He said to me, 'Even if you're right ... I mean, you're giving Chet a lot of credit for being some kind of genius ...'

'He's out of his fucking mind,' I assured everyone. 'But he's smart. I, however, am smarter.' I asked my seatmate, 'Right?'

She didn't reply. Clearly Kate was upset, and she was obviously worried that I'd slipped over the edge.

Brenner, in fact, said, 'Look, we've all been under a lot of stress—'

'All right,' I said, 'drive on.' I promised everyone, 'We'll see what happens.'

But Brenner didn't drive. He asked me, 'What do you *think* is going to happen?'

I replied, 'I think that a Predator drone, under the command of the Central Intelligence Agency, and under the operational control of Chet Morgan in his fish van, is going to launch a Hellfire missile at this vehicle and kill everyone inside it.' I added, 'The Predator pilot, wherever he is, will be clueless, or at least unsure, but he'll do what the operational control guy on the scene – Chet – tells him to do.'

It was Zamo who spoke first. 'Yeah. That could happen.'

It sure could. I also said, 'The Company has picked this method of a friendly fire accident to send a clear message that it wasn't friendly and it wasn't an accident.'

Brenner stayed quiet awhile, then said to me, 'Okay . . . what are *we* supposed to do?'

'What we're not going to do is drive down that slope and head cross-country toward the Marib road, because if we do, we're not going to get to the Marib road.'

Brenner asked, 'Then why are we even in this Land Cruiser? Why didn't you tell us this back in the Crow Fortress?'

'If I had, what would we have done?'

'Tell Chet and Buck what you just told us.'

I replied, 'At least they would believe me. But here's the deal – the mission comes first. Chet is poised to kill The Panther. And we will let him do that. But we will not let him have a friendly fire accident on our way to Marib.'

Brenner sort of nodded.

I said to him, 'Let's go.'

As we moved toward the rock pile and the Bedouin guarding the approach to the plateau, I said, 'Chet has not directed a Predator to watch us because the Predator pilot and other ground controllers would see that it was us who got into this Land Cruiser, and they would not fire on it.' I explained, 'Chet will get a Predator on station when he thinks we're traveling cross-country toward the Marib road. He will tell the pilot to keep us in his sight, then at some point he will inform the pilot that the Land Cruiser is a confirmed target. And then Chet will execute the assassination stage of the flight and order the pilot to take out the target.' I added, 'Kate's balto and our shiwals will be mentioned in the incident report as one reason for the misidentification of the people in the Land Cruiser as a target.' I added, 'Souvenirs can be dangerous.'

No one had anything to say about that, so I asked, 'Would anyone have a problem with asking one of those Bedouin to drive this vehicle down the slope and toward the Marib road?'

Zamo replied in a heartbeat, 'Not me.'

Brenner said, 'I would have a problem with that ... but ...'

Kate didn't reply, and I said to her, 'If nothing happens, then you're right and I'm crazy.'

She hesitated, then replied, 'I ... would not want to see an innocent person killed ...'

I pointed out, 'You said I was wrong.'

'I'm not making that decision.'

'Okay. I'll make it.'

The Bedouin around the rocks were watching us, and Brenner pulled close to them.

I said to him, 'I need your Arabic.'

Brenner and I got out of our Land Cruiser and everyone did their peace thing.

There were five Bedouin with AK-47s and they had one white Land Cruiser with them.

I said to Brenner, 'Tell them we will give them mucho rials if one of them will take our vehicle to the airstrip and pick up an Amriki who is waiting there for us.'

Brenner glanced at me, hesitated, then began speaking in halting Arabic.

The five Bedouin nodded in understanding, and Brenner said to me, 'This gentleman' – he pointed to a bearded guy in his thirties or forties – 'will go for us.'

I nodded and smiled at the guy.

'He says he'll take his own vehicle.'

'No.' I took Brenner's arm and we stepped onto a small flat rock. I said, 'See that?'

Brenner stared at the roof of our Land Cruiser, whose dusty white paint was smeared with what looked like blood, probably goat blood. He kept staring at the smear, then said, 'Jesus . . .' He looked at me.

I stepped down off the rock and asked him, 'So what do you think, Paul?'

He seemed at a loss for words, but then reminded me, 'Yasir told us to take *any* vehicle.'

'Right. Pick a card. Any card.' At the risk of stating the obvious, I said, 'They're all marked.'

He nodded.

I said to him, 'We can wipe the red target off, or since all the Bedouin vehicles are communal, we can swap cars with these gentlemen, and we can proceed to the Marib airstrip, and hopefully not get vaporized on the way. But I don't think there's anything or anyone waiting for us at the airstrip. So I suggest we go back to the Crow Fortress and deal with this.' I checked my watch. 'We should be there about the time The Panther is in Chet's sights.'

Brenner, who has seen lots of death, has probably not seen lots of treachery and double-crosses, and he still looked a little out of it. Hello, Paul?

Kate and Zamo were out of the Land Cruiser, and Kate glanced at Brenner, then asked me, 'What's happening?'

I said to Brenner, '*You* tell her.' She never believes me.

The Bedouin were watching us, curious about what the crazy Amriki were talking about, so we didn't want to go look at the roof again and put ideas into their heads. But Brenner said to Kate and Zamo, 'There is a red marking – looks like blood – on the roof of the Land Cruiser.'

Zamo, who'd painted lots of people red with a red laser beam before he sent them to Paradise, got it in a heartbeat, and said, 'Holy shit.'

Well said.

Kate is quick, but stubborn, and she reminded us, 'But Yasir said—'

'They're *all* marked,' I informed her. 'They weren't marked when we were up in the diwan or I'd have seen that, because I was looking for it. But when we went down to burn our civilian passports on the ground level, the Bedouin, at the prior request of Chet, marked all the roofs with goat blood, probably thinking that they were putting some kind of holy protection mark on the SUVs.

645

You know, like the Passover thing with the lamb's blood.' I added helpfully, 'Exodus.'

Well, maybe that was a stretch, but close enough. Or Yasir and his buddies had no idea why Chet gave them a few rials to do something weird. But they did know to keep their mouths shut about it. I further informed my teammates, 'Chet also asked Yasir to give us the shiwals, which will be mentioned in the incident report.'

Kate looked at me, and I thought maybe she'd say, 'Sorry I doubted you,' but she didn't. She asked me, and all of us, 'What do we do now?'

I explained to Kate and Zamo that a road trip to Marib airstrip might not be productive, and I suggested, 'We can let this kind gentleman here take the vehicle marked for death, and absolutely confirm that Chet was planning to whack us.' I asked, 'Anyone need to see that?'

No one apparently did.

I suggested, 'Let's go back to the Crow Fortress and talk to Chet and Buck.'

Brenner agreed, but said, 'They will deny everything.'

Kate agreed, and so did Zamo.

Indeed, Chet and Buck would deny everything, and we had no proof that I wasn't totally crazy. And if we disobeyed orders and went back to the Crow Fortress and I accused Chet and Buck of plotting to kill us, that could get very weird, and I'd be the one answering charges back in the States. Not to mention that the Company would definitely see to it that Kate and I met with a fatal accident. So we couldn't go back to the Crow Fortress without proof, we didn't want to drive to Marib, and we couldn't stay here.

Zamo said, 'Let the guy drive.'

No one responded to that.

The guy in question, whose name was Emad, said something to Brenner, who didn't reply.

Okay, someone has to make life-or-death decisions, and like Brenner, I too get paid for that. And yet ...

Finally, I said, 'Let Emad drive to Marib airstrip.'

Neither Kate nor Brenner seconded that, but neither did they object. Zamo, however, said, 'Otherwise, you'll never know for sure.'

Brenner hesitated, then said something to Emad, who smiled and got into our Land Cruiser. Emad didn't ask for his money up front, but Brenner pressed a handful of rials on him and said something to him in Arabic.

In truth, we were becoming more callous and more like the bad guys, but at least we had a conscience.

Emad waved and took off down the slope.

Well, part of me hoped I was wrong, but the blood on the roof said I was right. In fact, everything said I was right.

One of the Bedouin said something to Brenner, and Brenner said to me, 'He wants to know if we need a ride back to the Crow Fortress.'

I looked at my watch and said, 'Ask him if we can borrow his vehicle.'

Brenner asked, and it was no problem, and I tipped them with the last of my rials.

I drove this time, and Zamo rode shotgun. Kate and Brenner sat silently in the rear.

After a few minutes we could see the Crow Fortress ahead, and I spotted a pile of rocks on the left. I pulled over and said, 'We can watch from here.'

We got out of the Land Cruiser and climbed onto the rocks, which gave us a clear view of the flatlands below.

Zamo put his sniper rifle to his shoulder, adjusted his scope to full power, and said, 'I got him.'

Brenner, Kate, and I did the same with the weaker-powered scopes on our M4s.

I could see the white Land Cruiser driven by Emad kicking up dust about a mile away, heading north toward the Marib road.

There wasn't much vehicle traffic on the dirt roads that cut through the dry fields, and it was easy to follow the lone dust trail even as the Land Cruiser grew smaller.

The more time that went by without the SUV erupting into a ball of flames, the more I began to think that maybe I was missing my flight out of here.

No one spoke, but I could imagine what Kate and Brenner were thinking: Poor John has gone gaga. Zamo, however, was looking through his scope like he was tracking a Taliban general. He was as still as a statue and his breathing was so controlled that I thought he'd gone into a trance.

I was half hoping that I hadn't sent an innocent man to his death, but as the seconds ticked by, I also hoped that a Predator pilot had the Land Cruiser in its crosshairs and was waiting for Chet to say, 'Engage the target.'

After three or four minutes I lost sight of the SUV in my scope, and so did Kate and Brenner, and they put their rifles down. But Zamo still had him and kept looking through his scope.

I said, 'Maybe this will happen later.'

No one replied.

Zamo said, 'Lost him,' and put his rifle down.

Brenner asked me, 'What do you want to do now?'

I replied, 'Sit here and wait for the streak of white smoke.'

Again, no one replied, but Zamo was staring out at the distant horizon without his scope, so we did the same.

Kate said to everyone, 'Let's ask one of the Bedouin back there to drive us to the Marib airstrip.'

Brenner suggested, 'Or let's walk back to the Crow Fortress and say our car broke down and we need another one.'

Did I detect a note of sarcasm in his voice?

I said, 'We can see the smoke trail for over twenty miles from up here.'

Brenner informed me, 'I'm not waiting half an hour for that.' He said to Kate, 'Please talk to your husband. We need to make a decision.'

'John.'

'Quiet.'

So we sat on the rocks and stared out at the blue sky. The crazy guy was in charge. Or he needed to be humored until he came to his senses — or until they could get the drop on me.

So we continued to wait, but only Zamo and I were giving the sky our undivided attention. Kate and Brenner were exchanging glances.

Please, God, let me be right about the CIA wanting to kill me and my wife. That's not too much to ask.

Less than two minutes after we'd lost sight of the dust cloud, a white trail of thin white smoke cut across the blue sky. An instant later, there was a flash of orange light on the horizon, but no sound.

Zamo said, 'Target killed.' He added, 'Holy shit.'

Brenner stood, but said nothing.

Kate, too, stood, and stared as a column of black smoke began rising above the horizon. She said, 'Oh my God . . .' I didn't know if she was addressing me, but she looked at me and said, 'I can't believe this . . .'

Birds in the fields below suddenly took flight, then a muffled sound like distant thunder reached us and died away, leaving a stillness in the air.

Brenner was still staring at the rising smoke, and he said, 'Those bastards.'

Zamo said, 'I guess John was right.'

I guess so.

Kate said softly, 'That poor man . . . he's dead.'

No one responded to that.

Brenner said, 'Okay, let's go back and talk to Buck and Chet.'

I said, 'They'll think they're seeing ghosts.'

We got into the Land Cruiser and headed back to the Crow Fortress.

CHAPTER SEVENTY-SEVEN

I drove fast, but not so fast as to attract the attention of the Predator pilot whose job it was to watch the immediate vicinity of the Crow Fortress. But even if he saw us as we approached the fortress, all he'd see was the Bedouin Land Cruiser from the rock pile, so no reason to call Chet.

As for Chet and Buck, both their monitors would now be tuned in to the two Predators flying above the goat herder's hut. One of their screens would have been split to direct another Predator to follow the suspected target in the Land Cruiser – us – and Chet had just given the order to destroy the target. I wonder if Chet had a lump in his throat when he saw his teammates getting blown up.

We were now a few hundred meters from the Crow Fortress, and as I'd noticed since we'd been here, the Bedouin rarely posted a lookout on the walls of the courtyard – guard duty was the job of the Amriki in the tower – and I didn't see anyone as I looked at the wall in front of us.

When I got within fifty meters of the fortress, I retraced my route to come around to the gate on the east side.

Brenner asked, 'Do we have a plan?'

I replied, 'There is no plan possible for this situation. Sometimes you just have to shoot from the hip.' Literally.

Zamo suggested, 'They need to die for what they did.'

Good plan.

Brenner reminded Zamo and all of us, 'I give the order to fire – but you can fire if fired upon.'

Or if I feel like emptying a full magazine into those two bastards. But first we had to make sure that Chet had completed his mission and killed The Panther.

I pulled up near the gate, which was closed, and I turned the vehicle around, pointing it toward the edge of the plateau that we'd driven up on the night we landed in this shithole. I kept the engine running, and we all got out quickly, leaving the doors open.

Kate pulled off her balto for better mobility and access to her spare magazines, and Brenner said, 'Rock and roll,' meaning move your selector switches to full automatic.

I insisted on going in first and alone, and I lifted the latch handle, swung the gate in, and slipped into the courtyard.

The Bedouin were still where we'd left them, sitting along the shade of the west wall, chatting and chewing. I noticed also that all the vehicles were still there, so Chet and Buck had not yet left here to drive to the scene of the attack, meaning it hadn't happened yet. I checked my watch: 6:15 P.M., so apparently The Panther was late – or he wasn't showing up at all.

The Bedouin noticed me, but none of them looked surprised, though a few of them seemed to be discussing my return.

The doors of the van with the Predator monitors were closed, and the engine wasn't running, but I could hear the hum of the gasoline-powered generator.

I motioned to Kate, Brenner, and Zamo to come in, and I said, 'Act normal,' which meant walking casually across the courtyard to the van. The Bedouin were looking at us, and maybe they were unhappy that Kate was dressed like a man.

We stopped at the closed doors of Moses' Red Sea fish van and I saw that the padlock was not there, meaning someone was inside, which I expected. Hopefully it was both of them.

Well, I didn't want to interrupt Chet while he was in his stealthy assassination mode, but we couldn't stand here smiling at the Bedouin.

Brenner nodded toward the door and whispered, 'Let's go.'

Right. Chet and Buck would be unhappily surprised to see us, but they had a job to do and they'd do it, and then we could discuss other matters.

I leveled my M4 as Brenner and Zamo swung both doors open, and I jumped into the van.

Unfortunately, no one was there.

Brenner and Kate came into the van, and Zamo stayed outside to keep an eye on the Bedouin.

Kate asked, 'Where are they?'

Definitely not here. But the consoles were fully lit and the monitors were both on, as though they'd just stepped out for a minute.

We moved to the front of the van and looked at the screens. The left-hand screen – Chet's screen – showed the close view of the goat herder's hut, and the right screen had a split view, a higher and wider shot of the area around the hut, and another high shot showing a white SUV traveling on a dirt road.

As we watched, an electronic crosshair came onto the split screen over the SUV, and a few seconds later the white SUV was gone, replaced by a bright orange flash, followed by swirling black smoke and debris. A message came on the screen that said, 'Target engaged.'

Then I saw another, smaller message in the left-hand corner of the screen that said, 'Replay.' Then the original image appeared again and our SUV with the blood mark on the roof and Emad driving was vaporized again by the Hellfire missile. Ouch.

Brenner said, 'Those *bastards*.'

Kate said, 'Look.'

We focused on Chet's screen, which was also on replay, and watched silently as Sheik Musa, surrounded by about half of his fifteen men, walked from left to right toward another group of men who were moving from right to left.

Both groups stopped in the middle of the carpet, and after a hesitation, Sheik Musa took the hand of The Panther and kissed it. The Panther then did the same to Sheik Musa.

I don't know if they embraced or not, because the crosshair on the screen brightened, then an electronic message flashed 'Fire,' and the screen brightened again in an orange glow, followed by black swirling debris, then smoke and fire. The words 'Target engaged' flashed on the screen.

Everyone, I was sure, including Sheik Musa and all the men around him, were dead or mortally wounded. Same for Mr Bulus ibn al-Darwish – The Panther was dead.

I said, 'Mission accomplished.'

Brenner said, 'Chet killed the sheik, too.'

Kate pointed to the electronic clock counter and said, 'At six-ten ... seven minutes ago.'

Right. And these images had been broadcast to people in Washington – to the mission planners in Langley, and maybe even to the White House. And everyone was celebrating. The Panther was dead. Congratulations, Chet and Buck. And then Chet and Buck left the van. But where did they go? Maybe to gather some things in the diwan, then they'd jump in an SUV and get out of here.

I looked at Buck's screen and I saw the replay again, but from a higher and wider perspective, which showed all the vehicles that had arrived – Bedouin and Al Qaeda – parked away from the hut. Two more Hellfires hit almost simultaneously, blowing up the two groups of men and vehicles. The secondary explosions of the fuel tanks sent fiery wreckage and burning gasoline into the air. A third Hellfire hit the roof of the goat herder's hut, just in case anyone was inside, and the stone walls of the hut collapsed.

Kate asked again, 'Where are Chet and Buck?'

I didn't know, but I knew that they got out of here quickly, in case there were any Bedouin survivors at the scene of the attack who would call the Bedouin here saying that the Americans had killed their sheik. But where did our teammates go? I pointed out, 'All the vehicles are here.'

Kate concluded, 'So they have to be in the tower.'

'Maybe ... but we need to get out of here in case the Bedouin here get those calls ...' And then I remembered how Chet was going to get rid of this million-dollar van and I said, 'The Predator over the Crow Fortress is about to vaporize this van.'

We quickly exited the target, but we didn't want to spook the Bedouin so we didn't run. Brenner turned toward the gate, but I grabbed his arm and said, 'We need to see if Chet and Buck are in the tower.'

He hesitated for half a second, then nodded, and we began walking quickly toward the tower. Indeed, hate and revenge cloud your judgment. We should have been in the Land Cruiser now, tear-assing down the ravine to get away from here. But first we needed to settle up with our two teammates.

CHAPTER SEVENTY-EIGHT

As we got within thirty feet of the door of the tower, I noticed that two of the Bedouin were on their cell phones, and I knew what those calls were about; some of the Bedouin had indeed survived the Hellfire attack and were now telling their buddies in the Crow Fortress that the Amriki missiles had fried their sheik and everyone around him.

A few of the Bedouin started looking at us, then they all began standing. There was absolutely no reason now to act normal, so we began running toward the tower.

We let Kate in first through the narrow doorway, followed by Zamo, then Brenner. I took a quick look over my shoulder and saw the Bedouin running toward us, and a few of them were shouting and pointing their AK-47s at me.

Just as I slipped into the doorway, a deafening explosion filled the air, followed by the secondary explosion of the fish van's fuel tank, and the shockwave knocked me down. I could feel the earth shake under me as I got to my feet, and without anyone saying anything, we all ran for the staircase.

I don't remember hitting any of the stone steps, but within a few seconds we passed through the windowless storage level and we were all in the diwan, weapons at the ready.

Zamo ran to the indoor outhouse and kicked the door in, but no one was there. What was also not in the diwan was the washstand, and I pointed this out to everyone, who drew the same conclusion: Our missing teammates had headed for the roof.

Kate, Brenner, and I looked out the window into the courtyard. The van was a burning heap of twisted metal, and clouds of black smoke billowed from the wreckage. The courtyard was strewn with burning debris, and it appeared that three of the Bedouin had been killed or injured. The other ten seemed stunned as they wandered around the courtyard or stood dazed and silent.

Then one of them looked up and noticed us in the window, and he pointed and shouted.

Someone fired a full burst of rounds, which hit the stone above us, and without waiting for Brenner to give the order, Kate and I fired back with our M4s on full automatic, then Brenner pushed Kate away from the window and emptied a full magazine at the Bedouin down in the courtyard.

We didn't wait around for an accurate body count, but it looked to me as though we'd taken out about five of the remaining ten guys, including Yasir, who I'd seen fall. I said to myself, 'Sorry.'

The other Bedouin, unfortunately, had made it into the tower, and they were now right below us. Time to go, and there was only one way to go.

We raced up the stone steps and I could hear the shouts of the Bedouin behind us.

Brenner got to the next level first, and he called down, 'Clear.'

Kate and Zamo, with me bringing up the rear, charged up the stairs just as a burst of AK-47 fire came up the stairwell. Another burst ripped through the thick floorboards, close to where we were standing.

I fired a burst of rounds back through the floorboards as Kate fired down the stone stairwell. That seemed to quiet down the Bedouin, and we charged up the next flight of steps, then the next, which put us on the level below the mafraj.

So far, no sign of Chet and Buck, but they had to be in the mafraj or on the roof. Or they were up to their old tricks, so I fired a full burst of rounds into the wood outhouse, then kicked in the door and looked down the shaft through the holes, but I didn't see anyone.

I then looked up and I could see through the squatter hole in the floor of the mafraj, up to the vent hole in the ceiling. I thought I saw a shadow pass through the sunlight and I fired a short burst up through the vent, but I didn't draw any return fire.

I exited the outhouse and said, 'I think they're on the roof.'

As I said that, we heard a huge, thunderous explosion off in the distance, and we all turned toward the west-facing window. There was another explosion, then another, and in the far distance we could see black smoke rising into the blue sky.

Brenner said, 'That's the airstrike on the Al Qaeda base camp — probably a flight of F-15s from Najran, dropping two-thousand-pound bombs.'

Wonderful. Can they drop a smaller one on Chet and Buck?

The sound of the explosions kept rolling through the windows, and I counted twelve before it got quiet.

So that was the end of the Al Qaeda base camp — but there were more of them, and there'd be more coming. The Panther, however, was dead, and badasses like that were not as easy to replace as a camp full of jihadist recruits.

I said to everyone, 'We need to get up to the mafraj.'

Before we could make a move toward the stairs, Kate shouted, 'Look!' and pointed to the window on the north side of the tower.

We looked out at the sky and in the far distance we could see a helicopter coming toward the Crow Fortress.

Brenner was covering the stairwell, firing single rounds down the stone staircase, but not drawing any return fire from the Bedouin, who were probably watching the helicopter approaching.

The helicopter was getting closer, and Zamo took a look at it through his sniper scope. He said in a quiet voice, 'It's a Black Hawk ... no markings, but it's got to be US ... I see two door gunners ...'

Great. The cavalry had arrived. Unfortunately, it had not arrived to save us; it had arrived, as per schedule – or a few minutes late from Najran – to save Buck and Chet's treacherous asses. This was the part of the plan that Chet and Buck forgot to mention, though Brenner had thought about it – but a little late.

Well, when the Black Hawk got to the roof, what they'd find was two dead guys.

'Let's go!' I said, and we all ran for the staircase as a long burst of AK-47 fire came through the floorboards around us, followed by another burst that came up the stairwell.

I led the way up to the mafraj and we fanned out along the four walls with our backs to the stone columns that supported the large arches. I saw the washstand sitting against the wood wall of the excrement shaft, confirming what we already knew.

I pointed my M4 at the ceiling, and everyone did the same. No one seemed to have any qualms about doing to our teammates what they had tried to do to us. Also, we had five or six Bedouin trying to kill us, and we might not make it back alive to see that justice was done – so we had to do it here.

As we were about to fire into the ceiling, a voice shouted in Arabic, and it took me a second to realize it came through the vent hole.

I didn't know what Buck said, but Brenner apparently did, and he shouted back, 'It's not the Bedouin, Buck! It's us!' He added, 'Alive and well. Surprised?'

Silence.

Well, maybe it was a good thing to let Buck and Chet know that we were still alive and well, but not very happy with our teammates. Then we'd kill them.

I shouted through the vent hole, 'Come on down. We need to talk.'

It was Chet, who replied, 'Come on up.' He let us know, in case we didn't, 'There's a chopper inbound to get us out of here.'

Us? Bullshit, right to the end.

Meanwhile, another burst of automatic fire came through the floorboards, splintering the old wood and lodging into the ceiling above us. But we were hugging the perimeter of the mafraj, standing on the floor where the boards rested on thick beams and masonry below, so we were relatively safe – for the moment.

Brenner shouted up, 'Drop your weapons through the hole – pistols and rifles – then kneel at the hole with your hands on your heads.'

Brenner, ex-cop, was trying to make an arrest. Corey, ex-cop, was trying to make two corpses.

Buck shouted down, 'Paul, I don't know what you're thinking, or what—'

'Shut up, Buck!' suggested Paul. 'Shut your fucking mouth and get your ass down here. You, too, Chet!'

Buck replied, 'There are Bedouin down there. Are you all crazy? Get up here. We'll give you a hand.'

Buck was stalling for time as the Black Hawk approached, and Brenner was intent on making a bust, then getting on that helicopter with his prisoners.

I'd had enough of this and I shouted to Buck and Chet, 'You have three seconds to drop your weapons, or we ventilate that roof and you go on that chopper dead.'

No response.

'One, two—' Everyone raised their weapons at the ceiling, and Brenner said, 'At my command.' Then to Buck and Chet he said, 'Last chance!'

But before Brenner said, 'Fire,' someone else fired. In fact, it was the Black Hawk helicopter, which we could see through the big north-facing arch. It had gotten much closer, and the two door gunners were firing long bursts of machine-gun fire at the tower. We all hit the floor as red tracer rounds sailed through the arches. The rounds began hitting the columns and bullets started ricocheting around the mafraj. A spent round hit my arm, then a not-so-spent round hit the side of my Kevlar vest, knocking the wind out of me.

Chet was obviously in radio contact with the Black Hawk, and he'd told them there were bad guys below him and asked for protective fire. Psychos are smart.

I glanced up through the arch and saw the Black Hawk about a hundred yards away and coming fast. Another burst of machine-gun tracer rounds came through the mafraj and we all got into a fetal position as the bullets sailed above us or hit the stone columns and ricocheted around the stone walls.

I rolled on my back and emptied my magazine into the roof, hoping I'd see blood dripping down through the holes. But Buck and Chet were probably standing tight against the parapet now, and if they were smart, they'd also be standing on their Kevlar vests. Nevertheless, I slammed a fresh magazine into my M4 and fired again, and so did Brenner and Kate, but then another burst of machine-gun fire from the Black Hawk made us tuck in tightly against the floor and walls. Zamo, meanwhile, was lying flat at the top of the stairs, popping off rounds down the stairwell with his sniper rifle, just to let the Bedouin know we hadn't lost interest in them.

I couldn't see the Black Hawk any longer, and I knew the chopper was now flaring out above the tower and about to put down on the roof. The good news was that he couldn't fire through the arches at that angle, and he wouldn't fire through the roof with Buck and Chet there. The bad news was that we couldn't fire through the ceiling at Buck and Chet and take a chance of hitting the chopper. I mean, the four-man crew of the Black Hawk had no idea what the situation was except what Chet had told them, and Chet lies.

I could hear the rotor blades beating as the Black Hawk hovered above the roof. In about a minute, Chet and Buck would be airborne and on their way to Najran airbase, and we'd be left here to deal with the pissed-off Bedouin, whose sheik Chet and Buck had killed. Shit.

The chopper's rotor blades were getting louder, then I heard the thump of the wheels hitting the roof.

Chet and Buck would have some explaining to do at Najran and at every stop on their way to Washington – but they'd killed The Panther and that would make people happy, and happy people don't ask too many questions.

Unfortunately for Chet and Buck, the rest of the A-team was still alive, and we had a different story to tell. Now all we had to do was stay alive to tell it.

Brenner called out to everyone, 'When the chopper lifts off, he'll open fire again to cover himself.'

Correct. So let's get the hell out of here. The staircase was not an option, so without anyone saying the obvious, we ran in a crouch toward the excrement shaft.

As we got to the door of the shaft, we heard the Black Hawk's engine revving, and the pitch of the rotor blades changed as the big chopper began lifting off the roof. Almost immediately, two streams of red tracer rounds penetrated the roof and tore into the center of the floor.

We could now hear return fire from below – the Bedouin firing at the chopper through the windows. Then long bursts of machine-gun fire from the Black Hawk answered the Bedouin fire from below, taking the pressure off us for the moment.

We all quickly squeezed into the tight outhouse, and Brenner said he'd go first and establish a beachhead on the next level, where the Bedouin were hopefully not using the squatter. He squeezed himself into the hole, dangled by his fingers, and dropped as quietly as possible to the next level, then got down on one knee and covered the door with his M4.

We could hear more bursts of AK-47 fire as the Bedouin continued to fire at the chopper, which must have been almost out of their range by now. There wasn't much good news at the moment except that the Bedouin undoubtedly thought that all the Americans were on that helicopter. No such luck.

It took a few minutes for each of us to drop, level by level, squatter hole by squatter hole, to the last level below the diwan, right above the excrement level, which was pungent.

We were all jammed into the indoor outhouse now and

Brenner put his ear to the door, saying softly, 'I don't hear anything.'

The surviving Bedouin were either still on one of the higher levels, or they'd taken the stairs down and were in the courtyard, which would not be good.

Our choice now was either to get out of the outhouse and go down the stairs, or drop through the last hole and land in the pile of shit, which didn't seem so bad at this point. Both ways would get us to the ground floor, but not get us to our Land Cruiser and out of here. To do that, we might have to knock off the rest of the Bedouin, and to be honest I didn't want to kill any more of them. But neither did I want them to kill us. Actually, since we'd wasted a bunch of them, and since our Hellfires had vaporized their sheik and their buddies, we'd be lucky if they only killed us.

Kate whispered, 'We can't stay here. The Bedouin from the rock pile could be on the way.'

Good point. We didn't want to deal with more pissed-off Bedouin.

As we were contemplating our next move — stairs or free fall into the shit pile — we heard footsteps above us in the diwan, and voices in Arabic. If I had to guess, I'd say the Bedouin thought we were gone and they were rummaging through the stuff we'd left behind.

Well, before they took the stairs down, this was our chance to get out of here, and we all knew that.

The staircase was quicker and cleaner than the excrement route, so I threw open the door and we moved rapidly across the dark, windowless tower room, which was used to store hay, straw, and whatever. Zamo paused long enough to light a pile of hay.

I hit the stairs first and bounded down three and four at a time, then shoulder-rolled across the earth floor and got on one knee and covered the narrow doorway with my M4.

Kate came down next, followed quickly by Brenner and Zamo.

I stood, moved quickly to the door, and peered out into the devastated and body-strewn courtyard. Some of the wreckage was still smoldering, and the only people out there were dead.

I signaled all clear, pointed in the direction of the gate, and charged into the courtyard, with Kate, Brenner, and Zamo right behind me.

I got to the gate, stopped short, and spun around in a crouch to cover the courtyard and tower. I could see smoke seeping through the stone walls of the tower.

Just as Kate was getting to the open gate, a figure appeared in the diwan window and fired. Kate went down and lay sprawled on the ground. I got between her and the tower and fired long, rapid-fire bursts at the window, glancing back at Kate, who was getting to her feet. No blood, so she'd taken a round in her Kevlar, and I yelled to her, 'Move! Move!'

Kate and Zamo ran through the gate, but Brenner spun around and emptied his magazine at the window. The smoke was pouring out of the tower now, and I could see flames in the windows of the diwan.

I slammed a fresh magazine into my M4 and emptied it at the five vehicles in the courtyard, blowing out the tires and shattering the windows. Brenner did the same and one of the Hiluxes burst into flames. Time to go.

We ran through the gate and I saw that Zamo was already behind the wheel and Kate was in the rear, leaning out the window covering us. I jumped in beside her and pulled the door closed as Brenner jumped in the front. Before his door was even closed, Zamo was pushing pedal to the metal and we were shooting across the flat terrain toward the ravine.

Brenner and I lowered our windows, leaned out, and turned back toward the gate.

Two Bedouin came charging through the gate and all three of us opened fire, hitting one of them and making the other dive back behind the stone wall.

Within a few minutes we were at the edge of the plateau, and Zamo was slowing up, looking for the ravine. He spotted some tire marks and cut the wheel sharply to the right, then hit the brakes as the Land Cruiser's front wheels slipped over the edge of the plateau and into the ravine.

Zamo navigated down the steep, twisting terrain, going faster than was safe. But back there wasn't too safe either.

The sun was low on the horizon behind us, and the ravine, which was on the east side of the plateau, was in shadow, making it hard to see up ahead.

After a few minutes of escape-and-evasion driving, Brenner said to Zamo, 'We shot up the SUVs, so anyone behind us is on foot.'

Zamo let up on the gas and said, 'Now you tell me.'

We didn't exactly relax, but we were all breathing again.

I looked at Kate, who actually seemed fine, all things considered. She's cool under fire, and only loses her cool with me. I asked, 'You okay?'

'Knocked the wind out of me ... I'm okay ...' She looked at me and said, 'You can say it now.'

A bigger man would have said, 'I love you,' but I'm not that big so I said, 'I fucking told you so.' And I meant it.

Kate said, 'I love you.'

Brenner, who had more important things on his mind, asked, 'Anybody have any ideas?'

I asked him, 'Can we get to the Marib airstrip?'

He replied, 'Maybe. Maybe not. The airstrip has only a few charter aircraft going in and out, and there's usually no one there.'

Kate asked, 'Would the Bilqis Hotel be safe?'

Brenner replied, 'Only if you want to run into someone like Colonel Hakim, or maybe Hakim himself if he came to Marib.'

We didn't want to do that, and Kate asked, 'How far is it to Sana'a?'

Brenner replied, 'About four hours, but it might as well be on Mars. There are checkpoints all along the route, and we'll never make it without getting stopped by somebody who we don't want to meet.'

Forget Plan C. Or was that D?

Zamo continued down the ravine, which was getting wider and less steep.

It went without saying that we were in the middle of nowhere, and the closest safe place might be the Saudi border, which, based on where Najran airbase was, would be about 175 miles north of here, as the crow flies, and we weren't flying – Chet and Buck were flying.

I asked Brenner about the border and he said, 'Good thinking, but we'd never get past the Yemeni soldiers who patrol the border.'

'We have our diplomatic passports,' I reminded him.

He ignored my attempt to lighten the moment and said, 'The

best thing we can do right now is find a place to hide out and think about how to get out of here at dawn.'

Kate had a better idea and said, 'Let's use our cell phones to make contact with the embassy.'

Eureka.

I pulled out my cell phone and lowered my window to stick my head out, but Brenner informed me, 'Sorry to tell you, but Buck and Chet have by now notified the NSA that our sat-phones are probably in enemy hands, and the NSA will have called the carrier to discontinue service immediately.'

Holy shit. I turned my sat-phone on and it lit up, but I couldn't get a tone.

To be sure, we all tried to get service, but all the phones were dead.

Plan D – or E – was a bust, so I suggested, 'How about the Hunt Oil installation?'

Brenner didn't reply for a moment, then said, 'That may be our only play. It's about two hours northeast of Marib town, and it's the only place in this province where we'll find other Americans – Americans with guns.' He added, 'But travel at night here is unsafe, and the Hunt people will shoot at night if we tried to approach. So we need to wait until dawn.'

That sounded promising, but it barely lifted the dark mood in the Land Cruiser. I mean, we'd just exited hell with our shirttails on fire, and we were happy to be alive. But we'd only managed to pass from the center of hell to the next circle. This totally sucked. We'd gotten this far by our wits and our balls, without any help from anyone, and we deserved a break. Something good had to happen.

But this is not the land of good; this is the land of *not* good. We came down out of the ravine, and ahead of us, on the dirt road that we'd landed on — the road to the goat herder's hut — was what looked like a convoy of military vehicles.

Zamo said, 'Shit.'

The beginning of the road looked like the end of the road.

CHAPTER SEVENTY-NINE

When there's a military convoy coming at you, and the road you're on is the only road around, you don't have too many ways to avoid an encounter, except off-road, but that could end in a hail of bullets.

I could see three American-made Humvees in the front of the convoy, followed by four troop carriers that could hold up to a hundred soldiers.

Obviously, they'd responded to the Hellfire attack, and now they were headed toward the Crow Fortress. But why? And who, exactly, were they?

Brenner, Kate, Zamo, and I decided we had to meet them head-on, so to speak, then play it by ear. I reminded everyone, 'We're supposed to have a deal with the Yemeni government, and we're supposed to have a free hand here in Marib.'

Brenner pointed out, 'That information came from Chet and Buck.'

'Good point.' Maybe the deal expired when Chet and Buck got on that helicopter.

Zamo moved to the right, and the convoy continued toward us hogging the middle of the road. When we got within a hundred yards of the lead Humvee, Brenner told Zamo to stop.

Brenner said, 'Hopefully someone will speak English, but if not, I'll do the best I can.'

The convoy also came to a halt, and we could see now that the vehicles were not painted with the brown and tan of the Yemeni Army; they were the camouflage blue of the National Security Bureau, a.k.a. the Blue Meanies.

Brenner said to me, 'You and I will get out to meet them. Kate and Zamo will stay in the vehicle and cover us.'

Kate said to me and Brenner, 'Clip your sat-phones to your vests.'

Good idea. They didn't work, but only we knew that.

Without Buck along to be diplomatic, we decided to carry our M4s, which we slung across our chests, ready to rock and roll. Take a few of them with you.

Brenner and I got out of the Land Cruiser and began the walk toward the lead Humvee, paid for with my tax dollars.

I noticed now in the far distance black smoke rising into the sky. That would be the scene of the Hellfire attack – men and vehicles still burning, and, of course, this convoy had already been there to see the carnage. I said to Brenner, who was also looking at the smoke, 'Think about how to tell these assholes in Arabic that we have a dozen Predators with Hellfires watching us and the pilots have twitchy fingers.'

He nodded.

Someone got out of the second Humvee and began walking toward us. Even from this distance I could see that it was Colonel Hakim of the dreaded secret police. He was wearing cammies and carrying an AK-47, all ready for action. I love armed confrontations. They don't usually last too long.

We got within a few feet of Colonel Hakim and stopped. Brenner gave Colonel Hakim a half-assed salute, and Colonel Hakim returned the salute in a similar half-assed manner. He also eyeballed the sat-phones clipped to our vests, probably thinking about the American Embassy, or better yet about Predator pilots watching their monitors with itchy trigger fingers.

Brenner and Hakim exchanged peace greetings in Arabic, without much sincerity, and I said, 'Buenos días,' using my only second language.

Hakim ignored me and asked Brenner, 'What are you doing here?'

Brenner replied, 'You know what we're doing here, Colonel.'

'Yes? Why would I know?'

I said to Brenner, 'Just cut to the chase.' I mean, these fucking people could beat around the bush until the bush died of annoyance.

Brenner asked Hakim, 'What are *you* doing here?'

Colonel Hakim took offense at the question and snapped, 'It is *my* country, Mr Brenner. Not yours. And I will ask the questions of you.'

Brenner, following my suggestion, got to the point and replied, 'We are on a Yemeni-government-sanctioned mission to find and apprehend the Al Qaeda leader Bulus ibn al-Darwish, known as The Panther.' He asked Hakim, 'Don't you know that?'

Hakim replied, of course, 'It is my business what I know.'

Total asshole. But he'd come to meet us alone, and he was talking and not shooting, so that meant he thought he might be on shaky ground. Also, it might mean he wanted something from the Americans. Hey, everybody does. And it's not advice or love that they want; it's money.

So I got right to that subject and said, 'I assume you were at the scene of the attack' – I nodded toward the black smoke rising behind him and continued – 'and if you escort us there, and assist us in identifying the Al Qaeda bodies, we will see to it that you share in the five-million-dollar reward for the death of The Panther.'

That seemed to be what he wanted to hear, and his shitty demeanor softened ever so slightly.

He asked me, not Brenner, 'And are you in that position to make such an offer?'

No, but you've got a hundred guns with you so I'll lie all day.

Brenner said, 'We will do everything in our power to see that you are compensated for your assistance.'

What kind of lie is that? Come on, Paul. Tell him the check's in the fucking mail. I mean, this is *not* the time for truth, justice, and the American way.

Colonel Hakim seemed to like me more than Brenner now, and he asked me, 'How much?'

How about a mango up your ass? No? Then how about … 'Two and a half million.'

He'd have to work until he was about two thousand years old to make that kind of money, but he was a greedy shit and countered, 'Three million.'

'No,' I replied, 'we have to pay the Bedouin. Half for them, half to you.'

He asked me, 'And you?'

'Not a penny.' I explained to him, 'We get a paycheck every two weeks.'

He didn't seem to believe that, but it was the sad truth.

Colonel Hakim thought about my offer, then said, 'I will take you where you wish to go.'

I want to go to New York, and maybe Hakim could help me get there. I informed him, 'We are under surveillance by Predator drones. Capisce?'

He did, and he said, 'Let us now go.'

Colonel Hakim told us to follow his Humvee, and Brenner and I got back in the Land Cruiser.

Kate asked, 'What's happening?'

I replied, 'Colonel Hakim is taking us to the scene of the attack.'

I explained to Kate and Zamo about the great deal we made and Kate reminded me, 'You're not authorized to promise money, amnesty, immunity from prosecution—'

'I just don't feel like getting arrested and shot today.'

Brenner said, 'Hakim is our ticket out of here, or he's our worst nightmare. Either way, let's keep him happy and interested in our well-being.'

Kate pointed out, 'He's not going to let us out of here now until he gets his money.'

I asked her, 'Do you have a blank check on you? Or do you have a better idea?'

Zamo thought that was funny. Just like old times.

Brenner assured Kate, 'We'll work something out with the embassy.'

I also informed Kate, 'Hakim thinks we're all on Predator TV.'

'Good,' said Ms. Mayfield. 'And maybe we are.'

Maybe. But hopefully Chet was no longer directing the show.

Anyway, Hakim's Humvee turned around, followed by another Humvee, and we all squeezed past the troop carriers and headed east on the straight dirt road, toward the smoke in the distance.

The third Humvee and the four troop carriers were moving now, and they continued on, west toward the plateau. I asked Brenner, 'Why do you think they're headed toward the Crow Fortress?'

'They must be acting on information.'

'What information?'

Brenner replied, 'We'll ask Colonel Hakim.'

Who was as honest and forthcoming as Chet and Buck. Everyone here carried a large sack of bullshit.

Bottom line, this was not the plan that Chet had laid out for us in Aden, but as I said then, and as we discovered, there was more to Chet's plan than he was sharing with us. And as Chet discovered, I had a few plans of my own. And as we all discovered, man plans, God laughs.

But part of Chet's plan had worked out. The Panther was dead, and Chet and Buck were heroes — and better yet, I was going to see what was left of Bulus ibn al-Darwish. I came a long way for this.

CHAPTER EIGHTY

On the way to the goat herder's hut, I said to Brenner, 'We can take some evidence at the scene.' We'll stop at a 7-Eleven for Ziploc bags.

Brenner replied, 'We'll let the PSO and NSB do that and also take photos for us, and that will make Colonel Hakim think he's earning his two and a half million.'

'Right.' Just like Sheik Musa thought he was earning his five million. I mean, even I wasn't trusting the Americans anymore.

It took us less than twenty minutes to get to the scene of the attack, but I could see it and smell it before we got there.

Hakim's two Humvees pulled onto the path to the goat herder's hut and stopped.

We all got out of our vehicles and walked up the path to what remained of the stone hut. As we got closer, the smell of burnt tires and gasoline got stronger, and so did the smell of charred bodies. Kate wrapped her hijab over her face.

Despite my enthusiasm for seeing this, it was a bit jarring. Most of the bodies were intact, though they'd been ripped up by shrapnel — Bedouin bodies in their blood-drenched robes, and Al Qaeda bodies in their foutehs. The ground was strewn with AK-47s, sandals, shiwals, and even cell phones.

Where the direct hits from the Hellfires had landed, the ground was blasted away, and the human remains were scattered in all directions, making me remember what an old Vietnam vet had told me about getting an accurate body count after an air or artillery strike. 'Count the arms and legs and divide by four.'

Brenner, who'd seen things like this, didn't seem fazed, and neither did Zamo. Kate, however, was a bit shaken, and the NSB guys were eyeing her, so Zamo walked her back to the Land Cruiser.

Colonel Hakim spoke first and said, 'You see what has happened here. I have secured the area and I will cooperate with the American authorities in any way they wish.'

Brenner said to Hakim, 'We would like photographs of everything, and we will need your men to collect tissue samples of all the dead Al Qaeda who are identifiable by their clothing.'

Hakim didn't seem to understand and he asked, 'Why do you need that?'

Brenner explained, 'We have DNA of Bulus ibn al-Darwish.' He informed Colonel Hakim, 'His family lives in America.'

Colonel Hakim did not reply, and Brenner further explained, 'We can identify al-Darwish by this means, and also by his fingerprints if you would be kind enough to include as many fingers as possible.'

Again, Colonel Hakim had no reply, so I took a shot at it and said, 'We need a positive, scientific identification. Proof that al-Darwish died in this attack.'

Colonel Hakim nodded this time and said, 'Everyone has died. None escaped.'

Well, not true. At least one Bedouin had survived and called his Bedouin buddies at the Crow Fortress. So it was possible that other Bedouin and maybe Al Qaeda guys survived. But probably not The Panther, who was in the crosshairs of the first Hellfire missile.

Hakim said, 'The Panther is dead.'

Brenner and I exchanged glances. Something was not right here.

I asked Hakim, 'Were you able to identify al-Darwish?'

Colonel Hakim waved his arm around at the bits and pieces of men, as though saying, 'Are you kidding?' He did say, however, 'I have found the shiwal of Sheik Musa. That is all the proof I need of his death.'

Musa's nose would clinch it for me, but, okay, the sheik was dead – score a hit for President Saleh. But we're talking about *The Panther*, Colonel. The bad guy.

I moved slowly through the blast area, and there were lots of heads intact, on and off their bodies, but about half of them were bearded, and most of the faces were disfigured by shrapnel or burns. The Panther's own mother wouldn't recognize him. Also, I was looking for Nabeel, who had a scruffy beard the last time I saw him, but people look different when they're dead.

One head was lying facedown on a shred of carpet, and I gave it a kick to turn it over. Most of the face was missing.

Brenner came over to me, away from Hakim, and said softly, 'Either he doesn't get what I'm saying, or we have a problem with positive ID.'

I nodded, then I remembered the video replay – Sheik Musa had hesitated for a second before taking The Panther's hand and kissing it. Was Musa unsure of his guest's identity? I mean, to me, most fully bearded men looked alike, and forget bearded Arabs.

They may as well be wearing veils. Musa, too, apparently had a moment of doubt.

Colonel Hakim came over to us and said, 'You can congratulate yourselves on a successful attack.'

Okay. Congratulations to us.

Brenner said to him, 'I suggest you collect what we need and get it to the airport in Sana'a as quickly as possible. You will be met there.'

I also suggested, 'Get some ice from Marib. Maybe the Bilqis Hotel.' They don't need the ice for cocktails.

Colonel Hakim informed us, 'It is a sacrilege to do what you are asking.' He told us, 'All these remains must be buried as quickly as possible, according to our religion.'

I figured that was coming, and I didn't want to argue religion with this guy, so I said, 'Tell you what, Colonel, let's make this clean and easy for everyone. You get a hunk of hair from each head or beard here, number it, and deliver it to the embassy. We'll do a DNA match, and you get your money. How's that sound?'

Colonel Hakim couldn't think of any objection to that, so he said, 'I think you are trying to change our arrangement.'

'Not at all,' I assured him. 'We pay top dollar for dead Al Qaeda chiefs. But you can't tell me which of these heads belongs to al-Darwish. Right?'

'You know he was here. And you know that everyone here is dead.'

Ergo, and so forth. I pointed out, 'We don't know he was here. And neither do you.' And I was starting to think he wasn't. Holy shit.

So we stood there, trying to figure out how to get this resolved.

The stench of open body cavities and burnt flesh was overwhelming, and that smell, mixed with the acrid smell of smoldering vehicles and fuel, made my stomach heave. Anyone who thinks war is exciting should see and smell something like this.

I reminded Colonel Hakim, 'We just need some hair. Like, no disrespect to the dead. Okay?'

'That is not possible.'

Hokum, Hakim. I said to Brenner, 'We have a problem.'

Brenner nodded, then asked Colonel Hakim the question that had come up in the Land Cruiser. 'Where were you going with your convoy?'

'That is my business, Mr Brenner.'

He reminded Hakim, 'We are in business together.'

Colonel Hakim did not reply, and he was probably thinking that his two and a half million bucks was slipping away. He might also be thinking that if he was going to lose the money, he might as well get rid of us. Or maybe kidnap us for ransom and make it look like a tribal kidnapping. In Yemen, anything was possible.

Finally Colonel Hakim said, 'I was going to the Crow Fortress.'

Brenner nodded and asked, 'Why?'

He confessed, 'There was a survivor of the attack. An Al Qaeda man. He has told me that a Bedouin in the Crow Fortress, a man called Yasir, who you may know from your stay there, has told Al Qaeda by cell phone that the Americans were not kidnapped, and that they were in fact guests of Sheik Musa at the Crow Fortress.'

Brenner and I looked at each other, and Brenner said to me, 'Like I said, all it takes is one rat, and there's always one rat.'

Right. And usually the guy you least suspect. So what was in it for Yasir to rat us out? Probably the hundred thousand bucks that The Panther was going to pay to Sheik Musa to buy the Americans. And that would be a lot more money for Yasir than his share of his sheik's five million. Well, greedy Yasir was dead, and I was feeling not sorry about whacking him.

I said to Brenner, 'Chet's ingenious plan actually sucked.' I added, 'He didn't factor in the human element.' And how could he? He wasn't human.

Brenner agreed and added, 'Even his plan to kill us didn't work.'

That was almost funny.

Bottom line here, if The Panther knew we were actually guests of Sheik Musa, he also knew that the Americans would not be in this goat herder's hut at the meeting between him and Sheik Musa, and The Panther further knew this meeting was a sham and a trap.

I said to Brenner, 'The Panther is not here and not dead.'

Brenner nodded and looked at Colonel Hakim, saying to our new partner, 'I'm not understanding why you were going to the Crow Fortress.'

Colonel Hakim, probably trying to salvage a smaller reward, replied, 'The Al Qaeda survivor has also told me that the jihadists from the Al Qaeda camp in the hills were preparing to attack the Crow Fortress and take the Americans.'

I said to Brenner, 'I think we always knew that.'

Brenner nodded and said to Hakim, 'And what were you going to do at the Crow Fortress?'

He replied, 'It was my intention to come to your rescue.'

What a nice man. Doing his duty. Actually, if Colonel Hakim

was in business to make money, that was a good way to do it. But I doubted if he wanted a fight with Al Qaeda. More likely he was trying to get to the Crow Fortress before Al Qaeda got there, then he could arrest or attack his traditional enemy – the Bedouin – and say he rescued the Americans from the Bedouin. And that was worth some American dollars.

That didn't work out for him, but Colonel Hakim was still trying to figure out how to make a buck here. The dead Panther thing wasn't working out either, and rescuing the Americans from the Bedouin was a bust, so what was left?

Brenner said to him, 'We appreciate your intentions, but as you can see, we don't need to be rescued.'

Colonel Hakim said to us, 'I am told by the Al Qaeda man who survived this attack that the Bedouin, Yasir, told him there were six Americans at the Crow Fortress.'

Brenner informed him, 'Two have left.'

Hakim thought about that, then said, 'I believe I saw smoke coming from the top of the plateau.'

Well, that's a long story, but I shortened it and said, 'We had a problem with the Bedouin.'

He nodded and informed us, 'They are treacherous.'

They're amateurs, Colonel, compared to you.

Colonel Hakim also informed us, 'According to this Al Qaeda survivor, the jihadist attack on the Crow Fortress was to begin after the meeting with Sheik Musa – but only if the Americans were not at the meeting.'

'Right. Sorry we missed the meeting.' Sorry, too, The Panther missed it. Bottom line here, The Panther was willing to sacrifice his men to see if the meeting was a trap – which it was – and The

Panther was elsewhere. I asked Hakim, 'Is The Panther supposed to lead this attack on the Crow Fortress?'

Hakim replied, 'I asked that very question of the Al Qaeda survivor, but he did not know.'

Right. The Panther kept things to himself. Which was why he was still alive.

Hakim said to me and Brenner, 'I have no radio message from my men that they are encountering any Al Qaeda forces on the way to the Crow Fortress.'

That's because the Al Qaeda forces in the camp have been turned into hamburger by the US Air Force, but that was none of Hakim's business.

Recalling that the Bedouin in the courtyard of the Crow Fortress had taken a sudden dislike toward us, I said to Hakim, 'We know that there was also a Bedouin survivor of this attack who called his friends at the Crow Fortress to report what happened here.' I asked, 'Where is this man?'

Hakim informed us, 'Unfortunately, he died of his wounds.'

I asked, 'Hellfire wounds or a bullet wound in his head?'

To set the record straight, and set me straight, Colonel Hakim replied, 'It makes no difference.'

This guy was a cold, hard sonofabitch.

Colonel Hakim continued, 'We have made this arrangement – the Americans and my government – and it has been a successful arrangement.'

I replied, 'You have your dead sheik, but I don't think we have our dead Panther.'

Hakim replied, 'I think you do, but if you do not, that is no fault of mine and no fault of my government.'

Right. It's Chet's fault. In fact, Chet got hustled by the Yemeni government. They knew they'd get their dead sheik, and they didn't care if the Americans got their dead Panther. Now we were on the Bedouin shit list forever, and The Panther was still out there.

I said to Hakim, 'Is this Al Qaeda survivor still alive or did he die of a bullet wound?'

Hakim replied, 'I believe he is still alive.'

Hakim was still trying to work the deal, but he didn't have much left to offer. Nevertheless, I said, 'If the Al Qaeda man is still alive, and if we can speak to him, then our arrangement has not changed.' You're still not getting shit.

Colonel Hakim nodded and led us toward one of the blue trucks.

We climbed into the open truck and on the floor was an older man with a white beard who didn't look as lucky as he was. Also, he didn't look like a jihadist. He looked more like a Bedouin, but he was naked, so it was hard to tell by the clothing.

Someone had bandaged him up, and his wounds didn't look too bad, and he had no burn marks on him, so he hadn't been too close to the blasts. He seemed to be shivering, and I thought a blanket would be a good idea, but the NSB and the PSO weren't famous for taking care of wounded prisoners, as I saw at Ghumdan.

There were bench seats in the truck, and Colonel Hakim invited us to sit, which we did, and he sat opposite us.

The wounded man was semi-conscious, but Hakim got his attention by kicking him.

The man opened his eyes, and Hakim said something to him in Arabic, and the man answered.

The man apparently wanted water, and Hakim called out to an NSB guy, who came in with a canteen and poured water on the old guy's face, then Hakim took the canteen.

Hakim said to us, 'This man calls himself Altair, which means soaring eagle.'

The guy looked more like a dying duck, but whatever.

Hakim told us, 'That is his Al Qaeda name, and he will not give his true name unless he believes he is going to die. Then he asks that we tell his family of his fate.'

Altair was looking at me and Brenner now, and I had the impression he didn't like us. Probably something to do with the Hellfire missiles.

I said to Hakim, 'He doesn't look like a jihadist.'

Hakim informed us, 'Altair, who I know by name, is a senior advisor to al-Darwish.' He added, 'A friend of the al-Darwish family. And perhaps not truly Al Qaeda.'

Interesting. And what did he advise The Panther about taking this meeting?

Brenner had the same thought and said to Hakim, 'Ask him why he came here if he thought the Americans were not here and that this meeting could be a trap.'

Hakim informed us, 'I have already asked that of him, and he tells me that he did not believe that information from the Bedouin called Yasir.'

I guess not, or he wouldn't be lying here all fucked up.

I asked Hakim, 'Did Altair get that call directly from Yasir?'

Hakim again said, 'I have asked him and he says no, he received that message from one of his jihadists who received the call from Yasir.'

Right. And where would Yasir get the cell phone number of an Al Qaeda jihadist? Let me think. Well, maybe from the same person who gave Yasir those photographs. I asked, 'Did Yasir make this call to a man named Nabeel al-Samad?'

Hakim replied, 'In fact, it was that man.' He added, 'How do you know this?'

'I'm a detective.' I asked Hakim, 'Was this message, this warning, passed on to al-Darwish?'

Hakim replied, 'Of course. Altair told me he delivered it personally.'

'And were the jihadists told of this warning?'

Hakim looked down at Altair, then said to me, 'He has told me that the jihadists were told, but I am not sure of Altair's truthfulness.'

Right. The Panther kept this to himself, and the only one who acted on this warning was The Panther. In fact, he sent a double in his place, and he used his men to see what would happen at the meeting. If it wasn't a trap, and if the Americans were at the meeting to be bought, then all was well. If, however, it was a trap, then all it cost The Panther to discover that was about a dozen of his men. No big deal for The Panther, who wasted his men's lives for the cause — the cause being Bulus ibn al-Darwish's greater glory.

But The Panther had sent at least one senior advisor — Altair, a friend of the family. Why would al-Darwish do that? Maybe he was willing to risk the senior guy for appearances at the meeting. And Altair, apparently, was willing to take the risk for his boss. And if the meeting was legit, then Altair would advise The Panther's double on how to do the deal with Sheik Musa.

Brenner, too, concluded, 'Altair was willing to take a big risk for his boss, and his boss was willing to send Altair and his men into what was sounding like a trap.'

Right. The Panther really wanted the Americans, and he didn't care who he had to put at risk to get them — as long as it wasn't himself.

Recalling what Rahim ibn Hayyam told us at Ghumdan Fortress, about his boss's leadership style, I said to Hakim, 'Tell this guy that his chief is a coward. That he sends his men into danger, but he hides in a cave, like he did when his jihadists attacked the Hunt Oil installation. Tell Altair he owes no loyalty to al-Darwish.'

Hakim nodded and translated that, and Altair replied by spitting at me. And then he had the nerve to ask for more water. So Colonel Hakim, the soul of compassion, poured the rest of the canteen on Altair's face. Good practice for waterboarding.

I said to Hakim, 'I assume you've asked this guy where The Panther is right now.'

'Of course, and he tells me he does not know.'

'You believe that?'

Hakim shrugged and said, 'Only a very few people would know the hiding place of The Panther.'

Right. And a guy like Altair might be one of those people. I changed the subject and said to Hakim, 'Ask him if Nabeel al-Samad was here.'

Altair understood the name and so understood the question, and replied to Hakim, who told us, 'Nabeel al-Samad was not here.'

Bummer. I wanted Nabeel's balls in a Ziploc bag. But I'd find him someday. Maybe back in New York.

Brenner, combat vet, wanted to know, 'Where was Altair when the Hellfires hit?'

Hakim asked and Altair replied. Hakim smiled and said, 'The old man had the need to urinate and so he went off behind the stone fence to do this. He says he was spared by God.'

Or a bad prostate gland. Or he had a last-minute thought that standing on the carpet near The Panther look-alike and near Sheik Musa might not be the safest place around. Time for a piss.

Brenner asked Colonel Hakim, 'What will you do with this man?'

Hakim replied matter-of-factly, 'Probably I will shoot him.'

I suggested, 'You may want to bring him to Ghumdan, get him patched up, and continue the interrogation.'

Hakim assured us, 'He has nothing more to say.'

Brenner informed me, 'The Yemeni government doesn't like to have Al Qaeda prisoners.' He explained, 'The Al Qaeda guys have a way of breaking out of jail and embarrassing the government, or they radicalize the other inmates.' He concluded, 'So most of them are shot when captured, or die under interrogation.'

Sounds a bit harsh, but I had a better idea and said to Hakim, 'If, as you say, you know Altair is a senior advisor to The Panther, then I'm certain he knows where his boss is hiding.'

Hakim replied, 'This could be true, but he will not tell us this, even under torture.' He added, 'Or even if you tell him unkind things about his chief.'

'Try another approach,' I suggested. 'Offer him his freedom and, let's say, a hundred thousand dollars. The Americans will guarantee his freedom and the money.'

Hakim thought about that, and maybe he saw a chance to get

that money for himself, then shoot Altair anyway. He made the offer to Altair, who didn't respond, but neither did he spit.

I said to Hakim, 'Remind him again that al-Darwish sent him and his men like sheep to the slaughter.'

Hakim shrugged and spoke to Altair, who did not respond. When they don't respond, you're making progress.

I also suggested, 'Maybe The Panther thinks such an old man is expendable. Maybe he doesn't like Altair.' I said to Hakim, 'Tell him that.'

Hakim did and Altair closed his eyes, indicating he had no more to say.

Well, what now? I guess if you're partners with a PSO colonel, your options open up. And I had an idea.

I announced, 'I have to take a pee,' and jumped out of the truck. Brenner followed and I asked him, 'What do you want to do?'

He replied, 'We need to contact the embassy as soon as possible to report our status and to report what happened here.'

'That's the right thing to do,' I agreed.

'Then we need to get to the embassy first thing tomorrow.'

'Right. But I'm thinking that Chet and Buck are bad-mouthing us wherever they are, and we may have some problems at the embassy.' Like being locked in the basement bomb shelter waiting for the CIA station chief.

Brenner replied, 'I don't think that's true — about having a problem ... but in any case, Zamo and I need to report in person to the embassy.' He thought a moment and said, 'You and Kate, however, could probably go directly to Sana'a Airport and take the first flight out that's heading anywhere except Sandland.'

'Good thinking. But here's another idea. Ready?'

He nodded tentatively.

'We throw Altair into the Land Cruiser and take him into the hills. He shows us where the Al Qaeda camp is, and we show him what two-thousand-pound bombs can do. We tell him that if The Panther was in the camp, he's probably dead, but if not, he should be because he's an asshole, a coward, and an incompetent fuck-up. And then we ask Altair nicely to show us where The Panther's hideout is. And if he does that, we'll save him from Colonel Hakim, give him a nice reward, and send him to the Bahamas.' I asked Brenner, 'What do you think?'

'I think you're crazy.'

'Good. Look, Paul, Altair is our one and only link to The Panther, and I'm sure that old bastard knows where that asshole is hiding. We gotta give this a shot.'

Brenner thought a moment, then said, 'It's actually not a terrible idea, but we are definitely not authorized to make up our own missions.'

'Why not? Someone authorized Chet to bump us off, so we can do whatever the hell we want.'

Brenner took a deep breath and said, 'We have no backup, no logistical support, no commo, and we're low on ammo.'

'But we have a new partner. He's got what we need and we'll take him along.' I added, 'Hakim is authorized to do whatever he wants to do.'

'Actually, Hakim should do this on his own.'

'Hakim,' I pointed out, 'is incompetent, probably lazy, and he doesn't give a rat's ass about Al Qaeda or Bulus ibn al-Darwish.'

'But he cares about the reward.'

'Right. So he'll come with us. We need an interpreter anyway.'

Brenner went into thinking mode, weighing the pros and cons of getting out of this shithole or getting deeper into it. He pointed out, 'Altair may not be able to make the trip.'

'He looks fine. He's a tough old goat. Or eagle. And if he dies, he dies. Better than Hakim's bullet in his head.'

Brenner said to me, 'I think you've been here too long.'

'I've been crazy for years.' I suggested to him, 'When you get home, you'll realize how crazy *you* were here.'

He forced a smile, ruminated, then said, 'All right ... if Hakim says okay to this, and if he comes with us, we'll go.'

'Good. We're going to complete this mission.'

Mr Brenner asked, 'How about Kate?'

'She wouldn't miss this for the world.'

Brenner was about to say something about that, but Colonel Hakim, who wanted to see what his new partners were up to, hopped out of the truck and asked us, 'So what do you do now?'

'Glad you asked.' I explained my plan to him and he listened, nodding a few times. I assured him, 'If we can kill or capture The Panther, I'll see to it that you get the three million you asked for.' I pointed out, 'The Bedouin were helpful to us, but one of them betrayed us, and we don't have a dead Panther.' So fuck them.

Colonel Hakim nodded, but said, 'The old man is perhaps not well enough to make this journey.'

'Have your medic give him something to perk him up.' But not Viagra. We've been fucked enough today.

Hakim nodded again, but said, 'He may not be as cooperative as you wish. He will protect his chief.'

'We won't know what he's going to do until we get up there.'

Colonel Hakim asked us, 'Do you know where this Al Qaeda camp is?'

'Altair knows,' I assured him.

'He will not tell us.'

'I'm sure you can make him tell us.'

'Perhaps.' He let us know, 'I have some idea where it is.'

'Good. And I happen to have map coordinates.' I asked Hakim, 'Do you have a map of the area?'

'Of course.'

'Well, then, between you, me, and Altair, we're practically there.'

Colonel Hakim excused himself, and Brenner and I walked toward our Land Cruiser. I asked Brenner, 'How about Zamo?'

'He likes looking for jihadists in the mountains.'

'Right. Doesn't everyone?' So Operation Clean Sweep, sans Chet, Buck, and Washington, continues. No complicated plans, no high tech, and no John and Kate for bait; just a bunch of guys in the hills trying to kill each other the old-fashioned way.

CHAPTER EIGHTY-ONE

B renner and I explained the plan to Zamo and Kate, who signed on without a lot of questions. I mean, the more you think about bold ideas, the more problems you find. And if you keep going down that path, you'll come to an unpleasant truth: This is fucking dangerous. So why think about it? Just do it.

We had to do some fast talking to convince Colonel Hakim to take only one Humvee and not a hundred men with him, explaining that this was a stealth mission and not an invasion.

Hakim was in his Humvee with his driver now, along with two PSO thugs, plus Altair, who didn't want to take a ride with us, but one of Hakim's PSO goons hit him with a taser, then threw him in the rear compartment. On the plus side for Altair, he was now clothed, fed, watered, and alive.

Hakim had provided us with hand-held radios, and we left the scene of the Hellfire attack and headed into the sinking sun, back toward the highlands.

Hakim was in the lead, and we followed in the Land Cruiser. Zamo drove, I rode shotgun, and Kate and Brenner sat in the rear.

The basic plan was to first find the Al Qaeda base camp, because we all agreed that The Panther's cave couldn't be too far from his camp, so that was a good starting point, and a good place to encourage Altair to point the way to his boss's hideout.

Colonel Hakim had also provided us with a military terrain map, and Brenner, who knew how to read these contour maps, was looking at it with Kate. I'd given them the coordinates of the Al Qaeda base camp that I'd taken from the Predator monitor, and we'd put a mark on the map. Brenner said, 'Very inaccessible terrain ... no roads, but maybe some mountain trails that aren't shown here.'

I reminded Brenner, 'We saw a few vehicles on the Predator video monitor, so there's some kind of vehicle access.'

Brenner agreed, but said, 'The airstrike may have caused rock-slides.'

'So we'll walk. Meanwhile, we don't have a lot of daylight left. Call our partner and tell him to step on it.'

Brenner called Hakim on the hand-held radio and suggested, 'We need to move faster, Colonel.'

Hakim replied, 'This is a good speed.'

Brenner insisted, 'A little faster.' He signed off and said to me, 'That's the story of the Yemeni Army, police, and government — too slow, too cautious, and too late.'

'I don't think Hakim has much enthusiasm for this,' I said.

'I can't imagine why not.'

'He's a government worker.'

'So are we,' Brenner reminded me. He also reminded us, 'He wants the money. But he doesn't want to get killed earning it.'

'Same here.'

So we continued on the long, straight road toward the plateau where the Crow Fortress sat, and where the highlands began. Smoke still rose into the air from the burning tower and I asked Zamo, 'Why did you set the hay on fire?'

'Because it burns.'

'Right.' Well, so much for Buck's Sultan Crow Fortress Bed & Breakfast. And so much for American-Bedouin relations.

As we continued on, I thought about what was going on in our absence, and I had no doubt that Chet had concocted a good story about the friendly fire mishap to the Land Cruiser, though that would be a hard sell. The only people he could level with were the people in his Company who'd sent him on Operation Clean Sweep. And they'd cover his ass because Chet was a hero in Langley, and Buck was a hero at Foggy Bottom. The news release of this incident was already written, and the American public would be pleased to learn that Bulus ibn al-Darwish, the American traitor and a mastermind of the *Cole* attack, was taken out with a Hellfire missile. Unfortunately, in a separate but related incident, four unnamed Americans are missing in Yemen.

But if these Americans got back alive, they'd have, as I said, a different tale to tell, ending hopefully with me throwing The Panther's head on the table.

We were approaching the base of the plateau, and after a quick radio conference with Hakim, we decided not to go into the highlands via the Crow Fortress approach. Instead, we'd go cross-country and skirt around the plateaus from the north, then we'd head into the highlands forty kilometers west of here, closer to where the Al Qaeda camp was hidden in the bad terrain.

We went off-road and the ride got a little rougher, and Hakim's Humvee slowed up. I said to Zamo, 'Give him the horn.'

Brenner chose his radio instead and urged Hakim and his driver to push it.

We continued on, across the arid fields and pastures, and whenever we came to a stone fence, Hakim in the lead found the gate and smashed through it, liberating hundreds of goats.

It took us an hour to travel forty kilometers along the base of the highlands, and we could see up ahead that the plateaus were now extending farther north, blocking us.

Brenner consulted his map and said, 'The highlands get higher up ahead, and the only way through them is the Sana'a–Marib road, which takes us off course. So we need to head into the highlands around here ... but I don't see any trails or paths on this map ...'

I reminded him, 'Rahim ibn Hayyam said he got to the camp by vehicle.'

Brenner replied, 'If you knew the uncharted trails, you could do it ... but I do see some ravines that a four-wheel drive might be able to navigate.'

'Great.' I saw this in a TV commercial for a Jeep. 'Let's do it.'

Brenner radioed Hakim, who stopped, and we all got out for a map conference.

Zamo, too, was a good map reader, and even Kate had taken a map-reading course. I can read a subway map, and I can easily find my ass with both hands, but I had no clue about scoping out a terrain map. My contribution was reminding the A-team that we'd seen vehicles in the camp, and they weren't made there.

As the map committee was deciding on a route, I went to the Humvee to check on Altair, who was lying in the back compartment, covered with a blanket, holding a bottle of water. He didn't look great, but his color wasn't pre-croak, and his breathing seemed okay. 'Hang in there, old man. God saved you to help us find Bulus ibn al-Darwish.'

At that name, Altair shook his head.

Everyone got back in their vehicles and we took the lead now. Brenner sat up front with Zamo still driving, and he directed Zamo toward a shallow depression in the ground, saying to us, 'The map shows a wadi here, and there it is.' He further explained, 'This is a stream which comes out of the highlands during the rainy season, and I'm thinking that this has to be flat from erosion all the way up into the hills.'

Kate, who was born and raised in the great outdoors, said, 'The streambed should be a layer of small stones, which will give us good traction.'

I offered, 'Just like the wadi highway that cuts through the middle of Sana'a.'

'Correct,' said Mr Brenner.

Maybe I *have* been here too long.

So we drove into the wadi, and Zamo headed into the hills. It was easy to follow the dry streambed, and within fifteen minutes we were in a sort of gorge or valley between two towering plateaus. The streambed got very steep as we climbed farther into the highlands.

I kept checking to see if Colonel Hakim's Humvee was still behind us. I mean, I wouldn't put it past that bastard to throw it in reverse and go backwards all the way to Sana'a. But he kept right behind us, driven forward by duty, honor, country, and money.

The sun was definitely sinking, and the eastern sky was darkening, but there was daylight left to the west. After about an hour, we were driving in near darkness, but the half moon started to cast some light on these dead, dry hills, which almost shone in the moonlight.

No one had too much to say, and now and then Brenner and Hakim would exchange a few words on the radio. It occurred to me — a few times — that if there were any jihadists left in these hills, we were sitting ducks down in this wadi with high terrain all around us.

I asked Kate, 'How you doing?'

'Still fine.'

I was sure her ribs were very sore where that AK-47 round

punched her Kevlar vest. Sometimes you get a broken rib, and always a big, ugly bruise. But, as we say, better red than dead.

The status of Zamo's arm was not his favorite subject so I didn't ask, but I could see by how he handled the wheel that his arm was stiff. Hopefully, we didn't need him to blow al-Darwish's head off from a kilometer away. Or take out some asshole firing at us.

The wadi was getting very narrow now, and the terrain was getting steeper and rougher. Brenner said, 'We're coming to the end of where the rainwater drains into the wadi.'

And?

'And the terrain ahead is unpredictable. It could rise up like a wall and that's as far as we go.'

'Then we walk,' said Kate.

'Right,' I agreed. As my mother used to tell me, 'God made feet before He made cars.' There's no actual proof of that, but if it's true, then that's the reason for the gas pedal. On another subject, what the hell was I thinking?

We continued on, and we were in luck because there was no wall of rock as we crested the top of the rising terrain.

And there it was.

We stopped, and everyone got out of the vehicles and stood at the edge of a slope. Below us in the distance was a flat basin, maybe the size of four or five football fields, nestled among the rising hills around it. Just like we saw on the Predator monitor.

But the camp looked different now. The whole expanse of flat ground was smoldering, like the earth was cooking, and I counted twelve huge bomb craters, about thirty or forty feet across, and deep enough that I couldn't see the bottoms.

Brenner said, 'Good bomb pattern.'

I was just thinking that myself. *What?*

He continued, 'See how they're evenly spaced? No overlap. The crew pretty much covered the target with twelve two-thousand-pounds.' He also said, 'Beautiful. Haven't seen that in awhile.'

'Looks great,' I agreed. I asked him, 'Anyone alive down there?'

'No.' He explained, 'The blast sucks the oxygen out of the air, and the shockwaves burst your lungs, and sometimes turn your brain into jelly.'

Wow.

He continued, in a faraway voice, 'Sometimes you do find people alive, but they're zombies ... blood coming out of their ears, nose, and mouth.'

'Yeah ... well ... good bomb pattern.'

Zamo added, 'We don't want to go down there.' He explained, 'There'll be, like, unexploded ordnance, like mortar rounds, or grenades, and they get sensitized by the shock, and if you step on something, they could blow and you're toast.'

'Good to know that.'

Meanwhile, Colonel Hakim and his three PSO goons were standing off by themselves, looking down at what the Americans had wrought. I had no idea what was going through their minds, but I thought that they had to be impressed, but also troubled, like they'd seen the future.

An acrid odor drifted up from the destruction, like burnt fuel and melted metal, and it took me a few seconds to recognize that smell. The Towers.

Kate, who hadn't said a word so far, now said, 'Payback.'

So we stood there and looked at the smoldering fires and the black gaping holes in the earth, lit by a bright rising moon; a little bit of heaven, and a lot of hell.

Now we find The Panther's lair, and if he's home, we kill him.

CHAPTER EIGHTY-TWO

The PSO goons dragged Altair out of the Humvee and they sat him on the ground facing his Al Qaeda camp in the basin below.

No one said anything to him, and we let him look. He showed no outward emotion, but instead he stared quietly at the moon-lit landscape of bomb craters and smoldering rubble. Finally, he lowered his head.

Brenner said to Colonel Hakim, 'Tell him this is what the Americans will do to all Al Qaeda camps in Yemen.'

Hakim, who probably had a foot in those camps, hesitated, then translated.

Altair had no response.

Brenner continued, 'Everyone down there is dead. Everyone who went with Altair to meet Sheik Musa is dead. Many jihadists who attacked the Hunt Oil installation are dead.'

Hakim again translated, and again Altair did not respond, but kept staring at the ground.

Brenner then said, 'But The Panther who caused all this death is still alive.'

Hakim translated, but this time Altair responded, and Hakim told us, 'He says The Panther was in this camp, so he is also dead.'

I said, 'Bullshit. Tell this sonofabitch that the next time he lies to us, he gets tasered.'

Hakim nodded and passed on the good news.

Altair did not respond.

I also said, 'If The Panther is dead, then Altair can tell us where his hideout is.'

Hakim nodded, and translated, but Altair again had no response.

Okay, the taser was the stick, and here's the carrot. 'Tell him if he shows us where al-Darwish's hideout is, the Americans will pay him one hundred thousand dollars, and send him anywhere he wants to go.'

Hakim translated that and the other three PSO thugs looked interested themselves. I mean, if *they* knew where The Panther was hiding, they'd give him up in a heartbeat for a hundred large and a ticket out of here.

Altair, however, was not interested, and Hakim told us, 'He says first that al-Darwish is dead in this camp, and that he does not want your American money, and that he will die in Yemen.'

'That can be arranged.' Well, so much for the carrot. Back to the stick.

Hakim had the same thought and he nodded to one of his goons, who hit the old man in the neck with a jolt of juice.

Altair screamed and toppled to the ground, thrashing around, then he lay still.

Kate turned away and walked back to the Land Cruiser.

Brenner said to Hakim, 'Keep asking him the same question and if you get the same answer, repeat the process. Eventually he will tell us where al-Darwish's hideout is.' Brenner cautioned, 'Don't kill him.'

Hakim, who didn't need much advice or encouragement on the subject of torture, asked Altair the question again, but Altair did not respond, and Hakim's goon shoved the taser prod into Altair's nuts.

Hakim went through the routine two more times until Altair passed out. Hakim said to us, 'It is possible that he has no knowledge of where this hideout is located.'

Well, that *was* possible, but we hadn't gotten there yet.

Brenner looked at Altair lying unconscious on the ground, then bent over and took his pulse, announcing, 'He's ... okay.'

Maybe a little gray.

Well, if Altair didn't die here, Hakim would kill him anyway. We were trying to save the old guy's life, but he was making that difficult.

I moved away from Hakim and his goons, and Brenner followed.

Zamo, who'd told us about six times in the SUV that he didn't trust Hakim or his men, stood off near the vehicles with his rifle at the ready. I didn't trust Hakim either, but we were all here to do business.

I said to Brenner, 'Altair knows where al-Darwish's hideout is and he'd tell us if he really thought al-Darwish was dead.'

'Correct.'

I continued, 'He's not responding well to the carrot or the

stick, so …' I thought about this and said, 'So we need to try another approach.'

'Maybe more carrots and a bigger stick.'

'No. We're thinking the way we think, but Altair thinks differently.'

Kate saw that the taser session had ended and she came over to us. 'Any progress?'

'No. He's hanging tough.'

'That's enough taser.'

I agreed and said, 'This guy doesn't want to rat out his chief and go to hell. Right? He wants to take the express elevator to Paradise.'

Brenner nodded and said, 'It's not a choice between living and dying. It's a choice of what kind of death he's looking for.'

'Correct. So we have to help him become a martyr.'

Kate asked, 'How?'

'I don't know. But Hakim does.'

The gentleman in question came over to us and asked, 'What do you want to do?'

I said to Hakim, 'It seems to me, Colonel, that Altair does not want to die a traitor and a coward. Right?'

Hakim, who was probably both, had to think about that, but then he nodded and said, 'This may be true.'

'So? How do we make a deal with Altair that lets him tell us what we want to know, but also lets him into Paradise?'

Again, Hakim had to think about that, and he replied, 'That is difficult.' He informed us, 'You are the reason for his stubbornness.' He explained, unnecessarily, 'You are … infidels. He cannot betray his chief to you, or he will go to hell.'

'Right. We get that.' In fact, Altair should have mentioned that himself between tasers to his nuts. He would have saved himself a lot of pain, and saved us a lot of time. Not to mention saving all of us some discomfort. Well, the PSO guys didn't care – they did this stuff on their coffee breaks. Maybe, though, the pain was part of the process on the road to salvation.

Hakim interrupted my thoughts and said to me and Brenner, 'There is also an issue of the money. Altair rejects it, but he will want this for his family.' He explained, 'It is a thing which worries the martyrs for Islam. Their families. So, Altair will give me his family name and I will promise that his family receives the money – in exchange, of course, for the information you need.'

Hakim thought a lot about money, but he might be on to something.

'Okay,' I said, 'so how do we make all this work?'

Colonel Hakim replied thoughtfully, 'First, we must offer Altair two kinds of death. The one will be a bullet in the head, right here, and he will die a defeated man, a prisoner, and not a martyr who has died in jihad and who would ascend directly to Paradise. And also there is no promise of money to his family.'

Got it.

Hakim continued, 'The other death, to die in jihad, a martyr to his faith, that is more difficult to arrange.'

Maybe I should challenge Altair to a knife fight, but the old guy could get lucky and I'd be the one heading for Paradise.

Zamo, who was standing near the vehicles and who had spent some time in Islam, said, 'Let the old guy go into the camp.'

Yeah?

Hakim thought that might be a good idea and said, 'Yes, he

can be with the dead martyrs, his jihadists. He will pray among them, and find peace.'

Great. But first he has to do the open sesame thing with the cave.

Hakim continued, 'When I spoke to him earlier, he believed two things — that God spared him for a purpose, but also that he had not achieved martyrdom as his jihadists had.'

Right. A little survivor's guilt. We can help him with that.

Brenner said to Hakim, 'Speak to him. But don't forget what we need from him.'

Hakim said he certainly understood, and he reminded us, 'Do not forget what I need from you.'

How could we forget?

So Brenner, Kate, and I joined Zamo near the Land Cruiser to get out of Altair's sight.

Hakim's goons sat the old man up, gave him some water, and Hakim began talking to him.

About ten minutes later, Hakim came over to us and said, 'Altair has told me that he believes Bulus ibn al-Darwish was in this camp, and that he died here.'

That was not what I wanted to hear.

Hakim continued, 'But he has also told me that because he believes his chief is dead, he can now reveal the place where al-Darwish once lived.'

That's more like it. I think we all understood that Altair was bullshitting himself, but sometimes you gotta do that to save your soul, like me eating hamburgers on Good Friday and calling them veggie burgers. I mean, you can't bullshit God, but you can bullshit yourself.

We walked back to the edge of the basin and there was Altair, stumbling down the slope toward the Al Qaeda camp, going home.

Colonel Hakim told us, 'He will die here. And that is good.'

Very good.

'Or, perhaps, God will again spare him, and we may hear from him someday.'

'I hope not.' But a deal is a deal, and on that subject, I asked Colonel Hakim, 'Where is The Panther's hideout?'

Hakim looked off at the distant hills beyond the basin and pointed. 'There.'

'Can you be a bit more specific?'

He got specific and asked, 'Do you see that peak? The one that resembles the sail of a ship?'

Were we getting directions to Noah's Ark?

It was hard to see much in the moonlight, but I thought I saw what Hakim was pointing to. Zamo, however, had his nightscope on it and he said, 'I see it. It's about three klicks, across some rough terrain.'

Kate and Brenner were also looking at it through the lower-powered daylight scopes on their rifles, and they said they could see it clearly in the moonlight. Great.

Colonel Hakim informed us, 'Altair says there is a trail which begins on the far side of the camp. If you can locate that trail, it will take you to the other side of that mountain where the trail will ascend to the cave of Bulus ibn al-Darwish.'

Piece of cake. Or a sack of bullshit. I asked Hakim, 'Are you sure Altair was telling you the truth?'

'One can never be sure. However, he swore this to me, and I

believe he was truthful.' Hakim nodded to himself and said, 'Altair understood that the thing I was giving to him needed to be repaid.'

This place is starting to make sense.

Brenner said to Hakim, 'I assume you are not coming with us.'

The colonel replied, 'I see no reason for that, and I have duties elsewhere.'

Right. Like a swim in the pool at the Bilqis Hotel. I didn't want Hakim and his goons with us anyway, and neither did anyone else. We could handle this ourselves unless The Panther had a platoon of jihadists with him. I asked Hakim, 'Would you guess that al-Darwish is alone?'

Hakim replied, 'Al-Darwish is dead, according to Altair. But if he is not, then he is in that cave, and he is alone, or perhaps he has one or two trusted jihadists with him. But no more.' He motioned toward the camp, indicating that there weren't many jihadists left for The Panther to invite to his hole.

Well, the only thing left to talk about was money, and I said to Hakim, 'Whether or not we find The Panther if we find his cave, you will be rewarded as we discussed.'

'Three million dollars.'

And a small mango up your ass. 'Correct.'

Brenner confirmed that, and said to Colonel Hakim, 'We will arrange to meet in Sana'a, perhaps at the American Embassy, or in your office. The appropriate people will be there from my government to arrange for your reward.'

I lifted my foot, because the bullshit was up to my ankles.

But maybe Brenner would try to get *something* for Hakim, and I guess that was okay. As with Altair, you do a little bullshit and a little chocolate ice cream. Point is, we weren't out of here yet, and Hakim could be the problem or the solution.

Hakim said to Brenner, 'If you should capture al-Darwish – or find him dead – and you find yourself without means to transport him to Sana'a, I am at the Bilqis Hotel.'

Of course you are. And the hotel is not charging a PSO colonel a rial for the room. Life is good if you're a policeman in a police state. It occurred to me that I had the right job, but in the wrong country.

Brenner said, 'Thank you, Colonel. I'll let you know.'

Actually, if we found The Panther, the only thing we'd have to transport was his pinky finger, and the rest of him could rot in these hills.

I hate long goodbyes, so I said, 'Goodbye.'

But Kate, a compassionate lady, asked Colonel Hakim, 'Did you tell Altair that his family would be taken care of?'

'Ah, yes, I did that. So we will need to discuss that as well.'

I didn't think Uncle Sam was going to pay a terrorist's family a hundred grand, but they might pay Hakim something and Hakim could take care of that. Goodbye.

But Hakim had more to tell us, and he said, 'The family name of Altair – it is al-Darwish.'

I hardly knew what to say, so I said, 'See you later.'

Colonel Hakim and Mr Brenner exchanged salutes, and the PSO guys got back in the Humvee I bought for them.

So, here we were. Alone at last.

They say the journey is the destination, but it is not. The journey is the journey; the destination is the end. And we were near the end of this journey – and so was Bulus ibn al-Darwish.

CHAPTER EIGHTY-THREE

We took what we needed from the Land Cruiser and began hoofing it.

The direct route to the head of the trail, if the trail existed, was through the Al Qaeda camp, but the camp was a hellish landscape of bomb craters, smoking earth, and dead bodies, not to mention unexploded munitions. So we began our way around the rim of the flat basin with the sloping hills to our right and the smoking camp to our left.

Every hundred yards or so, Zamo would look through his nightscope, checking out the terrain around us. He also looked down into the camp and told us, 'I see the old man. He's wandering around.'

Just as Zamo said that, there was a loud explosion and we all hit the ground.

Zamo said, 'The old guy set something off.'

Well, I hope he's on his way to a better place than this.

We continued on and the terrain was a challenge, with ridges of loose shale-like rock that gave way under our feet.

It took us half an hour to circumvent the Al Qaeda camp, and we were now approaching the far side of the camp where the trail was supposed to begin, according to Altair, who could not be re-questioned about that.

We stopped and took a break. Zamo passed his rifle around so we could look through the nightscope and do what he called 'terrain appreciation and orientation.'

I looked through the scope, which lit up the night with a weird green glow, like I was wearing tinted glasses. I'd trained on a similar nightscope, so my eye and brain adjusted to the monochromatic image, and I was able to fully appreciate that this whole place was a wasteland, deader than the moon. Not even a goat. Also no sign of Noah's Ark.

I looked across the smoking basin at the place where we'd started, and I could see our white Land Cruiser still there, which was a good sign that our deal with the devil was intact.

I passed the rifle to Kate, who focused on the sail-shaped peak and said, 'Maybe another two kilometers.'

We moved on, looking for the trail that we would have to intersect as we continued around the rim of the basin, but the ground was so rock-strewn that a foot trail wouldn't be noticeable. Also, the thought occurred to me, and probably to everyone, that Altair had pulled a fast one on Colonel Hakim, or Hakim himself had pulled one on us so he could get out of here and go someplace nicer and safer. Did I promise him the money for services already rendered? Or for results?

The A-team separated and doubled back, looking for the trail, but we kept one another in sight as we closely examined the rocky ground in the dim moonlight.

I realized that this trail, if it existed, would not be well trodden. I mean, I doubted if The Panther invited a hundred jihadists up to his cave every night to play bridge and have a cigar, and I doubted, too, if The Panther made the trip down to the camp very often. So we weren't looking for an actual trail but more of a starting point into the hills.

It was Kate, with her obsessive attention to untidy floors, who spotted something, and she said in a quiet, enemy-territory voice, 'Look here.'

We went over to where she was standing and she pointed the muzzle of her M4 at something that would not be noticeable or remarkable in most places, but which here, on the moon, showed evidence of human presence; it was, in fact, a plastic bottle cap.

Kate picked it up and passed it around like a found diamond, and we all agreed that it was fairly new, and that the litterbug, whoever he was, had left us a trail marker.

So with our backs to the Al Qaeda camp, we had our starting point for the route that would take us where we needed to go.

We moved away from the basin and toward the hills to our front.

Kate, who'd kept the bottle cap as a souvenir, was looking for more, like Hansel and Gretel looking for shiny pebbles in the moonlight.

We also looked for the plastic water bottle that had been attached to the cap, but that seemed to be it for litter.

We had no second point to connect to the bottle cap, but as we moved on, the route became more clear because the terrain started to narrow between two ridgelines, like the narrow end of a funnel.

The ground rose more steeply and the loose rock was making noise as it slid beneath our feet, and noise was not what we wanted, so we slowed up.

As we came around a bend in the rising trail, it suddenly ended, and in front of us was a huge pile of rock, blocking the way.

We approached the rock pile and it was obvious that this was a recent slide, caused either by God telling us to go back, or by twenty-four thousand pounds of high explosives shaking the earth like an erupting volcano.

Zamo volunteered his rock-climbing skills, and Brenner held his rifle as Zamo picked his way up the broken rock with his Colt .45 automatic in his hand.

There was no doubt that The Panther, if he was in his cave when those bombs hit, had heard and felt the airstrike, and I imagined that he knew he'd lost a base camp and everyone in it. His unanswered sat-phone call to the camp would confirm that.

I had no idea what this psycho was thinking or feeling when his cave started shaking around him, but I hoped he realized that his world had gotten much smaller. That, and the lack of news from the goat herder's hut, told him he was alone, with a problem. Maybe Perth Amboy wasn't so bad after all.

Zamo called down in a loud whisper, 'Clear.'

Brenner slung Zamo's rifle across his back and we all picked our way up the rockslide.

At the top we could see the continuation of the trail and the sail-shaped peak off to our right.

Zamo took his rifle and scanned the terrain, saying, 'Nothing moving ... no scope looking back at me ... There's like a deep gorge ahead that cuts through the trail ... about six hundred meters ... I see a stone hut ...' He focused in and said, 'Nothing moving around the hut ...'

Brenner took the rifle and looked through the scope, saying to us, 'It could be a sentry hut — between the base camp and the cave . . .'

'Could be,' which meant we were on the right track.

Brenner said, 'We can go around it.'

I suggested, 'Let's see if anyone is home.'

We scrambled down the rock pile as quietly as possible and continued along the route.

There was nothing moving in this dead zone except us, and the night was silent, except for the crunch of brittle rock beneath our feet. The high terrain around us made me start to imagine that there were people looking down on us, and I was expecting the silence to be shattered any second by blasts of submachine-gun fire. Whose idea was this?

We were spread apart as we walked, but I moved closer to Kate and gave her an encouraging pat on the back, then continued on.

Zamo was on point now and he raised his arm, indicating halt. We stopped and everyone got down on one knee, rifles at the ready.

Brenner moved up to Zamo and they took turns looking through the nightscope.

Brenner motioned me and Kate forward, and we moved in a crouch to where he and Zamo were kneeling.

About fifty meters in front of us was the gorge we'd seen, and sitting in the gorge was the stone hut.

Brenner whispered, 'I'll check it out.'

Well, if you insist, go ahead. But I remembered whose idea this was so I grabbed Brenner's arm and made it clear that I was going. Kate wanted to come along, but that wasn't happening. I whispered, 'Cover me.'

I moved forward quickly in a crouch and got to the edge of the gorge, keeping my eyes on the stone hut. I flattened out on the ground and looked through my four-power scope to the right where the gorge descended between two hills. The moon was higher in the southern sky, and it cast good light on this south-facing slope. Nothing seemed to be moving uphill, and to my left was the hut at the bottom of the gorge.

I focused my scope on the hut. Like most of these huts it had no windows, only a narrow, doorless entrance. There was a crude ladder going up to the flat roof, and from here I could see that there was no one on the roof, so if this was a sentry post, the sentry was inside, which didn't make much sense in terms of vigilance.

I made my way on my butt down into the gorge, dividing my attention between the hut and everything else.

At the bottom, I crouched between two rocks and looked at the hut. There is the cautious approach, favored by most, and the let's-do-this-fast approach, favored by me. I sprang out of my crouch and charged across the rocky ground directly for the door of the hut.

I really didn't expect to find anyone inside, so when I tripped over a body lying on the dirt floor, I was as surprised as the guy I tripped over.

It was pitch dark inside the hut, except for a little light coming through the door, and I saw the guy getting to his feet at the same time I did. He'd just been rudely awakened, so he wasn't at the top of his game, but he instinctively kicked out and caught me in the gut. I grabbed his bare foot, twisted it, and he fell to the floor, then scrambled toward the door, grabbing what looked like his rifle on the way.

I dove on top of him, and he collapsed to the ground, but then he tried to lizard-crawl out the door. I gave him a roundhouse punch in the face, then another that broke his nose, and he was down for the count.

I stood, yanked his AK-47 away from him, and smacked the butt against his head to see if he noticed.

I heard something outside the hut, and I flattened my back to the left side of the door and held my M4 by the pistol grip.

It got quiet outside, and I waited, knowing that my team was covering me from the top of the gorge.

'John?'

'I'm here. Abdul is on the ground.'

My teammates came into the hut, stepping over the other guy.

There wasn't much to say except that the guy on the ground was probably Al Qaeda and not an innocent civilian, and that he had been sleeping on the job.

We pulled the guy away from the doorway and sat him up in a corner.

Zamo frisked him while Brenner held a red-filtered flashlight on him. The guy had a 9mm Browning automatic and a satphone on him. He also had a cracked nose and a split lip, and his face was bloody. Before Brenner shut off the light, Kate took it and shined it closer to the guy's face. She's really good with faces, even when they've had a nose and lip job, and she said, 'Nabeel.'

Indeed it was. That called for a drink. Zamo opened a bottle of water and splashed it in Nabeel's face, then poured some between his lips as he slapped him around.

Nabeel coughed up some water, then half-opened his eyes.

We didn't have a lot of time to get to the point, so I drew my jambiyah and put the blade to his throat, noticing the bandage on the left side of his neck, like he'd cut himself shaving, or maybe someone else had tried to get his attention with a knife. I said to him, 'You owe me for that bagel.'

He focused on me and there was real terror in his eyes, which made me feel bad, like *I* was the terrorist.

I said to him, 'Here's the deal, Nabeel. You have your choice of living or dying, and by dying I mean I'm going to open up your throat like a ripe melon. Understand?'

He nodded his head without moving his neck.

I asked him, 'Where is al-Darwish?'

He knew that was coming, and he said, 'Please not to kill me and I say where is he.'

'No, asshole, *I* say where is he. *You* say where he is. Where is he?'

'He … he is in … maghara …'

Brenner said, 'Cave.'

'Where is this cave?'

'Here. Close.'

'Can you be more specific?'

'I tell you … not far. You go … go to where sun go—'

'West?'

'Yes. West. You see where to go. Up.'

Brenner took over in Arabic, then said to us, 'He says there are two people with al-Darwish. A sentry who he says sits on a rock, and a person inside the cave with al-Darwish.'

Hopefully the sentry didn't have a nightscope, though he

probably did, but maybe he, too, was asleep on the job. If not, we had to put him to sleep.

I said to Brenner, 'Do you believe him about only two guys?'

Brenner replied, 'We're about to find out.'

Brenner asked Nabeel a few more questions in Arabic and English, and Nabeel claimed he'd never actually been to the cave, but he did confirm that the entrance to the cave was on the hill with the distinctive ship's sail peak. So that jibed with what Altair had said, making it a little less likely to be bullshit.

I was surprised that Altair and Nabeel gave up the boss, and I was getting the feeling that those who knew Bulus ibn al-Darwish did not love him. Just like back in the States.

Zamo asked, 'Is this guy supposed to make a sit-rep?'

Brenner asked in Arabic, then told us, 'He says yes, and he's happy to make that call now to al-Numair.'

We all agreed that it was better if The Panther didn't hear from Nabeel that all was well, because there was a chance that Nabeel would give the code word for 'I have a gun to my head.' No news from the sentry sometimes just means the sentry is asleep.

Nabeel, trying to firm up his life-or-death deal, also offered to help us find the way to his boss's hideout, but it's never a good idea to take the enemy with you on a stealth mission.

Anyway, if we had time, we could have happily tormented Nabeel with the news about his buddies getting vaporized at the Sheik Musa meeting. Not to mention his camp being turned into a toxic waste dump. I would also have liked to take those photos of the Belgians, which I had with me, and shove them, one by one, down Nabeel's throat. But bottom line on Nabeel al-Samad was that he'd come to the end of his usefulness.

Well, the moment that we would have liked to avoid had come, and it was time to say goodbye to Nabeel.

Zamo said, 'I'll tie and gag him.'

We all nodded and left the hut. A second later, I heard the cough of the muzzle silencer, and Zamo stepped out of the hut, bolting another round in the chamber.

No one said anything as Zamo slung Nabeel's AK-47 over his shoulder and we moved on.

Kate noticed that the gorge was littered with plastic water bottles and similar evidence that a lot of people had been there, and we concluded that this was a meeting place, like an amphitheater, maybe where The Panther rallied his troops. If so, his cave couldn't be far off.

We climbed out of the gorge and continued on. I had point now, but Zamo was close behind me, scanning the terrain to our front, sides, and rear.

We were about a hundred yards from the base of the high hill where the cave was supposed to be, and I felt Zamo's hand press down on my shoulder. I dropped to one knee and glanced back to see him focusing on something up the slope of the hill.

He passed his sniper rifle to me and pointed, like a bird dog. I followed his outstretched arm and scanned the hill. About halfway up, sitting on a rock, was a man in dark cammies with what looked like a rifle across his knees. As I focused in, the man raised the rifle and began scanning the ground below him. I caught a brief flash of his nightscope lens as it swept past us, and Zamo and I hit the ground and rolled behind a flat rock.

As I passed the rifle back to Zamo, Kate and Brenner inched forward, and I said, 'Sniper.'

They both nodded and kept completely still.

Zamo was now refocused on the sniper, and Brenner inched closer to him.

Zamo said, 'We can't move without that guy seeing us.'

Meaning, permission to fire.

We all understand that if Zamo took that guy out, there'd be another dead sentry who was not reporting in. On the other hand, there seemed to be no way around that.

Brenner thought a moment, then said to Zamo, 'Take him out.'

Zamo seemed pleased with the assignment.

Zamo knew, and we all knew, that he had literally one shot at this. The sound of his shot would be muffled by the silencer, but the bullet, if it missed the target, would hit rock and even the most clueless sniper would know that he'd been shot at and missed. And by the time Zamo chambered another round and re-aimed, the enemy sniper would be behind a rock and raising the alarm. Then he'd start shooting back.

It looked to me like the sniper was maybe five or six hundred meters up the side of the hill, still within the nine-hundred-meter effective range of Zamo's scope and rifle. But it wasn't an easy shot because it was a night shot, and because rising or falling terrain distorts your perception of the target's distance.

We all sat as still as the rocks around us while Zamo steadied his aim from a kneeling position. There wasn't a rock around that was high enough for him to use to steady his rifle, so he was aiming freehand, and I could see he was having a problem with his injured left arm, which couldn't hold its position long. In fact, Zamo lowered the rifle, then sighted again, then lowered it again.

Jeez. Come on, guy. You can do it. And do it fast before that bastard starts scanning the terrain again.

Zamo took a deep breath, then actually stood, took another breath, held it, then fired.

He dropped to one knee and chambered another round.

Brenner was the one to ask, 'Hit?'

Zamo glanced back at him as though he couldn't understand the question. Finally, he said, 'Yeah. Hit.' Like, why bother to fire if you're going to miss?

Well, Zamo was feeling good about himself, and I was feeling that we were very lucky and that The Panther was not.

I suggested, 'We really need to move it before The Panther hears all this silence.'

Everyone agreed and we dispensed with stealth and caution and double-timed it up the trail that curved around the base of the high hill with the sail on top. We kept an eye out for what could be a climbing path up the hill, and after about a hundred yards Zamo spotted a small pile of loose rock on the trail.

We all dropped to one knee and hugged the side of the hill as Zamo scanned straight up and confirmed, 'This is the way.' He also said, 'I don't see an entrance to a cave ... but I see, like, over-hanging flat rocks ...'

I peered through my scope at the high hill and I could see rock strata jutting out, casting moon shadows across the face of the hill. The entrance to the cave would be under one of those overhangs.

So what's the plan? If Chet and Buck were with us, we'd sit here for a week with charts and diagrams, then call Howard and ask him to call Washington for clearance. But I had a better plan – go up the hill, find the cave, kill The Panther, go down the hill.

Brenner, however, had a few add-ons — Zamo was to stay here and cover our backs, then he, me, and Kate would go up and look for the entrance to the cave, but only one of us would go in. And who would that be? Well, whoever thought of this.

Brenner whispered, 'Watch for tripwires — flares or booby traps.' Thanks for that.

I went first, Brenner was behind me, and Kate brought up the rear as we began our ascent. The climbing path was mostly rock ledges, like a steep staircase cleared of loose stone. But now and then a piece of stone would fall and make a very loud noise, which I knew wasn't as loud as I heard it in my head.

I was happy with the small M4, which, as advertised, was light and compact, and I was sure it would be excellent in caves. The moonlight was bright enough to see the way, but not bright enough to see a tripwire, so I felt my way carefully, brushing my fingers around the stone ledges to feel for a wire.

This was slow going, but the idea was to surprise The Panther, without being surprised ourselves by tripping a wire and getting blown to pieces. Or at the very least, tripping an illumination flare that would light us up like deer in the headlights, followed by a long burst of AK-47 fire.

We had no way of knowing for sure if there were any such devices on the approach to the cave, but if I was living in a cave, I'd damn sure put something on the path to alert me to visitors.

And there it was. I felt it with my hand — a taut metal wire about six inches above the wide ledge I was about to crawl onto.

I turned and motioned to Brenner, who was about ten feet behind me, using the hand signal for tripwire, which if you're interested is like pantomiming stretching a rubber band.

Brenner nodded, and I turned back and did a crab walk carefully over the wire. You can't cut it because it could also be set to trip if the tension is released. So you leave it, mark it, and move on. I draped the wire with my white handkerchief and kept climbing.

Brenner got over the wire, followed by Kate, and we continued on.

We were about halfway up the hill, which was maybe fifteen hundred feet high, and the slope was becoming less steep, and this had the effect of making it more difficult to see ahead to what was over the next strata of rock.

Then something caught my eye to the right and I froze. It was a man about fifty feet away sitting on the same rock ledge that I was on. It took me a few seconds to realize that this was the sniper's perch, and that the man, who was leaning back against the rock, was not moving because he was dead.

I signaled to Brenner, who passed the signal along to Kate. They climbed to the ledge below me where they could see the dead man.

I moved sideways to my right and got to the sitting man, whose head was tilted back as though he was moon gazing. I could see that Zamo had hit his target full in the chest, slightly right of the heart, but fatal nonetheless.

The man's rifle, lying to his side, had the distinctive shape of the Soviet-made Dragunov sniper rifle, which it probably was. More importantly, the rifle had a nightscope whose lens was still illuminated, and I reached out to take it.

All of a sudden the silence was broken by a loud, piercing noise, like an alarm, which made me jump. Ringing phones always make me jump, and the phone rang again, then again. Well, it wasn't my sat-phone, which was dead, so it was the guy's phone and he was dead. If my Arabic was better, I'd have answered it and reported all was dead quiet here.

The phone finally stopped ringing, and I looked at Brenner and Kate below me. Obviously the sniper had missed his situation report, as had Nabeel, and whoever was calling — maybe The Panther himself — was getting a little worried. And with good reason. We, however, also had a problem now. But there was nothing we could do about it except continue on and get rid of the problem.

Brenner was signaling insistently that he would take the lead, and Kate was nodding in agreement and motioning me to come toward her. But I had come too far to drop back this close to the finish line, and I continued up the slope with my new sniper rifle. I got to the next ledge and used the nightscope to scan up the hill.

Less than thirty feet in front of me was a huge overhang, a long slab of rock that formed the roof of a deep, dark shelter — a cave. I focused the nightscope and saw something move in the darkness.

A figure suddenly emerged from under the overhang, carrying an AK-47, and I took aim with the sniper rifle. As I pulled the trigger, I realized the figure was wearing a balto. My shot hit her where I'd aimed, right through the heart, and her arms flew up, sending her rifle into the air as she fell backwards and hit the ground.

The bastard who was still inside the cave had fixed my position, and before I could take cover I saw the muzzle flash a half second before I heard the hollow popping sound of an AK-47 on full automatic. A tracer round clipped my hip and another round hit my Kevlar and knocked me backward off the ledge to the ledge below, and I lost the sniper rifle. It took me a few seconds to catch my breath, and when I looked up I could see green tracer rounds streaking down the slope right above where I was lying.

Kate and Brenner were returning fire, but they were probably low on ammunition from the shootout at the Crow Fortress and they weren't on full blast. The firing from the cave stopped, and Kate and Brenner ceased fire. It suddenly became quiet.

I was lying flat on my back on the rock, and I couldn't see Brenner or Kate, but I'd be able to see anyone who appeared on the ledge above me, and I had my M4 on full automatic across my chest, ready to fire at anything that moved.

Only one AK had been firing and I assumed that was The Panther. The other person that Nabeel had mentioned must have been the woman. I don't know who she was – girlfriend or wife – but like all women around here, she was expendable, and al-Darwish had used her to draw my fire. Nice guy. And now The Panther was wondering if I was dead or alive. The name of this game is patience, deception, and surprise, and I was good at two out of three.

The minutes ticked by, and I was concerned that al-Asshole was flanking around to our sides, or worse, he could be hightailing it up the hill, heading for someplace far away. But if Zamo was in a good spot, he should be able to see that kind of movement and take care of it. Still, The Panther had the immediate advantage of the higher ground.

When you get hit, you don't always feel it at first, and I didn't, but now I could feel the pain where the bullet grazed my left hip, and the throbbing in my chest where the Kevlar had absorbed the second hit. I also felt some warm blood, but it wasn't gushing. Still, the hip would start to stiffen up when the initial shock wore off and the body said, 'You got hit, stupid.'

Another minute passed, and I was starting to think that maybe Brenner or Kate had been hit, but I couldn't think about that now. And I couldn't lie here all night waiting for The Panther to make a move – or a full retreat. So I took a deep breath, sat up quickly, and fired a long, sweeping spray of rounds up the slope. Bullets ricocheted from the rock as I dropped down, slapped another magazine into the M4, rolled down the slope, got up, and repeated the recon by fire.

But no one returned the fire and it got quiet again. I reached for another magazine in my bush vest and discovered that I was out of ammunition. Shit.

I drew my Colt .45 automatic and lay very still. I couldn't figure out what this asshole was up to, but he'd gone from panic-fire to very cagey silence. Or he was in the next province by now.

I yelled out, 'Bulus! Asshole! Shithead!'

He didn't respond to his name, so I moved as far as I could along the ledge, still on my back, which was the only way to see what was above me without raising my head. I yelled out again, 'Asshole! I'm talkin' to you, Bulus. You speak English?'

No response.

Okay, time to do it. I yelled, 'Cover fire!' and I charged up the slope as Kate and Brenner, off to my right, opened up with their M4s. I zigzagged across the flat ledges toward the mouth of the wide cave in front of me, popping off a few rounds from the

Colt. Brenner and Kate were firing full, long bursts of suppressing fire into and around the cave, and the bullets were ricocheting around me, but I wasn't drawing any return fire, so the bastard was either gone, ducking, or dead.

I got to the overhanging ledge, jumped over the dead woman, then shoulder-rolled into the mouth of the cave. I lay still on my side and peered into the darkness.

I realized I was lying on a very funky blanket. Some moonlight was penetrating the space under the ledge, and as my eyes adjusted to the darkness, I could see that the carpeted floor was strewn with what I guessed was camping equipment. So this stinking shithole was the lair of The Panther, the mastermind of the *Cole* bombing, the head of Al Qaeda in Yemen, and the target of the greatest power on earth. I mean, I expected something like this, but now that I was here, it was hard to believe that this crap hole was where Bulus ibn al-Darwish, al-Numair, The Panther, lived and plotted and ruled from.

Mr al-Darwish pressed the muzzle of his AK-47 against the back of my head and said, in perfect English, 'Throw your gun on the ground. Now!'

I threw the Colt .45 a few feet away.

He had backed off so I couldn't grab the barrel of his rifle, and he said, 'Hands on your head.'

I put my hands on my head. Where were Kate and Brenner?

'Who are you?' he asked.

'Your worst nightmare.'

'No, I am *your* worst nightmare.'

'I'm taking you back home, Bulus.' I reminded him, 'Your momma's waiting for you.'

He gave me a kick in the back of the head and asked, 'How many people are with you?'

'More than are with you. Everyone you know is dead.'

He had nothing to say about that, and there was a long silence. Then he asked me, 'How did you find this place?'

'A soaring eagle told me.' I translated for him, 'Altair.' He didn't respond to that, so I went into my police mode and said, 'You're trapped, Bulus, and you're going to die unless you surrender.'

'Do not use my given name.'

Shithead? I said, to make it official, 'You're under arrest.'

He thought that was funny and asked, 'What is my arresting officer's name? That's my right as an American citizen to know your name.'

Asshole. I told him, 'John Corey, Anti-Terrorist Task Force.'

'So you finally found me. Or have I found *you*?' He asked, 'Where is your wife, Mr Corey?'

'Where's yours? Dead?'

I thought that would send him over the edge and he'd try another kick, which would not go as well for him as the last one, but he didn't react. Maybe he had more wives.

He asked me, 'Do you think this cave has only one entrance? Do you think I'm stupid?'

Yes, I do think you're stupid, and yes I thought this cave had only one way in and out. But I guess it had two. Shit.

He let me know, 'I will be on the other side of this hill in ten minutes, you'll be dead, and anyone who follows me through the cave will step on a pressure mine and be blown up.'

Holy shit.

'So I will say goodbye to Mr Corey, and to Mrs Corey in absentia.'

I was certain he wouldn't fire, because he knew there were other people out there who would come charging in, firing – so he was going for his jambiyah to do it quietly.

I spun around on my buttocks and as I did I saw that he had his knife in his right hand, his rifle was slung, and his left hand was reaching for my hair. My legs caught him below the knees and he lost his balance and fell sideways.

I pulled my jambiyah, which he didn't see as he scrambled away from me and unslung his rifle.

Before he could level it, I was on top of him and I pressed my full weight down on him. He thrashed around, trying to get his rifle into a firing position, but I wasn't going to let that happen. He'd dropped his jambiyah, but now his right hand reached out for it, and he got hold of the handle and brought the tip around and buried it into my back. He realized it wasn't penetrating, and he brought it up again to stick it into my neck or head.

I gave him the old knee in the balls, which refocused his attention, then I put the curved blade of my jambiyah under his full beard and on his throat and said, 'Remember the Cole, asshole.'

Our eyes met for a second, then I pressed hard and drew the blade across his throat, which opened his jugular vein and both carotid arteries, causing his warm blood to spurt over my hand. I told him, 'You have the right to remain silent.'

I kept at it, sawing through his flesh, windpipe, muscles, and tendons until I got to his spine, which I separated with the blade, then I kept going until the blade hit the dirt floor.

I sat up, drew a long breath, then grabbed his hair and held up his head. I said to The Panther, 'Payback, you fucking bastard. Payback for the men on the Cole, payback for the men, women, and children you murdered, you piece of shit. Payback—'

Kate said, 'John … John … it's okay … it's okay … stop …'

Brenner grabbed the severed head by its hair, pulled it out of my hand, and threw it across the floor of the cave. He said, 'Time to go.'

Kate took my arm and I stood.

Time to go home. That's the plan.

— PART IX —

New York City

CHAPTER EIGHTY-FOUR

The big, four-faced stanchion clock read 6:50. Most of the commuters had departed for the suburbs, but arriving trains brought fresh blood – theatergoers, partiers, and others from near and far who poured into Manhattan every night through Grand Central Station.

Maybe, I thought, it was a little hokey to meet under the clock that had been used in so many movies as a rendezvous for lovers. But the clock had also served as a meeting place for tens of thousands of soldiers, sailors, and airmen coming home to their families, so this was okay.

Buck could not join us, but he was a gentleman of the old school, and he had sent his regrets, demonstrating not only good manners, but also tremendous chutzpah.

In other news from the front, Kate and I had been notified, officially, that Mr Chet Morgan of the Central Intelligence Agency had been struck by a Bedouin bullet as he tried to rescue us in the Black Hawk helicopter. That's not quite how I remembered it, but in any case Mr Morgan had died of his wound before the helicopter reached Najran airbase.

This was the second CIA officer whose death had been announced to me, the first being the aforementioned Ted Nash, who actually died twice, officially, before Kate whacked him for real. And I had the feeling that Chet Morgan, too, would experience a resurrection, and that I'd hear from him again. If not, he would hear from me.

Zamo, too, couldn't join us because he was on extended medical leave, recuperating from his injury, in Las Vegas. I hope his luck holds out.

We'd also invited Howard Fensterman and Clare Nolan, who had grown closer in the three weeks since we'd seen them, and they would have loved to be in New York with us, but their new duties in Sana'a prevented them from taking home leave at this time. They did promise, however, to be in New York for the holidays, all of which Howard probably celebrates.

Reunions sound good in theory, like my high school reunions, but in reality you don't always want to see the people who you bonded with at certain times and places in your life journey. The memories are good and they should be preserved and acknowledged with a holiday card or a quick email and not be spoiled by actually having to see those people again. Clare, however, might be an exception.

Also, I was looking forward to seeing Paul Brenner. Mr Brenner was home on leave, in Virginia, but as I predicted he was returning to Yemen. Some people can't get enough fun. I mean, this is the guy who did a second tour in Vietnam. One day, some tour in some shithole would kill him, but for now he was happy to feel alive by daring death. I suppose I could say the same about myself, and maybe even Kate, but ... Well, no buts. We're back at 26 Federal Plaza, me with a new three-year contract, and Kate with a guarantee of three more years in the city she's grown to love with the man she loves, and tolerates. That's me.

But if we get bored or restless or tired of Tom Walsh's act, there are a dozen other hellholes where the Anti-Terrorist Task Force operates, and we may volunteer for one of them. Hopefully we won't have to take another State Department course in cultural awareness. The last one didn't work too well.

Kate and I watched Paul Brenner and his lady walking across the marble floor of the Main Concourse. They spotted the tall clock, then spotted us, and Brenner and his lady made their way through the crowd.

Kate said, 'She's very attractive.'

I wouldn't have expected less from a man who has good taste in women.

We waved, they waved, we all met and shook hands or hugged, and Brenner introduced us to his lady, who said to Kate and me, 'I've heard a lot about you.'

I couldn't say the same, but she seemed like a nice woman and we went up to Michael Jordan's Steak House on the mezzanine, where I got silly and asked the waiter for a Pink Panther, on the rocks.

When the ladies went to freshen up, Brenner said to me, 'Buck.'

I didn't reply.

Brenner asked, 'Are we supposed to let that go?'

'We're supposed to believe that Buck was an unwitting accomplice.'

'He wasn't unwitting.'

Right. But Buckminster Harris had served his country well and honorably since I was a milk drinker, so I said, 'I don't want to see him disgraced in public.'

Brenner nodded, then inquired, 'How about dead in private?'

'Whatever you decide, I'm with you.'

Brenner said, 'I'm not buying that Chet is dead.'

'Seems a little suspicious,' I agreed. 'When we see Buck, we'll get the truth.'

Brenner leaned toward me and said softly, 'I want both of them dead.'

I nodded.

The ladies returned and we ordered another round. I could see that Kate liked Brenner's lady, whose name was Cynthia, and we learned that Paul and Cynthia had met on the job, just as Kate and I had. Cynthia Sunhill was Army, Criminal Investigation Division, and she'd requested a posting in Yemen. Good luck.

When the waiter came around, I, of course, inquired about any goat specials. Kate rolled her eyes. Brenner laughed.

It was a good evening and we parted, promising to stay in touch, which was inevitable because of the scheduled CIA post-op meeting in Washington. That should be interesting.

As for the thanks of a grateful nation, that hadn't yet been scheduled.

Hey, we were lucky we had jobs. Right?

ACKNOWLEDGEMENTS

First, my sincere thanks to Jamie Raab, Executive Vice President and Publisher of Grand Central Publishing, for taking on an additional job as editor of this novel. Jamie has been tireless, patient, and precise during the entire process, and this is a better book because of her keen editorial judgment and sage advice. We don't always agree on what I've written, but we always agree that the end product is a smooth combination of Jamie's yin and my yang.

Thanks, also, to Harvey-Jane Kowal, a.k.a. HJ, who came out of retirement from Hachette Book Group to work on another DeMille book. HJ is a master of grammar, punctuation, spelling, and fact-checking, and she saves me from looking uneducated. Our tradition for the last eleven books has been to celebrate the editing of the last page with a few Bloody Marys. Here's to you, HJ.

A book needs many editorial eyes and minds, and I thank Roland Ottewell, who has worked with care and precision on my last several manuscripts. And because my manuscripts are always late and due at the printer yesterday, Roland also works long hours to make the manuscript printer-ready. Thanks, Roland, for another job well done.

On the corporate level, I'd like to thank David Young, Chairman and CEO of Hachette Book Group. David takes the time from his busy schedule to read my manuscripts, though that isn't in his job description. David either enjoys my writing or he wants to see what he's paying for. I thank David, too, for his friendship and for his good taste in Scotch whisky.

As in all my novels, I've called on friends and acquaintances to assist me with technical details, professional jargon, and all the other bits and pieces of information that a novelist needs but can't get from books or the internet.

First in this category is Detective Kenny Hieb (NYPD, retired), formerly with the Joint Terrorism Task Force and currently doing something similar, though I can't be specific. Kenny has been to Yemen in real life with the JTTF, and his experience there and his memories, notes, and photos of Yemen have all been invaluable to me as I constructed the world of this book. Thanks, Kenny, for your help, but more important, thank you for your work in keeping America safe.

I should say here that any errors of fact or procedures regarding police work, Anti-Terrorist operations, and related matters are a result of either my misunderstanding of the information given to me, or a result of my decision to take dramatic liberties and literary license.

Another eyewitness to Yemen was Matt Longo, who was in that country for more peaceful reasons than John Corey was. Matt, a college roommate of my son, Alex, is well traveled in many Arabic countries and he has been of great help to me in regard to the Arabic culture and the religion of Islam. I have included Matt as a character in this book with the thought that Matt represents a younger generation who may help define our future relations with the world of Islam, and bridge the cultural gap that exists between the two worlds. Thanks, Matt, for your help and your insights.

Many of my novels have benefited from the assistance of my childhood friend Thomas Block, US Airways Captain (retired), columnist and contributing editor to aviation magazines, and co-author with me of *Mayday*, as well as the author of seven other novels. Although Tom has retired as an international captain, he has not retired from writing, which does not require good eyesight or quick reflexes, and Tom has recently published his seventh novel, *Captain*, available on his website: www.thomasblocknovels.com.

Many thanks, too, to Tom's lovely wife, Sharon Block, former flight attendant for Braniff International and US Airways, for her timely and careful reading of the manuscript and her excellent suggestions, as well as her keen eye for typos and bad punctuation. Sharon's reading skills have been invaluable to both me and Tom, as our minds tended to wander in high school English class. What we were thinking about is another story, but we both knew we'd someday have a lady in our lives who knew how to proofread.

Thanks, too, to John Kennedy, Deputy Police Commissioner, Nassau County (NY) Police Department (retired), labor arbitrator, and member of the New York State Bar. John has read and assisted with all my John Corey novels, and he comes to this task with a unique combination of skills and knowledge as a police officer and an attorney. John is my reality check, and if he says something is not legally or procedurally correct, then I rewrite it — or I invoke the novelist's right to make up stuff.

This book would not have existed without the dedication and hard work of my two assistants, Dianne Francis and Patricia Chichester. I write my novels longhand, but for years no one could read my handwriting and it seemed that I had to learn to type or never be published again. But then along came Dianne, then Patricia, who could understand my illegible scrawl and put it into type form so I, too, could read what I wrote. Dianne and Patricia also read the manuscript, page by page, and their comments, fact-checking, and proofreading are nothing short of amazing. Thank you for that and for keeping my life and schedule organized.

As with dessert, the best is last, and that's my wife, Sandy Dillingham DeMille, who has shared with me all the agonies and ecstasies of book writing. Sandy's support and encouragement have pulled me through some tough writing periods, and her editorial suggestions and marginal notes are literally the last word on my manuscript before it gets sent to the publisher.

Sandy and I are celebrating our tenth year together, and it's all been one well-plotted and beautifully written romance novel. The following people have made generous contributions to charities in return for having their name used as a character in this novel:

Howard Fensterman, who contributed to the Crohn's & Colitis Foundation of America; and **John 'Zamo' Zamoiski**, who contributed to the Irvington Education Foundation.

I hope they enjoy their fictitious alter egos and that they continue their good work for worthy causes.

CATCH UP WITH THE OTHER
JOHN COREY THRILLERS

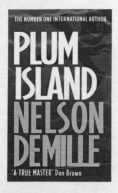

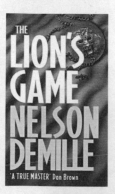

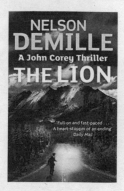

THE FIRST BOOK FROM THE
MASTER STORYTELLER

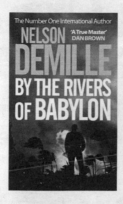

They were forced to meet by the rivers of Babylon . . .

In Israel, two Concorde jets take off for a UN conference that will
finally bring peace to the Middle East. Covered by F-14 fighters,
accompanied by security men, the planes carry warriors, pacifists,
lovers, enemies, dignitaries – and a bomb planted
by a terrorist mastermind.

Suddenly they're forced to crash-land at an ancient desert site.
Here, with only a handful of weapons, the men and women of the
peace mission must make a desperate stand against an army of
crack Palestinian commandos – while the Israeli authorities
desperately attempt a rescue bid.

*

'Not since *Exodus* has there been such a raw powerful story
of the Middle East' Harold Robbins

978-0-7515-4179-3